PETER McLEAN

PRIEST OF BONES

Jo Fletcher
BOOKS

First published in Great Britain in 2018
This edition published in 2019 by

Jo Fletcher Books
an imprint of Quercus Editions Ltd
Carmelite House
50 Victoria Embankment
London EC4Y 0DZ

An Hachette UK company

A CIP catalogue record for this book is available
from the British Library

PB ISBN 978 1 78747 349 2
EB ISBN 978 1 78747 350 8

10 9 8 7 6 5 4 3 2 1

Typeset by CC Book Production
Printed and bound in Great Britain by Clays Ltd, Elcograf S.p.A.

For Diane.
Always.

'If you must break the law, do it to seize power.'

—Julius Caesar

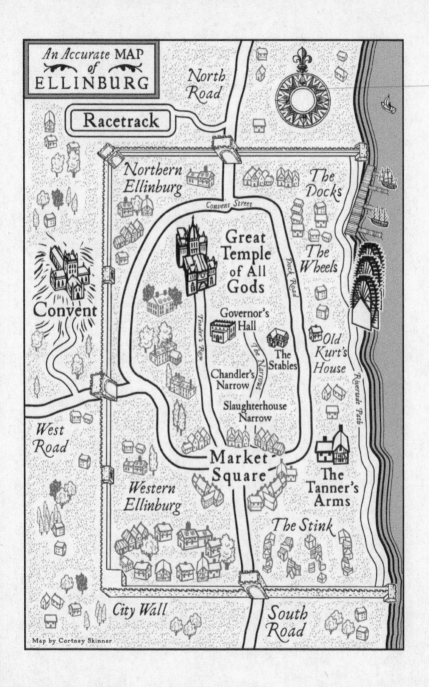

Dramatis Personae

The Piety Family

Tomas Piety: An army priest, a veteran, and a businessman. Leader of the Pious Men. Your narrator.

Jochan Piety: His younger brother, a very disturbed man.

Enaid Piety: Their loving aunt, sister to their da. A spinster of some sixty years. She had been a soldier in the last war, and she took no shit from anyone.

Tomas' Crew

Bloody Anne: A sergeant, a good soldier, and a loyal friend. Anne always had preferred the close work; that was how she got her name in the first place.

Sir Eland: A false knight with the eyes of a weasel. Not a man you'd trust.

Kant: A corporal and a psychopath. Kant the Cunt, the crew called him, but never to his face.

Brak: Kant's second, a young thug of some twenty years. He was only tough when he had the big man in front of him.

Cookpot: A cook, a forager, and a thief. Cookpot had grown up in Ellinburg, but he didn't know how business was done any more than Simple Sam did.

Fat Luka: Another Ellinburg man. If he had managed to stay fat on army rations then it was just his natural shape and he'd be fat for life.

Simple Sam: A slow lad but a faithful one, and he certainly had a good size to him.

Black Billy: Black Billy was proud of his arms, and rightly so. Good with his fists too.

Billy the Boy: An orphan of twelve years, touched by the goddess. A very strange young man.

Grieg: A conscript with some unpleasant habits.

Nik the Knife: Not such a bad fellow, despite his name. Nik was well liked in the crew.

Stefan: A soldier. There was little more to be said about Stefan.

Borys: A thoughtful, older man who said little. He could move quiet when he wanted to, for a big man.

Erik: He was good at the close work, was Erik.

Three other ruffians whose names are not recorded here.

Jochan's Crew

Will the Woman: We called him that because every time Will kills a man he weeps afterward, but he's killed so many men it ain't funny no more.

Hari: Not a natural soldier, but a man of hidden talents.

Mika: He could think for himself, could Mika, which is more than some of the lads could.

Cutter: A professional murderer with a mysterious past.

Ganna: A shithead.

Their Friends, Acquaintances, and Enemies in Ellinburg

Governor Hauer: The city governor of Ellinburg. A frugal man, or so he let it be thought. Overly fond of wine.

Captain Rogan: Captain of the City Guard. A hard man and a ruthless bully, but he was greedy and he had his vices.

Ailsa: An Alarian barmaid. Among other things.

Rosie: A whore with a heart of secrets.

Doc Cordin: A barber-surgeon. He had always been a better surgeon than he was a barber.

The Mother Superior: Head of the convent of the Mother of Blessed Redemption. Can't take a joke.

Sister Jessica: A nun at the convent. Good with a halberd.

Old Kurt: People called Old Kurt a cunning man, and that had two meanings.

Ernst: A barber.

Pawl: A tailor.

Georg: A baker.

Desh: An Alarian lad from Hull Patcher's Row. As far back as he could remember, he always wanted to be a Pious Man.

Captain Larn: A career army officer and a pain in the arse.

Ma Aditi: A gangster and an enemy, the head of the Gutcutters down in the Wheels.

Gregor: A gangster who sits at Ma Aditi's left hand.

Bloodhands: A very, very scary man.

Part One

Part One

Chapter 1

After the war we came home.

Sixty-five thousand battle-shocked, trained killers came home to no jobs, no food, and the plague. What the fuck did Her Majesty *think* was going to happen?

'Drink up, lads,' I said. 'It's on the house, now.'

'That it is,' Bloody Anne said as she threw the innkeeper out of the door and locked it behind him.

He had wanted silver, for food and beer barely worth half a clipped copper. That was no way to welcome the returning heroes, to my mind, and it seemed Anne had agreed with me about that. She'd given him a good kicking for his trouble.

'That's done then,' she said.

Bloody Anne was my sergeant. Her hair was shorter than mine and she had a long, puckered scar that ran from the corner of her left eye down almost to the tip of her jaw, twisting the edge of her mouth into a permanent sneer. Nobody messed with Bloody Anne, not if they knew what was good for them.

'You drinking?' I asked, offering her a tankard.

'What do you think?'

She had a gravelly voice that had been roughened by the smoke of blasting powder and too many years of shouting orders. No amount of beer would soften that voice, but that didn't stop her trying every chance she got. We sat at a table together and she took the cup from me and drained half of it in a single swallow.

A couple of the lads were dragging the innkeeper's daughter up some splintery wooden stairs while the others tapped a fresh cask. Kant grinned at me from those stairs, his hand already thrust down the front of the girl's kirtle. I shook my head to tell him no. I don't hold with rape and I wasn't allowing it, not in my crew.

I'm a priest, after all.

Over Anne's shoulder, I watched Kant ignore me and drag the girl up onto the landing and out of sight. Those were the times we lived in.

All the same, there were limits.

I got to my feet and shoved the table away from me, spilling our tankards of warm beer across the sawdust-covered floor.

'Oi,' Anne complained.

'Kant!' I shouted.

Kant stuck his head back around the rough plaster arch at the top of the stairs. 'What?'

'Let the girl go,' I said.

'Good one, boss.' He grinned, showing me his shit-coloured teeth.

Bloody Anne turned in her seat and saw what was going on. 'Enough, Corporal,' she growled, but he ignored her.

It made me angry, that he thought he could ignore Anne like that. She was a sergeant and he was only a corporal, although that sort of thing didn't matter much any more. Kant was a head taller than me and maybe thirty pounds heavier, but I didn't care. I knew that didn't matter either and, more to the point, Kant knew it too. There was a devil in me, and all my crew knew it.

'No,' I said, letting my voice fall into the flat tone that warned of harsh justice to come.

'You're joking,' Kant said, but he sounded uncertain now.

'Come here, Kant,' I said. 'You too, Brak.'

Spring rain blew against the closed shutters, loud in a room that had otherwise plunged into nervous silence. A smoky fire crackled in the grate. Kant and his fellow would-be rapist came back down the stairs, leaving the girl crying in a heap on the top step. She had maybe sixteen or seventeen years to her, no more than that, putting her at barely half my age.

4

I could feel Anne and the rest of my crew looking at me. Men set down their tankards and bottles to watch. Even Fat Luka put his cup down, and it took a lot to stop him drinking. The crew knew something had been ill done, and when something was ill done in my eyes there was *always* harsh justice.

Bloody Anne was giving me a wary look now. Sir Eland the false knight just stood there sneering at everyone like he always did, but he was watching too. Billy the Boy was halfway to drunk already, but then he was only twelve so I supposed I had to let him off not being able to hold his beer. Grieg and Cookpot and Black Billy and the others just watched.

I met Kant's eyes and pointed at a spot on the boards in front of me. 'Come here,' I said. 'Right now.'

A log popped in the grate, making Simple Sam jump. Kant glared at me but he came, and Brak followed in his wake like a little boat trailing behind a war galleon.

'Would you like someone to fuck, Kant?' I asked him.

Kant was bigger than me, huge and ugly. Kant the Cunt, the crew called him, but never to his face. His chain-mail byrnie strained across his massive barrel chest over a jerkin of boiled leather. The scars on his face stood out livid and red as he started to get angry right back at me. I remembered how he had earned those scars at Abingon, forcing his way through the breach in the west wall when the citadel fell. Kant had led his squad over a mound of corpses, and never mind the archers waiting for them. He had taken an arrow through the cheek for his trouble. He had kept fighting, had Kant, spitting blood and teeth as he swung his mace into this head, that shoulder, those balls, crushing and bludgeoning and forcing his way forward. Bludgeon and force, that was how Kant the Cunt made his way in the world.

Kant was a war hero.

But then so was I.

'Course I want someone to fuck,' Kant said. 'Who don't?'

'You want to fuck, Kant?' I asked him again, and this time my voice went soft and quiet.

All the crew had been with me long enough to know what *that* tone meant. That tone meant the devil was awake and there was harsh justice coming for sure, and soon. Kant was drunk, though – not booze drunk but rape drunk, power drunk – and I knew he wasn't going to take a telling. Not this time.

'Yeah, I fucking do,' he said.

I didn't like Kant. I never had liked Kant, truth be told, but Kant was a good soldier. In Abingon I had needed good soldiers. Now I needed good men, and the Lady only knows the two ain't necessarily the same thing.

'Come here,' I said again. 'If you want to fuck, come here and fuck me.'

I held Kant's gaze. I wouldn't have put it past him, under different circumstances. If I had been some other man, some peasant lad, I doubted Kant would have been picky. A hole was a hole as far as he was concerned, and if he could stick his cock in it then it made him happy.

'Tomas . . .' Anne started to say, but it was too late for that and I think she knew it.

The Weeping Women hung heavy on my hips. They were a matched pair of beautifully crafted shortswords that I had looted from a dead colonel after the last battle of Abingon. I had named them Remorse and Mercy.

My crew knew all too well what the Weeping Women could do in my hands.

'You didn't ought to force yourself on lasses. It's not right,' Black Billy said. He nudged the man beside him with his elbow. 'Ain't that so, Grieg?'

Grieg grunted but said nothing. He was a man of few words, was Grieg.

'Lady's sake,' Brak muttered, scuffing his foot at the beery sawdust underfoot while Kant tried to stare me out. 'We was only having a bit of fun, like.'

'Does she look like she's having fun?' I asked.

Kant saw me point to the girl, he saw my eyes and hand move away from him, and he took his moment. I had thought he might, for all that I hoped he had more sense. He was quick, was Kant, and he was brutal, but he wasn't any kind of clever.

He lunged at me, his hand going to his belt and coming up with a long knife. I dipped and turned, and swept Remorse out of her scabbard and across his throat in a vicious backhand cut. Kant dropped in a great spray of red foam, bubbling and cursing as he fell.

I could feel Billy the Boy watching me.

'Good fucking deal,' he said, his voice not yet broken, and he drained his tankard.

'Fuck,' Brak said.

'That's what you wanted, Brak,' I said. 'The offer's still open. My arse, if you can come and take it.'

He looked at me, and at Kant bleeding out on the floor and at the length of dripping steel in my hand. He shook his head, and that was as I had expected. Brak was Kant's second, but he had barely twenty years to him and he was only tough when he had the big man in front of him.

'Nah,' he said at last. 'I ain't in the mood no more.'

'Didn't think so,' I said.

I wondered where this left Brak now in the pecking order of my crew. Truth be told, I didn't care. That was Brak's problem, not mine. Staying boss was my problem – how they sorted out their own hierarchy was up to them.

Matters of rank and the chain of command had gone to the whores after Abingon, but I had been the company priest. That put me in charge of the crew by default after the captain died of his wounds on the way home. That and I was used to leading men, and no one else was.

Simple Sam stood looking down at Kant for a long moment, then gave him a hefty kick as though checking to make sure he was dead.

He was.

'What's the colonel going to say about this, Mr Piety?' Sam asked.

'We ain't got a colonel any more, Sam lad,' I told him. 'We've been disbanded, remember?'

'What's disbanded?'

'Means they've stopped paying us,' Anne grumbled.

She was right. Our regiment had gone from being three thousand paid, organised murderers to three thousand unpaid, disorganised murderers.

That had gone about as well as might be expected.

'Bollocks,' Sam muttered, and kicked Kant again to show us what he thought of that.

The Lady only knew what had happened to our colonel, but the rest of us had stayed together in a loose mass of independent crews as a matter of habit more than anything else. There were nearly three thousand men camped in and around this town, but no one was really in charge any more. No, I wouldn't be getting court-martialled for killing Kant. Not these days.

I looked down for a moment and gave thanks to Our Lady of Eternal Sorrows for my victory. She hadn't guided my hand, I knew that much. Our Lady doesn't help. Not ever. She doesn't answer prayers or grant boons or give a man anything at all, however hard he might pray for it. The best you can hope for from Her is that She doesn't take your life today. Maybe tomorrow, aye, but not today. That's as good as it gets, and the rest is up to you.

She was a goddess for soldiers and no mistake.

'Well done,' Sir Eland the false knight said in my ear. 'You've kept the men this time, at least.'

He was a sneaky bastard, was Sir Eland. I hadn't known he was there until I felt his hot breath on the back of my neck. I turned and looked at him, carefully keeping a bland expression on my face. Sir Eland had been the captain's champion, this man who called himself a knight. He was nothing of the sort, I knew. He was just a thug who had stolen himself a warhorse and enough ill-fitting armour to carry off the lie. He was about as noble as my morning shit. All the same, he was dangerous and he needed watching.

'Sir Eland,' I said, and forced myself to smile at him. 'How gratifying to have your support.'

I turned away before he could say anything else. I could feel his eyes on my back, boring through my hooded black priest's robe and my chain-mail byrnie and boiled leather jerkin and linen shirt all the way to my heart. Oh, yes, Sir Eland the false knight would stab me in the back the first chance he got. It was my job to not give him that chance. That was what it was, to be a leader of men like these.

At least Anne hated him as much as I did, that was something. I knew

8

she had my back; she always did. I made my way to where Billy the Boy was sitting. Kant was still lying on the floorboards in a spreading pool of his own blood, but no one seemed to be in any sort of hurry to move him. I sat down at the scarred trestle table across from Billy and nodded to him.

The lad looked up, light catching the smooth planes of a face that had never seen a razor. A slow smile crept across his moist, young lips.

'Speak, in the name of Our Lady,' he said.

'I killed Kant,' I confessed to him, keeping my voice low.

'It was his time to cross the river,' Billy said. 'The Lady knows Kant needed killing and She forgives you. In Our Lady's name.'

He'd needed killing, all right. No one would miss Kant, I knew that much.

Billy was only twelve years old, but he wore mail and a shortsword like a man. I might be a priest, but Billy was my confessor, strange as that may seem. I bowed my head before the child.

'In Our Lady's name,' I repeated.

Billy the Boy reached out and brushed the cowl back from my face to put a hand on my forehead. It looked ridiculous, I knew, me giving confession to this child-man. I was the priest there, not him, but Billy was special. Billy was touched by Our Lady, all there knew that. That was the only reason the crew left a young lad like him alone. I remembered when Billy first joined us, an orphan refugee from the sack of Messia. The regiment had been recruiting by then, replacing its losses, and had accepted Billy, even young as he was.

Sir Eland had taken a shine to him at once. He liked lads, did Sir Eland. He tried to get into Billy's bedroll one night, to have his way with him. To this day, I don't know exactly what happened, and to be sure Sir Eland was never likely to raise the matter in conversation. All I remembered was a campfire by the roadside. I'd had the watch that hour, and the rest of the crew were curled up asleep in their blankets as close to the fire as they could get. I remembered a sudden shrill scream in the darkness.

It hadn't been Billy who'd screamed, but Sir Eland. Whatever he had tried to do to Billy – and I suppose that was his business really – his attention hadn't been wanted. Billy had done . . . something, and that was the end of it. That was how the pecking order got worked out, and no one ever mentioned it again. The crew adapted and moved on, and after that Billy the Boy was one of us.

The one touched by the goddess.

'Thank you, Billy,' I said.

He shrugged, indifferent. So simply was atonement given. There was no expression at all in his flat brown eyes, and Lady only knew what went on in his head.

I got up and looked around the room, my gaze taking in the rest of the crew. They were drinking and laughing and cursing once more, throwing dice and stuffing their faces with whatever Cookpot had found in the kitchen. At some point the girl had run away, and I thought that was wise of her. Simple Sam was being noisily sick in a corner. I went to join Bloody Anne at her table. All was well.

Right up until several armed men kicked the door in, anyway.

'Fuck!' Brak shouted.

It was his favourite word, I had to give him that.

I sat quiet and stared at the newcomers as my crew drew steel. I knew the one who led them, but I hadn't thought to see *him* again. I kept my hands on the table in front of me, well away from the hilts of the Weeping Women.

Six men shouldered their way inside with the rain blowing in behind them. Their leader shoved the hood of his sodden cloak back from his face and showed me a savage grin.

'Fuck a nun, Tomas Piety!' he said.

I stood up.

'Brother,' I said.

Chapter 2

My brother Jochan looked around him and roared with laughter. He was four years younger than me but taller and thinner, with wild hair and a three-day growth of beard on his prominent, pointed chin.

'Fucking priest?' he said, staring at my robes. 'How are you a fucking priest? If I'm any judge, half your crew are puking shitfaced and you've fucking killed one of them yourself.'

Thanks to the mercy of Our Lady, Jochan wasn't a judge. Still, I had to admit he had the right of it this time. I showed him a smile that I didn't feel.

'Those are the times we live in,' I said.

'Fucking right,' Jochan agreed, and turned to his crew. 'Lads, this is my big brother Tomas. I ain't seen him since the war started but he's a fucking priest now, apparently. Still he's all right, despite that. His boys won't mind sharing, will they?'

That last was pointed at me, of course. I shrugged.

'Be our guests,' I said. 'Ain't like we paid for it.'

If my crew could feel the tension between my brother and me they had the sense not to show it.

Jochan's lads started helping themselves to beer and food, while he came and joined me and Bloody Anne at our table. I didn't know any of his crew. Jochan and I had ended up in different regiments, and if he was here now I could only assume he had led his handful of men cross country from wherever they were supposed to be to join us.

'Oi!' he shouted. 'Woman! Bring us beer.'

Anne's head snapped around in anger, but he didn't mean her.

One of Jochan's men came over with tankards for us, then went to rejoin the others. He was as rough-looking as the rest of them and there was nothing remotely womanly about the fellow, to my mind. I raised an eyebrow at Jochan.

'Woman?' I asked.

'Aye, that's Will the Woman,' Jochan said. 'We call him that because every time Will kills a man he weeps afterward. Mind you, he's killed so many fucking men it ain't funny no more, but you know how a name sticks.'

I did.

'He must have wept a lot, at Abingon,' Anne said.

'Aye,' Jochan said, and fell silent.

We had the war in common, us brothers, if little enough else. The war and the memories of it, of home before it and of childhood things long past and best forgotten. We were nothing alike, me and Jochan. We never had been. We had worked together before the war, but I wouldn't have called us friends. My aunt always told me that I didn't feel enough, but to my mind Jochan always felt far too much. Perhaps between us we made a whole man. I wouldn't know. That was a philosophical question, I supposed, and this was no time for philosophy.

I looked across the table into my brother's eyes, and in that moment I realised what the war had done to him. Jochan had always been wild, but there was a feral quality to his stare now that I hadn't seen before. I could almost see the flare of the cannon in his pupils, the clouds of dust from falling walls rolling across the whites of his eyes into corners that were as red as the rivers of blood we had waded through. Whatever little sanity Jochan possessed before the war, he had left it in the dust of Abingon.

'Brother,' I said, and reached out a hand to him across the rough tabletop.

Jochan lurched to his feet and drained his tankard in a long, shuddering swallow, spilling a good deal of it down the front of his rusty mail. He turned and hurled the empty vessel into the fire.

'What now?' he bellowed. 'What now for the glorious Piety boys, reunited at the outskirts of Hell?'

He leaped up onto the table and kicked my tankard aside, spraying beer carelessly across Kant's cooling body. He'd have looked drunk to anyone who didn't know him, but Jochan wasn't drunk. Not yet, anyway. Jochan was Jochan and this was just his way. He'd never been quite right in the head.

'What now?' he roared, arms outstretched as he turned in a circle before the assembled men.

His own crew were obviously used to this sort of thing, whereas my lads watched him with a mixture of suspicion and barely concealed amusement. Best they keep it concealed, I thought. One thing you didn't do was laugh at Jochan.

Simple Sam obviously didn't get that note, not that he could read anyway. He sniggered. I remembered this sort of thing from the school-rooms of our shared, lost youth. I remembered how some of the other boys had laughed at Jochan, once.

Only once.

No one laughed at Jochan a second time. Not ever.

He launched himself off the table without a word, without a warning, and ploughed into Simple Sam. Sam was a big lad, but he was slow in body as well as mind, and Jochan caught him full in the chest with his elbow and slammed him back into the wall beside the fireplace. He had Sam on the floor a second later, and then the beating started. His fist rose and fell in a merciless rhythm.

I couldn't let that pass, brother or not. Bloody Anne began to rise, to make something of it. I put a hand on her arm to tell her to be still. Sergeant she might be, but Jochan was my brother and that made him my problem, not hers.

'No,' I said, in that special voice even Jochan recognised.

He knew what harsh justice looked like, and he'd felt it once or twice himself when we were young.

He let Sam go and turned to face me, blood dripping from his knuckles as he stood up. 'No, is it, war hero?' he sneered. 'You think you can order me about? What's your big fucking plan then, Tomas?'

He was testing me, I knew that. Testing the limits of that harsh justice, with his men around him and mine with me. I'd like to say no one wanted a bloodbath, but I wasn't sure that was true. Even though we outnumbered them better than two to one, I didn't think Jochan realised that, or that he would care even if he did. I knew I didn't want blood, though, not now. That wouldn't help anyone.

'We go home,' I said. 'We go home with my crew, and yours, and any of the rest of the regiment who'll follow us. We go home and pick up where we left off.'

'Pick up *what*?' Jochan demanded. 'The county is on its fucking knees, Tomas. There's plague. There's famine. There's no fucking work. And we *won* this fucking war?'

'Aye, we won it,' I said. 'We won, and Aunt Enaid has been keeping the family business for us while we've been away.'

'Away?' he roared at me. 'We've been in *Hell*! We come home as devils, tainted by what we've seen.'

I looked at him, at the tears in his mad eyes.

Jochan had always felt too much, and I not enough. If the war had changed me I had noticed it little enough. Running the business back home, running a crew in Abingon, it was all the same to me save that the food was better back home and there was more drink to be had. I spread my hands in a gesture of conciliation.

'You have a place at my side, Jochan,' I told him. 'You're my brother; you'll always have a place. Come home with me.'

He spat on the floor in empty defiance, then sniffed and looked down at his boots.

'Aye,' he said, after a moment. 'Aye, Tomas.'

He had always been like this, after his rages left him. Quiet, contrite. Sometimes tearful, like now. I could see he was fighting to hold that back in front of his men, and that was wise of him. Will the Woman might get away with weeping among that lot, but I didn't think Jochan would. Not if he wanted to stay the boss of them, anyway.

I looked at Simple Sam, sitting half unconscious in front of the fireplace with blood streaming from his broken nose and one eye already swollen shut. Anne got up and handed him a rag for his nose, but held her peace about what had happened. Sam had been lucky, all things considered. He wouldn't have been the first man Jochan had beaten to death with his fists.

So there we were, the Piety boys.

I had been intending to return home anyway, with my crew and any others I could raise from what was left of the regiment, return home and reclaim what was mine. Jochan's lads would follow him, I was sure, and in time they would become *my* lads.

I might well need them. Aunt Enaid was keeping the family business for us, I had told Jochan. I hoped that was true, but I wasn't prepared to bet on it. I wouldn't have bet a clipped copper on it, truth be told, not with the state of what I had seen so far since we returned. That was only in the countryside, mind. The Lady only knew what the city looked like by now.

'Good,' I said. 'That's good, Jochan. Have another beer, why don't you? There's plenty.'

There *was* plenty, and that was good too. There was famine, as I have written, and the land south of here had been foraged to within an inch of its life. This inn, though, this nothing little country inn in the middle of this nothing little market town, this place still had barrels in the cellar and stringy meat and a few root vegetables in the kitchen. That meant we were ahead of the main march of the army, and for that I gave thanks to Our Lady.

I sat back in my chair, thinking on it while the boys drank themselves silly all around me. After a while Bloody Anne joined me again, a fresh tankard in each hand. She put them down on the table and gave me a look. Anne wasn't as drunk as the others, perhaps wasn't drunk at all. It was hard to tell, with her.

She was my second, in my eyes anyway, for all that Sir Eland assumed that role was his. I didn't know how much I could trust Anne, not really, but I couldn't trust Sir Eland at all. Oh, I would trust Anne with my life on the battlefield, make no mistake. I had done in fact, many times, and had been pleased to call her my friend. But now we were almost home and business was calling, that might be a different matter.

'Have a drink, boss,' she said.

She pushed one of the tankards toward me. I nodded and took a swallow to say thank you even though I didn't really want it.

'Did you notice what this town was called, Anne?' I asked her.

She shrugged. 'Someone's ford,' she said. 'Harrow's Ford? Herron's Ford? Something like that.'

'Anything strike you as queer about it?'

Again, she shrugged. 'Market town,' she said. 'All the same.'

She was right; they *were* all the same. Burned out or starved out or everyone dead from the plague, every single one we had come across on our long, slow march back home. Until this one.

'This one isn't,' I said. 'This one's not dead.'

'Soon will be,' she said. 'There's three thousand hungry men here.'

She had a point there, I had to allow.

Those were the times we lived in.

We might as well make the most of it while the inn was still there.

Chapter 3

I woke up the next morning, my face pillowed on my arms on the table, stiff and sore and with an aching head. I sat up and swallowed spit that tasted of stale beer. Most of the crew were still lying where they had passed out, all but Bloody Anne. She was sitting by the door, picking at her nails with the point of her dagger and obviously keeping watch. She was a good soldier, was Anne.

Someone had to be.

'Morning, boss,' she said.

I nodded to her and got up, heading out the back for a piss. The kitchen had been ransacked; all the cupboards opened and anything fit to eat already taken. Cookpot knew how to give a place a thorough foraging, I had to give him that.

I stood in the muddy yard behind the inn, pissing into a thin morning rain. It was cold, and everything seemed to have taken on the colour of fresh shit. This town might not have been dead yet, but I could see now that it wasn't far off, and the arrival of our regiment would surely be helping it along its way. I looked up at the overcast sky and guessed it was an hour past dawn.

I laced my britches back up and leaned against the door for a moment, thinking. We were three, maybe four days' march from Ellinburg. The regiment would break up here, I knew. This was farming country and most of them were farm boys, with land and wives and pigs and sheep to get back to. If they were lucky, those things might even still be there waiting for them.

Jochan and I, we were city boys, the same as Fat Luka and Cookpot. We had grown up together, the four of us, been in school together. Those two knew what my business was, and before the war Luka had even helped out now and again. He was a good man, handy in a pinch. He might be fat but he was strong with it and he could fight. Lady, but could he fight. Cookpot couldn't, not worth a spit, but he could steal and he could cook, and those things made him useful too. In a regiment where almost everyone could fight and hardly anyone could cook, it had made him very useful indeed. I had been glad to have him in our company then, and I was glad to have him in my crew now.

I wondered what the rest of them would make of the city, Sir Eland and Brak and Stefan, Bloody Anne and Borys and Nik the Knife and the others. Sir Eland said he'd been to Dannsburg, to court even, although that part was about as believable as him being a knight at all. Court was where the queen lived, this queen we had gone through Hell for, and they didn't welcome the likes of Sir Eland there.

I didn't even know what the queen looked like.

All the same, Sir Eland had spun a yarn you could almost half believe if you were drunk and stupid, so I supposed he must at least have seen a city somewhere along the line.

Not Ellinburg, though. He wouldn't have been there. His accent spoke of the south and the west, and we had been going north for weeks now. North was home, far away from the border. Away from the war. Our regiment had been founded there, among those cold, wet hills, and there it would break apart again. I didn't know what would happen to them. Those lads who thought they were going back to their old lives were in for a hard surprise, so far as I could see. They'd find their wives starved or dead of the plague or run off with anyone who had food to give them, most like. They'd find their sheep fucked and their pigs eaten and their lands burned.

Those were the times we lived in.

We had won the war, but at what cost? The queen had beggared the country to do it, and trade had died out and then the weather turned and the crops failed and the plague came. A superstitious man might say those things were related, but I wouldn't know. I was a priest, not a mystic, and Our Lady gave no answers.

I pushed the cowl back from my head and ran my hands through my hair, letting the rain dampen it. It felt good just to stand there, to breathe the fresh morning air, to feel the rain on my face and listen to it pattering into the puddles. I remembered days of choking dust and tearing thirst, the bellow of the cannon and the acrid fumes of blasting powder.

The rain felt good on my skin, clean and fresh. There had been nothing clean or fresh at Abingon, nothing but fire and dust and shit and death, men dying of wounds and burns and the bloody flux. What we would have given for a cool rain, there.

What we would have given . . .

I felt a touch on my shoulder and whipped around. Remorse flashed from her scabbard and I laid steel against flesh. I had the blade against the side of Jochan's neck before I knew it was him. He just stared at me, the fires of my memories reflecting from his haunted eyes.

I stood there for a moment, my heart pounding and my sword at my brother's throat. A horse whinnied, somewhere in another street, and broke the spell. I sheathed the blade and pulled my cowl back up over my wet hair.

'What?' I said.

Jochan shook his head. He said nothing as he walked past me and out into the yard where the rain was falling harder now. He unlaced and took his piss out in the open, careless of the weather or anything else.

'Home,' he said, when he was done. He laced up and looked at me, the rain dragging down his wild hair. 'We're going home, then. You said Aunt Enaid has been holding the business?'

I shrugged. 'She told me she would,' I said. 'We'll see, won't we? When we get there. You and me, Jochan, and your crew and mine.'

'And if she fucking ain't?'

I gave him a look. 'Then we'll have two crews, and we'll take back what was ours.'

He nodded. That was the answer he wanted to hear. Jochan wasn't done fighting, I could see that much. The enemy might have been defeated, but that thing inside that drove him, that violence of the soul our da had left him with, that would never be overcome. We were different in that respect. Our da had left me with a cold devil inside, but Jochan's was hot and wild. He started to laugh. I don't know what at, but he laughed, standing there in that yard that was more horse-shit than mud.

'The lads are going to fucking love Ellinburg, ain't they?' he said.

I shrugged. I had to allow that they wouldn't, but they'd get used to it. City life had its advantages, after all, and it would be my job to make them see that.

'Fucking tell me something, Tomas,' he said, after a moment.

It was pouring now, and I took a half step back into the open doorway to keep the worst of it off me. I didn't think Jochan had even noticed the rain that was now plastering his wild hair to his face in wet straggles.

'What's that?' I asked him.

'How are you a fucking priest?'

'I said the words,' I told him. 'I took the vow.'

'And that's all there is to it?'

'Pretty much,' I said.

The ministry of Our Lady of Eternal Sorrows had little in the way of doctrine, or scripture. She wasn't a goddess for learned men, for mystics or merchants or politicians. She was a goddess for soldiers, and most soldiers can't even read.

It's funny how people always think soldiers worship a god of war. Do we fuck as like. The knights had one, of course. Real knights, that is, not frauds like our Sir Eland. They had an iron god of glory and honour, with a big long lance and a mighty beast between his legs. Us conscripts don't want glory or honour. We just want to not die today. That was what Our Lady offered, if you were lucky and you fought your balls off.

That was all we had, all we could hope for in this world.

Jochan shook his head, his wet hair showering droplets of water into the falling rain. 'Why?'

I shrugged. 'Why not? The company needed a priest, once ours crossed the river with an arrow through his neck. A priest listens to people. A priest leads people. I can do that.'

'But you don't *care* about people,' Jochan challenged, taking a step toward me. 'You never fucking have!'

'No one ever said you had to,' I said. 'Listen and lead, the captain said. He never said care.'

Jochan laughed so hard he blew snot out of his left nostril. 'Fuck a nun, Tomas,' he said. 'You, a fucking priest?'

'Aye,' I said. 'Me, a priest.'

He looked at me then, sensing the change in my tone. I wasn't angry with him, but he was close to saying something that I couldn't let pass. I could tell he knew it too.

He pushed his sodden hair back from his face and shouldered past me into the inn without another word. I let myself relax against the doorway once he was gone, just breathing in the clean smell of the rain.

I was going to have to watch Jochan.

I gave him a minute or two and then followed him back into the common room. Most of the boys were awake now, his crew and mine, and there was an uneasy divide down the middle of the room. I strode straight into that empty space and stood with a wall behind me where I could see both sides of the matter. Jochan was sitting with his own lads, I noticed, dripping wet onto the floor.

'Right,' I said. 'Have a listen, my boys. For those as don't know me, my name is Tomas Piety. I'm Jochan here's big brother, and I'm a priest of Our Lady.'

I paused for a moment to let that sink in with the two or three of Jochan's lads who had been too drunk or too stupid to realise it last night.

'The war's done,' I went on. 'We won, for all that it doesn't feel like it. We won and now we're nothing, disbanded and unwanted. Well, I say fuck that.'

I paused again, watching the nods and listening to the grunts of approval from both sides of the room. I hadn't broached this with my own crew yet, but it seemed like now was the time. They might as well all hear it at once. The regiment would break up in this town, as I have written. Most of them would want to be off back to whatever was left of their past lives, but I needed to keep my crew with me. My crew and Jochan's as well, if I could.

'Three or four days north of here is Ellinburg,' I said. 'We grew up there, me and Jochan, and Fat Luka and Cookpot too. I've got a business in Ellinburg, a good one. Good money to be made. Lady knows the army don't want you no more, but I do. I'm no noble, to be looking down my nose at you, and I haven't always been a priest. The army made me that, but I came from the same place you did. My da was a bricklayer, and I was a bricklayer's 'prentice. That was until I decided breaking my back carrying a hod to build rich folks' houses was no way to live. Those who follow me to Ellinburg will have jobs when they get there, food in their bellies, and money in their pockets. Does that sound good, lads?'

I saw nods all around the room, nods from everyone but Sir Eland. He was just watching me, I noticed, his eyes narrow and weaselly. It would have felt like justice to kill Sir Eland, right then. I made myself ignore him, and carried on.

'Good,' I said. 'I welcome you all, my crew and my brother's. If you're with me, that pleases Our Lady and it pleases me. If you ain't, there's no bad feelings but the road's out there and you know the way back south. Best be going.'

I watched them, and nobody moved toward the door. That gave me just over twenty men, all told. Part of me wished Sir Eland had taken up his stolen shield and ridden off on his stolen warhorse, but he just sat there looking at me with a mug of morning beer in front of him. I nodded.

'Good,' I said. 'Have a drink and a piss and be ready to march in an hour.'

Chapter 4

We rode into Ellinburg three days later, as the sun was going down.

Jochan was at my right hand on his skinny rowan gelding, Bloody Anne at my left on her grey mare and Sir Eland behind on his stolen warhorse, leading a column of nineteen men on foot. The gate guards eyed us suspiciously as we approached the city walls at the south gate, but soldiers returning from war could hardly be turned away. Certainly not when they were led by a robed priest, they couldn't. The sound of our horses' hooves echoed in the gatehouse tunnel that cut through the wall, and then we were past the gate and into the city proper.

The smell hit me like a fist in the face. Ellinburg is an industrial city, home to tanneries and smelting works and forges beyond counting. The river that ran along the east side of the city was a polluted nightmare of effluent from the factories that lined its bank. I had grown up here, and yet during the three years of the war I had still managed to forget how it smelled. I patted my mare's glossy black neck to calm her. I had been given her by the captain when I took my holy orders. She was no city horse, and I could tell the noise and the smell were bothering her.

I glanced back over my shoulder at the column of men behind us. Fat Luka had a big grin on his face and Cookpot was staring with wide eyes in his round face, drinking in the familiar sights. Two or three of the other lads had gone a bit green, and one of Jochan's country boys was actually bent over and vomiting into the gutter.

I smiled. 'Welcome to Old Reekie,' I said. 'Welcome to Ellinburg.'

They didn't look too welcomed, most of them. Jochan and me, Fat

Luka and Cookpot, we were home. The rest of them looked like they were seeing the second worst thing of their lives. The very worst, of course, had been Abingon. We all had Abingon in common and that was what had forged the bond. That was what held us together. Men who have been through Hell together tend to stay together, if they can. The shepherds and pig farmers of the regiment might have left but these lads, these ones who had been made of the sort of stuff that held men together under Jochan's chaotic leadership or under my cold harsh justice, these were lads who would stay together through anything.

I hoped so, anyway.

We rode out from the long shadow of the walls and I looked around properly. The more I saw, the more I lost faith in the thought that Aunt Enaid might have kept things in her grasp for the last three years.

Ellinburg had never been a handsome city, it was true. This was no capital, and there were few grand buildings here. There was no palace, or great library, or theatre, or house of magicians, or any of the other things Sir Eland said he had seen in Dannsburg. If he had ever been there.

All the same, Ellinburg had been prosperous, before the war. There was a grand Great Temple of All Gods on the hill at the top of Trader's Row. That still stood, at least, but now half of the shops were boarded up, and I could see broken windows and alleys mounded with decaying refuse. There were beggars in the streets, far more than there should have been, displaying stumps of missing limbs or bandaged eyes to uncaring passers-by. Too many looked like veterans for comfort.

We turned our column off the main street and headed down into the Stink, the warren of slums that lay close to the river and the tanneries. This was our neighbourhood, this was home, and it was well named. The stench we rode into was like a living thing, cloying and vile. That was normal, but down here there had been life too. The narrow streets of close-packed homes had been alive with wives scrubbing their steps, unwashed children chasing each other and whooping and shouting in the gutters. Now there was barely a soul in sight, and those we did see looked starved to the edge of death. The streets smelled of bitterness and despair. It seemed every fourth door had the sign for plague on it in cheap, faded white paint.

'Lady's sake, Tomas,' Jochan said beside me. 'What the fuck happened?'

I squeezed my eyes shut and immediately I saw the flames leaping in the streets of Abingon, the diseased, starving people being dragged out of their homes and put to the sword. I remembered mounds of corpses shovelled into mass graves by soldiers with scarves tied over their mouths and eyes gone numb to horror.

'They brought it back with them,' I said, thinking of the veterans begging near the city gates. 'The wounded and the maimed. The plague followed them home from Abingon and Our Lady's face was turned to the south at the time.'

Jochan looked at me like he thought I was mad. Perhaps he did, but then it takes one madman to recognise another.

'If Aunt Enaid was running the business she'd have fucking sorted this,' Jochan said. 'These are *our* streets, Tomas.'

'How do you suppose she'd have sorted the fucking plague?' I snapped, as close to angry now as I dared let myself get with him.

'Aye, well,' he muttered. 'You know what I mean. There should be . . . I dunno. There should be food, at least. And doctors. And . . .'

He trailed off, and I knew he had remembered that every doctor who had less than sixty years to him had been forced into the army. Most of them died of plague in Abingon, and the country was the poorer for it.

'These are our streets,' he said again, and he sounded helpless now.

I nodded. That they were.

I owned a tavern half a mile away, and I led the column there. It was called the Tanner's Arms and it had been a fine old place, before the war. It wasn't looking so fine now, though. The windows had been the new sort – thick glass in square panes instead of the little leaded diamonds of older buildings – but now half of them were broken and boarded over. The sign was hanging at an angle and, most worryingly, there was no one on the door. All the men with less than forty years who could stand upright and hold a spear at the same time had been conscripted, of course, but Alfread had still been a fierce one at fifty-two and I had left him on the door when we went away. He wasn't there now.

I dismounted and hitched my horse to the dry, splintery rail outside, remembering when it had been smooth and gleaming with oil. The other three riders followed suit and I motioned Jochan, Anne and Sir Eland to come with me.

'The rest of you stay out here, for now,' I told the assembled crews. 'You'll know if we need you. Luka, you're boss.'

The fat man nodded and hooked his thumbs self-importantly into the top of his straining belt. I didn't really want Eland with me, but I wanted Fat Luka in charge outside, and if I had put him over the false knight there would have been trouble about it. A leader has to think of these things. Besides, Eland looked the part well enough in his stolen armour.

I led the three of them into the tavern. Any hope I might have had of seeing Alfread or Aunt Enaid or any familiar face behind the bar died as soon as the door swung closed behind us. The place was dim with half the windows boarded up and only a few lanterns lit against the gloom. The fireplace was cold despite the chill of the early evening. A man looked up at us from behind the bar, and his face went pale as I met his eyes.

'Who the fuck are you?' I demanded in the soft, flat tone of danger.

There was a big brass ship's bell hanging over the bar, something I had acquired from a merchant sailor years ago, and now this man who was standing behind my bar lunged for it and pulled the rope hard, making it clang fit to raise the gods.

Jochan lost his temper all at once. He picked up a chair and hurled it over the bar and into the man's face. The fellow went down cursing, smashing bottles and glasses as he fell. A door at the back opened and six ruffians ran in with knives and cudgels in their hands.

We drew steel, and Bloody Anne put two fingers to her mouth and whistled loud. The front door burst open as Fat Luka led his first charge, and a moment later there were nineteen men at our backs. The strangers froze, wild-eyed, as they stared at my crew spread out around them.

I took a step forward. 'My name is Tomas Piety,' I said, 'and you're in my fucking tavern.'

'I am Dondas Alman,' one of them said, 'and this is my tavern now.'

I looked at his men, then very deliberately turned in a slow circle to look at mine. Once I was sure I had his full attention, I smiled at him.

'Can you not count?' I asked him. 'This is *my* tavern.'

'I know people,' he said, and that sounded too much like a promise for comfort. 'I know important people.'

'We fucking *are* important people!' Jochan bellowed. 'We're the Pious Men, and we've come home!'

Chapter 5

Dondas Alman and his boys weren't stupid enough to try to fight us. We threw them out into the street, and then Fat Luka took half a dozen lads into the back and threw all of their stuff out into the street after them.

'There's a stable yard round the back,' I told Luka. 'Bring our horses off the road before it gets full dark and give them a rubdown and some oats.'

He did as he was told, and I sat at the bar with a glass of brandy and watched the room. The Pious Men. That was a name I hadn't heard since before the war. That was what we had called ourselves when we were up-and-coming young men, Jochan and me. I couldn't remember now which one of us first thought of it, but when your family name is Piety you might as well make something out of it. I'd never thought to become a priest as well, but it completed the picture nicely.

Once Alman and his meagre crew were out of sight I let the lads loose behind the bar. I hadn't paid for the stock, after all, and I thought some of them probably needed a few drinks to help them get over their first sight and smell of Ellinburg.

The tavern was a good size, with a kitchen and three storerooms out the back that would be large enough to sleep the boys, and a couple of rooms upstairs in the loft space too. I reckoned one of them would do for me. It's not like anyone in the crew was used to luxury.

Someone had got the fire going and lit a few lamps, restoring a little of the old cheer to the Tanner's Arms. I caught Bloody Anne's eye and motioned her toward me.

'Round up four lads and keep them sober,' I said. 'I don't want those fools coming back in the night and finding everyone passed out drunk.'

Anne nodded and turned away without a word. She walked across the room, picking men and taking the drinks from their hands with short, hard words. Anne had been a sergeant, and the boys in my crew respected her. I noticed she didn't choose any of Jochan's crew, and I thought that was wise. I didn't know them, and that meant I didn't trust them. Not yet, anyway. It looked like Bloody Anne thought the same way.

I poured myself another brandy and sat alone at the bar, watching the revelry. Jochan was drinking with his men, roaring with laughter, even louder than they were. We had different ways of leading men, Jochan and me.

I felt someone beside me and turned to see Billy the Boy staring at me.

'They're coming back,' he said.

I nodded. 'I guessed as much,' I said. 'When?'

Billy looked at my drink. 'Can I try that?'

I nodded again and poured a measure of brandy into a spare glass for him. He only had twelve years to him but he had fought in battles and he had killed men, so I didn't see why he shouldn't drink like a man too. He took a big gulp of the dark amber spirit and gasped, almost choking as it burned his throat.

'Do you like that, Billy?' I asked him.

'Beer's better,' he said.

'Then drink beer.'

'I just wanted to try it,' he said.

'And now you have. When will they come back?'

'Tonight,' Billy said. 'She didn't say when, exactly.'

She didn't say, exactly. Billy was touched by Our Lady and sometimes she spoke to him, or through him, or he thought she did anyway. Perhaps he was just mad, I wouldn't know, but he was right often enough that I wasn't about to reject the idea out of hand. He was *always* right, come to think on it. I reached across the bar and pulled the rope to ring the big brass bell.

'No more drinking,' I said when everyone turned to look at me. 'Those bloody fools will be back tonight, with their "important friends" no doubt. We need to be ready for a fight.'

'I'm always up for a fight!' Jochan bellowed, raising a bottle of brandy in his hand.

He took a long, deliberate swallow from the neck, as though to show me what he thought of my orders. His lads laughed. Mine didn't.

I couldn't let that pass, not now. Not when I needed them to be coming together, and Jochan seemed to be trying to keep them apart. We were brothers, after all, and we needed to stand as one on this.

I got to my feet. 'Listen,' I said. 'Most of you are new to the city, so you don't know how this works. We're the Pious Men. You're *all* Pious Men now. That means you do what I say, and you get rich. These are Pious Men streets, round here, and Pious Men businesses. I own taverns and boarding-houses and inns, racehorses and gambling houses and brothels and all the good fucking things in life. You can be a part of that, but you *do what I say*. Understand?'

Heads nodded, but not all of them. Sir Eland, I noticed, was just staring at me. Jochan was giving me that look of sullen resentment I knew too well, but I'd worry about him later. I met Sir Eland's eyes and held his gaze. He took his sweet time, obviously weighing his options, but eventually he nodded too.

'Good, that's settled then,' I said. 'Four-man watches, three-hour rotation. You know the drill, boys. It's just like the army. The rest of you get some sleep while you can.'

It was another three or four hours before they came, and by then I was dozing in a chair near the fire. The sound of shattering glass woke me. I opened my eyes in time to see something hurtle through the broken window and land in the middle of the tavern floor, fizzing.

'Flashstone!' I shouted, and dived off the chair and under a table.

That cry woke everyone, veterans all of them. A flashstone is like a hollow cannonball packed with blasting powder and nails. There's a fuse sticking out of it that you light, and then you throw the whole thing into a confined space. Most of us had used them in the war, and been on the receiving end of them too. I pulled the table over in front of me, putting a two-inch thickness of solid oak between me and the flashstone just in time.

It went off with an almighty noise, hurling shards of red-hot iron around the room and producing a choking cloud of acrid smoke. Someone screamed, hit by a flying chunk of metal, and then all Hell broke loose. The front door of the tavern exploded into splinters, and I could only guess that they'd put a charge of powder outside there as well. More smoke boiled across the room and flames licked at the door frame, lighting the face of Cookpot, who had been sitting nearest the entrance.

He went berserk.

I think only those who had not been at Abingon could fail to understand the effect that using blasting weapons on us would have. Cookpot wasn't even a fighter, not really. He had been in charge of stores and foraging and the cook fire, but he had been there. He had seen almost as much as the rest of us, and Lady knew he never wanted to see it again. The first of the attackers charged through the door, and Cookpot rammed his shortsword into the man's side with a bellow of tormented rage. He pulled the blade out and stabbed him again, and again. In that moment, Cookpot was back in Abingon.

'Breach!' Jochan roared, and then he was over the table where he had taken cover, an axe in his hand. 'Breach in the wall!'

Men stormed into the tavern over the body of the one Cookpot had stabbed, and Jochan met them with a bestial fury. We were all up now, steel flashing in the light of the fire in the grate and the other that was licking up the wooden door frame and trying to eat its way into the walls.

The Tanner's Arms was timber and daub at the front, and that fire could take with frightening ease if we didn't put it out soon. Smoke filled the room, and shouting, and the clash of blade against blade. I had the Weeping Women in my hands now and I slid into the battle beside my brother. I killed a man with a straight thrust of Mercy through his kidneys, then found myself driven back by a huge, red-bearded stranger with a battle-axe. I could only dodge and parry, unable to get inside the reach of his swings in the boiling, confused mass of fighting, cursing men. He forced me back almost to the bar before he went rigid, his face twisting in sudden shock. He dropped his axe and sagged to the floor with blood gushing from the inside of his thigh, and Billy the Boy grinned up at me.

'In Our Lady's name,' the lad said, a dagger dripping red in his hand.

Sir Eland ran a man through and kicked the corpse off the long blade of his sword. His eyes found mine across the room. Had he seen? Had he judged me weak, in that moment? I didn't know, but I would have to keep an even closer watch on him from now on.

The fire was threatening to take hold now, but we had won the fight. Jochan was holding the doorway, and all these *important people* were trapped inside the same as us. There were five of them on the ground, and eight still standing facing us. They slowly lowered their weapons in surrender.

'Put the blades down, all of you,' I told them. I pointed to a lad who couldn't have had more than eighteen years to him. 'You, come here.'

He dropped his shortsword and took a hesitant step toward me. I touched the point of Remorse to his throat.

'Kill the others,' I told the men.

It was butchery, but sometimes that's what harsh justice looks like. I held the lad in front of me at sword-point and met his terrified eyes with a level stare until all of his friends were dead on the ground.

'Now you,' I said, 'you I'll let go. You're going to go back to your boss, and you're going to tell him that the Pious Men are home from the war. If he sends any more fools into any more of my businesses, they won't come out again. You tell him Tomas Piety made that promise. You understand?'

He nodded, as much as he could with a sword under his chin.

'Kick him out,' I said.

Once the lad was gone into the night my boys set to putting the fire out, passing buckets down a line from the hand pump in the kitchen behind the bar. It was piped river water, too filthy to drink, but it served.

I stood in the sodden, smoky room and took stock. There were twelve men dead on the floor, and none of them were mine. Black Billy was holding a bloody rag to a wound in his bicep, the blood bright against his dark skin, but he'd live. One of Jochan's men didn't look too good, though – he was sitting slumped in a chair with both blood-slick hands clutching a cut in the top of his thigh. It wasn't in the killing place where Billy the Boy had got the axe man or he'd have been dead already, but it was close enough. His face was waxy pale and sweaty.

I went to him.

'What's your name?' I asked him.

'Hari,' he whispered.

'Keep the pressure on it, Hari.'

'There's metal sticking out of my leg,' he said. 'Please take it out.'

I shook my head. He'd been hit by a bit of the flashstone, and that meant the shard was in there good and deep. The lump of iron stuck in the wound was probably all that was keeping the rest of the blood in his leg, and taking it out would most likely have killed him.

'Leave it alone, and keep the pressure on it,' I told him.

I beckoned Fat Luka over to me.

'You remember old Doc Cordin, from Net Mender's Row?' I asked him in a quiet voice.

'Aye,' Luka said, trying hard not to look at Hari's leg.

'Right, go and find him and bring him here. Drag him out of his bed if you have to, but you bring him.'

Luka nodded and hurried out of the tavern. I sent Billy the Boy to find some rags to bind Hari's leg while we waited.

'Fuck a nun, can we have a fucking drink now?' Jochan shouted from behind the bar, and a couple of the lads cheered.

I ignored him the same way he was ignoring Hari. We had different ways of leading men. I looked at the bodies on the floor again. Only twelve of them, and the one I'd let go. They had obviously thought that their blasting powder would give them enough of an advantage to make up for the numbers, and no doubt they had expected to find us passed out drunk as well. I looked at Jochan, swigging from the neck of a brandy bottle. We would have been, I thought, if he had been the boss instead of me.

'We need to get rid of these bodies,' I said. 'Cookpot, you remember the short way to the river, don't you?'

Cookpot was staring blankly into space with a dazed look on his face.

He only came back to himself when I said his name a second time. He needed something to do, I realised. Something to bring his mind back from Abingon and into the here and now. After a moment he nodded.

'Through the alleys,' he said. 'There's steps down to the water.'

'That's right, Cookpot,' I said. 'I want you go and find a cart and hitch one of our horses to it. Not Sir Eland's monster, take mine or Anne's. Then I want you and Brak and Simple Sam to load these bodies into the cart and take them through those alleys and roll them down the steps into the river. Can you do that, Cookpot?'

He cleared his throat, licking his lips nervously. I didn't really think he could, but it would give him something to do. Once they had been shown the way, Brak and Simple Sam would take care of the rest of it anyway. Brak had never been one to be bothered by dead men, and nothing much of anything seemed to bother Sam.

'I can do that,' he said after a moment.

'Good lad,' I said. 'Best get on with it, then.'

Cookpot nodded again and headed out the back to the yard where Luka had stabled the horses. I knew there was a dray cart out there, to fetch the barrels behind the bar from the brew house. I'd let Cookpot find that by himself, and feel important for it. It would do him good.

I set a couple of the lads to boarding up the broken window and barricading what was left of the doorway. It would need replacing in the morning, but anything would do for now.

Fat Luka came back while Brak and Sam were dragging the bodies out of the tavern to the waiting cart, and he had Doc Cordin with him. Cordin was only sort of a doctor, more of a barber-surgeon really, and he had seventy years to him if he had a day. All the same, he knew how to clean and dress a wound. I'd seen him cut a crossbow bolt out of a man before; I couldn't think a shard from a flashstone would be much different. Cordin was wearing a nightshirt and a pair of old boots under a patched and grubby cloak, and he didn't look happy to be there. He looked even less happy to see me, truth be told, and he gave the dead men a hard stare.

'Tomas Piety,' he said. 'I never thought I'd see you again.'

35

I shrugged. 'It takes more than a war to finish the Pious Men,' I said. 'I've got a couple of wounded here for you.'

The doc crouched down beside Hari. He was now the colour of a cheap tallow candle, sick-looking and breathing in shallow gasps of shock and pain. Black Billy wasn't so bad off, so he'd have to wait.

'He's lost a lot of blood,' Cordin said, as though that weren't obvious. The left leg of Hari's britches was soaked with it, and it was pooling on the floor around his boot. 'Someone carry him into the kitchen and find him something to bite on.'

I looked down at Hari and saw that he had passed out in the chair. I let a couple of Jochan's lads see to him, and they disappeared into the kitchen with the doc. Jochan himself was still drinking. I went over to him.

'That's your man in there,' I said quietly. 'That's your man about to scream for his ma when the doc starts cutting. Maybe you should be with him.'

Jochan gave me a look, and I held his stare until he backed down and followed his lads into the kitchen. He took the bottle with him, I noticed.

Different ways of leading men, as I said.

Chapter 6

The next morning Hari was still alive, and I gave thanks to Our Lady for that. Black Billy was sporting a row of neat stitches in his arm, and in a few weeks he would have another fine scar to show the girls. Billy was a good man. He was the bastard son of a merchant trader from Lady only knew where, someplace across the sea where men are black as night. He grinned at me when I went to check on him.

'I'm fine, boss,' he said, flexing his muscular arm to prove it.

'Don't burst those stitches or they'll only have to be done again,' I warned him, and clapped him on the shoulder.

He was the first of my crew to be wounded as a Pious Man rather than as a soldier, and his lack of reaction was telling. That was a good sign – I didn't want anyone feeling like too much had changed, at least not yet. I went through to the kitchen to see Hari for myself.

He was lying on a straw-stuffed pallet bed on top of the long table, his leg swathed in bandages. He was breathing, but he was deathly pale and clammy-looking. There was blood soaking through the cloth, but not too much. Doc Cordin was still there, which surprised me. Jochan was passed out drunk in a chair, and that didn't surprise me one bit.

'Is he going to keep the leg?' I asked the doc.

Cordin pursed his crinkly old man's lips and drew his shabby cloak closer over his threadbare nightshirt. 'If the wound doesn't go bad, aye,' he said. 'If it does, he'll die. It's too high up for me to take his leg off. If that wound does go bad, Tomas . . . you might have to do him a kindness.'

I nodded. A quick death from a knife in the heart was better than a slow one from gangrene and madness, after all. If it came to it, that was what would be done. Sometimes a man needed help to cross the river peacefully. We had done it for friends before, in Abingon. It's a hard thing, but sometimes it's for the best.

'Aye,' I said. 'I know you'll want paying, and you will be paid. I just need to find my aunt.'

'Enaid?' the doc said. 'You'll find her at the convent.'

I gave him a look. 'Are you being funny with me?'

'No, Tomas, I'm not,' he said. 'Your aunt took holy orders a year ago.'

'Then who the fuck,' I said softly, 'is running my businesses?'

'I don't know,' Cordin said, 'but they ain't yours no more. You saw what happened here. The boarding-houses are still open, and the inns and the Golden Chains, but there's new faces in them. The brothel burned down, and traders are paying their taxes elsewhere now.'

'What about my fucking racehorse?'

'It broke a leg,' he admitted. 'They cut its throat. I . . . I'm sorry, Tomas.'

I stared at him.

Everything was gone, that was what he was telling me. That I had lost all my businesses, everything except this one tavern that I had just taken back. That was hard news, but what had been built once could be built again, to my mind. The Tanner's Arms had been the important one. This was the first business I had taken on, when I turned my back on bricklaying. The Tanner's Arms was special.

I left the doc watching over Hari and went to find Bloody Anne. She was in the main room where the crew were tucking into salt pork and breakfast beer, even Billy the Boy. At least Alman had managed to keep the place stocked during the shortages. That meant the black market was still healthy if nothing else, and that was good.

'Come with me,' I murmured in Anne's ear. 'Nice and quiet.'

She got up without a word and followed me through to the back, into the brick-built part of the building. I led her down the corridor to the smallest of the three storerooms.

'What is it, Tomas?' she asked.

I looked at her for a long moment, weighing her in my mind.

'I need to trust you with something,' I said at last.

'I was your second, before your brother came back. I'd like to think you can trust me with anything.'

In battle I could, I knew that. In the army I could. This might be different. This was vitally important.

'I want you to watch the door,' I said. 'Be subtle about it, but don't let anyone in here till I come out. Not even Jochan. Can you do that for me, Bloody Anne?'

She nodded. It was the measure of her that she didn't ask why, or for how long. She just stepped back out into the narrow corridor and closed the door behind her.

It was dim, with only one tiny window letting in grey light through its filthy pane, and I wished I had thought to bring a lamp with me. All the same I found what I was looking for, a pry bar of the sort used to open crates and dry storage barrels. It was covered with dust and cobwebs, but it would serve. I weighed the iron bar in my hand and turned to the back wall of the room. It was a good wall, that.

It ought to be; I had built it myself.

If the room was a little bit smaller than it should have been for the shape of the building then it would have taken a keen eye to spot it, and thank Our Lady no one ever had. I counted the bricks, twenty-three along from the door and sixteen up. That one.

I pushed the end of the pry bar through the thin skin of dry, crumbling mortar and wiggled it until I got some purchase. The brick started to move and I worked the bar back and forth, trying to be quiet about it. The crew were making plenty of noise over their breakfast beer out in the main tavern and I didn't think they'd hear me unless I started shouting, but I didn't want Anne hearing me either. I didn't trust her *that* much, not with this. If this went wrong, then I was done. I had promises to keep to the men, after all.

I worked the loose brick far enough out of the wall to get hold of it, then pulled it out and set it carefully down on top of a barrel of pickled fish. I stuck my hand into the cavity and stretched my arm down to the hidden shelf, feeling among the bags of coin.

The first I touched was gold, a bag half full of gold crowns. This was the secret of the Tanner's Arms. This was why I had led my crew straight there, why I had fought and killed to retake this business above any of the others, even the Golden Chains. I didn't trust banks. Banks came with tax collectors and questions, and so the Tanner's Arms had become the golden heart of the Pious Men. No one knew that but me.

I didn't want the gold, though. I groped blindly, my hand at an awkward angle, through the narrow gap in the wall. I could feel the thick weight of gold crowns through the leather bag, heavy and difficult to move with so little mobility. Eventually I wormed my hand around enough to find another bag full of thinner coins. Silver marks; those were what I wanted. I lifted the bag, worked it out through the gap, and weighed it in the palm of my hand.

There were between two and three hundred silver marks in that bag, by my reckoning. A skilled craftsman might earn two marks a month in Ellinburg, if he was doing well for himself and had steady work. I nodded and dropped the bag into the big pocket in the inside of my robe. It was heavy, but I reckoned it would be getting lighter soon enough.

I worked the brick back into the gap in the wall and smeared as much of the loose mortar as I could into the cracks around it, then swept the rest carefully out of sight with my boot. It wasn't perfect, but it would have to do. I hid the pry bar behind a cask of salt pork and opened the door.

Bloody Anne was leaning casually against the wall, picking her nails with a dagger and watching the corridor.

'Done?' she asked.

I nodded and reached into my robe. I took ten marks out of the bag and pressed them into her hand.

'You *are* my second, Anne,' I said. 'There's no *was* about it, and that means you get second's pay. Just, for the Lady's sake, don't let Jochan hear about it. He hasn't replaced you, but right now I need to let him think he has. You understand that, don't you?'

She looked down at the ten silver coins in her hand and back up at me. Her eyes narrowed. It took a sergeant a good long while to earn ten marks in the army, half a year or more. She pursed her lips like she was about to say something, then thought better of it. The coins disappeared into her pouch and she nodded.

'Appreciate it,' she said, and that was how Bloody Anne became my second for real.

I wanted a word with my aunt, but first there were things to take care of.

In the kitchen I paid Doc Cordin a silver mark. That was too much, but I didn't have anything smaller except a few coppers, which wouldn't have been enough. It wouldn't hurt to have him in my debt. Hari was staring up at me with a confused look on his death-pale face. I didn't think he knew who I was, right then.

'Go home and put some clothes on,' I told Cordin, 'then come back and look after Hari. I don't know him but he's my brother's man, and he got hurt fighting for me. That makes him *my* man.'

Truth be told, Hari had got hurt waking up when a bomb went off, but that wasn't the point. The point was, if he lived he'd be mine forever now. That would be one of Jochan's crew I had taken, at least.

I looked at Jochan, still slumped and snoring in the kitchen chair. The empty brandy bottle was on the floor beside his boot. He had fought well the night before and I knew I shouldn't take ill against him, but just having him back here under this roof again was reminding me of how little we got on. We had the horror of our childhood in common, but that had never made us friends as adults.

I went back into the common room and gave every man there three silver marks.

'Welcome to the Pious Men,' I told them. 'You did well last night, all of you, and I won't forget that. I told you there would be work for you here, and there is. It'll be harsh work sometimes, I won't lie to you, but harsh work pays well and it's no worse than you did in the army.'

There was a moment of stunned silence before grins started to spread across their faces.

'Thanks, boss,' a lad called Mika said.

He was one of Jochan's crew, and he had just called me boss. That was good. That might just have made it two. I clapped him on the shoulder and gave him another mark.

'Take that and find some tradesmen,' I said. 'I want a new front door by the time I come back, and those broken windows replaced too.'

He nodded. It was enough responsibility to make him feel trusted and valued, but not enough money to be worth running out on me for. That was how it was done, to my mind. A little trust, a little responsibility, increasing bit by bit until they were yours.

Cookpot and Brak and Simple Sam had been up half the night rolling corpses into the river and they were still snoring in the stable, so I let them be for now. I'd pay them later, and another mark each on top for losing those bodies for me. Once word got about that there was more money to be had for some of the harsher jobs, volunteers would be easier to come by. I knew I'd be needing them soon.

I gave Sir Eland a look.

'I'm going out,' I told him. 'Chuck a bucket of water over Jochan and tell him he's in charge till I get back.'

The false knight nodded, but I could see the resentment in his eyes. He thought *he* should be my second, I knew that. Maybe if I had trusted him then he might have been, but I didn't and that was because he had never given me a reason to.

Bloody Anne had saved my life more than once in Abingon, and I hers, and that had forged a bond between us. Anne was my right hand. Jochan was my brother, for all that we didn't get on, and that was a different sort of bond. Maybe it wasn't a good one, but it was a bond none the less. He would never be my second, whatever he thought, but I wouldn't see him without a place at my side. I owed him that much, at least. That put him at my left hand, then. That didn't leave Sir Eland a place at either of my hands, as far as I could see. He would follow behind a woman and like it or he could fuck off; it was all the same to me.

'Anne, Luka, come with me,' I said.

I led Anne and Fat Luka out into the yard behind the tavern. Anne and I saddled our horses, and Jochan's as well for Luka.

'Where're we going, boss?' Luka asked once we were done buckling the tack.

I shaded my eyes against the cold, watery morning sun and pointed to the hill that loomed over the west side of Ellinburg.

'Up there,' I said. 'There's a convent up there. Nuns of the Mother.'

'Why?' Anne asked.

'Apparently my aunt has taken holy orders,' I said. 'If it's true, that's where she'll be.'

'And you need a woman with you, to get you in,' she said.

'Maybe, maybe not,' I said. 'You're coming because I trust you, Anne, not because of what's between your legs.'

She gave me a sharp look. 'And that's why you're bringing me and not your brother?'

'I'm not bringing my brother because he's passed out drunk, and "fuck a nun" is one of his favourite expressions,' I said. 'He wouldn't be an asset.'

Fat Luka sniggered, and even Anne cracked a rare smile.

'All right,' she said.

She swung up into her saddle. Fat Luka and I followed suit, and the three of us rode out into a fine Ellinburg morning. A fine morning in Ellinburg means it's not raining yet.

'Keep your eyes open,' I said quietly as we rode out of the alley and onto the narrow street, into shadows cast by the overhanging upper floors of the houses. 'I can't say for sure if last night's message will have been understood.'

When I had given that message to the young lad I let go the night before, I had still assumed that I *had* other businesses. Now that I had discovered that apparently I didn't any more, I wondered if the threat might have sounded a bit hollow.

We were armoured, all three of us, and I was wearing my priest's cowled robe over my mail and the sword-belt that held the Weeping Women. Fat Luka rode like a sack of turnips, unused to the saddle, but he had a big axe at his belt, and Bloody Anne had her daggers and her crossbow. I didn't think anyone was likely to misunderstand our purpose that day.

'We're making a stop on the way,' I said.

'We are?' Anne asked.

'We are,' I said. 'Chandler's Narrow.'

I led them off the road and up a winding alley between two towering tenements, our horses picking their way over the wide, shallow steps. Most of Ellinburg is hills, with steps and narrow passages between dark, looming buildings that seem almost to touch overhead. Near the top of the alley was a courtyard, with a boarding-house on one side and a chandler's shop on the other. I cocked my head at the boarding-house.

'Anne, go in and see about renting a room for tonight,' I told her. 'I want to know who's behind the desk.'

She gave me a look. 'Why me?' she said. 'They'll only think I'm a whore.'

I didn't think they would. Anne was sitting on her horse like she had been born in the saddle, wearing mail over boiled leather with two daggers at her belt and a crossbow and quiver hanging from her tack. I didn't think anyone would be mistaking Bloody Anne for a whore any time soon.

'Because you're not from Ellinburg, and they won't know your face or your accent,' I said, and she had to nod at that. Luka and me were both Ellinburg men, after all.

She grumbled, but dismounted and pushed open the door of the boarding-house. Luka and I sat and waited, holding our horses and hers around the corner out of sight. When Anne came back she had a look like murder on her face.

'You're a cunt,' she told me.

I raised my eyebrows at that. Anne was my second and she could get away with it, but only just.

'Why's that?' I asked her.

'He thought I *wanted* a whore, and he told me I was too ugly for any of his girls. So thanks for that, boss. That's made me feel good about myself.'

That was a lot of words at once, from Bloody Anne. That told me she was upset, and I couldn't let that pass.

'Right,' I said. 'Stay here.'

I threw my reins to Luka and got off the horse.

'Wait—' Anne started, but I ignored her.

Anne was a good soldier, and a good woman, and this had been my place of business. Even if it wasn't mine any more – and we would see about that – I wasn't having her spoken to like that. She was my second, and I liked to think she was my friend as well.

I kicked the door open and marched into the dingy little room with my hands on the hilts of the Weeping Women, ready to deliver justice for the insult. There was only one person in there, a balding fat man of fifty or so years. He was face down over his desk in a spreading pool of fresh blood.

It looked like Bloody Anne had already pronounced her own harsh justice.

Very harsh, to my mind.

I turned and went back outside to where they were waiting.

'I can fight my own fucking battles,' Anne growled.

She turned her horse and rode up the alley without looking at me. I mounted up and followed her. She could, at that. Bloody Anne had earned her name at Messia, and I knew what she could do. Coming home, going back to my old ways, had perhaps made me forget who I was with. She had been harsher with the man than was deserved, and under other circumstances I might have been angry about that, but I had made her feel small and that was ill done of me. Fat Luka kept his eyes on his horse and held his peace, and that was wise of him.

We rode up through the Narrows, leaving the Stink behind us as we wound our way into the more affluent parts of the city. Even there it was obvious that hard times had come to Ellinburg. The market square had barely half the traders it should have done at that time of year, and the prices I heard being cried for simple food were ridiculous.

'The fuck has happened?' Fat Luka wondered aloud.

'War happened,' Anne rasped, and I knew she had the right of it.

'Aye,' I said, but she ignored me.

We carried on through the city and out of the west gate. We turned off the West Road and headed up the hill, the horses plodding as the way grew steeper. Anne's silence was a cloak of anger around her, and I knew better than to disturb her. Later I would have to apologise to make it right between us, but now wasn't the time. The convent loomed above us on its hill, and that was where my attention needed to be.

It was time to have words with my aunt.

Chapter 7

We were met at the convent gates. Those gates were never closed, except when there was rioting in the city, but that didn't mean all were welcome. There were two nuns standing guard, big burly women in grey habits with halberds in their hands. Their weapons moved together to bar the way ahead of us.

'What's your business here, Tomas Piety?' one of them asked.

It seemed I hadn't been completely forgotten in my own city, and that was good.

'I'm here to see my aunt,' I said.

The nun looked from me to Luka to Anne, assessing us and the weight of our weapons and armour. Her lips tightened into a hard line.

'Sister Enaid is doing penance and is not allowed visitors,' she said.

I couldn't help but smile. That didn't surprise me, knowing my aunt as I did. She had been a soldier in the last war, and she took no shit from anyone.

'Perhaps you could make an exception,' I said. 'Her favourite nephew has just come back from the war. She'll want to know I'm alive, if nothing else.'

'We'll be sure to tell her,' the other nun said, 'when she has finished her penance.'

Bloody Anne looked up then and took her cue. She was no fool, was Anne, and she had been right in part. There *had* been one reason in particular why I had wanted her along for this.

47

'I seek sanctuary, sister,' she said. 'I am a woman returned from war, and I wish to take holy orders. These men are my witnesses.'

The first nun scowled at her. She was obviously no fool either and could quite clearly tell that Anne didn't mean it, but those were the words and I knew she couldn't refuse them. This was a convent of the Mother of Blessed Redemption, the goddess of female veterans and the survivors of war. If Anne said she wished to take their holy orders, then they had to let her in, and her witnesses with her. Traditionally her witnesses were supposed to be women too, but nothing said they absolutely had to be, and Anne had known that. So had I, of course.

The nuns grudgingly uncrossed their halberds and allowed us through the gate.

'You'll have to put your case to the Mother Superior,' one of them called after us. 'That won't be so easy.'

Thankfully it didn't matter. Once through the wall we found ourselves in a wide open space where vegetable patches and fruit trees were laid out in front of the grey bulk of the convent itself, and there on her knees in the dirt was Aunt Enaid.

I dismounted and left Fat Luka holding the reins of my horse, still sitting his saddle like a sack of turnips with Anne beside him. I approached my aunt, who picked up her stick and got to her feet slowly and with obvious pain. Her grey habit was bunched up into her belt to spare it the worst of the muck, and her bare knees were muddy. She leaned on her stick and looked at me. I stared into her twinkling blue left eye, avoiding the stained brown leather patch that covered the missing one.

'Hello, Auntie,' I said.

She puffed her cheeks out with a sigh. She was a heavyset woman with some sixty years to her, short-haired and one-eyed and with a limp from a broken ankle that had never healed properly.

'You're dressed like a priest, Tomas,' she said, taking in my cowled robe.

'That's because I am a priest,' I said. 'And now apparently you're a nun.'

'I am a fat old woman being forced to weed a vegetable patch because the Mother Inferior can't take a fucking joke,' she said. 'How was the war?'

I could feel her weighing and measuring me, looking for the thing that I didn't feel. The battle shock. Jochan felt it, of course, and Cook-pot and maybe even Anne for all I knew. But I didn't.

'I came back, thanks be to Our Lady,' I said, and waved a hand toward the horses. 'This is Bloody Anne, and you might remember Luka.'

Enaid gave them a short nod. 'Well and good,' she said. 'You'll want to know what's happened.'

'Aye, I will,' I said. 'I'll want to know who these people are who are running my businesses. I'll want to know who we had to fight to take back the Tanner's last night.'

Enaid sighed again. 'It all went to the whores, Tomas,' she admitted. 'With you and Jochan and all the lads gone off to war. We found poor Alfread floating in the river. Your horse was nobbled in a fixed race. They took the boarding-houses and stormed the Golden Chains and burned the brothel, and I couldn't stop them. I held out for two years but . . . One fat old woman and a bunch of beardless boys and old men, what could I do?'

'Who?' I demanded.

Of course we Pious Men weren't the only businessmen in the city, but the other gangs had been dragged into the war the same as we had. No one should have been in a position of strength in Ellinburg for the last three years, and certainly not strong enough to overthrow Enaid. She might say she was a fat old woman, and perhaps she was, but she was also a veteran soldier who I had personally seen break heads open with a mace. Unseating Enaid hadn't been done easily, I knew that much.

She shrugged. 'Men from off,' she said, and spat on the ground. 'With all the fighters gone from the city, we looked a ripe old prize. They came down the road from some town or another, I suppose. I didn't really get the chance to ask, busy as I was not getting fucking killed.'

'Aye,' I said. I supposed it made sense, for all that I didn't like it. 'And now you're here, a nun.'

'Mmmm,' she said. 'A roof over my head, food in my belly, and strong walls around me looked appealing at the time.'

'And have they lost that appeal?'

'Oh, what do you think?' she snapped, gesturing irritably at her mud-spattered habit. 'Do I look like a fucking nun to you, Tomas Piety?'

'You most *certainly* do not sound like one, Sister Enaid,' a voice said, cracking like a whip across the open space.

I turned to see a thin, shrewish-looking woman in a white habit striding toward us with one of the nuns from the gate at her side. She had perhaps forty-five years to her, with a long, pointed nose and a thin-lipped mouth that looked designed to express disapproval. She was obviously the Mother Superior who couldn't take a joke.

Aunt Enaid turned to face her as she drew up. The woman in white was visibly quivering with anger.

'I don't know *why* you let them in, Sister Jessica,' she snapped at the burly nun beside her. 'Words or no words, this was quite obviously a falsehood. Sister Enaid is *not* allowed visitors while she is serving penance, and she will be serving penance for a *very* long time.'

'This is the Mother Inferior,' Aunt Enaid said to me.

'How *dare* you!' the other woman screamed at her. 'I'll have you switched to within an inch of your life for that!'

'Switch this,' Aunt Enaid said, and punched the Mother Superior full in the face.

The thin woman landed on her arse in the dirt, blood from a broken nose spattering the front of her habit. Anne snorted laughter and lifted the crossbow from her saddle. She pointed it at the big nun.

'Don't,' she said, covering Enaid as she hobbled toward them.

'Off the horse, boy,' Aunt Enaid told Luka. 'You might be fat but I'm sure you can run, and I can't.'

Fat Luka dismounted in a flustered hurry, and Aunt Enaid hauled herself up into the saddle and held her stick across her knees.

'Well?' she demanded of me as the Mother Superior struggled to her feet, spluttering with rage and streaming blood from her face. 'I think we should be going, don't you?'

I swung up into my own saddle and we spurred for the gates with Fat Luka panting along behind us on foot.

That was how Aunt Enaid left the convent.

Chapter 8

When we got back to the Tanner's Arms it was to find that Jochan had finally stirred himself from his stupor and there was a fight in progress. Cookpot was raging about how the others had been paid and him and Brak and Simple Sam hadn't, while Jochan was just raging because he could. Sir Eland was leaning back with both elbows on the bar, watching the scene with an amused smirk on his face.

We had already stabled the horses and left Fat Luka weeping and vomiting in the yard after his unaccustomed run, so it was Bloody Anne, Aunt Enaid, and I who came into the tavern through the back door and found the chaos waiting for us. Cookpot had a hand around Mika's throat and his fist raised, an uncharacteristic snarl on his round face.

'Oi!' Bloody Anne roared in her best sergeant's voice.

They knew that voice, these men of mine, and Jochan's lot might not have done but they recognised a sergeant when they heard one. The shouting stopped, and Cookpot let go of Mika's neck.

'What the fuck,' I said quietly, 'is going on here?'

'You're paying the men?' Jochan demanded. 'What fucking with?'

'With good silver, brother,' I said. 'And there's pay for you three too, and a mark on top for the night's work.'

Cookpot nodded at that, looking shamefaced at his outburst. Him and Brak and Simple Sam I gave four marks apiece, in full view of the others. Harsh work was well rewarded, and I wanted them all to understand that.

'Where the fuck did that come from?' Jochan wanted to know. 'Doc

Cordin's been telling me how the land lies out there, Tomas, and you haven't got it from any of our other places because they're all *fucking gone!*'

He was shouting again, at me this time, in front of everyone. I couldn't let that pass, and I could see that Aunt Enaid knew it.

'Haven't you got a hug for your fat old aunt, you silly drunken boy?' she said before I could speak, putting herself between Jochan and me with a practiced ease. 'Come on through to the kitchen with me and we'll catch up, my lad.'

She steered him deftly away from me and out of my sight. That wasn't the first time Aunt Enaid had rescued my younger brother from his own actions and the harsh justice they would have earned him, and I doubted it would be the last. Hari would still be in there, of course, lying unconscious on his pallet on the kitchen table, but I knew a thing like a near-fatal wound wasn't likely to bother my aunt. She had been a soldier herself, after all.

I took a breath, forcing my anger down. I looked around the tavern and for the first time I noticed the two carpenters who were bent over their work at the front door, their heads down as they tried hard to be invisible. I nodded at Mika.

'Well done,' I told him.

'They reckon it'll be done by sundown, boss,' he said. 'It'll be tomorrow before there's glass for the window, though.'

'That's good enough,' I told him. 'The door is the important thing.'

Truth be told, I was glad to be able to give them work. The streets around there had always been poor, but they had been my streets, Pious Men streets, and no one had gone hungry. That had changed while I was away at war, and I couldn't let that pass. I wasn't going to watch my people starve, whatever it took.

I went behind the bar and poured myself a brandy, and one for Bloody Anne as well. The crew were settling down now, going back to whatever they had been doing before the fight started. There were men sewing up holes in their clothes, while others sharpened weapons or cleaned rust from their mail. Brak was giving Nik the Knife a rudimentary haircut. Black Billy was arm wrestling with Will the Woman like a fool, his stitches standing out angry-red against his bulging bicep. Black Billy was proud of his arms and rightly so, but if he burst those stitches it would be his own fault. If it came to it, he'd have to pay Doc Cordin out of his own pocket to stitch him up again. I wasn't paying for stupidity.

Anne came to join me at the bar and nodded her thanks as she picked up her brandy. Some of the lads were shouting bets at each other over the arm wrestling match now, and Anne leaned closer to speak quietly under the noise.

'About the money,' she said, her voice a low rasp.

I gave her a level look. 'What about it?'

'I don't know what you were doing in that back room,' she said, 'and I know it's none of my business, but you went in with nothing and you came out with silver. Watch your brother.'

I drained my glass and poured another. 'What do you mean?' I asked her.

'You *know* what I mean,' she said. 'If you're hiding something, and I think you are, then Jochan will make it his business to find it.'

I nodded. 'Aye, I know my brother.'

I started to turn away, but she reached out and touched my arm to check me. 'And your aunt,' she said.

'My aunt?'

That made me pause. Aunt Enaid had all but raised the two of us.

'She's been in that convent for over a year, Tomas, and I doubt she's been enjoying it,' Anne said. 'If it turns out she needn't have been, I think she'll take it ill.'

That was as many words as I usually heard from Bloody Anne in a day, and they had all been said in the space of a couple of minutes. I looked at her, and took in the serious look on her face. She was worried, I could tell. Well and good, she was my second and worrying for me was part of her job, but she was wrong about Enaid. Jochan, yes. I didn't need her to tell me I couldn't put my faith in my little brother. That was why she was my second and not him. But my aunt?

'I found Alman's strongbox, that's all,' I lied. 'The takings from the tavern. My tavern, my silver.'

Anne nodded and turned away to watch the arm wrestling match, her brandy in her hand. It was obvious that she didn't believe me, and that she could tell that I knew she didn't. It didn't matter. That was the story, and that was what she would tell Jochan and Enaid if she was pressed. I could trust Anne, out of all of them. I sighed and touched her arm.

'About earlier,' I said. 'The boarding-house. I'm sorry, Anne. About what he said, and about not trusting you to make it right. That was ill done of me, and I apologise.'

She gave me a look, then nodded. The long scar on her face twisted as she turned the corner of her mouth up into a sour smile.

'If I want a whore I'll fucking well have one, ugly or not,' she said. 'I've got money now, and money beats looks every time.'

She got up then and walked across the room to join the men at the wrestling table. Black Billy had Will the Woman almost pinned, the back of his wrist barely an inch from the wood. I frowned after her. I had never known Bloody Anne to lie with a woman, but then come to think of it I'd never known her to lie with a man either. I supposed that was her business, either way.

I swallowed my brandy and went into the kitchen after my aunt.

Hari looked terrible but he was still alive, and the doc was with him. Jochan was pacing up and down with a bottle in his hand, and Aunt Enaid was slumped in a chair with her stick beside her, watching him.

I ignored them both and spoke to Cordin. 'How is he?'

Doc Cordin looked up at me and shrugged. 'The wound don't smell rotten, so there's that,' he said. 'He's in a bad way, though. Don't know who he is half the time, and every time I've tried to sit him up he's all but passed out. I'm giving him small beer and he's taken a few oats, but he won't be able to digest much. He lost so much blood, I . . . I don't know, Tomas. Truly, I don't.'

I nodded. Hari was ghost white and his breathing was shallow and uneven. There was a fresh bandage around his leg with a fresh stain on it, but the stain was red like good blood and not the greenish yellow that would have meant death. I'd seen wounds go bad before, and if it had I knew I would have been able to smell it from where I was standing.

'Captain?' Hari croaked. 'I'm so thirsty, sir. Is the oasis near?'

'He wants water, but that filth from the river will kill him quicker than the wound could,' Cordin said. 'It's small beer or nothing, but he's struggling with it.'

'Keep trying,' I said, and put a hand on the doc's shoulder as I passed him.

Cordin might not be a real doctor but he was a good man, and he was doing his best. I looked at Jochan, at the angry expression on his face and the brandy bottle in his hand, and I had to admit that neither of those things could be said of my brother.

'Jochan,' I said.

'Where the fuck is mine?' he demanded before I could say anything else. 'Everyone's paid, with silver you shouldn't have, but not me. Not your own fucking brother, Tomas.'

I held up a hand for peace, and took five silver marks out of my robe.

'Here's yours, brother,' I said. 'More than I paid any of the other men, so I didn't want them to see me give it to you. That's all.'

He held my gaze for a long moment, then took the money from my hand.

'Aye,' he said at last, and the anger drained out of him as it usually did.

More than I gave any of the other men, I had said, and that was true enough. Bloody Anne was no man, after all.

Jochan shoved the coins into his pouch and took a long swallow of his brandy. I gave another five marks to Aunt Enaid, out of respect and for her trouble. She sat there with the coins in her open hand and said nothing.

'Where did it come from, then?' Jochan said after a moment. 'You never answered me that one, Tomas.'

'Alman's strongbox,' I said. 'I found it, and I kept it. The silver he made from my tavern is my silver.'

'It's funny,' Aunt Enaid said, looking up at me.

'What is?' I asked her.

'It's funny that Alman had any money. This place wasn't his, the way I heard it. He was just running it for his boss. You wouldn't think there would have been much coin kept here.'

I shrugged. 'Then I suppose he was stealing,' I said, and I turned away to make that the end of it.

This wasn't going to do for long, I knew. I was going to need to spend more money soon, a lot more, to feed those streets outside my new front door. That meant I was going to have to be able to come up with an explanation for where it had come from, because Lady knew I couldn't tell them the truth.

There was no other way, to my mind. I was going to have to take back my businesses.

Chapter 9

The next morning I called a council of war. Bloody Anne and Jochan and Aunt Enaid joined me in the largest of the three storerooms, the big windowless room where most of the men slept. I had debated with myself whether I should invite Sir Eland as well, and decided against it. Part of me said I didn't trust him and that meant I should keep him close, but the bigger part of me said he thought too much of himself and needed reminding that he was just one of the crew. Maybe I was wrong about that.

'We need to talk,' I told them, sitting on a bedroll in the light of a flickering oil lamp. 'Jochan, you're my brother. Bloody Anne, you're my sergeant. Aunt Enaid, you all but raised Jochan and me after Da died. You're the ones I trust.'

They looked at me in that dim light, and no one said anything. I *didn't* trust Jochan, not nearly as much as I should have been able to, but he was my brother. I owed him a debt from the past, one I couldn't repay, and there wasn't anything I could do to change that. I sighed and pulled my robe around me against the morning chill. It didn't get warm in Ellinburg until later in the year, and it never stayed that way for long.

'Out there,' I said, 'on streets that belong to the Pious Men, there are people who don't have anything to eat. There are people who are sick and can't afford a doctor. On my streets, people are starving for want of work. I can't let that pass.'

'We grew up on those streets,' Jochan said quietly, a distant look on his face. 'You chased me down those alleys, when we were lads. People went hungry then too.'

'Aye, they did,' I said, 'and when we became Pious Men we put a stop to it. My streets, my people. My responsibility.'

'Our streets,' Jochan said.

I gave him a look, but nodded. 'Our streets, then,' I said. 'Pious Men streets. I lifted them up once before and I can do it again, if you're with me.'

I looked around at their faces. Bloody Anne had no history here, had never set foot in Ellinburg before in her life, but I knew she would be with me.

My aunt cleared her throat. 'The way I recall it, Tomas Piety, is that the way you lifted up these streets was to tax each house whether they liked it or not and spend the money as you saw fit on those you decided deserved it,' she said.

That surprised me, I had to admit. She wasn't wrong, of course, but I hadn't expected her to voice that opinion now.

'Aye, that's right,' I said. 'And for that they received my protection. No one robbed a house on Pious Men streets and got away with it, and after a while word went around and they stopped trying. Time was a woman couldn't walk alone after dusk, and I put a stop to that as well. I made these streets safe.'

'It wasn't too safe for anyone who didn't want to pay for your protection, though, was it?'

I stared into Aunt Enaid's single eye and wondered why she was going out of her way to make me angry. I was about to say something I probably shouldn't have done when Jochan did it for me.

'What the fuck is your point, old woman?' he demanded. 'Our streets, our fucking rules!'

'My point, Jochan, is that you can't do it again,' she said, still holding my gaze. 'You can't tax people who have got *nothing*.'

'I know that, Auntie,' I said. 'I've come back from war, not from the madhouse. I've got money all over this city, tied up in businesses that have been stolen from me. Well, I'm taking them back. We'll start with the boarding-house up in Chandler's Narrow. Bloody Anne showed her face in there yesterday morning and it's not held by anyone we know. I want it back.'

'Fucking right,' Jochan said. A slow grin spread across his face, and he slapped me on the shoulder like a real brother might have done. 'Fucking right, Tomas!'

I glanced at Anne, and she shrugged. 'I'll go where you lead,' she said.

Aunt Enaid slipped a finger under her eyepatch and scratched for a moment, sucking her teeth. She couldn't have looked less like a nun if she had tried, and it occurred to me that we'd need to get her some different clothes before anyone saw her in public.

'Do what you think is best, Tomas,' she said after a moment.

'Right then,' I said. 'That's good. Anne, get ten of the men together, and make sure the rest know they're to hold this place while we're about it. We'll go tonight.'

'Aye,' Anne said, and got to her feet.

She left us, and Jochan followed her a moment later. My aunt fixed me with that steel-hard glare of hers.

'This fucking tavern,' she said quietly, 'wasn't making a copper and you know it. You had that silver stashed somewhere, Tomas Piety, and don't you try to tell me otherwise. Your brother might be a fool, but I'm not. Is there more where that came from?'

'That's my business,' I said.

'If you've got money and you want to help those people, then just spend your bloody money,' she hissed.

Truth be told, there was enough gold hidden behind that wall to feed my streets for a year or more, but that was no more Enaid's business than it was Jochan's. If I started spending gold I would face hard questions about where it had come from, and I couldn't risk that. The gold had to stay my business and no one else's.

'I haven't got any more money,' I said. 'And even if I had, what would I do when it ran out? If people start to depend on me to feed them, I have to be able to *keep* feeding them, and that won't do. I need to give them work, not handouts, and to do that I need income. As you say, I'll not be taking it in tax for a good long while to come, so I need those businesses back. And I'm going to go out and fucking take them.'

Enaid didn't speak to me for the rest of the day, not even when I had Cookpot go out and buy her a woollen kirtle to replace her nun's habit. It was used, of course, but there would be time enough later to have new clothes made up for her. I was glad when night fell and I joined Bloody Anne and Jochan in putting our mail on, alongside Sir Eland and Fat Luka and Will the Woman and five of the others. Will was the only one of Jochan's old crew who looked to be coming with us, but that suited me fine.

'My aunt is in charge until we get back,' I told the others. 'No more drinking. I need this place held and held firm, understand me?'

There were nods and mutters, and I led my ten out through the new front door and into the street. We only had four horses between us, and they would have been in the way anyway, up in the Narrows. We went on foot.

It was full dark by then, and when we got to the top of the steps the chandler's shop was closed. The courtyard was thick with shadow, the only light coming from a single lantern hanging above the door of the boarding-house.

'How do we do this?' Bloody Anne asked me.

'We do it like Pious Men,' Jochan said, and before I could reply he lifted his axe and kicked the door in.

It looked like that was how we were doing it, then.

The others bundled in after Jochan, all except Bloody Anne and me. I kept a hand on her arm to hold her back, letting the crew follow Jochan's reckless charge.

'When you lead, Anne,' I told her, 'sometimes the front isn't the right place to be.'

I heard glass shatter inside, followed by a scream. There was a crash, and the sound of boots thundering up poorly made wooden stairs. I pulled Anne back into the doorway of the chandler's shop, and sure enough a moment later one of the second-floor windows of the boarding-house exploded into the courtyard in a shower of glass and broken lead as a body was thrown through it.

Whoever it was hit the cobbles in front of us with a wet thump. I could feel Anne's eyes on me in the gloom.

'Are we not fighting, then?' she asked me.

I shook my head. 'Not tonight,' I said. 'Tonight we are making a fucking entrance.'

I gave it another five minutes, until the sounds of chaos and violence had subsided. I could hear a voice from the lobby of the boarding-house, someone with a strange accent begging for his life. *Now* it was time.

'Come on,' I said, and stepped over the pool of blood that was leaking from the broken body on the cobbles.

I walked through the doorway with Bloody Anne at my side, my priest's robes drawn closed over my mail. There were three people on their knees inside, and blood and broken glass everywhere. Two men were dead that I could see, and neither of them was mine.

Jochan was standing behind his three prisoners with a mad grin on his face and an axe clutched in his hand, dripping blood on the floor.

'That's done then,' he said.

I nodded and looked at the three kneeling men. I didn't recognise any of them, but one of them was definitely not native to Ellinburg. He was too pale and too tall to have been from these parts, and he wore his hair long in a dirty blond plait. No Ellinburg man had long hair.

'My name is Tomas Piety,' I said, addressing them. 'This is Bloody Anne. And this, my friends, is *my* fucking boarding-house.'

The tall, pale man spat at me, and I kicked him in the face. Jochan's blade was at his throat a moment later, the broad shape of the axe forcing his chin up.

'How many of them did you kill?' I asked my brother.

'Four, in all.'

I nodded. 'Seven men,' I said to the pale man. 'Seven men to guard a boarding-house. That seems like a lot.'

'Someone killed our bookkeeper yesterday,' he said, his voice sounding thick through his split lips.

'So they did,' I said. 'Now, you're not from this city, so I'll do you

61

the courtesy of explaining something to you. We are the Pious Men, and we're in charge. You're in one of my businesses, and I'm throwing you out. But first you're going to tell me who you work for.'

The blond man shook his head. One of his fellows looked like he was about to speak, then thought better of it.

'Well?' Jochan demanded.

He pressed his red blade to the kneeling man's throat but got no answer. Jochan growled and yanked the man's head back by his long plait of hair, the axe-head digging into his neck and drawing a trickle of blood.

'We can't,' one of the others said. 'Our families, please . . . he'll kill our families if we talk!'

'Shut up,' the blond one gasped. 'Say *nothing*!'

'Let him go,' I said, and Jochan reluctantly withdrew his axe from the man's neck. 'If that's the lay of things, then I understand. You're brave men, but know that you've crossed me. I'm not going to kill you, not tonight, but if I see you again I will. Do you understand me?'

The long-haired man gave me a sullen nod.

'Kick them out,' I told Jochan, 'and start making the place secure.'

'Aye, Tomas,' Jochan said.

Anne pulled me aside as the three men were booted out into the alley. Jochan disappeared into the back.

'Why did you do that?' she asked me quietly.

'Let them live?' I asked. 'Same as the one at the Tanner's – so that they can spread the word.'

'Not that,' she said. 'You come in like death walking, making your entrance like you said, and you gave your name and mine. You never mentioned Jochan, Tomas. You never named your own brother.'

'You're my second, not him,' I said. 'If he starts to realise that for himself, nice and slowly, maybe it's gentler than flat-out telling him.'

'And when he does?'

I looked at her and shrugged. It would be how it would be, to my mind.

Jochan blundered out of one of the back rooms just then, a bottle of brandy in his hand and his other arm around a half-naked woman.

'There's new whores, Tomas.' He grinned at me. 'We ain't killing them, I fucking hope!'

'No, we ain't,' I said, 'but we ain't taking advantage either. Round them up in the parlour.'

Anne gave me a look, but I ignored her. Business was business. A few minutes later, I went in to address them. There were seven women in total, most of them with no more than eighteen or nineteen years to them. They wore anything from thin shifts to demure kirtles, depending on what they had been doing when we burst in, I supposed, but each one had the bawd's knot on her left shoulder in yellow cord. There were city ordinances about that, after all, and any licensed whore had to show the knot. A couple of them saw my priest's robes and dipped clumsy curtseys. A redhead who looked to have a year or two more than the others laughed at them.

'He's no fucking priest,' she sneered. 'He's just another gangster.'

'I am a priest,' I corrected her, 'and I'm a businessman as well. You all worked here, and I assume you lived here as well?'

There were nods among the women, and some of them looked worried at my use of the past tense. That was good. That was the point I was making.

'My name is Tomas Piety,' I said, and I could see that more than a few of them knew that name. 'This was my stew, before the war, and now it's my stew again. Those that want to stay here and keep working are welcome to. Those who want to leave, leave.'

'Where would we go?' the redhead challenged me. 'We're not street scrubs. We're better than that. We all wear the knot, here.'

I shrugged. 'That's your affair,' I said.

I could see I was going to have to keep an eye on her. She was obviously the boss of them, and she had the look of trouble about her. She scratched her ribs idly and flicked her dirty hair out of her face, her insolent gaze finding Bloody Anne standing beside me.

'You his woman?'

'No,' Anne rasped. 'I'm my own woman.'

The redhead nodded, as though the answer pleased her. 'What terms?' she asked me.

Truth be told, Aunt Enaid had always run this side of Pious Men business, but she wasn't there and I was. I didn't know how high my terms of commission should be. I was about to say something to stall her when Will the Woman spoke up.

'I'll take care of it if you want, boss,' he said. 'I used to run a bawdy house back home, before the war. I know how it's done.'

I gave him a nod. I wasn't too sure how far I could trust Will, not yet anyway, but he had fought for me and when Black Billy had beaten him at the arm wrestling he had taken it good-naturedly enough. Those things went a way toward building that trust, to my mind.

'Aye,' I said. 'This is Will. He's the boss here, now. You do what he says and everyone will get along.'

I left the men to get acquainted with the Chandler's Narrow girls and walked back out into the courtyard. One of the lads would have to stay there with Will, of course, to keep the place guarded. I was sure none of them would mind that duty, but Sir Eland would be ideal for it. He might give the place a bit of fake class, for one thing, and more importantly I knew he didn't like women in that way so at least he would leave the girls alone. The duty would keep his sneer out of my face as well.

I stood in the gloomy courtyard and stretched my back under the weight of my mail. That body would need shifting before long, I thought. I was aware of Bloody Anne standing beside me.

'Thank you,' she said.

I glanced at her. 'For what?'

'For not assuming I know how to run a bloody bawdy house just because I'm a woman,' she said. 'I wouldn't know where to start.'

I shrugged. It had never crossed my mind that she would. 'Help me with this?'

Anne nodded, and between us we dragged the body back into the boarding-house and threw it in a corner with the others. As my memory served, there was a dirt-floored cellar under the building. Some of the lads would be digging graves down there tonight.

Anne looked at the pile of bodies and shook her head. 'I need some air,' she said. 'Coming?'

We went back out into the courtyard again. Eleven men were out there waiting for us. Anne was about to yell for the crew when I held up a hand to say be quiet. This lot were from the biggest, best-armed and meanest gang in Ellinburg – the City Guard.

I knew the one who led them. Captain Rogan was the city governor's chief thug. I should have been honoured to warrant a visit from him in person, I supposed. He had almost fifty years to him, and was a strong, solidly built man who wore a plain steel breastplate over his mail, with a gold star on each shoulder to show his rank. It was a running street joke that those stars looked like the bawd's knot, but it would be a brave lad who called Rogan the governor's whore in the hearing of a guardsman. Heads had been broken for less, and sometimes people just disappeared and weren't seen again.

'Captain Rogan,' I said. 'What a pleasure.'

He met my eyes and scowled. 'Piety,' he said. 'You're coming with us. Hauer wants a word with you.'

I had thought he might, sooner or later. Looked like it was sooner.

'It's all right, Anne,' I said. 'Tell Jochan I've gone to see Grandfather.'

'Right,' she said.

She didn't move, though. She just stood there with her hands hanging by her sides, near the hilts of her daggers. There were eleven of the Guard, but I knew she would have waded in if she'd had to, buying me time until the crew could get to us. Bloody Anne was the best second a man could want and no mistake.

'It's all right,' I said again, and let Captain Rogan and his men lead me away.

Chapter 10

The governor of Ellinburg wasn't really my grandfather, of course – that was just street cant. 'Going to see Grandfather' meant you had been taken in, but it wasn't bad. If it was bad you were 'going to see the widow', and that was a different matter. If I had said that, there would have been a pitched battle between my crew and the Guard, and I wasn't sure how that would have ended. Our numbers were roughly even, but the guardsmen were sober and well fed and their mail was in good order, and each one carried steel along with his club, as well as a whistle that would bring more men running.

No. All in all I was glad to be going to see Grandfather.

'I wasn't sure you'd be back,' Rogan said as we marched through the narrow by the dim light of a couple of lanterns. 'I heard it was rough, down south.'

'Aye, it was rough,' I said.

Rogan had fought in the last war, in Aunt Enaid's war, and I knew his understatement wasn't meant as an insult. It was just how veterans spoke of things, in terms that made them seem less than they had been. You don't dwell on the memories so much, that way.

'Aye,' he said. 'Well, here you are, Tomas Piety, and the big man wants to see you.'

Of course he did. Word travels fast on the streets of Ellinburg, though, and my face was remembered.

'And see me he shall, Captain,' I said. 'I've no quarrel with the Guard, you know that. I'm just finding my feet and putting my house in order. Then regular payments will resume, and we'll all go back to how we were.'

Of course I'd had an arrangement with the City Guard, one that had involved my silver in exchange for their blind eyes. A fair quantity of that silver had gone to Rogan himself.

'We'll see,' he said, but I could see the corner of his mouth curling slightly with avarice.

Captain Rogan was a hard man and a ruthless bully, but he was also greedy and he had his vices. Gambling was chief among them – before the war, on a good week at the racetrack, I could take back the bribes I had paid him and more besides.

'I hope we will, Captain,' I said. 'I hope we will.'

I let them lead me out of the narrow and on up the hill toward the governor's hall that lay in the shadow of the Great Temple of All Gods. There was no castle in Ellinburg, but the governor's hall was the closest thing to one that a building could be. A great lump of grey stone with narrow windows and iron doors, it squatted near the end of Trader's Row like a war elephant from Alaria.

Lanterns on iron hooks projected from the walls, casting a yellow glow on the ground outside where the uneven cobbles gave way to good flagstones. A single royal standard flew from the rooftops, the red banner looking almost black in the darkness. There were two of the City Guard stationed at the front doors at all times, and regular patrols around the building day and night.

Rogan greeted the men on guard duty, and they opened the heavy double doors to admit our party. We trooped up the steps and into an echoing stone hall. Lamps burned in there, but not many. The hour was late and the governor was a frugal man, or so he let it be thought.

'You know the drill,' Rogan said.

I unbuckled my sword-belt and handed over the Weeping Women, Remorse and Mercy heavy in their scabbards as I held the belt out to Rogan. He passed it to one of his men and looked at me with narrowed eyes.

'Is that everything?' he asked me.

'I was out on business, not riding to battle,' I said. 'That's everything.'

They searched me anyway, but I hadn't been lying. Eventually Rogan grunted and sent half his men back to their barracks. The other five escorted me down a long corridor and up a flight of narrow stairs meant for servants. The grand staircase in the main hall wasn't for the likes of me; that message was plain enough.

Governor Hauer was in his study on the second floor, sitting behind a large desk with a glass of wine in his hand. He looked paunchy even in his expensively tailored clothes, and he was already half bald. The governor lived well, whatever he liked to put about regarding his frugal ways. He lived to excess, in fact, and his health was the poorer for it. He looked like he had ten more years to him than he actually did.

Rogan bade his men wait outside and followed me into the study alone. The look on the governor's face gave me pause. I had thought I knew what this meeting was about – bribes and taxes and how they had no doubt gone up while I was away. Now I wasn't so sure.

'Tomas Piety,' Hauer said.

'Lord Governor,' I replied. 'This is an unexpected pleasure.'

'No, it isn't, unexpected or a pleasure,' he said. 'Give me one reason why I shouldn't have Rogan break your neck.'

'And why might you want to do that?'

He glared at me. 'You're only a few days back in Ellinburg, and the place is already a charnel house. Corpses found floating in the river, a disturbance at the convent – and don't think I haven't heard all about *that* from the Mother Superior – and now a battle in Chandler's Narrow. You're more trouble than you're worth, Piety.'

'I've been to war to fight for queen and country, and I come home to find myself robbed blind and my people starving in their own homes. You think I can let that pass?'

'You've been to war because you were conscripted and forced to go, so don't give me all that horseshit,' he said. 'Queen and country mean no more to you than they do to me, and we both know it.'

He was wrong about that, to an extent anyway, but I didn't see a need to tell him so. Not yet, anyway.

'I see,' I said instead. 'Do you expect me to sit meekly by and watch while other men profit from the businesses I built with my own hands?'

'No,' Hauer said. 'No, I don't, and that's why you're still breathing. Sit down, Tomas. Have some wine.'

I sat in the chair across the desk from him, all too aware of Rogan looming behind me. Rogan's big, callused hands were made for wringing necks, and I was there unarmed. Not defenceless, no, but I've never been as good with my fists as Jochan was. If it came to it, I knew I'd struggle against Rogan. I sat and offered a silent prayer to Our Lady that tonight wouldn't be the night I crossed the river.

I reached for a goblet and the flagon and poured myself a drink. I prefer brandy to wine, but hospitality extended should never be refused. The wine was strong and cloying, too sweet for my taste, but I drank it anyway.

'You've something on your mind,' I said.

The governor took a long draft from his own goblet and cleared his throat. 'What've you noticed, about these people you've been killing?'

'They're scared,' I said, thinking of the three in the boarding-house. 'Whoever's in charge of them, they're more scared of him than they are of me and my crew. One of them said something about their family being held hostage. That and I've lived in Ellinburg all my life aside from the war years and I don't recognise a single one of them.'

'Someone's got a knife held to their children's throats,' Hauer said. 'Who?'

He ignored the question. 'Have you seen any foreigners among them?'

'One,' I said. 'Long haired and blond and tall. Not from these parts.'

'From Skania,' Hauer said.

'If you say so,' I said.

I had only spent a few years in school; enough to learn my letters and how to figure simple accounts, but that was all. History, geography, those were mysteries to me. I knew Skania was somewhere across the sea to the north, but no more than that.

'I do say so,' he assured me. 'Most of the men you're fighting are petty scum like you, little people made to feel big by violence and stolen silver. Men from country towns by and large, and a few billy-big-bollocks they've brought up from Dannsburg to stiffen them. They've been careful not to recruit any Ellinburg chaps, who might have other loyalties. A man called Bloodhands leads them, so folk say, and where he came from is anyone's guess. No one even fucking knows who he is.'

I let the insults slide and thought about it. 'What about the other crews?'

The Pious Men had been influential in Ellinburg before the war, but of course we hadn't been the only street crew doing business or paying off the Guard. The Gutcutters, the Alarian Kings and all the other crews had seen their men dragged off to war just like we had.

'Much the same,' Hauer told me. 'Our northern friends have been busy, while Ellinburg men have been at war.'

The governor hadn't been at war, I noted, for all that he was of an age. He might not look it, but he only had a few more years than me. Not too old to fight. No man with less than forty years to him was called too old to fight when the recruiting parties came calling.

'And who are they then, these mysterious northern friends?' I asked him.

He paused to refill his goblet, and all the while Captain Rogan stood just behind my chair with his big, hard hands not so very far from my neck. This was the point of the interview, I realised. This wasn't about the violence I had caused, or even about the bribes I owed. Whatever the governor really wanted to say to me was about to come out.

'Foreigners, as I say,' Hauer said. 'From Skania like the one you met, although he sounds like he was no one. They're not people like you, Tomas; don't ever make the mistake of thinking that they are. No, they're people more like me. They're people like the Queen's Men, in their own land. And now they're here.'

That gave me pause. The Queen's Men were a semi-secret part of the royal government. They were *nothing* like the governor, and he was flattering himself if he thought otherwise. They were a particular order of the knighthood whose weapons were not sword and lance but diplomacy and gold and a knife in the dark. The Queen's Men were subtle, unseen and officially non-existent. They were the thing businessmen like us frightened our children with. Never mind the boggart with its long twisted fingers, that was just in stories – the sort of scary stories that children enjoy because they know they're not real. Do what your father says or the Queen's Men will come and take you away. Now *that* was something to be frightened of.

'Is that right?' I said.

'It is,' Hauer assured me. 'I need to be honest with you now, Tomas, and to trust you with something. Can I do that?'

I looked at him for a moment, at his drooping jowls and the faint sheen of sweat on his broad forehead. I doubted very much that he was going to be honest with me, and I knew that he didn't trust me any more than I trusted him. All the same, this was a change from the way our conversations usually went, and that held my interest if nothing else.

'Of course,' I said.

'There's a Queen's Man in the city right now,' he told me. 'Well, a Queen's Woman, I suppose you might say.'

'Is there, now?'

'There is,' he said.

'And why's that, then?'

And why are you telling me that, more to the point?

'There are things afoot, Piety. Political things, which I can't expect a cheap thug like you to understand,' he said. 'That's all right, you don't have to understand. You just have to do what you're told. When the Queen's Men say jump, you jump, you understand me? You'll do what she tells you, if you're wise.'

'Why me?' I asked him.

I had a strong suspicion I knew exactly why me, but I wanted to find out if *he* did.

He shrugged. 'I was told to put them in touch with the first gang boss who made it home from the war,' he said. 'That would be you.'

I wasn't sure how far to believe that. From what I had seen of Ellinburg, I probably *was* the first boss to make it home, but it sounded thin to me. I thought this might be more to do with history than anything else. History that the governor still didn't seem to know about.

'All right,' I said. 'Who do I expect, and when?'

'I don't know,' he said, and for the first time he sounded shaken. 'A woman, that's all. She's a Queen's Man, Tomas – for the gods' sake, I never saw her face. She'll find you.'

I could see the fear in his eyes now and couldn't help wondering if he had woken one night to find this woman in his bedchamber, holding a knife to his balls while she made her demands. From what I knew of the Queen's Men it wouldn't have surprised me.

Not one bit it wouldn't.

Chapter 11

It was late when I got back to the Tanner's Arms. Most of the men were asleep by then, but Simple Sam was on the door and Bloody Anne was inside waiting for me.

'What in the Lady's name happened?' she asked me.

'It's all right, Anne,' I said. 'I got taken to see Grandfather, that's all.'

'Taken in,' she said, and I knew someone had explained what that meant, 'but they let you go again. Why, and what for?'

I sighed and poured myself a brandy. 'The governor wanted a word,' I said. 'You have to understand the way this works, here in Ellinburg. We're a crew and I'm a boss, and the City Guard are a bigger crew and the governor is a bigger boss. I have to pay him taxes, the same way my people pay me taxes. It's just business.'

Anne frowned at me. 'The governor is corrupt?'

'He's a businessman,' I said. 'We're all businessmen, Anne.'

Bloody Anne was a soldier, not a criminal. I didn't know much about her past, where she had lived or what she had done before the war, but she was honest and she was faithful. Those were admirable qualities in a sergeant, but now she was my second in the Pious Men and it was time she learned how things really worked.

'I'm not a fucking idiot, Tomas,' Anne said. 'A bribe is a bribe, so call it that.'

'All right, we'll call it that,' I said. 'I bribe the Guard to keep them out of Pious Men business, and so do the bosses of the other crews in the city. Captain Rogan gets a cut of that money, the guardsmen get a

73

pittance and the governor keeps the rest of it for himself. That's just how it works.'

I shrugged, making light of it, and looked around the room. Mika and Brak were sitting by the fire playing cards and looking reasonably sober, but everyone else appeared to have turned in for the night.

'Where's Jochan?' I asked.

Anne was my second but Jochan still thought that *he* was, so by rights it should have been him waiting up for me and not her. But it hadn't been. That said a lot, to my mind.

'Asleep out the back,' she said. 'He's had a drink.'

He'd had a bottle of brandy or more and passed out, was what she meant.

I nodded. 'How's Hari?'

'Better,' Anne said, and now she looked uncomfortable. 'Much better.'

'That's good,' I said.

She stared down at her boots and didn't say anything for a long time. I knew that face. She had looked like that in Abingon, when she had needed to tell me someone else had died. That was the face Anne got when there was hard news, but if Hari was getting better then I couldn't see what that news would be. I sipped my brandy and waited, giving her the time she needed to put her words together.

'He's a lot better,' she said at last. 'Doc Cordin had to leave, so Billy the Boy sat with him a while, and then he was sitting up and eating and he seemed to know who he was again. Tomas, this morning he called me Colonel and asked how far it was to Abingon. He was so far gone, so nearly dead from all the blood he'd lost, and now . . . he isn't.'

'Well, that's good,' I said. 'Isn't it?'

I gave Anne a look, and she nodded.

'Aye, it's good,' she said. 'I know he's not part of our crew but he seems like a good man.'

'He *is* part of our crew,' I said. 'Now, he is. They're all Pious Men, Anne.'

'Aye,' she said again. 'Just like Billy the Boy is.'

I nodded. I could tell that Anne was scared of Billy the Boy, and that didn't surprise me. I knew that Sir Eland certainly was, and had been ever since that first night in the woods outside Messia. Sometimes I was scared of him too, although I'd have been hard pressed to put my finger on exactly why.

Touched by the goddess, I thought.

No twelve-year-old child should be a confessor and a seer, but Billy was.

'Is there something you're not telling me, Bloody Anne?'

'Maybe you ought to see for yourself,' she said.

I followed Anne through to the kitchen and there was Billy, watching over Hari as she had said. Hari did look better, I had to allow. He was asleep again now, but that awful waxy sheen was gone from his face and he almost had some colour back in his cheeks. Billy was sitting cross-legged on the table staring at him, unblinking. Billy had an intense way about him sometimes, and this was nothing out of the ordinary for him.

'What am I not seeing?' I asked her.

'Tomas,' Anne said slowly, 'he's not touching the table.'

I looked again, and realised that she was right. There was a good inch of clear space between Billy's arse and crossed legs and the top of the table.

He was floating in the air.

'By Our Lady's name,' I whispered.

I swallowed. Billy was touched by the goddess, I knew that. I knew that, but knowing it and seeing it weren't the same thing.

Billy didn't look like he realised we were in the room. He just floated there, staring at Hari, and he gave no sign that he could see or hear us. Perhaps he couldn't. He was in some sort of trance, to my mind, although how and why were anyone's guess. Was the goddess really working through him, healing Hari? Perhaps. I didn't discount the idea, but if that was the case then I had no explanation for it. Our Lady didn't heal men, that I knew of.

'We should send for a priest,' Anne said.

I gave her a look. 'I *am* a fucking priest,' I said, 'and it's more than I can explain. We'd need a magician to explain this.'

Of course I didn't know a magician, no more than I knew a real doctor. There was Old Kurt, though, who people called a cunning man.

He was to a magician what Doc Cordin was to a doctor, I supposed. Not book-schooled, maybe, but what he did worked well enough. Most of the time, anyway. Perhaps *he* could explain it.

Still, if Billy the Boy had done something to Hari, or if Our Lady had done something through Billy, then it didn't seem to have caused anyone any harm. Quite the opposite, to my mind. A man of mine who had been dying wasn't any more, and I wasn't going to argue with that.

'It's late and I'm tired,' I said. 'If Billy wants to float in the air, then I can't see it's hurting anyone.'

'You're just going to let it pass?' Anne asked.

I shrugged. I couldn't see what else I could do about it, short of getting hold of him and physically dragging him down onto the table. I had a feeling that wouldn't have been wise.

'It's witchcraft, Tomas.'

'I'll pray on it,' I said. 'Then I'm going to sleep.'

I left Anne in the kitchen, watching Billy the Boy while he floated above the table and stared down at Hari, never blinking.

I wouldn't pray on it.

Our Lady didn't answer prayers, after all, and I had more pressing things to concern me than Billy the Boy.

I made my way up the rickety stairs to the garret room I had claimed as my own, and shut the ill-fitting door behind me. I could hear my aunt snoring in the next room.

Billy the Boy would keep, I told myself, whether it was witchcraft or not and how the fuck was I supposed to know either way? I was a priest, not a mystic, but the last thing I wanted was Anne worrying about witchcraft in our crew. I took my sword-belt and mail off and flexed my shoulders, aching from the weight of the armour. She would have to keep as well; other things wouldn't keep at all.

There were Queen's Men in the city, and they wanted me to work for them.

Again.

I woke early the next morning, despite not having laid my head down much before dawn. I needed to piss. I kicked my bedroll open and got up, feeling the cold morning air around my bare shins. I found the pot and stood over it in my smallclothes, thinking while I did my business. There's nothing like a good piss in the morning to clear the head. That was better than prayer any day, to my mind, and certainly more productive.

The Queen's Men.

I thought I had seen the last of them, but it seemed like I had been wrong about that.

I have written that I'm a businessman, and I am. I'm a priest as well, and that's true enough. But perhaps I'm something else too. That gold hidden in the wall of the storeroom downstairs hadn't come out of thin air, after all. I had earned that gold, and no one knew about that. Not Governor Hauer, not Jochan, not even Aunt Enaid.

No one.

I had earned that gold from the Queen's Men, before the war. That was what I had been worried that Governor Hauer might have discovered. From what he had said last night it seemed that he hadn't, and that was good even if nothing else was.

They paid well, the Queen's Men, I had to give them that. They had paid me very well indeed, to spy on the governor. Oh, he thought he was untouchable, did Hauer, here in his reeking industrial city where none of the fine lords and ladies of Dannsburg would ever want to set their silken feet.

Incomes were what he said they were, to Hauer's mind, and taxes were paid accordingly. He never thought anyone in the capital would trouble themselves to question his accounts, but then of course at the time he didn't know there was a war brewing. Wars need to be paid for, in gold as well as blood. Blood might be cheap but gold had to be wrung out of the provinces, by force if necessary. I'm no politician, but even I knew that.

A man contacted me maybe a year before the war broke out. He was no one I knew, just a trader from the east offering good terms on tea and silk and poppy resin. We made some deals, that man and I, and once he had my trust he showed me the Queen's Warrant and offered me another deal – work for the Queen's Men or face the queen's justice for the dodged tea taxes and the unlicensed poppy trade.

I knew the queen's justice was even harsher than mine, so of course I agreed.

I never thought I'd be a spy for the crown, but then I never thought I'd be a priest either. Working for the crown had stuck in my throat like a fish bone, though, and it almost choked me. To work for the crown, to be an informer and a spy, that went against everything I believed in, and I hated it.

Better that than hang, though, or so I told myself so I could sleep at nights.

I worked for that man for five months, passing him information on everything from the bribes that the Pious Men paid the City Guard to the number of boats that came down the river and how many bales and barrels each unloaded and what each one had contained.

It cost me silver to find those things out, of course, but for every mark I spent it seemed the Queen's Man was happy to repay me with a gold crown. I was careful, and circumspect, and I made sure that my eyes and ears were no one that we knew. This wasn't Pious Men business; I had known that from the start. If I had made it Pious Men business, then Jochan would have known about it and got himself involved, and it would all have gone to the whores. Even then, I realised as I finished my piss and buttoned my smallclothes, even before the war I had known I couldn't trust my brother.

That was over and done, or so I had thought, but it looked like I had been wrong about that. It seemed that the Queen's Men weren't done with me yet. I've heard it said that the only way to leave the service of the crown is at the end of a rope, and it seemed that that might just be true after all.

I splashed water from the basin into my unshaven face. I needed to see a barber, I thought. It wouldn't do to greet a representative of the queen with a rough chin.

I got dressed and headed downstairs to the kitchen, buckling my sword-belt as I went. I found Hari sitting in a chair with a bowl of oats in his hands and a mug of small beer on the table in front of him. He was spooning oats into his face like he hadn't eaten in a month. He was still a bit pale, but otherwise his recovery was nothing short of miraculous. I wasn't sure that I believed in miracles, but I believed what I could see with my own eyes.

'Morning, boss,' Billy the Boy said from beside the fireplace.

I gave him a look, noting how pale and drawn he seemed.

'Morning, Billy,' I said. 'Hari, it's good to see you up and about again.'

'Aye, boss,' Hari said. 'I'm feeling a lot better. Just needed some sleep, I reckon. I've been awful tired, of late.'

I wondered how much he remembered but decided to let it pass.

'You take it easy,' I said.

I reached into my pouch and gave him four silver marks. He stared at me in open astonishment.

'You missed out on the accounting,' I told him. 'It's three marks a man for joining the Pious Men, and there's another for you on account of being grievously wounded in my service. I look after my crew, Hari, and I reward loyalty. You remember that.'

'Yes, boss,' he said, making the money disappear swiftly into his sweaty shirt. 'Thank you.'

The men would need new clothes, I thought. They were all filthy and ragged, every one of them, and I wasn't much better myself. Conscripts usually were, of course, but that wouldn't do any more. Not now we were home it wouldn't. The Pious Men had a certain appearance to maintain, after all.

'Billy,' I said, and the lad looked up at me with expressionless eyes. 'Boss?'

I didn't want to do this, I realised. Not now, anyway. It would keep, as I had told myself the night before.

'Stay out of Bloody Anne's way today,' I said. 'I'm going out.'

I went back into the common room and found Fat Luka returning from the shithouse in the yard.

'You're coming into town with me,' I told him.

He just nodded and went to get his weapons. Luka was a good Ellinburg man, and he knew how things worked. Bloody Anne was my second, no mistake about that, but I had known Luka a lot longer and he knew the city. There were some tasks he'd be better suited for.

I knew I could trust him.

Chapter 12

I put Luka on Jochan's horse again and the pair of us rode up out of the Stink toward Trader's Row. I didn't need anyone with me, not really, but a man in my position should never ride alone. If nothing else there are expectations to be met, and it wouldn't look right for Tomas Piety to be about in Ellinburg without at least one bodyguard.

Three years of war was a long time, and if people had started to forget about the Pious Men, then it was my job to remind them who we were. We were back, and I needed the whole city to know that. These Skanians that Hauer was so worried about were only half the problem, to my mind. I needed my own people, the people of Ellinburg, to respect me. That wasn't going to happen while my men and I looked like vagrants.

Many of the streets in Ellinburg were named after the trades that had first claimed them, hundreds of years ago. Net Mender's Row, where Doc Cordin lived, was what it sounded, a squalid street near the river in the heart of the Stink where the poor worked on the nets with their gnarled and arthritic hands until they could no longer afford to feed themselves. It backed onto Fisher's Gate, where the river water seeped into the foundations of the houses and men pulled sickly fish from the polluted river to feed their equally sickly wives and children. Trader's Row, half a city away and near the governor's hall and the Great Temple, was another matter.

Trader's Row was home to the halls of the guilds, and there was money there. Even these days, even with how the city was now, there was money on Trader's Row. There was a barber's shop near the hall of spicers that I had frequented before the war, and that was where we went first. It was expensive, of course, but as I say, there were expectations to be met. Doc Cordin had always been a better surgeon than he was a barber, and I wasn't letting him near my face with a razor.

We hitched the horses outside and Luka pushed the door open for me. An elderly, aproned man was halfway through shaving a well-dressed stranger, and he gave Luka a disdainful look before his eyes found me. A look of shock blossomed on his pink face.

'Mr Piety,' he said, and if his hand trembled on the razor just a little it wasn't enough to cut his customer's throat, so there was that.

'Hello, Ernst,' I said. 'I'm home, and I need a shave and a haircut.'

I have never seen a barber finish a shave so fast. Ernst had sixty or more years to him, but he could work quickly when he needed to. Whoever the man in the chair was, he was smooth and dry and out the door in less than five minutes.

'Sorry to keep you waiting, Mr Piety,' Ernst said, wringing his plump, pink hands. 'So sorry. It's just me here now, you see. My apprentice boy went off to war and he hasn't come back, not yet he hasn't, so I'm rushed off my feet all day. Sit down, sir, sit down.'

I shrugged out of my robes and he ushered me into the chair in my shirtsleeves, all the while fussing around me like he had a prince of the realm in his shop. Good. That was what I wanted.

I was Tomas Piety, and in Ellinburg I *was* a fucking prince.

Luka stood by the door while Ernst worked, keeping guard. Before long I was shaved smooth and my hair was cut short and neat, the way it should be. Ernst passed me a moist towel, the water scented with rose petals. This water hadn't come from the river, that was for sure. There were good wells around Trader's Row, for the servants of the rich folk to draw their water.

'I'll take tea while you see to my man,' I said.

Ernst nodded and bustled into the room behind the shop, returning a few minutes later with a shallow, steaming bowl cradled in his hands. Ernst loved his tea, and there was always a pot ready. Tea was expensive, though, very expensive, and he didn't make a habit of offering it to customers. Only princes don't wait to be offered, do they? Princes demand what they want, and are given it. Expectations to be met, as I have said.

I stood by the window and sipped my tea while Luka had his shave and his haircut. He looked better for it, I had to admit, although he was still fat. There was little enough to be done about that – if he had managed to stay fat on army rations then it was just his natural shape and he'd be fat for life, to my mind.

When we were done, I paid Ernst and told him to expect my brother and some of my friends over the next few days. He looked uncomfortable about that, but he nodded anyway. Jochan frightened him, I knew, but then Jochan frightened most people. That was what he was best at.

We left the barber's and headed farther up Trader's Row, past the hall of mercers and the temple of the Harvest Maiden to the shop of a tailor I knew. He looked a good part more pleased to see me than Ernst had, and he took our measurements and showed me the bolts of cloth without any unnecessary conversation. A good tailor has to be discreet, after all, and Pawl was certainly that. He was old too, older than Ernst, and he had seen enough of life to understand how it worked. I thought Pawl might have been a soldier once, but if so he had never spoken of it in my hearing. He agreed to come by the Tanner's Arms the next day and measure up the rest of my crew. I wasn't having any member of the Pious Men seen looking like that lot did, not now things were starting to happen.

They might not like it, but they had money now and they were going to start spending it in the right places and on the right things. Soon enough they would learn what those were.

I would insist on it.

Luka and I returned to the Tanner's Arms shortly before noon, and I found there was a whore waiting for me. She stood at the bar chatting to Bloody Anne, her back to me and her long red hair loose, but I could see the bawd's knot on her shoulder clear enough. We didn't run whores from the Tanner's. We never had done, and I wasn't about to start now.

'Who's this then?' I asked.

Anne was about to speak when the other woman turned around and gave me an insolent grin. It was her, I realised; that redhead who seemed to be the boss of the Chandler's Narrow girls. I had known that one was going to be trouble the moment I first saw her.

'Well now, don't you smarten up fine-looking?' she said.

She tossed her hair off her shoulder, proudly displaying the bawd's knot. Her hair was clean now, I noticed, which was probably why I hadn't recognised her at first. That and she was wearing a kirtle that looked new. Will the Woman had obviously started spending money on his girls now that he was in charge up there, and that was good. That was investment, and it showed initiative and that he knew what he was doing. Maybe he was one to watch.

'What do you want?' I asked her.

'He's a silver-tongued devil, ain't he?' the redhead said to Anne, and I noticed my second's scar twitch as she tried not to smile. 'What a charming man! My name's Rosie, Mr Piety, seeing as you didn't ask before.'

'And?'

'And I'm here to see you.'

She held my stare bold as brass and gave her hips a suggestive wiggle, and a thought struck me.

There's a Queen's Man in the city right now, the governor had told me. *Well, a Queen's Woman.*

It wasn't impossible, I realised, that I was looking at this Queen's Woman right now. The bawd's knot would make a fine disguise for a spy. A licensed whore comes and goes where she pleases, just about, and is seldom questioned. How far did duty to queen and country extend? I wondered. Enough to wear the knot, and do what that entailed? Perhaps it did. I wouldn't know.

'Then see me you shall,' I said. 'I think I'll see you in my chambers, Rosie. As I'm such a charming man.'

Bloody Anne gave me a look, but I ignored that and ushered Rosie up the rickety stairs and into the room I had taken as my own. I closed the door behind us and turned to face her.

'You'll have been spoken to,' Rosie said, and all the flirting ended. This was *her* talking now, not what she wore on her shoulder. 'I don't know by who, but someone's told you.'

'People tell me a lot of things,' I said. 'I'm a priest, after all.'

She snorted. 'You're a thug and a gangster,' she said, 'but someone's got your balls in a jar, haven't they, Mr Piety? I don't know who and it's none of my affair, but here's what I'm to tell you: she'll give her name as Ailsa. She'll be here tonight, and you're to give her a job when she asks you for one.'

'How do I know she's the one?'

'She'll say she can be trusted with money and with words alike. You hear her say that, she's the one.'

'Is that all?'

She shrugged. 'It's what I was told to tell you. Don't know what it means, and I don't much care.'

So this Rosie wasn't the one, then. I was glad about that, although I couldn't have said why.

'Told by who?'

Rosie sucked her teeth for a minute and shook her head. 'I ought to get back,' she said. 'Will don't want us being out and about on our own.'

I blocked her way. 'You'll tell me if I insist,' I assured her.

'Do you hit women, Mr Piety?' she asked me, and I saw a sudden flash of anger in her eyes. 'You probably do, but never the merchandise, I'm sure. That'd be bad for *business*, wouldn't it, and you wouldn't never want that. Get out of my way.'

Chapter 13

Rosie shoved past me and out the door, a furious set to her shoulders. She might not be the Queen's Man I had been told to expect, but I didn't think she was quite an ordinary whore, either. Someone important trusted her enough to carry messages, anyway. I followed her down the stairs and reached the common room in time to see her pulling a good woollen cloak around her. It seemed new as well, and all in all she made Bloody Anne look like she had just escaped from the poorhouse. That wouldn't do, not for my second it wouldn't.

'That was quick.' Anne smirked when I came into the room.

'I'll be seeing you,' Rosie said to Anne, and blew her a kiss. 'I hope.'

She ignored me completely and stalked out of the tavern, letting the new door swing shut behind her.

I looked around the common room, at the general state of the men in there, and shook my head. I rapped my knuckles on the bar to get their attention.

'We've been to see Ernst the barber, Fat Luka and me,' I said.

'Ain't he pretty now?' Black Billy laughed, reaching out to pinch Luka's smooth-shaved cheek.

'He's presentable is what he is, unlike you lot,' I said as Luka slapped Billy's hand good-naturedly away. 'Ernst is expecting the rest of you, so you'll get yourselves up there and get made presentable too. Jochan knows the way. And there'll be a tailor calling by tomorrow to measure you all up for some proper clothes. You're paying for your own,

87

but old Pawl discounts deep when he's stitching for the Pious Men, so treat yourselves to something nice.'

'I ain't wasting my beer money on clothes,' Simple Sam complained. 'I'm all right how I am, like. I ain't naked, Mr Piety.'

'Not this time,' someone said, and got some laughs for his trouble.

Simple Sam might not be naked but his britches had holes in the knees and it was a wonder I couldn't smell his shirt from where I was standing. I shook my head.

'Listen to me,' I said. 'You're Pious Men now, and in Ellinburg Pious Men look and act a certain way. When word gets around who you are, you'll be treated like lords, mark my words. That comes with some expectations, one of them being that you look and act like fucking lords. Isn't that so, Jochan?'

'Fucking right it is,' my brother said, and treated the men to his grin. 'You won't be paying for your own beer, my boys, not on our streets you won't. The Pious Men get the finer things in life.'

I nodded. 'That's settled then,' I said, making an end to it. 'Go five at a time; I don't want to frighten Ernst too bad all at once.'

Hari would have to wait, of course – he might be better than he had been, but he was still a long way from healed, and I knew he wouldn't be walking more than a few steps at a time on that leg for a long while yet. I'd have Cordin give him a shave, at least; that would have to do.

I went behind the bar to get myself a drink while the men argued over who was going first and with who, and I found Bloody Anne waiting for me. She put her thumbs through her belt and hitched up her britches.

'Don't think I'm wearing a dress, because I'm not,' she growled. 'I can't fight in a dress or ride in one neither, so I've no use for them.'

I shrugged. What she chose to wear was her business, to my mind, so long as it wasn't what she was standing in now.

'So have Pawl make you up some new britches and shirts, then,' I said. 'I don't think a woman in britches will bother him any.'

I started to turn away before she got to what she really wanted to say, but she put her hand on my wrist and stopped me.

'We need to talk about last night,' she said in a low voice. 'About Billy.'

'No, we don't,' I said.

I shook my hand free and poured myself a brandy. I hadn't had time to think about it, or rather I had but I had chosen not to. Something about Billy the Boy had always made me uneasy, but all the same I had accepted him as my confessor. I tried to remember why I had done that, back in Abingon, and found that I couldn't. It was a long time ago now, lost in the mists of blood and smoke and horror.

Eventually five of the crew got themselves out of the door with Jochan in the lead. He was busy telling them tall tales about the high life the Pious Men had lived before the war. There was some truth in his words, but I noticed that he hadn't mentioned that by the time war came there had only been him, me, Enaid, Alfread and Donnalt left. Pious Men lived well, it was true, but not necessarily for very long.

'Come and see Hari with me,' Anne said.

She wasn't going to let it pass, I could tell that much. I followed her through into the kitchen, where Hari was eating another bowl of oats and a hunk of salt pork, a fresh mug of small beer on the table in front of him.

'How are you, Hari?' she asked.

He looked up and grinned around a mouthful of pork. 'Good, Sarge,' he mumbled, and stuffed oats into his face to follow the pork.

'That your fourth bowl now, Hari?'

He shrugged, his brow furrowing in thought for a moment before he nodded. 'Aye.'

'That's good,' I said. 'You eat if you want it, there's plenty. Get your strength back.'

'Where's Billy?' Anne asked.

Hari jerked his head toward the fireplace, where the lad was curled up asleep on a threadbare rug by the hearth. For a moment I thought he was dead, he was so pale.

'He looks tired,' Anne said.

I shrugged. Perhaps he was. If he had been awake all night watching over Hari then it wasn't surprising, to my mind. I steered her out into the corridor to let Hari eat in peace and leaned close to speak to her.

'Is there a point you're getting to, Bloody Anne?'

'You know what point I'm getting to,' she hissed. 'Yesterday Hari was almost dead and today he's sitting up and eating enough for three men, and now Billy looks like he's crossed the river himself. Last night, Tomas, we saw him doing *witchcraft*!'

'No, we didn't,' I said, for all that I had no idea what we had seen. 'We saw him floating in the air, and who's to say how and why that happened. Do you know what witchcraft looks like, Anne? Because I don't. Maybe we saw a miracle.'

'Does Our Lady work miracles now, Tomas? *Does* she? Because we could have fucking done with some in Abingon, and I never saw any.'

I took a breath. Anne was making me angry, and I didn't want to get angry with her. I looked down the corridor into the common room and frowned.

'Where's my aunt?'

'Gone home,' Anne said. 'Jochan took her and a couple of the lads to her house this morning while you were out making yourself beautiful. They were going to see who was living there now, and to kick them out.'

'Right,' I said. 'Well, that's good.'

It was. It wouldn't have been good for whoever had decided they could help themselves to Aunt Enaid's house, I was sure, but whatever Jochan had done to them was deserved, to my mind. No one stole from the Pious Men, or from their families. Not in the Stink they didn't, not if they knew what was good for them. And this way I wouldn't have Enaid under my feet, with her looks and her awkward questions, and that was good too.

Jochan and I had never bothered getting homes of our own, even once we had enough money. It was easier to just live out of one of our boarding-houses, but for a long while after our da died we lived with Aunt Enaid in that house. I was glad she had it back now.

'I trust someone's staying with her, in case they come back,' I said.

Anne nodded. 'Brak is,' she said, 'and stop trying to change the subject.'

'What do you expect me to do about it, Bloody Anne?' I snapped. 'I'm an army priest, not a fucking mystic. I don't know what he was doing.'

'There must be someone,' she said. 'You said we'd need to talk to a magician.'

'There aren't any magicians; this isn't Dannsburg,' I said. 'There's no house of magicians here. As far as I know they never stir themselves far from the capital and the queen's favour. The closest thing I know to a magician is Old Kurt. People call him a cunning man, but he's about as much a magician as Doc Cordin is a real doctor.'

Magicians were very respectable, of course, whereas witches were to be hated and feared. The cunning folk fell somewhere between the two, but I wasn't sure I could see the difference. Magic was magic, whoever did it.

'Cordin knows what he's about,' Anne said, and from the stubborn set to her jaw I understood we weren't going to resolve this without shouting. 'I'm not letting it pass, Tomas.'

I could see that she wasn't. I had never thought Bloody Anne to be a particularly superstitious woman, no more than any other soldier is, anyway, but this idea she had got into her head that Billy the Boy was a witch was obviously troubling her more than she wanted to let on.

'All right,' I said. I'd let her have this, to keep the peace if nothing else. 'All right, Bloody Anne, if it'll make you happy we can go and talk to Old Kurt.'

'It would ease my mind some,' Anne admitted.

Old Kurt lived down in the Wheels, north of us between the Stink and the docks, on the edge of the river where the great waterwheels turned day and night. The waterwheels powered bellows in foundries, churns in tanneries, grinding stones in mills, anything that could be hooked up to gears and spindles. With most all the men of working age in the city dragged off to war at once, it was those wheels that had kept Ellinburg alive for the last three years. Those wheels, and women and old men. Ellinburg men age tough, like old roots, and if you ask me our women are born that way.

Ellinburg owed its life to the Wheels, but that didn't make it a nice part of the city.

'You and me, then,' I said. 'We'll go down to the Wheels and find Old Kurt. You'll want weapons and mail, and we'll be going on foot.'

'Should we take a couple of the crew with us, for guards?'

I shook my head. 'Old Kurt wouldn't like that,' I said. 'Me he knows, although we're not friends. You he'll tolerate just because you're a woman, and he likes women. All the same, he doesn't like strangers, and the Wheels is the sort of place where a band of armed men will draw more attention than we want.'

'I thought these were your streets?'

'*These* are,' I said. 'The Wheels ain't. I don't own all of Ellinburg, Anne. The Wheels is Gutcutter territory. I don't think their boss is back from the war yet, and Our Lady willing she won't be *coming* back, but even so it's no place for the Pious Men to go in force until we mean it.'

Bloody Anne nodded thoughtfully and went to don her leather and mail. She was still learning the city, I reminded myself. Yes, we were the Pious Men who were treated like lords, but only in the right places. The Stink was my territory, and the Narrows. Trader's Row and the wealthy streets around it were neutral ground, under the control of the City Guard, and western Ellinburg belonged to the Alarian Kings and the Blue Bloods. They were no one much and too far away for our territories to overlap, so we left each other alone. The Wheels, though, that might as well have been a foreign country. One that we weren't quite at war with, not at the moment anyway, but we seemed to be always on the brink of it. The Wheels belonged to the Gutcutters, and they were no friends of mine.

I got into my own leather and mail and buckled the Weeping Women around my waist. I looked at my priest's robe and decided against it. I told Fat Luka he was in charge until Jochan got back. Anne and me went out the back way, through the stable yard and along the alleys that led toward the river. We found the steps down to the water, where I had sent Cookpot with the cart and the bodies that first night back in Ellinburg.

The steps were stone, so old each one was worn into a shallow bowl by the passing of thousands of feet over more years than I knew how to count. Those steps were death in winter, I knew that much, when the hollows filled with water and froze into ice, and a careless man could slide all the way down into the merciless cold of the river.

'Right here,' I said to Bloody Anne, 'this is the edge of Pious Men streets. South of us is the Stink, and that's mine. Southwest is the

Narrows, and that's mostly mine too up as far as Trader's Row. That way, north, that's the Wheels, then the docks, and it ain't.'

Anne followed me down the steps to the narrow stone path that edged the riverbank and looked the way I was pointing. Upstream, the great waterwheels ceaselessly turned, dozens of them, casting their long afternoon shadows across the water. Most of the city's industry lay that way, all those lovely factories with all their profits, just waiting to be taxed. The filth they pumped into the river ran downstream into the Stink and gave the place its name. The Wheels wasn't going to stay Gutcutter territory forever. Not if I had my way.

Before the war, Ma Aditi had run the Gutcutters, and moving into her territory was unthinkable. But Ma Aditi had gone off to war with the rest of us, leading her men like some sort of empress. Women didn't get conscripted, but they could volunteer and she had, just like Bloody Anne, and so far she hadn't come back. I would be very happy if it stayed that way.

Ma Aditi was Ellinburg-born, but her skin was the same deep brown colour as the men off the tea ships. Her parents must have been from somewhere in Alaria, I could only assume, not that it really mattered. Ma Aditi was very clever and very cruel, and to my mind Ellinburg was better off without her. I knew *I* was, anyway.

'Are we safe then, going up there?' Bloody Anne asked.

I shrugged. 'Are you ever safe, Bloody Anne?' I asked her, and I was mocking her now even though I knew better. 'A Pious Man lives life on the edge. You could get run over by a cart tomorrow. You could get a curse put on you by a witch.'

I don't think I've ever seen Bloody Anne move so fast.

Before I could draw breath I was up against the slimy stone wall with her hard hand around my throat and the point of her dagger pressed into the corner of my eye.

'You take that back!' she hissed in my face, and I could see she was pure fucking furious. 'You take those words back, Tomas Piety, or I'll fucking blind you, I mean it!'

I didn't move a muscle.

'All right, Bloody Anne,' I said, offering a silent prayer to Our Lady that I wouldn't cross the river today. 'It's all right. I'm sorry, and I take my words back. I didn't mean anything by it.'

'No,' Anne said, and she eased the dagger back from my eye and took a step away. 'No, I know you didn't. I'm sorry. It's . . . doesn't matter. It's a long story, and not for telling now.'

She looked shaken, though, and it takes a lot to shake Bloody Anne. I blew out a breath and straightened my mail where she had grabbed me.

'Right,' I said. I'd let it pass, but I was curious all the same. Still, that would keep for later. 'Shall we?'

Anne nodded without speaking, and followed me along the path beside the river and into the Wheels.

Chapter 14

The Wheels was squalid and damp, but then it always had been. Although this was one of the worst parts of Ellinburg, it was also one of the most profitable territories to control. No one wanted to live near a tannery, no, but they might well enjoy the money from one.

Ma Aditi and the Gutcutters owned the Wheels, but I knew that she wasn't back from the war yet, so I hoped that meant most of her boys weren't either. Even so, we went carefully, keeping our hands close to the hilts of our weapons as we made our way along the treacherous path with the oily-looking river lapping at its bank a few feet below us.

It was quiet down by the water, and as we drew closer we could hear the great wooden wheels themselves turning on their axles, groaning rhythmically. Scummy white froth drifted downstream toward us where the river had been churned up by the movement, and in places I could see things floating in it. Turds, mostly, but there was the odd dead rat too.

We were in the Wheels all right.

'Keep your eyes open,' I said quietly, 'and don't draw attention.'

I could feel eyes on me like the flies on a hot Abingon night, making my skin crawl. There were high buildings on our left, their damp timber flanks rearing above the path and keeping us in shadow. Across the water to the east was nothing. It was just open marshland stretching into the distance. The river formed the fourth wall of Ellinburg, and they would be desperate raiders indeed who tried to cross the marshes, and then that wide expanse of flowing filth.

'Someone's watching us,' Anne said.

'I know,' I murmured. 'Someone always is, in the Wheels. It's probably just children.'

It probably was, but even children are dangerous if there are enough of them and they're armed. I didn't know how many there were, but they would be armed all right. You could bet on that. The path ended in a sheer drop down to rotting wooden pilings that had once supported a jetty, but on the left there was a cobbled alley leading up between two buildings. About twenty feet ahead of us was the first of the great wheels.

'There's folk up there,' Anne said.

I turned and looked up the alley toward Dock Road, where three cloaked figures were hiding in the shadows at the top in a way that said *murder* as loud as if they had been shouting it.

'Stinkers and Wheelers don't get on,' I explained. 'We didn't come along the riverbank for the fresh air. Going through the streets wouldn't have been good for our health. I don't think those fine fellows know who we are, but they're giving us the hard eye just because of which direction we've come from. The river path is all right, though, usually – Old Kurt insists there's free access to his door for everyone, wherever they're from.'

'And these Wheelers listen to him, do they?'

'Yes, Anne, they do, and more to the point so do the Gutcutters. Old Kurt is . . . well, I told you that people call him a cunning man. He's that all right, in both senses of the word. He knows how to win respect and get his own way, and I admire that. Whether he knows how to do magic, though, that's another matter.'

'I don't want him to *do* magic,' Anne said, somewhat sharply. 'I just want him to tell us about it.'

'Aye, well, he can do that,' I said. 'Some of what he says might even be true. I wouldn't know.'

I led the way into the alley, keeping my eyes on the fellows at the far end. Halfway along the narrow cobbled space, set into the side of an otherwise blank brick wall, was Old Kurt's door.

The building he lived in had been a workshop of some sort once, but many years ago Old Kurt had paid my da to brick the frontage up for him and seal it off from the street. He'd had Da bash a hole through the alley wall and make a new entrance there instead, so that Wheelers and Stinkers alike might have access to his door without having to fight their way there.

That was how I had first met him: as a ten-year-old 'prentice boy mixing lime mortar in this alley for Da and trying not to get my head kicked in while I was doing it. Kurt had made a point of picking a Stink man to do the work instead of a Wheeler, although that had caused some hard words at the time.

Kurt had been old even then, or had looked it to my young eyes anyway, and I had over thirty years to me now. Old Kurt was still there, though; I could tell that from the rat that was nailed to the outside of his front door.

He always nailed a fresh rat to his door every fifth day, and this one didn't look to be more than two or three days old. As to why he did it, well, I supposed that was his business, but it told folk he was still alive if nothing else.

I rapped on the door and called out the words. 'Wisdom sought is wisdom bought, and I have coin to pay,' I said loudly.

A moment later the door creaked open and Old Kurt's face peered out at me from the shadows inside.

'You'd better have, Tomas Piety,' he said. 'Oh, and this fine lady too! Welcome, welcome. Come you in, and mind your heads.'

I looked at Bloody Anne with her scar and her daggers and her stained, dirty men's clothes, and wondered if Old Kurt had ever seen a fine lady in his life. Probably not, I thought. We followed Kurt into his house, which was dimly lit with lamps on account of most of the windows having been boarded up. The place was squalid and it stank, but there were treasures in there too. Odd things, things you wouldn't necessarily notice if you didn't know to look for them.

The sword hanging over the mantel, its scabbard thick with cobwebs, had once belonged to a king. The skull on the windowsill, the one with its temple bashed in, had supposedly belonged to the same king. That brass candlestick with dried crusty tallow all over it was really solid gold. Or so Old Kurt had told me when I was a boy, anyway.

I smiled at the memories. He was a horrible old man with a house full of shit, to my mind, but he had been the one who had chased those Wheeler boys off me while I had been mixing my mortar in the alley outside. Not my da. Old Kurt had done that. Da had thought fighting was good for a boy, that it made a man of him. Although considering what went on in our house at nights I'd have thought that was the last thing Da wanted. I didn't want to think about that now, though. Or ever.

There had been three boys, and all of them old enough to shave, but Da hadn't stirred himself while Kurt chased them away. I had told Anne that Old Kurt and me weren't friends and that was true enough, but I would always have time for him, for that.

He took his chair by the fireplace and waved us to a pair of rickety stools.

Kurt must have had almost eighty years to him, by my reckoning, but he still looked the same as I remembered him from when I had been a boy. He was a narrow, spare man, his pointed face and whiskered chin making him look much like the rat nailed to his door. His thin white hair was short but dirty, pushed up in all directions by his darting, ratty hands.

'Show me your silver and tell me your troubles, Tomas,' Kurt said.

I looked at Bloody Anne. 'This is your question, not mine,' I said to her. 'It'll be your silver that buys an answer to it.'

She took a mark out of her pouch and put it in Old Kurt's grubby outstretched hand. He looked down at the coin, back at Anne, and grinned.

'Fine silver from a fine lady,' he said with a leer. 'I'm a lucky boy, ain't I?'

She cleared her throat. She looked uncomfortable, did Bloody Anne, and I noticed her eyes kept wandering to the skull on the windowsill, the bound herbs that hung in bunches from the ceiling, the thick dusty books that were scattered around the room. Some of the books had rat shit on them, I saw.

'There's this boy,' she started. 'He—'

'A boy, is it?' Kurt interrupted. 'Might have known you'd be wasting my time, Piety. I don't do love spells, nor potions neither.'

I said nothing and let Anne speak for herself. The lesson of the boarding-house was still fresh in my mind, and I don't believe in making the same mistake twice.

'I don't want a fucking love spell,' Bloody Anne snarled at him. 'I've paid you silver for wisdom, so you'll have the good grace to shut up and listen to the fucking question without interrupting me again or I'll nail you to your door with your fucking rat, you understand me?'

Old Kurt stared at her for a moment, then laughed his thin, reedy old man's laugh. 'That's me told, ain't it,' he said. 'I'll listen, my fine lady. I'll listen to you.'

He was quiet then, but something in his eyes and the way he was looking at Anne made me wary. You didn't cross Bloody Anne, not if you knew what was good for you, but you didn't cross Old Kurt either.

No, you didn't do that.

'This boy,' Anne started again. 'He's an orphan, with twelve years to him. We found him near Messia, after the sack. In the war, this was, way down in the south. A strange boy, but he wanted to join up and the regiment took him and any others they could get. He's touched by the goddess.'

'Which one?' Kurt asked. 'And who says so?'

'Our Lady of Eternal Sorrows. Tomas is her priest, and *he* says so.'

Old Kurt turned a stare on me. I wasn't wearing my robes that day, and this was obviously the first he'd heard of it.

'A priest, is it?'

'It is,' I said. 'This boy, Billy. He's a confessor and a seer. The goddess speaks to him, or through him. I don't know which.'

'Well and good,' Kurt said, 'if a *priest* says so.'

He smirked when he said it, though, and I remembered why Old Kurt and me weren't friends.

'One of our crew was wounded,' Anne went on. 'He nearly died from all the blood he lost. *Should* have died, to my mind, but he didn't. He didn't because Billy sat up all night floating in the air and staring at him, doing magic at him. Now he's awake and alive and eating for six men, and I want to know if we have a *witch* in our crew.'

Her scar tightened and twisted when she said *witch*, I noticed.

'Witches now, is it?' Old Kurt said. 'Messia, is it? Well, what could that mean?'

'You tell us,' I said. 'You're the cunning man.'

Old Kurt thought on it for a moment, then got up and went over to a big chest by the back wall. He rummaged inside for a moment, then straightened up and handed Anne a long iron nail.

'You put this under where the boy sleeps at night,' he said, 'and we'll see.'

'What is it?' Anne asked.

'A nail,' I said.

'It's a witchspike, you ignorant thug,' Old Kurt snapped. 'Priest my hairy arse, or you'd know what it was. That there's a witchspike, and if he's what you fear he'll feel it. Put that under his blankets and wait. If he wakes screaming in the night then he's a witch, and you can deal with that as you see fit. If he doesn't, though, then you bring him here. You bring him to see Old Kurt and I'll have a look at him. Is that a deal, my fine lady?'

Anne nodded and slipped the nail into her pouch.

'Deal,' she said.

Chapter 15

We left Old Kurt's after that, having no reason to linger. I stepped back out into the alley and there were the three cloaked figures waiting for us.

'You're away from your streets, Piety,' one said to me.

I nodded slowly. 'That I am,' I said. 'I've been visiting with the cunning man, as you can well see. All have free passage to Old Kurt's door. You know that.'

The man stepped closer to me, and I could see the jut of an unshaven chin poking out of the hood of his cloak. He looked to have perhaps thirty years to him and he sounded like an Ellinburg man, and those things together made him a veteran.

'How long have you been back?' I asked, before he could say anything else.

He paused, looked at me. I heard his sigh and knew I had found common ground. Men who had shared the Hell of Abingon would always have that in common, if little enough else.

'Three days,' he said.

'And no Ma Aditi,' I said.

'Not yet. She'll come.'

'Will she?'

I was conscious of the other two, who had the back of the one I was talking to, and of Bloody Anne, who as always had *my* back. Common ground or no, that made us three to two, and we were on their streets where they might have mates just a shout away. I didn't know what they were carrying under those cloaks, but I wouldn't have bet a clipped

101

copper against it being steel. We might have shared the same horrors, but that alone wasn't going to make us friends. That was three to two against us at the very best, then. Not good odds, not when we'd be betting with our lives.

'She will,' he said.

I nodded at that, and decided that honour would keep for another day.

'We'll be on our way, then,' I said.

'Back to the Stink.'

'Aye, back to the Stink,' I agreed. 'The Wheels belong to the Gutcutters, everyone knows that.'

'That it does, Piety,' he shouted after us as we walked back down to the path at the riverside. 'That it does, and see you remember it!'

When we returned to the Tanner's Arms it was starting to get dark and we were both hungry. I found Hari limping around in the kitchen, leaning on a stout stick he had picked up somewhere. He was tidying cupboards and taking what looked like an inventory of what he found in there.

'How're you feeling?' I asked him.

'Not so bad, boss, thank you,' he said, although I could see the pain and weariness etched in the lines of his pale face.

'You look at home, in here,' I said.

He shrugged. 'Just trying to keep busy,' he said. 'I want to be useful to you. I . . .'

I don't want to be thrown out into the streets to starve because I can't fight no more, his face said.

'You're all right, Hari,' I assured him. 'Don't you worry. Have you seen young Billy?'

Hari shook his head, but some of the tension went out of his face at my words and he allowed himself to sink into the chair with a wince of pain.

'I think he went in the back to sleep some more,' Hari said.

I nodded and helped myself to something to eat, then left him to it. I dumped my mail and leather upstairs in my room but buckled the Weeping Women back around my waist again over my shirt tails.

I didn't think the Gutcutters would bother us, not on our own streets. Not without Ma Aditi here to say so, anyway, but one of them had seen me and by now they'd all know I was back in Ellinburg.

The war in the south might only just have ended, but all that meant was that the war in Ellinburg was about to start up again. It was a quiet sort of war, by and large, but it was a war all the same, and now we had this man they called Bloodhands and his Skanians added to the broth. If Hauer was to be believed we did, anyway, and I couldn't think that he wasn't. He had no reason to lie about it, that I could see.

I went back down to the common room and found Bloody Anne waiting for me behind the bar with two glasses of brandy already poured for us. She nodded to me cordially enough, but I couldn't help noticing the way her fingers kept touching her pouch. Billy the Boy was going to come between us if I wasn't careful.

'You're going to use that, then?' I asked as I picked up my drink and leaned forward with my elbows on the bar opposite her.

'The witchspike? Yes, Tomas, I am.'

I nodded. 'Well, that's your affair,' I said. 'Your silver bought you wisdom from Old Kurt, so it's up to you whether to believe what he told you.'

'Don't you?'

I shrugged and took a swallow of brandy. 'People call him a cunning man,' I said, 'and that has two meanings, like I said before. Maybe he knows about magic and maybe he doesn't, but he's the other sort of cunning too. Old Kurt is very good at making people believe in him, Anne. Very good indeed. He's *that* sort of cunning, you mark me.'

'I'll put it under Billy's bedroll,' she said, sounding firm about the notion, 'and then we'll see.'

I just nodded. If that made Anne happy, then who was I to judge, but to my mind all that would prove was that a boy who was exhausted and would probably go to bed drunk anyway wouldn't notice that there was a lump under his blankets.

The front door creaked behind me, and I turned to see who it was coming back from wherever he had been. My eyebrows rose as I realised that this wasn't one of my crew at all. I leaned back with my elbows on the bar behind me and my hands hanging loose within easy reach of Remorse and Mercy.

She walked into the tavern with her hood pushed back to bare thick dark hair and a face the dusky brown colour of an Alarian's. A patched and frayed green cloak hung from her shoulders, open over her white linen shirt and servant's skirts. There was a leather travelling bag in her hand.

'How do?' I said.

She smiled shyly and bobbed a clumsy curtsey. 'Good evening, sir, Mr Piety,' she said. 'My name's Ailsa. I heard the tavern was opening again, under new management as you might say, and I wondered if you had any work going? I need the coin and I ain't afraid of hard work, with my hands nor my head. I can keep a bar and I can tally books, or I can scrub a floor and wash glasses, and I can be trusted with money and with words alike.'

She had perhaps twenty-five years to her and she looked like a trader off one of the tea ships, but I realised she wasn't. Oh, she was young and very pretty, but I wasn't fooled. Her dark eyes met mine and I knew *exactly* who she was.

She'll give her name as Ailsa, Rosie from Chandler's Narrow had told me. *She'll be here tonight, and you're to give her a job when she asks you for one.*

That had sounded a lot like an order to me, the sort of order that I knew I had to obey. I didn't fucking like it, but then I hadn't liked it the last time either. Serve the crown or hang; that had been the choice before me, and to my mind that was no choice at all.

She'll say she can be trusted with money and with words alike. You hear her say that, she's the one.

I nodded. 'Aye,' I said. 'The Tanner's Arms is back under its rightful management, to set the matter straight, but aye. I reckon there might be work going, as you asked so nicely.'

I heard Bloody Anne draw breath to speak, then obviously think better of it. She poured herself another brandy, and if she put the bottle down harder than was strictly called for then that was her affair.

Ailsa bobbed another curtsey and showed me a smile that was a little bit more than friendly. 'Thank you, Mr Piety, sir,' she said. 'You won't regret it.'

I wasn't too sure about that, but I knew what the choice was. Ailsa might appear common and clumsy, but she was a Queen's Man and I was swimming out of my depth in dangerous waters.

Billy the Boy came through from the back just then, and he stood there staring at Ailsa with his mouth open. I frowned at him, and he looked at me and nodded.

'She'll be staying,' he announced.

'Aye, Billy, she will,' I said, but it hadn't sounded to me like he was asking a question.

'Who's this young man then?' Ailsa asked.

'I'm Billy,' he said.

'Billy the Boy, we call him,' I said, 'and this here's Bloody Anne.'

'A soldier's name,' Ailsa said, giving Anne a long look.

'What of it?' Anne snapped.

'Nothing at all.'

'There's a room upstairs, next to mine,' I said, cutting in before the two of them fell to hard words over nothing, as strangers sometimes can. 'My aunt doesn't need it any more so you might as well take it.'

Ailsa nodded. Jochan and Anne were both happy enough sleeping with the crew, but obviously I couldn't put Ailsa in there with that lot. That wouldn't have ended well, for someone. Whichever of my boys stupid enough to put his hands where they weren't welcome, I suspected, but I knew someone would have been bound to try it. Best if that didn't happen.

'Much obliged,' Ailsa said.

I had Billy show her up to the room, and the lad even took her bag for her like a proper young gentleman. Anne waited until they were gone before she rounded on me.

'What in Our Lady's name are you doing, Tomas?' she demanded.

'I need a barmaid,' I said. 'It's time we opened the Tanner's to the public again. I've a mind to put Hari in charge of the business as he seems to have a feel for it, and he can't do much else. Even so, he can't be behind the bar all night on that leg of his. She can keep the bar and he can run the business side, with one of the others on the door.'

'And where are we supposed to sleep, and live?'

'We'll fit round it, for now,' I said. 'Later on, we'll have more places to choose from.'

'Billy likes her, I see,' Anne noted, and something in her tone made me give her a look.

'You haven't proved anything about Billy yet,' I reminded her, 'and I don't believe that you will. Don't jump to justice until you know if it's deserved, Anne. That's no way to lead.'

She patted her pouch, the one that held Old Kurt's witchspike.

'I'll know tonight,' she said. 'And then we'll see.'

I supposed that we would, at that.

Chapter 16

I let Ailsa settle in, and told Hari and Jochan what I had in mind. Hari was overjoyed, obviously glad to feel useful and even more glad to know he'd be keeping a roof over his head. Jochan just leered at me.

'The room next to yours, is it?' he said. 'Boss gets first go, is that the way of it?'

I snorted. If he wanted to think that, if all of them wanted to think that, then it made my decision to hire a stranger at a moment's notice a lot more believable. I'd rather they believed I was keeping Ailsa as my fancy woman than that they started wondering who she might really be. That way she'd be left alone too. It was for the best, to my mind, and I can't say that the idea was without its charms. You didn't see many women who looked like her, not in the Stink you didn't.

'If you want a woman, you know where Chandler's Narrow is,' I said. 'But see that you pay for it.'

Jochan winked at me. 'Might be that I will, Tomas,' he said.

I made a mental note to check with Will the Woman that Jochan and any of the others who went up there had paid their way. You can't keep a stew and tell men like these they're not to visit it, but they were going to pay full price like anyone else. Taking for free was stealing from the girls, and indirectly it was stealing from me as well. There would be harsh justice for anyone who thought he could do that and look me in the eye afterward.

Ailsa was in the kitchen with Hari now, being shown the ropes. Hari had even found himself an old stained white apron in one of the storage chests out the back, and made himself look like a proper tavern keeper. He could hobble about on his stick for a few minutes at a time but that was all, and I knew I'd have to make sure there were always a couple of the crew on hand once we opened up properly.

These were my streets but that didn't mean there was never trouble, and when folk have beer and brandy inside them and dice or cards in front of them the chances of that always go up. Hari wasn't going to be stopping any fights by himself. That was for sure.

I was standing at the bar thinking on who might be best for that job, who looked the part and who I could trust not to get too drunk of a night, when Fat Luka strolled over.

'The new lass seems nice,' he said, drawing himself a beer from one of the big barrels behind the bar.

'Aye,' I said.

Luka wouldn't do – he drank too much, and besides as an Ellinburg native he would be more useful doing other things for me. I didn't want him stuck in the Tanner's every night.

'She knows her figures too, and she can read well enough,' he said, sounding impressed. 'She could do the books and that.'

Luka hadn't even spent as long in school as I had, and while he could read after a fashion it was hard work for him. All the same, apart from me and Jochan, he was the only one of the crew who could read and figure at all, to my knowledge. I knew Cookpot couldn't, school or not. Sir Eland said he could, of course, but no one had ever seen him do it. I think Luka had been dreading being asked to keep books.

'She could,' I agreed. 'Tell me something, what's your opinion of Mika?'

Mika was one of Jochan's original crew and I didn't know him well yet, but he was the one I had sent to find carpenters when I had needed them and he had managed that all right.

'He can think for himself, which is more than some of the lads can,' Luka said.

I nodded. That was what I had thought too.

'Him and Black Billy, then,' I said, thinking out loud. 'They can keep the peace here when the Tanner's opens for business again.'

Black Billy was a big lad and he was good with his fists. Black faces weren't unknown in Ellinburg, but they were a lot rarer than brown ones, and certainly not so common that he wouldn't be noted. I'd put him on the door where he could be seen, I decided, and have Mika inside keeping a quiet eye on things. That would work.

The right man for the right job, that was how I led men.

Luka took a long drink and put his tankard down on the bar. 'Can I say something?' he asked.

'What?'

'It's Jochan,' he said.

I had thought it might be.

'What about him?'

Luka had another drink while he picked his words carefully. 'Well, he ain't said anything, not to me,' Luka said, 'but I've known him since . . . ever. You too, of course.'

I nodded. 'Out with it, Luka,' I said. 'I know what my brother's like, and I don't think you're about to tell me anything I'd call a surprise.'

'The Tanner's Arms,' Luka said. 'He'll think it should have been his. You've put Hari in what he'll think was his rightful place, and Hari's crippled as well so you've got to set another two men to mind the place where one would have done. He'll think that, is all I'm saying.' Luka coughed and gulped beer, looking worried that he'd said too much.

'I'm disappointed that you think I don't know that, Fat Luka,' I said. 'Jochan all but has brandy for breakfast, these days. Lady knows the last thing he should be doing is running a fucking tavern.'

'I know, boss,' Luka said, 'and I didn't mean you wouldn't, like. I'm just saying, is all.'

I nodded, and looked at Fat Luka. I had known him since we had all been in school together, him and me and Jochan and Cookpot. He hadn't been a Pious Man before the war, but he had been around, on the fringes of our life. He had done bits and pieces of work for me even back then, and I knew I could trust him. I wondered if perhaps he was working around the edges of saying he thought *his* part in things should be bigger now, and maybe he had a point about that.

I considered that for a moment, and I made a decision.

'I want to ask you to do something for me, Luka,' I said. 'I won't take ill against you if you say no, but there's silver for you if you'll do it.'

'Course,' he said. 'I'm a Pious Man now, ain't I?'

He was, and he knew better than most of the others what that meant. He had seen enough of how things worked before the war to know what he was getting into, and he had been happy to join us just the same. Luka was greedy, I knew that, but he could be trusted. To a point, anyway. Knowing your men, knowing which levers move them, is a big part of leadership, to my mind.

Fat Luka was moved by silver.

'You are,' I said. 'You're all Pious Men now, but you're an Ellinburg man too and you know how things work. How they *really* work, I mean, which might not always be how I explain things to the rest of the crew. They're still learning the city, all except Cookpot anyway, but he was never one of us before the war. He doesn't know how business is done any more than Simple Sam does.'

'That's true enough,' Fat Luka said. 'What do you need, boss?'

'Eyes and ears, and a supportive voice,' I said. 'I want you to watch the men and listen to them when I'm not here. I want you to listen to their talk over dice, and when they're in their cups. If anyone starts disagreeing with me or questioning my orders, I want you to explain to them why they're wrong. Then I'll want to hear about it, and who said what. Can you do that, Fat Luka?'

He took a moment, and a long swallow of beer, then put his empty tankard down on the bar and nodded.

'I can do that,' he said.

I took a silver mark out of my pouch and slid it across the bar to him, and he made it disappear.

The right man for the right job, as I said.

It was late by the time I had the chance to talk to Ailsa in private. There had been enough nudges and winks and gossip exchanged throughout the evening that no one passed further comment when I went up to her room, and by that time half the crew had taken themselves off to

Chandler's Narrow to find a girl of their own. Bloody Anne had gone with them, I noticed.

Ailsa opened her door at my knock and let me in. She turned a smile on me as I stood leaning against the inside of the door with my arms crossed. She had unpacked her few things, hung some spare clothes from nails in the beams and spread herself a bedroll on the floor. There was a neat row of little bottles and small flat cases lined up on the windowsill above the washbasin.

'Welcome to the Pious Men,' I said. 'We live in luxury, as you can see.'

'You did before and you will again,' she assured me as she sat in the room's only chair.

She sounded completely different than she had earlier, I noticed. Her voice now carried the inflections of Dannsburg aristocracy instead of a common girl from the countryside, and if she had seemed clumsy before, then that was gone too.

'What do you know about me?' I asked.

'Everything,' she said. 'Assume that I know absolutely everything, and you will never be surprised or caught in a lie that you would regret.'

'Well, I don't know the first thing about you, so there you have me at a disadvantage.'

'Yes.'

'Tell me this, then,' I said, lowering my voice. 'How does a slip of an Alarian girl become a Queen's Man?'

She smiled, and this time it was without warmth. 'I was born and raised in Dannsburg,' she said. 'My parents may have come from Alaria, but I have never set foot in the place. And "a slip of a girl", Tomas? Is that what you think?'

'You've what, twenty-five years to you?'

She snorted. 'Paints and powders are worth their weight in gold,' she said, and showed me that humourless smile again. 'I'm a good deal older than I look, and if you're underestimating me based on my face and the colour of my skin then you are a fool and I am pleased, because that means it's working.'

'I'm not a fool,' I said. 'This is new to me, that's all. I only saw a Queen's Man once before, and he had over sixty years to him.'

'Had he? Paints and powders, Tomas. False hair and mummer's scars. Perhaps he was your age. Perhaps you and Luka walked past him on Trader's Row this morning on your way to the barber's and the tailor's, and you never knew him.'

I shrugged. I supposed she had a point, but that didn't matter. She was telling me that she knew where I had been that morning, before I even met her, and who I had been with and what I had done. That wasn't lost on me.

'Perhaps,' I admitted.

'You didn't, he's dead.'

'Those are the times we live in.'

'One of his informers betrayed him a year ago,' she said. 'Someone sent him back to Dannsburg on four different trade caravans, a piece at a time. This is "harsh work" we do, as you would put it, and our enemies are every bit as harsh as we are.'

I cleared my throat and looked at her. Now that she had told me, I could almost see her age. There was something in the way she held her head, keeping her neck out of the light of the lamp with an ease that spoke of practised skill. Something in the way her hands were neatly folded in her lap that was helping her hide the telltale signs of age on the backs of her knuckles. She was good, though. She was very, very good, and I would never have guessed if she hadn't told me and I hadn't been trying hard to look for those signs.

'Tell me about the Queen's Men, then,' I said. 'I thought you were supposed to be knights.'

'We are,' she said. 'A particular order of the knighthood, one that answers directly to the crown. You won't have seen any of us on the battlefield, though, not and known who we were. The sort of knight you're thinking of, their weapons are the sword and lance and battle-axe. My weapons are gold and lace, and paints and powders. And the dagger, when it's needed. You can hide a dagger very well indeed, behind enough lace.'

I supposed that you could, at that.

The right man for the right job, I thought. I wondered exactly what job Ailsa was here to do.

Chapter 17

I was still awake and sitting in the common room with Black Billy when those of the crew who had gone out came blundering back from Chandler's Narrow in the small hours of the morning, drunk and looking pleased with themselves. Bloody Anne looked the most pleased with herself of all, and I hoped that she had found what she was looking for up there. I remembered how her and Rosie had been talking in the Tanner's, and I thought that she probably had. It was only then that I noticed Billy the Boy was with them.

I snagged Jochan's arm as he swayed past.

'Tell me you didn't get Billy a woman,' I said.

Jochan laughed. 'He's too young for that,' he said. 'He'll have a pecker like your little finger. He said he wanted to come with us so I let him, but he just sat there staring at Sir Eland all night while we had our fun. Fuck knows why. The lad's strange in the head, Tomas.'

I saw Anne's scar twitch at that, and her hand go to her pouch again. She'd be putting that nail under Billy's bedroll tonight. I knew she would. I just hoped that Our Lady was kind and Billy didn't wake up screaming from some nightmare, or I dreaded to think what Anne was likely to do.

'Eland must have been pleased to see him,' I said, knowing he would have been nothing of the sort. 'How's Will the Woman getting on?'

Jochan shrugged. 'He knows what he's about,' he said. 'The place is the cleanest I can remember it, and the girls too. None of them have taken ill against him, anyway, so he must be doing right by them.'

'Good,' I said.

Licensed whores don't grow on trees, and you have to keep them happy. Rosie might have said they had nowhere else to go, but I knew Ma Aditi's Gutcutters would have taken them in tomorrow, and I thought that she probably knew that as well. The bawd's knot has to be earned and paid for, and it's what sets them apart from common street scrubs. That meant higher prices and more money all round. It sounded like Will was working out well up there in Chandler's Narrow.

'Go to bed, the lot of you,' I said. 'It's Godsday tomorrow, and I'll be taking confession from those that want to give it.'

Godsday fell every eighth day, the day when all the temples were opened and the priests of the various gods held confession and gave absolution to their faithful. Traditionally, no one worked on Godsday. When times were as hard as they were now in Ellinburg, though, and folk had to work if they wanted to eat, most priests let that pass. In the army it had been irrelevant anyway, and sometimes it had been hard to even keep track of what day it was.

At Abingon I had taken confession whenever someone wanted to give it. There was no saying they would still be alive come the appointed day, after all, but now we were back home it seemed only right that I put some formality into it. People expect certain things from a priest, in the same way they expect things from a businessman. They expected certain ways of being, and of acting. I'd need to remember that. Being a priest in a city in peacetime was different to being one in the army during a war. I knew that much, and I had never done it before.

I shrugged and finished my brandy as the crew jostled their way through to the back to wait their turns at the shithouse and get into their bedrolls. Black Billy was on the door, his new post, and I gave him a nod.

'You can lock up for the night now,' I told him. 'Get yourself a drink, if you want one.'

'Thanks, boss,' he said.

He seemed pleased to have a regular posting, and had taken to wearing a big wooden club at his belt that left no one in any doubt that the door was his.

Things were starting to come together quite well, to my mind. I thought of Ailsa, asleep upstairs in the room next to mine, and I frowned.

She was a Queen's Man, and sleeping under my roof at that. What did that make me? I wondered. An informer, I knew, and the very word made my tongue curl up in my mouth like I wanted to spit at someone.

You've no choice, I told myself. *It's this or hang, and that won't help those streets outside your door. It's just business.*

Perhaps not quite everything was coming together, but most things were.

The next morning Bloody Anne had a sore head and dark circles of tiredness under her eyes.

'All night I sat up, and he never screamed,' she said. 'The lad slept like a fucking baby on top of that witchspike.'

'Told you so,' I said, while Ailsa brought us mugs of small beer and hunks of black bread to break our fast.

She had donned a clean white linen apron that put Hari's to shame, although where hers had come from was anyone's guess. I could only assume she had brought it with her in her bag.

'You did,' Anne admitted. 'I was wrong about him, Tomas.'

I just shrugged. A nail from a crazy old man didn't prove water was wet, to my mind, but if it quietened Bloody Anne down on the subject then I would take that and be grateful for it.

'No shame in that,' I said. 'Magic is a tricky thing, so I hear.'

'We saw what we saw,' she said, and I could see she still wasn't going to let it pass. 'If he's not a witch, then what?'

'I don't know, Anne. Old Kurt said to bring Billy to him, if he slept on the nail and didn't wake, so I suppose we'll be doing that. But not today. Today is Godsday, and I'll be busy and so will Kurt.'

'He's no priest,' Anne said.

'No, he ain't, but he's the closest thing a lot of folk have, especially down in the Wheels. He hears confession too. He shouldn't, to my mind, but he does.'

'And you'll be taking confession today?' Anne asked. 'Here, I mean?'

'I could throw open the doors of my magnificent golden temple and do it there instead, but it's a long fucking walk to dreamland,' I said. 'Aye, I'll be doing it here.'

There was no temple of Our Lady in Ellinburg, but she had her shrine in the Great Temple of All Gods along with all the others. That wasn't my place, though, I knew that. My place was here in the Stink, with my crew.

Anne cleared her throat. 'Aye,' she said. 'I . . . I might speak to you, then.'

'As you like,' I said. 'Our Lady listens to everyone.'

Anne had never come to me before, and I had always assumed she had some other god she held to, but perhaps not. She nodded and left me there, thinking on the day ahead.

When I had finished my breakfast I put it about that I would be hearing confessions, and I went up to my room. I put my robe on and sat in the chair under the small window, and waited.

Cookpot was first.

He came into the room, looking nervous for all that he had said confession to me enough times before. Perhaps it felt more formal like this, alone in a room together on Godsday instead of in a tent behind the lines whenever the chance came up. Whatever it was, he couldn't meet my eyes as he shuffled into the room and knelt awkwardly at my feet with his round face cast to the ground.

'I wish to confess, Father.'

They only used the title when I was hearing confession, but it still sounded strange in my ears. 'Father' was Da, to my mind, and Our Lady knew I wasn't him.

Anything but that.

'Speak, in the name of Our Lady,' I said.

'I killed a man,' Cookpot said. 'I never done that before, not ever. That night, here, when they came. The flashstone went off and then the door blew in right beside me and I . . . I . . .'

He choked into silence. I waited, giving him his moment. That was how this was done. Some men found confession easy and some found it hard, and some treated it like a joke. It was all the same to me. They were speaking to Our Lady, not to me, and it was on their consciences how they went about it. Every man in his own time and his own way. That was how I held confession.

'I ain't a fighter,' Cookpot said at last. 'I was at Abingon with everyone else, but I never killed no one. That doesn't mean I never saw it, though,

116

or heard it. I'm just a fucking cook, but I remember when they brought Aaron back on a stretcher with his guts hanging out all blue and slimy and him screaming for his ma. I remember when the surgeon took Donnalt's arm off at the shoulder and he still went mad and died from the rot in his blood. I remember the noise, Tomas. The fucking *noise*! Them cannon, all fucking day, and the walls coming down, and the smoke and the dust.

'When that door blew in, I just . . . I thought we was done with it, you know? I thought it was over and I weren't dead after all and it might be all right now, but when that door came in I was right back there and Aaron was screaming again and I could hear the cannon roar and that man come through the door and I just . . . I just had to stab him. I *had* to, do you understand?'

Cookpot was weeping now, and I reached out a hand and put it on his head.

'It was his time to cross the river, and Our Lady forgives you,' I said. 'In Our Lady's name.'

Truth be told, I didn't know what Our Lady of Eternal Sorrows would have thought of that. Not much, I suspected. She had decreed that that wasn't Cookpot's day to die, and that had been the end of her part in the business, to my mind.

Cookpot wiped a sleeve across his eyes and nodded, still sniffling. 'In Our Lady's name,' he repeated. He got to his feet and looked at me, snot running out of his left nostril. 'I don't know that I can do this,' he said. 'Be a Pious Man, I mean.'

I nodded slowly. 'Well, you think on it, Cookpot,' I said. 'If you can't, then I won't take ill against you for it, but I'll need to know soon.'

'Aye,' he said. 'And thank you, Father.'

I would have to have Luka keep a close eye on him until he made his choice, I thought. Cookpot left, and I had Simple Sam after that.

Simple Sam grinned and confessed that he had pissed in Jochan's brandy bottle one night when Jochan had passed out, then Jochan had woken up and drank it and not noticed the difference. Simple Sam held that that was funny, but he felt he ought to confess it anyway, and I told him that I thought it was funny as well, but he didn't ought to do it again or Jochan would hurt him, and I forgave him and sent him on his way.

Most of the others came, one after another, to confess to cheating at dice or stealing something they shouldn't have done, and I forgave them all in Our Lady's name. Petty crimes from petty criminals didn't interest me, and I dare say they interested Our Lady even less.

Grieg from my original crew confessed that he had hurt his girl last night, in the house at Chandler's Narrow, and that was how he liked it. I stood him up and I belted him in the face, and felt his nose shatter under my knuckles.

When he stopped choking on the blood, he admitted he didn't like it when someone did it to him, and I forgave him and sent him on his way. I made a mental note to have Will the Woman find out which girl that had been and make sure she was all right, and to pay her a week off by way of apology from me.

That was how I held confession that day, until at the very end Bloody Anne came to my room and knelt in front of me.

'I wish to confess, Father,' she said.

'Speak, in the name of Our Lady,' I said.

Anne spoke, and what she told me wasn't what I was expecting to hear.

'Last night I lay with a woman,' she said, and that part I had been expecting, at least.

'I don't think Our Lady cares who we lie with, so long as both are willing,' I said. 'There's no need to confess that, Bloody Anne.'

Her head snapped up, and there was a look of fury on her face. 'Don't tell me what I need to confess!' she snarled. 'A priest listens to people, so you'll fucking well listen to me.'

That made me blink, but I nodded. 'As you will,' I said. 'Confess, then.'

Bloody Anne drew a shuddering breath and lowered her head again. 'I grew up in a little village in some hills, northwest of here,' she said. 'Nowhere you'd have heard of. We raised sheep and traded wool, and we held to the Stone Father there, not Our Lady, and we didn't have no priest. There was just Mother Groggan.'

I sat quiet and waited for her to work her way around to her point.

'Mother Groggan very much cared who lay with who,' Anne went on. 'One day my brother caught me and Maisy the cooper's daughter out in Da's barn together. He raised the gods over it, and we were both dragged in front of Mother Groggan to confess how we had sinned with each other in the Stone Father's eyes.'

I nodded, understanding. I didn't know this Stone Father, but a god who had nothing better to worry about than who you might choose to fuck didn't sound like he was worth much, to my mind.

'It was Mother Groggan,' Anne went on, her voice going very quiet. 'She was the one.'

'The one what, Anne?'

'The witch!' she spat. 'How do you think I got *this*, Tomas?'

She threw her head back and gestured angrily at the long scar on her face.

I had never given it any thought. Anne had been at war for a year before I ever met her, and a lot of soldiers had scars. I shrugged.

'Fighting, I'd always thought,' I said. 'The road to Messia, maybe.'

'Being held down by my own brothers and cut by a witch called Mother Groggan, when I had only sixteen years to me,' she said, and now her voice was flat and quiet. 'Cut open for the crime of being in love with a girl. She cut my face, and she cut me in the other place too. Me and Maisy, both. I was pretty once, Tomas. Can you believe that?'

I nodded slowly. I could.

'She cut my face so I wouldn't be pretty enough for anyone to want me no more, and she cut me down below so I wouldn't be tempted even if they did. She did the same to Maisy and she put her witch's curse on us so we wouldn't never love again. Love another woman, Mother Groggan cursed us, and she'll die. Only I never stopped loving my Maisy because how could I, and then her wound went bad and she died from it and that was my fault.' Anne paused to choke back tears before she could go on. 'Last night I . . . it was the first time, in all those years. I lay with Rosie, from Chandler's Narrow, because I like her a lot. I can't . . . with a woman, or a man neither. Not since Mother Groggan cut me. But I can touch someone, and take pleasure from doing it. And now I think it's going to happen to her too, like it did to Maisy, and it will be my fault again. I shouldn't have done it, put her at risk like that. So I'm confessing that, whether you think Our Lady cares or not.'

I swallowed. I had never known, never even suspected, what Bloody

Anne had been through. She was my second and my friend, and I had never had the slightest idea. I found that I didn't have any words to say to her, and that shamed me.

'I never,' Anne said, like she had to fill the silence somehow. 'I never lay with anyone else, after Maisy, not until last night. I was a long time healing from what Mother Groggan did to me. Once I was healed I went back to the fields and I watched the sheep like I was supposed to, but I was dead inside just like my Maisy was dead, because what right did I have to be alive when she wasn't? Even with my scar, a boy from the village tried to court me, once, very properly, and I said I'd kill him if he touched me and I meant it and he knew I did. When the recruiters came through our village I almost begged them to take me off to war.'

'Did you expect to die, in Abingon?'

'I did.'

'Did you hope to?'

She shrugged. 'Perhaps. To start with. But you see things, in war. I don't have to tell you, Father, you were there. Among all the pain and the suffering, you see things that give you hope.'

You did, at that. I remembered witnessing acts of bravery and of kindness that you'd never see in Ellinburg if you lived there your whole life. I just nodded. That wasn't something we needed to talk about.

'So you found hope,' I said. 'And you came back to life.'

'I did,' Anne said. 'I came back to life, and I came back to the world, and then I saw witchcraft in our own fucking crew and then I broke my promise to myself and I lay with Rosie. Now I'm terrified I've brought it down on her too, what happened to Maisy.'

I reached out and put my hand on Bloody Anne's head.

'What happened to Maisy wasn't your fault, and it won't happen to Rosie,' I said. 'I promise, Anne. Our Lady forgives you your guilt. In Our Lady's name.'

Bloody Anne looked up at me, and there were tears in her eyes. 'And that makes it right, does it?'

'No, Anne,' I had to admit. 'It doesn't, but it's all I have to offer.'

Chapter 18

Bloody Anne's confession was the hardest I'd ever heard, and I'd heard confession from rapists and murderers and men so battle-shocked they couldn't do more than stare into space and cry. I could see now why she was scared of Billy the Boy, but I knew the lad wasn't a witch. Not the way Anne thought of witches, anyway. If he could do magic, and perhaps he could, then he wasn't doing it in the name of any cruel god who wanted to maim and mutilate folk for who they loved.

I thought that one day, once I had time and money and resources again, I might find out where Anne had been born and head up there with her and some well-armed men. I thought Mother Groggan and I might have some points of theological difference to discuss, priest to witch. I thought Bloody Anne might like to settle those points.

All told I was glad Anne's was the last confession I heard that Godsday.

It doesn't sound difficult, being a priest of Our Lady, not when the captain knows he needs a replacement and he's talking you into it. Listen and lead, the captain said, and he never said care. He never said it, but sometimes I did, whatever Jochan might think of me. Not often, no, but sometimes. If I had been hearing the confession of strangers in a temple, then no, he was right.

I wouldn't have cared.

Why would I care about people I didn't know? But these were my crew and some of them were my friends, like Bloody Anne. Some like Cookpot I had known most of my life, and if we weren't friends then

121

we were at least a part of each other's lives. That goes a way to building a trust, to my mind, if not necessarily a friendship.

I took my priest's robe off and hung it up, and only then did it occur to me that Fat Luka hadn't come to say his confession. That was his affair and I never insisted any of the men came to me, Godsday or otherwise, but Luka had often knelt in front of me in Our Lady's name before. Not today, it seemed.

I shrugged the thought off and headed down to the common room, where Pawl the tailor was just finishing taking measurements while his boy made notes of who wanted what. The tavern was open by then, open to the public for the first time since I had kicked Dondas Alman and his boys out into the street and put his 'important friends' to the sword. Trade was slow, as might be expected after that, but there were a few folk in there from the surrounding streets. No one had much coin to spend, I knew, and I had Hari selling beer below cost just to get bodies through the door. I was still selling Alman's stock, of course, so I could do that for a while and not show a loss, but I knew it wouldn't do forever. Not at the rate my own lads were getting through the taproom it wouldn't, anyway.

Black Billy was on the door how he should be, and I could see Mika at a table in the far corner with two walls at his shoulders where he could keep a watchful eye over the whole room. Ailsa was a vision behind the bar in her clean white apron, smiling and flirting and sweeping coppers into the lockbox as she served mugs of beer and the occasional glass of brandy. I kept an eye on those who were buying brandy. They were the ones who had coin to spend, and on these streets that made them conspicuous.

Hari limped out of the kitchen on his stick and smiled at folk, shaking the hands of those he didn't know and introducing himself. He looked the part as the tavern keeper, and word soon got around who he was and who he worked for.

When I made my entrance and Ailsa brought me a brandy I didn't pay for, everyone in there knew *exactly* who I was.

It might be Godsday but everyone who was likely to visit a temple and say their confession would have already done so by then, and I had put away my priest's robes for the day. Father Tomas was done, for now, and it was time to be Tomas Piety again. I stood up, the glass in my hand, and cleared my throat.

'Everyone shut up!' Jochan roared.

Silence fell over the room, and I took my moment.

'Welcome to the Tanner's Arms,' I said. 'Most of you here know me, but for those who don't my name is Tomas Piety and I own this place, among others. I've been away to war but now I'm back, and the Tanner's is back to being how it should be.'

'And are taxes back to being how they were?' someone said, his voice carrying more than I thought he had meant it to.

'Taxes are suspended,' I said. 'I know times are hard. The war has been hard on everyone, those who fought and those who stayed behind alike. Whatever you were paying Alman is gone now, and what you paid me before the war we can discuss later. For now there are no taxes on these streets, and if anyone comes asking for them you come and tell me or my brother about it, and we'll make them go away.'

There was a cheer at that, albeit a half-hearted one. I doubted that anyone there had much of anything to pay taxes with, other than the few conspicuous brandy drinkers. I watched each of those carefully, noting their faces, and I hoped Fat Luka was doing the same. There were some I knew by sight, and if they were doing that much better than their fellow men then I wanted to find out how and why.

I remembered what Governor Hauer had told me about this mysterious Bloodhands and his Skanians, who had supposedly overrun the city while we had been at war, and about how they had gold to spend. I remembered the men in the house at Chandler's Narrow too, and how they had been scared for their families. These men with brandies in their hands were playing a dangerous game, to my mind.

Ailsa stood behind the bar, drawing tankards of beer and smiling and flirting, but I would have bet a gold crown to a clipped copper that she was noting who had money for brandy too. Oh, she was no fool, that one, that was for sure.

No, Ailsa was nobody's fool, and whatever tricks she could perform with paints and powders and lace, I was sure that the Queen's Men didn't take in anyone who wasn't shrewd at business as well. I gave her a look and she nodded back at me, and I could see that we understood each other.

She had a way with people, I could see that too. Upstairs in her room she had spoken to me like a Dannsburg aristocrat, with her accent like cut glass and always making me feel like she was looking down her nose at me. Down here behind the bar she was everybody's sweetheart, common and charming and funny with a wink and a smile and a joke. Oh, yes, she was good. A spy has to blend and mix and mingle until they could have been anyone, and no one thinks anything of a flirty barmaid, do they? Flirty barmaids are two a copper penny, and who's to remember which tavern they know her from?

I sat and watched the room for an hour or so, then told Ailsa to take her break in the kitchen and had Fat Luka stand a turn behind the bar while I went after her. We were left alone to talk in peace, which was another advantage of having the crew think she was my fancy woman.

'The ones with money for brandy are spies, more than likely,' she said as soon as we were alone, 'or at least in their pay. Do you recognise any of them?'

'A few faces I've seen before, but not to put names to them,' I said. 'I thought you might have noticed that.'

'I notice everything, Tomas, it's my job,' she said. 'You realise the one the men call Cookpot has battle shock, don't you?'

'I know,' I said. 'He's having a think about whether he wants to stay.'

'You'd be better off without him,' she said. 'He'll be unpredictable.'

I knew that. Jochan was unpredictable too, but then he always had been.

'He's my man, and he stays my man unless he chooses otherwise,' I said. 'I'll take your say on whatever your business here may be, but don't you tell me how to lead my men.'

She held my gaze for a moment, then nodded. 'Very well,' she said. 'We'll keep to the subject of the spies, the Skanian agents. That should interest you well enough. The Skanians are the ones who have taken over your old business interests. It's high time you started taking them back again.'

'I know that,' I said. 'What I don't know is why they're doing it.'

'Ellinburg is corrupt to the core,' she said. 'From Governor Hauer on down, the city all but stands on the shoulders of its underworld. People like you and Ma Aditi are key to the real economy of this city, or at least you were before the war. The bulk of the gold might be in the hands of the merchant guilds and the factories, but they survive only so long as they have a workforce. Those who control the streets control that workforce, in the main. Hauer managed to get a little of that control back during the war years, but then he lost most of it again to the Skanians. If they were to take over the street economy of Ellinburg, they could be in a position to break Hauer's authority and the wealth of the merchant guilds together. With control of the city in their hands, they could prepare an advance staging point here, ready and waiting for a possible invasion that might threaten Dannsburg itself. We won the last war but only just, truth be told, and the country is weak and ripe for invasion. They keep slaves in Skania, Tomas, did you know that? Do you have any idea what it is like, to be a Skanian slave? If we fail here, you could well find out.'

I looked at her and frowned. I'd die before I would be any man's slave, but, that aside, it seemed to me she had told me much that was supposition and little that was certain.

'That's an awful lot of *could* and *might* and *possibly*, to my mind,' I said.

'Yes, it is,' she agreed. 'You'll find that we deal mostly in *could* and *might* and *possibly*, Tomas. By the time something becomes a certainty it is often too late to do anything about it.'

'So you could be wasting your time with—' I started, before she interrupted.

'And don't be shy about it, my handsome,' she giggled in her barmaid's voice just as the door opened and Mika stuck his head into the room.

'Sorry to interrupt, boss,' he said. 'Only there's an old geezer in the bar asking for you. Says his name's Kurt.'

I frowned at that, but I got up. 'Keep it warm for later,' I told Ailsa, following her lead and wondering just how good her hearing must be to have known there was someone outside the door.

Hearing that wasn't deadened by years of cannon fire was bound to be better than mine, I supposed. She giggled again and I followed Mika into the bar. Old Kurt was there right enough, leaning on a gnarled length of wood and with a shabby cloak around his shoulders. I gave Luka the nod.

'Give him a beer on the house,' I said.

I let Kurt have a sip of his beer, then took him by the elbow and steered him to a table in the corner. Mika came and stood with his back to my table and his arms crossed in front of him, sending a clear message that we weren't to be disturbed. Mika could think for himself, as Fat Luka had said, and that was good.

'What are you doing here?' I asked the old man.

'Having a drink' – Kurt grinned at me – 'and I thank you for it. I came to see how this boy of yours slept last night, of course.'

'Well enough,' I said, and Old Kurt nodded his narrow, ratty head.

'I thought as much,' he said. 'You'll want me to look at him, then.'

'I will,' I said, 'but not here. Never here, Kurt. This is Anne's worry and only her and I know about it, and I want it kept that way. I don't want you at the Tanner's, spreading fear and superstition among my men.'

'So Old Kurt's not welcome among your finery, is that the lay of things?'

'It is,' I said. 'I have respect for you, to a point, but these are simple men and if they get wind of magic in their midst they'll raise the gods over it, and then there's bound to be trouble. I don't want that.'

Kurt shrugged. 'That's your choice, but if you keep it from them and then they find out for themselves, you'll be sorry, you mark my words.'

He drained his beer in one long, greedy draft, the lump in his scrawny neck working as he swallowed. He thumped the tankard down on the table and got to his feet.

'Thank you for your hospitality,' he said.

With that he picked up his stick and left the Tanner's Arms, leaving me to think on what he had said.

Chapter 19

By the next day I had made a decision on that.

Old Kurt was right, I knew. If I hid Billy's gift from the crew and something gave it away, then all my attempts to instil order and discipline would have been wasted. There would be panic, and anger, and then there would probably be blood. The men knew Billy was touched by the goddess, and that was one thing, but it would only take someone else to say 'witch' and it would all go to the whores in a heartbeat.

These were religious men, in their way, and acts of the goddess were all well and good, to their minds. I doubted a single man of them had ever seen a magician, but they knew they existed and they were well and good too, and even folk like Old Kurt got a wary sort of respect. Breathe the word *witch*, though, and there was fear and violence. I wasn't sure I could see a difference, myself, but then it wasn't something I much cared about. Priest I might be, but if I'll confess anything it's that I'm a sight less religious than most of my crew were.

Of course, if we had been in Dannsburg this would have been easy. I could have taken Billy to the house of magicians and told them he had the gift, let them test him, and paid them for his schooling. Talented children were always in demand in Dannsburg, so I had heard, but we were in Ellinburg and there was no house of magicians here. There was just Old Kurt, and I knew that would have to be how I sold this to the crew.

I took Fat Luka out to the stable for a quiet word. Cookpot was grooming the horses and Simple Sam was mucking out, so we kept on walking until we were in the alley behind the tavern. I was starting to feel how cramped it was at the Tanner's with so many men sleeping there, and it was chafing at me. Will the Woman and Sir Eland were living in the house on Chandler's Narrow now, of course, and Brak was with my aunt, for which I could almost feel sorry for him. Even with that, though, we were still too many under one roof.

'What's the lay of things?' I asked Luka once we were finally away from listening ears.

'Jochan's brooding, like I said he would, but he hasn't made trouble yet,' Luka said. 'Grieg had some hard words to say about you breaking his face until some of the others got to the truth of why you did it, and now he's got more bruises than he can count. Everyone took that ill, I reckon, and he got a good kicking. You shouldn't ought to hit whores, and I reckon even Grieg knows that now.'

I nodded. That was well enough.

'How's Cookpot?'

'Fat-faced and stupid, same as usual,' Luka said. 'He's been a bit quiet, though.'

'You keep a close eye on Cookpot,' I told him. 'He's got the battle shock worse than he lets on. I'm not sure he's suited to this life.'

'Right,' Luka said. 'Anything else you need?'

'There is,' I said, 'and this is important. It's about Billy the Boy.'

'What about him?'

'You know Billy's touched by the goddess,' I said, and Luka nodded. 'Well, I think he has a bit of the cunning in him, too, and that's good. It's good but it's not something I know how to help him learn. So Old Kurt, the man who came to see me yesterday, he's a cunning man. You remember Old Kurt from back when we were boys, Luka?'

'I know the name,' Luka said, and now he looked a bit uncomfortable. 'Can't say I've had anything to do with him. People say . . . well, you know how folk are. People say things.'

'He's a cunning man,' I said again, 'and all that means is he's a magician who hasn't had the schooling. Like Doc Cordin is to a doctor, you understand? There's nothing wrong in it.'

'I heard he did witchcraft, down in the Wheels,' Luka said.

I leaned very close to Luka, and put my hand on the back of his neck while I spoke softly in his ear. 'If I hear that word again, Fat Luka, I won't be able to let it pass,' I said. 'That's the very word I don't want to hear spoken, not by you or anyone else, do you understand me? Billy is touched by the goddess and he might have it in him to become a magician if he gets some teaching, and those are good things. Those things are good for Billy, and they're good for the Pious Men too. I need to know that you understand that.'

I heard Luka swallow, and he nodded.

'Right, boss,' he said.

'Good,' I said, and let go of his neck. 'Now, Billy is going to learn from Old Kurt, and he might have to go to the Wheels to do it. I know that isn't ideal, but there it is. If there were a house of magicians in Ellinburg he'd be going there, but there's not and that's not something I can change. What I need from you is to make sure everyone in that tavern understands what a good thing this is, and how nobody wants to make any fuss over it. Can you do that for me, Fat Luka?'

Luka nodded, and I patted him on the shoulder and pressed a silver mark into his hand. Luka might fear magic, but he loved silver more.

We went back through the yard as Cookpot and Simple Sam were finishing up in the stables. I put my hand on Cookpot's shoulder to keep him back.

'A little word,' I said.

The others left us in peace, standing there among the smell of freshly raked stables and clean horseflesh, and I looked into Cookpot's round, sweaty face.

'I set you something to think on, yesterday,' I reminded him. 'Have you made a decision yet, Cookpot? Only I can't have a man here who's not committed to what we do, I'm sure you understand that.'

'I . . . I don't know that I can do it,' he admitted, 'but I don't want to leave, neither. I went to war and back with you and Jochan and Luka, and we met Anne and all the lads. You . . . you're all I've got, Mr Piety.'

I knew Cookpot didn't have any family. His ma had died just before we went off to war, and it had only ever been the two of them since we were children. I could understand what he was getting at. All the same, he wasn't from my streets and if he couldn't be a Pious Man, then why should I feed him? I thought on that for a moment, and I looked around the yard. My gaze settled on the stables, and Our Lady gave me my answer.

'I saw you grooming the horses earlier,' I said. 'It needed doing but I never told you to do it, so that was well done. Do you like horses, Cookpot?'

'I do,' he admitted. 'I've never rode one, but I like them all the same. They're noble beasts, are horses.'

I wasn't sure about that, but I nodded to keep him happy. I had seen enough horses torn to pieces by cannon to think that they were no nobler than men were, and that was to say not very. That wasn't anything Cookpot needed to hear, though.

'Might be I need a groom,' I said. 'That could be you, Cookpot. You won't be a Pious Man, and you won't earn silver like those who are, but you'll have a place here and a job and a roof over your head. Does that sound good?'

He looked up at me, and there were tears in his eyes.

'It does, Mr Piety,' he whispered. 'It sounds very good indeed.'

'That's done, then,' I said. 'Be sure to tell the crew, so everyone knows the lay of things.'

Cookpot nodded and hurried off into the tavern, and he looked like a great weight had been taken off his shoulders.

The weight of a cannon, maybe.

I looked at our four horses and I knew very well that I didn't need a groom. Not for four horses I didn't. I was being soft on Cookpot, I knew I was, but then I felt like he had earned it. He had kept us fed at Abingon, when the supply lines were cut and some companies were starving. A forager like Cookpot had been worth five fighting men, to my mind, and I owed him for that. He was hurt because of it, hurt in the mind where it doesn't show to a casual eye.

He had made it all the way home and then he had killed a man, because of a situation I had put him in. I knew that had hurt him even more. I owed him a soft job, and some peace.

That was how I made it right with Cookpot, the only way I knew how.

·

The tavern was open again that evening, but we didn't have so many customers as the day before. The brandy drinkers were all gone, no doubt having seen what they needed to see and gone off to whisper in their masters' ears. The few patrons left were all faces I recognised from the surrounding streets.

Sir Eland came to see me that night, and that surprised me. I still didn't trust Sir Eland, and truth be told, I had been greatly enjoying his absence. The false knight joined me at my table and I could feel his narrow, weasely eyes on me.

'Can we talk?' he asked.

I nodded.

He had something on his mind, I could tell.

'A bunch of the crew came to Chandler's Narrow, night before last,' he said.

'Aye, I know.'

'Billy the Boy was with them.'

Again I nodded, and waited for him to work his way around to his point. If he had some sort of complaint about the crew, then he should be taking it to Bloody Anne, to my mind, not bothering me with it, but he was there now so I'd hear him out.

'What of it? Jochan said they didn't get him a woman anyway.'

'No, they didn't,' Sir Eland said. 'They left him with me.'

'And?'

The false knight swallowed, and looked down at the table, and I could see the fear in him.

'You can trust me,' he said, so quiet I almost didn't catch his words. 'I know you think you can't, but you can. Maybe I was jealous when your brother came back, I'll admit that. Maybe I haven't shown you as much respect as I should have done, and I apologise for it. I might not be a real knight, I'll accept that you know that, but I'm a real Pious Man now. I'll prove it to you somehow, when I get the chance. Just . . . just don't send that boy to me again.'

I frowned at that, and wondered what the fuck Billy the Boy had said or done to Sir Eland that night, while Anne and the men were whoring. Whatever it was, Sir Eland seemed to be of the mind that it had been my doing. Billy seemed to have frightened some honesty into him anyway, and that was good. Whether it would last remained to be seen.

I nodded slowly, and fixed him with a look. 'I appreciate your words, Sir Eland,' I said, 'and I hope you get that chance soon.'

He sighed and got up. 'I'll prove it to you somehow,' he said again. He turned away then and left the Tanner's Arms, alone.

I circulated after that, shaking hands and listening to what people had to say for themselves while Hari played dice with a couple of local men at another table. I heard nothing new, by and large, but folk appreciate being listened to. There wasn't enough work to go around, and some of their neighbours were going hungry. They'd like to help, of course they would, but they had families of their own to feed, surely I understood that.

The streets weren't as safe as they had been before the war, when the Pious Men were running things properly. I heard that as well, and I knew it was meant to carry my favour. There was still disease. They weren't ill, oh no, not them, so no need to be throwing them out of the tavern, but they'd heard of people who were. No one they knew, though, of course, but they'd heard things.

Sometime in the middle of the evening when trade had all but died and I was sitting at a corner table with Mika, Ailsa came over to speak to me.

'Quiet night,' I said.

She nodded, still wearing her barmaid's face for the sake of the remaining men in the common room.

'There's sickness in the streets again, so I heard,' she told me. 'The plague all but burned itself out these last few weeks, but people are saying how maybe it's coming back again. A lad on Sailcloth Row come down with a case of the boils, and there's all but panic. Folk don't want to mix too much, if you take my meaning, Mr Piety.'

I frowned at that. 'The plague we had doesn't give you boils,' I said. 'The lad's probably just been washing in bad water.'

'Or he's caught the pox off some street scrub,' Mika put in, and immediately looked like he wished he hadn't. 'Begging your pardon, Ailsa.'

132

'I hope that's true, sir,' she said, and gave me a look that said she knew very well that it wasn't.

The plague was all but gone from Ellinburg, and thank Our Lady for that, but folk were bound to still be nervous at the first sign of disease of any sort. It was the same sort of nervousness they got at the first sign of magic, too, and that made me think of something.

'Have you seen Billy the Boy tonight?' I asked her.

'He's away in the back, with some of the lads,' she said. 'Luka's been telling them all about how the lad's going off to learn to be a great magician, and now they can't get enough of looking at him. I've never seen so many men look so impressed about something that weren't a horse or a woman.'

Luka was good at this sort of thing, I was coming to realise, very good indeed. He was good at making people see what I wanted them to see and in the right way, a way that meant them never getting around to thinking there might be a different way to see a thing. They'd had a word for that in the army, but I couldn't remember what it was. This was the same sort of thing, to my mind, and it seemed Fat Luka had the knack for it.

'That was skilfully done,' she whispered to me in her own voice.

She was right, it *had* been well done. I had chosen very well, giving that task to Luka.

The right man for the right job, always.

She gave me a knowing tip of the head and sauntered off back behind her bar.

It was only later that night, when I was lying in my blankets trying to sleep, that I realised I had never spoken to Ailsa about Billy's magic.

Not even once.

Chapter 20

I spent the next morning thinking on what I had heard the night before. A lot of it had been what folk thought I wanted to hear, I knew that, but some of it hadn't. The streets really weren't safe at night, and there was nothing like enough work to go around and keep everyone fed. Those things were true enough, and I needed to do something about them.

Finding work for all those people was out of my reach, at the moment anyway, but the other thing wasn't. To my mind the Pious Men streets weren't safe because there were crews other than the Pious Men operating on them. That was something I could change, and it suited me well enough to do so. If I had to do other things later, to feed and employ people, I would need gold.

Ailsa would have gold, or at least access to it, and of course there was the fortune I still had bricked up in the back of the small storeroom from the last time I had worked for the Queen's Men. That was the problem in front of me, of course. I hadn't been able to spend much of that gold back then and I couldn't spend *any* of it now, not without facing too many hard questions about where it had come from.

I needed to get my businesses back and push some of the gold through them to make it look like it had been earned in commerce and honest crime and wasn't the queen's money, dirty money that I should never have taken. Then things could be different. There was little enough I could move through the Tanner's Arms, not with trade how it was at the moment.

I thought on what I had owned, where each business was in relation to the Tanner's and how I needed to consolidate my strength into one area to keep it defensible. I wanted the Golden Chains back, but that was out of the question for now. The Chains was a gambling house, a very private one, where only the wealthiest of the city were welcome. The place made a fortune, but I knew it was guarded hard and I didn't have the strength yet to take it. That and it was almost on Trader's Row, too far away from my other businesses.

That brought the decision down to a simple one. There was another boarding-house I had owned, in Slaughterhouse Narrow. That one was an actual boarding-house, not a thinly disguised stew, a legitimate place that mostly took in travelling slaughtermen and the labourers and skinners who followed them. It wasn't the Chains, but it made money well enough. If I started with that one, I could use the Chandler's Narrow house as a staging point, with an easy supply line back to the Tanner's if needed. I had learned a thing or two in the army, I realised, even if I hadn't much appreciated it at the time.

Jochan was happy with the idea when I told him, and Bloody Anne still looked preoccupied but she nodded agreement anyway. The three of us were in the back room, having our council of war while Luka kept the door and listened in.

That was good. He'd need to know what the plan was anyway, so he could explain to the lads why it was a good one that would see everyone make money and not get hurt in the process. He knew his job, did Fat Luka, and if I hadn't quite explained to Jochan and Anne what that job was then I think they had mostly worked their way around to figuring it out for themselves by then.

'Slaughterhouse Narrow it is, then,' Jochan said, and his face twisted into a savage grin that put me in mind of a wild animal. 'We'll make it a fucking slaughterhouse all right, Tomas. These pricks think they can steal from us? Well, they fucking can't!'

'Well said, brother,' I said. 'Well said.'

I tasked Jochan with picking the men for the job, and Luka with putting some fire in their bellies. I kept Anne back for a moment as the two men left the room.

'I have to ask you something, and I hope you won't take it ill,' I said.

'Go on.'

'When you went to Chandler's Narrow the other night, did you talk much with Rosie? Afterward, perhaps?'

Anne shrugged. 'Some,' she said, looking uncomfortable.

'Did you tell her about Billy the Boy?'

'I . . . I might have done,' she said. 'I was drunk and happy and scared, Tomas. I can't rightly remember what I said. Why do you ask?'

'No matter,' I said, shrugging it off as a casual thing, but I had learned something.

Rosie hadn't just been a messenger – she was actually working for Ailsa and the Queen's Men. That might matter or it might not, but it was a good thing to know. It stood to reason that Ailsa wouldn't be alone, not in a nest of vipers like ours. Oh, I was sure she could take care of herself and then some, but she had to have some way of passing information back to Dannsburg. No spy works truly alone. I had learned that much in the army. Of course she had someone else attached to my business, and now that I knew who it was I felt a little bit more secure. Once you know who the spy is, you're halfway to controlling the flow of information.

I'd have to keep a close eye on Rosie from Chandler's Narrow from now on.

We went that night. Ten of us rallied at the Chandler's Narrow house, slipping through the darkened streets between the Tanner's and the stew two and three at a time until we were all together. Everyone had their leather and mail on, and weapons hidden under their cloaks. Sir Eland was ready and waiting for us in the parlour of the boarding-house. He was wearing his stolen armour, with his long sword hanging at his belt.

Jochan and I disagreed over this, but I had made it his business to pick the men for the job and he had chosen Sir Eland as one of them, so I had to let it pass. I still didn't trust the false knight and I wouldn't until he gave me a reason to, but Jochan didn't know him the way I did and he didn't know about the words we had exchanged in the Tanner's Arms the previous night. All he saw was a fighting man with good harness and a keen blade and nothing better to do with his night.

Truth be told, I think Sir Eland was getting bored at Chandler's Narrow. Women didn't interest him, and to hear him tell it there had only been three fights, all of which he had ended in seconds with his usual arrogant ease. Will's version of events differed slightly, but not enough that I had to make something of it. Nothing was ever as easy as Sir Eland made it sound to people who hadn't been there to see, and that was another reason I still didn't trust him, but he had done what was needed all the same and that was good. So was the house, I had to admit.

The house at Chandler's Narrow was spotless, in fact, well repaired and all the furniture polished while the women walked around clean and neatly dressed. Will admitted to me that he had sunk all the money I had given him into the business, but when I offered to cover his expenses he shook his head.

'I'd like to think we were partners now,' he said. 'I've made my investment, and I think a quarter of the returns for me would be a fair deal on that.'

I looked at him for a long moment. Will the Woman was more shrewd than perhaps I had given him credit for, I realised. He said he had run a bawdy house before the war and I believed him, but now he was talking about moving out of working for me and into working with me, and they were very different things. That showed ambition, and ambition is always to be admired.

Within reason.

'We'll see,' I said. 'If you can show me you've taken five marks by next Godsday and turned at least a mark profit on it, you can keep a quarter of that profit. Any less and I'll cover your expense but take all your profits. Does that sound fair, Will the Woman?'

He nodded. 'That sounds fair,' he said. 'Do me a favour, though, boss?'

'What's that?'

'Stop calling me "the Woman". Your brother Jochan came up with that name and I've never cared for it. Maybe I wept when I done hard things, but who hasn't? It ain't only women who weep.'

I nodded. He was right about that. All the same, names were given, not chosen, and they weren't always given kindly. That was the way of soldiers, and he knew that as well as I did.

'Will the Wencher, then. Does that suit you better?'

He snorted. 'I'll take what I can get,' he said. 'Suits me now, I suppose.'

It did, at that.

Jochan hadn't picked Grieg for tonight's work, and I thought that was wise. I doubted he was welcome at Chandler's Narrow at the moment. I spoke to Will about that while I was there, and he agreed to make it right with the girl that Grieg had hurt. The crew had already made it right with Grieg, with their boots by the sound of things, and I didn't think he'd be doing it again.

That done, I gathered the crew together in the parlour. Jochan and Bloody Anne were both there, and Sir Eland and Fat Luka and Nik the Knife and the others.

'You know what we're doing and why,' I said. 'Slaughterhouse Narrow belongs to the Pious Men, and we're taking it back. The slaughterhouse itself is at the bottom of the narrow. We'll go around the side and up the steps there toward the boarding-house. It'll be dark behind the slaughter yard, so watch your footing.'

'And it fucking stinks,' Jochan added with a grin. 'I hope none of you ladies has a dainty nose.'

There were a few half-hearted laughs, but that was it. Men were checking weapons and mail, preparing to fight and kill for me, and few were in the mood for humour. I caught Luka's eye and looked at Jochan. Luka gave me a nod. He would keep an eye on my brother, that nod said.

We headed out, me and Jochan at the front and Bloody Anne keeping the rear of our column with Sir Eland beside her. Our route led us down Chandler's Narrow to the main street, then through the shadows of an alley and into the darkness behind the slaughterhouse. Jochan had been right, to be fair; the stench was appalling even by the standards of the Stink. I heard someone gagging, and a muffled thump as someone else hit them to tell them to shut up.

Slaughterhouse Narrow itself led up the hill between two tenement buildings, the steps steep and in utter darkness at that time of night. The blank sides of the buildings loomed over us, robbing us even of moonlight. I felt my way along the damp wall beside me, aiming for the dim glow of a single lantern hanging outside the entrance to the boarding-house in the small courtyard. As I climbed I realised I could see a shadow under that lantern where a shadow shouldn't be.

I stopped and put a hand on Jochan's arm to hold him.

'There's someone on the door,' I whispered, right close into his ear.

Jochan looked, nodded. He turned and picked a man out of our group, one of his old crew, who I had only ever heard called Cutter. This fellow was lean and wiry, dark haired and bearded, and he hardly ever spoke. He slipped through the men and joined Jochan and me at the front. Jochan pointed to the shadow under the lantern and made a hand gesture that I didn't recognise, some sign cant of their crew. Cutter nodded. He had a shortsword hidden under his cloak, but he ignored that and produced two small knives from his belt. He held them backward, to my mind, one in each hand with the top under his thumb and the flat of the blade against the inside of his wrist. When he lowered his hands, the knives were invisible.

I watched as he slipped past us and up the steps. He stumbled drunkenly, although he wasn't drunk.

'Fuckin' steps,' he slurred, loud enough to be heard. 'I fucking hate these . . . fucking steps.'

The shadow under the lantern moved, became the shape of a man. 'Who's that?'

'Wha'? I'm fucking lost, pal. How d'you get to fucking Trader's Row from here? I gotta . . . got a woman waiting for me and I can't . . . fucking find the place.'

The man who should have been on the door laughed and pointed, half turning away from Cutter to indicate the way up through the narrow. Cutter moved fast, his hands crossing the sides of the man's neck in a blur of movement and steel. Blood sprayed black in the dim light, and Cutter lowered the dead man silently to the cobbles.

'Thanks, pal, you're . . . you're a pal,' he said, and stumbled on a few steps farther for the benefit of anyone listening.

That done, he crouched down at the edge of the light and beckoned us on.

I didn't know this Cutter but it seemed that he had his talents, for all that he hadn't really made any friends among the men. We hurried to join him. A man on the door meant they were expecting trouble, but after what we had done at Chandler's Narrow that wasn't a surprise. I searched the blood-slick body and came up with a key, and I smiled.

'I'm first in,' Jochan whispered. 'I'm always first in.'

I nodded. I remembered Kant from my old crew, who I had killed with my own hand before we even reached Ellinburg. He had always been first too, leading his squad with his mace in hand, crushing and bludgeoning and forcing his way forward. Bludgeon and force, that was how Kant the Cunt had made his way in the world, and I couldn't think that my brother Jochan was much different. Still, it was good, for now.

We'd do this the same way as last time, then. What had worked once would work again, to my mind. I gave Jochan the key and stepped aside as he unlocked the door to the boarding-house.

'The fuck are you—' someone started, and Jochan's axe rose and fell.

He charged into the house with Sir Eland and the others at his back. I kept Bloody Anne with me in the narrow until they were all inside, and then we dragged the dead body farther into the shadows and followed a minute later.

There were five of them already dead in the main room, and I could hear fighting from upstairs and in the back. Too much fighting. Nik the Knife was slumped on the floor with his back against the wall, white as a sheet and clutching his stomach.

'How bad is it?' Anne asked him.

He heaved in a breath, and when he exhaled blood ran out of his mouth and down his chin.

'Bad enough, Sarge,' he said, and I saw that it was.

His mail was slick with blood around his hand, where a sword-thrust had gone straight through it and deep into his guts. A man doesn't survive a wound like that, not without a surgeon and usually not even with one. He looked up at me.

'I wish to confess, Father,' he whispered.

I nodded and turned to Anne. 'I'll stay with him,' I said. 'Go and help the others.'

She drew her daggers and followed the sounds of violence into the

141

boarding-house, a hard set to her scarred face. It would go badly for the first stranger Bloody Anne laid eyes on.

I crouched down beside Nik. 'Speak, in the name of Our Lady,' I said.

'I'm dying, I know that,' he said. 'I'm dying and I'm scared, Father. I've done wrong in my life, and I ain't always confessed it. I . . . I don't know that I've the time or the strength to confess it all now, and I'm scared what that means.'

'It's your time to cross the river, and Our Lady forgives you,' I said. 'In Our Lady's name.'

'In Our Lady's name,' he repeated.

I reached out to put my hand on his head, but he had already died.

I stood up, and drew Remorse and Mercy.

I started up the stairs.

Chapter 21

I met a man on the first landing. He was no one I knew, so I rammed Remorse into his groin even as I took the last step. He screamed and fell, clutching at himself, and I gave him Mercy through the throat.

'Pious Men, call out!' I bellowed.

I heard a shout from the room ahead of me, followed by a curse and the sound of a crash. I kicked the door open and found Fat Luka hard-pressed by a stranger with a mace. Luka dodged and ducked as best he could, keeping his blade up, but it's a difficult thing to fight a mace when you've no shield. The man swung again and Luka dodged, and the weapon smashed into the door I had just thrown open, splintering it.

Remorse slashed out and up, and took his hand off at the wrist. The mace tumbled to the floor with the severed hand still gripping it, and Luka lunged with his sword and that was done.

'Fuck, but there's a lot of them,' Luka panted, red-faced and sweating from the unaccustomed exercise. 'This ain't like the last bunch of cunts – these are fucking soldiers.'

I nodded. That had been my thought too – no civilian carried a mace, or would have much idea what to do with one if they did. This Bloodhands or whoever he was had obviously started recruiting from among the veterans who were beginning to trickle back into the city. That was bad, but it gave me an idea.

'Where's Jochan?'

'He took the top floor, with Sir Eland,' Luka told me.

That was as I had hoped.

'Hold here,' I said. 'You'll know what do when the time comes.'

I bolted back down the stairs and into the back room. I found Bloody Anne working one of her daggers out of a dead man's eye socket. She was red to the elbows, and there were three corpses in the room with her. Anne always had preferred the close work. That was how she got her name in the first place.

'Call the hammer,' I told her. 'How we took the east cloister at Messia, remember?'

Bloody Anne nodded and pulled her dagger free with a satisfied wrench. She marched into the main room with me beside her, and she threw her head back and took a great breath.

'Company!' she roared, her leather-lunged sergeant's voice filling the building with ease. 'The hammer!'

Anne was no tactician but by Our Lady she was loud, and on the battlefield a loud commander is worth two clever ones any day. What's the point of clever orders if no one can hear them?

Three of the lads rushed out of other downstairs rooms and joined us, red blades in their hands. From upstairs came an answering roar, Sir Eland's war cry. I heard boots stamping on wooden floors, thundering down the stairs toward us.

There were six of them left and they fled down the narrow corridors before Jochan and Sir Eland's insane charge, and as they passed his door Fat Luka leaped out to join the pursuit. They were the hammer. The enemy had thought to make a stand in the main room where they'd have space to make their numbers count, but they found our steel waiting for them. We were the anvil that the hammer met, with those men between us.

It was bloody slaughter.

We had used the tactic before, in the sack of Messia, and I couldn't take the credit for it. It was the captain's design, but what had worked then would work again. In narrow spaces, such as corridors or cloisters or tunnels, numbers count for little. It's ferocity that matters, and when two men decide to charge like wild beasts they can drive a whole squad before them. That was what Jochan and Sir Eland did, and the enemy panicked and ran, looking for space enough to spread out and fight as a group. The trick was to have that space prepared for them, with armed men waiting. Drive them into the trap, and you'll crush them between your two forces.

The hammer and the anvil, that was how we took back the house on Slaughterhouse Narrow.

It was a victory, but not without its cost. Nik the Knife was already dead on the floor behind me, and in the melee another of our men had joined him on his river crossing. He was one of Jochan's, and to my shame I didn't even know his name.

'Ganna's done,' Cutter said, not sounding like he cared one way or the other about it.

Jochan looked at his fallen man, lying prone with a shortsword still lodged between his ribs and his mail drenched in blood.

'Aye,' he said, and it seemed like that was all the opinion he had on the matter.

Jochan's crew had never seemed close like mine had been, but that felt cold even for his way of leadership.

'Who was he?' I asked.

Jochan shrugged. 'A soldier, a conscript. They only sent me the shit-heads, by and large. Cutter here's a good man, and Will the Woman can handle himself, but the rest of them aren't worth spit.'

I thought of Mika and Hari back at the Tanner's, both men from Jochan's original crew, and found that I disagreed with him on that. All the same, I held my peace on it. That wasn't the time to debate the merits of men, after all. There was one thing, though.

'I gave Will a new name,' I said. 'Now he's running the stew, he won't be weeping any more. He's Will the Wencher now.'

Jochan laughed at that, and Cutter turned and spat on the floor to show what he thought of it, but it broke the mood as I had intended. I was pained by the death of Nik the Knife, but I hadn't known Ganna, and Jochan obviously hadn't cared about him, so grief for him was a waste of emotion, to my mind. There was work to be done.

There was a good deal of work, to remove the bodies and secure the house on Slaughterhouse Narrow before dawn came. Moving bodies was harsh work, but Fat Luka said he had heard where there was a plague pit not far away that hadn't been filled in yet. A few more corpses stripped and shovelled in with the others would never be noticed.

Harsh work, as I say, but we had done worse before.

Every one of us had done worse.

When it was done, I turned the house over to Jochan to see to. It was time he had some responsibility, and I still remembered what Luka had said to me about his views on Hari running the Tanner's Arms. He had fought well, too – being the hammer is hard and dangerous, and Jochan had stepped up and done it the same as Kant had back in Messia.

There was a good deal of likeness between my brother and Kant, but he was still my brother all the same. He chose Cutter to stay with him, which didn't surprise me, and Sir Eland as well, which did. Eland had been part of the hammer too, I reminded myself, and I wondered if perhaps him and Jochan might be starting to find a trust between them. We could see to a more permanent arrangement in the morning, so I just nodded and let him have it his way.

Anne and I led the rest of them the quiet way back to the Tanner's Arms.

Ailsa was waiting up for us with Mika and Black Billy when we came in, although she'd had the sense to close up for the night before then. That was good. We shed our cloaks to reveal clothes and hands almost black with blood, although little of it was our own.

'You've had a night of it, Mr Piety,' Ailsa said, in her barmaid's voice.

She went to pour brandies without being asked. There was a look of approval on her face, although I was sure she could see we were fewer than we had been. We were fewer than we should have been, even accounting for setting guards at Slaughterhouse Narrow, but she didn't mention that. She took it in her stride like any businessman's woman would have done, and that was good. I respected her for that.

Anne set Simple Sam to heating water in the kitchen for washing, and we drank in the sort of shaky silence that always follows harsh work. There would be jokes and boasting in the morning, and tales grown tall in the telling of who had killed the most men and how, but that was for later. These were hard folk used to hard deeds, but shock is shock and no one is immune to it. Not even Jochan, for all that he might pretend otherwise.

Perhaps it's different for archers, or the crews who work the great siege cannons, men who barely see the faces of the people they kill. I wouldn't know. What I do know is how it feels to look into the eyes of a man not a foot in front of you as you pull a length of sharpened steel out of his guts and take his life away.

You don't feel like joking about it afterward.

I sat at my usual table in the corner with my brandy and nodded at Mika across the room. He hadn't been with us, of course. His place was in the Tanner's with Billy now, but he had been at Messia, and at Abingon. He knew what harsh work felt like, and he knew I'd want leaving alone. He nodded back and left me be.

Bloody Anne joined me a minute later, a brandy of her own in her hand. Now we were in the light I noticed she was walking stiffly, favouring her right leg. She lowered herself into the chair across from me with a grimace that made her scar writhe.

'It's a sad thing to lose Nik, and Jochan's man,' she said. 'We're spreading thinner.'

I nodded. That was true enough. With Will and Sir Eland and now Jochan and Cutter holding the boarding-houses, Nik the Knife and Ganna both dead and Brak still guarding my aunt, Hari wounded, and Cookpot effectively retired, I was down to eleven men stationed at the Tanner's Arms, not counting Billy the Boy or Anne herself.

That was enough, for now, and it was still a lot to have sleeping under one roof. All the same, the more businesses I took back the thinner I would be spread, and a business once taken had to be held or I wouldn't keep it for long.

'Those are the times we live in,' I said. 'We'll do, for now. Later, perhaps I'll put the word about the streets that there's work for likely lads who can follow orders and know which end of a blade to hold.'

'How will the others take that?' Anne asked. 'We have a trust, a comradeship. Losing comrades is hard, and Nik at least was well liked. Bringing new faces into that . . . I don't know, Tomas.'

I shook my head. 'I don't mean as Pious Men,' I said. 'Not straightaway, certainly. Perhaps in time, but that would have to be seen. Door guards and runners and watchmen, though, they can be hired lads.'

'I suppose they can,' she said, obviously giving the matter some thought. 'It'll be like Messia. We took in new men there, to fill the holes in the line.'

She frowned, and I knew she had remembered that we had also taken in Billy the Boy at Messia. She winced again, rubbing her leg under the table.

'How bad are you hurt?' I asked her.

She shrugged. 'I got clipped in the thigh with a mace,' she said. 'It only got the meat, though. Nothing's broken. I'll heal.'

'You'll have a good black bruise to show Rosie tomorrow.' I smiled, but when Anne looked up at me I wished I had held my peace about that.

'I don't . . .' she started, and trailed off.

'Our Lady forgave you your guilt,' I reminded her, keeping my voice low. This was a private matter, after all, a matter between a priest and one of his faithful, and nobody should be overhearing that. 'You didn't cross the river in Abingon, and you didn't cross it tonight, but I can make no promises for tomorrow. Live, Bloody Anne, while you have the chance.'

She put her head down and took a long, shuddering breath. 'Aye,' she said after a moment, and lifted her face again. 'Perhaps I will.'

She drained her brandy in a single swallow and went through to the kitchen to wash the blood from her hands at last.

Chapter 22

Things settled down after that, for a few days. Anne wasn't the only one who'd been hurt at Slaughterhouse Narrow, and everyone needed time to rest and heal. There was grief for Nik the Knife, but he wasn't the first friend these men had lost, and they knew he wouldn't be the last. Pawl the tailor and his boy came by again, with a cart this time, and everyone collected their fine new clothes. With that, and regular trips to Ernst the barber up on Trader's Row, I had the lot of them looking like proper Pious Men. That was good.

We had taken back the two boarding-houses, in addition to the Tanner's Arms, and money was starting to come in. I had fresh supplies brought into the Tanner's, food and beer and brandy, and Will the Wencher kept good on his promise; when Godsday came around again and he presented me with his accounts, I had to admit that he had done what he said he would do. He had taken six marks, not five, and turned a good profit on them. A quarter of that profit was his, then.

I heard confessions in the morning, and that afternoon I made Will a partner in the Chandler's Narrow house. Anne hadn't come to say confession, but I knew she had been up to Will's place every day since the battle at Slaughterhouse Narrow and she looked the better for it. I was pleased to see her happy.

All was well, except one thing.

I had told Old Kurt that I would bring Billy the Boy to him, and I hadn't done that.

Billy seemed happy enough, and he and Hari had found a friendship

149

somewhere. Whether it was born that night when Billy floated over Hari's dying body and done whatever it was he had done, or whether it was rooted in the extra treats that Hari produced for him in the kitchen I didn't know, but then I dare say it didn't matter either. It was good to see and I didn't like to take it away from either of them, but I knew the thing had to be done.

The day after Godsday, Anne and I took Billy the Boy through the stable yard and along the alleys to the path beside the river. Anne was still limping from the blow she had taken at Slaughterhouse Narrow and I had suggested that she didn't need to come, but to her mind I was wrong about that.

That made the going slow, but we walked to the Wheels anyway with Billy the Boy between us. We might have looked like a family, if Anne had been wearing a kirtle under her cloak and not the men's britches and shirt and coat that she insisted on. I looked down at Billy, and thought that perhaps it would be no bad thing, to have a family. Not with Bloody Anne, though; I knew that could never happen and truth be told, I wouldn't have wanted it to. We were friends, and that was all. My thoughts wandered to Ailsa, and I thought perhaps that might be a different matter.

That was a fool's thinking and no mistake. Working for the crown sickened me enough without starting to think about a Queen's Man in that way. It was out of the question, I knew, yet I seemed to keep doing it. I turned my attention to the alley that led up to Old Kurt's door. There was a fresh rat nailed to the door, I noticed, not more than a few hours old by the look of it.

'He's in, then,' I said, nodding to the rat.

'Aye,' Anne said.

I knocked on the door and called out the words. 'Wisdom sought is wisdom bought, and I have coin to pay.'

Old Kurt opened the door and grinned at us. 'Tomas Piety and the fine lady,' he said, 'and this young gentleman too!'

Billy the Boy watched Old Kurt, his face expressionless. After a moment he turned and looked up at me. 'I'll be staying here,' he announced.

I blinked at him. That was the same way he had decided in his mind that Ailsa would be staying at the Tanner's Arms. He had been right about that, but this might be a different matter. It wasn't something I had intended to bring up so soon, or quite so abruptly as that.

'I said I'd have a look at him,' Old Kurt said. 'No more than that, Tomas.'

'The lad needs teaching,' I said, 'and he's keen to get started, that's all. You know how boys are when they've an idea in their heads. Can we come inside?'

Kurt nodded and led us through to his dusty parlour where the sword of a king hung over the fireplace. So he said, anyway. Billy sat down on a low stool in front of the cold grate and drew his knees up to his chin. He looked at home there.

'Hmmm,' Kurt said, looking down at the lad.

'We proved he's not a witch,' I said, although to my mind we had proved nothing of the sort, 'but he's something. Touched by the goddess, aye, but Our Lady doesn't heal men. Apparently Billy does, and that must mean he's got the cunning in him.'

'Perhaps he has,' Kurt admitted. He sat down and looked at Bloody Anne. 'What does the fine lady say?'

'She says she'll stab you if you call her that again,' Anne growled. 'My name's Bloody Anne.'

Kurt snorted but made no more of it. 'Well and good,' he said. 'And what do you say, Bloody Anne?'

She took a breath and shook her head. This didn't sit well with her, I knew that, but she knew what needed to be done.

'Teach him,' she said.

'This is no house of magicians,' Kurt said. 'He won't learn no philosophy from me, nor mathematics beyond his 'rithmetic. I don't scry the stars like they do in Dannsburg, nor summon up demons and make pacts with them neither. That's high magic, and I don't do that.'

I doubted that the magicians in Dannsburg did that either, but then I wouldn't know. I nodded and held my peace about that.

'What *can* you teach him, Old Kurt?'

Kurt snorted again and waved at the fireplace. There was a sharp crack, and the coals in the grate caught and burned with an acrid smoke that his chimney did a poor job of removing. Anne hissed and took a step back, her hands going to her daggers.

'Easy, Bloody Anne,' I cautioned her. 'This is what we're here for.'

'I can teach him the cunning, if he has the wits and the will to learn,' Kurt said. 'Cunning is about real things in the real world, not stars and demons and debating high ideas. Sorcery, the magicians call that. Low magic. They look down their noses at it as being beneath them. Maybe it is, with all their money. A man as rich as a magician has servants to lay his fire for him, but a cunning man don't so he makes his life easier the best way he can. A cunning man can set fires and quench them, mend hurts and cause them. A cunning man can tell you things you've forgotten you knew, and divine what tomorrow might bring.'

'What do you think, Billy?' I asked the lad. 'Do you want to learn from Old Kurt here?'

Billy glanced at the fire and it abruptly went out, the last of the smoke curling slowly into the room.

'I'll be staying here,' he said again, and it seemed his mind was set on it.

I nodded and looked at Kurt. He had a frown on his face and was staring hard at Billy. It occurred to me that perhaps it hadn't been Kurt who put the fire out. The old man cleared his throat like he was about to say something, perhaps change his mind, and I couldn't have that.

'You'll want paying,' I said.

'I will,' Kurt agreed, and maybe it was talk of money that swayed him in the end. 'A silver mark a week, for my time and his keep. Not a copper less, and I won't dicker on this. If I'm teaching the lad I'll have little time for anything else, and why should I be short of pocket? A mark a week, Piety, and I'll take six weeks up front or you can fuck off.'

That was a lot of money, but I had it. The price wasn't something anyone else needed to know about, which meant I could draw on my hidden coin for it and no one would be the wiser. I nodded.

'All right,' I said. 'But you keep this between us, Old Kurt. The Pious Men know Billy is coming to learn from you, but the price has to be kept a secret and it has to stay that way. Does that sound fair?'

Kurt nodded. 'That's fair,' he said.

He stood and spat in his palm, and I spat in mine and we shook hands on it, the old way. I dug in my pouch and took out six silver marks, and gave them to him. He nodded again, and it was done.

That was how Billy the Boy started on the path to becoming a magician.

Chapter 23

When we got back to the Tanner's Arms my aunt was waiting for me, sitting in the common room with a mug of beer in her hand. She had the same look on her face that she had always got when I was a child and about to receive a switching.

'Aunt Enaid, what a pleasure,' I said.

Brak was standing behind her chair like a bodyguard, and his expression said he felt somewhere between proud and foolish to be doing it. I hadn't seen him since Enaid had got her house back, and I could only wonder what old stories she had been filling his head with of an evening.

'Come and sit down, Tomas, and talk to your fat old aunt,' she said, and it wasn't so much an invitation as an order.

I did as she said, while Bloody Anne disappeared into the back to put her weapons away.

'How are you, Auntie?' I asked her. 'I hope the house is adequate.'

'My house is fine and never mind that,' she said, fixing me with a glare from her one bright eye. She lowered her voice and leaned forward across the table toward me. 'Who is that tart behind our bar, and where the fuck did she come from?'

I cleared my throat and offered up a silent prayer to Our Lady that Ailsa's hearing wasn't good enough to catch Enaid's words.

'Ailsa is a barmaid, not a tart,' I said. 'She's working here, and she's doing a good job.'

'That's not all she's doing, to hear your men talk,' Enaid said.

She grabbed her crotch for emphasis in a way that immediately reminded me that she had been a soldier herself. All the same, that wasn't what I wanted to see from my own aging aunt.

'Men talk,' I said, trying to shrug it off. 'What of it?'

'I'm disappointed in you, Tomas Piety,' she said. 'I thought perhaps you and Anne, yes, but this? You and some foreign tart off the tea ships?'

'She's not a tart,' I said again, starting to get angry with her now, 'and she's not off the tea ships. And you thought it would be Anne? No, Auntie. Never Anne.'

'If you can't see past a scar, then I raised you wrong, Tomas,' she growled at me. 'Anne's a good woman, I can see that.'

'Aye, she is,' I agreed, 'and she's a good friend too. Anne doesn't enjoy male company, Auntie, not in that way.'

Aunt Enaid looked at me for a moment, then turned and spat on the floor. 'Bugger,' she said.

'The fuck is it to you, anyway?'

'I know how strange women can get to a man,' she said. 'I don't want that one whispering ideas into your ear on the pillow at night and making you soft in the head.'

My head had never been on the same pillow as Ailsa's, but as I watched her serving drinks and moving among the men I had to admit to myself that I wished it had. There was something about her that fascinated me, and it wasn't just her looks. I was impressed by the way she had adapted so smoothly to our way of life, and by the easy way she had with the crew and the customers alike. All the lads seemed to love her, and that was how it should be. If she were really my woman, I thought, that would be a good thing for me and for the Pious Men. She would make any boss a fine wife. It was out of the question, I knew that, but that didn't stop me wanting it to be otherwise.

It was a long while before I got rid of Aunt Enaid, nearly midnight, and by then Brak was having to help her walk. She had one hand on her stick and the other on his arm, and she was still swaying visibly as she tottered toward the door. It was amazing how much one old woman could drink, when she put her mind to it and it was free.

As the door started to close behind them I saw Enaid's hand move from Brak's arm to his arse, but I pretended that I hadn't. She was almost thrice his age, but that was between them, to my mind, and none of my business. I knew what my aunt was like, and I just hoped that Brak understood what sort of woman she was. I sighed and looked around the room. There were no customers left in there now, just Pious Men and Ailsa. I nodded to Black Billy and told him to close up for the night.

Ailsa was racking dirty glasses and taking them through to the kitchen, and I got up and followed her. When I came in Hari picked up his stick and limped out, giving us our privacy.

'Your aunt doesn't like me any, Mr Piety.' Ailsa giggled.

I kicked the door shut behind me and looked at her. 'No,' I said. 'She doesn't, but she'll learn to live with it.'

'She had better,' Ailsa said, using her own voice now that the door was closed – or at least what I assumed was her own voice. Perhaps it was another act. I didn't know. 'The last thing I need is that old warhorse making trouble. Everybody else has accepted our pretence, and she needs to learn to do the same.'

'She will,' I said.

'Never mind that now,' Ailsa said. 'There's news. The Skanians have noticed your return, which by now is hardly surprising. I don't think they'll try to retake the boarding-houses, but only because they don't care about them and you've chosen too good a defensive position for them to do it easily, which I'm pleased about. They still hold the Golden Chains and I think that's the only one of your businesses they really wanted. They'll try to draw you out, though, to stretch you and force you to overreach until your supply lines break and you suddenly find you haven't got enough men to hold your territory any more.'

I nodded. 'I worked that out for myself,' I said.

'What are you going to do?'

'Consolidate,' I said. 'Build up the three businesses that I have, maybe recruit some more men if I think I'll need them. Now that there's income again I can start to trickle some of my stored funds through the businesses, make the money look legitimate. It's a slow game, but I know how to play it.'

'No,' Ailsa said, her voice turning sharp and cold. 'You really don't.'

That made me look at her, and I noticed the hard set to her jaw as she sat down at the kitchen table. She waved me to a seat as though she were receiving me in her own parlour. *This* was what working for the crown was like, being fucking bossed around and made to feel small in my own place of business, and a pretty face didn't change that.

It was this, or hang.

I swallowed it like bitter medicine, but that didn't mean I liked it. 'How so?'

'You think small, Tomas, but then you're a small man,' she said. 'We play on a greater stage than you can imagine. The *last* thing you should do is consolidate. You need to expand, fast and hard, while they don't expect it.'

'Which is the opposite of what you just said,' I pointed out.

'No, it isn't,' she snapped. 'What I said was that they will *try* to draw you out and overstretch you, not that you should allow it to happen. Let them think you're playing into their hands. Take back everything you had, as hard and as fast as you can. I have the means to fund it, if you need to hire men and buy weapons. I have access to men, for that matter, trained men we can slip in among the new recruits if we have to. *Dangerous* men. The Skanians must be stopped, Tomas.'

I like to think that I'm not a fool, but Ailsa seemed to be trying to make me feel like one. I didn't care for it. Not at all.

I leaned across the table until I was very close to her. 'I hate to tell you this,' I started quietly, 'but I don't give a *fuck* about your Skanians!'

She didn't even blink when I shouted in her face. She just held my gaze and slowly put a finger to her lips. 'Shhhhh,' she said, as though she were speaking to a child. 'I understand, Tomas. This is my business, not yours, and you've been dragged into it against your will. But know this – things have changed, and we have moved beyond *could* and *might* and *possibly* and into uncomfortable certainty. If we cannot stop this infiltration, there will be another war and *we will lose*. There will be another Abingon, right here in our own country. If you think that what you did in the south was harsh work, you have no idea what the Skanians would do to *us* in war. In war, and after they have *won* that war.'

I swallowed, my mouth suddenly gone as dry as dust.

I would never forget Abingon, but it was over and done with and it had been so far away it almost felt like a dream now, some nightmare from which I had awoken. I looked into Ailsa's dark eyes, and it seemed I could see the flames of battle reflected in them, the mouths of the cannon looking back at me from her inky pupils.

I reached out for my brandy.

I managed to stop my hand from shaking, but only just.

'Tell me what you want me to do,' I said, 'and I'll think on it.'

Ailsa started to talk, and I to listen.

I couldn't sleep that night. My thoughts kept going back to what Ailsa had said. *There will be another Abingon, right here.* I couldn't allow that, not if it was in my power to help stop it. These were my streets and my people, and I wouldn't see them reduced to the smoking rubble and rotting corpses that we had left behind us in the south.

That was well enough, but I knew my crew wouldn't agree.

These weren't imaginative men, and to their minds they were good and done with this queen who had dragged them off to war against their will. When the time came for me to announce that we would be taking back another business, I knew the crew would set to it. If word got out we were doing it because an agent of the crown said so, though, then they'd raise the gods over it and I would lose half of them at least. These men weren't patriotic, or overly concerned with what the law might or might not say. They'd have been little enough use to me as Pious Men if they had been. No, these were men out for themselves, trying to put the war behind them and make something fresh of their lives.

I had promised them they would get rich and have all the good things in life. Perhaps I could still keep that promise, but if they thought I was working for anyone but myself they would come to doubt my words, and fast. People expect things of a businessman. One of those things is self-interest, and if I did this I would have to make sure it looked like I was acting for myself and the Pious Men, and no one else.

Whatever happened, this wasn't a decision I could share with Anne or Jochan or anyone else, not even Aunt Enaid. Sometimes a leader has to keep things to himself and make the hard decisions alone. We had come together as soldiers, and in the army you don't get to vote on decisions. Orders come down the line and they are obeyed, and that's just the way of things.

It was nearly light. I kicked my blankets off and padded to the window, looking out into the pre-dawn grey of the street below. Dew glistened on the cobbles, making them shine like dark pearls. I leaned forward and rested my forehead on the inside of the pane, feeling the cold glass against my skin.

Abingon.

I remembered smoke and dust and noise, the siege cannon firing day and night to bring down the great walls. There had been flames everywhere, in the city. Disease was rampant. Wounds got infected and men died screaming in their beds. Supplies were lost or looted, and men starved. Even Cookpot couldn't produce forage from thin air, but he had caught rats for us to eat rather than see us go hungry. The water was almost always bad, and it wasn't uncommon to see men fighting with liquid shit running down their legs from their poisoned guts.

Abingon, where I had seen men driven so mad by the constant noise of the guns that they didn't know their own names any more. I remembered a fellow brought before me for confession, dragged between two of the colonel's bullyboys. He was a man broken with battle shock who had fled the field the day before when he simply couldn't stand it another second longer. They brought him to me to say his confession, but all he could do was weep.

Afterward, they executed him for cowardice.

No, there couldn't be another Abingon. Not here, not now.

Not ever.

It had been horrific and yet we had been on the winning side, those of us who had laid siege to Abingon. What it had been like for the defenders, the besieged, I couldn't even bring myself to imagine. They were eating their own dead in Abingon, before it was over, and we'd heard tales of children being killed for meat by the starving soldiers.

We will lose.

You haven't truly known Hell until you have seen a city under siege. *That* was what would happen here, if the Skanians got their way.

I would do *anything* to prevent a repeat of Abingon, especially here in my own city. Sometimes a man has to balance two evils in his hands, and choose the lighter one. If that meant working for the crown, then so be it.

Those were the times we lived in.

The decision made, I went back to my blankets and I managed to sleep at last.

That was how I gave my loyalty to the Queen's Men.

Part Two

Part Two

Chapter 24

Winter had come to Ellinburg, and brought bitterness with it. It was six months since we had returned home from the war.

I was sitting at one end of a long table in the private dining room of a fine inn on Trader's Row. That was neutral territory, outside of my streets and anyone else's bar the governor himself. At the other end of the table, staring back at me, was Ma Aditi.

She was a fat woman with perhaps forty years to her, richly dressed with thick black hair that framed her dusky brown Alarian complexion. She styled herself Mother, but if she had ever borne a child I didn't know of it.

Bloody Anne sat at my right hand and Jochan at my left. The arrangement wasn't lost on him, I knew, but he was becoming used to it. Bloody Anne had earned her place ten times over, these last six months. Fat Luka stood behind my chair, draped in his fine new clothes, and he leaned forward to whisper softly in my ear.

'The one in the purple shirt,' he said. 'Gregor.'

I nodded without taking my eyes off Ma Aditi, and Luka straightened again and rested his big, strong hands on the back of my chair.

I glanced at the man he had indicated, the one seated at Ma Aditi's left hand. He was the one who was taking Luka's bribes, then. Our man inside the Gutcutters. I wondered if Aditi had anyone inside the Pious Men yet, although I was sure she must have. More to the point, I wondered who it was.

One of the new recruits, I was certain. The old crew was getting thin now – we had lost another three men in the bitter fighting to reclaim my businesses, and those who were left were loyal to the bone. Even Sir Eland the false knight had finally proven himself when an agent of the Gutcutters offered him gold to betray me. Sir Eland had brought me his head in a wet sack, and when I clapped him on the shoulder and thanked him for his loyalty he almost wept. I thought that perhaps all Sir Eland really wanted was a place in the world, and to my mind now he had found one.

To date we had had no open blood on the streets with the Gutcutters, though, and I wanted to keep it that way. For now, at least. I tried to gauge Ma Aditi's mind on that and found that I couldn't. Her face was expressionless, her plump hands folded on the table in front of her, where the light of the oil lamps made her many golden rings shine softly.

'Ma Aditi,' I said, breaking the silence at last. 'I am glad to see you returned safely from the war.'

I was glad of no such thing, of course, and truth be told, I had prayed that she had died in Abingon. Our Lady doesn't answer prayers, though, and Ma Aditi had returned to Ellinburg a month after I had, riding in at the head of her surviving men. This was the first time we had spoken, in a carefully brokered meeting that had taken Fat Luka three months to arrange to his satisfaction and that of her agent.

She nodded slowly. 'Mr Piety,' she said. 'I give thanks to the Many-Headed God for your life.'

I showed her a thin smile. The Many-Headed God was an Alarian god, not one I knew, but there was a temple to him up by the docks that served the traders off the tea ships. Perhaps Aditi held to him. I wouldn't know, but I doubted it somehow.

'Let those be the last two lies we tell each other today,' I said. 'Are we not both people of business?'

Aditi frowned, her fleshy face creasing until her small black eyes seemed almost to disappear into the folds that surrounded them. 'We are,' she agreed.

I could feel her thinking, trying to work out my intentions. The form of these rare meetings between rival bosses was usually to tell pleasant lies while each plotted how best to stab the other in the back. I had come close to being candid, then, and I think that surprised her.

'Then let us speak like people of business,' I said. 'We are no nobles of the court, you and I, to be hiding our knives behind smiles and sharp courtesies. I have my interests and you have yours, but as long as they don't conflict, then I see no reason why we can't exist together in Ellinburg. Do you?'

'The Stink is yours, the Wheels is mine,' she said. 'That hasn't changed.'

'No, it hasn't,' I agreed. 'But tell me this – how many of your businesses did you find had been taken away from you when you returned from the south?'

Her mouth tightened in an angry line and the man seated to her left, this Gregor, who was wearing a purple shirt under his fine black coat, leaned close to whisper in her ear. She thought for a moment, then nodded.

'I know the Pious Men weren't to blame in that,' she said.

'No more than the Gutcutters were to blame for the businesses *I* lost during the war,' I said. 'We have a mutual enemy.'

'Hauer,' she spat. 'Always that fat slug wants more, and more. Taxes and bribes, permits and inspections and fees for this and fees for that. Always more, every year.'

I shook my head slowly. 'The governor is the same man we knew before the war,' I agreed, 'but why would he take businesses away from us that he would then have to staff and run himself? Far easier to just tighten the screw on taxes, instead. Hauer isn't behind this.'

'Then who?'

I recited the carefully prepared speech Ailsa had given me before the meeting. 'There are new people in the city,' I said. 'Opportunists, from far northern towns that the recruiters never got to. They're backed by someone else, though, someone big from outside Ellinburg who wants to take our livelihoods away from us.'

'Do you know who?'

'No,' I lied. 'But that doesn't mean we can't hurt them. I've taken back all but one of my businesses now, and from what I hear you have been doing much the same thing. How have you fared with that?'

Ma Aditi narrowed her eyes, as though she suspected a trap. Again, the man in the purple shirt leaned close to whisper in her ear, feeding her the version of the truth that Fat Luka had bought and paid for with my gold.

'I have lost men,' she admitted, after a moment. 'You?'

I nodded solemnly. 'There have been deaths,' I agreed. 'Too many Pious Men have crossed the river this last six months.'

I had lost five men since my return to Ellinburg, all told. Six, if you counted Hari, who would never fight or walk properly again. From what Luka's whisperers told me, Ma Aditi's losses had been heavier, though. Much heavier, I suspected.

The Skanians had concentrated their efforts more in her territory than mine, in the Wheels where the factories and the tanneries were. They wanted the infrastructure of the city, Ailsa had explained to me, and they wanted its workforce. They had taken my businesses because they could, but they never much wanted them. Except for one, anyway. The one they still held.

Ma Aditi sat back in her chair and gestured to the man at her right hand, a big scarred brute in a voluminous coat and silver-studded black leather doublet whom I didn't recognise. He was new to the Gutcutters, Luka had told me. I could only assume she had brought him back from Abingon with her, a recruit from whatever crew she had ended up in charge of down there, but I didn't know for sure.

Strange that he should be at her right hand, if so.

He reached into his fine coat and produced a long clay pipe, passing it to her. She lit a taper from the lamp on the table between us and puffed her pipe into life, and the sickly sweet smell of poppy resin reached my nose.

The man obviously wasn't the only thing that had come back from Abingon with her. I saw Bloody Anne's eyes narrow with disapproval. Poppy resin had been a problem in Abingon, and we all recognised the smell of it.

It had been known in Ellinburg before the war – I had traded in unlicensed resin myself, of course, with the first Queen's Man I had known, which was how the bastard snared me in the first place – but it had been rare, and I had only sold it to doctors who used it for treating those in unbearable pain. In Abingon it had been used for the same purpose, to start with, until men discovered that smoking it when you weren't half dead from wounds made you feel good.

Men smoked resin to make themselves feel good, to escape the horrors in their minds, to let them sleep at night. Eventually they discovered that once you start smoking poppy resin, you can't stop.

Then there had been problems.

Since the war we had been seeing more and more of it in Ellinburg, and seeing what it did to people. There were resin smokers driven onto the streets, having sold everything they owned to feed their habits. Petty crimes were the highest I had ever seen them, and even on my own streets my newly recruited watchmen were hard-pressed to keep honest households safe.

Those who smoked resin and turned to crime to feed their habits, I ejected from the Stink.

Those I caught selling it, I killed.

I looked down the table at Ma Aditi, at the tendrils of blue smoke curling up from her nostrils, and I knew this meeting had been a waste of time.

'She wouldn't have helped us take the Golden Chains even if I could have brokered a truce between the Pious Men and her Gutcutters,' I explained to Ailsa that night, in her room next to mine above the Tanner's Arms.

It was after midnight by then, and the tavern had closed over an hour ago. Snow swirled over the stable yard below Ailsa's window and settled gently on the wooden frame.

'So what did you say to her?' Ailsa snapped in her cut-crystal Dannsburg accent. '"I'm terribly sorry but you seem to be a poppy smoker so we can't work together, goodbye"?'

She was sitting in the only chair in the room, knitting by the light of an oil lamp on the windowsill.

I took a swallow from the brandy bottle in my hand and glared at her.

'No, Ailsa. I didn't,' I said. 'I spoke the platitudes to her, how I was supposed to. I used the backup speech you gave me in case it all went to the whores, which it fucking well did. "Yes, Ma Aditi, we're all friends and fellow businessmen. No, Ma Aditi, I'm not looking to take over the Wheels. Thank you, Ma Aditi, it was an honour. Bend over, Ma Aditi, and I'll kiss your fat fucking arse." When I think how much Luka paid that purple-shirted bastard Gregor and he never mentioned she was a *fucking* resin smoker . . . !'

I turned and slammed a fist into the wall beside the door, cracking the plaster and hurting my hand with equal success.

'Be calm, Tomas,' Ailsa said, which irritated me so much I could almost have thrown the bottle at her.

Almost.

Her knitting needles clicked together, the sound boring through my head and making me feel like live things were crawling around inside my ears. I took a long swallow of brandy and a shuddering breath.

'It wouldn't have worked. You see that, don't you?' I said. 'She's probably their best fucking customer by now.'

'Yes, of course I see that,' Ailsa said. 'I'm thinking, that's all.'

'Well, think quickly,' I said. 'We're supposed to be taking the Chains back next Godsday, and now we've no Gutcutters to support us and no fucking plan.'

'Godsday is still five days away,' Ailsa said. She sighed and put down her knitting. 'Without the Gutcutters, an all-out assault like we had planned is out of the question. We simply don't have the numbers for it.'

I clenched my teeth. I knew by then that Ailsa often thought out loud, but to my mind a lot of the time that sounded like she was explaining my own business to me as though she were addressing a simple child. I knew that was just her way, but all the same I had to remind myself not to take ill against her for it.

'I realise that,' I said, forcing my voice to stay calm.

'There are ways and means, Tomas. There always are,' she said. She looked up at me then, and smiled brightly in the way that she did when she was about to change the subject with a lurch so hard it gave me a headache. 'You should go and see Billy tomorrow.'

'Aye,' I said, happy for anything that steered the conversation away from the evening's failure of a meeting with Ma Aditi. 'Perhaps I'll do that.'

'Take him seriously, Tomas,' Ailsa cautioned me. 'You haven't seen him since he began his time with the magician and he may seem different to you now, but see that you take him seriously. The time may come when we might need him.'

We were back to *may* and *might* again, I noticed. The habit of the Queen's Men of never speaking in certainties was chafing at me, I had to admit.

I said good night to her and went to my own room to sleep.

That wasn't easy, but with the help of the rest of the brandy I managed it in the end.

Chapter 25

I don't know why I took Bloody Anne with me the next morning, but it seemed like the right thing to do. She was the one who had a problem with Billy the Boy in the first place, of course, and without her worries he would never have ended up at Old Kurt's.

Going alone was out of the question, especially after my useless meeting with Ma Aditi the day before, but I could have taken any of the men with me as a bodyguard. I didn't, though. I brought Bloody Anne and no one else.

That was risky, these days. The last time we had trod the riverside path into the Wheels I had only been back in Ellinburg a short time and word about that had yet to completely get around. That was then, though. Anne and I had managed to pass for any scruffy returning veterans wandering the bad parts of the city, but I couldn't do that any more.

Now I was Tomas Piety again, head of the Pious Men, and *everyone* knew who I was. By rights I should have had six armed men at my back wherever I went, but we were heading into Gutcutter territory and it wasn't on official Pious Men business. I had told Anne once before that the Pious Men wouldn't enter the Wheels in force until we meant it, and that was still true. All the same I could feel the eyes on us, watching us from the grimy windows of the wooden tenements we passed.

The river path was treacherous in the winter, and thin skins of ice floated downriver past us. It was freezing down by the water, and despite our fine coats, cloaks and gloves, both of us were chilled to the bone by the time we reached Old Kurt's front door. The rat nailed to it looked to be frozen solid.

I raised a hand to knock, drawing breath to call out the words, but the door opened before I touched it. Billy the Boy stood in the entrance looking up at us.

'Tomas,' he said. 'Bloody Anne.'

I nodded. 'How are you, Billy?'

He had the first fluff of a moustache on his upper lip, I noticed, and he looked to me as though he had grown almost an inch for each of the months he had been with Old Kurt. Not literally perhaps, but truth be told, the lad wasn't all that far off my height already. All the same he looked to be painfully thin under his loose shirt and britches. I thought perhaps his thirteenth nameday had come and gone unmarked while he was away, and it pained me to have missed his coming of age.

'Well enough,' he said. 'You'll be coming in.'

As always with him it was a statement, not a question, and I wondered just how prescient Billy the Boy was. Did Our Lady truly speak to him, telling him what was to come? I wouldn't know. Perhaps it was the cunning in him, or perhaps he was just a good judge of human nature, or just mad. Whatever it was, he was right.

'We'd like that, Billy,' I said.

He nodded and stepped back to let us into Old Kurt's house.

He led Anne and me through into Kurt's parlour, where the old man was sitting in his chair close to a fire that burned fiercely in the grate. Kurt looked older than I remembered, pale and drawn. That was passing strange, to my mind, as he seemed to have aged little in the years between my childhood and my return to Ellinburg. Life catches up with all men in the end, I supposed.

He looked up at us and grinned his ratty grin.

'Tomas Piety and the fine . . . and Bloody Anne,' he said, and I knew that he had remembered Anne's words. 'How fare you?'

'Well enough,' I said.

I took the stool across from him, there being no other chair in the room, and Anne stood behind me with her hands never far from her daggers. I knew she didn't trust Kurt even now, and I thought she still wasn't easy in her mind with what was being done in this house.

Kurt laughed, a sound full of phlegm and age. 'Well enough,' he repeated. 'Well enough that you're dressed like a lord and have the whole of the Stink bowing and scraping to you again. You and Aditi both, back from your war, and it's as though nothing ever happened.'

I thought of Jochan, and Cookpot, and my own bleak memories, and I shook my head. 'It happened,' I said. 'We survived it, that's all.'

'Well and good,' Kurt said. 'You look rich. Maybe I should put my prices up.'

'We agreed on the price,' I said. 'A mark a week for his tuition and keep. That's more than fair.'

'Well, growing boys eat a lot,' Kurt said, and he looked evasive now. His gaze shifted from the fire to his boots to me to the door, his eyes moving like restless animals.

'What is it, Kurt?'

He coughed, and I realised Billy was standing in the doorway listening to us.

'Boy,' Kurt said, his voice quavering a little despite his attempt to put authority into it. 'Go upstairs and fetch your notes.'

Billy nodded and left the room, and a moment later I heard his footsteps on the stairs. I looked at Kurt and raised my eyebrows as he beckoned me close with a surprising urgency. I leaned toward him to listen.

'Three marks a week or you're having him back.'

'What's the problem?' I asked him.

Kurt grabbed me by the back of the neck and dragged me closer, so he could whisper in my ear. I held up a hand to tell Bloody Anne to be calm, and I listened.

'Touched by a goddess, my wrinkly cock,' Kurt hissed in my ear, so quiet I was sure Anne couldn't hear him. 'He gives me the fear, and I don't say that lightly of anyone. No unschooled lad should be that strong. The boy's fucking *possessed*!'

I remembered the day we had first brought Billy to Kurt's house, how Kurt had lit the fire with cunning and a gesture and how Billy had put it out again with just a look. I hadn't known he could do that, and it had been clear that Kurt hadn't expected it either. I wondered what Billy could do now, after half a year of teaching.

I had always been a little bit scared of Billy myself, truth be told, although I could never have clearly said why. I knew Sir Eland walked in fear of him too, even more so after Billy's visit to Chandler's Narrow, but I didn't know what had happened that night and I never expected to learn the answer. I had said my confessions to Billy, during the war, and that was because one night in Abingon after I had done things that troubled me he had come to me in my tent and told me that I would confess.

He had *told* me.

There was never any question, with Billy. If he said a thing would happen, it did. He said I would confess to him, and I did, and I still didn't know why. Touched by the goddess, I had thought. That was how I had explained it to myself, and to the men, and that was well enough. That made Billy holy, in their eyes.

Holy and possessed were perhaps two sides of the same coin, but one was acceptable, laudable even, and the other very much wasn't. I knew I couldn't let this pass, not when that would mean the risk of others hearing it.

'I don't want to hear that word again,' I whispered in Kurt's ear. 'Three marks a week if that's what it takes to keep your mouth shut but not a copper more, and that price will never go up again, whatever he does. Don't test me on this, Old Kurt. The boy is *holy*, you mark me on that, and that's the way it's staying. Understand?'

Old Kurt nodded sharply and let go of me just as Billy started back down the stairs. Three marks a week was enough money to make me wince. All the same it was coin well spent, to my mind. I turned to see Billy standing in the doorway clutching a great black leather book in his arms, his unblinking stare taking in the three of us.

Where is the difference between holy and possessed? I wondered. When does miracle become magic, magic become witchcraft? Is it in the nature of the deed itself, or in the eye of the beholder? Is it decided in the telling after the fact, and if so does it depend on who does that telling? Magic was magic, but then I wouldn't know. That was a philosophical question, I supposed, and this was no time for philosophy.

'What have you got there, Billy?' I asked him.

'Show your Uncle Tomas what you've been working on, boy,' Kurt said.

Uncle Tomas. That was something I had never been called before. Jochan was my only sibling and he had never fathered a child, any more than I had myself. It sounded well to my ears, I had to admit. It would be a good thing, to be an uncle. Perhaps a better one, to be a father.

I got to my feet and Billy opened the book and held it for me to see. The thick vellum pages were covered in his childish handwriting, scrawled with notes and diagrams that I didn't have time to read before he turned the pages. All I could think was that that book must have cost a pile of silver, even unprinted. A book like that was well out of the reach of a common man, that was for certain. It was the sort of book that guildmasters wrote in, and that I supposed nobles did as well. Perhaps Old Kurt wasn't overcharging me all that much after all, if he was giving Billy things like that.

I nodded as though I knew what I was looking at, wanting to please Billy. The lad had obviously been working hard, although I couldn't divine what at. The cunning was as far beyond me as it was most other people and I've no shame in admitting it.

Maybe one person in ten thousand has it in them to learn the cunning, if that. There had been sixty-five thousand of us at Abingon and we had had two cunning men and three women among us that I knew of. The magicians of Dannsburg hadn't gone to war, of course. War magic was sorcery, and as Old Kurt had said, they looked down on that as beneath them. Our five cunning folk had all died in battle, fighting for their country. It hadn't been beneath *them* to serve the crown, I noted.

'Look at this one, Uncle Tomas,' Billy said, turning the page to show me a diagram of almost impossible complexity.

I stared at it, trying to work out exactly what I was looking at. I found I couldn't really focus on it. Billy had just called me Uncle like it was the most natural thing in the world. I kept hearing that word in my head, rolling over and over like distant thunder. The image on the page seemed to squirm and shift even as I looked at it. I blinked and put a hand to my head.

Uncle.

The image moved, the lines redrawing themselves across the vellum before my eyes. I saw words I couldn't pronounce, fading as fast as I made them out. I saw maps, contours and hills and buildings, lines of supply and attack and defence. I saw strategic plans and armies arrayed across sketched terrain. I saw Ailsa's face, staring up at me. I saw a bird's-eye view of the Stink, of the Narrows and the houses that bordered them.

I saw cannon, positioned on the hill by the convent.

I saw what would happen to Ellinburg, if Abingon came here.

Ailsa.

Cannon.

Smoke boiled across the page, lit red from within by the cannon's murderous roar.

Uncle, they bellowed.

Uncle!

I saw the face of Our Lady, looking back at me.

Merciless.

Uncle!

Anne caught me before I hit the floor, her strong hands in my armpits. She lowered me back onto the stool by the fire and crouched down in front of me, looking intently into my face.

'Tomas? Can you hear me?'

I shook my head and blinked. I could see Anne's face, her scar puckering as she frowned with concern. I pinched the bridge of my nose between thumb and forefinger, squeezing my eyes closed for a moment before I opened them again and nodded at her.

'I hear you, Bloody Anne,' I said.

I looked up at Old Kurt and saw him staring back at me, a bleak look on his face. 'Billy drew that one himself,' he said. 'I never showed him how.'

'What is it, Billy?' I asked.

The lad shrugged. 'A picture,' he said. 'I drew it.'

'It's a wyrd glyph,' Old Kurt said. 'In three years, maybe a bit less if he was clever and learned fast, it would have been time for me to have started teaching him how to draw those. He done that one himself, two weeks ago, and I never showed him how.'

Old Kurt swallowed, the lump in his scrawny neck working up and down, and he said no more on the subject.

'Well done, Billy,' a man said, but his words sounded hollow, as though he was a long way away, at the end of a tunnel. 'It seems like you're ahead of your studies. I was never very good at school, myself, but it looks like you're making up for my failings there.'

Had *I* ever been to school? I couldn't remember. Perhaps that man had been, but I wouldn't know. I didn't know who he was.

Billy just looked at me. 'You fell down,' he said, after a moment. 'I knew you would.'

He turned and walked out of the room then, his book under his arm, and I heard his footsteps climbing the rickety wooden stairs.

Had I fallen down?

I had no idea.

I stared into the fire and shivered. I was frozen to the bone. I pulled my cloak around me, huddling for warmth in my coat and all my fine warm clothes as sweat ran tickling down my back.

I was so cold.

I leaned closer to the fire, until I could feel its heat making my cheeks tighten.

So.

Fucking.

Cold.

'What is it?' Someone said that, somewhere. I think it was a woman's voice, but it was so raspy it was hard to tell. I wondered who she was. 'What's wrong with him?'

'Battle shock.'

That was a man's voice, an old man by the sound of him.

I wondered who they were talking about, but my thoughts were drifting now and I found that I didn't really care.

I was so cold, and the fire was so far away. Why were they keeping the fire so far away from me when I was so cold?

177

'He's never shown signs of it before.'

'Sometimes it comes out later. Sometimes, when it's bad, it takes a long time.'

'And you'd know about that, would you?'

She sounded aggressive now, the raspy woman. Challenging.

'Aye, I would,' the old man said, and the sorrow in his voice told me that he knew from bitter experience.

I wondered who he was.

Chapter 26

'We had to come and fucking get you,' Jochan said.

I blinked up at him. I was lying in my bed above the Tanner's Arms, and Jochan was standing over me. Cold morning light was shining through the window, and my little brother was giving me a telling.

'Bloody Anne sent a runner, some Wheeler girl she found and paid,' he went on. 'I dunno who she was. Urgent it is, she said. Send men and a cart. Well, fuck that, we both know you being carried through the Wheels in a cart would have been the end of the Pious Men. Me and Black Billy and Fat Luka came for you, and we waited until it was full dark, and then we carried you back between us down the river path where no one could see, with Bloody Anne watching our tail. So you're home now, Tomas. It's all right. It's over. You're home now.'

I looked up into Jochan's face, and I could see from the pain in his eyes that he understood.

Battle shock.

That thing that I didn't feel, or so I had thought. I never had felt it, not until Billy the Boy had shown me his drawing or his glyph or whatever it had been. I had . . . lost my way, for a while there.

I knew that, but this was no time to show weakness.

'I'm well,' I said, and sat up in my blankets. 'I'm well, Jochan, and don't let anyone think otherwise of me.'

'It was me and Luka,' he said, 'and you know you can trust Black Billy. We won't say anything, none of us.'

I nodded, but it left a sour taste in my mouth all the same. Was it

179

a secret that needed keeping, that I had been affected by the war like every other man who had fought? I had been strong all the way back from Abingon, keeping my crew together until we reached Ellinburg. I had been strong for the last six months, leading them and taking back my businesses one by one, watching men die and still doing what needed to be done.

I had been strong right up until I just couldn't do it any more.

Billy the Boy had done something to me, I knew that. Something that had opened the strongbox in the back of my mind where I kept the horrors locked away. That was the place where I never went, the part of my mind where I had parcelled up the memories called *Abingon* and vowed never to look again.

Whatever Billy had drawn in that book, it had been something magic. Ink on vellum can't do that to a man, not by itself. There was magic woven into the picture Billy had drawn. I knew that much, and I was starting to understand why Old Kurt had looked so scared of the lad. They were living under the same roof, after all.

But of course, Billy had been at Abingon too.

Billy had killed men in battle under the crumbling walls of the citadel. Billy had endured the noise of the cannon the same as the rest of us. Billy had done his part when it came to giving mercy to the wounded and shovelling corpses into the plague pits.

I wondered how much of what I had seen in that picture had come from my mental strongbox, and how much from Billy's own. Of course the lad was scarred by what he had seen, and by what he had done. We all were, but the rest of us were grown men.

Billy was a child. A scared and scarred and broken child, who was touched by a goddess and learning magic at a frightening rate.

I got out of my bed and took a long and deliberate piss into the pot, to show Jochan that I could. We all start the day the same way, after all, and once you've seen that you might not notice the otherness in someone quite so much.

'Right,' I said as I buttoned my smallclothes. Someone had obviously undressed me and put me to bed the night before, but I didn't know who. 'Let me get dressed, and then we'll see how the land lies.'

'No better than it did yesterday,' Jochan said. 'The Chains is still held like a fucking fortress, and without the Gutcutters we still ain't got the men to take it.'

No, we hadn't, but I remembered one thing from yesterday. When Old Kurt had greeted us he had almost made the mistake of calling Bloody Anne a 'fine lady' again, and that had given me an idea.

'Are you taking the piss?' Anne demanded when I told her.

We were sitting in the kitchen of the Tanner's Arms, and Ailsa was washing glasses and listening.

'No, Anne, I'm not,' I said. 'I need the Chains back, you know that. We've been planning this for weeks.'

'We've been planning to do it with the Gutcutters' help, and that's in the shithouse now,' she said. 'What makes you think we can still do it at all?'

'You remember what the captain told us about battle, don't you, Bloody Anne? "Always cheat, always win," he said. Well, if I haven't got the men to do this in an honest fight, then I'm going to fucking cheat.'

'And even supposing I say yes, which I haven't, how would this make us look to the other gangs?'

I shrugged. The only unfair fight is the one you lose, to my mind. In a year's time nobody would remember the details of what had happened or how it was done. They would only remember who had lived and who had died.

'It'll make us look like the people who own the Golden Chains,' I said. 'This will work, Anne.'

She fixed me with a stare and jabbed a finger pointedly at the long scar on her face. 'What sort of "fine lady" has a face like mine, Tomas Piety?'

'We might be able to do something about that,' I said. 'Ailsa? Come here a minute.'

Ailsa came over to the table and put her hand on my shoulder as naturally as if she really were my fancy woman and not just playing a part. She was very convincing, in everything she did. I had to keep reminding myself that playing a part was *all* she was doing.

'What can I do for you, my handsome?' she asked, and giggled.

Anne gave her a look but held her peace.

'How good are paints and powders, really?' I asked her.

'Oh, but they can work wonders,' she said. 'And there's other things too. Resins and dyes and . . . oh, oh, I see! Oh, why Anne, I can make that scar go away, my lovely, if that's what you're asking me. For a little while, at least. It'll take a bit of filling so you didn't ought to be smiling or you might crack, but Ailsa can make that look just—'

'What about everyone else?' Anne interrupted.

She thought Ailsa was no more than a foolish barmaid and my bit of fancy, and she made no pretence at liking her. Ailsa took that in her stride, of course, like she did washing glasses and flirting with drunks and everything else needed to keep up her false face.

'These lovable louts?' she said. 'Oh, I can make them look like new men, with a little touch of this and that. If that's what you're wanting, Tomas?'

I nodded. It was.

I hadn't had the chance to discuss my plan with Ailsa yet, but I could tell she had already worked out what I had in mind. She was no one's fool, whatever Bloody Anne might think.

'That's good, then,' I said. 'We stick to the original plan. Godsday evening. That gives us enough time to get clothes and things bought as well. Can you do everyone in a day, Ailsa? It'll be Anne, me, Jochan, Grieg, Cutter and Erik.'

Ideally I would have liked to have had Black Billy with us, but black faces weren't so common in Ellinburg that someone wouldn't have recognised him whatever Ailsa did. Grieg and Erik from my old crew were both good at close work, though, and Jochan's man Cutter was a devil at it. More to the point, no one would know them.

'What about Luka?' Anne said. 'He's hardly the only fat man in the city, and he plays the lute. That might be useful.'

He did, at that.

Luka had played before the war, and once he had some coin in his pocket again he had bought himself a beautiful instrument that he kept in a big leather case. It was that case that interested Anne, I realised, not the lute itself. I gave her a nod of approval. She was no one's fool either.

'Aye,' I said. 'Luka too, then.'

'Well, I'll be busy, but I can do it,' Ailsa said. 'For you I can, Tomas.'

I patted her on the arse, something I could only get away with when she was playing her part, and smiled at her.

'You're a good lass,' I said.

She went back to her glasses and I pursed my lips in thought.

'We'll need to get you a proper dress,' I said to Anne. 'Something fine, like a real noble lady would wear. Footmen's outfits for the men, I think, and finery for Jochan. I'll be your consort.'

'Oh, will you?' Anne said, but smiled to take the sting out of it. 'That'll be the day, Tomas Piety.'

I returned her smile. We understood each other, Anne and I. She was still one of the best customers of the house on Chandler's Narrow, and I think Rosie seldom saw anyone but her these days.

'Is that a yes, Bloody Anne?'

She sighed. 'I suppose so,' she said, 'but don't expect miracles. I'm no actress, and I've told you before I can't fight properly in a fucking dress.'

'Keep Luka close and you won't have to,' I said. 'If we do this right, and we will, they won't know what's fucking hit them.'

Chapter 27

Godsday came at last, and I held confession upstairs in the Tanner's Arms while Ailsa worked her magic on Bloody Anne in the room next to mine. I had been cultivating a moustache for the last week, and it finally looked almost presentable. As presentable as a moustache can ever look, anyway. I had kept it thin and neat, the way nobles wore them. I hated it, but it was the last thing that Tomas Piety would ever have chosen to wear on his face.

Tonight I didn't want to look like Tomas Piety.

When Simple Sam had finished telling me how he had farted on Erik's face three nights ago while he was sleeping and I had forgiven him for it, I took off my priest's robe and went down to the common room. The Tanner's was closed today, as there was too much happening to have people from the neighbourhood coming in and maybe carrying tales away with them.

Grieg was already dressed in his footman's clothes, prancing about the room and making a fool of himself practising his bow. If Pawl the tailor had been surprised by my request for three sets of footman's livery, a fine lady's dress and the clothes of a Dannsburg dandy he had kept it to himself, and he had delivered exactly what I wanted. A good tailor should be discreet, as I have written, and Pawl was certainly that.

Grieg just looked like himself in foolish clothes, but that was well enough. No one at the Golden Chains would know Grieg, after all, or Erik or Cutter. It was Jochan and me, and maybe Luka, that someone might recognise. I would be dressed as a lord and I had clothes enough for that already. Jochan was to be the dandy, and posing as my friend. Grieg, Erik, and Cutter had footman's livery, and Fat Luka was to be a bard.

Ailsa came down after a while with her pots of paints and powders in one hand and a bag in the other.

'Now, my lovely boys, who's first?'

I went first, to show them there was no shame in it.

Ailsa could have opened a theatre company with the things she had in that bag. Two hours later I had greying hair, a faded scar on my cheek and lines around my mouth and eyes that made me look like I had twenty more years to me than I had in truth. She held the looking glass up for me and smiled.

'You look like some old duke, with a boyhood duelling scar,' she said.

I did, at that.

'Thank you,' I said. 'That's fine work, Ailsa. Very fine.'

'Oh, I have my talents, Tomas. You of all people should know that,' she said, getting a laugh from the men for her sauce. 'Now then, my lovelies, who's next?'

Jochan went next. Yesterday he'd had Ernst style his wild hair into a pomaded swirl that the barber had assured us was how the fine gentlemen of Dannsburg were wearing theirs this season, and he had grown a fashionably thin strip of beard on his pointed chin. He looked ridiculous, to my mind, but more importantly he looked like a different man. Ailsa didn't have to do much work on him, just some darkness around the eyes that somehow made him look like he lived an overly dissolute lifestyle and slept for too few hours a night, which wasn't all that far off the truth. She was so skilled with her paints and powders it was almost witchcraft.

Luka was the hardest.

He had always been fat but he had got even fatter over the last six months, and there was no hiding that. He had tried to grow a beard but with little success, and the patchy stubble on his plump cheeks just made him look like there was something wrong with him. Ailsa tutted and fussed and opened her bag, and started to work with a pot of glue and a little brush.

I watched, transfixed, as Luka's beard took shape. She had all the tools of the mummer's trade in that bag, false hair and glues and dyes and things I couldn't even put names to, things to hide scars and things to raise them, things to make beards and to cover baldness.

When she was done with Luka I could have walked past him in the street and not known him. He now had a thick, full beard, and he looked older and somehow more important than he had before. He looked ready to take the stage at a grand theatre in Dannsburg and act a part from one of the great tragedies. How do you make a man look like an actor? I wouldn't know, but Ailsa obviously did.

By the time the painting was done it was dark outside so the rest of us got into our clothes, and then Bloody Anne came down the stairs and joined us.

I was pretty once, Tomas, she had told me, and I saw now that it was true.

Her hair was still short, but Ailsa had styled it with wax so that it curled around her face, and she was wearing the magnificent green silk gown that I had paid Pawl a small fortune for. Her scar was invisible, and if the side of her face didn't move much then I doubted anyone would notice. Noble women weren't renowned for smiling, after all.

'Fuck a nun,' Jochan said when he saw her. 'Is that really you, Bloody Anne?'

'Fuck yourself, Jochan,' she said. 'It's me, all right, and bugger if this dress isn't sending me half mad already.'

If I looked hard, *really* hard, I could just about see the line of her scar under the thick coating of powder on her face. Anyone who didn't know it was there would never have noticed, I was sure of that. I had no idea what Ailsa had used to fill it with but I only hoped it wouldn't fall out before the evening's work was done.

'Right,' I said. 'Listen to me. You all know the plan, but now it's time to put it into action so we're going to go over it one more time. The captain always said you can't be too prepared, and he had the right of that. Just remember that no plan survives first contact with the enemy, and tonight we're going right into the heart of them. The Golden Chains was my business before the war, but these bastards who've stolen it from me have made it their stronghold. There's money in the Chains, not just silver marks but real gold crowns money. This is where the rich folk go to play their games of cards and smoke their fucking poppy resin, and it's guarded tight as a virgin's arse. We stick to the plan, boys, but as soon as it goes off we take them hard and fast. They'll have the numbers but we'll have surprise, so we've got to be quick and brutal about it. You understand?'

Heads nodded around the room, and that was good. Brutal was something these men understood, I knew that. Jochan flourished what he thought was a courtly bow, lace spilling from his cuffs as he moved his arm.

'My dear sir, we shall kill them all most terribly fucking politely,' he said, and the men laughed.

'Just remember who you're supposed to be, and try not to say *fuck* too much,' I said. 'The carriage will be here in a minute. Luka, have you got your lute case?'

'Yes, boss,' he said, his expression serious under his mummer's beard as he picked up the heavy instrument case and hefted it in his hand.

Jochan might not be taking this very seriously, but I could tell that Luka was, and that was good. I could see that this felt like a grand caper to Jochan and Grieg, an excuse to dress up and play the fool, but it wasn't. The Golden Chains was important to me, and more than that it was important to Ailsa.

There were actual Skanians there, she had told me, not just their hired agents. This was the one business of mine that they had really wanted: the place where the rich folk went. The Golden Chains was a gambling house just off Trader's Row where hands of cards were played for more money than a working man made in a year, and now it was a place where aristocrats smoked the finest poppy resin to escape the tedium of their privileged lives.

The place had always been strong, but since the poppy trade began the Skanians had made the Golden Chains into a fortress, beyond my means to simply storm. I wouldn't be doing this the way I had taken back my other businesses, I knew that. My original idea had been to make a deal with the Gutcutters, to take it between us through sheer force and split the business, but when I had seen Ma Aditi smoking resin I had known that idea had gone to the whores. The Chains was the centre of the resin business in Ellinburg, everyone knew that. Aditi would hardly be likely to want to kill her own supplier, after all.

No, that plan was dead and in the shithouse, as Anne had said. That left cheating, and the captain had taught me well how to cheat.

Chapter 28

'Lady Alicia Lan Verhoffen,' Anne announced herself to the five guards on the door of the Golden Chains. They looked frozen, all of them huddled in heavy cloaks against the winter night. 'My consort, Baron Lan Markoff, and his friend the honourable Rikhard Spaff. My bard, and three footmen of no account.'

Ailsa had coached her well, for all that Bloody Anne had struggled to take instruction from a barmaid she regarded as no more than a tart. Her accent was passable Dannsburg, if nowhere near as sharp as Ailsa's was when she spoke with her own voice. I nodded to the head doorman and palmed a silver mark into his hand by way of introduction.

My own accent is so strongly Ellinburg that there was nothing to be done about it, so we had agreed that I would say as little as possible. *Keep a disdainful silence*, Ailsa had advised me, and from what I knew of nobles that didn't seem so far from the truth.

'Your bard?' the man asked, his breath clouding the air in front of him. 'It's not usual to bring your bard to a gaming house.'

'I enjoy music,' Bloody Anne said, her mouth held in the tight line that was all that the filler Ailsa had set into her face would allow. 'I may wish for a tune, later, after I have wiped your tables clean of coin.'

I could see the doormen looking at us, obviously scanning us for weapons. Of course, there was nowhere to hide anything larger than a pocketknife in any of the ludicrous clothes we were all wearing.

'My lady enjoys music,' I repeated, giving the man a look.

I was dressed in my finest clothes, and the grey in my hair and the false duelling scar on my cheek made me look every inch a Dannsburg noble. If my accent was wrong then surely that only spoke of a man widely travelled, or so I hoped. I was very cold, and standing out in the street wasn't helping.

The doorman fingered the coin I had given him and nodded. 'As you will, my lord baron,' he said, and finally let us in.

'Wait by the door, boy,' I told Cutter. 'My lady may wish for something from her carriage during the evening.'

Cutter nodded, and loitered in his footman's costume next to the two men on the inside of the great oak-and-iron front door. They exchanged the sympathetic looks of put-upon servants.

The remaining six of us walked down the corridor and into the warmth of the main gaming hall. There were no more guards along the way, as I had suspected there wouldn't be. I knew the Golden Chains, and I knew how it was run. I used to run it myself, after all.

There was only one way in or out, and that was the door we had just come through. There used to be a tradesman's door at the back, once, but I had bricked that up myself. One door is easier to guard than two, and guarded it was. There were five men outside that door, as I said, and from what Ailsa's spies had reported there were another five patrolling around the building, watching the narrow windows.

The whole idea was to keep prospective threats out of the business. Once inside, the wealthy patrons didn't want a horde of thugs with weapons standing over them. There were only five men in the gaming hall who were conspicuously armed, although I suspected the card dealers and footmen probably had blades of some sort hidden about their persons as well. Storming the Golden Chains by brute force would have been virtually impossible even with the Gutcutters' help, I realised now.

This way was better.

The warm air in the main room was thick with the sickly smoke of poppy resin, and the light was dim. There were maybe a dozen patrons at the gaming tables, all of them playing the same complicated game with cards and stacks of wooden counters. I understood nothing of it, but Jochan had assured me that he knew how the game was played.

'Cards,' he announced with a joyful smile that I didn't think he had to feign.

'Not for me,' I said, taking a glass of wine from a tray held by a footman in the livery of the house.

'My friend the Baron Lan Markoff is a terrible bore,' Jochan went on as he drew up a chair at one of the card tables, pushing his way between a man in elegantly cut grey wool and a woman in a russet silk dress. He was affecting a ridiculous accent that made him sound somewhere between a rich drunk and a simpleton. 'Never plays a bloody hand. Name's Spaff, the honourable, et cetera. I bloody love cards. No good at it, though, but it's only money and I've got shitloads of that. What's the buy-in?'

One of the other players grinned at him and silver moved from Jochan's purse to the banker's box to be replaced by a small stack of wooden counters. Why they didn't just play for coin I didn't know, but I suspected they may have regarded it as being beneath their honour or some such nonsense. One thing I have noticed in life is that the men who speak the most of honour are usually those who have the least of it.

'How very tedious,' Bloody Anne said loudly, in her best Dannsburg accent. 'All these silly people, playing games with cards. It pleases me that you do not indulge, my lord baron.'

I made a noncommittal noise, looking out the corner of my eye at a tall man in an extremely expensive-looking coat who was heading our way. This was the one, I was sure. This had to be the Skanian who Ailsa had told me was running the Chains.

'Baron . . . ?' he asked, letting the question hang in the air.

'Lan Markoff,' I said in as gruff a tone as I could manage without sounding too Ellinburg.

'A pleasure,' the man said, although I noticed he offered no name of his own. 'I cannot place your accent, my lord baron.'

'The accent of ships and caravans,' I said with a shrug. 'I am a merchant speculator. My home is Dannsburg, although I've not seen the city in years.'

I had no idea what a 'merchant speculator' was, but Ailsa had assured me it was a plausible occupation for a minor noble such as a baron.

The man's smile widened a little, and I could only assume she had been right about that.

'Have your travels taken you to Skania, my lord baron?'

'Not as yet,' I said, 'although who knows what the future may bring? I'm not here to discuss business, not tonight.'

I looked around the gambling house, affecting boredom in an attempt to steer the conversation away from this supposed occupation of mine that I didn't know the first thing about. The Skanian obviously caught my mood.

'If cards are not to your liking, Baron,' he said, 'perhaps I might offer you and your lady something . . . a little more relaxing?'

He meant resin, of course, and I wanted no part of that. All the same, we had to stick to the plan. I turned away and coughed into my fist, taking the opportunity to glance over my shoulder. Fat Luka was two paces behind me, where he should be, with his heavy lute case in his hand. He met my eye and nodded a fraction.

'A pipe would be most soothing,' Bloody Anne said. 'Don't you think, my dear?'

'Aye,' I agreed. 'Pipes it is.'

The man turned away from us and clicked his fingers at a footman, and I shot Jochan a look.

Now, I mouthed at him.

'Fucking *cheat!*' Jochan bellowed.

He surged to his feet with a roar and flipped the card table over, scattering drinks and counters and cards all over his astonished fellow players.

That was the signal.

I heard a grunt from down the corridor as Cutter's tiny blades, no larger than pocketknives, sent the men inside the door on their way across the river. I could only offer up a prayer to Our Lady that Cutter could get the key turned in the lock and the heavy beam down across the inside of the door before the men outside stormed in to see what the shouting was about.

If not, we were done.

Jochan punched the man next to him full in the face, sending him reeling backward into his fellows. Anne yanked up the skirts of her dress to reveal her daggers, one sheath strapped to each pale thigh. She drew her blades and hammered one into the Skanian's chest without word or hesitation.

Fat Luka flipped open his lute case, took out a compact crossbow and shot the nearest guard through the gut even as he tossed my sword-belt to me with his free hand. I grabbed it out of the air and drew the Weeping Women, letting the leather fall to the floor as the armed men in the room charged us with bared steel in their hands.

I was hard-pressed for a moment before Jochan vaulted the overturned card table and grabbed his axe from Luka's open case. We felled three men between us. Grieg and Erik took up their weapons and waded in. Even Luka wasn't strong enough to have carried enough weapons for everyone in one hand, so this had been the plan. The surprised guards fell before us.

Our Lady smile on me, it was working.

It kept working until another Skanian came out of the back room. This one was older than his dead fellow, his long blond hair bound back from his gaunt face with a silver clasp. He was wearing robes not unlike my priest's garb, but I knew this was no priest. His eyes were as hard as any soldier's, his thin lips drawing tight with fury as he saw his countryman lying dead on the floor in a spreading pool of blood.

Grieg took a step toward him with a guard's shortsword held ready to do murder, and the Skanian raised his hand. A great gout of fire burst from his fingers and took Grieg full in the face.

He fell shrieking, the meat cooking from the bones of his skull even as the rest of us hastily took cover behind overturned tables. A moment later Grieg exploded as though he'd had a flashstone sewn up inside him.

'Lady save us!' I gasped, although I knew She wouldn't. 'Magician!'

Sudden panic gripped the room. The other patrons had seemed almost bemused by the earlier violence, as though armed men fighting were beneath them and none of their affair, but now they were cowering along with the rest of us and that was good. That added to the confusion.

The magician, who hadn't seen the initial eruption of violence and didn't know who was who, wasted precious moments burning a young man with foolish hair who had nothing to do with anything.

Anne took aim with one of her daggers and let fly in a long overhand throw, but the blade seemed to swerve in the air as it neared the Skanian magician. The dagger made an impossible turn and ended up embedded harmlessly in the wall behind him.

'Bloody witchcraft!' Anne spat.

Something moved behind me, just outside my vision. It seemed to scuttle along the wall like an oversized rat, but it was gone before I could take it in. I had to duck again as a new blast of flame washed across the room from the magician's hands, setting a tapestry on fire behind me. I didn't have time to think about what the moving thing might have been. There was only one way in or out of the Chains, as I have said, and I could hear the guards outside pounding on that door even now. If the fire took we would all burn alive in there. It could be minutes before the second half of my plan bore fruit, and I didn't think we had minutes to spare.

'Reload the crossbow and give it to Anne,' I hissed at Luka. 'It's the only way we'll get that fucking—'

I stopped in astonishment as the sides of the magician's neck burst open in a spray of blood that decorated the wall beside him and the low ceiling over his head. He twisted and fell with a gurgling rattle, blood still gushing from his neck, and I saw Cutter standing behind him with his tiny knives dripping gore.

'Fuck a nun, you took your time,' Jochan said. 'Scuttle quicker next time, you little bastard.'

Oh, yes, Cutter had his uses all right. I could see that now.

Jochan got to his feet and laughed. There was a single guard left alive in the room with us, white-faced with fear. Jochan planted his axe in the man's head without comment and showed me his savage grin. I could still hear pounding on the front door, and however strong it was I knew it wouldn't hold forever.

'Where have those fuckers got to?' Luka wondered aloud, voicing my own thoughts.

A moment later there was a thud, then a scream, and I heard the thump of crossbows and the sound of more impacts. The ten lads I had hired from around the Stink and armed with crossbows had finally come out of the alleys they had been hiding in, then.

Thank the Lady for that.

Someone pounded on the door and called out, 'Pious, in Our Lady's name!'

Those were the right words. I nodded to Luka. 'Go let them in,' I said. 'Erik, get that fucking fire out before it takes in the plaster and we all burn to fucking death.'

Bloody Anne was staring at the dead magician, and at the tattered shreds of cloth and flesh and the huge red stain on the floor that had once been Grieg.

'I don't . . .' she started to say, before Jochan kicked a table back the right way up and jumped up onto it.

'We're the Pious Men!' he roared, arms outstretched and his axe in his hand with bits of the guard's head still clinging to the blade.

I counted eleven of the wealthy patrons left alive, all of them staring at Jochan as though he were some sort of devil, escaped from Hell. This wouldn't do, I realised. I picked up my sword-belt and buckled it on, sheathing the Weeping Women as the first of the hired crossbowmen came into the room with reloaded weapons in their hands. Luka was still outside in the cold, directing the defence of the building. I took a step into the centre of the room and gave Jochan a look that said to be quiet.

'My name is Tomas Piety,' I said. 'I don't normally look like this, but I'm sure you'll make allowances under the circumstances. I am a businessman, and I own the Golden Chains.'

'Gangsters,' a woman said, fanning herself rapidly with her hand.

'Businessmen,' I corrected her. 'The Chains was mine before the war, and now it is mine again. This has been a business disagreement, no more than that, and now it's settled.'

'That man *exploded*!' a weak-chinned fellow shouted, waving vaguely at the stain where Grieg had been.

'Aye, he did,' I said. 'They had a magician, and I didn't expect that. It won't happen again.'

'I dare say it won't,' the woman said. 'The magician appears to no longer be with us.'

She tittered, then giggled, then fainted into the arms of the man beside her.

'For fuck's sake,' I heard Bloody Anne mutter to herself.

Still, it was done. Not done easily perhaps, but as I had told the men, no plan survives first contact with the enemy.

Chapter 29

There was no chance that an assault with crossbows would have gone unnoticed in the middle of the city, especially not so close to Trader's Row. I let the patrons go and sat down with a drink to wait for the City Guard to arrive. There were far too many bodies for us to attempt to hide them, so we didn't bother.

Captain Rogan came in person, as I had thought he might, leading a full troop of twenty men armed with crossbows as well as their shortswords and clubs. I was paying taxes to Governor Hauer again by then, of course, large ones, so I wasn't overly concerned what Rogan might think of the evening's events.

All the same, he was furious, and he made no attempt to hide it.

'What in the name of all the gods do you think you're doing, Piety?' he demanded. 'I know who you are, all of you. No amount of mummer's paint will change that.'

He was standing in the main gaming hall with ten of his men around him while the rest of them dragged corpses out into a waiting cart, and he was far too close to me for my liking. I looked into his ugly, brutish face and held his stare.

One thing you didn't do in front of a bully like Rogan was back down or show weakness, not ever. Back down once and you'd never stop doing it, I knew that. My da had taught me that much, at least.

'I am conducting a business takeover, Captain Rogan,' I said. 'The Golden Chains is now back under its rightful management and will be open for business again in a few days' time.'

'You've conducted a fucking massacre, in full view of half the city!' he roared at me. 'Take him in.'

We had done it in view of some of the city's nobility was what he meant, of course. Now he had to be seen to do something, and that inconvenienced him. Being inconvenienced meant having to do some work, and that put Rogan in a foul temper at the best of times. I had been expecting this.

'I'm going to see Grandfather,' I told Jochan, who nodded back at me.

'You're too sure of yourself by far, Piety,' Rogan growled at me, but I ignored him.

I was untouchable, and we both knew it.

'We'll be open for business again soon,' I said instead. 'I don't recall that you used to be a member here, Captain. Perhaps that could change.'

Rogan shot me a look. He had his vices, as I have written, and none so strong among them as gambling. He was a regular face at the racetrack, where I had often won back the bribes I paid him, but he had never had enough social status to earn an invitation to the Golden Chains. Letting him in might slightly lower the tone, I knew that, but after what had happened there this evening I thought the reputation of the Golden Chains might have suffered somewhat already. At least I knew he had plenty of money to lose.

'That . . . that would please me,' he said. 'I still have to take you in, you know that.'

'I know,' I said.

He nodded, and led me from the Golden Chains with his men surrounding me, but I wasn't in irons and I knew I'd be out again by morning.

That was how business was done in Ellinburg.

I had expected to be thrown into one of the cells under the governor's hall, for appearance's sake if nothing else, but instead Rogan brought me before Governor Hauer himself once more.

It was late, but the governor was still up, although obviously much the worse for wine. He received me in his study on the second floor as he had six months ago when I was newly returned to Ellinburg. He looked even more unhealthy than I remembered, florid of face and fat, with ugly pink patches on his scalp that showed through his thinning hair.

'Business is going well, I see,' Hauer said.

He was all but reeling in his chair, and wine sloshed from his goblet onto the polished wooden surface in front of him as he gestured at me.

I pretended not to notice that.

'The Pious Men have always paid their taxes, Governor,' I said.

'Not for three years they didn't,' he said, and laughed.

The war was nothing to make jokes about, to my mind, not by a man who hadn't even been there. I held my peace, but I think he could see in my eyes that I had taken that ill. He cleared his throat with obvious embarrassment, and I was aware of Rogan moving that little bit closer to the back of the chair I had been pushed into.

They had taken the Weeping Women from me when I was brought before the governor, of course, and once again I wondered if I could best Rogan in a bare-handed fight. He had ten or more years than me at least, but still I doubted it. With swords perhaps, but not fists.

'This evening's events were regrettable, but necessary,' I said. 'The Golden Chains was mine. The last time we spoke, you said you didn't expect me to sit meekly by while men stole my businesses from me, and I haven't. That's all this was.'

'You really haven't, have you, Tomas?' the governor said, and laughed into his wine. 'Oh, no, not at all you haven't. Between you and Aditi, we've never had so many murders in Ellinburg in less than half a year.'

'I pay my taxes,' I said, 'and I assume Ma Aditi does the same. I wouldn't know, but that's between you and her. What I *do* know is how our arrangement works, and I can't see that I've broken the terms of that arrangement.'

'Perhaps not,' Hauer said. 'Perhaps not the letter of them, anyway, but certainly the spirit. No amount of taxes can allow you to conduct open warfare on my streets.'

'Tonight was an exception,' I assured him. 'A regrettable one, as I said. I don't intend for it to happen again.'

'It had better not.'

He thumped his goblet down on the table, spilling more wine, and put the elbow of his expensive silk shirt in the resulting sticky mess. His doublet strained over his gut as he leaned toward me.

Here it comes, I thought. *This is why I'm here, not just to take a telling. There's something he's been working his way around to saying to me.*

'Did she come to you?' Hauer asked, his voice dropping to a hoarse whisper. 'The Queen's Man?'

I nodded, seeing no gain in lying. 'She came,' I said.

Hauer's complexion visibly darkened as he realised I wasn't about to say anything more on that. I remembered our previous conversation, and the fear I had seen in his eyes when he had spoken of the woman I knew as Ailsa.

That gave me an idea.

'And?' he demanded. 'What did she want? What did you do for her?'

'I did what she wanted,' I said, and forced myself to swallow. 'I don't know if I'd still be here if I hadn't, Governor, do you?'

'And where is she now?'

'I really couldn't say.'

I really couldn't, I knew that.

If Hauer realised I had a Queen's Man living in my tavern, serving behind my bar even, then Lady only knew what he would do. So far I wasn't doing anything that he hadn't expected, and the fact that I had only struck as hard and fast as I had on Ailsa's insistence wasn't something that he needed to know, to my mind. All the same, I wondered how well he knew me, and whether he might be working it out for himself.

'It seems to me that you've taken your businesses back very quickly,' Hauer said.

I nodded. 'I won't sit meekly by and be robbed,' I said. 'My men are soldiers, and they know what they're doing. I have men under me who fought at Messia, and at Abingon, and came home to tell of it. They are trained, experienced, *ambitious* killers. Men like that need to be paid, to keep them at heel. They need to be paid well. You realise what would happen if I couldn't pay them any more, don't you?'

Hauer coughed and gulped his wine. I thought that we understood each other now. The thought of my crew unleashed on the city, leaderless and feral, was enough to give the governor pause.

'And the Queen's Man isn't behind this?'

I met his eyes. 'I don't even know her name,' I said, and that was true enough.

She called herself Ailsa, but I could call myself the Baron Lan Markoff and that didn't make it true. I knew nothing about her, I realised, not even her real name. I was the only one of the crew who had heard her speak with that beautiful Dannsburg voice, but who was to say that was really her own and not just another act? I had never seen her without her paints and powders, and I didn't even know how old she really was.

I had to admit to myself that that bothered me.

Hauer sighed and looked over my shoulder at Rogan.

'Who saw?' he asked.

'Hard to say, my lord governor,' Rogan admitted. 'The patrons were gone by the time my men arrived so I don't have their names, but nobles aren't like to gossip about something that would mean admitting they had been there with resin pipes in their hands. It's the fight outside that's likely to have been seen, but there's no way of knowing by who.'

'What to do?' Hauer wondered aloud. 'I should lock you up and leave you to rot, Piety.'

'An imprisoned man pays no taxes and earns no money to pay his men,' I said.

'I *fucking well* know that!' Hauer shouted. 'You're a thorn in my side, Piety, you and Aditi both. The gods only know what will happen when the rest of your sordid peers finally drag themselves home from the war.'

I held my peace at that.

To date, Ma Aditi and me were still the only bosses to have come back from Abingon, but the rest of them led only minor gangs anyway. The Pious Men and the Gutcutters were the main businesses in Ellinburg, as the governor well knew. He was drunk, I could see that, but I could also see that he was scared.

His grip on order in the city depended on maintaining good relationships with people like me, and he knew it. If he lost that grip, then Dannsburg would notice and they would send people to help him regain control. The sort of *help* that a failing governor would get from the Queen's Men was probably the stuff of his nightmares, and I knew I could make something of that.

I looked at him, and I could see he was measuring me with his bloodshot eyes, trying to work out through the haze of wine how much of what I had told him was true. I prided myself that I hadn't told him a single lie that night, although of course many truths are open to interpretation.

I should know.

I'm a priest, after all.

It was fear of the Queen's Men that drove him, in the end, as it had driven me. For him it was fear of failure, and of intervention from the capital. Fear of an investigation that would expose his accounts and the queen's ransom in taxes that he had withheld from the crown over the years. For that he would hang, just as surely as I would for the poppy trade. Under that, I could see, was a deep-rooted fear that perhaps there was still a Queen's Man in Ellinburg.

No, he didn't know that I was working for Ailsa, but I thought that he might be beginning to suspect it.

I would have to do something to change that.

Chapter 30

I spent the night in a cell, as I had expected. There were appearances to be kept up, I understood that, and I didn't take it ill. Rogan made sure I was fed, at least, and that I was brought drinkable water from the good wells off Trader's Row and not the river filth that they gave to normal prisoners. I used most of it to wash the paint and powder from my face until I looked like myself again. Apart from that hideous moustache, anyway.

I had been in the cells before, but not since I was a young man. I hadn't missed it. The room was two floors below the entrance to the governor's hall, a cramped and windowless stone space lit by a brazier in the corridor outside that shed a feeble light through the bars of the door. It stopped me from freezing to death, too, but only just. There was a straw pallet on the floor, crawling with lice, and a wooden bucket already half full of someone else's shit. It stank down there.

I ignored the pallet and sat on the cold, damp floor with my back to the wall, huddled in my coat, and waited. Hauer would have to let me go in the morning, I knew, and anything can be endured for a little while. It can when you know there will be an end to it, anyway. Every soldier knows that.

My chin sank down onto my chest, and I started to think on what the governor had said.

At some point I must have dozed, and after a few hours Rogan came and shook me awake.

He looked tired, with dark circles under his heavy eyes, and I didn't think he had slept at all. He told me that the workings of the governor's operation had spread the word that we were honest businessmen who had been attacked and robbed and had merely been defending ourselves within the extent of the law.

I just nodded.

Stories like that didn't have to be true, or even particularly believable, so long as they came from the right source. If the governor said a thing was so then it was so, as far as the majority of the population were concerned.

The nobility simply didn't care.

I knew there would be trouble over the young dandy who had died, but luckily it had been the Skanian magician who had killed him and not one of my crew. That meant that the outrage of society was directed toward the mysterious foreigners who had so imposed themselves on a fine and upstanding member of the Ellinburg business community like me, and that was good.

I was fed again, and come the dawn the Weeping Women were returned to me. I was released from the cells with the governor's official apology and his public vow to maintain the peace in Ellinburg against the corrupt influence of foreigners.

That was how business was done.

Captain Rogan himself showed me from the governor's hall that morning, and I got a surprise when the doors opened. I was cramped and cold and dirty from my night in the cells, but I found Bloody Anne waiting for me in the packed square outside. The mummer's paint was gone from her face and she looked herself again, in her men's coat and britches with her scar standing out against her pale face. She had Jochan and Fat Luka and five of the lads with her, and a crowd of perhaps two hundred Stink folk around them. Two hundred or so people from my streets, all turned out in the cold to see me walk free with the governor's pardon.

There was a cheer when the morning sun touched my face, the face of a good Ellinburg man who had been wronged by outsiders and had put matters right for himself. A truth can be interpreted in many ways, and the people from my streets had obviously chosen the way in which they would hear this one.

That or they had been told.

Rogan looked at them all, counting heads and not liking what he saw. I could tell he was wondering what might have happened if I hadn't been released. Riots are ugly things, and far from unknown in Ellinburg.

If that gave Rogan something to think on, then that was good.

Business in Ellinburg is one tenth violence to nine tenths posturing, and it was in everybody's interest to bring down the ratio of violence. Blood is bad for business, everyone understood that, but all the same sometimes it's necessary. The threat of it, at least, can be a strong bargaining tool.

Bloody Anne stepped forward from the crowd and clasped my arm as I walked down the steps from the governor's hall. We shook hands in that manner, each holding the other's wrist in the traditional greeting between second and boss. I squeezed her arm for a moment and nodded to her in appreciation.

I wondered who had taught her that.

Ailsa, I assumed, or possibly Fat Luka.

I looked over her shoulder and my eyes found Jochan in the crowd. He knew that Anne stood above him in the Pious Men, and if he hadn't fully accepted that truth before, then now there was no way he could avoid it any longer. She had publicly greeted me as my second, and I had returned the greeting in front of too many people for it to be undone.

That might make trouble later, but I knew it had needed to be done. Anne had obviously known that too, or more likely Ailsa had.

I walked out into the square with Anne at my side, and accepted claps on the shoulder and pats on the arm from my men. Only Jochan hung back, a brooding hurt in his eyes that I knew I wouldn't be able to ignore for long.

Luka had brought the fine carriage we had hired the previous night, and I can only think that we made a lordly sight as I stepped up into it with Anne and Jochan behind me. Luka got in after us and closed the door. He thumped on the roof, and the carriage driver flicked his reins, and then we were moving. I sat back against the padded leather bench and sighed.

'Well done,' I told them. 'Bringing the common people with you was a good touch, and not one that the governor will be able to ignore.'

'They came by themselves,' Anne said. 'Perhaps Luka put the word around, but we didn't force anyone.'

I nodded. That was good, better than I had expected, in fact.

Luka just smiled and said nothing.

He had removed his mummer's beard and shaved at some point in the night, I noticed, and his eyes crinkled in his smooth, plump face. I would have bet good silver that he had been behind the enthusiasm of the common folk, and I wondered how much that had cost me. Still, it was coin well spent, if only to see the look on Rogan's face.

'How are the men?' I asked Anne.

'There was some grief for Grieg,' she said, 'although in truth less than there might have been before word got around about what he did in Chandler's Narrow back in the spring.'

I nodded. Grieg had lost a lot of friends over that, I knew, and never recovered them. Now he had crossed the river that was between him and Our Lady, to my mind.

'Aye,' I said, and left it there.

'The foreign witch has some of them worried,' she went on, 'but Cutter proved that witches can die like everyone else, so it isn't panic. Mostly they're just glad to see you released unharmed.'

'Everyone fucking loves you, Tomas,' Jochan said, but he was looking at his boots as he said it and I couldn't read the expression on his face.

When we got back to the Tanner's Arms I found Aunt Enaid there waiting for me, with Brak beside her. Ailsa was behind the bar, and there was a hostile tension in the air between the two women that I could feel the moment I walked into the tavern.

Mika and Black Billy led the boys in a cheer when I walked in, and I grinned and sketched a mock bow that got a laugh.

'The Golden Chains is ours again,' I said to my aunt, and got another cheer for my trouble.

My aunt was not cheering.

'I hear you're quite the hero,' Enaid said. 'The local boy who stood up to the villainous outsiders and won. What a load of fucking *horseshit!*'

The room went quiet when she shouted at me, and I narrowed my eyes as I met my aunt's piercing one-eyed glare.

'Of course it's horseshit, Auntie,' I said. 'Horseshit makes things grow, and the legend of the Pious Men is even now growing, out there on our streets. That's good.'

'Is it?' she snapped. 'Is it good, Tomas? The Pious Men are *businessmen*, but you've turned them into soldiers. A pitched fucking battle on the streets, with crossbows? On the edge of Trader's Row, of all places? How's the governor supposed to take that?'

My aunt was giving me a telling in front of almost my entire crew, and I couldn't let that pass.

I slammed the flat of my hand down onto the table in front of her to shut her up. I leaned over her and I spoke quietly but in a voice that I knew the whole room could hear.

'He'll take it with his taxes and keep his nose out of my business, like he always has,' I said. 'Do not, my dear aunt, tell me how to run my business. Don't ever do that.'

I stood up and straightened my coat, and I walked across a tavern that was utterly silent.

I went upstairs to my room, and Ailsa followed.

She closed the door behind her and stood there looking at me as I stripped off my coat. It was stained and damp from the cells, and it smelled of shit. I tossed it on the floor and turned to face her in my shirtsleeves.

'What was that all about?' she demanded in her sharp, Dannsburg voice.

Just then I would have welcomed common, funny, flirty Ailsa, but it seemed I was getting the other one. I was getting Ailsa the Queen's Man whether I wanted her or not.

I met her dark eyes and had to admit that I *did* want her. There was no fooling myself on that score any longer, however far out of the question it might be. Ridiculous, I know, but there it was.

'I can't have my aunt give me a telling in front of the men, you understand that,' I said. 'I have—'

'Certain expectations to meet, yes, I grasp that,' she interrupted. '*Why* was she giving you a telling, I mean? I thought that old harridan was part of your operation, before the war?'

'Aye, she was,' I said. I sat down in the chair and sighed. 'Things are different now, Ailsa. Before the war . . . Aye. The Pious Men were businessmen, as she said. Jochan and me, her and Alfread and Donnalt and the others. Me and Jochan were the violent ones, when we had to be, and that wasn't often. Since we came back things have changed, and not to her liking.'

'Your business was built on violence,' she said.

'No, it wasn't,' I said. 'It was built on the *threat* of violence, and the capability for it, but very seldom the reality of it. In Ellinburg it is enough to be seen as violent, as *potentially* violent. People are weak, Ailsa, and the poorer and more oppressed they are, the weaker they become. When I gave up bricklaying and became a businessman, me and my brother and two friends walked into this tavern and we made them an offer. We offered to protect them from having their business burned down, in exchange for a weekly tax. They paid. So did the baker, so did the chandler, so did the cobbler. Soon half the Stink was paying us to protect them.'

'To protect them from yourselves, yes, I understand that,' she said. 'And when someone else threatened them?'

'Aye, then we did what we had said we would do. Protection is protection, after all. The Gutcutters were a new outfit then as well, down in the Wheels, and when they sent lads down the river path to try their luck in the Stink, we showed them how unwise that was. Twice that happened, no more, and then a border was drawn up and everyone went back to doing business in their own neighbourhoods and leaving each other alone. That was just how it worked. When I had enough money I came in here and I told the owner I was buying his tavern, and he didn't refuse me. No violence was done. It wasn't necessary. Do you see what I'm saying?'

'That the past was glorious, that the sun always shone, and you were firm but fair and you never really hurt anyone,' Ailsa said, the sarcasm dripping like venom from her beautiful lips. 'Yes, Tomas, I know very well what you're saying and it's about as true as the face I gave Bloody Anne last night. The past is as scarred and bitter and ugly as your second is, and you know it.'

That was going too far.

I was on my feet in a moment, my hand around Ailsa's throat as I forced her back against the wall.

'Don't you *ever* insult Anne like that,' I hissed in her face. 'Don't you *fucking* dare!'

I felt the unmistakable pressure of steel against the inside of my thigh, in the killing place.

'It would be very wise of you to take your hands off me, and never put them back,' Ailsa said.

We stood there for a moment, me with my hand around her throat and her with a dagger I hadn't even known she had, held a whisker away from taking my life. She had me at the disadvantage there, I had to admit.

I let go and took a step backward, and Ailsa made her blade disappear again.

You can hide a dagger very well indeed, behind enough lace.

I remembered her telling me that, once, but it seemed a barmaid's apron served well enough. I had underestimated her, and I wouldn't make that mistake again.

Chapter 31

I slept for a few hours after Ailsa stalked out of my room, making up for the fitful night I had spent in the cells. When I woke I shaved with the cold water in my washbasin, which was uncomfortable but better than wearing that moustache any longer. By the time I went back downstairs my aunt had left, for which I was glad. I didn't want more harsh words between us, but I could see no other way it would have gone that day. I had a late breakfast in the kitchen with Hari, who fussed around me as though being taken in by the Guard and released the next day were some great event. Perhaps it was, to him. I had no idea where Hari was from or what he had done before the war, and I was happy to keep it that way. He was a Pious Man now, to my mind, and that was all that mattered. The past was the past, and it was best for everyone to leave it there. Some things in the past didn't want looking at too closely. I knew that all too well.

When I returned to the common room, Ailsa was there waiting for me.

'You look brighter for some sleep, my poor lovely,' she said, wearing her barmaid's face in front of the other men in there.

No one would ever have guessed we had been moments from killing each other just a few hours before.

'I feel it,' I admitted, and it was true.

I leaned closer to her, hiding my thoughts behind a smile. She smiled back up at me and ran a flirtatious hand along my arm until Mika looked away and Simple Sam went bright red and left the room.

'I'm sorry if I spoke harshly to you before,' I murmured. 'Not enough sleep, and after a fight . . . no one's quite themselves.'

'Oh, don't you worry, my handsome,' she said, 'it takes more than hard words to upset Ailsa.'

I thought perhaps a hand around the throat might do it, though, and I felt bad about that now. All the same, if I had pressed it I knew she would have killed me and disappeared without a backward glance, and no one would ever have found her even if they had been of a mind to look. I had to remind myself who I was dealing with here.

Do what your father says or the Queen's Men will come and take you away.

This was a Queen's Man right here, her hand lying seductively on my arm, and I knew she was one of the most dangerous people I had ever met in my life.

'Aye,' I said, and cleared my throat. 'We'll say no more about it, then.'

'Let's not,' she whispered, her own accent cutting me across the face sharp as a whip.

'I can take the bar, boss,' Luka volunteered. 'If you two want to, you know, have some time.'

I looked at him for a moment and nodded. Fat Luka was a good deal cleverer than I had ever given him credit for before the war, I had to admit. He saw things that other men didn't, and he knew how to use the things he saw, and that made him useful. It made him dangerous too, in his way, but I knew I could trust him.

'That sounds good,' I said, and caught Ailsa's eye.

She giggled on cue, and let me chase her up the stairs to my room.

'What?' she said once we were alone.

'Ailsa, I've said I'm sorry and I meant it,' I said. 'Let's not have harsh words between us.'

'That's done,' she said dismissively. 'There's something on your mind, though.'

'Aye, there is,' I admitted. 'Hauer is suspicious. He thinks I've done too much too fast, and he's right. I was thinking on it in the night, and he *knows* me, Ailsa. He knows that my instinct would have been to consolidate, the way I told you I was planning to, but I didn't. I went all out, and he'll know that idea didn't come from me. He doesn't know who you are but he knows you came to me, and I think he suspects that you're still here.'

Ailsa frowned, and for a moment she looked much older. 'That is not acceptable,' she said.

'No, I know,' I said. 'There's more too, although it's more my problem than yours. My brother. Anne openly declared herself my second this morning, in front of half the Stink. That's how it is and it's well and good, but Jochan's taken it ill. I haven't seen him since we got back, and come tonight I dare say I'll have to send the lads out to pour him home from some tavern somewhere. He'll make trouble, if I'm not careful.'

'Then *be* careful,' Ailsa said. 'Your brother is your problem, not mine, but the governor worries me.'

I nodded. I had given this a lot of thought during my night in the cells.

'I need to fuck something up,' I said. 'If I do something rash, something poorly planned that fails, then Hauer will know you weren't behind it. That would work, but I also can't be seen to look a fool when I'm just now winning the common folk over to my side.'

Ailsa smiled at me then, a smile that was neither the barmaid's nor that of the Dannsburg aristocrat. It was truly beautiful, that smile. For one brief moment, I thought perhaps I had seen her real face.

'Well, that's simple, then,' she said, and all at once the aristocrat was back. 'Put your brother in charge of something, and let nature take its course.'

I stared at her.

Of course, I could see the sense in her words. Everything Jochan touched with an unguided hand went to the whores, just about. Could I hang him out like that, though? Could I give him a job just to watch him fail, because it would put the governor's mind at ease?

I knew I had to. This was war, and in war sometimes sacrifices have to be made. Again I felt my respect for Ailsa growing. She had the ruthlessness of a businessman, I had to allow. I liked that about her.

I liked it a lot.

I wouldn't see Jochan get hurt, of course, but people knew what he was like and I knew he could fail without making me lose face. It would still be a failure for the Pious Men, though, and no crew with a Queen's Man backing them would ever make mistakes. Yes, it made sense, for all that it left a bad taste in my mouth.

'Perhaps that's the answer,' I admitted.

Jochan rolled into the Tanner's late that evening, after we had closed. I was in the middle of saying a few words to the men in memory of Grieg.

My brother was stinking drunk, as I had expected, but I had sent Fat Luka out to find him an hour earlier and Luka had at least brought him home unbloodied. Jochan shoved his way through the circle of men in front of me, reeking of brandy and vomit, and he leered at me with mad eyes.

'Grieg was a cunt!' he shouted. 'Fuck him. Fuck anyone who hits whores.'

'We've covered that,' I said. 'He said his confession and we made it right with him, in our way.'

'We kicked the fucking piss out of him,' Jochan slurred, and laughed. 'Fucking right we did.'

'We did, and now that's done,' I said. 'Grieg has crossed the river. May he sleep in peace.'

'May he sleep in peace,' the men echoed.

'May he fucking rot,' Jochan muttered, but Luka was steering him away toward the door behind me now, and I don't think anyone else heard.

I turned to Bloody Anne to say something, I don't remember what, when Jochan suddenly lurched around in the doorway, almost dragging Luka back with him.

'That's another fucking thing!' he bellowed, his words so thick with drink he was barely intelligible. 'You fucking . . . your own fucking brother, Tomas. We always stuck together, didn't we? We fucking used to, anyway. When Da was . . . when . . .'

'Go to bed, Jochan,' I said, lowering my voice into the tone that always got through to him whatever state he was in. He didn't want to argue with that tone, I knew, and he *really* didn't want to bring up our da in front of everyone. That wouldn't have been fucking wise. 'Go and sleep it off, before you say something you'll regret.'

He glared at me, his bloodshot eyes wide and staring. No one spoke.

Anne was by my side, and I didn't think that was helping. This was about that morning, I knew it was, and how Anne and me had greeted each other in front of hundreds of the common folk from our streets. This was about him feeling betrayed, although if he couldn't see why he wasn't suitable to be my second, then I wasn't sure I knew how to explain it to him.

It was about all that, and about the past. About Da.

Luka whispered something in Jochan's ear and put an arm around his shoulders that was part comforting, part restraining. Luka knew what would happen if Jochan pushed this too far in front of the crew, I realised. He was a clever man, and he had known us both for a very long time. He might not have grasped the truth of the matter, but he understood all too well what was happening between the Piety brothers.

'Go to bed,' I said again, in the quiet tavern.

'Our own da . . .' Jochan said.

A sob caught in his throat, but he said no more and I gave thanks to Our Lady for that. He slumped against Luka's chest as his knees buckled. The big man tightened his grip around my brother's shoulders to keep him from falling on his face and all but dragged him out of the room.

I turned away.

Anne kept a distance between us, perhaps sensing something private between brothers, something painful, and she made sure the others kept their distance too.

I needed some air.

I headed for the front door, which Black Billy hastily unlocked and opened for me without a word. I shouldered past him and stepped out into the freezing cold darkness of the street, out of sight.

Only then did I allow myself to weep.

I have written of the strongbox in the back of my mind where I keep the horrors locked away, the place where I never go.

Part of that box is called *Abingon*, but part of it has another name. Part of it is called *Da*.

Chapter 32

I stayed out in the street until I had myself under control again. Fifteen, perhaps twenty minutes had passed by the time I went back into the tavern, red-eyed and shivering with the cold, and with flakes of snow in my hair. I found the common room empty except for Bloody Anne.

She was sitting at a table in the middle of the room, a bottle of brandy and two glasses on the scarred wood in front of her. She didn't speak, just lifted the bottle in her hand and raised her eyebrows in a silent invitation.

I locked the door behind me and took the chair across the table from her. She poured for us both and pushed a glass toward me. I drained it in a single swallow, and she poured again. I lifted the glass and stared into the dark amber spirit, avoiding her eyes.

'I don't want to talk about it,' I said.

'Then don't. Just drink.'

'Aye.'

We drank together, neither of us speaking, until the bottle was half empty. It had been like that in the war, sometimes. When we had managed to get our hands on some drink, anyway. At first you think you want to pour out your feelings into the bottle, but you come to realise that you don't. You just want to drown them, to burn them away with alcohol until it stops hurting.

Anne knew that. She had been there.

It had been like that after Messia, I remembered. We had sacked the city when it fell and we looted what little they had had left. I remembered sharing a bottle with Anne and Kant, in the ruins of the great temple. None of us had said a word all night, just passed the bottle back and forth between us until it was done. After what we did that day, even Kant's bravado had deserted him. For a little while, at least. There's a comradeship in that, in drinking together and saying nothing, because no words need to be said.

'I think,' Anne said at last, when the bottle was half gone, 'I think I'm in love with Rosie.'

I looked up at her, at the expression on her face. That expression was half joyous, that she had someone she could tell, and half terrified by what she was saying. I nodded.

'That's good,' I said.

'Be better if she felt the same,' Anne said, and swallowed her drink. 'I'm still fucking paying for it.'

I shrugged. 'There's no shame in that.'

'There's no future in it either, though, is there?'

'Who can say? Perhaps there is.'

Anne nodded, and poured again. She could drink, could Bloody Anne, I had to give her that.

'Perhaps,' she said. 'She's got to make a living, I understand that, and time she's with me is time she's not with anyone else, earning. I have to . . . cover her lost income, I suppose.'

'That's between you and Rosie,' I said, 'but you don't have to justify it to me, Anne. If she makes you happy, then it's good.'

'She does,' Anne admitted. She swallowed her drink and looked at me. 'What about Ailsa, Tomas? Does she make you happy?'

I dare say she could have done, if she had ever shown the slightest interest in trying. I felt things for Ailsa that I knew were foolish and unwise, but knowing that a thing is foolish and doing something to change it are different matters. Ailsa thought nothing of me, I knew that. She was my fancy woman as far as everyone in the crew was concerned, though, including Anne. I didn't want to lie to her about this, not after she had opened up to me, but I knew I had to.

'She's a good girl,' I said, and forced a smile I didn't feel.

'She's got more to her than I thought at first, I'll admit that,' Anne said. 'I haven't been kind to her, and I regret that now. She's no fool, Tomas.'

'That she's not,' I agreed. I reached for the bottle and poured us both another drink, emptying it. 'I don't enjoy the company of fools.'

Anne laughed and swallowed her drink. 'Your brother must chafe you some,' she said.

I stopped the glass halfway to my lips and bit back a harsh reply that Anne didn't deserve. Jochan *was* a fool, I knew that, and Anne certainly wasn't, so of course she knew it too. I put the glass down again, untouched, and looked at her.

'It's difficult, sometimes,' I said. 'With Jochan. He's my little brother. Our childhood was . . . difficult too. I looked after him, in my way, as best I could.'

I remembered what Anne had told me about her own youth. What Jochan and I had suffered didn't compare to that. Not quite, anyway.

'I never meant—' Anne started.

She looked embarrassed now, and I didn't want that.

'No, it's all right,' I said. 'He *does* chafe me, you've the right of that. I . . . I owe Jochan a debt I can never repay, Anne. From the past, from when we were children. I should have done a thing . . . I did do it, but not soon enough, and he suffered for that. He suffered a great deal, and I could have stopped it and I didn't until it was too late. I'll always owe him a place at my side, for that. Not at my right hand, no, that's your place, but *a* place none the less.'

Anne just nodded.

'I'll get another bottle,' she said.

The next morning I had a headache like all the guns of Abingon were firing in the back of my skull. I lay in my bed with an arm over my eyes and suffered it. I had earned that sore head, I knew. I think Anne and me had almost emptied the second bottle before we finally admitted defeat and crawled to our respective blankets. *Crawl* was right, as well. I still had the splinters in the palms of my hands from dragging myself up the rough wooden stairs to my room on all fours, like an animal.

I groaned, and tried to remember where the conversation had gone once the second bottle was open. I know from experience that I'm a quiet drunk, not a talkative one, so I could only hope I hadn't said anything that I might regret. I didn't think I had, and even if so I doubted Anne would remember any better than I did.

Snatches of memory floated back to me as I lay there in my sweaty bedding. Anne had opened up to me, I recalled. She *was* a talkative drunk, which made me think again about what she might say to Rosie of an evening. I'd have to keep that in mind, I knew. She had told me more about what went on in their bed than I had really wanted to know, I remembered now, but I supposed it was no more than any other soldier boasts about their woman.

That made me smile despite the pain in my head, and I forced myself to sit up. Bloody Anne was a good friend, and I'll not record what she told me that night. Those things were her business, to my mind, and no one else's.

I made myself have a wash and a piss and put some clothes on, and I headed unsteadily down the stairs to the tavern. Mika and Hari were sharing small beer and black bread in the common room, and I joined them.

'Late night, boss?' Mika asked.

'Aye,' I said.

Hari picked up his stick and limped off to fetch me a mug of small beer, and I sipped it reluctantly. It would do me good, I knew, but truth be told, it was a struggle.

'Where's Ailsa?' I asked, after I had choked down half the mug.

'In the kitchen,' Hari said. 'She's got a visitor. That Rosie, from up Chandler's Narrow. I think they're friends, like.'

That gave me pause. I was certain by then that Rosie was Ailsa's contact in the Queen's Men, and I wondered what business they could have together at that time in the morning.

'I hope Bloody Anne don't take it ill,' Mika said, and I could see that he had a point there.

Mika could think for himself, as I have written, and Ailsa's tastes were something I had never even given thought to. Just because Ailsa had shown no interest in me didn't mean she preferred women, of course, but I had never even considered the possibility until then. I didn't want to see Anne hurt, I knew that much.

'Course she won't,' I said, making light of it. 'I know my Ailsa, and Anne's got no worries there.'

The lads gave me a laugh for that, and I excused myself and went through to the kitchen to see for myself.

'Oh, he's a devil, ain't he?' Ailsa was saying when I opened the door, and I knew she had heard someone coming and switched to her barmaid's voice without a second thought.

She giggled, and I gave her a look that said I knew very well what she had done. Rosie was sitting across the table from her, chewing on a hunk of bread.

'Good morning,' I said.

'Oh, you do look rough, you poor thing,' Ailsa said, and laughed her barmaid's laugh. 'You will sit up drinking with other women, my lover, you ought to expect to suffer for it in the morning.'

I closed the door behind me.

'Drinking's all we were doing,' I said, more for Rosie's benefit than hers.

'I know that,' Ailsa said in her sharp Dannsburg voice. 'Sit down, Tomas. We need to talk business.'

I looked at Rosie, and her gaze was like razors.

Chapter 33

'If you haven't worked it out for yourself yet,' Ailsa said, 'Rosie works for me.'

'Aye,' I said. 'I'd just about found my way to that.'

'Well and good,' she said. 'Now be quiet and listen, there's news.'

'There is,' Rosie said. 'Ma Aditi's pure furious with you, Mr Piety. Her new second had ties to the Golden Chains, and now it's yours again he's raising the gods over it. Well, I say he's her second but I'm not so sure that's even the lay of things down in the Wheels any more. From what I hear, Ma Aditi's a slave to the poppy now, and he's where her resin comes from. He's only been with them a couple of months but it might be he has more influence over the Gutcutters than she does, these days.'

That made me think. I remembered the man who had been sat at Ma Aditi's right hand. He was a big brute of a fellow, with the scarred face of a soldier. Someone she had found in Abingon, I had assumed, as he was no one I knew from Ellinburg. How he had ended up her second I still didn't know, but I suspected that the poppy had a good deal to do with it. I wondered who he was, and where his allegiances really lay. To the north, if I was any judge. To Skania.

The Skanians wanted the infrastructure of the city, as I have written, and they wanted its workforce too. Perhaps, it came to me, instead of continuing to fight the Gutcutters as they were fighting me, the Skanians had simply found the means to take them over from within. That would make sense – no general would choose to fight a war on two

225

fronts if he didn't have to, and if the Skanians had truly taken over the Gutcutters, then that was a lot more soldiers they had at their command.

'And what does she mean to do?' I asked.

Rosie snorted. 'Aditi means to smoke her poppy resin and fuck her young lads and get even fatter, the way I hear it. It's this man of hers you want to be thinking on, Mr Piety. What he wants is the Chains, and he's making no secret of it. There's a good deal of gold to be had from the Chains these days, selling poppy resin to nobles and those who deal down the line and onto the streets. Ruthless bastard he is, too, from what I hear. Bloodhands, they call him, though I've not managed to hear why.'

I almost fucking choked, and Ailsa's face told me this was news to her too.

'I *beg* your pardon?' Ailsa said.

Rosie gave her a blank look, and I realised she wasn't privy to all of Ailsa's business after all. So she was just a spy then, and not a Queen's Man herself. For Anne's sake, I was glad about that.

'What I said, ma'am. They call him Bloodhands, but—'

'Never mind.' Ailsa cut her off, but her eyes bored into mine across the table and I knew that we were thinking the same thoughts, but I wasn't to speak them in front of Rosie.

Ma Aditi's new second was Bloodhands, the boss of the Skanians in Ellinburg. Bloodhands, who commanded the loyalty of his men by threatening their children's lives. Bloodhands, who had murdered a Queen's Man and sent him back to Dannsburg in four fucking pieces on four separate trade caravans.

I had been sitting at the same table with the cunt, and I hadn't known him.

'We must take the poppy trade before he does,' Ailsa announced.

I shook my head. 'I'm not doing that,' I said. 'Not resin.'

'You sold resin before the war,' she said. 'That was how we approached you the first time. Tea taxes alone wouldn't have done it.'

Fucking *approached* me? *Blackmailed* was the word for it, to my mind, and whatever I felt for Ailsa I still took that extremely ill.

'Aye, I did,' I said through clenched teeth. 'I sold it to doctors who couldn't get it any other way, so they could help desperate people who needed it to ease their suffering. I'm not supplying the street trade. Lady's sake, Ailsa, I'm doing everything I can to *stop* the fucking street trade.'

'There's gold to be made,' Rosie said again.

I thumped the flat of my hand down on the table and glared at both of them. 'I don't give a *fuck* if there's gold to be made,' I said. 'I've *got* gold, and I can't spend half of it. Poppy resin is ruining my people. I won't have it.'

Ailsa ignored me. 'Thank you, Rosie,' she said. 'I think it's time for Tomas and me to speak alone.'

Rosie nodded, dismissed, and got up from the table. We sat in silence while she put her cloak on, and then she was out of the kitchen and the door closed behind her.

'Bloodhands is Aditi's fucking second?' I said, once we were alone.

'So it would appear,' Ailsa said.

'I was sat at the table with the fucker,' I said. 'I could have—'

'But you didn't,' she interrupted me, 'because we didn't know. Now we do, and we must use that knowledge and move on. By its very nature the battlefield is ever shifting, Tomas, and it's no good dwelling on what *didn't* happen. The poppy trade is what matters now.'

'I'm not having that filth around my people.'

'Not your people, then,' Ailsa said. 'Forget the street trade. You're right; that causes more problems than it solves. The nobility, though, think on that. They know what they're doing, and they don't need to turn to crime to feed their habits.'

I put my head in my hands and drew a long breath. My head was still pounding from last night's drink and I was struggling to make sense of what Ailsa was saying.

'If you don't supply them they'll simply go to someone who will,' she went on. 'They'll go to Bloodhands, and through him to the Skanians. Do you want to put gold in his pockets so he can buy more soldiers and threaten more children?'

'I won't have it on my streets,' I said. 'I won't have it near working people, nor children either.'

'The nobles,' Ailsa said again. 'The nobles who come to the Golden Chains, at least. They expect it, Tomas. They *need* it.'

'I don't know anything about the fucking poppy trade,' I said. 'Where would I even get poppy resin to sell to them?'

'From me, of course.'

It took me two days to come up with a job that I could be confident Jochan would botch, but not badly enough to get himself hurt. By the time I was satisfied with my plan, I didn't need it any more. The Gutcutters broke the peace themselves.

Rosie had all but told us that they would, of course, but I hadn't expected it so soon. This Bloodhands wasn't a man to take his time, it seemed.

I was in the kitchen at the Tanner's after closing up for the night. Ailsa and me were having another argument about selling poppy resin through the Golden Chains when Simple Sam burst in on us. Thank the Lady he was too worked up to have overheard anything he shouldn't have done.

'Boss! Quick!'

I hurried after him into the common room to find a breathless Aunt Enaid leaning heavily on the bar, her fallen stick on the floor at her feet and snow melting from her cloak. Brak was slumped in a chair, his right hand clutching his left shoulder. Blood seeped between his fingers, and his sleeve was soaked with it. He had a long cut on his face too, and burns on both hands.

Jochan was there before me, reeling drunk and shouting.

'What the fuck happened?' he demanded.

'Gutcutters,' Enaid wheezed. 'I can't . . . curse it to the whores, I can't run on this fucking ankle. They stormed my house, four of them. Brak tried to fight them, bless his silly young heart. They—'

'Cunts!' Jochan bellowed.

He grabbed his axe from behind the bar and was off and running out the door a moment later, his mail forgotten and his shirt tails flapping behind him in the freezing wind and blowing snow of the winter night.

'Sam, Billy, Mika, get after him,' I snapped. 'I'll see to my aunt.'

The boys hastily grabbed weapons and set off after my brother's reckless charge. Ailsa was helping Enaid into a chair now, and I had a proper look at Brak.

'I'm sorry, boss,' he said. 'I tried me best.'

'I know,' I said, and frowned. 'How are you burned?'

'They had blasting powder,' he said. 'That's how they took the front door off. There was a fire. I couldn't . . . I tried.'

His face and hands were a mess, but a few more scars wouldn't kill him. It was that shoulder I was worried about. The cut was deep, right through the meat and almost to the bone. That's not a killing place, not in itself, but if it went bad he'd be done.

'Ailsa, rouse Cookpot out of the stable and send him to get Doc Cordin,' I said.

She nodded and went, and by then Anne and Erik had joined us. I put Erik in Billy's place on the door to watch for more trouble, with Stefan and Borys in the alley behind the stable yard. That was it; that was all the crew I had left at the Tanner's, what with the men I had off guarding my other businesses. I didn't count Hari in that, but he could still barely walk. I found I actually missed Sir Eland, which wasn't a thought I'd ever had before. He was a Pious Man in truth now, and his heavy armour and long sword would have been welcome if the Gutcutters came in force. I considered sending a runner to Chandler's Narrow to fetch him back, but what if they struck there instead? Will couldn't hold the place alone, and Cutter was still at Slaughterhouse Narrow.

'Cookpot's off on his errand,' Ailsa said.

I looked around and saw her standing there with my sword-belt in her hand. She passed it to me and I nodded thanks as I buckled it on.

'Keep the pressure on that shoulder,' I told Brak. 'The doc's on his way.'

Brak nodded, pale now with shock.

'Fucking blasting powder,' he whispered, and I could only nod.

It seemed to me that if Ailsa could supply me with poppy resin, then she ought to be able to get her hands on powder too. That was a thought for later, though. I turned to Anne.

'I need to go after my brother before he gets himself killed,' I said. 'Can you hold the Tanner's with just three men, if it comes to it?'

'Aye,' Anne said. 'If it comes to it.'

'I can work a crossbow,' Ailsa said, and smiled at me. 'If it comes to it.'

I was sure she could, at that.

'My thanks,' I said. 'Anne's in charge.'

With that I threw a cloak around my shoulders and headed out the door in pursuit of Jochan.

Chapter 34

Aunt Enaid's house wasn't far from the Tanner's Arms, and by the time I had run the length of three streets I could hear fighting. It had stopped snowing by then, but as I dashed around a corner my feet still almost slipped on the wet cobbles. I drew the Weeping Women. The house was on fire, the house that I had mostly grown up in, and Black Billy and Mika were back to back and fighting three men in the street outside. There was no sign of Jochan or Simple Sam anywhere. I stepped up behind one of the Gutcutters and rammed Mercy through his left kidney, dropping him to ground. Billy pressed the advantage and finished his man with a swing of his heavy club that smashed the fellow's head like an egg.

'Where the fuck's my brother?' I demanded.

Billy jerked a thumb toward the burning house and turned to help Mika. I left them to it and ducked through the shattered doorway, where a charge of blasting powder had torn half the front wall down. Inside was chaos.

Enaid had said there were four of them, but either she had been wrong about that or more had followed – there were two Gutcutters dead on the floor in the main room, and Sam and Jochan were fighting another three who were holding them off while one of their fellows wrestled a barrel upright in the space under the stairs.

Jochan had cuts and grazes and blood all over him, one sleeve of his shirt torn off and a long sooty burn up his exposed arm. He was roaring like a madman as he fought. Sam was favouring his right leg

231

and had a hand held to a bloody gash in his thigh as he slashed wildly about him with the shortsword gripped in his other.

The damn fool had obviously charged straight into the house in his rage, and poor, faithful Sam must have followed him. I coughed in the thick smoke and joined them in the fray. Now we were evenly matched, Pious Men and Gutcutters. Cinders fell from the ceiling as we fought, and the wooden stairs were on fire. It felt like Abingon in there, choking smoke and flames all around us, the desperate clash of steel in the firelit darkness.

I parried a cut with Mercy and took my man through the throat with Remorse. A moment later Billy and Mika joined us, and the last Gutcutter still fighting chanced a desperate look over his shoulder at the man with the barrel.

A barrel.

A burning building, and a barrel . . .

'Run!'

I grabbed Jochan by the shoulder and almost dragged him after me as I sprinted for the hole in the wall. The others followed, trusting my instinct and the voice of command that they remembered from Abingon. When I saw that the two Gutcutters were fleeing with us, I knew that my instinct had been right.

We all but threw ourselves into the nearest alley, and a moment later the house exploded with a deafening roar as the barrel of blasting powder went up. A great rush of hot air and dust and smoke burst past the mouth of the alley, choking us even as we covered our heads against the rain of shattered timbers and burning laths.

The last timber clattered to the cobbles, the following silence broken only by the faint crackle of flames.

'Fuck a nun,' Jochan whimpered. He was slumped on the ground with his back against the wall, visibly shaking. His breath came in short gasps that spoke of a violent bout of battle shock. 'Oh, fuck a nun, Tomas, when will it ever end?'

He put his head in his hands and started to weep.

I rubbed a hand over my face and it came away black with soot and sweat. Billy and Mika were both obviously shaken too, and I saw Sam hurrying down the alley away from us.

No, that wasn't right – Sam was wounded in the leg but he wasn't limping. This man was balding on the crown of his head, too, and Sam wasn't.

'Oi!' I shouted.

Billy's head whipped around and he took off on his powerful legs, quickly running down the Gutcutter whom I had taken to be Simple Sam in the dark confusion of the alley. There was a thud and I saw Billy's knife rise and fall once, twice, and it was done.

'Where the fuck's Sam, then?' Mika asked.

I doubted Sam could have run, not on that wound. I swallowed bile and looked away.

'Stay here,' I said. 'Watch my brother.'

I ducked out of the alley and back into the street, Remorse in my hand. The house was gone, and only flames and a few of the heavier timbers remained of the place I had called home after my da had died. People were out of their houses now that the fighting had stopped, passing buckets from their pumps and trying to keep the flames from reaching their own homes. Everything was still wet from the earlier snow, thank the Lady, and I didn't think the fire would spread.

There were two bodies lying on the cobbles.

No one paid me any attention as I stood over them. These were my streets, the heart of the Stink, and if anyone there saw me they would know well enough to pretend that they hadn't. One man lay on top of the other, his back raw and blackened with burns. He was quite dead, but he was no one I knew. I rolled him to one side and bent over Simple Sam. He was breathing, at least, and with no time for niceties I slapped his face until his eyes opened.

'Come on, Sam lad, up with you now,' I said.

Sam grinned up at me. 'Hit me head, boss,' he said. 'I knew I couldn't run none so I stabbed that arsehole and pulled him down over me, but I hit me head on the cobbles.'

'Aye,' I said. 'You're alive, thank the Lady, but we need to go.'

Simple Sam was alive because he had had the good sense and the plain ruthlessness to use the fleeing Gutcutter as a shield from the explosion, even if he had managed to knock himself out in the process. I wondered if Sam was quite as simple as we all thought.

Mika and Billy helped Sam back to the Tanner's between them. He had both his arms over their shoulders, and his wounded leg dragged behind him in the patchy snow as the three of them walked awkwardly down the road. I led Jochan, my hand on his arm to steer him. He was meek as a child now, his eyes downcast and his breathing steady once more.

As we approached the tavern I caught a glimpse of Ailsa at my upstairs window, with Bloody Anne's crossbow in her hands. Erik let us in and locked the door again behind us as Anne hurried over to help the lads get Sam into a chair.

Doc Cordin was there, finishing sewing up Brak's shoulder.

'I brought you another one, Doc,' I said.

The doc just sighed and nodded, and I sat Jochan down and put a bottle of brandy on the table in front of him. I thought he had earned it.

'What happened?' Anne asked.

'We killed them,' I said, and that was enough. I looked up and met my aunt's flinty stare. 'Your house . . . I'm sorry.'

She shook her head and said nothing.

Jochan had the bottle open now and was drinking straight from the neck, the lump in his throat working as he swallowed brandy like it was beer. I saw Ailsa come down the stairs with the crossbow still in her hands. It looked at home there.

'We blew your fucking house up, Auntie,' Jochan said.

He laughed, brandy dribbling from the corner of his mouth. He laughed, and once he had started he didn't seem to be able to stop. I helped him out of the chair, and as I did I saw that he had pissed himself. I picked his bottle up for him and led him through to the back where the others couldn't see him any more. Hopefully he'd drink himself to sleep soon enough.

When I came back Ailsa had put the crossbow down on the bar and donned her barmaid's face.

'Are you hurt, my lover?' she asked, fussing around my sooty face with a damp cloth.

'I'm fine,' I said. 'Doc, how's Sam and Brak?'

'I'm all right, boss,' Brak said, but he was ghost white and clutching a brandy bottle so hard with his good hand that I thought the glass might shatter. Enaid was sitting with him now, her hand resting on his knee.

Sam was biting down on a folded belt while the Doc sewed up the long gash in his thigh, but to my mind he'd got off lightly. It's not often a man walks away from an explosion like that.

'This isn't too deep,' Cordin said. 'Keep it clean and he'll be all right. Your other man's shoulder worries me, though.'

'I'm all right,' Brak said again, but he obviously wasn't.

'The silly boy's being strong for me,' Enaid said.

'I'm not a boy,' Brak said, for all that Enaid must have had forty more years than him. 'I'm your man.'

'Hush now,' she said, and I realised she thought I didn't know.

'Auntie,' I said in a low voice, taking a chair beside her, 'who you choose to bed is your affair, not mine. Brak, you're *not* all right. You need to rest. Take my room tonight, you and Enaid. I'll sleep with the men.'

'You can sleep with me, my handsome,' Ailsa said, putting a hand on my shoulder.

It must have looked like an affectionate gesture to anyone watching, but I could feel the strength in her grip and I knew it wasn't meant that way. Ailsa wanted words, I could tell.

'Aye,' I said. 'Aye, why not.'

Mika and Black Billy hid their grins as best they could, and I let it pass. Ailsa was supposed to be my fancy woman, after all, so why not indeed?

Chapter 35

Borys and me helped Brak up the stairs to my room, and we left him there with Enaid looking after him. Alone together at the top of the stairs, Borys gave me a level look. He was older than most of the others, a big, thoughtful man who said little. He looked like he was about to make up for that, to my mind.

'It's going wrong, boss,' he said in a low voice. 'We're running out of men in a fit state to fight. They've got blasting weapons and we ain't. What's going to happen if these Gutcutters come at us in force?'

'I can get blasting weapons,' I said, and thought on what Ailsa had told me. 'More men too. Trained men, who can handle themselves. This is my city, Borys. I can get men.'

Both those things were true, if unrelated. I had raised the crossbowmen we had used at the Chains myself, admittedly, but they wouldn't do. They weren't men I knew and they weren't veterans, and I wouldn't trust them with anything more than a simple ambush. Ailsa's men, though, I thought they would be useful.

'Are you lovely boys having a private chat, or can anyone join in?' Ailsa said, startling me.

The stairs were old and splintery and creaked like a sign in the wind, but I hadn't heard her climb them. That explosion obviously hadn't done my ears any good.

'Sorry, Miss Ailsa,' Borys said, moving out of the way of her door.

'How many times do I got to tell you? Just Ailsa's fine,' she said, and showed him her barmaid's smile.

She went into her room and beckoned me to follow with a saucy wink. Borys nodded and clumped off down the stairs, leaving us alone in her bedroom.

I closed the door behind me and turned to face her.

'Well, you said you wanted to fuck something up,' Ailsa snapped at me. 'Blowing up your own aunt's house certainly qualifies.'

'That's not . . .' I started to say, and sighed. I slumped against the wall and put a hand over my eyes. 'That's not exactly what happened. They had a whole fucking barrel of powder in there, Ailsa. Blowing the house up was what they intended. They were making a statement, going after my family to show me that they can.'

'And you just didn't stop them, is that it? Oh, it's well and good, Tomas. Hauer will never believe *I* orchestrated a disaster of that magnitude, so at least your brother's incompetence should have thrown him off my scent. That is what we wanted, after all.'

'I didn't want Jochan to get hurt,' I said.

'He's in a better state than Brak and Sam are.'

'No, he's not,' I said. 'I saw him in that house, fighting in the flames. He was back in Abingon, Ailsa, back there in truth. When the blast went off I think he nearly lost his mind.'

'Tomas,' she said, and came to me. She took my hand and looked into my eyes. 'Your brother's mind is probably beyond your power to save, you have to realise that. You can't cure him, but you do have to control him.'

'I know,' I said.

'He can still be useful,' she went on. 'He fights like a wild animal, and he's dangerous, and men fear him. Those traits can be used, but they must be used *carefully*.'

'I know,' I said again, and sighed. 'He's my brother, Ailsa, not a war dog.'

'The right man for the right job, isn't that how you lead men?'

It was, but I couldn't recall ever having said it to her. I supposed I must have done, and forgotten it.

'Aye,' I admitted.

'And how are *you*?'

'Well enough,' I said, although I wondered if I really was.

I still remembered what Billy the Boy had done to me at Old Kurt's house, and I wondered if my own mind was so very much stronger than Jochan's. I walked over to the window and stared out of it, into the stable yard behind the tavern. Stefan was keeping watch at the alley gate, wrapped in two cloaks over his heavy coat. Bloody Anne was coming out of the shithouse, hitching her britches up with one hand and trying to hold her cloak around her with the other against the freezing night air. It might be cold, but other than that Ellinburg didn't feel so very different to Abingon, that night.

That was the very thing I was trying to avoid, and it seemed to my mind that I was failing at it.

'You need to sleep,' Ailsa said.

'Aye,' I said, but my voice sounded hollow in my own ears.

'Tomas,' she snapped. 'Look at me.'

I turned from the window and tried to focus. Lady knew Ailsa was beautiful, but I was struggling to see her face. The shadows in the room looked all wrong, and that was making me nervous. Anyone could be hiding in those shadows. My hands went instinctively to the hilts of the Weeping Women and I bent my knees into a half crouch, my gaze darting around the room. I felt exhausted but too alert, my senses stretched taut yet at the same time also strangely numbed. I drew a sharp breath.

I was ready.

Ready to kill.

'It's all right, my handsome,' Ailsa said in her barmaid's voice. 'There's no one here but Ailsa.'

She came and took my face in her hands, and looked deeply into my eyes. She breathed steadily, slow and deep, and unconsciously I found my own breaths matching her rhythm. My hands slowly relaxed, slipping off the hilts of my swords until they hung limp at my sides. That awful tightness of the senses drained away and I felt myself calming.

I was so tired.

She backed up a step and I went with her, feeling the warmth of her hands on my face. She held my stare and never broke it until we were right beside her bed. She breathed slow and deep, and so did I. Just then I was fighting to keep my eyes open, as though I hadn't slept in days. I wondered if perhaps she was doing something to me, some magic, but I was too tired to think about it.

'You need to sleep,' she said again, her voice low and soothing.

My knees buckled and I slumped sideways onto the mattress. She stroked my forehead with her fingertips and my eyes closed. Her touch lulled me like . . . a charm.

I was dimly aware of her pulling her blankets over me. As sleep took me, I wondered just what hidden skills the Queen's Men had.

When I woke it was to see Ailsa dozing in her chair with a spare blanket wrapped around her. I took care to be still, not wanting to wake her. She was sitting under the window, and the dawn light lit her face in a way that she would never have chosen. Some of her paints and powders had rubbed off in the night, and I could see then that she had a good many more years to her than I had first thought. She had forty, perhaps forty-five years to her, I could see now, and not all of them had been kind. It made sense. I had thought when I first met her that she was too young for the position she held, and she had told me herself that she was a good deal older than she looked. But I didn't recall her ever telling me that she was a cunning woman.

Perhaps she wasn't that, not exactly anyway, but she had done something to me the night before. Some sort of magic, I was sure. Truth be told, I was glad that she had. I had been slipping, I knew, starting to lose my way again. Perhaps my battle shock wasn't the same as Jochan's, or Cookpot's, but it was there all the same. Men could react to a thing in different ways, to my mind.

I eased the blankets off and Ailsa's eyes snapped open at once.

'Morning,' I said.

'How do you feel?' she asked, and it was the Queen's Man talking again now.

'Better,' I said, and it was true. Whatever had started to take hold of me last night had gone, or at least faded away in the night. 'What did you do to me?'

'I just helped you to sleep,' she said. 'You needed some rest.'

'Was that magic?'

'No,' she said. 'No, not in the way you mean it. I'm not a magician, Tomas, nor do I have what you would call the cunning. There are things that can be learned, though. Ways of speaking, rhythms of breathing and tones of voice that can make a person . . . receptive to suggestions, shall we say.'

I didn't really understand what she meant, but I couldn't see that she had reason to lie to me about it. Making a man 'receptive to suggestions' had obvious uses when it came to asking questions, and it was common knowledge that the Queen's Men asked questions on behalf of the crown.

'I see,' I said.

I sat up and swung my feet out of bed. She had taken off my sword-belt and boots at some point after I fell asleep, but other than that I was still dressed in the soot-stained clothes I had fallen down in the night before. I had left a fair amount of that soot in her bed, I realised.

'Sorry about your blankets.'

'The washerwoman can see to them,' she said. 'Never mind that now. I need to repair my face – go downstairs and see who's awake. Hopefully your brother is still unconscious, but if not you may need to keep an eye on him this morning.'

'Aye,' I said, biting back my irritation at being dismissed from her room like a servant.

I put my boots on and left her to her paints and powders, buckling on my sword-belt as I headed down the stairs. It was early but Bloody Anne was up, taking the morning watch in the common room.

'Who's about?' I asked her.

'Borys has the back,' she said. 'I let the rest sleep. It seemed to me that as you slaughtered the lot of them at Enaid's house last night they might not be in a hurry to try again.'

I nodded. I had the same hope. The Gutcutters might have succeeded in destroying my aunt's house, but it had taken them nine men to do it and we had left no survivors. That wasn't a good result for them, to my mind, and I doubted that this Bloodhands thought otherwise. He was ruthless, yes, but as the governor had told me he was something like a Queen's Man himself so he must understand strategy, and when losses were acceptable and when they very much weren't.

'That's good,' I said, and took the seat opposite her. 'I hope you got some sleep yourself.'

'Aye, some,' Anne said. 'I'm working the men on short watches, like we did in the mountains. It's too cold out there for a man to stand a full watch in the yard and not freeze to death.'

'Aye,' I said.

Bloody Anne knew what she was about. This was sergeant's work, not Pious Men business now, and Anne had been the best sergeant in our regiment.

The Pious Men are businessmen, but you've turned them into soldiers.

I remembered my aunt telling me that, and I knew then that she was right. These *were* soldiers, every one of them, so why not use them that way? The right man for the right job, always.

'Word will have got round the streets about last night,' I said, after a while. 'If you need to go up to Chandler's Narrow and show Rosie that you're safe, I'll understand. Once some of the men are awake I'll send a bodyguard with you.'

Anne gave me a bleak look. 'I don't know that she's been up all night worrying,' she said. 'I'm her best customer, but I'm not fooling myself that I'm any more than that to her.'

I shrugged and looked away. I wouldn't know, and I didn't want to say the wrong thing.

'Ailsa couldn't wait to get you in her bed last night,' Anne went on, a bitter note in her voice now. 'That must be nice, to have someone who wants you back.'

'She doesn't,' I said, although I hadn't meant to. I was supposed to be keeping up a pretence that Ailsa was my fancy woman, after all, but I was sick of lying to the only real friend that I had left. 'I slept in her bed, that's all. She didn't join me.'

'I thought you two . . . ?'

'No,' I said. 'No, but that's between us, Bloody Anne.'

'Of course.' She surprised me by putting her hand on mine, on the table. Her scar twisted as she formed a wry smile. 'Who'd want either of us, Tomas?'

I returned her smile and gave her hand a squeeze. In a different world, perhaps one where Anne liked men and I didn't regard her almost as a brother, we might have been good for each other. Not in this world, though; we both knew that.

A knock on the front door had us on our feet and sent my hands to my sword hilts. I shot Anne a questioning look. She frowned and slipped one of her daggers from its sheath and into her sleeve, then got up and went to the door. She pushed back the small sliding hatch that let her see outside, and then her face split into a wide grin and she hastily unlocked the door and threw it open.

Rosie was in her arms a moment later.

'Thank the gods,' Rosie gasped, visibly out of breath. 'I just heard what happened. I ran all the way here from Chandler's Narrow.'

I turned away and found that my eyes were stinging.

Chapter 36

After a week of arguing, I made a deal with Ailsa.

The Gutcutters had caused no more trouble, and according to Luka's spies they were barricaded in the Wheels awaiting my reprisal for the attack on Aunt Enaid's house. They could wait, to my mind, although I thought my aunt disagreed on that. Jochan was still in a bad way with the battle shock, drunk every day and barely coherent. That, and I had too many men wounded to be able to move against the Gutcutters yet, whatever Enaid said. Brak was healing slowly, and I had temporarily moved the two of them to the house on Slaughterhouse Narrow where they would be out of my way. Cutter had the guard there, and I didn't think anyone would get past him easily.

'It won't do, Tomas,' Ailsa said, yet again. 'You have your old businesses back, but that isn't enough. It won't be enough for the Skanians to merely control the Gutcutters and their part of the city. They want all of it. They will come after you again, and still you sit here and do nothing.'

'I know that,' I said, pacing to her window to stare down into the stable yard. 'I know that, and I've told you that I don't have the men or the weapons to attack the Wheels. If you want me to expand, I need blasting powder, and flashstones, and men who know how to use them. I need crossbows and bolts and swords, and skilled hands to wield them.'

'Men and swords are easy to come by; military weapons are not. Flashstones are illegal outside of the army.'

'So's fucking poppy resin!'

245

'That's different,' she said, although I couldn't see how. She sighed and sat down on her bed. 'A stalemate is no use to me; I need to drive the Skanians from the city completely.'

'Aye,' I said, 'and if you want me to do that for you then I need the fucking weapons to do it *with*.'

'Then you'll do what I ask,' she shot back at me. 'You're asking me for a miracle, Tomas. Well, miracles are not free, and this is the price.'

I had been hiring staff, mostly through Fat Luka, and I was about ready to open the Golden Chains again. Ailsa's price was that I continue the poppy trade through the Chains, selling to the nobility and rich merchants who would be my customers there. She wanted the lever that moved them, of course, and addiction is a strong enough lever to move anyone. With her hand controlling the supply of poppy resin that these powerful people were becoming dependent on, she would gain a great deal of influence in the upper levels of Ellinburg society. I knew that, but that didn't mean that I liked it. I didn't like it one fucking little bit, truth be told, but I couldn't see that I had a choice. It seemed I seldom did, where the Queen's Men were concerned.

All the same, I couldn't see any other way to break the deadlock between us. Ailsa owed me nothing. I knew that. Our relationship only stood while we were useful to each other, for all that I would have had it be otherwise. I hated what she represented, it was true, but I had to allow that I was a long way from hating *her*.

'Aye,' I said at last. 'I'll make a deal with you, then. You bring me the weapons and men that I need to take the fight to Ma Aditi and the Skanians who move her, and I'll sell your filthy poppy resin for you. Only through the Chains, mind, and only to the rich folk. I'm not having it on my streets, Ailsa. I mean it.'

'Well and good,' she said. She sighed. 'You're a stubborn and difficult man, Tomas Piety.'

I supposed that I was, at that.

'How long?' I asked her.

'To bring you men and swords and crossbows, blasting powder and illegal military weapons? Do you think I have them under my skirts?'

I cleared my throat and turned back to the window. I had been giving too much thought of late to what lay under Ailsa's skirts, and I knew talk like that wouldn't help.

'I accept it may take time,' I said.

She laughed. 'A week to send a rider to Dannsburg, perhaps two for the wagons to make the return trip with what you ask. No more than that.'

I stared at her, and realised she had been making fun of me.

'So simply?' I asked.

'If I want men and weapons, I will have them,' she said. 'I have the Queen's Warrant, Tomas. I can do anything.'

'Not so much of a miracle, then, is it?'

'Is it not miracle enough that the crown is prepared to give you the means to take over almost the entire underworld of Ellinburg? "When you are gifted a horse, count not its teeth". I believe that is the expression.'

I didn't know much about horses, or their teeth. I could ride one, but that was it. I was no idle noble, to have time on my hands to spend on horse breeding, and I had hired the people who used to look after my racehorse. Again, I suspected she was making fun of me, and I didn't care for it.

'Three weeks, then,' I said, pushing the conversation back to where I wanted it. 'In three weeks I'll have the men and weapons to take the Wheels?'

'Three weeks or thereabouts,' she said. 'My rider might be waylaid on the road. There could be a shortage of blasting powder in Dannsburg. We deal mostly in *could* and *might* and *possibly*, as you may recall. Nothing is certain in this life until it is too late, but yes. Plan for three weeks, and be prepared to hold off if required.'

'Aye,' I said, and started to turn to the door.

'Oh, and Tomas? Have someone run up to Chandler's Narrow and bring Rosie to me, would you?'

Of course it was Rosie she would give this request to, and Rosie who would no doubt pass it to someone else, some other agent of the Queen's Men in Ellinburg. That person would set a rider on their way to Dannsburg, and soon enough what I had asked for would arrive. I had no idea who Rosie might speak to, and I wondered if Ailsa herself did. From what I had seen of the Queen's Men, it wouldn't have greatly surprised me if she didn't.

The day before Godsday, Old Kurt came calling at the Tanner's Arms.

He had Billy the Boy with him, and the lad had a bag in his hand.

It was a little after sundown, and snowing outside. The tavern was busy, full of local men drinking away their wages or gambling them on the turn of the dice. That was how life was lived, in the Stink. Godsday was traditionally a day of rest, as I have written. Even where that rule wasn't strictly observed, the night before was usually the night when men did most of their drinking. The day before Godsday was Coinsday, and it was when working folk who were paid by the week received their wages. A man might give two thirds of his pay to his wife, to keep their house, but the rest was his and it was usually gone by Godsday morning. People are weak, as I had told Ailsa, and the poorer and more oppressed they are, the weaker they become. Working men, above all others, have a weakness for drink.

The Stink was a good place to keep a tavern.

I was sitting at my corner table in the common room, with Simple Sam standing between me and the customers to keep folk away from me. His leg was mostly healed by then, and since the night of the explosion he had taken it upon himself to become my personal bodyguard. I think he felt indebted to me for bringing him home that night. Sam was a slow lad but a faithful one, and he certainly had a good size to him. No one bothered me without an invitation, not with Sam standing in front of my table.

The job suited him, I had to admit. I believe in putting the right man in the right job, but if a man chooses that job for himself and is suited for it, then I won't argue with him.

I poured myself another brandy from the bottle on the table in front of me and was just raising the glass when Old Kurt walked into the Tanner's. Black Billy had the door, and he shot me a look as the old man shambled into the common room, leaning heavily on his stick. I saw the boy beside him, in a hooded cloak that was too big for him and flakes of snow melting off the thick wool around his shoulders. I nodded to Billy to let them in and reached out to tap Sam on the arm.

'Let those two join me,' I said. 'And they drink on the house.'

Sam nodded and ushered Kurt and Billy the Boy to my table. A moment later Ailsa was there with mugs of beer for them both, without needing to be asked. She missed nothing, I had to admit, however busy the tavern might be.

'Kurt,' I said. 'This is an unexpected pleasure. And young Billy, how are your studies progressing?'

'Well, Uncle Tomas,' Billy said, pushing his hood back from his head.

He needed a haircut, but the fluff on his upper lip was gone, I noticed, and he had a faint shadow on his jaw that said he had started shaving.

'That's good,' I said, and caught Kurt's eye.

The old man had a bleak expression on his face, and I could tell that he wanted to speak to me alone.

'Billy, why don't you run into the kitchen and see if Hari can find you something to eat?'

The lad grinned at me and nodded, and did as I said. He took his beer with him, I noticed, as a grown man would have done. I raised my eyebrows at Old Kurt.

'You're having him back,' the cunning man said.

'Pardon?'

'You heard me. I can't handle him no more, and that's that.'

'Three marks a week and not a copper more, that's what I told you. I said that price would never go up again whatever he does, and I stand by those words.'

Old Kurt turned and spat on the floor beside his chair. 'You could offer me ten marks a week and I'd turn you down,' he said. 'I don't want him in my house no more. The boy's fucking possessed, like I told you.'

'And I told you, the boy is *holy*.'

'No,' Old Kurt said. 'He fucking well ain't.'

He met my stare without blinking, and I saw that he meant it.

'What did he do?' I asked at last.

'I came down one morning and there must have been fifty rats in my parlour,' Kurt said. 'Not running around, mind, nor nibbling on nothing. Just sitting there, they was, staring at me with their little ratty eyes. Accusing, like. Billy said it was on account of the rats I nail to my door, and how they didn't like it when I did that. I allowed that perhaps they didn't, and asked him if he knew how they had got there.'

'And?'

'Well, he didn't say he had brought them, but then he didn't say as that he hadn't, either. He just sort of smiled at me. That smile made me feel cold, Mr Piety, I have to admit. I asked him if he could get rid of them, and he nodded. I went through the back for my morning piss and when I come back . . . when I come back they was all dead. Fifty dead rats lying on my parlour floor and all of them with their backs broken, and your Billy didn't look like he'd moved an inch. He shouldn't . . . he shouldn't ought to be able to do that. Not yet. Maybe not ever.'

'And you didn't teach him how?'

'I don't fucking *know* how,' Kurt hissed at me.

I nodded slowly. Old Kurt couldn't keep Billy the Boy any longer, I could see the truth of that. Not now he was this afraid of the lad. Besides, it seemed to my mind that Billy might have outgrown his teaching already.

'All right,' I said. 'I'll have the lad back and we'll call it square. What else can he do?'

Kurt just shrugged. 'He learned the basic things fast enough,' he said. 'The quenching of fires he had before we even started, and he picked up the setting of them fast enough, and then the calling of them. He can mend hurts, but you knew that, and now he can cause them too. Divination's a strange one, with him. Sometimes he knows a thing will happen, however outlandish it may seem, and the thing happens just how he said it would. But ask him what time the sun will rise in the morning and he has no answer to give you. He can write and he can draw a glyph, but he seems unable to read any hand but his own, and he can't read a printed book at all. How you can learn to write when you can't read is beyond me, but there it is.'

'The goddess moves through him,' I said, thinking out loud.

'Something does, aye,' Old Kurt said. 'Whether it's your goddess or some devil from Hell is another question.'

'You be quiet with that,' I said, sharply. 'You listen to me, Old Kurt, and you mark me. The boy is *holy*. Do you understand me? If you've a different opinion, you'd be wise to keep it to yourself. Very wise indeed.'

'Aye,' Old Kurt muttered, and took a long swallow of his beer. 'Aye, I mark you, Tomas Piety.'

I nodded. 'Well and good,' I said. 'See that you do.'

Chapter 37

Billy the Boy seemed happy enough to move back into the Tanner's Arms, and he took to Ailsa immediately. Once word reached him that she was my woman, he took to calling her Auntie.

For all that that caused some merriment among the crew, she didn't seem to mind it any. I was glad about that. I remembered walking along the river path with Anne and Billy on our way to Old Kurt's house, back in the spring. It had seemed to me at the time that we might almost have been a family, and I remembered that I had thought then that perhaps it would be no bad thing. Not with Anne, no, but with Ailsa I thought it might well be a different matter. I was being a fool there, I knew that, but still the thought lingered.

Aunt and Uncle, I would take that if it was offered.

Hari and Billy renewed their friendship, largely based on pastries though it may have been, and a few days passed merrily enough. Jochan still worried me, but there was little I could do about that. He would come out of it or he wouldn't, I supposed. Fat Luka was away a lot, out in the streets doing what he did best.

'The Gutcutters are laid in for a siege,' he told me one night, sharing my table in the Tanner's while Simple Sam loomed in front of us and kept flapping ears away. 'I think they don't understand why there's been no reprisal for Enaid's house. Some of them say it's because you're too weak to strike back, but the prevailing word is otherwise. I've paid well for that word, and so far it's working. Our man Gregor sits at Ma Aditi's left hand, and he whispers in her ear whatever I tell him to.'

I remembered that man from our sit-down with the Gutcutters, sitting there in his purple shirt and whispering to her as Luka said. Whether or not Bloodhands listened to him remained to be seen. I nodded.

'Well and good,' I said, 'but it won't do forever, will it?'

'No, boss, it won't,' Luka said. 'Is there any word on the . . . the thing we talked about?'

'It's coming,' I said, and I hoped that was true.

Ailsa might well like to deal in *could* and *might* and *possibly*, but I preferred cold certainties. I needed those weapons and men, and I needed them soon. It had been over a week now since I had made my deal with Ailsa and sent a boy to fetch Rosie to her, so I could only hope that her rider had already reached Dannsburg. All being well, there were wagons rolling up the West Road toward us even as we spoke, laden with trained men and army weapons.

If not, then there would be hard times ahead. Luka's gold could only keep the Gutcutters sitting tight for so long, and if they came at us again I knew we would be sorely pressed. They had blasting weapons and I didn't, and through Bloodhands they had the backing of the Skanians.

If the Skanians had had one magician then I dare say they had another. I didn't have a magician, but perhaps I had something else. I had Billy the Boy, and from what Old Kurt had told me I thought that might be a good thing.

It may seem harsh, to use a boy so young in battle, but he had fought and killed men in Abingon, and before that. We had found him as an orphan in Messia, but he was alive and unharmed and that meant he had fought there, too, alone among the ruins. He'd have been dead if he hadn't.

Billy the Boy was a soldier, in his way, and he was of age now. Aye, if it came to it, Billy would fight. Whether his cunning was strong enough to defeat a Skanian magician was another matter, of course. I remembered the one we had faced in the Golden Chains and how flames had sprung from his fingertips like living things. I remembered how Grieg had burned and then simply exploded before my eyes. Could Billy really stand up against that?

The boy's fucking possessed, Old Kurt had said. *Whether it's your goddess or some devil from Hell is another question.*

If those weapons didn't arrive soon, I would take whichever I could get.

Another week went by, and I knew it wouldn't keep any longer.

Luka's spies reported that the Gutcutters were restless, and nothing that his man said could keep them in fear of us now. I had sat too long without acting, and I knew that I couldn't wait for Ailsa's men. I had to do something, and at once.

'Word is, they'll try us tomorrow,' Luka told me that morning. 'Something to test our defences. Bloodhands has Aditi's ear, and he controls her poppy supply. I don't know where he's getting it from so I can't cut it off, but he has more say over her now than my man does.'

I would have bet good gold that Bloodhands was getting that resin from his Skanian masters the same way I was getting mine from Ailsa, but I couldn't tell Luka about that. He certainly wasn't getting it through the Golden Chains, I knew that much. We were open for business again by then, but the membership list was small and select and drawn only from the upper class of Ellinburg, such as it was. And Captain Rogan, of course. I had had to honour that agreement, although all he did was play cards and lose money. Rogan wasn't the type to smoke the poppy, whereas Ma Aditi very much was.

I was sitting with Luka and Bloody Anne at my table in the common room, keeping our voices low although we weren't open for the day yet. I hadn't invited Jochan to this council of war. He was my brother, yes, but he was still too far gone from himself to be of much use at the planning table.

'Very well,' I said. 'Then we hit them tonight, while they're busy planning for tomorrow. That should put them off the idea.'

'Boss,' Luka said, and shifted his bulk in his seat the way he did when he was about to say something he thought I might take ill. 'I don't know that we can. The new men are untried and I don't trust a one of them, not yet. Sam's only just fit, and Brak's still useless with his shoulder. We could swap out Cutter and Sir Eland for a couple of the new lads just for a night, I suppose, but you need four to hold the Tanner's and that still only leaves us . . .'

His brow furrowed as he tried to figure it, and I cut him off.

'I know how many men I've got, Fat Luka,' I said. 'You're right, it's not enough for a frontal assault on the Wheels and that's not what I'm suggesting.'

I turned to Bloody Anne and noted the thoughtful expression on her face.

'You remember the road from Messia, when we were ahead of the main march of the regiment and we caught up with the enemy baggage train?' I said. 'Well, the captain didn't have us attempt to storm it, did he? That would have been madness, and the captain was no fool. Small raiding parties, coming in the night from all directions, that was how we did it. Hit and run and hit again, until they thought we had ten times the numbers that we did. Do you remember that, Bloody Anne?'

She nodded. 'Aye,' she said. 'I remember.'

'Well and good,' I said. 'What worked once will work again, to my mind.'

Anne nodded, and even Fat Luka started to smile.

'Who, and where?' Anne asked me.

I trusted Sir Eland enough to have him running security at the Golden Chains now, where his airs and graces could be put to good use, while Will the Wencher was breaking in a couple of the new lads for me in his place up at Chandler's Narrow. That was good and Eland needed to stay there, but Cutter was wasted babysitting a boarding-house full of harmless slaughtermen and skinners.

'Jochan, with Stefan and Erik,' I said. 'Leave Sir Eland where he is, but take Cutter and put him with Jochan's crew. Some of the new boys can look after Slaughterhouse Narrow for a bit. Me, with you and Borys. Mika, Billy and Luka with Sam to hold the Tanner's.'

'Which Billy?' Luka asked.

I blinked at him. 'Black Billy, you fool. The door's his, and he won't want anyone else taking it. Billy the Boy . . .' I paused for a moment, and remembered my thoughts of the previous week. 'Aye, I'll take Billy the Boy with me.'

Anne gave me a look, but I ignored that.

'A bit of experience will do him good,' Luka said.

I nodded, but that wasn't what I had meant.

Not at all.

Chapter 38

That night we didn't open the Tanner's to the public, and I assembled the three crews in the common room to address them.

Jochan, Stefan, Erik, and Cutter made up one raiding party. Me, Bloody Anne, Borys and Billy the Boy were the other, leaving Fat Luka, Simple Sam, Mika and Black Billy to hold the Tanner's. Sir Eland and his squad of hired men had a good grip on the Golden Chains, I knew, and I could only hope that Will the Wencher had his new lads in good enough shape to keep the house on Chandler's Narrow safe. Slaughterhouse Narrow wasn't likely to be at risk, to my mind, being the farthest from the Wheels and the least valuable. The rest of my businesses just paid me protection and weren't permanently guarded. That was well and good, then.

Everyone was mailed and fully armed, and Bloody Anne had made sure no one was drunk. Except for Jochan, of course. There was nothing to be done about that.

'Right,' I addressed them. 'Tonight we take the fight into the Wheels. There's two ways up there from here, the river path and Dock Road. Jochan, I want your squad to head along the river path. Slip up the alley past Old Kurt's house and come out at the top of Dock Road where they won't expect you. Kill anyone who tries to stop you. I'll lead my lot right up the road from here, where they'll see us coming. That should put the fox in the fucking henhouse, and once they're up and at us you can come running and take them in the rear. Everyone clear on that?'

There was a chorus of grunts and ayes, and I nodded. Ailsa was standing behind the bar, for all that we weren't open. I looked over and caught her eye. She gave me a short nod, and it was done.

We pulled up the hoods of our cloaks and set off into the blowing snow.

Dock Road was a good mile long, from the edge of the Stink to the top of the alley that ran past Old Kurt's house, but no one had noticed that flaw in my plan. Not that it was a flaw, as such, not if what I believed turned out to be true. Expecting Jochan's crew to creep along the river path and join up with us before we were overwhelmed would have been a fool's thinking, of course, if it had just been the four of us with blades marching into Gutcutter territory. I had hoped for it to be the four of us with a cart full of flashstones, and another five men who knew best how to use them, but it seemed that wasn't going to be the case tonight. I had something almost as good, though.

I had magic, or so I very much hoped.

'How do you feel, Billy?' I asked the lad as we approached the edges of my streets.

'We're going to fight,' he said. 'Good fucking deal.'

'Aye, we are,' I said. 'We're raiding tonight, though, not going into battle. Do you know what raiders do, Billy?'

'Strike fast, strike hard, burn everything and run away afore we're caught,' Billy recited, quoting the captain's words from memory.

'Good lad. That's right,' I said. 'That's exactly what raiders do. They strike fast, and they burn everything. If I ask you to burn something, Billy, can you do that for me? A workshop maybe, or an inn?'

He looked up at me, although truth be told, he wasn't all that much shorter than I was, by then.

'With the cunning?' he asked.

I nodded. 'Aye, lad, with the cunning.'

'I can do that,' he said, and he grinned at me. 'Old Kurt never let me burn nothing big, but I know I can if I try.'

'Good lad,' I said again.

I could feel Bloody Anne giving me the hard eye in the darkness, but I had to ignore it. Billy the Boy was of age now and he was one of us, whether Anne liked it or not. If I was right, he was the most dangerous man I had.

Apart from Cutter, perhaps. I remembered the fight in the Golden Chains, and how the Skanian magician had sent us all cowering behind tables. I remembered how Cutter had crept up behind him and opened his neck, magic or no fucking magic. Cutter was very dangerous too, I had to remind myself.

That, and he was still Jochan's man, not mine.

All my attempts to build a trust with Cutter had fallen on stony ground. He had been content to move into the house on Slaughterhouse Narrow and I had seen little of him since. The man said next to nothing, and I had no idea what levers moved him. Something tied him to my brother, some bond of loyalty forged in the war, although I hadn't managed to find out what it was. I didn't even know where he was from, but he had skills that conscripts don't get taught.

I would have bet a gold crown to a clipped copper that Cutter had been a professional killer before the war, but where and for who remained a mystery. So long as he was a Pious Man, that was well and good, but I trusted him even less than I had trusted Sir Eland before he proved himself to me, and that was quite some statement to be making.

'Right,' I said, and squared my shoulders under my cloak. I could feel the weight of the mail dragging against them, over the thick layer of leather beneath. 'This is the last street of the Stink. Up there is Dock Road, and that runs all the way through the Wheels to the docks. That's Gutcutter territory, all of it. What we're going to do is walk up that street, nice and slow. Billy, I want you to leave the houses alone but burn every business I tell you to. Anne, Borys, we're going to kill every bastard who comes out and tries to stop us. When we meet up with Jochan and his lads, we're going to turn and run back to the Stink like the very gods of war are behind us. Everyone understand?'

They all nodded, and the smile on Billy the Boy's face told me how much he was looking forward to it.

'Yes, Uncle Tomas,' he said.

We set off up Dock Road, and the first place we passed was a baker's that I knew paid protection to Ma Aditi. I pointed to it, and Billy's smile widened. He stopped in the street and stared at the shop front, the snow settling on his cloak. A moment later a dull glow began to light the windows from within. It brightened by the moment, until I could see flames licking at the inside of the panes.

'It's done,' he said.

I nodded, and we moved on.

'Witchcraft,' I heard Bloody Anne mutter under her breath.

'Magic,' I said, correcting her. 'It ain't the same thing, Anne.'

I wasn't sure I could see a difference, but I needed *her* to.

There was shouting behind us, the crash of breaking glass and the sound of panicked voices as the baker and his family fought the fire. They weren't my enemies, no, but then the people of Messia had done nothing to me either. This was war, the same as Messia had been.

The same as Abingon.

Civilians suffer in war, and there was nothing to be done about that. I couldn't meet the Gutcutters in formal battle any more than our generals had been able to draw the garrison at Abingon out from behind the city walls. Instead we had smashed those walls with our cannon and stormed the city, killing and burning as we went. This was the same thing, to my mind.

'There,' I said, indicating a chandler's shop.

That went up even better than I could have hoped, and it took the tailor's shop next door with it. A lot of Ellinburg is timber and daub, and even in the cold wetness of winter that burns well. We hurried on, hearing the shouts and chaos building behind us. These were just protected businesses, though, and for all that we were making a nuisance of ourselves in the Gutcutters' eyes, we hadn't really hurt them yet. To do that, we had to reach the Stables.

The Stables was nothing to do with horses.

It was Ma Aditi's favourite place in all of Ellinburg: a brothel that specialised in boys. She liked young lads herself, and there were enough men who felt the same way for it to be a lucrative business. The Stables was near the top of Dock Road, where it could attract incoming sailors who had got too used to their cabin boys while aboard ship.

I wanted to burn the Stables to the ground.

We had to be careful about it, though, I knew that much. Those lads hadn't hurt anyone, and for all that civilians have a hard time in war I wouldn't see it happen to them. Those boys had seen enough hardship.

This was where the second part of my plan came to life, the part I hadn't shared with anyone.

Chapter 39

I led my raiding party through the alleys, leaving Dock Road behind us. The Gutcutters would be out in force now, with fires burning the length of their main street, and I wasn't looking for open battle. Not with only two soldiers and a boy at my back I wasn't.

I knew the Wheels better than most Stink men did, and I had my da to thank for that if for little enough else. He had worked for Old Kurt when I was a boy, as I have written, and had taken me up there with him. I had been chased by Wheeler lads more times than I could remember, and I had learned those alleys while fleeing for my life. Memories like that stay with a man, it has to be said.

Anne, Borys and Billy followed me through the narrow ways, keeping quiet and listening to the din of fires being fought on the main street. I led them roughly parallel to Dock Road, through the twisting wynds behind workshops and between tenements. Only once did we stop, when I pointed to the back of a cobbler's shop and had Billy set it alight from the rear. We hurried on after that, until our alley opened up onto the courtyard behind the Stables.

'Right,' I said. 'This is it. This is Ma Aditi's favourite business, and I want it burned down. But first, there's work. There are lads in there, and we need to get them out.'

'What lads?' Borys asked.

'Boy whores,' I said. 'Young ones. Too fucking young for whoring. We're getting them out.'

'How?' Anne asked.

I looked at the back of the Stables. There was a single guard out-side the back door, leaning against the wall and picking his nose with obvious enthusiasm. With him gone, we could slip inside and up the stairs to the rooms where the boys worked, and lead them out before anyone knew what was happening.

'The man on the door,' I said to Anne. 'Can you drop him from here?'

Anne lifted her crossbow and sighted along the bolt, her eyes nar-rowed against the snow that was blowing into the mouth of the alley.

'Perhaps,' she said. 'It's dark and the angle's for shit. I can't make any promises.'

That wasn't what I wanted to hear. If she missed he would raise the alarm and then it would all be in the shithouse, I knew that much. I was about to speak when Billy beat me to it.

'I can, Uncle Tomas,' he said.

I frowned at him. 'I need him dead, Billy, you understand?' I said. 'Fast and quiet, without anyone seeing.'

The lad nodded. 'I know,' he said. 'He'll die.'

Anne and me exchanged a look, but I knew that when Billy said a thing would happen he was always right. If he said he could do this, then . . .

I knew I had to trust him.

'Do it, then,' I said.

Billy narrowed his eyes and stared at the man outside the door. He was maybe thirty yards away, and as Bloody Anne had said the angle was for shit and that was without the dark and the wind and the snow. I couldn't have made that shot with a crossbow, I knew that much, and if even Anne doubted herself then it was a difficult shot indeed. Billy didn't have a crossbow, though.

He didn't need one.

Billy's fists clenched at his sides, hard and sudden, and he made a sharp hissing noise like he had pushed all the air out of his lungs at once. The man on the door jerked forward, one hand scratching des-perately at his throat, then pitched onto his face on the icy cobbles. He kicked once and was still.

I waited for him to rise, but he didn't. Falling snow settled on his back as he lay there under the glow of the single lantern above the door.

'What did you do, Billy?' I whispered.

'I crushed his lungs and took his breath,' Billy said. 'All of it. He don't need it no more, Uncle Tomas. He's dead.'

'Aye,' I said. 'Aye, that he is.'

We slipped through the shadows to the back door of the Stables. The snow was falling heavier now, already beginning to cover the body of the fallen man. I eased up the latch and opened the door an inch, putting my eye to the gap. There was no one in sight, just a patch of bare wooden floor at the bottom of the stairs that led to the upper floor.

The Stables was a tavern, officially, and only a certain few knew what was upstairs. The way up was in the back, and when there were no ships in and no sailors to entertain like there weren't at the moment, the back was kept curtained off.

I could hear laughter and revelry coming from the common room, but the back of the building was quiet. That was how I had hoped it would be. I eased Remorse out of her scabbard and pushed the door open.

Bloody Anne followed with her crossbow slung and her daggers in her hands, and Billy came behind her. Borys brought up the rear, closing the door silently behind us. He could move quiet when he wanted to, for a big man, and I didn't think anyone had heard us. I made my way up the stairs as softly as I could, trying to figure how long it had been since we all set off from the Tanner's Arms.

Jochan would be making slower time than us, I knew. The river path was treacherous in the snow and they would have had to take it carefully, and I was sure they would have met at least some resistance coming that way. I thought I had perhaps ten minutes until they reached the alley beside Old Kurt's house. They would have to fight again there, as that way was always guarded.

Then they'd be out onto Dock Road, only a hundred yards or so north of the Stables. I had to have the place burning by then. I hadn't explained this part of my plan, as I said. I should have done, I knew that, but I just couldn't bring myself to speak of it in front of the men. All the same, Jochan would know what to do. Once he saw the flames at the Stables he would realise that I had set them, and why. That would bring him running, and his men with him.

We slipped into the corridor at the top of the stairs and I paused outside the first door. I eased it open and saw the lad inside. He had perhaps twelve years to him, and he was sitting on the bed wearing a pair of tight red velvet britches and nothing else. He looked up at me and showed me a seductive smile that I knew he didn't feel.

I put a finger to my lips. 'I'm not a customer,' I whispered. 'Come on, boy, I'm getting you out of here. Do you have any more clothes?'

His eyes went very wide, and for a moment I thought he might panic and start shouting. Just then Billy popped his head around the door and grinned at the other boy. He gave him a wink and an encouraging wave, and quick as that the lad was off the bed and stuffing his feet into a pair of old boots.

He dragged a patched cloak out of a small chest beside the bed and pulled it around his thin, naked shoulders, and he was as ready as he was going to get. I ushered him quickly out of the room to where Bloody Anne was waiting with as reassuring a smile as her scarred face could manage. She gave the boy a brief, brusque hug and passed him back to Borys, who took him down the stairs and out the back door. Borys stayed outside with the lad, and I went to the next door.

We brought out six boys in all, sending them down to Borys one at a time, before I reached the last room and found one who was working.

The poor little bastard couldn't have had more than seven or eight years to him. He was face down on the bed and sobbing, with a naked man grunting away on top of him.

Memories crashed into my head hard enough to make me vomit.

The man's head whipped around at the sound, his face red and sweaty and outraged at the intrusion. He looked just like my da.

I swung Remorse so hard I nearly took his fucking head clean off.

Blood erupted up the wall and across the ceiling, and the force of my blow made his corpse roll off the bed and hit the floor with a heavy thump. That was bad.

I wiped sick from my chin with the back of my left wrist and held out a hand to the whimpering boy.

'Come on, lad, quickly now,' I said.

The boy just wept and stared at me with wide, terrified eyes. He was naked and bleeding, and I realised that he was in no state to run. I ripped my cloak off and wrapped him in it, and bundled him over my shoulder.

'It's all right,' I said. 'You have to keep quiet, though, you understand me?'

The lad nodded against my back, still sniffling. I hurried back into the corridor and pushed past Anne and Billy on my way to the stairs.

'Burn it all,' I snarled at Billy the Boy as I passed him, and I found that I was weeping. 'Burn it to the cunting ground.'

Chapter 40

It seemed Billy the Boy had formed his own opinion about what went on in the Stables. The fire that consumed the building was apocalyptic.

I sent Borys back to the Stink with the boys we had rescued, leading them through the alleys behind him. He had the youngest lad cradled in his arms, still wrapped in my cloak. I took Bloody Anne and Billy around to the street to meet the Gutcutters as they came boiling out of the tavern entrance into the swirling, firelit snow, shouting and cursing with blades in their hands.

Anne dropped the first with the bolt from her crossbow, and then they were too close and there was no time for her to reload. Remorse and Mercy took their toll, and Billy the Boy stood back and concentrated with a fierce look on his face, and here and there a man dropped clutching his throat as Billy stole his breath. There were too many of them, though, and even as Anne took a man's throat out with her dagger two more stepped up to take his place. I gave one Mercy through the ribs and kicked out at another, almost losing my footing on the treacherous, icy cobbles.

'Tomas!'

I heard Jochan's roar and looked up to see him charging, his bloody axe raised high. I had never been so glad to see my brother in my life. He crashed into the rear of the mob of Gutcutters like a man possessed, like a berserker. The flames from the burning Stables reflected in his eyes, and I knew that he understood all too well why I had done what I had. Cutter slipped into the melee and men died around him, falling back from the evil little blades in his hands while Stefan and Erik fought with the stolid, determined competence of veterans.

I was beginning to think we might just take them all, when a man came out of a house across the street. He put a hand to his mouth and whistled. He whistled a long, shrill note that made my ears first hurt and then scream. I stumbled back a step and clapped my hands to my head, the Weeping Women tumbling from numb fingers as I sagged to my knees. I could feel hot blood against my palms.

The magic was indiscriminate, though. Gutcutters and Pious Men alike were on their knees in the snow as the Skanian magician walked slowly into the street with his long hair blowing around his face.

Everyone was on their knees except Billy the Boy.

The magician stopped and stared at Billy, a frown creasing his pale brow. Billy stood with the fire at his back, outlining him in flame like the devil Old Kurt had feared him to be. He took a step toward the magician and raised a hand.

'No,' he said. 'I won't.'

The Skanian stumbled back a step, his own hands moving in a complicated sequence in front of him. Something invisible seemed to rush through the air between them, but Billy made a chopping gesture with his left hand and whatever it was dissipated like mist on a summer morning.

'No,' he said again. 'I'm going to hurt you now.'

He can mend hurts, Old Kurt had told me, *and now he can cause them too.*

The magician screamed.

I don't have the words in me to describe that scream, save to liken it to a lamb being slaughtered the slow way, like they do in some of the temples. He clutched his hands to his stomach and doubled over, and blood gushed out from the bottom of his robe and darkened the snow around his feet. He pitched to his face on the ground, vomiting more blood, and his entrails left his body through his arsehole at great speed.

The spell broke at once, and I snatched up Mercy and stabbed the nearest man within reach before he could react. Bloody Anne threw herself on top of the fellow beside her and her daggers rose and fell, rose and fell.

Jochan and Cutter made short work of the rest of them, and it was done.

The Stables was a blazing ruin behind us, but I could hear running men, coming closer. Lots of them.

'We need to go,' I said. 'Right fucking now.'

We fled back to the Stink through the alleys, taking wild turns and doubling back on ourselves until I was sure we had shaken off the pursuit. Billy collapsed on the way, ghost pale and shaking like he had contracted the falling sickness. I scooped him up and threw him over my shoulder, and we ran again.

By the time we made it back to the Tanner's Arms I was exhausted, gasping for breath from the boy's weight and frozen to the bone under the sweat that covered me. Mail is not a good thing to wear in winter without a cloak to cover it, and mine was still wrapped around the young lad I had rescued. At least, I very much hoped it was. If Borys had lost those lads I vowed I would kill him myself.

Black Billy let us into the Tanner's with a grin of visible relief as he saw we were all there. Ailsa came bustling over, a worried frown on her face.

'Is young Billy hurt?' she asked, when she saw me carrying him.

'The lad's exhausted, that's all,' I said, and I hoped it was true. 'He fought hard tonight.'

He had done that all right, and no mistake. I remembered the day after he had healed Hari, and how he had looked near death and slept for a whole day afterward. I wondered what this night's work had cost him.

'I'll put him to bed,' Ailsa said, and took the lad from me as though he weighed no more than a newborn.

She disappeared into the back with the unconscious boy, and I sank into a chair and pulled off my frozen mail and leather. Anne brought a coat and wrapped it around my shoulders, and I huddled into it and nodded my thanks.

'Where are the boys?' I asked.

'Borys brought them in about twenty minutes ago,' Luka said. 'They're in the kitchen with Hari, eating us out of house and home.'

He smiled when he said it, though, and I nodded. That was good.

Mika came around with brandies for everyone, leaving a couple of bottles on the tables for us. I drank and shivered, and I saw the others doing the same. That night had been harsh work indeed, the sort of work we had done at Messia, and I knew it would have brought back memories for everyone.

'Get Doc Cordin up here tomorrow to have a look at the lads,' I said, and Mika nodded. 'Some of them aren't in great shape.'

I would worry about what to do with them in the morning. Since the Chains had opened up again I had proper money coming in, and that allowed me to move some of my hidden gold through the business without anyone raising hard questions about where it had come from. Now that I could spend money, I could do things. If I needed to pay some families to adopt the young lads, to raise them and teach them a trade, then I could do that.

And I would.

I sat back in my chair and swallowed brandy, and poured myself another. There was a tap on the door a while later, and Black Billy slid the hatch aside and peered out. He turned and beckoned to Fat Luka.

'One of yours,' he said.

Luka went to the door and opened it, just a little. I could see him talking to someone outside, but their voices were too low to overhear. A moment later Luka nodded and coin changed hands, and then the door was closed and locked again.

'All the Wheels is in uproar,' he said, a satisfied smile on his plump face. 'The traders of Dock Road are asking why they should pay protection to the Gutcutters if they aren't protected, and Ma Aditi is in a fury over losing the Stables and her little boys. There's other talk too, of a powerful man who was supposed to help them and didn't, or did and failed, or died trying. It's confused, is that, but word is the Gutcutters have been let down bad by someone.'

I nodded, and thought of their Skanian magician shitting out his own intestines into the gutter as Billy the Boy pulled him inside out with his mind. I thought that might give Bloodhands something to think on, and no mistake.

'Good,' I said. 'It's been a good night's work for the Pious Men.'

There was a cheer for that, and glasses were raised and brandy downed.

'Fuck a nun, Tomas,' Jochan said, and he started to laugh. 'You burned down the fucking Stables! That's wanted doing for a long time.'

'Aye, it has,' I said. 'Too long. I left it too long.'

I met his eyes, and he blinked back a tear and nodded.

'Aye well, it's done now and done well,' he said.

I felt like a weight had lifted from my heart, to hear him say that.

Chapter 41

A week passed, and I found homes for the Stables boys. Gold opens many doors, after all, and I had gold to spare. The poppy trade was bringing in a fortune, as Ailsa had said it would. Taxes were coming in again too, from all the businesses under my protection, and Will the Wencher had turned the house on Chandler's Narrow into the best and most profitable stew in Ellinburg. It was doing so well, in fact, that I had Sir Eland return there, and put Erik in charge of security at the Golden Chains in his place.

It was a fine morning, cold and crisp, and the sun was shining. Anne and I walked the streets of the Stink together, partly to see how the land lay but mostly so that we could be seen. We looked like lords of the manor in our fine coats and doublets, and we had Stefan and three of the new lads with us as bodyguards. The Gutcutters were still licking their wounds from our attack on Dock Road and the Stables, so that wasn't strictly necessary, but I had to be seen to be guarded and guarded well. Perhaps I should have brought Jochan along, but Jochan was still stinking drunk from the night before and snoring in his blankets.

Billy the Boy had wanted to come too, and I indulged him. He was recovered now, but it had taken him three days to regain his strength after his battle with the Skanian magician. He looked quite the young lordling himself, since I had lavished him with new clothes by way of thanks for his efforts.

'What's that place, Uncle Tomas?' he asked, indicating a baker's shop.

The sign above the door said clearly what it was, but I remembered Old Kurt telling me that Billy seemed unable to read any hand but his own. All the same, the good smells wafting from the open door of the shop were enough to tell anyone what the owner's trade was. He grinned at me to say he was making mischief, and I returned his smile.

'Are you hungry again?' Anne asked in mock surprise.

The lad had done nothing but eat since he regained consciousness, but still he remained painfully thin.

'I could fancy a pastry,' he admitted.

'Then you shall have one,' I said, and ducked through the low doorway of the shop with Anne behind me.

'Mr Piety!' the baker exclaimed when he saw me, his plump, floury hands fluttering nervously at the front of his apron. 'I'm not late, am I, sir? I swear I paid my taxes not three days ago.'

'That you did, Georg,' I assured him. 'Our lad is hungry, that's all. You know how growing boys are, I'm sure. You've two of your own, as I recall.'

'I have, sir, and it's good of you to remember,' he said.

Georg flustered and fussed about behind his counter, and a moment later he presented me with two dried fruit pies and a spiced pastry, wrapped up in waxed paper. Those were his best wares, I knew, but he waved away my coin.

'No charge for you, Mr Piety,' he said. 'There's no charge for the Pious Men, not in here there isn't.'

I nodded and accepted the wrapped package. 'My thanks, Georg,' I said.

We left the shop and I let Billy bury his face in the pastries. It was good to have my streets back again, and I wouldn't forget the respect that Georg had shown me.

It may sound strange, that I taxed these people and they still gave me their wares for free, but that was how respect worked in Ellinburg. They knew that I taxed them fairly, and that my protection actually *would* protect them. Also, I wouldn't see a family starve in the Stink, and that was known too. I had found work for many of their sons and brothers in my businesses, and their daughters too, as guards and messengers and card dealers, as doormen and draymen and cooks and porters. Those who were sick and couldn't afford even Doc Cordin's services had been treated at my expense. Those who were hungry had been fed. That was how I protected my streets, and that was how I earned the respect of the folk who lived there. It was a closed system, to be sure, and participation wasn't optional, but it worked well enough once everyone accepted that.

Anne cadged a mouthful of pastry from Billy and stood on the street corner, munching thoughtfully.

'We should check on your aunt,' she said, brushing crumbs from her chin as she spoke.

'Aye,' I said. 'I suppose we should, at that.'

I had arranged a new house for Aunt Enaid, to replace the one we blew up, and she and Brak had recently moved in. Brak was most of the way to healed by then, although whether his left arm would ever work properly again was still in some doubt.

I saw that he was well paid for his troubles, of course, and everyone else too. The Pious Men were rich again, richer now than we had been before the war. All my crew were dressed like lords, although they were still a long way from learning to act like them.

The new house was down at the end of Cobbler's Row and it was twice the size of her old place. I had hired a maid for her too, one of Doc Cordin's granddaughters, and put a couple of the new boys on duty there to make sure there was no repeat of what had happened last time.

An Alarian lad called Desh had the front door when we came strolling down the row, and he stood up smart when he saw me coming. I think he would have saluted if he had known how, but he had been just slightly too young to be conscripted and had missed the war by a matter of months. He was almost a grown man now, though, and he had a shortsword at his hip and a crossbow hidden behind the garden wall where he could reach it easily.

'Morning, boss,' he said.

He was a good lad, from a poor family down on Hull Patcher's Row. When I had been recruiting new men he had been among the first to take my coin. I thought perhaps Desh might well have grown up wanting to be a Pious Man.

I nodded to him. 'Is my aunt in?'

'Yes, sir,' he said, and opened the front door for us.

Anne and I went inside, but Billy was still eating and spraying crumbs everywhere so I left him outside with Stefan and the guards. It wouldn't do to have him making a mess all over Aunt Enaid's freshly swept floors, I knew that much.

She met us in the hall and ushered us into her parlour, where Brak was taking his ease in front of the fire with his left arm still bound up in a sling.

'Morning, Auntie,' I said.

She squinted at me with her one bright eye. 'That it is,' she said. 'What brings you here, Tomas Piety?'

'Can't I pay a social call on my favourite aunt?'

She snorted and waved us to seats. I spoke briefly with Brak, and then Aunt Enaid picked up her stick and hauled her bulk back out of her chair again.

'Anne and Brak will have a lot to discuss, I'm sure,' she said, although I couldn't think what. 'Come through to the kitchen with your fat old aunt.'

There was something on her mind she wanted to say in private, that was clear enough, so I got up and followed her. Once in the kitchen she chased Cordin's girl out and closed the door behind her.

'What is it, Auntie?' I asked her.

She sat at the kitchen table and I joined her there, letting her take her time.

She didn't take her time at all.

'What the names of the gods are you playing at?' she demanded, as soon as I had sat down.

That made me blink.

'In what way?'

'You attacked the Wheels last week. You burned down the fucking Stables, the way I heard it.'

'Aye, I did,' I said.

'You've got the business *back*, Tomas,' she said. 'It's done. Why go making more blood with Aditi? Everything worked well enough before the war, didn't it?'

'Did it? Was anything well enough, while that filthy place was open?'

'That was never your affair,' she said. 'You run the Stink your way, Ma Aditi runs the Wheels *her* way, that's just how it is.'

'Maybe that's not enough,' I said. 'Maybe I want the Wheels too. Maybe, my dear aunt, I just couldn't stand the thought of that fucking place staying open another week.'

She turned and spat on the floor, and never mind that we were in her own kitchen. Enaid would always be a soldier at heart.

'They'll make fucking war over it!' she hissed at me. 'I should have found a way to keep myself out of that bloody convent. I should have kept a hand on the tiller while you were away, like I said I would. Then maybe we wouldn't be in this mess.'

'You should have married,' I said. 'A long time ago. Made some poor man a terrifying wife, and left me alone.'

'And done what, raised brats?' She snorted. 'This country has twice the mouths it can feed already; that's why we're always at bloody war. No, no brats for me, Tomas. My brother raised two and that's more than enough Piety boys in the world, to my mind.'

Her brother was my da, of course, and I didn't want the conversation going that way.

'This is a good thing for the Pious Men,' I said instead. 'I've got money coming in now, lots of it, and I'm spending it wisely. There's new weapons on their way from Dannsburg, and the men to use them. I mean to clean Ma Aditi out of the Wheels and take them for myself.'

'That's blood for blood's sake,' she said. 'You don't need the Wheels.'

I shook my head. 'It's for the sake of the Pious Men,' I said. 'It's to secure everything we've always worked for.'

It was because Ailsa and the Queen's Men said so, of course. It was to save us all from the horrors of another Abingon, from siege and starvation and slavery, but that was nothing my aunt needed to hear.

'There's a devil in you, Tomas Piety,' Enaid said. 'There always has been, and there's no blaming the war for it. I remember how you were, even as a lad. You were twelve years old when you came to my house in the dead of night with your little brother at your side and you said "Da's dead", and there was no sorrow on your face.'

No, there wouldn't have been.

It seemed there was no keeping the talk away from that subject now. I wondered if Aunt Enaid even remotely suspected what had really happened to Da. I didn't think that she did.

I didn't want to think about it, but her words had opened that strongbox in the back of my mind now and the horrors were crawling out whether I wanted it or not. I felt sweat on the palms of my hands, felt my throat wanting to close up. I could see my da's face all over again.

He'd hit me often enough, hit me and worse beside. Ma died two years after birthing Jochan, and times had been hard. Da was violent and he drank, but that was often the way of men in the Stink. He was still my da, and most fathers had heavy hands. That was nothing in itself but Da did more than hit me. Da put his rough bricklayer's hands where they weren't wanted too. No one wants their own da stuffing his hand down their britches, but I was young when that started. I had only had six or seven years to me, and I thought that perhaps most fathers did that too. I was wrong about that, of course, but I hadn't known any better. By the time I learned different, I was too shamed to tell anyone.

When I turned nine, he came into my bedroom one night and he forced himself on me and used me like boys were used at the Stables.

That went on for three fucking years, and I suffered it.

I suffered it because I had to, because I was a little boy and he was my da and I still loved him, despite everything. He told me that if I loved him then I'd let him do it. He told me that I deserved it, and that I owed it to him, and he made me believe that those things were true. I was only young and he was my da and I loved him and I trusted him, so of course I believed him. But eventually he grew bored with me, or I got too old for him, and he left me be and started on little Jochan, who had just turned eight.

I heard his wails, night after night, and I suffered that too. That was the debt I owed Jochan, the debt I could never repay. I should have done a thing and I didn't, not until it was too late. I remembered lying in my bed one night listening to Jochan cry out in pain in the next room and I *knew* it was wrong and still I didn't fucking do anything. I didn't do anything because he was my da and if I told anyone then they'd know it had happened to me as well, and I couldn't face that. I couldn't face the fucking thought of how they would have looked at me, and the pity and the shame. So I hid my face in my pillow and I wept, and next door my little baby brother sobbed and suffered because I was a coward.

Eventually, though, a thing happened that broke something inside me, something that has never healed. It had been well after midnight, and Da was passed out drunk in the parlour downstairs. Jochan crawled into my blankets with me, crying for what Da had done to him. I tried to comfort him, and Jochan . . . Jochan offered to let me use him, how Da did.

He wanted to please me, I think, his big brother, and that was the only way he knew how. That made me sick to my stomach, and I said it was enough. Fuck the shame, and the pity, and what people might think. People didn't have to know, I realised. I had twelve years to me by then, almost a man grown, and to my mind a man solved his own problems. Something cold woke in my head that night. This was going to stop, that cold thing said to me, and it was going to stop right fucking now.

I got out of bed and I went into the parlour where Da was snoring. He was asleep in his chair, red-faced with drink and sweaty, his mouth half open and dribble on his chin. The hammer had been right there, in his work bag, the hammer he used to tamp down his bricks.

I picked it up and I stood there with it in my hand, and I looked at my da for a long time. I looked at him and I felt the shame in me, the shame of what he had done to me, and more than that the shame of what I had let him do to Jochan while I looked the other way. No one was ever going to know about that, the cold thing said to me. No one ever needs to know.

I lifted the hammer and I broke Da's head with it.

I hit him again, and again, and again, until his head was wet mush and I couldn't see for the tears in my eyes.

If it had been the first time he had done it, perhaps I could have forgiven myself. But it hadn't been, not by a long way. I would always owe Jochan for all the nights of his suffering when I had lain in my bed and done nothing because I was a coward. I knew I could never forgive myself for that.

When I came back to myself I roused Jochan from my bed and told him what I had done, and that it was a secret and that he had to take that secret to the grave with him. I made him promise on Ma's memory, and together we had dragged Da's body to the top of the stairs and pushed him out of his window onto the cobbled street below.

Da drank, everyone in the street knew that, and a drunk man could fall from his bedroom window taking a piss in the night without raising too many hard questions. So that was how it was, and that was how it had stayed. Jochan and I never spoke of that night.

That's where the devil in me came from, the cold thing that killed my da, and it has never left me since.

I looked up at Aunt Enaid, and I clenched my fists and forced the past back into the broken strongbox in my head where it belonged. I loved my aunt, but all the same my voice dropped into the flat tone that meant I was close to violence.

'Don't ever talk about my da,' I said.

Enaid stared at me, and she swallowed. No, she had no idea, but she recognised that voice when she heard it and she must have realised there was *something*. Something she didn't understand, and Our Lady willing never would.

She nodded. 'Aye, Tomas,' she said, and that was wise of her.

Chapter 42

Two days later word reached Ailsa that the wagons from Dannsburg were finally on their way with the men and weapons I had asked for. I started to plan my next move.

I was holding a council of war in the kitchen of the Tanner's with Anne and Luka at the table, and Ailsa unobtrusively listening as she swept the floor.

'Are we going to hit them with the explosives straight away, boss?' Luka asked.

I shook my head. 'No, we're not. I don't know these men. They come from someone I trust, but I don't know a one of them. They're not just bringing flashstones and powder, though. They're coming with swords and crossbows, and we'll try them with those first. I don't want the Gutcutters realising I have blasting weapons until we're ready to go to war, and we're not doing that until I'm sure of every man in my crew.'

Ailsa paused in her sweeping for a moment, a thoughtful look on her face.

'That sounds wise,' Bloody Anne said, and Luka nodded.

'Aye,' he said. 'What, then?'

I pursed my lips in thought for a moment. 'At the top of the riverside path there's a factory,' I said. 'Just beyond the alley that leads up to Dock Road. You know where I mean?'

'Aye,' Luka said again. 'They make . . . broadcloth, I think. I'm not sure. Something with looms, anyway, running off the big wheel at the end of the path. They're weavers, under the mercer's guild.'

'That's right,' I said. 'Ma Aditi takes a lot of protection money from that factory, and I know the mercers think ill of that. If we can take it, kill her guards and smash the machines, the mercers will turn against the Gutcutters. Losing the faith of a major guild will hurt her, and hurt the . . . hurt her backers.'

I coughed to cover my slip. It was getting taxing, remembering who knew what and who didn't, and I had nearly said 'Skanians' in front of two people who shouldn't have ever heard that name.

Luka just nodded, and if he had noticed my mistake he made nothing of it.

'We can do that,' Anne said. 'If we have the men take some planks and rope with them, they can get across from the pilings at the end of the path and go in under the waterwheel. They'll need hammers, too, for the looms. It won't be pleasant work, not at this time of year, but it can be done.'

'Good,' I said. 'Anne, I'll leave it to you to pick who goes with the new lads.'

'Cutter,' she said at once, without hesitation. 'This is sneak-and-kill work, and that's what he's best at. I'd have another couple of lads go with them, but we want to keep the crew fairly small for a job like this.'

Bloody Anne knew what she was doing, so I just nodded. That sounded right to me. Cutter was the obvious choice, as she had said.

'Are any of us going?' Luka asked.

I thought on that for a moment, then shook my head. 'No, we're not,' I said. 'Not this time. Cutter's good at this sort of thing, as Anne says. Put him in charge. I can't keep risking my top table on simple raids.'

Anne nodded. 'Aye, Cutter then, in the corporal's role.'

That sounded good, to me. The right man for the right job.

The wagons finally arrived on Queensday afternoon. There were two of them, with canvas covers over their cargos and ten men in all between them. Rosie was there to meet them, and although she was making a show of having come to see Anne on her afternoon off, somehow we all ended up in the stable yard of the Tanner's. We stood there watching these strange, hard-faced men unload crates and barrels and carry them into the storeroom.

'Well, this is a to-do, Tomas,' Ailsa said. 'I'm sure I don't know where we'll sleep all these fine lads, but then I doubt they'll be staying long.'

I didn't get to keep them, then. That was what she was telling me. I supposed that shouldn't have surprised me. These men were trained soldiers, professional career army by the look of the way they carried themselves, not just conscript veterans like us. This was a loan from the Queen's Men, nothing more.

'No,' I said. 'They probably won't.'

Once the weapons were stowed, Ailsa distracted Anne with some chatter or other while the leader of the new men spoke to Rosie, and I saw a purse move from her hand to his. Then it was done, and she was back at Anne's side.

'Don't you go making eyes at her,' Rosie teased Ailsa, and she and Anne set off arm in arm together for an afternoon stroll while the weather was still fine.

I followed the leader of the soldiers into the storeroom, and a moment later Ailsa joined us.

'My name is Tomas Piety,' I said, holding out a hand to him.

He looked at it for a long moment, and he didn't move. 'So what?' he said.

'So he's the man you're here to serve.'

Ailsa's voice cracked like a whip in the dim room. She took a step toward the soldier and opened her belt pouch. Her fingers dipped inside and came out holding a thick piece of folded leather. She unfolded it and showed the man what was inside, and he visibly paled.

He saluted and clicked his heels, the great fool, right there in my storeroom.

'Captain Larn, ma'am. Queen's Own Third Regiment, sapper company,' he said.

'You're just Larn, here,' she said. 'No ranks, and no saluting. And *definitely* no heel clicking. Take the broomstick out of your arse, Captain. You're supposed to be a criminal.'

'Yes, ma'am,' he said.

'Ailsa,' she corrected him, and her voice changed all at once. 'Just Ailsa, sir, a simple barmaid and Mr Piety here's fancy woman, begging your pardon.'

Larn narrowed his eyes at me, and I showed him an emotionless smile. I was going to have to watch this one, I could tell.

'Let's try again,' I said. 'My name is Tomas Piety.'

I held out my hand once more, and I knew that if he didn't take it this time I was going to stab him.

Larn took my hand and gave it a brusque shake. 'Larn, sir,' he said.

I nodded. That was good. One step at a time.

'Get your men settled in, Larn,' I said. 'It's cramped, but we'll manage. It's no worse accommodation than we had at Abingon, I promise you.'

He looked at me then, and I saw something in his eyes that said I had made a start toward common ground between us. That was how it was done.

'That's good to know,' he said.

I nodded. 'Aye,' I said. 'You'll have had a long journey, I know. There's beer and brandy in the tavern, food in the kitchen, and no charge for my friends. Let your men rest. Tomorrow night there'll be work for you.'

Larn gave me a short nod and stalked out of the room. He wasn't quite marching, but it wasn't far off it.

I gave Ailsa a look. 'Are they all going to be like him? Because if they are, it'll be a fucking miracle if there isn't a fight before sunset.'

'No, I doubt it,' she said. 'His men are sappers, tunnellers and demolition experts. They are most likely as, ah, earthy, shall we say, as your own men are. Captain Larn is a professional commissioned officer and the second son of a minor noble in the capital, with nothing to inherit, everything to prove and no one to prove it to. He is what I believe you would call a pain in the arse.'

I snorted laughter. Hearing Ailsa speak like a barmaid in her aristocrat's voice struck me as funny, but I could see from the expression on her face that she wasn't joining me in amusement.

'Are you listening to me?' she went on. 'These are demolition experts, not rangers. You want to send them on a knife job, to infiltrate this factory of yours? That's *not* the right man for the right job, Tomas.'

'It's a job any soldier should be able to turn his hand to,' I argued. 'These are just Gutcutter scum, not army sentries. If they can't do this, then I won't trust them with the explosives. Anyway, I'm putting Cutter in charge – he'll see them right.'

'Captain Larn will take that extremely ill,' she cautioned me.

'Let him,' I said.

I already disliked Larn, but if he was any sort of soldier at all, then to my mind he would respect the chain of command and do what he was fucking told.

Chapter 43

I sent them out the next night. It seemed strange to send a raid off and not be with it, but then this wasn't Abingon any more. This was Ellinburg, and in Ellinburg I was a prince. Princes don't lead raiding parties, and they don't crawl under waterwheels in freezing temperatures to smash weaving looms with hammers.

The Stables had been different. I had been lacking men, then, and that had been personal. This was just business, and I had good men to take care of business for me. Cutter had briefed his crew in short, hard sentences that left even Captain Larn in no doubt as to who was in charge. Larn might be a career officer but Cutter was a professional murderer, and this sort of work was his bread and beer.

They headed out in a silent column, wearing leather but without their mail, wrapped in old cloaks that they could throw away before they went into the water. I saw Anne watching them leave from across the tavern, and once the door was closed behind them she came and sat with me.

'Rather them than us, I have to say,' she admitted. 'It's fucking freezing out there.'

It was, but sappers are hardy men and once they had done the job there would be no shortage of good cloth in the factory to dry themselves on and wrap around them until they got their warmth back. This late there would be no one there but Gutcutter guards, so their instructions were simple.

Kill everyone, break everything.

That would cripple the factory, enrage the guild of mercers, and turn the workers against the Gutcutters. That last was important, to my mind. From what Ailsa had told me, a large part of the Skanians' plan involved gathering the street-level support of the workers of Ellinburg. Put them out of work, and where would that leave their loyalties? Not with the Gutcutters, that was for certain.

I knew it would mean hardship for some, in the Wheels, but if everything went to plan that would only be for a short while. Anything can be endured for a little while, every soldier knows that, and they weren't my people. Not yet, anyway.

'Aye,' I agreed. 'It's harsh work, but it wants doing.'

'Does it?' Anne asked me. 'I thought we'd be done, once you had the Stink back.'

I didn't need Anne starting on me the way that Enaid had, but just then Fat Luka joined us at the table and showed Anne a wide smile.

'That's a lovely coat, Anne,' he said, nodding to her latest purchase, which hung draped around her shoulders.

It was, at that.

'What of it?'

He shrugged. 'Nothing, nothing. I'm just observing that you've bought yourself a very nice coat. You'll have bought that with money you earned in the Pious Men, I don't doubt. I saw that Rosie had a new necklace around her throat too, a fine piece of goldwork. I'd be surprised if she bought that for herself, or accepted it as a gift from anyone but you.'

Anne scowled and said nothing.

'That money you're spending comes from the business, and the more businesses we have, the more money we all make, isn't that right, Tomas?'

'It is,' I allowed.

Luka was right, of course, but I was surprised all the same.

If anyone starts disagreeing with me or questioning my orders, I want you to explain to them why they're wrong.

I had told Fat Luka that, back in the spring, but I'd never thought to see him argue the point with Bloody Anne. Luka was a good man, and he took his job very seriously. He could be persuasive, too, I knew that. Very persuasive indeed.

'I know,' Anne said, and swallowed her brandy. 'It's just . . . it's more violence, Tomas. More killing. I thought once we had your old streets back we'd be more like a ruling garrison than a fighting force, that's all.'

The Pious Men are businessmen, but you've turned them into soldiers.

'We will be,' I promised her. 'We will be, once Aditi is done. I can't share the city with her, Anne, not any more. You've seen what sort of businesses she runs, and the sort of men her backers have brought against us. The foreign witches.'

That was cheap of me, I knew. I hated having to manipulate Anne, of all people, but the crown's will had to be served and if that meant doing things that I didn't like, then so be it. That was the lighter of the two evils balanced in my hands. It was cheap of me, but it worked. Anne's jaw tightened at the very word, and she gave me a sharp nod.

When you lead, you have to know the levers that move a person.

Cutter and his men came back an hour before sunrise. I was waiting up, with Ailsa and Black Billy for company, and we had kept the fire burning high. I had thought it would be welcome, later. The others had long since gone to their beds, save for Stefan, who had the watch out back.

There was a soft rap on the door and Billy looked through the sliding hatch, then opened the lock and let them in. Cutter and his crew filed into the room, and I counted them all back safe. They were bedraggled and damp and frozen, and they smelled bad from the river water, but they were all back and that was the important thing. Captain Larn had a look on his face that told me he had done things that night that he had never done before.

A professional officer he might have been, and a sapper too, but I'd have bet good silver that he had never met a man quite like Cutter before. I knew that I hadn't. Sappers were brave men and they had done some of the harshest work, in Abingon. Undermining the walls to set charges, fighting in the stifling confines of narrow, crumbling tunnels, that was the stuff of nightmares.

But so was Cutter, to my mind.

The man seemed to have no emotions, no desires, no *soul*. I still had no idea what levers moved Cutter, but if you wanted someone killed quietly and without anyone seeing, then he was the right man for the job.

Black Billy locked the door behind them and they started stripping off sodden leather and ruined wool in front of the fire. They huddled around the warmth in fresh, dry blankets, shivering.

'It's done,' Cutter said, and he spat on the floor to show me what he thought of that.

'How many were they?' I asked.

Cutter frowned. 'Ten, twelve. Dunno. All dead. Smashed the looms like you said, broke the gears and spindles and threw the hammers in the river afterward. Place is fucked.'

That was all he had to say, and he made that plain by walking away to warm himself in front of the fire with the other men. The sappers made room for him there, and I noticed they left a respectful distance around him that spoke of a quiet, underlying fear. When *sappers* fear a man, that man is to be feared indeed.

I wondered again exactly where Cutter had come from, and how he had ended up in Jochan's crew.

Ailsa took my arm and ushered me through to the kitchen.

'You did well not to go with them,' she told me, using her own voice now that we were alone. 'You need to distance yourself now, Tomas, and you need to do it at once.'

I frowned at her. 'Distance myself? How do you mean that?'

'This is a war fought on two fronts,' she said. 'On the streets, yes, but also in the arena of politics. You have men enough to fight in the streets; you don't need to join them any more. What you *don't* have is anyone you can put in front of the governor and the nobility. You'll need to do that yourself.'

'How am I supposed to do that?' I asked. 'I don't move in their circles.'

'Then start,' she said. 'You're a rich man now, Tomas. You need to enter society.'

'Has Ellinburg *got* society?'

'Not particularly, but it's a place to begin. Governor Hauer is a bloated warthog of a creature who thinks he is thrice the man he is, but obviously his position has connections to Dannsburg. Attend a reception here, a ball there, at which I shall dazzle and you shall intrigue, and before you know it we will be in the capital and you will find the ears of more important men.'

'I see,' I said. 'And how would I go about that?'

'The important thing is that you remove yourself from the immediate business of the Pious Men before things start exploding all over the Wheels,' she said. 'There will be no coming back from that, if you or your family are implicated in the resulting carnage. We need to move fast. We will need a house, of course. Something grand, off Trader's Row. And obviously we shall have to marry.'

I stared at her in astonishment. *'Marry?'*

'Yes, of course,' she said. 'I am a lady of court, or at least I am when I choose to be. I can hardly be seen to entertain a provincial bachelor out of wedlock. If I were to produce a husband, though, with mysterious wealth and connections to industry, then yes. That would be entirely acceptable.'

'I see,' I said again. Marry Ailsa? The idea wasn't without its obvious charms, I had to admit, but I hadn't expected this. 'I need to think about this.'

'No, you don't,' she said. 'You just need to do it. We're *already* doing it, in fact. One of my representatives completed the lease of a suitable house yesterday. Servants are being hired, and furnishings purchased. The date of the wedding has been set.'

'Now wait a minute,' I started to say, but she cut me off with a look.

'I don't *have* a minute,' she said. 'I have the Queen's Warrant, Tomas, and you will *do what I tell you*. I can't keep those sappers forever, and we have to hit the Skanians soon. You *cannot* be implicated in that if you are to become a respectable member of society. Which you will.'

There was a first time for everything, I supposed.

Ailsa started to explain exactly what she meant about us getting married, about timing and about how people needed to be able to prove they had been in a certain place at a certain time, and I felt a grim smile form on my face.

Oh, yes, she was a Queen's Man all right. If I had ever met anyone more dangerous than Cutter, I realised, it was Ailsa.

Chapter 44

Three nights later all Hell broke loose.

We had no warning. The first I knew of anything wrong was when a man charged into the Tanner's Arms with his face bloodied and the coat on his back in scorched tatters.

'Gutcutters!' he shouted, and never mind that the tavern was full of customers. 'They're attacking the Chains!'

'Fuck!' I shouted, and rounded on Fat Luka. 'Where was our intelligence?'

Luka had gone pale in the face, and he had no answer to give me.

Bloody Anne was already on her feet and shouting orders. Black Billy and Simple Sam were throwing customers out as fast as they could while men ran around getting into their leather and mail and fetching their weapons. Captain Larn and his men I tasked with holding the Tanner's, and guarding the precious weapons they had brought with them. I had Luka stay there too, and Black Billy. Everyone else was armed and ready in record time.

'Jochan, you'll lead the counterattack,' I said.

He nodded, and I saw the savage gleam in his eye. He was the right man for the right job, I knew that. It was time to unleash the mad dog whether I liked it or not. Jochan picked eight men, Cutter included, and they charged out of the tavern and were on their way to the Chains no more than ten minutes after the alarm had been raised. I looked at Bloody Anne.

'You're with me, with young Billy and the rest,' I said. 'Larn, hold here at all costs.'

Ailsa grabbed my arm as I buckled the Weeping Women around my waist.

'What do you think you're doing?' she hissed at me. 'Distance yourself, I said.'

I gave her a hard look. 'Fuck. That.'

I wrenched my arm free and led my crew out into the biting cold.

'Chandler's Narrow?' Anne said, and the look on her face was almost pleading.

I nodded. 'Aye.'

It was their obvious second target, and of course Anne knew that. Her Rosie was there, and all the other women, with only Will the Wencher and Sir Eland to protect them.

We ran.

As we came up the steps of the narrow I could see we were too late. The front door of the stew was hanging open on one hinge and there was a body sprawled in the courtyard outside the closed chandler's shop, lying half in the light of the single lantern. He was no one we knew, so I simply stepped over him and went inside with Remorse and Mercy in my hands.

There was a stranger in the entrance, leaning on the counter with his hands clutching a wound in his side. I gave him Mercy without breaking stride. The sounds of fighting were coming from down the corridor. Bloody Anne kicked the door open with her daggers drawn.

Sir Eland had retreated to the parlour door, and there he was making his stand.

He hadn't had time to get into his armour when they attacked, of course, and he was standing there in his shirt and britches and bleeding from a dozen cuts, his long sword running scarlet in his hands. Four more men lay dead on the boards, but there must have been another six facing him. One man can hold a narrow space against many, until his strength deserts him or he is overcome by his wounds. It looked like Sir Eland was close to both of those things.

Just as Anne stormed into the corridor a crossbow bolt burst through the neck of one of the Gutcutters, and I heard a ratchet being cranked from behind Sir Eland as someone frantically reloaded. Anne and Mika and me waded into the rear of the Gutcutters while the rest of our crew spread out through the building, searching the bedrooms and killing every stranger they found.

Eland's face split into a savage grin when he saw us, and he attacked.

The hammer and the anvil, that was how we cleared the corridor in Chandler's Narrow. That's a terrible thing in such a confined space, and we butchered them until all of us were red to the elbows and it was done. The floor was littered with corpses, just like it had been at Messia.

'Rosie!' Anne shouted.

She shoved past Sir Eland and into the parlour, and now I could see the women he had been protecting. Rosie was at the front of them, with the crossbow in her hands. Three of the bodies on the floor had bolts in them, I noticed. Rosie had given a good account of herself while Eland held the door.

I clapped Sir Eland on the shoulder. 'You fought well,' I told him.

'I really did,' he said, and collapsed at my feet.

'Boss!' someone shouted from behind me.

'See to Eland,' I snapped at Anne, and turned back down the corridor.

Stefan led me up the stairs and into one of the bedrooms. There were more dead Gutcutters there, who I supposed had been looting the building, and two customers whom the Gutcutters had obviously killed themselves. I saw two of the women dead too, and that pained me. Will the Wencher was sprawled on the floor out cold with an ugly purple bruise on his temple. It looked like he had been trying to protect the girls who had been working when the Gutcutters attacked, but he had been unarmed at the time and had never stood a chance. I respected him for trying, all the same.

Billy the Boy was waiting in that room, and he had something for me.

I recognised the man at once. He wasn't wearing his purple shirt that night, but I recognised him anyway. This was Gregor, Luka's man in the Gutcutters. *My* man, bought and paid for. My man, who should have given us ample warning of this attack, and who had said nothing.

He was backed against the wall, and Billy was staring at him. I didn't know what Billy was doing, but it was plain to see that Gregor was pinned there as helpless as he would have been if four strong men had been holding him in place.

'You'll want this one alive,' Billy said, and as always he was right.

I walked slowly toward the helpless man, Remorse and Mercy dripping red in my sticky hands.

'Hello, Gregor,' I said, my voice taking on the tone that meant harsh justice was coming, and soon.

'Mr Piety, I can explain,' he said.

I nodded slowly, and turned and used Remorse to point at the half-naked woman lying dead on the floor with her guts hanging out of a ragged wound in her stomach. She couldn't have had more than twenty years to her.

'Explain that,' I said. 'Explain to me why two of my girls are lying dead because I didn't know there was going to be an attack on my stew. Explain to me why no *cunt* told me that.'

'I can't—' Gregor started, and I dropped and rammed Mercy through his calf hard enough to smash his shin bone.

He howled.

'Try again,' I said.

'He's got my son!' he gasped around the agony. 'I couldn't . . . he found out I was informing . . . I *couldn't*!'

Some people aren't your friends, however much you pay them. They're just scared to be your enemy. If someone finds a way to scare them more than you do, someone like Bloodhands, then you'll lose them. I knew that well enough.

'I grieve for those two women,' I said. 'I grieve for them, but I didn't know them. You're very lucky, very lucky indeed, that it wasn't a different woman who died here tonight. If Bloody Anne's woman had been killed, Gregor, I would have given you to her. I want you to understand what that would have meant. Bloody Anne would have started at your feet and filleted you like a fish, if you had got her Rosie killed. Do you understand me?'

He nodded, his teeth clenched against the fire in his ruined leg and the pain making flecks of spit bubble between his teeth.

'I don't think you do,' I said, and I smashed Remorse down hilt-first into his kneecap.

He shrieked that time, and a moment later Bloody Anne came through the door behind me.

'Tomas?' she asked me. 'What in Our Lady's name are you doing?'

'This is the man who almost got your Rosie killed tonight,' I said. 'This is the man who Luka pays to tell us what the Gutcutters are doing. This is the man who didn't. Fucking. Tell us.'

I swear to Our Lady that I heard Bloody Anne growl, low in her throat like an animal. I held up a hand to stay her.

'Is Sir Eland still alive?' I asked her.

'Aye,' she said. 'He's weak, but he'll live.'

'Good,' I said. 'I want you to do something for me, Bloody Anne. I want you to go downstairs and borrow Sir Eland's sword from him, and bring it up here to me. Will you do that for me?'

'Aye,' she said again, and left the room.

I looked Gregor in the eye, and I held his fearful stare. Remorse and Mercy are beautifully crafted weapons but they are shortswords, and they're not designed for taking a man's head off.

Sir Eland's heavy war sword, though, that was.

Chapter 45

It was a long night, and it didn't end with the dawn.

Will the Wencher came round in the end, and although he was groggy and having trouble standing I didn't think his skull was broken, so that was good. We put him to bed and left him weeping over his dead girls.

Anne didn't want to let Rosie out of her sight after what had happened, but there was too much to do for me to allow that. Besides, I knew Rosie could take better care of herself than Anne credited her for. Mika and me and a couple of other lads set to repairing the door, and I told Anne to patch up Sir Eland. She was no barber-surgeon like Doc Cordin, but in Abingon everyone had turned their hand as best they could. Anne could clean and stitch a wound well enough, when she had to. There was little enough love between the two of them, I knew, but he had fought well that night. Very well.

It seemed, to my mind, that when Sir Eland had found himself the only thing between those women and death, he might finally have become the hero he had always pretended to be. He had found his place in the world at last.

Billy the Boy was in charge of the big leather bag, and he seemed to take a pleasure in that. It was leaking, of course, but he guarded it well all the same. We held the house on Chandler's Narrow all through the long, tense night, waiting for another attack that didn't come. I wanted to go to the Golden Chains, but that was almost on Trader's Row and I couldn't get Ailsa's words out of my head.

You need to distance yourself, she had told me. *Remove yourself from the immediate business of the Pious Men before things start exploding.*

No blasting weapons had been used, so far as I knew, but a night that bloody was as good as the same thing. If my face were seen at the Chains I wouldn't be able to undo that. I had to put my faith in my brother, for all that the thought made me uneasy.

The sky was just beginning to get light when Borys came to the house and banged on the newly shored-up door. Mika brought him to me, and I looked at the weary expression on his face.

'What happened?' I asked him.

Borys had been with the crew Jochan had taken to the Chains, and he looked like he had seen hard fighting that night. His mail was rent in two places, and he had dried blood splattered over his face and a seeping cut on the back of his forearm.

'It's done, boss,' he said. 'We drove them off and secured the Chains. A lot of them got away, though. Too many.'

'Fuck,' I muttered. 'Where's my brother?'

'The City Guard are all over the Chains like flies on shit,' he said. 'Jochan slipped away back to the Tanner's, to see the lay of things.'

To find a bottle more likely, I suspected.

'Who's got the Chains, then?'

'Cutter, with enough men to hold it and enough coin in the strongbox to keep the Guard from looking at us too hard.'

I nodded, but I didn't like it. My brother put too much trust in Cutter, to my mind.

'Well and good,' I said. 'I'll meet him at the Tanner's, then. Come with me. You too, Anne. Billy.'

They nodded, and the four of us slipped out into the narrow and away down the steps. I left Mika in charge at the bawdy house for the time being, and we returned to the Tanner's Arms as the sun was rising over the riverside streets.

I found Jochan pacing the common room with a brandy bottle in his hand, as I had expected, but when he saw us he put it down and embraced me. That surprised me, I had to admit, but I didn't think it was a good sign. Ailsa was up already, or more likely she had been up all night again. She gave me a smile too, and a hug for appearance's sake. All the same I could tell she was furious with me for going off to fight with the crew.

Luka came over and clapped me on the shoulder. I shot him a hard look.

'Billy,' I said, 'give Luka the bag.'

Billy passed the wet sack over to Fat Luka, and I held his stare.

'Get one of your little spies over here,' I said, 'and have him take that up to the Wheels and dump it in Ma Aditi's breakfast porridge.'

'What's in it?' Luka asked, but I think he knew.

'Gregor's head,' I said.

Luka cleared his throat. 'Aye,' he said.

I could see he felt that he had failed me. That was harsh, I knew. This wasn't Luka's fault, for all that intelligence was his responsibility. I reached out and put a hand on his arm as he turned away.

'It's all right,' I said. 'They had his son. No amount of gold could have prevented this.'

Luka nodded, understanding, and went to send Cookpot out to rouse one of his spies from their bed. I wondered what Aditi would make of my little gift. Truth be told, I hoped she choked on it.

'How bad was it?' I asked Jochan.

He gave me a bleak look and took up his bottle again. 'Bad,' he said. 'We had to storm the place. Erik's dead, and six of the new lads with him.'

Erik had been a good man.

'In Our Lady's name,' I said.

'What the *fuck* has Our Lady got to do with it?' Jochan roared. He turned and hurled his bottle across the room to smash against the wall. 'You're no fucking priest of Our Lady, Tomas, not no more you ain't! All you want is more blood, and more fucking death, and it's never enough for you, is it? You've become a fucking priest of *bones*!'

He rounded on me with fury on his face, fists clenched and the battle shock shining bright in his mad, tear-filled eyes.

I hit him.

I hit my own little brother, who had once crawled weeping into my blankets and offered me the only thing he had to give. I've never been as good with my fists as Jochan was, but I caught him just right. My knuckles slammed into the tip of his prominent chin and sent him reeling backward into a table. He lost his balance and fell on his arse on the floor.

He started to cry.

I was suddenly aware of Captain Larn standing in the doorway to the storeroom, watching us. If he had said a single word right then I would have murdered him with my bare hands, but he was wise and he held his peace, and he turned away.

He had a brother too, I remembered.

An hour later they came at us again.

A runner reached me to say that Georg the baker's shop was on fire, and there were Gutcutters on the streets of the Stink.

I doubted that my little gift had reached Aditi's table by then, so I figured this must have been part of their original plan. It seemed the Gutcutters were throwing everything they had at us. We were all tired, and a lot of us were carrying wounds of some sort by then. I pressed Larn and his men into service.

'It's your watch,' I told him. 'My lads have been fighting all fucking night.'

Larn shook his head. 'We'll carry out planned missions but we're not brawling in the streets,' he said. 'It's too dangerous. If the City Guard were to capture even one of my men and find out who we really are, the implications could reach Dannsburg itself. That is out of the question. I have my orders.'

I wanted to hurt him, right then. I hadn't slept in far too long, and I couldn't get the image of the dead women at Chandler's Narrow out of my mind. Captain Larn was a donkey's shrivelled prick, to my mind, but I knew that I needed him, and more to the point I needed his men and their weapons and their expertise.

I took a deep breath and made myself nod. 'As you say,' I said. 'Hold here, then, and see that you hold fucking hard. Don't forget you're sitting on enough explosives to send half the Stink across the river. It wouldn't do for you to let anyone set fucking fire to the place.'

Larn's jaw tightened at that. All sappers have a healthy respect for the tools of their trade, I knew. He would see that no Gutcutter got inside the Tanner's with fire in their hands, if nothing else.

I went to Jochan and put an arm around his narrow shoulders. 'We have to do it again, brother,' I told him. 'I know you don't want to, but there it is.'

Jochan looked up at me, and the tears were gone from his eyes. There was a hatred there now, not for me but for the whole world, a burning bloodlust that I hadn't seen in a man's face since the walls of Abingon finally fell.

He nodded. 'Get my fucking axe.'

Chapter 46

We stormed onto the streets of the Stink, exhausted and wounded but fuelled by brandy and anger, and our memories. The Gutcutters were attacking the businesses I had sworn to protect, and I couldn't let that pass. Georg the baker was a good man. He had given me three treats for young Billy when I had only asked for one, and taken no coin for them. I have written that I wouldn't forget that, and I hadn't.

By the time we got there the shop was blazing, but Georg and his family were out in the street and safe and that was all that truly mattered. He gave me a stricken look as we marched past, and I stopped to speak to him.

'I will make this right,' I promised him, and I meant it. 'I'll bring harsh justice to those who did this, Pious Men justice, and I won't see you out of pocket for what has happened. There'll be a new shop for you, Georg, and all the coin you need to replace what you've lost.'

'Bless you, Mr Piety,' he said, bobbing his head in something that was almost a bow.

I was a prince, in Ellinburg, and, to my mind, a prince looks after his people. That was how I ruled my streets.

We turned a corner and now we had caught up with them. There were perhaps fifteen Gutcutters on Net Mender's Row, breaking windows and setting fires. This was the poorest part of the Stink, here and Fisher's Gate below it. The folk here had nothing worth taking from them, and I knew very well that the Gutcutters were making a deliberate effort to hurt those who had the least to spare. They wanted to make me look weak, I knew that, like the sort of man who would protect his gambling house and his stew and let his streets burn while he did it. They wanted to turn the very poorest of my people away from me, and in that I saw the hand of the Skanians. This plan had come from Bloodhands, not Aditi – I knew that much and I hated him for it. These people had done *nothing*!

I drew Remorse and raised her above my head to catch the dawn light.

'Company!' Bloody Anne bellowed at my side, in her sergeant's voice. 'Charge!'

We fell upon them like the wrath of Our Lady.

A glorious charge, in the light of the rising sun.

It sounds so grand.

It sounds like the stuff of legends, the act of heroes. Well, we were no heroes, and we were outnumbered and exhausted and hurt, and it was a fucking disaster.

These were fresh men we were facing, and there were just too many of them. Five minutes of battle was enough to tell me that we were going to lose. Two of the new lads were down already, and Jochan was spitting blood from where someone had caught him in the mouth with the pommel of their shortsword.

'This ain't good,' he hissed at me when we found ourselves fighting back to back in the middle of the street.

He was right, I had to allow. It wasn't.

'Anne!' I shouted over the clash of weapons. 'Break and scatter!'

'Break!' Anne roared at the top of her leather-lunged voice, a voice that carried better than mine ever would. Our Lady, but she was loud. 'Company, break and scatter!'

The men did as they were ordered, every man who could, disengaging from his fight and fleeing into the alleyways around us. I found myself in a dank, narrow space with Jochan and Anne and young Billy beside me, watching the rest of my crew split in five different directions as the Gutcutters looked about themselves in bewilderment. These were *my* streets, and I knew them blindfolded. I had been born here, after all, and although most of my crew hadn't been, they had had half a year and more to learn the lay of the area.

The Gutcutters might know the Wheels but they didn't know the

Stink, not like we did, and some of them were young. They weren't all veterans, that was for sure, while most of my crew were.

I was back in Messia, right then. I remembered the close fighting in narrow alleys where numbers counted for nothing, with daggers and the volleys of crossbows that left no one standing.

We had no crossbowmen that day, but we had Billy the Boy.

We caught some Gutcutters ahead of us in an alley between two crumbling warehouses. I pointed, and Billy raised his hands and sent a wash of flame down the alley that turned half of them into screaming, burning travesties of life. I had seen men burned like that before, in Abingon, and I knew there was no coming back from it.

We led them on a wild chase through the alleys of our own neighbourhood, splitting them into small groups to break up their strength. Jochan, Anne, Billy and me stayed together, harrying a group of Gutcutters down toward Fisher's Gate.

'Take them down the narrow to the river!' I shouted to Jochan as we headed into the warren of alleyways behind Hull Patcher's Row. 'Cut them off!'

We needn't have hurried, as it turned out. When we rounded the corner it was to see the remaining Gutcutters surrounded by thin, sick, angry people with barrel staves and kitchen knives in their hands. They looked at Jochan and me, these people of the Pious Men streets, and they fell on the intruders like a pack of wild animals.

When they were done, there was nothing left alive.

Was that shocking?

I supposed that it wasn't, in Our Lady's eyes. When people have run out of food, and hope and places to hide, do not be surprised if they have also run out of mercy.

When it was done I walked among them, and they bowed their heads and competed with one another to kiss my hand.

'Mr Piety,' someone said, and there was a sort of reverence in his voice. 'We don't want their sort down here, not on Pious Men streets we don't.'

Pious Men streets.

That was where we stood, and there could be no more argument about that.

Chapter 47

'It's enough, now,' Ailsa told me, after I had finally managed to get some sleep, and her tone brooked no more argument about *that*, either. 'No more, Tomas. No more violence, not with you involved. I had to spend a lot of money this morning to turn the Guard away from you and your streets.'

'Aye,' I said. 'I thank you for that, Ailsa, and I hear you about the violence. I remember the other things you said too. Did you mean them?'

We were in my room above the Tanner's Arms, where no one could overhear us, and this was Ailsa the Queen's Man I was speaking to now.

'Oh, I meant them,' she said. 'We will marry, and soon. This Godsday afternoon, in fact.'

I stared at her. 'That's only five days away.'

'Yes,' she said. 'Captain Larn and his men have to return to Dannsburg next week, and the timing must be right if you're not to be implicated in what they do.'

'I see,' I said. 'I'll need . . . everything.'

'Everything has been arranged,' she said. 'Your tailor has our clothes ready, and suitable outfits for Jochan and Anne and Enaid as well. Your family *have* to be there, and I assumed you would want Anne to be present as well.'

I nodded. She was right about my family having to be there, and Anne as well. This wasn't just a matter of propriety or respect, I knew. This was deadly serious now. It felt like I was back in the army again, with orders to follow and all the planning done for me. The decisions had already been made and the supplies arranged, and there were no choices left.

'She'll not wear a dress,' I cautioned Ailsa.

'I know,' she said, 'but Rosie will and I need her to be there as well. They will make a handsome couple, to bear witness to our union.'

Our union. I barely knew the woman, even now, and I had no way of telling if what little I did know of her was true. Ailsa was a master of the false face, after all.

'What about the Gutcutters?' I asked. 'If they attack again before Godsday . . .'

'Billy says they won't,' she said, 'and my spies and Luka's agree with him. You hurt them badly last night. Very badly indeed. Now let them wait on our wedding day, and *my* justice.'

Ailsa's justice was the queen's justice, and I knew that was even harsher than mine.

That was good. Once justice was done, all of the Wheels would be mine for the taking and the Skanians would be without their foot soldiers. Whether marrying Ailsa was good remained to be seen. She was certainly pleasing to the eye, but what use is that in a stranger?

'You said something about a house,' I reminded her.

'Would you like to see it? It wouldn't be proper for us to move in until we are married, but it's ready now.'

I paced over to the window and looked out into the street below. This was the Stink; this was my home. I'd lived all my life in Ellinburg save for the war years, and all of it in these streets. Even when I'd had money before, I had never felt a need to move up to the area around Trader's Row. That wasn't for people like me.

I tapped my fingers against the windowsill, and realised I was nervous. Not about the marriage, as I knew that didn't truly mean anything. I was nervous about moving, and about society, and how I wouldn't fit into it. I listened to Ailsa talk about this house she had arranged for us, but I wasn't paying attention to her words. I was listening to the sound of her voice, the way she spoke and how she turned her phrases. I didn't talk like that, and I couldn't see that I ever would. Oh, I could dress like a lord, and spend money like one too, but I would never sound like one. I had seen nobles in the army. Most of the senior officers had been nobility, after all. They didn't even walk like normal people.

And then of course there was my brother. I wondered if Ailsa had given any thought to how we were going to explain Jochan. Truth be told, I didn't care. If this let me do what needed to be done without being dragged off to see the widow afterward, then that was good.

I would worry about everything else later.

The house was splendid, I had to admit. We went to look at it the next day, Ailsa and me, with Jochan and Luka in tow. It was set on the far side of Trader's Row from the Stink, in the shade of the hills below the convent, and with a view of the magnificent Great Temple of All Gods where we were to be married. The house must have had thirty rooms, and all the ones we saw were elegantly furnished and decorated in what Ailsa told me were the latest fashions.

I wouldn't know.

'Fuck a nun, Tomas,' Jochan said, turning around and around in the hall and staring up at the gallery and the high ceiling above him. 'This is a fucking palace!'

'Aye,' I said. 'That it is.'

The servants were lined up in the hall to greet us, and if any of them thought anything of Jochan's language or of my accent they had the grace not to show it. That was wise of them, to my mind.

Ailsa had them introduce themselves to me, the steward and the housekeeper and the cook and the undercook and the valet, the lady's maid and the scullery maid and the three footmen and four household maids and two housemen. What I was supposed to do with them all I had no idea, but I assumed Ailsa would. I was paying more mind to how many guards I would need to put on the house, and where best to station them.

'I'll have a few of the lads come up,' Luka said, as though reading my mind.

I nodded. 'Have them bring crossbows, and plenty of bolts,' I said. 'The high windows have a good position over the approaches.'

Ailsa cleared her throat and gave me a look. 'Tomas,' she said.

'No,' I said. 'No, it's not that simple. Business doesn't stop just because I buy a fucking big house, Ailsa. We're still Pious Men.'

'We're getting *married*,' she said pointedly. 'You know what that means.'

'We are,' I agreed, 'and I hear you, Ailsa, but that won't change everything. Not in one day it won't, not in Ellinburg.'

Jochan frowned at me in obvious confusion, but I ignored him. He would see what she meant, in due course.

Everyone would see what she meant, on Godsday afternoon.

Chapter 48

Godsday came at last. My wedding day.

Pawl the tailor had come by in his cart the day before and delivered all the fine new clothes Ailsa had commissioned from him, and that Godsday morning I didn't hear confessions. We were all too busy getting ready. The place was packed, and almost everyone was there apart from Larn and his men, and Cutter. They had all gone off together the night before, and they hadn't come back.

Ailsa had been gradually changing her voice over the last week, slowly becoming less common, but she did it so smoothly that I didn't think a soul had noticed. The barmaid act was almost a distant memory now, and I suspected it would stay that way. I wanted to see her, to make sure everything was in hand, but that would have been ill luck on the morning of our wedding. I wouldn't see Ailsa again until we stood before the priest together, so all I could do was trust to Our Lady that everything was going to plan.

I was eating an early lunch with Jochan and Anne and Luka, all of us dressed up for the occasion in our magnificent new coats and doublets and britches. Even Billy the Boy looked like a young lord. He would be coming too, of course, as my adopted nephew. Everyone had to be there and, more importantly, to be *seen* to be there.

Aunt Enaid would be joining us later at the Great Temple of All Gods, and Brak with her. She had pitched a fit when I told her I was marrying Ailsa, and all but thrown me out of her house, but I had insisted that she come whether she liked it or not. I had insisted very

317

hard indeed. I couldn't tell her exactly why she had to be there, of course, but my aunt was no fool and eventually she got the general idea about what I meant. All my family and my top table *had* to be seen to be there around me. That was very, very important. Even Sir Eland was coming, to escort Rosie from Chandler's Narrow and give my retinue a bit of class.

Fat Luka was to play the ceremonial part of Ailsa's father, as he sadly couldn't be with us in person. Truth be told, I had no idea if her father was even still alive. She had said that he was and I accepted that, but I knew that it might well not be true. Still, Luka had learned the ceremony, as had I, and that was all that mattered.

It was hot in the common room with the fire burning and all of us wearing too many heavy clothes, and after I had eaten I took my glass of brandy and walked out the back to the stable yard to take a breath of air. Anne joined me a moment later.

'Congratulations on your wedding,' she said.

I looked sideways at her, unable to gauge whether she was making fun of me.

'I wanted you beside me, as my Closest Man,' I said. 'I hope you understand that I had to ask my brother. Appearances.'

'I know.'

'I'm sorry,' I said. 'I wanted it to be you.'

'I know,' she said again. 'Appreciate the thought.'

I nodded and put my hand on her shoulder for a moment. Anne grunted and swallowed her brandy.

'Do you know what you're doing?' she asked me.

'Yes,' I said. 'No.'

Bloody Anne put her empty glass down on the wall beside the back door and silently examined her fingernails, giving me the moment I needed.

'I know what I'm doing *today*,' I said. 'Today is vitally important, Anne. You'll see why, this afternoon. A thing will happen, this afternoon, and then you'll understand. After that, though? No. I don't think that I do.'

She sucked her teeth for a moment, then turned and spat over the wall into the stable yard. 'Didn't think so,' she said.

*

The air in the Great Temple of All Gods was thick with incense and overly hot from the sheer number of candles that burned in there. I knelt briefly to pay my respects before the shrine of Our Lady, one of many shrines in the temple to the great number of gods and goddesses that were held to in Ellinburg. That done, I made the long, echoing walk to join my brother in front of the altar. The worst of the incense was burning there, on that huge stone slab under the tall windows with their thousands of leaded, diamond-shaped panes. I looked briefly over Jochan's shoulder and out those windows. My eye was drawn to the shapes of the great waterwheels turning in the haze from the factories where the river ran along the eastern side of the city. From its vantage point on the hill at the end of Trader's Row, the Great Temple of All Gods commanded an impressive view of the Wheels.

That was going to be interesting.

A moment later the priest joined us there, a Father Goodman who, if the words of the Chandler's Narrow girls were to be believed, was nothing of the sort. There were several of the women among the wedding guests, in fact, sitting in the row of pews behind Anne and Rosie. Each had the bawd's knot proudly displayed on her shoulder, and I could see them looking at the priest and giggling to each other as they waited. Father Goodman was holding his face very still as he made a point of not looking at any of them.

'Is it time?' I asked him.

'Almost,' he said.

There was no clock in the temple, of course, and good clocks were a rare enough thing anyway. I fidgeted, wondering what was keeping Ailsa. This *had* to happen at the right time. Everything did, or we were done.

'Getting nervous?' Jochan asked me.

He winked and passed me his pocket flask. The priest wasn't looking so I took it and had a swift gulp of brandy. Truth be told, I *was* nervous, if not for the reasons Jochan thought. Ailsa would have understood, I knew, but no one else did yet. I wished I could have confided in my brother, and in Bloody Anne even more so, but it was out of the question. The fewer people who know a secret the more secret it stays, to

319

my mind, and there was too much at stake today to risk a wrong word or an overheard conversation anywhere.

I pressed the flask back into Jochan's hand and he pocketed it, and a moment later the doors at the far end of the huge temple opened and the drummers took up their beat.

Ailsa looked breathtaking as she stepped into the Great Temple in a magnificent dress of cream silk that set off her dusky brown complexion perfectly. At that moment I wished with all my heart that I were marrying her for real, in a way that would mean something between us as man and wife.

Her gown shimmered in the light of a thousand candles as she walked slowly down the nave with Fat Luka at her side. She stopped the requisite five paces away and dropped me a low curtsey. Jochan and I bowed respectfully to her in return, and again to Fat Luka, in his place as her father.

The forms obeyed, Luka brought her to my side in front of the priest who was waiting with his back to the altar. Luka and Jochan, my Closest Man, both took two steps backward, leaving us there together. We turned to face the priest, so that we were looking directly out the great windows behind the altar. The drums stopped all at once, leaving an echoing silence that seemed to portend what I and Ailsa alone knew was to come.

'Faithful of the gods,' the priest proclaimed, 'you have come together in this temple so that the most holy ones may seal and strengthen your love in the presence of the temple's ministry and this community. The gods most abundantly bless this love. Let them now bear witness so that you may assume the duties of marriage in mutual and lasting fidelity. And so, in the presence of the gods, I ask you to state your intentions unto one another.'

There was a flash of light somewhere over in the Wheels, and then an almighty bang shook the glass panes in the windows behind the altar. It sounded like a siege cannon firing, but I knew it wasn't. I knew *exactly* what it was.

It had begun, and right on time.

Father Goodman almost jumped out of his robes, and I could hear startled whispering among the congregation behind us.

'Thunder,' I muttered. 'Carry on.'

'Ailsa and Tomas, have you come here freely and without reservation to give yourselves to each other in marriage?' he asked.

'I have,' Ailsa said.

Another roar rattled the glass, and this time I could see flames rearing up in the distance as the first row of factories caught fire. A column of thick, choking smoke rose into the air and spread over the Wheels like the shadow of Our Lady.

This is what happens, I thought, *when you cross me.*

'I have,' I said.

'Will you love and honour each other as man and wife for the rest of your lives?'

'I will.'

Smoke boiled up from a dozen places in the Wheels as merciless fires tore through the timber-and-daub buildings. Another almighty explosion shook the lead in the stone mullions and a warehouse collapsed, sending clouds of dust over the water.

'I will,' I said.

'Will you accept children lovingly from the gods and bring them up according to the laws of the temple and the land?'

'I will.'

A factory exploded like the wrath of the gods. I could see beams and burning laths raining down onto the surrounding streets, spreading the fire and the carnage. Our Lady Herself walked those streets that Godsday afternoon, and Our Lady has no love in Her heart.

'I will.'

Again the priest tried to turn toward the windows.

'Thunder,' I hissed at him. 'Continue.'

The whispering in the congregation behind us was getting louder, more urgent. I shot Jochan a look over my shoulder, and I could see the grim smile form on his face as he worked out what was happening. His eyes gleamed in the light of the candles, mad with battle shock but seeming to welcome the thunder of the explosions, to embrace it as I did.

Another roar, and now the flames had reached the great waterwheels themselves. The wheels might have been wet but the gantries that held them weren't, and they burned. Oh, how they burned! I watched in fascination as the first wheel pitched forward and fell into the river in a great cloud of steam.

'Since . . . since it is your intention to enter into marriage,' Father Goodman stammered, 'join your hands, and declare your consent before the gods and this temple.'

I reached out and took Ailsa's hand in mine. 'I, Tomas,' I said, 'take you, Ailsa, to be my wife. I promise to be true to you in good times and in bad. I will love you and honour you for all the days of my life, for I am an honourable man, as no one here gathered will deny.'

A sixth explosion rocked the Wheels, sending another great cloud of fire and smoke up into the sky. A rippling line of smaller explosions followed, racing down the length of a street and tearing houses apart as they went. The warehouse at the end of the row went up with a roar, and I thought perhaps the fires had found the Gutcutters' hidden cache of blasting weapons. The flames spread in the wind like the wings of devils.

All was death and destruction, and Ailsa squeezed my hand.

'I, Ailsa, take you, Tomas, to be my husband. I promise to be true to you in good times and in bad. I will love you and honour you for all the days of my life, for I am an honourable woman, as no one here gathered will deny.'

The sounds of shouting could be heard through the thick stone walls of the temple now, of screams and running feet and ringing bells even up here on Trader's Row. A fire like that was to be feared indeed, and there would be panic spreading on the streets.

The smoke reached up to touch the heavens, and below it the Wheels had become Hell.

Father Goodman was white as a fresh linen shirt above his black robes now, but my brother held him pinned with a stare that brooked no argument.

'You have declared your consent before the temple,' the priest said, his voice trembling in fear of what was happening outside his walls. 'May the gods in their goodness strengthen your consent and fill you both with their blessings. What the gods have joined, no man may divide. May you both walk in righteousness until the end of your days.'

With that we were married, and all the Wheels burned bright as though in celebration of our union. It was done.

All of it.

Chapter 49

It was the custom in Ellinburg to hold a party after a wedding, and we held ours in the Tanner's Arms. The grand house could wait until tomorrow.

The common room was packed with all the Pious Men and everyone who could be spared from the businesses. So many people from the streets of the Stink came to pay their respects that Sam and Black Billy were serving beer out in the street. Ailsa wasn't working behind the bar, of course, not on her wedding day. Not ever again, in fact, now that she was to be a lady of society once more.

I was standing there laughing, with a full glass of brandy in my hand and my arm around my new wife's waist, surrounded by my family and my closest friends. My brother was making a fool of himself, drunkenly trying to give a speech while standing on a table and waving a bottle around in his hand.

That was when the City Guard arrived.

Captain Rogan himself shouldered his way into the Tanner's with ten armed and armoured men behind him and a look like murder on his face.

'Tomas Piety,' he growled.

I turned to face him, and so did the better part of two hundred other folk. I think that was when Rogan began to wonder if perhaps he had miscalculated.

'Captain Rogan, what a pleasure,' I said. 'Have you come to wish me well on my wedding day?'

'I've come to take you in,' he said. 'I mean it this time.'

'You want to take me to see the widow, Captain?' I asked, my voice quiet and flat but sounding loud in the sudden hush. 'On what charge?'

'What charge?' Rogan spat. 'Half the fucking Wheels is on fire! Blasting weapons were used; flashstones and the gods only know how many barrels of powder. There are whole streets gone! I can't let that pass, not in my city.'

'I'll allow that I'm sure you can't, Captain,' I said. 'However, I have spent the afternoon getting married, in the Great Temple of All Gods. The most reverend Father Goodman officiated, with all my family and friends around me as everyone will tell you. *All* of them. The Pious Men had no hand in this terrible thing, Captain, I can assure you of that. They were all at my wedding.'

Captain Rogan had ten men with him and I had half the Stink with me, and he couldn't prove a fucking thing. Everyone was quite drunk and in a celebratory mood, but a crowd that size with drink inside them can turn ugly very quickly, and an ugly crowd can fast become a riot. I knew no one there would see their prince dragged off in chains. Not on his wedding day they wouldn't.

No one.

I could see that Captain Rogan knew it too.

'One day, Piety,' he said. 'One day I'll fucking have you for this.'

'For something perhaps, Captain, but not for this,' I assured him.

That got a laugh from the crowd, and that laugh turned into some ugly looks pointed at the Guard. Rogan finally decided that he could count after all, and he ordered his men to withdraw. They turned and trooped back out of the Tanner's with jeers following them down the street, and Ailsa gave me an approving look. I raised my glass and bade Jochan continue with his speech.

I never did see Captain Larn and his men again, but the company of army sappers had served me well.

Ailsa and me moved into our splendid new house the next day, as man and wife.

Luka was directing the unpacking, not that either of us had brought much with us from the Tanner's Arms. We hadn't needed to. Ailsa must have been keeping Pawl the tailor and his 'prentice boy in full-time work all by herself, what with the amount of new clothes that were waiting for us in the chests and wardrobes in our bedrooms.

Two bedrooms, I had to accept that. Adjoining to be sure, for the sake of appearances, but we wouldn't be sharing a bed. That didn't surprise me, and truth be told, it didn't sadden me either. Ailsa was clever and fine to look at and she could be good company, when she chose to be, but I didn't know her. I still felt . . . something, I supposed, for her, but I couldn't rightly have said what.

Respect, I supposed. Fascination too, I won't lie about that, but it was the sort of fascination you might feel toward a lioness seen in a travelling menagerie. You admire the power and the grace of the lioness, yes, but no sane man would choose to lie down with her. I remembered thinking how she had the ruthlessness of a businessman and how much I admired that, but this had been something more than business.

Much more.

The attack on the Wheels had been Ailsa's idea, and timing it to coincide with our wedding had been Ailsa's plan. Captain Larn and his men had been utterly ruthless in their efficiency. They were professionals indeed. I had been able to see that even while I said my wedding vows.

The Wheels was a burned and blackened wasteland of devastation.

I had no idea how many had died in the explosions and the fires that resulted from them, but I had no doubt that it was a lot. Too many, to my mind. The blasts had been targeted at the factories and the businesses, and it had been Godsday when those places should have been empty. All the same, fires spread quickly in a timber-and-daub city like most of Ellinburg was, even in late winter. No businessman would have done that.

The butcher's bill for our wedding day was horrific.

I had finally got Ailsa alone late the previous night, after the party had died down and we retired upstairs to keep up the appearance of consummating our marriage. Once the bedroom door was closed she just smiled at me.

'The Skanians will have been hurt by that,' she said.

I would allow that they probably had been, but not so much as the people of the Wheels had. The Gutcutters were all but wiped out, from what Luka's spies told me, and that was good, but the slaughter had been on a scale larger than I had ever imagined.

The Pious Men are businessmen, but you've turned them into soldiers.

I remembered my aunt telling me that, and she had been right. And when specialists had been needed, and weapons that only the army should have, then real soldiers had been found, and they had been used.

This wasn't business, I knew that. I was still fighting a war, for all that it was now a hidden one.

I watched Ailsa, wearing her fine new kirtle as she bustled around our fine new house directing her new servants as though she had no cares in the world, and truth be told, I wasn't sorry that we wouldn't be sharing a bed that night.

There had been a time when I had thought I was falling in love with Ailsa, but I realised now that I had been wrong about that.

If we cannot stop this infiltration, there will be another war and we will lose. There will be another Abingon, right here in our own country.

Ailsa had told me that, and she had swayed me to her cause with those words, but when I thought of how the Wheels had looked that morning I wondered if perhaps Abingon hadn't followed me home after all.

I have written that those were my streets and my people, and that I wouldn't see them reduced to the smoking rubble and rotting corpses that we had left behind us in the south. Perhaps I had spared the Stink from that fate, but it seemed to me now that I had done so only at the cost of the Wheels.

I had brought the horrors of Abingon to the Wheels myself, in the service of the crown.

No, on balance I didn't think that I wanted to lie down with the lioness any more.

Not at all.

Late that evening, after we had dined and most of the servants had retired to wherever they went, Ailsa and me were sitting in our parlour. She called it the drawing room, for no reason that I understood, and apparently I was to call it that as well. I couldn't draw to save my life, and I only hoped that I wouldn't be expected to try.

A hearty fire crackled in the grate, and we were making light conversation about nothing in particular while I drank brandy and she worked at some embroidery. The big house was quiet around us, and I found that I was already missing the noise and rude camaraderie of the Tanner's Arms. I heard a thump on the front door and made to rise, but Ailsa lifted a hand.

'Footman,' she hissed at me. 'The steward will come to us if it is important.'

I nodded and sat back in my chair once more, feeling something of a fool. I had no idea how to live in a big house, with servants.

I heard one of the footmen open the door, then some muffled conversation coming from the hall. A minute or so later the parlour door opened and our steward coughed politely.

'Mr Piety, there is a gentleman here to see you. He gives his name as *Cutter*.'

The steward's tone in itself was enough to tell me what he thought of that. I hadn't seen Cutter since the day before the wedding, but I had a fair idea of where he had been. I nodded and waved a hand in what I thought was a suitably noble gesture.

'Show him in,' I said.

The steward coughed again, this time in a way that said I shouldn't be receiving the likes of Cutter in the parlour or drawing room or whatever the fuck it was called, not in front of my lady wife, but he had the grace to do as he was told.

Cutter strolled in with a big wooden box in his hands. 'Evening, boss,' he said.

I nodded to him. 'Cutter,' I said.

'Brought you a wedding gift, ain't I?' he said.

He dumped the box down on the finely inlaid table in front of us that held our drinks, and stood back with an expressionless look on his bearded face. I reached out and flicked back the hinged lid of the box.

'Well done,' I said. 'You'll forgive me if I don't mount it over the fireplace.'

Cutter snorted. 'I'll get rid of it,' he said. 'Just thought you'd want to see.'

'Aye,' I said. 'My thanks, Cutter. You've done well.'

'Right,' he said, and nodded. 'I'll feed it to the pigs then, now that you've seen it.'

He picked up his box again and left with it under his arm.

The box that contained Ma Aditi's head.

Chapter 50

With the Gutcutters crushed and Ma Aditi dead, all of eastern Ellinburg was mine. I would have been happier if someone had brought me Bloodhands' head, truth be told, but I settled for what I had.

No one could tell me what had happened to the Skanian leader who had pretended to be Aditi's second. Captain Larn and his men had done their evil work and vanished like wraiths the way sappers do, never to be seen again. Cutter had been the only one of my crew to go with them, the night before the wedding. I think he was the only one they respected, and after the raid on the factory that didn't surprise me. There was something about Cutter that could give nightmares to the hardest of men.

When I questioned him about it in the Tanner's Arms a few nights later, he just shrugged.

'We killed all that was there,' he said. 'Set the charges and hid. Lit them at the appointed time and legged it. If he ain't dead, then he weren't there.'

'Be happy, Tomas.' Jochan grinned at me. 'That fat boy-fucking whore-monger has finally been kicked across the river where she belongs.'

I nodded. 'Aye, she has at that,' I had to agree.

Ma Aditi wouldn't be mourned by anyone I knew, that was for sure. Least of all not by the boys I had rescued from the Stables.

They were doing well, so I heard, going to school and starting to learn the trades of their adopted parents. That was costing me a pretty penny but it was coin well spent, to my mind. In a way I felt like I was finally paying back an old debt, one I owed to my own little brother.

All the same there was great hardship in the Wheels, now. The Gutcutters were gone, or close as made no difference, but so were a lot of people's jobs and even their homes. Many more than I had bargained for.

I broke open my treasury in the back of the Tanner's to make that right. It was a simple thing now, with the Gutcutters gone, to ride into the Wheels like a conquering prince. I came with open hands and I offered protection, and jobs, and the coin to rebuild what had been taken away from them.

They received me like a saviour.

All but Old Kurt, anyway. I saw him, once, standing at the end of the alley between Dock Road and the river path. I had ridden past on my black mare with ten men around me, and I caught sight of the cunning man out of the corner of my eye. He lifted a dead rat by its tail and held it up toward me, and the look on his face was unreadable.

I didn't think Old Kurt regarded me as any kind of saviour at all, but to my mind that was a conversation we didn't need to have.

A month after the wedding, the Pious Men streets stretched from the bottom of the Stink up through the Wheels and across the docks beyond, all the way to the northern wall of the city. All of that was mine, now, and the people of those streets were *my* people.

I reckoned that might give Bloodhands and the Skanians something to think about.

Two months after my wedding, there was to be a spring ball held at the governor's hall. All the great and the good of Ellinburg were invited, which meant all of us who had lots of money. That was the definition of what passed for society in Ellinburg, after all. There was no way that Governor Hauer could overlook Ailsa and me when he was sending out his invitations, much as I was sure he would have liked to.

We arrived outside his hall in a grand carriage, wearing our most fashionable finery, where we were met by his footmen. The fact that our own 'footmen' that night were scarred and uncouth and heavily armed drew no comment, as though the governor's staff had been prepared in advance for what sort of guest I was. I dare say that they had been, at that.

We were ushered into the hall and this time I *was* allowed to climb the great staircase, with Ailsa on my arm in a beautiful dark-green gown with diamonds at her throat. There was no servant's stair now, not for Tomas Piety there wasn't.

Not any more.

I was a man of consequence, a wealthy businessman wed to a noble lady. Even though Ailsa was obviously of Alarian descent and no one seemed to have actually heard of her, she was unmistakably from an aristocratic Dannsburg family. That carried a lot of weight out here in the provinces.

That alone was enough to secure our place in what passed for Ellinburg society. The open secret that I was the owner of the Golden Chains didn't hurt, either. That had enough of my wealthy patrons looking sideways at me in fear that I might mention poppy resin in polite company to ensure that we were treated with nothing but cordiality and respect.

There was a ballroom on the main floor of the governor's hall. It was grand enough, to my eye, but obviously not to Ailsa's. She looked around herself with barely concealed disdain and wafted a feathered ivory fan in front of her face. That fan had cost more than a carpenter in the Stink made in a month.

'I see little here to entertain me, Tomas,' she said, her tone sounding bored and yet deliberately loud enough to be overheard. 'The Earl Lan Klasskoff throws such wonderful balls that I fear I am completely spoiled for the provinces.'

That may or may not have been the case, but her mention of upper-level Dannsburg aristocracy had the effect she had no doubt intended. Heads turned in our direction, eyebrows rising at the thought that this Alarian woman had attended social functions that they quite obviously hadn't been invited to.

'Perhaps we should retire to the Golden Chains,' I said.

I spoke the words she had given me in the carriage on the way from our house, which was all of ten minutes' walk away, but I felt a fool doing so. My voice was like a clod of wet earth dumped among the fine crystal of those others there. I would never learn to sound like a noble, I knew that much.

'Tomas, where are your manners? I'm sure our lord governor has a most splendid evening's entertainment planned for us,' Ailsa said, in a tone carefully crafted to mean the exact opposite.

I looked across the expanse of the ballroom and saw Governor Hauer glaring back at me with a murderous look on his face. He had a man standing at his right hand, a big scarred brute in a fine coat. I looked at that man, and I felt cold to my bones.

I caught the attention of a footman.

'The man standing with the governor,' I said. 'Do you have his name?'

'The gentleman's name is Klaus Vhent, sir,' the footman said.

The footman's tone said he thought I should have known that, but I ignored him.

I knew that man by another name.

I knew him as Bloodhands.

Tomas Piety will return in

PRIEST OF LIES

Acknowledgements

This book was a real departure for me, and I had a lot of help for which I am eternally grateful.

I'd like to thank my wonderful agent, Jennie Goloboy of Red Sofa Literary, and my equally wonderful editor Rebecca Brewer at Ace. I couldn't have done it without you.

As always thanks are due to my long-suffering beta readers, Nila and Chris, who have helped birth every one of my books so far.

I'd also like to thank Lisa L Spangenberg for her invaluable assistance with historical research and for putting up with my endless weird questions.

Thanks are also long overdue to Mark Williamson, who taught me everything I know about leadership – thank you, sir!

And always, of course, the biggest thanks are for Diane for putting up with me when I'm writing, and for everything else. Love you, hon.

Peter McLean lives in the UK, where he grew up studying martial arts and magic before beginning a twenty-five-year career in corporate IT systems. He is also the author of the Burned Man urban fantasy series.

Find him on Twitter (@PeteMC666), on Facebook (@PeterMcLeanAuthor) and at his website https://talonwraith.com.

JOEL F. HARRINGTON

The Faithful Executioner

Life and Death in the Sixteenth Century

VINTAGE BOOKS
London

Published by Vintage 2014

6 8 10 9 7 5

First published in Great Britain in 2013 by
The Bodley Head

Vintage
Random House, 20 Vauxhall Bridge Road,
London SW1V 2SA

www.vintage-books.co.uk

Addresses for companies within The Random House Group Limited can be
found at: www.randomhouse.co.uk/offices.htm

The Random House Group Limited Reg. No. 954009

A CIP catalogue record for this book
is available from the British Library

ISBN 9780099572664

Printed and bound in Great Britain by Clays Ltd, St Ives plc

For my father, John E. Harrington, Jr.

Contents

Maps   ix

Preface   xiii

1. THE APPRENTICE   3

2. THE JOURNEYMAN   45

3. THE MASTER   91

4. THE SAGE   137

5. THE HEALER   185

EPILOGUE   227

Notes   239

Acknowledgements   265

Index   269

Illustration Credits   285

THE WORLD OF FRANTZ SCHMIDT

North Sea

Baltic Sea

Elbe

Rhine

FRANCONIA

Danube

A l p s

SAXONY

Saale

Gräfenthal

Steinach

Hof

Kronach

Presseck

BOHEMIA

Lichtenfels

Main

Kulmbach

Weyer

(Bad) Staffelstein

Weismain

Main

Eschenau

Bayreuth

BAMBERG

Hollfeld

WÜRZBURG

F R A N C O N I A

Forchheim

Pegnitz

Betzenstein

Regnitz

Gräfenberg

Velden

Neustadt an
der Aisch

Herzogenaurach

Pegnitz

Hersbruck

Langenzenn

Fürth

Lauf

MARGRAVATE OF
BRANDENBERG-
ANSBACH

NUREMBERG

Altdorf bei
Nürnberg

Amberg

Ansbach

Schwabach

Feucht

Pyrbaum

UPPER
PALATINATE

Lichtenau

Roth

Heilbronn

Regnitz

Sulzbürg

Hilpoltstein

Heideck

Altmühl

Danube

Scale of miles

10   20   30   40

DUCHY OF BAVARIA

Map by Gene Thorp

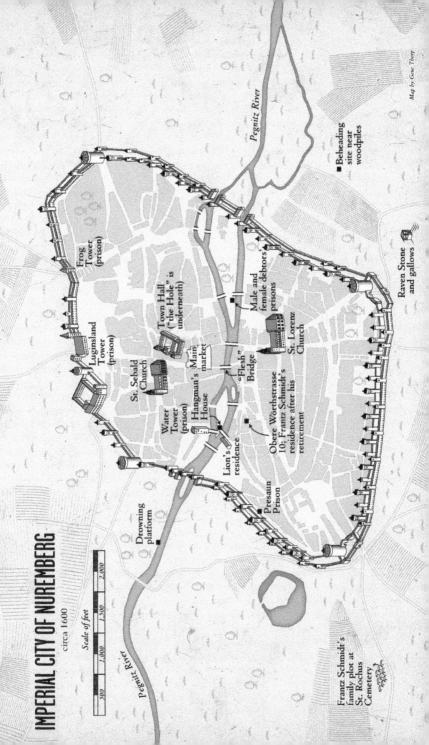

IMPERIAL CITY OF NUREMBERG

circa 1600

Scale of feet

500   1,000   1,500   2,000

Pegnitz River

Drowning platform

Frog Tower (prison)

Luginsland Tower (prison)

St. Sebald Church

Water Tower (prison)

Town Hall ("the Hole" is underneath)

Hangman's House

Main market

Lion's residence

"Flesh" Bridge

Male and female debtors' prisons

St. Lorenz Church

Obere Wörthstrasse 10; Frantz Schmidt's residence after his retirement

Presaun Prison

Pegnitz River

Beheading site near woodpiles

Raven Stone and gallows

Franz Schmidt's family plot at St. Rochus Cemetery

Map by Gene Thorp

Preface

Every useful person is respectable.

—Julius Krautz, executioner of Berlin (1889)[1]

The sun has barely cleared the horizon when a crowd begins to form on the chilly Thursday morning of 13 November 1617. Yet another public execution awaits the free city of Nuremberg, renowned throughout Europe as a bastion of law and order, and spectators from all ranks of society are eager to secure a good viewing spot before the main event gets under way. Vendors have already set up makeshift stands to hawk Nuremberger sausages, fermented cabbage, and salted herrings, lining the entire route of the death procession, from the town hall to the gallows just outside the city walls. Other adults and children roam the crowd, selling bottles of beer and wine. By midmorning the throng has grown to a few thousand spectators and the dozen or so town constables on duty, known as archers, are visibly uneasy at the prospect of maintaining order. Drunken young men jostle one another and grow restless, filling the air with their ribald ditties. Pungent wafts of vomit and urine mix with the fragrant smoke from grilling sausages and roasting chestnuts.

Rumours about the condemned prisoner, traditionally referred to as the "poor sinner", circulate through the crowd at a dizzying pace. The basics are quickly conveyed: his name is Georg Karl Lambrecht, age thirty, formerly of the Franconian village of Mainberheim. Though he had trained and worked for many years as a miller, he most recently toiled in the more menial position of wine carrier. Everyone knows that he has been sentenced to death for counterfeiting prolific amounts of gold and silver coins with his brother and other nefarious figures, all of whom successfully got away. More intriguing to the anxious spectators, he is widely reputed to be skilled in magic, having divorced his first wife for adultery and "whored around the countryside" with an infamous sorceress known as the Iron Biter. On one recent occasion, according to several witnesses, Lambrecht threw a black hen in the air and cried, "See, devil, you have here your morsel, now give me mine!" upon which he cursed to death one of his many enemies. His late mother is also rumoured to have been a witch and his father was long ago hanged as a thief, thereby validating the prison chaplain's assessment that "the apple did not fall far from the tree with this one."

Shortly before noon, the bells of nearby Saint Sebaldus begin to ring solemnly, joined in quick succession by Our Lady's Church on the main market, then Saint Lorenz on the other side of the Pegnitz River. Within a few minutes, the poor sinner is led out of a side door of the stately town hall, his ankles shackled and wrists bound tightly with sturdy rope. Johannes Hagendorn, one of the criminal court's two chaplains, later writes in his journal that at this moment Lambrecht turns to him and fervently asks for forgiveness from his many sins. He also makes one last futile plea to be dispatched with a sword stroke to the neck, a quicker and more honourable death than being burned alive, the prescribed punishment for counterfeiting. His request denied, Lambrecht is expertly shepherded to the adjoining market square by the city's longtime executioner, Frantz Schmidt. From there a slow procession of local dignitaries moves towards the site of execution, a mile away. The judge of the "blood court", dressed in red and black patrician finery, leads the solemn cortege on horseback, followed on foot by the condemned man, two chaplains, and the executioner, better known to residents, like all men of his craft, by the honorific of Meister (Master) Frantz. Behind him walk darkly clad representatives from the Nuremberg city council, scions of the city's wealthy leading families, followed by the heads of several local craftsmen's guilds, thus signalling a genuinely civic occasion. As he passes the spectators lining his way, the visibly weeping Lambrecht calls out blessings to those he recognises, asking their pardon. Upon exiting the city's formidable walls through the southern Ladies' Gate (Frauentor), the procession approaches its destination: a solitary raised platform popularly known as the Raven Stone, in reference to the birds that come to feast on the corpses left to rot after execution. The poor sinner climbs a few stone steps with the executioner and turns to address the crowd from the platform, unable to avoid a glance at the neighbouring gallows. He makes one more public confession and a plea for divine forgiveness, then drops to his knees and recites the Lord's Prayer, the chaplain murmuring words of consolation in his ear.

Upon the prayer's conclusion, Meister Frantz sits Lambrecht down in the "judgment chair" and drapes a fine silk cord around his neck so that he might be discreetly strangled before being set on fire – a final act of mercy on the part of the executioner. He also binds the condemned tightly with a chain around his chest, then hangs a small sack of gunpowder from his neck and places wreaths covered in pitch between Lambrecht's arms and legs, all designed to accelerate the body's burning. The chaplain continues to pray with the poor sinner while Meister Frantz adds several bushels of straw around the chair, fixing them in place with small pegs. Just before the executioner tosses a torch at Lambrecht's feet, his assistant surreptitiously tightens the cord around the condemned man's neck, presumably garroting him to death. Once the flames begin licking the chair, however, it is immediately clear that this effort has been botched, with the condemned man pathetically crying out, "Lord, into your hands I commend my spirit." As the fire burns on, there are a few more shrieks of "Lord Jesus, take my spirit," then only the crackles of the flames are heard and the stench of burnt flesh fills the air. Later that day, Chaplain Hagendorn, now fully sympathetic, confides to his journal, based on the clear evidence of pious contrition at the end, "I have no doubt whatsoever that he came through this terrible and pitiful death to eternal life and has become a child and heir of eternal life."[2]

One outcast departs this life; another remains behind, sweeping up his victim's charred bones and embers. Professional killers like Frantz Schmidt have long been feared, despised, and even pitied, but rarely considered as genuine individuals, capable – or worthy – of being known to posterity. But what is going through the mind of this sixty-three-year-old veteran executioner as he brushes clean the stone where the convicted man's last gasps of desperate piety so recently pierced the thickening smoke? Certainly not any doubts about Lambrecht's guilt, which he himself helped establish during two lengthy interrogations of the accused, as well as the depositions of several witnesses – not to mention the counterfeiting tools and other incontrovertible evidence found in the condemned's residence. Is Meister Frantz perhaps re-envisioning and ruing the bungled strangulation that made such an embarrassing scene possible? Has his professional pride been wounded, his reputation besmirched? Or has he simply been hardened to insensitivity by nearly five decades in what everyone considered a singularly unsavoury occupation?[3]

Normally, answering any of these questions would remain a speculative endeavour, a guessing game without any chance of a satisfactory resolution. But in the case of Meister Frantz Schmidt of Nuremberg, we have a rare and distinct advantage. Like his chaplain colleague, Meister Frantz kept a personal journal of the executions and other criminal punishments he administered throughout his exceptionally long career. This remarkable document covers forty-five years, from Schmidt's first execution at the age of nineteen, in 1573, to his retirement in 1618. As it turned out, his gruesome dispatch of the penitent counterfeiter would be his final execution, the culmination of a career during which, by his own estimate, he personally killed 394 people and flogged or disfigured hundreds more.

So what was going through Meister Frantz's mind? Astonishingly, although his journal has in fact long been well known to historians of early modern Germany (c.1500 to 1800), very few, if any, readers have attempted to answer this question. At least five manuscript copies of the since-lost original circulated privately during the nearly two centuries after its author's death, with printed versions appearing in 1801 and 1913. An abridged English translation of the 1913 edition appeared in 1928, followed by mere facsimiles of the two German editions, both issued in small print runs.[4]

My own first encounter with Meister Frantz's journal occurred some years ago in the local history corner of a Nuremberg bookshop. While considerably less dramatic than, say, the discovery of a long-lost manuscript in a sealed vault that opens only after you solve a series of ancient riddles, it was nonetheless a eureka moment. The very idea that a professional executioner from four centuries ago might be fully literate, let alone somehow motivated to record his own thoughts and deeds in this manner, struck me as a fascinating prospect. How could it be that no one to this date had made significant use of this remarkable source to reconstruct this man's life and the world in which he lived? Here, consigned to a back shelf as a mere antiquarian curiosity, was an amazing story begging to be told.

I purchased the slim volume, took it home to read, and made a few important discoveries. First, Frantz Schmidt was by no means unique among executioners in his self-chronicling – although he remains unsurpassed for his era in both the length of time covered and the detail conveyed in most entries. While the majority of German men in his day remained illiterate, some contemporary executioners could write well enough to keep simple, formulaic execution lists, a few of which have even survived to the present day.[5] By the beginning of the modern era, the executioner's memoir had become a popular genre in itself, the most famous being the chronicles of the Sanson family, an executioner dynasty that presided in Paris from the mid-seventeenth to the mid-nineteenth centuries. The subsequent decline of capital punishment across Europe prompted a final wave of published reminiscences from "last executioners", some of which became bestsellers.[6]

Still, the continued obscurity of this fascinating figure remained puzzling until I examined the journal more closely and made a second, more daunting discovery. Although Meister Frantz is undeniably riveting in his portrayals of the diverse criminals he encounters, he consistently keeps himself tantalisingly in the background – a shadowy and taciturn observer despite his vital role in many of the events he describes. In this respect, the journal itself reads less as a diary in any modern sense and more as a chronicle of a professional life. Its 621 entries, ranging in length from a few lines to a few pages, are indeed written in chronological order, but in the form of two lists, the first comprising all Meister Frantz's capital punishments from 1573 on, and the second covering all the corporal punishments he administered from 1578 on – floggings, brandings, and the chopping of fingers, ears, and tongues. Each entry contains the name, profession, and origin of the culprit, as well as the crimes in question, the form of punishment, and where it was administered. Over time, Meister Frantz adds more background information about the culprits and their victims, more details about the immediate crimes and previous offences, and occasionally fuller descriptions of the last hours or moments before an execution. In a few dozen longer entries, he provides still more information about the deviants in question and even re-creates certain key scenes, with colourful descriptions and occasional lines of dialogue.

Many historians would not even consider Schmidt's journal a proper "ego document" – the kind of source, such as a diary or personal correspondence, that scholars look to for evidence of a person's thoughts, feelings, and interior struggles. There are no accounts of moral crises brought on by long sessions of torture, no lengthy philosophical discourses about justice, not even any pithy speculations on the meaning of life. In fact, there are strikingly few personal references at all. In over forty-five years of entries, Schmidt only writes the words "I" and "my" fifteen times each and "me" only once. The majority of instances refer to professional milestones (e.g. *my first execution with the sword*), without expressing an opinion or emotion, and the remainder appear as random insertions (e.g. *I whipped her out of town three years ago*).[7] Significantly, *my father* and *my brother-in-law*, both fellow executioners, each appear three times in a professional context. There is no mention at all of Schmidt's wife, seven children, or numerous associates – not entirely unsurprising, given the focus of the journal. But there is also no acknowledgement of kinship or affinity with any of the crime victims or perpetrators, many of whom he demonstrably knew personally, including his other brother-in-law, a notorious bandit.[8] He makes no explicit religious statements and in general uses moralising language sparingly. How could such a studiously impersonal document provide any meaningful insight into the life and thoughts of its author? The ultimate reason why one had yet made use of Meister Frantz's journal as a biographical resource, I decided, might just be that there simply wasn't enough of Meister Frantz in it.[9]

My project too would have been doomed at the outset were it not for two important breakthroughs. The first occurred a few years after my initial encounter with Meister Frantz when, while working on a different project, I discovered in the city library (Stadtbibliothek) of Nuremberg an older and more accurate manuscript copy of the journal itself than any previously used. Whereas the editors of the two previous published editions relied on late-seventeenth-century copies, both modi- ʼd by baroque copyists for greater readability, this biographical portrait ʼ on a copy completed in 1634, the year of Schmidt's death.[10] Some ʼariations introduced in the later versions are minor: different spelling of certain words, numbering of the entries for easier reference, slightly divergent dates in a few places, syntactical improvements, and the insertion of punctuation in the later versions. (There is no punctuation in the 1634 version, and it's probable that Schmidt, like most writers of his educational background, used none in the original journal.) Many discrepancies, however, are significant. Some versions omit entire sentences and add completely new lines of moralising language, as well as various details culled from Nuremberg's city chronicles and criminal records. These later pastiche versions rendered the journal more appealing to the bourgeoisie of eighteenth-century Nuremberg, among whom these limited-edition manuscripts circulated privately. But at the same time they often robbed the journal of Meister Frantz's distinctive voice, and thus his perspective. In later editions, the final five years in particular diverge radically from the 1634 version, leaving out several entries altogether and omitting the names of most perpetrators, as well as details of their crimes. In all, at least a quarter of the older text varies to some degree from later versions.

The most interesting – and useful – difference appears at the very outset of the journal itself. In the 1801 and 1913 published editions, Frantz inscribes his *work begun for my father in Bamberg in the year 1573*. In the version used for this book, the young executioner instead writes *Anno Christi 1573rd Year* [*sic*]: *Here follows which persons I executed for my father, Heinrich Schmidt, in Bamberg.* The distinction, at first sight a subtle one, in fact sheds light on the most elusive question about the entire journal: why was Frantz Schmidt writing it in the first place? The wording in the later copies suggests more of a paternal imperative than a dedication, with the elder Schmidt dictating that his journeyman son begin building the equivalent of a professional curriculum vitae for prospective employers. But the older version of the journal specifies that it was the first five years of executions, not the writing itself, that Frantz undertook for his executioner father (also mentioned here by name). In fact, as a later reference in this version makes clear, the journal itself was begun not in 1573 but in 1578, the year of Schmidt's appointment in Nuremberg. Looking back, twenty-four-year-old Frantz can only remember his previous five years of executions and omits virtually all his corporal punishments, since *I no longer know which persons I so punished in Bamberg.*

This discovery immediately prompted several new questions, most notably, if Frantz Schmidt did not start writing for his father in 1573, who was he in fact writing for and why? It's doubtful that he intended the journal for subsequent publication, particularly given the sketchiness of most entries for the first twenty years. Perhaps he imagined that

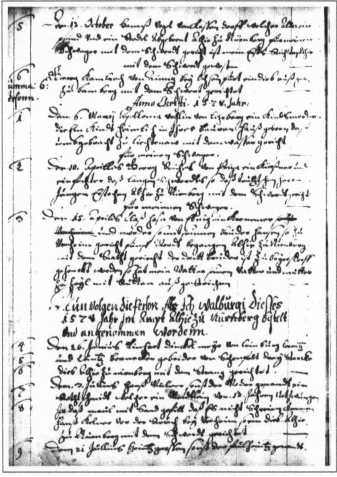

A page from the 1634 copy of Frantz Schmidt's journal, the oldest extant version, located in the Stadtbibliothek Nürnberg. The enumeration of executions in the left margin was likely added by the copyist.

eventually it might be circulated in manuscript copies – as was indeed the case – but again, the earlier years are far less detailed (or interesting) than the city's other competing chronicles and overall read more like a ledger than a genuine literary attempt. Possibly the journal was never meant for anyone but the author himself, but this raises the question of why he started it when he did, at the time of his appointment as Nuremberg's full-time executioner in 1578, as well as why he steadfastly avoided any mention of private matters.

The second key that unlocked the mystery of Frantz Schmidt's journal is a moving document from his later years, now preserved in the Austrian State Archives in Vienna. After spending his entire life in a profession that was widely despised and even officially designated as "dishonourable", the seventy-year-old retired executioner made a late appeal to the emperor Ferdinand II to restore his family's good name. The petition was clearly formulated and penned by a professional notary, but the sentiments expressed are highly personal, even surprisingly intimate at times. Most revealingly, the elderly Frantz recounts the story of how his family unjustly fell into their infamous profession as well as his lifelong determination to avoid the same fate for his own sons. The thirteen-page document includes the names of several prominent citizens healed by Schmidt, who maintained a sideline as a medical consultant and practitioner – a surprisingly common occupation among executioners – as well as an enthusiastic endorsement from the Nuremberg city council, his employer for four decades. His long service to the city and personal propriety, the councillors declared, had been "exemplary", and they urged the emperor to restore his honour.

Could it be that the council itself had been the journal's intended audience all along, with Schmidt's quest to have his honour restored the guiding motive? He might have been the first, but hardly the last German executioner to adopt this strategy.[11] Rereading Meister Frantz's journal entries with this foundational motive in mind, I began to see a thinking and feeling author step slowly from the shadows of what had initially seemed an impersonal account. Thematic and linguistic patterns emerged; discrepancies and shifts in style grew more significant; an evolving self-identity became ever more pronounced. Here was an author utterly uninterested in self-revelation, yet one who inadvertently exposed his thinking and passions in virtually every entry. The very subjectivity that later copyists had unintentionally expunged became a gateway, revealing the author's antipathies, fears, prejudices, and ideals. Well-defined notions of cruelty, justice, duty, honour, and personal responsibility emerged and, over the course of the journal, converged to provide the outline of a coherent worldview. The journal itself took on a moral significance, its very composition a testament to the author's unwavering lifelong campaign for respectability.

The complex individual who emerges from this reading, supplemented by extensive archival sources, is a far cry from the stereotypical emotionless brute of popular fiction. Instead we encounter a pious, abstemious family man who is nonetheless excluded from the respectable society he serves, forced to spend most of his time with convicted criminals and the thuggish guards who assist him.[12] Though effectively isolated, the longtime executioner paradoxically exhibits a high degree of social intelligence, a capacity that makes possible both his brilliant professional success and his gradual reversal of the popular stigma oppressing him. Thanks to the broad chronological scope of the journal, we witness the literary and philosophical evolution of a minimally educated autodidact, whose journal entries progress from laconic summaries of his criminal encounters to virtual short stories and in the process reveal ever more of their author's innate curiosity – particularly on medical matters – as well as his moral cosmos. Despite his repeated exposure to the entire gamut of human cruelty and his own regular administering of horrific violence, this apparently genuinely religious man seems never to waver in his belief in ultimate forgiveness and redemption for those who seek it. Above all, we vicariously experience a professional and private life dually animated by a man's bitter resentment of past and present injustices as well as by his unshakeable hope for the future.

The book that has resulted from all of this digging contains two intertwining stories. The first is that of the man Frantz Schmidt. Starting with his birth into an executioner family in 1554, we follow him through a youthful apprenticeship at his father's side to his independent travels as a journeyman executioner. Moving back and forth between his own words (always in italics) and a re-creation of his historical world, we become familiar with the necessary skills of a professional executioner, his uneasy social status, and Frantz's early efforts at self-advancement. As he matures, we encounter the legal and social structures of early modern Nuremberg, the middle-aged executioner's relentless attempts to advance socially and professionally, and his concepts of justice, order, and respectability. We also meet his new wife and growing family as well as a motley assortment of criminals and law enforcement associates. Finally we witness the blossoming in later life of two increasingly dominant identities – moralist and healer – and in the process catch a glimpse of the inner life of this professional torturer and killer. The accomplishments of his final years are rendered bittersweet by disappointment and personal tragedy, but the steadfastness of his solitary quest for honour remains in itself an object of wonder and even admiration.

At the heart of this book lies another narrative, a reflection about human nature and social progress, if there are such things. Which assumptions and sensibilities made the judicial violence that Meister Frantz regularly administered – torture and public execution – acceptable to him and his contemporaries yet repugnant to us in our own times? How and why do such mental and social structures take hold, and how do they change? Certainly early modern Europeans did not enjoy any

The only fully reliable portrait of Frantz Schmidt that has survived, drawn in the margin of a legal volume of capital sentences by a Nuremberg court notary with artistic aspirations. At the time of this event, the beheading of Hans Fröschel on 18 May 1591, Meister Frantz was about thirty-seven years old.

monopoly on human violence or cruelty, nor on individual or collective retribution. Judged purely by homicide rates, the world of Frantz Schmidt was less violent than that of his medieval forebears but more violent than the modern United States (no mean feat).[13] On the other hand, measured by state violence, the higher rates of capital punishment and frequent military pillaging of all premodern societies pale in comparison to the total wars, political purges, and genocides of the twentieth century. The continuing worldwide practice of judicial torture and public executions alone underscores our ongoing affinity with "more primitive" past societies, as well as the tenuousness of the social transformation that allegedly separates us from them. Is capital punishment truly destined to become extinct everywhere, or is the human drive towards retribution too deeply rooted in the very fibre of our being?

What was Meister Frantz thinking? Whatever we find out, the godly executioner from Nuremberg will always remain a simultaneously alien and familiar figure. It's hard enough to understand ourselves and those most intimate to us, let alone a career killer from a distant time and place. As in all life stories, the revelations from his journal and other historical sources inevitably leave many unanswered – and probably unanswerable – questions. In the only contemporary drawing of Schmidt that can be deemed reliable, the steadfast executioner is – fittingly – turned away from us. Yet in making the effort to understand Frantz Schmidt and his world, we experience more self-recognition and empathy than we might have expected when engaging with this professional torturer and executioner. The story of Meister Frantz of Nuremberg is in many ways a captivating tale from a faraway era, but it is also a story for our time and our world.

Notes on Usage

Quotations from Frantz Schmidt

All direct quotations from Schmidt are set in italics and are my own translations, based on the 1634 copy of his journal and the 1624 petition for restitution of honour.

Names

Spelling was not yet standardised during the early modern period and Meister Frantz, like other writers, often spelled the same proper names differently, sometimes within the same passage. I have modernised the names of towns and other locations as well as most personal first names; family names have retained their early modern orthography, albeit in a standardised form for the sake of clarity. I have also kept female surnames in their early modern form, typified by an occasional vowel shift in the penultimate syllable and the invariable *-in* ending. For example, Georg Widmann's wife would be known as Margaretha Widmänin or Widmenin, while Hans Krieger's daughter becomes Magdalena Kriegerin or Kriegin, and so forth. Popular nicknames and aliases have been translated from contemporary street slang (known as *Rotwelsch*) to their closest modern U.S. equivalents, thus permitting some artistic licence on my part.

Currency

There were many local, imperial, and foreign coins in circulation during the early modern era in German lands, and currency exchange values also naturally varied over time. For the purposes of scope and comparison, I have provided the approximate equivalent of each sum in florins (or gulden, abbreviated *fl.*), the largest denomination. A household servant or municipal guard during this period might earn ten to fifteen gulden per year, a schoolteacher fifty, and a municipal jurist three or four hundred. A loaf of bread cost four pence (0.03 fl.), a quart of wine about thirty pence (0.25 fl.), and a year's rent in a slum dwelling about 6 fl. The approximate equivalencies are as follows:

1 gulden (fl.) = 0.85 thaler (th.) = 4 "old" pounds (lb.) = 15 batzen (Bz.) = 20 schilling (sch.) = 60 kreuzer (kr.) = 120 pence (d.) = 240 heller (H.).

Dates

The Gregorian calendar was introduced in German Catholic lands on 21 December 1582, but not adopted in most Protestant states until

1 March 1700, or later. As a result, the intervening years saw a discrepancy of ten days (later eleven) between Protestant territories such as Nuremberg and Catholic states such as the prince-bishopric of Bamberg (e.g. 13 June 1634 in Nuremberg was 23 June 1634 in Bamberg. Contemporaries thus sometimes wrote 13/23 June 1634). Throughout the book I rely on Nuremberg's calendar, where (as in most places by this time) the year began on 1 January.

THE FAITHFUL
EXECUTIONER

1

THE APPRENTICE

A father who does not arrange for his son to receive the best education at the earliest age is neither a man himself nor has any fellowship with human nature.

—Desiderius Erasmus, "On the Education of Children" (1529)[1]

A man's value and reputation depend on his heart and his resolution; there his true honour lies.

—Michel de Montaigne, "On Cannibals" (1580)[2]

Neighbours in Bamberg had become accustomed to the weekly ritual getting under way in the rear courtyard of Meister Heinrich Schmidt's house and went about their business uninterested. Most of them were on cordial terms with Schmidt, the prince-bishop's new executioner, but remained wary of inviting him or any of his family members into their homes. His son, Frantz, the focus of his father's attention on this May day in 1573, appeared to be a polite and – if one could say this of the offspring of a hangman – well-bred youth of nineteen. Like many teenagers of the day, he planned to follow his father into the same craft, a path he began as early as the age of eleven or twelve. Frantz's childhood and adolescence had been spent in his native Hof, a small provincial town in the far northeast corner of modern-day Bavaria, ten miles from what is now the Czech border. Since the family's move to Bamberg eight months earlier, he had already accompanied Heinrich to several executions in the city and nearby villages, studying his father's techniques and assisting in minor ways. As he grew in size and maturity, his responsibilities and skills developed apace. Ultimately he intended to become, like his father, a master in the practise of "special interrogation" (i.e. torture) and in the art of efficiently dispatching a condemned soul in the manner prescribed by law, using methods that ranged from the common *execution with the rope*, to the less frequent death by fire or by drowning, to the infamous and exceptionally rare *drawing and quartering*.

Today Meister Heinrich was testing Frantz on the most difficult – and most honourable – of all forms of execution, *death by the sword*, or beheading. Only during the past year had father considered son capable and worthy of wielding his cherished "judgement sword", an engraved and elegantly crafted seven-pound weapon that spent most of its time hanging in an honoured spot over their fireplace. They'd begun their practise months earlier with squashes and pumpkins before moving on to sinewy rhubarb stalks, which better simulated the consistency of the human neck. Frantz's first attempts were predictably clumsy and at times endangered himself and his father, who held *the poor sinner* firmly in place. Over the weeks, his gestures gradually became more fluid and his aim more accurate, at which point Meister Heinrich deemed his son ready to ascend to the next level, practising on goats, pigs, and other "senseless" livestock.

Today, at Schmidt's request, the local "dog slayer", or knacker, had assembled a few stray canines and brought them in his ramshackle wooden cages to the executioner's residence in the heart of the city. Schmidt paid his subordinate a small tip for the favour and removed the animals to the enclosed courtyard behind the house, where his son was waiting. Though there was only an audience of one, Frantz was visibly anxious. Pumpkins, after all, did not move, and even pigs offered little resistance. Perhaps he felt a twinge of apprehension about killing "innocent" domestic animals, though this is likely an anachronistic projection.[3] Above all, Frantz knew that successful decapitation of the former pets before him, each requiring one steady stroke, would be the final step in his apprenticeship, a visible sign of his father's approval and of his own readiness to go out into the wider world as a journeyman executioner. Meister Heinrich again played the part of the assistant and held the first yapping dog fast while Frantz tightened his grip on the sword.[4]

A dangerous world

Fear and anxiety are woven into the very fabric of human existence. In that sense they link all of us across the centuries. The world of Heinrich Schmidt and his son, Frantz, however, was characterised by much more individual vulnerability than members of a modern, developed society might imagine bearable. Hostile natural and supernatural forces, mysterious and deadly epidemics, violent and malevolent fellow human beings, accidental or intentional fires – all haunted the imaginations and daily lives of early modern people. The resulting climate of insecurity may not account entirely for the frequent brutality of the era's judicial institutions, but it does offer a context for understanding how institutional enforcers like the Schmidts might simultaneously be viewed with gratitude and disgust by their contemporaries.[5]

The precariousness of life was evident from the very beginning. Having survived a combined miscarriage and stillborn rate that claimed at least one in three foetuses, Frantz Schmidt entered the world with only a fifty-fifty chance of reaching his twelfth birthday. (Childbirth also presented real risks for the mother, with one in twenty women dying within seven weeks of delivery – a significantly higher rate than in even the worst-off of modern developing nations.) The first two years of a child's life were the most dangerous, as frequent outbreaks of smallpox, typhus, and dysentery proved particularly fatal to younger victims. Most parents experienced firsthand the death of at least one child, and most children the death of a sibling and one or both parents.[6]

One of the most common causes of premature death was infection during one of the innumerable epidemics that swept through Europe's cities and countryside. Most people who reached the age of fifty would have survived at least half a dozen outbreaks of various deadly infections. Large cities like Nuremberg and Augsburg might lose as much as a third to a half of their entire population during the one-to-two-year course of an especially severe epidemic. The most feared disease, though not necessarily the deadliest by this point, was the plague. Outbreaks of the plague became especially frequent in central Europe during Frantz Schmidt's lifetime – occurring more often than at any other time or place in European history since the Black Death's first appearance in the mid-fourteenth century. They were also fearsomely capricious in their timing and their virulence.[7] Individuals' traumatic memories and experiences generated a shared cultural dread of all contagion, further underscoring the fragility of human life and the extent of individual vulnerability.

Floods, crop failures, and famines also struck at frequent – though rarely predictable – intervals. The Schmidts had the particular misfortune to live during the worst years of the period known to us as the Little Ice Age (c.1400–1700), when a global drop in year-round temperatures resulted in longer, harsher winters, and cooler, wetter summers, particularly in northern Europe. During Frantz Schmidt's lifetime, his native Franconia saw much more snow and rain than in previous years, resulting in flooded fields and crops left rotting in place. In some years there were not enough warm months for grapes to ripen, thus yielding only sour wine. Harvests produced desperately little, and the resulting famine left humans and their livestock prey to disease and starvation. Even wildlife populations shrank dramatically, with starving wolf packs increasingly turning their attention to human prey. The scarcity of all foodstuffs sent inflation soaring and, faced with starvation, many formerly law-abiding citizens turned to poaching and other stealing to feed themselves and their families.[8]

Pummelled by natural forces beyond their control, the people of Frantz Schmidt's day also had to contend with the violence of other humans, particularly the seemingly ubiquitous bandits, soldiers, and assorted lawless men who roamed the land freely. Most territorial states, including the prince-bishopric of Bamberg and the imperial city of Nuremberg, mainly consisted of virgin forests and open meadows, dotted with tiny villages, a few towns of one to two thousand inhabitants, and one relatively large metropolis. Without the protection of city walls or concerned neighbours, an isolated farmhouse or mill lay at the mercy of just a few strong men with modest weapons. Well-travelled paths and country lanes often lay far from help as well. The roads and forests just outside a city, along with all border territories, were especially dangerous. There a traveller might fall prey to bandit gangs led by vicious outlaws such as Cunz Schott, who not only beat and robbed countless victims, but also made a point of collecting the hands of citizens from his self-declared enemy, Nuremberg.[9]

The largest German state of the day was in fact – as Voltaire later

An early-sixteenth-century drawing of Nuremberg omits the poor suburbs outside the city's walls but captures the fortress character of town living, which promised protection from the many menaces of surrounding forests (1516).

famously quipped – neither Holy, nor Roman, nor an Empire. Responsibility for law and order was instead divided among the empire's more than three hundred member states, which ranged in size from a baronial castle and its neighbouring villages to vast territorial principalities, such as Electoral Saxony or the duchy of Bavaria. Seventy-plus imperial cities, such as Nuremberg and Augsburg, functioned as quasi-autonomous entities, while some abbots and bishops, including the prince-bishop of Bamberg, had long enjoyed secular as well as ecclesiastical jurisdiction. The emperor and his annual representative assembly (known as the Reichstag, or diet) provided a common focus of allegiance and held symbolic authority throughout German lands, but remained utterly powerless in preventing or resolving the feuds and wars that regularly broke out among member states.

Just two generations before Frantz Schmidt's birth, the reforming emperor Maximilian I more or less conceded that violent chaos prevailed throughout his realm, proclaiming in his 1495 Perpetual Truce:

> No one, whatever his rank, estate, or position, shall conduct feud, make war on, rob, kidnap, or besiege another . . . nor shall he enter any castle town, market, fortress, villages, hamlets, or farms against another's will, or use force against them; illegally occupying them, threaten them with arson, or damage them in any other way.[10]

In those days, feuding nobles and their entourages proved the greatest cause of unrest, conducting frequent small-scale raids against one another – and in the process burning many rural inhabitants out of their homes and property. Worse still, some of these nobles freelanced as robber barons, running criminal rackets based on robbery, kidnapping, and extortion (commonly referred to as *Plackerei*), further terrorising rural folk and travellers.

By the time of Frantz Schmidt, incessant feuding between noble families had largely ceased, thanks in equal measure to greater economic integration among the aristocracy and the rise of stronger princes.[11] However, having consolidated their power in large states such as the duchy of Württemberg and the electorate of Brandenburg (later Prussia), these powerful princes now set out to conquer still more territory, using much of their considerable wealth to raise large armies of soldiers for hire. This thirst for war coincided with a steady decline in the number of non-military jobs available to commoners during an exceptionally long period of inflation and high unemployment that historians have dubbed the long sixteenth century (*c*.1480–1620). The ranks of soldiers for pay accordingly ballooned twelvefold over the course of the sixteenth and seventeenth centuries, spawning a terrifying new threat to personal safety and property in German lands: the universally despised landsknechts, or mercenaries.

One contemporary characterised landsknechts as "a new order of soulless people [who] have no respect for honour or justice [and practise] whoring, adultery, rape, gluttony, drunkenness . . . stealing, robbing, and murder", and who live "entirely in the power of the devil, who pulls them about wherever he wants". Even the emperor Charles V, who relied heavily on such men, acknowledged the "inhuman tyranny" of the roving bands of landsknechts, which he considered "more blasphemous and crueller than the Turks".[12] While engaged, the mercenaries spent most of their time loitering in camps and sporadically pillaging the hinterlands of their contracted enemy – perpetrating countless acts of small-scale localised violence like that captured chillingly in an episode from Hans Jakob Christoffel Grimmelshausen's seventeenth-century novel *Simplicissimus*:

> A number of soldiers began to slaughter, to boil and roast things, while others, on the other hand, stormed through the house from top to bottom. Others still made a large pack out of linens, clothes, and all kinds of household goods. Everything they didn't want to take with them they destroyed. A number of them stuck their bayonets into the straw and hay, as if they didn't already have

A German landsknecht, or mercenary (c.1550).

enough sheep and pigs to stick. Many of them shook out the feathers from the bedcovers and filled them with ham. Others threw meat and other utensils into them. Some knocked in the oven and the windows, smashing copper utensils and dishes. Bedsteads, tables, stools, and benches were burned. Pots and cutting boards were all broken. One servant girl was so badly handled in the barn that she couldn't move any longer. Our servant they tied up and laid on the ground and rammed a funnel in his mouth and then poured a ghastly brew full of piss down his throat. Then they started to torture the peasants as if they wanted to burn a band of witches.[13]

Things were not much better in times of peace. When unemployed or simply unpaid (a frequent occurrence), some of these groups of mostly young men roved about the countryside in search of food, drink, and women (not necessarily in that order). Frequently joined by runaway servants and apprentices (known in England as "ronnegates") as well as by debt-laden wife deserters, banished criminals, and other vagrants, these "sturdy beggars" survived mainly by begging and petty theft. Some became more aggressive, terrorising farmers, villagers, and travellers with the same *Plackerei* as robber knights and professional bandits. The distinction between full-time and part-time extortionists and robbers was of course irrelevant to their many victims, as in the instance of two professional thieves flogged out of town by the adult Frantz Schmidt, who along with their companions, some begging mercenaries, *forced the people at three mills to give them goods and tortured [them], taking several hatchets and guns.*[14]

Among the many crimes associated with robber bands and other roving ruffians, one struck special terror in the hearts of the rural populace: arson. In an era long before fire departments and home insurance, the very word was incendiary. One carefully placed torch could bring a farm or even an entire village to ruin, turning prosperous inhabitants into homeless beggars in less than an hour. In fact, the mere threat of burning down someone's house or barn – often used as a form of extortion – was considered tantamount to the deed itself and thus subject to the same prescribed punishment: being burned alive at the stake. Some gangs – known as murderer-burners – actually thrived on the extortion money they extracted from farmers and villagers threatened with this terrifying crime.[15] Fear of professional arsonists was rampant in the German countryside, but most intentional house fires were the by-product of endemic private feuds and attempts at revenge, sometimes preceded by the warning figure of a red hen painted on a wall or a dreaded "burn letter" nailed to a front door. Fire prevention in most cities had advanced little since the Middle Ages, and rural

A lone pedlar is ambushed by highwaymen; detail from a landscape painting by Lucas I. van Valkenborch (*c.*1585).

dwellings and barns remained completely without protection. Only the wealthiest merchants could afford insurance, and even then it usually covered only goods in transit. Whether natural or man-made, house and barn fires spelled financial devastation to virtually all households.

Beset by all the dangers above, the people of Frantz Schmidt's day feared yet another unseen, lurking threat: the bewildering array of ghosts, fairies, werewolves, demons, and other supernatural attackers traditionally believed to inhabit field and forest, road and hearth. Clerical reformers of all religious denominations attempted in vain to quash such ancient beliefs, while at the same time generating even more widespread anxiety by trumpeting what they believed to be the greater supernatural threat of a genuine satanic conspiracy at work in their time. The spectre of witchcraft hovered menacingly throughout Frantz Schmidt's lifetime, often leading to the tragic real-world consequences we know today as the European witch craze of 1550–1650, during which at least sixty thousand people were executed for the crime.

Where did one turn for protection and consolation in this vale of tears? Family and friends, the typical refuge from the world's cruelties, might help an individual cope with misfortune but could offer little preventive help. Popular healers ("cunning people"), barber-surgeons, apothecaries, and midwives could offer occasional relief from some pains and wounds, but they remained helpless against serious diseases or most of the dangers of childbirth. Physicians, the modern medical expert of choice, were rare, expensive, and just as constrained by the medical knowledge of the day. Astrologers and other fortune-tellers might provide some sense of control and even destiny to troubled souls, but, once more, they could offer no protection from the world's dangers themselves.

Religion continued to serve as one of the main intellectual resources of the age, offering explanations of misfortune and occasionally putative preventive measures. The teachings of Martin Luther and other Protestants from the 1520s on repudiated any reliance on "superstitious" protection rituals, but otherwise reinforced the common belief in a moral universe where nothing happened by chance. Natural disasters and epidemics were routinely interpreted as signs of God's displeasure and even anger, though the cause of that divine wrath was not always self-evident. Some theologians and chroniclers identified a particular unpunished atrocity – an act of incest or infanticide – as the catalyst. Other times, collective suffering was interpreted more generally, as a divine call to repentance. Luther, John Calvin, and many other early Protestants retained an apocalyptic expectation that they were living in the final days and that the tribulations of the world would soon be at an end. And of course the devil and his minions remained a key component of every explanation of disaster, ranging from claims that witches caused hailstorms to stories of demons endowing criminals with supernatural powers.

The most commonly used preventive measure against the various "angels of death" was simple prayer. For centuries, Christians had collectively intoned "Protect us, O Lord, from plague, famine, and war!"[16] Petitionary prayer to Christ, Mary, or a specific saint against a specific threat remained widespread throughout the later sixteenth century, even among Protestants, who formally rejected any supernatural intercession other than Christ's. For many believers, magical talismans – such as gems, crystals, and pieces of wood – provided supplementary protection against natural and supernatural dangers, as did a variety of quasi-religious items known as sacramentals among Catholics: holy water, pieces of a consecrated host, saints' medals, blessed candles or bells, and supposedly holy relics, such as an alleged bone fragment or other bodily part from a saint or member of the Holy Family. Other more explicitly magical spells, powders, or potions – some of them officially proscribed – promised recovery from illness or protection from enemies. If consolation and reassurance were the primary goals, we cannot so readily dismiss the efficacy of such measures. Belief in an afterlife, where the suffering and virtuous would be rewarded and the evil punished, may have offered additional solace, though even the strongest personal faith remained powerless to prevent or avoid catastrophe itself.

Assailed by dangers on all sides, Frantz Schmidt and his contemporaries were desperate for some sense of security and order. Secular authorities – from the emperor to territorial princes to the ruling magnates of city-states – all shared this longing and were determined to do something about it. Their paternalistic outlook was far from altruistic – entailing by definition an expansion of their own authority – but their concern for public safety and welfare was for the most part genuine. Their efforts to mitigate the effects of earthquakes, floods, famines, and epidemics may have offered some small aid to victims. But even the most ambitious improvements in public hygiene had a minimal impact before the modern era. The quarantines that many governments imposed during epidemics, for example, slowed the spread of contagion somewhat, as did better-regulated refuse and waste disposal, but flight from urban areas during outbreaks remained the most effective measure among those who could afford it.

Law enforcement, on the other hand, offered an irresistible opportunity to demonstrate government's ability to curb violence and provide some measure of security for all inhabitants. It also ensured greater popular support and expanded power for secular leaders themselves. Frantz Schmidt and his contemporaries consequently shared a paradoxical attitude towards the violence that surrounded them. As we might expect, people resigned to regular assault by waves of unpreventable natural disaster and illness tended to regard the violence of their fellow humans with a similarly fatalist resolve. At the same time, the heightened aspirations of political leaders in reducing such violence – or at least extracting a heavy price for it – clearly raised popular expectations and hopes. When legal authorities urged aggrieved individuals to avoid private retribution and turn to their own courts and officials, they were scarcely prepared for the onslaught of petitions and accusations that flooded their chanceries. Requests for official intervention ranged from complaints about road repairs and refuse collection to requests to curb the public nuisance of aggressive beggars and rambunctious street children to reports of unruly or criminal activities among neighbours. The greater dominance these ambitious leaders sought came at the high price of having to listen to their subjects and provide visible proof that the people's confidence in official promises was not misplaced.

The skilled executioner was in that sense the ruling authorities' most indispensable means of easing their subjects' fear of lawless attacks and providing some sense of justice in a society where everyone knew that the great majority of dangerous criminals would never be caught or punished. The ritualised violence that the executioner administered on the community's behalf at once (1) avenged victims; (2) ended the threat represented by dangerous criminals; (3) set a terrifying

example; and (4) forestalled further violence at the hands of angry relatives or lynch mobs. Without the executioner's carefully orchestrated,
highly visible, and often brutal assertion of civic authority, secular
rulers knew that "the sword of justice" would remain an empty metaphor and that their self-proclaimed role as the guarantors of public
safety would be regarded as meaningless. As their representative, the
executioner undertook the precarious operation of achieving the desired semblance of orderly justice while in the process of physically
assaulting or killing another human being. An aspiring master such as
Frantz Schmidt would need to convince prospective employers not
only of his technical abilities but also of his capacity to remain calm
and dispassionate in even the most emotionally charged situation.
This was a daunting goal for one so young, but one that Meister Heinrich and his apprentice son embraced with singular and unflinching
resolve.

A father's shame

The relative social tolerance that Heinrich Schmidt and his family enjoyed in the spring of 1573 was itself a recent development, and one by
no means guaranteed to endure. Since the Middle Ages, professional
executioners had been universally reviled as cold-blooded killers for
hire and accordingly excluded from respectable society at every turn.
Most were forced to live outside the city walls or near an already unclean location within the city, typically the slaughteryard or a lazar
house (for lepers). Their legal disenfranchisement was just as thorough:
no executioner or family member could hold citizenship, be admitted to
a guild, hold public office, serve as a legal guardian or trial witness, or
even write a valid will. Until the late fifteenth century, these outcasts
received no legal protection from mob violence in the event of a botched
execution, and a few were actually stoned to death by angry spectators.
In most towns, hangmen – as they were most commonly known – were
forbidden to enter a church. And if an executioner wished to have his
child baptised or desired last rites for a dying relative, he depended
on the willingness of the sometimes less-than-compassionate local
priest to set foot in an "unclean" residence. They were also banned from

bathhouses, taverns, and other public buildings, and it was virtually unheard-of for an executioner to enter the home of any respectable person. People of Frantz Schmidt's era harboured such a pervasive fear of social contamination at the very touch of an executioner's hand that respectable individuals jeopardised their very livelihoods by even casual contact. Folklore abounded with tales of the disasters that befell those who broke this ancient taboo, and of beautiful condemned maidens who chose death over marriage to willing hangmen.[17]

The source of this deep anxiety seems obvious, given the distasteful nature of the hangman's trade. Even today, direct contact with dead bodies carries a polluting stigma in many traditional societies. In early modern Germany, the associated "infamous occupations" thus not only included executioners, but also gravediggers, tanners, and butchers.[18] Most people also considered hangmen a type of amoral mercenary and thus excluded from "decent" society in the same manner as vagrants, prostitutes, and thieves, as well as Gypsies and Jews. Contemporaries and even some modern scholars commonly supposed that any individual attracted to such an unsavoury occupation must be a criminal himself – even though the evidence of such a correlation remains inconclusive. It was likewise presumed that socially marginalised figures had been born out of wedlock, with the distinction between illegitimate (*unehelich*) and dishonourable (*unhehrlich*) often elided, so that even official documents might casually refer to "the whoreson hangman".[19]

Not surprisingly, hangmen and other dishonourable individuals tended to bond together, both professionally and socially. Executioner dynasties sprang up across the empire, built on both mutual exclusion and strategic intermarriage. Some of these families bore ominous surnames – such as Leichnam (corpse) – while most gained fame principally among their fellows in the trade, such as the south German families of Brand, Fahner, Fuchs, and Schwartz.[20] Over the course of generations, these interconnected families developed many of the same ritual initiations and other forms of corporate identity common to "honourable" crafts such as goldsmiths and bakers. Like the honourable craftsmen who spurned them, executioners also developed professional networks, oversaw the training of new practitioners, and sought to secure gainful employment within the trade for their sons.

The full extent of Heinrich Schmidt's ambitions for his own son at this moment, however, was far greater than either of them dared admit to anyone outside their own household. Together they sought to undo the family curse that had condemned them and all their progeny to the gutter status of the executioner – an audacious dream of social ascent that was virtually unthinkable in their rigidly caste-conscious world. The secret reason for the family's descent into shame – a story passed down from father to son – would only be revealed to the wider world by Meister Frantz in his old age. But on this day, as the young Frantz raised his sword over the trembling body of an unlucky stray, that secret shame burned fresh in his mind.

Until the autumn of 1553, Frantz's father, Heinrich Schmidt, had enjoyed a comfortable and respectable life as *a woodsman and fowler* in the town of Hof, situated in the margravate of Brandenburg-Kulmbach, the territory of a Franconian noble of middling rank. Schmidt and his family had survived and even prospered during several years of upheaval caused by the expansionist ambitions of their young lord, Albrecht II Alcibiades (b. 1522), popularly known as *Bellator* (warrior). Like his Athenian namesake, Albrecht Alcibiades frequently shifted allegiances during the religious conflicts of the 1540s and 1550s, ultimately alienating both Catholic and Protestant states with his savage raids of their territories. Most recently, the Warrior's aggression and duplicity had even succeeded in uniting against him troops from the Protestant states of Nuremberg, Bohemia, and Braunschweig, with those of the Catholic prince-bishoprics of Bamberg and Würzburg, in what would later be known as the Second Margrave War. Albrecht's act of unintentional ecumenism culminated in his enemies' joint invasion of his territory and their siege of many strongholds, including the city of Hof.

One of Albrecht's better-fortified towns, Hof was surrounded by stone walls twelve feet high and three feet thick. The margrave himself was not resident when the siege began on 1 August 1553, but the local militia of some six hundred men held their own against a surrounding army of more than thirteen thousand troops for over three weeks, until a letter from Albrecht arrived, announcing that reinforcements were on the way. The promised relief never came, however, and after four more weeks of daily bombardments, raiding parties, and mass starvation, the battered town capitulated. The subsequent occupation was mild. Nonetheless, the conquerors had to force Hof's angry citizens to formally

The universally reviled Albrecht Alcibiades of Brandenburg-Kulmbach, author of the Schmidt family's misfortune in Hof (c.1550).

welcome their own lord when he finally rode into town with an entourage of sixty knights on 12 October. Within a few weeks of his return to Hof, Albrecht succeeded in not only further alienating his resentful subjects but also reigniting hostilities with the victorious army still camped outside the city walls. This foolhardy campaign ended in disaster, with the conquerors inflicting a much more severe occupation on the city and the margrave himself forced to flee the city. Declared an imperial outlaw, he spent four years as a wandering exile in France, before dying in 1557 at the age of forty-five. By then, large parts of Albrecht's territory lay in ruins and his name was bitterly cursed among his former subjects.

Heinrich Schmidt and his son had a still deeper and more enduring grudge against the disgraced margrave than did other residents of Hof. It originated on Monday 16 October 1553, three days after Albrecht Alcibiades had returned to the devastated Hof with his retainers. Like other German towns of its size, Hof could not afford to maintain a full-time executioner. But when the widely despised Albrecht had three local gunsmiths arrested in an alleged plot on his life, rather than sending for a travelling professional to execute them – the usual course of action – the headstrong margrave invoked an ancient custom and commanded a bystander to carry out the deed on the spot. The man singled out for this terrible distinction was Heinrich Schmidt. Having lived as a respectable citizen of Hof, Schmidt vehemently protested to his ruler that this act would bring infamy upon him and his descendants – but to no avail. *Unless [my father] complied*, recounted the seventy-year-old Frantz, *[the margrave] threatened to string him up instead, as well the two men standing next to him.*

Why was the innocent woodsman singled out for this dreadful commission? The answer lies in another story that Frantz would not reveal until late in his life – a bizarre and improbable case of a dispute with a man about a dog. A few years before the fateful confrontation with Albrecht Alcibiades, Frantz's grandfather, the tailor Peter Schmidt, was approached by a weaver journeyman from Thüringen and asked for permission to wed his daughter. The young couple subsequently married and settled in a small farmstead near Hof. One day, as the weaver (named Günther Bergner, Frantz recalled eight decades later) was strolling the countryside, he was attacked by a large dog. In anger, Bergner picked up the animal and hurled it at its owner, a deer hunter, *to his misfortune and ours* (Frantz later recalled) *killing him*. Though not prosecuted, the weaver was thereafter considered dishonourable and barred from all crafts. *Since no one wanted to be around him, out of desperation and melancholy he became an executioner.* The stigma did not apparently carry over to his father-in-law Peter Schmidt, who continued to work as a tailor in Hof. A few years later, though, when the anxious margrave sought someone to dispatch his would-be assassins, the infamous occupation of Heinrich Schmidt's brother-in-law Bergner (who presumably was not himself available) sealed the choice of a new executioner.[21]

As Schmidt had predicted, from his moment of capitulation to Albrecht's order, he and his family were ruthlessly and definitively excluded from honourable society by their own neighbours and former friends, simultaneously tainted by their association with an odious trade and a reviled tyrant. The dishonoured Heinrich Schmidt could have attempted to escape ignominy by starting anew with his family in a distant town. Instead, he chose to remain in his ancestral home and attempt to earn a living from the only craft now open to him. Thus was a new executioner dynasty born – though if the plan that Heinrich would later share with his son, Frantz, succeeded, it would be a short-lived one.

Frantz Schmidt entered the world within months of his father's dramatic fall from grace, sometime between late 1553 and mid-1554.[22] The Hof of his childhood and adolescence remained a closed society of at most one thousand people, its insularity and social rigidity exacerbated by its remote location. Later known as the Bavarian Siberia, the region surrounding the town on the Saale River was wrapped in dense, ancient forests and overshadowed by mountains up to one thousand metres high. Long, brutal winters and a native soil riddled with chalk and iron made farming difficult. Weaving and other cloth-related trades dominated economic life in the town, cattle- and sheepherding in the countryside. Mining had provided another source of wealth for centuries, in the days of Frantz Schmidt yielding finds of gold, silver, iron, copper, tin, granite, and crystal.[23]

Hof was also a frontier town in the cultural sense. To Thuringians and Saxons, it was the far south; to Franconians their own far north. Just west of the Bohemian border, the town was shaped by a unique mix of Slavic and German influences and in 1430 had actually been

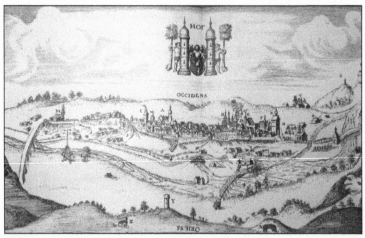

The town of Hof as seen from the east (c.1550).

sacked by invading Hussites, radical followers of the martyred religious reformer Jan Hus. The regional identity most closely associated with Hof was that of the Vogtland. By the sixteenth century, the territory originally named for its imperial *Vögte* (lord protectors) had become more of a vague cultural construct than a political entity, distinguished most by its dialect, sausages, and exceptionally potent beer. Much later, among nationalists of the nineteenth century, the scenic and pristine Vogtland would represent an ur-Germanic wilderness, possessing an idealised but also savage beauty. For the ostracised Schmidt family, the geographical isolation of Hof merely deepened their own state of internal exile and despondency.

Heinrich Schmidt's reasons for staying put after his disgrace are unclear. At least the political aftermath of Albrecht Alcibiades's disastrous reign was more favourable to his imposed profession. Upon Albrecht's death in 1557, his cousin Georg Friedrich, margrave of neighbouring Brandenburg-Ansbach, assumed control over Brandenburg-Kulmbach as well. Hof's new lord was as steady and circumspect as his kinsman had been rash. All the city's trees miraculously bloomed again that autumn, reported the local chronicler Enoch Widman, as potent an omen as the earthquake that had presaged Albrecht's disastrous rampage.[24] From his residence in nearby Bayreuth, Margrave Georg Friedrich immediately set about rebuilding Hof and other damaged towns while repairing relations with neighbouring states. He also initiated thorough financial and legal reforms, beginning with a series of new police ordinances and other criminal legislation. One immediate result was a sharp increase in the number and intensity of criminal prosecutions. In the twelve months leading up to May 1560, Heinrich Schmidt, the margrave's new executioner, was called on to perform an unprecedented eight executions in the district of Hof alone.[25]

Heinrich Schmidt's work for the margrave was consequently stable enough to provide him with a reliable income, which he was able to supplement with freelance execution work as well as the traditional executioner sideline of healing wounds. His chances of reversing the family's social misfortune while in Hof, however, were practically nil. He applied at least twice for executioner jobs elsewhere but not until 1572, when Frantz was eighteen, did he finally secure the position of executioner to the prince-bishop of Bamberg, a notable step up the career ladder.[26] After nearly two decades of being shunned by their former friends and neighbours, the Schmidts were finally free of provincial Hof, if still shackled to their painful memories and shameful legacy.

The diocese (later archdiocese) of Bamberg was one of the oldest and most prestigious sees in the empire. In 1572 its bishops had enjoyed four centuries of simultaneous secular and religious authority and, despite considerable losses to the Protestant Reformation during the previous four decades, still ruled over four thousand square miles of territory and approximately 150,000 subjects. The prince-bishopric's administration was relatively sophisticated and widely admired in the area of criminal law, particularly since the 1507 publication of its immensely influential code, the *Bambergensis*.[27] Bishop Veit II von Würtzburg, Heinrich Schmidt's new lord, was better known among his subjects for his heavy taxes, but it was in any event his vice chancellor who supervised the new executioner and other judicial personnel. When Heinrich Schmidt reported to the cathedral city for duty in August 1572, he celebrated a significant personal as well as professional achievement.

The Schmidt family enjoyed a materially comfortable life in their new town, with a healthy income that averaged 50 fl. a year – as much as a pastor or schoolteacher – as well as other benefits Meister Heinrich accrued as a municipal employee.[28] Their spacious house, located on a peninsula in the northeastern corner of the city today known as Little Venice, came rent-free for the duration of his work for the bishop. After the family's arrival in the late summer of 1572, the city undertook a thorough renovation and expansion of the house according to Heinrich's specifications.[29] Admittedly, the family was expected to share quarters with Hans Reinschmidt, the executioner's assistant (known in Bamberg as the *Peinlein*, or penaliser), but with Frantz the only child remaining at home, some degree of privacy was still possible.

Although still precarious, the family's social position became less oppressive than it had been in the smaller community of Hof. Bamberg was a relatively cosmopolitan town of about ten thousand, known principally (even today) for its magnificent thirteenth-century cathedral and the city's prolific production of a unique smoked beer. Locals proudly compared Bamberg's seven majestic hills, each crowned with its own distinctive church, to the seven hills of the Eternal City. At least in theory, the Schmidts' new home allowed them a much greater degree of anonymity in the streets and markets than provincial Hof, and perhaps even a degree of neighbourly acceptance. Some churches in cities of this size had begun to permit executioners their own pews, and a few taverns even provided them with their own stool – sometimes three-legged, like a scaffold.[30] The Schmidts' Protestant faith undoubtedly created some additional barriers in the overwhelmingly Catholic city, but it apparently made no difference to Heinrich's Catholic employers, despite the bishopric's public embrace of the Counter-Reformation.[31]

The surest sign of the executioner's relatively enhanced (or rather, less degraded) status in this era was the increasing frequency of reactionary legislation that attempted to restore "traditional values" and the "natural" social order. Like the so-called sumptuary laws of the previous century, imperial police ordinances of 1530 and 1548 required executioners (as well as Jews and prostitutes) to wear "distinctive clothing by which they could be readily identified."[32] Many local decrees similarly decried the blurring of traditional boundaries and attempted to reverse the perceived trend towards tolerance of all "dishonourable" people, imposing hefty fines or even corporal punishment on those who transgressed.

Popular prejudice always dies slowly, especially among those individuals most anxious about their own deteriorating economic situation and unstable social status. The second half of the sixteenth century saw the emergence of an increasingly global marketplace, a shift with especially dire consequences for traditional craftsmen and their products. But rather than direct their anger at the new breed of extravagantly wealthy bankers or merchants, most "poor but honest" artisans instead attacked seemingly prosperous executioners such as Heinrich Schmidt and other individuals (notably Jews) whom they considered rightfully beneath them. Obsessed with preserving their self-defined "dove-pure" honour, German craftsmen universally ignored the emperor's 1548 opening of guild membership to executioners' sons and continued to forbid their members any social contact whatsoever with them. Any artisan defying this sweeping ban – which also applied to butchers, cobblers, tanners, sack carriers, and a number of other "disreputable" occupations – risked social ostracism, loss of guild membership, or worse. One Basel artisan allegedly committed suicide because of his pollution by close contact with the local executioner; others so tainted felt compelled to leave town and start anew somewhere else. This rigid view of social status, based principally on birth, would continue to exercise enormous influence on how most people in Europe and in the German lands thought and acted for a long, long time – well into the modern era, in fact.[33]

Fortunately for the Schmidts, these heavy-handed legal attempts to single out marginal individuals and stymie their social advancement made no difference in day-to-day life and served little purpose other than to appease anxious artisans. Contrary to modern representations, for instance, Heinrich Schmidt and later his son, Frantz, were not compelled to wear any standard on- or off-duty uniform, and there is absolutely no evidence anywhere of the stereotypical black mask – likely an invention of nineteenth-century Romantics. A few cities required their executioners to don a bright red, yellow, or green cape, or wear a striped shirt, or perhaps a distinctive hat.[34] In illustrations from the second half of the sixteenth century on, though, they are invariably well dressed, sometimes to a dandified degree. In short, they dressed the same as any other middle-class burgher – and therein lay the problem for status-anxious craftsmen.

The toothlessness of such ordinances did not ease the uncertainty of the Schmidts' slightly improved social standing in urban Bamberg. Personal honour, based on both social rank and reputation, remained the most valuable – and fragile – commodity around. In Heinrich Schmidt's day, verbal insults to one's "name" – "rogue" or "thief" for a man, "whore" or "witch" for a woman – frequently led to physical assault or even homicide among individuals of every rank. "Whoreson of a hangman" remained a common curse (even appearing in Shakespeare's plays) and "it belongs to the gallows" was the most succinct way to condemn any frowned-upon practise. The Schmidts were likewise reminded of their lowly place with virtually every feast day, public procession, or other civic occasion, where both the reigning social hierarchy – and their own exclusion from it – were vividly reasserted. As in any racially or otherwise segregated society, law and custom still explicitly banned executioners and their families from many venues and severely constrained their opportunities for education, occupation, and housing, a condition that would persist for generations to come.

A Nuremberg chronicle's portrayal of Frantz Schmidt's execution of Anna Peihelsteinin on 7 July 1584, possibly drawn by an eyewitness. In the original, the executioner wears the unusual – and visually striking – combination of pink stockings, light blue hose with a pink codpiece, and a leather jerkin over a blue doublet and white shirt collar, the jerkin offering some protection from bloodstains (1616).

Perhaps the most insidious aspect of the stigma tied so deeply to Heinrich Schmidt's profession was its unpredictable effect, which created a fragile and always socially tenuous atmosphere in any interaction between family members and their Bamberg neighbours. Like other elastic social concepts – the famed notion of "middle class" comes to mind – the definition of the executioner's dishonour might be interpreted variously and selectively, and sometimes even spitefully, by different individuals and communities. A visiting merchant from Lübeck might express shock not only that the Augsburg "hangman" lived in the midst of town but also that honourable people regularly ate and drank with him and even entered his house. In another town, by contrast, there might be regret but also little surprise when the wife of one executioner died in childbirth because the midwife refused to set foot in their home. Even a widely respected executioner might be reputed to have "a great many friends in the village", and yet at his death have not a single soul willing to serve as a pallbearer.[35]

Heinrich Schmidt knew well that neither his position as a well-paid government official nor his bourgeois standard of living nor his personal reputation for honesty guaranteed any kind of lasting acceptance or secure future for him or his family. Social humiliation in minor or major ways remained a routine experience, a continual reminder of his shame. His contemporaries considered his predicament an unalterable fact of life. But for Meister Heinrich and his equally determined son, the disgraceful occupation thrust upon them both would provide the very means of their family's attempted salvation.

A son's opportunity

Timing and luck are important to any personal success. Frantz Schmidt had the good fortune to come to maturity in what historians now call "the golden age of the executioner". This development was itself the culmination of a very gradual yet profound transformation of German criminal law that had been under way for at least two centuries. Since the days of the Roman Empire, Germanic peoples had treated most crimes as private conflicts to be resolved by some form of financial compensation (wergild) or by a customary punishment, such as loss of a limb or banishment. State officials, who remained few in number until the later Middle Ages, typically played the role of referee, ensuring orderly procedures but leaving instigation, trial, and judgement to elders or other local jurors. The main goal in this approach was modest – to prevent blood feud and ongoing violence – certainly not to punish all malefactors, which would have seemed a simultaneously alien and impractical objective. Usually a male relative of a murder victim was allowed to execute the perpetrator himself; other state-endorsed killings used freelance hangmen or court beadles (low-level enforcers), paid on an ad hoc basis, by the execution.[36]

The late medieval origins of a more active, even interventionist, governmental role in criminal justice lay in two intertwined but distinctive impulses. The first was a broader, more ambitious definition of sovereignty itself that first surfaced in prosperous city-states, such as Augsburg and Nuremberg. Eager to make their jurisdictions safe and attractive havens for trade and manufacturing, municipal guilds and ruling patrician families began to issue ordinances governing a wide variety of behaviour previously left to the private sphere. Some of the new regulations appear odd, even quaint, to modern eyes, particularly the many sumptuary ordinances ostensibly aimed at preserving the public peace by restricting clothing and dancing of various sorts. Only noblemen might wear swords or fur, for instance, while their wives and daughters might possess exclusive right to don jewellery and certain multicoloured fabrics. More significantly, by the beginning of the sixteenth century, more than two thousand cities and other jurisdictions in Germany had sought and been granted the monopoly of high justice, or the right to try capital crimes. Most of these local courts continued to rely on private settlements for lesser offences but jealously guarded the privilege to perform their own executions. Lynch justice – whether by stoning, beating, or hanging – became almost as much a target as crime itself, since such spontaneous mob actions deeply undermined the authority that governmental officials sought for themselves.

Of course it is one thing to loudly proclaim new laws and state prerogatives and a different matter entirely to enforce them, particularly in a highly decentralised empire. At this point a new generation of reforming lawyers emerged, providing the second key element in the transformation of German criminal law and practise. These academically trained jurists convinced their more business-oriented magisterial colleagues that the increasing number and complexity of new laws and procedures rendered the old legal apparatus inadequate and instead required an ever-growing cadre of professional functionaries at all levels.

In a similar vein, the patrician magistrates of both Augsburg and Nuremberg became the first to conclude that in order to prosecute criminals more effectively, their cities needed to employ a full-time expert trained in the methods of judicial interrogation (including torture) and execution. Elevating the hangman to the position of a permanent civic employee helped legitimise his work, in theory associating him more with scribes and municipal inspectors than with mercenary soldiers and their "evil turbulent lust for spilling human blood".[37] Offering the city executioner a long-term contract also gave local authorities a greater sense of security and control over these presumably loyal implementers of their expanded legal ambitions. By the beginning of the sixteenth century, the trend throughout the empire towards permanent executioners appeared irreversible.

The full transformation of the part-time hangman into the full-time professional executioner, however, like the evolution of German criminal justice itself, required several generations and was still not complete by the time of Frantz Schmidt's birth in 1554. In some areas, officials continued to pay the hangman on a per-execution basis as late as the eighteenth century.[38] Many smaller jurisdictions simply could not justify the expense of a full-time executioner, while others selectively followed the medieval tradition of requiring a young male member of the community to carry out the odious task of judicial killing – a scenario intimately familiar to the Schmidt family. A few more isolated localities continued the still more ancient custom of bestowing the right of administering final justice to a male member of the victim's family. Even among the majority of German lands that employed a salaried executioner by the sixteenth century, prosecution and punishment of crime remained one part of a job description that also included a number of other distasteful tasks, ranging from oversight of the city's brothel to refuse disposal to burning the bodies of suicides.[39]

The mid-sixteenth century nonetheless inaugurated a new era of opportunities for the professional executioner. Even more fortuitously, Frantz's two future employers, the prince-bishop of Bamberg and the imperial city of Nuremberg, stood at the forefront of that very reform of German criminal justice. Jurists trained in civil (Roman) law were particularly influential in Franconia, leading to two exceptionally influential pieces of criminal legislation: the 1507 *Bambergensis*, officially titled the *Bambergische Halsgerichtsordnung* (literally, "neck-court-ordinance". because of its focus on capital punishment), and its 1532 successor, the imperial *Constitutio Criminalis Carolina* (or Criminal Constitution of [Emperor] Charles V), popularly known as the *Carolina*.[40] The older publication, compiled by the Franconian nobleman Johann Freiherr von Schwarzenberg, was intended as a manual for lay judges who, like Schwarzenberg himself, had not trained as jurists, and was thus written in a direct and unornamented German, accompanied by many illustrative woodcuts. Though the book lacked official endorsement, it became immensely popular, going through several editions within the first ten years.

The full-fledged, imperially sponsored offspring of the *Bambergensis*, the *Carolina*, incorporated much of the parent text's directness but was more ambitious in its political goals. By the early sixteenth century, territorial rulers and the emperor himself had come to appreciate the value of standardised legal procedures in governing their own realms, but they faced considerable opposition from many quarters on the use of Roman law in their attempted codifications. The *Carolina* hit upon a workable compromise between innovative jurists attracted by the substance and consistency of Roman law and conservative secular authorities suspicious of "foreign laws and customs" and jealous of their own prerogatives.[41] While "we would in no way detract from the old, lawful, and just customs of electors, princes, and estates". the authors of the *Carolina* sought to establish fair and consistent standards and procedures among the empire's diverse jurisdictions, involving trained legal professionals as much as possible. Rather than just proscribing a variety of crimes, the new code meticulously defined the scope and nature of the offences, provided standards for arrest and establishing evidence, and issued formulas for judicial proceedings themselves. Clarity and regularity in practise were the goals. With the notable exceptions of magic and infanticide (newly promoted to capital crimes), the *Carolina* did not alter customary definitions of serious criminal offences. Virtually all medieval forms of execution – including live burial, live burning, drowning, and quartering – likewise remained untouched in substance.

Most important for young Frantz Schmidt, the *Carolina* endorsed the *Bambergensis*'s detailed guidelines for the performance of each judicial functionary, including the individual formerly known as the hangman, now consistently referred to as the executioner (*Nachrichter*, literally, "after-judge") or the "sharp (i.e. sword) judge" (*Scharfrichter*).[42] The document strongly recommended regular salaries for "reputable individuals" to be supplemented by a sliding scale of compensation for different types of executions (with drawing and quartering earning the most). The *Carolina* also formally guaranteed a professional executioner immunity from all popular or legal retribution for his work and required that courts publicly reaffirm this status at each judgement. Cruel, corrupt, or otherwise unprofessional executioners were to be dismissed immediately and punished appropriately. Finally, to prevent the capricious or otherwise unjustified use of physical coercion, the new imperial ordinances set out copious instructions on what evidence might be considered sufficient to initiate torture (e.g. the testimony of two impartial witnesses), which crimes qualified for such "special interrogation" (most notably witchcraft and highway robbery), and how such duress was to be applied (listing the standard implements of torture on an ascending scale of severity, beginning with thumbscrews for women).[43]

The *Carolina*'s higher professional standards for executioners typically translated into better pay, but the law code's broader social impact enhanced Frantz Schmidt's position beyond anything its framers could have imagined. Within one generation of the *Carolina*'s proclamation, criminal arrests, interrogations, and punishments all spiked dramatically throughout the empire. The execution rate likewise skyrocketed, in some places by more than 100 per cent over the previous half century – and many times that if witch panics are included in the statistics – creating a huge demand for trained executioners. In fact, Nuremberg's average execution rate of nine per year during Meister Frantz's lifetime (in a city of forty thousand) was the highest per capita of any city in the empire. But many larger jurisdictions saw similar levels of activity. Heinrich Schmidt himself averaged nearly ten executions a year during his service in the more populous prince-bishopric of Bamberg, and the yearly total for the still larger nearby margravate of Brandenburg-Ansbach totalled nearly twice that during the same period.[44]

What accounts for this apparent surge in crime and punishment? Rising unemployment and inflation – which led to more theft and violence – naturally played a role in the perceived crime wave of Frantz Schmidt's day. But the most powerful reason for the increase in prosecutions was, paradoxically, the *Carolina* itself. The new imperial law code achieved much that was good. But like many well-intentioned reforms, the *Carolina* also yielded unintended consequences that exacerbated the situation in several unprecedented ways. First, the new codes inadvertently opened local authorities up to greater popular manipulation, most infamously in the case of the witch craze, when mobs or even a single individual could demand the prosecution of a suspected witch, who if convicted now faced the death penalty. Second, the *Carolina*'s attempt to eliminate arbitrariness and "unnecessary" cruelty in criminal prosecution produced exactly the opposite effect in the use of torture, the so-called last resort of the interrogator. Some jurisdictions, Nuremberg for example, adhered more closely to the *Carolina*'s prerequisites for administering torture. But elsewhere local authorities paradoxically perceived the imperial code's multiple guidelines and restrictions on the appropriate use of "special interrogation" to be a learned endorsement of physical coercion during questioning.

At the same time, another section of the *Carolina*, which was intended to prevent recidivism, unintentionally forced the execution of many repeat offenders – often for mere property crimes such as theft that, in an earlier time, would not have sent them to the gallows. How did this happen? To discourage criminals from returning to crime, the *Carolina* prescribed an ascending scale of punishment: public flogging for a first offence, banishment for a second offence, and in the event that an exiled offender returned and was convicted of a third offence, execution. This frustratingly narrow set of punishment options forced the hand of local governments with tragic consequences. Crimes against property, for instance, had previously resulted in less than a third of the executions in German lands, but during Frantz Schmidt's lifetime they accounted for nearly seven in ten executions.[45]

This seemingly inexplicable harshness was less the product of new cruelty than of deep frustration over the ineffectiveness of existing punishments. Most of the thieves that Meister Frantz hanged during his career had lengthy criminal records, comprising numerous imprisonments, various corporal punishments, and banishments. Occasionally flogging, both painful and humiliating, followed by banishment from the territory – the typical punishment for first- and second-time offenders – produced the desired effect. After the adult Meister Frantz publicly whipped two teenage brothers, who *stole here and there at the markets*, they disappeared from Nuremberg's criminal records.[46] More often, however, the publicly humiliated and exiled offenders – now permanently cut off from whatever kin and social network they had enjoyed – simply returned to the only life they knew and resumed stealing in another location, often nearby, or even in the city itself.

The obvious ineffectiveness of local banishment for non-violent crimes led some European states to adopt a more permanent kind of exile for thieves and other undesirables, known as transportation. But sending deviants across the ocean was not a ready option among landlocked German states such as Nuremberg and the prince-bishopric of Bamberg, which possessed neither fleets nor foreign colonies. The duke of Bavaria did persuade the city of Nuremberg to experiment briefly with leasing its convicted thieves out to Genoese galleys. But after five years its frugal leaders concluded that the venture was too unreliable. Forced enlistment in the emperor's Hungarian army was another frequently suggested solution but apparently also remained small-scale and short-lived.[47]

The modern-day solution to this problem – internal exile, or extended incarceration – entailed a much greater conceptual leap and was thus even slower to gain acceptance. Most governmental authorities considered long-term imprisonment – except in the case of the dangerously insane – too costly and too cruel. The popular precursor to modern prisons, the workhouse, would gain many adherents during the seventeenth century, largely because it was touted to be financially self-supporting. But Frantz Schmidt's Nuremberg superiors accurately determined early on that such an institution would in fact be a money pit, and thus resisted the new fad for another century.[48] Instead they embraced the allegedly more efficient punishment of chain gangs for begging and thieving youths and young men, a practise until then limited principally to France. Known as *Springbuben* or *Schellbuben* ("knaves" wearing foot irons and belled hats respectively), these prisoners typically faced several weeks of street cleaning and repairs, including the collection and disposal of human and animal waste and other refuse. Like banishment, the chain gang deterred some but not all young thieves from continuing in their criminal ways, as Meister Frantz would later note when many of them ended up before him on the gallows.[49] Perceiving themselves as out of options for dealing with recidivist thieves and other "unreformable" non-violent offenders, governmental authorities during the second half of the sixteenth century thus turned increasingly to the "last resort" of hanging.

The subsequent rise in demand and salaries for trained executioners was obviously good news for a budding young professional of Frantz Schmidt's background and aspirations. The *Carolina*'s elevation of his craft to the indispensable servant of justice further strengthened his hand. Protestant Frantz was probably most grateful for a blessing from the father of the Reformation himself. "If there were no criminals, there

Condemned Nuremberg prisoners on their way to serve galley sentences of two to ten years. This form of banishment was much more common in Mediterranean lands (1616).

would also be no executioners," Martin Luther preached, adding, "The hand that wields the sword and strangles is thus no longer man's hand but God's hand, and not the man but God hangs, breaks on the wheel, beheads, strangles, and makes war." Lest the implications for the reviled hangman be lost, Luther concluded,

> Thus is Meister Hans [the stereotypical executioner] a very useful and even merciful man, since he puts a stop to the villain so that he can do no more and warns others so that they do not do [the same]. The one has his head chopped off by him; the others behind him he admonishes that they should fear the sword and keep the peace. That is a great mercy.

While John Calvin remained content to acknowledge the executioner as "God's instrument", the ever-ebullient Luther went so far as to provide a celebrity endorsement for the profession: "If you see that there is a lack of hangmen, constables, judges, lords, or princes, and you find that you are qualified, you should offer your services and seek the position so that the essential governmental authority may not be despised or become enfeebled."[50]

The clerical elevation of the Schmidts' profession, while a welcome development for executioners, was slow to spread outside of learned circles. Luther's pleading tones still resonated in one famed jurist's 1565 defence that "although the name of executioner is still hated by many [and] it is perceived as an inhuman, bloody, and tyrannical office, he does not sin before God or the world if he acts on orders, not of his own will but out of justice, as God's servant." Like the judge, jurors, and witnesses in the trial, the executioner was himself blameless unless he acted "out of greed, jealousy, hate, vengeance, or lust"; otherwise, he was as indispensable to law and order as the princes themselves. Another legal scholar compared the disgust directed at the executioner's task to the shame associated with excretion – both distasteful but necessary parts of God's plan. The source of continuing popular opprobrium, all agreed, lay less in the office itself than in the job's tendency to attract "godless and rash people, [among them] sorcerers, robbers, murderers, thieves, adulterers, whoremongers, blasphemers, gamblers, and others burdened with coarse sins, scandals and troubles", when what effective courts needed were "pious, debt-free, kind, merciful, fearless men, well-experienced in such work and executions, who carry out their office more for the love of GOD and the Law than out of pre-existing hate and scorn for poor sinners".[51]

Frantz Schmidt thus entered the profession of executioner at a time of significantly greater remuneration and social acceptance than his predecessors, but also of higher personal standards and expectations. A generation or two earlier, secular authorities necessarily tolerated the unsavoury background of many recruits to the office and still saw some executioners who eventually ended up on the wrong side of the scaffold or pyre. By Frantz's day, professionals' reputations as "very orderly and law-abiding" had become a prominent part of their public profile, with any kind of criminal transgression resulting in swift dismissal and punishment. In return, the previously ironic designation of every practitioner as Meister took on a new dignity, with a few executioners even permitted to practise other arts or even granted their own coat of arms.[52]

Centuries of accumulated superstition, disgust, and fear were not easily erased, of course, and the relatively greater opportunities Frantz enjoyed must be weighed against the still heavy social cost. Whatever magistrates and ministers said, most of Frantz's contemporaries still considered executioners to be suspicious, if not sinister, figures. In a society obsessed with the ritualistic display of rank and honour, pious and honest hangmen were a welcome development, but the perception that these people would pollute others by their mere touch persisted.

Many doors would remain closed to the son of Heinrich Schmidt throughout his life. But the growing demand for a new kind of executioner provided young Frantz with an opening, one that he would gladly exploit to achieve the dream that eluded his father and die an honourable man.

The art of the executioner

We know nothing directly of Frantz Schmidt's childhood and youth in Hof. A surprising number of his experiences would have been similar to those of any middle-class boy in sixteenth-century Germany, despite his father's infamous occupation. His first six or seven years were spent mostly in the company of adult women as well as other children. Frantz's mother died sometime before his sixth birthday, possibly during or shortly after his birth – an all-too-common occurrence at the time – at which point an aunt or grandmother most likely stepped into the maternal role. In 1560 he acquired a stepmother, also a common experience for the day, when his widower father married Anna Blechschmidt, likely from an executioner family herself, in nearby Bayreuth.[53] Despite the bad press of the Brothers Grimm, many early modern stepmothers enjoyed positive, even loving, relationships with their stepchildren. We can only hope that this was the case for young Frantz.

If the family's social isolation in Hof was as severe as Frantz later suggested, his childhood must have been a solitary one. Toddlers and young children of the day were fairly unsupervised – at least by modern Western standards – and were free to explore open wells, cooking fires, and a multitude of other dangerous places that routinely claimed many young lives. Perhaps this liberty provided Frantz with some playmates, undaunted by the prejudices of their parents. We know that he had at least one older sister, Kunigunda, who reached adulthood; it's possible, even likely, that he had other siblings who were victims of the dreadful 50 per cent mortality rate for all children under the age of twelve.

About the time that Heinrich Schmidt remarried, Frantz probably acquired more household chores and began to learn the basics of reading, writing, and arithmetic. In some locations, executioners' children were permitted to attend a local Latin school or German grammar school, always on a fee basis. Frantz's Nuremberg kinsman Lienhardt Lippert later complained bitterly that other parents refused to let their children sit next to his own son in school, but city officials refused to intervene, suggesting instead that the boy be taught at home.[54] Hof maintained both a parochial (German) school and a Latin school (founded by a student of Philipp Melanchthon), but the matriculation records have not survived, so we can't be sure whether Frantz learned to read and write at school, from a private tutor, or from one of his parents. His adult writing, as well as his elegant signature, suggest rudimentary training in German and perhaps some Latin. But he writes completely without punctuation and employs idiosyncratic syntax and spelling, displaying no apparent awareness of literary or even plain notarial style. Like many "semi-educated" artisans of the day, Frantz Schmidt wrote as he spoke, without artifice. He was a practical chronicler who valued fact and expediency, sometimes even at the expense of clarity.

Frantz likely received his religious training at home, although a local pastor – if one would consent to enter the Schmidt household – may have instructed the boy in the rigours of the catechism. It was the Evangelical, or Lutheran, faith that informed the boy's earliest religious sensibilities. The city of Hof had broken with the Catholic Church and allied itself with the new Lutheran faith during the early, strife-ridden days of the Reformation in the 1520s. By the time of Frantz's birth a

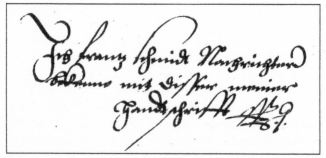

Frantz's signature on his 1584 employment contract. The form is exceptionally neat for the era but clearly distinctive from the notarial hand that drew up the document itself, thus likely a genuine autograph.

generation later, Hof had become a bastion of Lutheranism, with virtually every citizen adhering to its Protestant creed. The adult Meister Frantz held strong religious convictions, and it's likely that he learned to take his faith seriously from his parents or other members of the immediate household who did so as well. Many children of the era studied religion at home. In fact, church leaders preached that every *Hausvater* (literally, "house father") had a divine responsibility to ensure that children received proper instruction. As in most households, young Frantz and his sister, Kunigunda, would thus study the Lutheran perspective on the central doctrines of Christianity at an early age, learning of both original sin and divine forgiveness, of the centrality of faith in the human experience, and of the imperative to persevere in godly living.

Frantz's apprenticeship in the executioner craft probably began around the age of twelve. Whatever Heinrich Schmidt's presence in his son's life had been until this point, he now became the boy's most important personal and professional role model. Honourable trades – such as tailoring or carpentry – typically required a formal apprenticeship contract of two to four years with an acknowledged master, who received a sizeable annual fee from the young man's family. Some executioners' sons did leave to work for a kinsman or other master executioner on such terms. But such masters were relatively few, so most sons stayed at home and learned the craft "from youth on" under their own fathers' tutelage.[55] An executioner's son like Frantz was of course forbidden to train in another, respectable craft, nor could he pursue a university education or even seek to enter the ministry – all deeply entrenched prohibitions that were still widely in force two centuries later. Such realities could not prevent him, of course, from imagining a different life for himself or for his children.

What did the teenage Frantz learn from his father? Above all, he formed his fundamental notion of what it meant to be a man. Early modern masculinity was particularly focused on the notion of honour, both personal and collective. As Heinrich impressed upon Frantz from an early age, the hated margrave had robbed them of everything they held precious: an honourable profession, the right to citizenship, the company of friends, and their very name. The details that the seventy-year-old Meister Frantz would include in his own much later recounting – the full names of his late grandfather and uncle (in an era when most people never knew their own grandparents), the fatal encounter with the deer hunter and his dog, the exact words of the margrave to his father, the number of the would-be assassins, and so on – all bear the hallmark of a much-told family tale. Most early modern men were pre-occupied with attacks on their honour; the Schmidts were – understandably – morbidly obsessed with the subject, not least because of the daily reminders of their ignominy. Frantz's own understanding of personal honour evolved over his lifetime, but, like his father, he held fast to a burning anger over the fundamental injustice of his family's predicament. One wonders, in fact – was it mere coincidence that Heinrich and Frantz went on to serve the cities of Bamberg and Nuremberg, once the bitterest enemies of the hated Albrecht Alcibiades?

The only other knowledge we can be sure that Heinrich Schmidt imparted to his son concerned the practical side of masculinity – a craft. "The art of the executioner" in fact comprised several discrete skills. The sine qua non was technical competence: how to effectively administer torture and a range of corporal punishments, ranging from eye-gouging and finger-chopping to flogging with birch rods to several forms of execution. First, however, Frantz performed the menial tasks delegated to any apprentice: cleaning and maintaining his father's sword and torture equipment, gathering and preparing supplies for public executions (shackles, rope, wood), fetching food and drink for his father and his assistants, and perhaps even helping to dispose of the bodies (and heads) of decapitated felons.

As he grew older and stronger, Frantz advanced to helping restrain prisoners during interrogation or execution, and he began to accompany his father on trips to various execution sites throughout the Franconian countryside. By observing and listening to the experienced Meister Heinrich, Frantz learned where to place the double ladder at a hanging and how to manage both rope and chains with a resistant victim. He helped construct the temporary wooden platforms used for drowning in rivers and observed how to expedite this inevitably difficult and often prolonged ordeal. Most crucially, Heinrich Schmidt taught his son how to apply the various instruments of torture at his disposal during "painful interrogation", and how to judge a subject's capabilities of endurance, so as to avoid a premature death.

One area of expertise for the typical executioner often comes as a shock to modern observers: the frequent sideline as a popular healer. Some professionals exploited the magical aura of their craft to attract clients, but it was their familiarity with human anatomy – and particularly with various wounds – that ensured the reputations of the hangman healer. Thus Meister Heinrich also passed on to Frantz his own knowledge (likely learned from other executioners) of which healing herbs and salves to apply to the wounds of a torture victim and how to mend the broken bones of a prisoner in preparation for a public execution. Having mastered such skills, the adult Frantz Schmidt earned a significant supplementary income as a healer and medical consultant throughout his life – and finally went on to establish for himself an alternate professional identity after his retirement.

Finally, a successful executioner, especially in this era of heightened expectations, also needed what we would call people skills and a certain degree of psychological insight. Abilities of this nature were of course more difficult to teach, but Heinrich Schmidt at least provided an example of how to deal with both status-conscious patrician superiors and less-than-reliable lower-class subordinates, as well as agitated poor sinners in the torture chamber and at the gallows. For Heinrich's Bamberg employers, the key attributes of a successful executioner were obedience, honesty, and discretion – all explicit in his oath of office:

> I shall and will protect my gracious Lord of Bamberg and His Grace's diocese from all harm, conduct myself piously, serve faithfully in my office, judicially interrogate and punish as I am commanded each time by His Grace's secular authority; also not take more than the appropriate fee, all in accordance with this ordinance; also whatever I hear during criminal interrogation or am otherwise commanded to keep secret, the same I will not further disclose to anyone; nor will I travel anywhere without the explicit permission of my gracious Lords Chamberlain, Marshall, or House Steward and I will be obedient and compliant in all affairs and commands of the same, faithful and without trouble in all things. So help me God and the saints![56]

Frantz witnessed firsthand the transactional character of each capital case that came before his father, the difficult balancing of diverse interests and objectives, as well as the business dimension of criminal justice in practise. Whether Heinrich provided a positive or negative model in each of these areas we cannot know, but the teenage Frantz quickly realised that technical proficiency would in fact be less crucial to his professional success than would his ability to instil confidence in his employers, fear in subjects under interrogation, and respect among his neighbours. The performative aspect of his job, in other words, was not limited to those dramatic (and still important) minutes on the scaffold. The position of executioner would be an all-encompassing lifelong role, demanding unrelenting self-awareness and vigilance.

People skills also came into play in an executioner's relationships with his fellow professionals. Like all specialists, Meister Heinrich and his counterparts in other cities employed an insider lingo, often based on the street cant of the day, known as *Rotwelsch* or *Gaunersprache*. Among fellow practitioners, hanging was known as "lacing up" and beheading as "slicing". An especially skilled colleague might be admired for "making a fine knot", "playing well with the wheel", or "carving nicely".[57] Executioners also had their own word for a botched beheading (*putzen*), as well as their own nicknames for their craft, such as Punch, Killer, Crusher, Slicer, Freeman, and Cruncher. Though hardly flattering, these self-designations were at least less condescending (and colourful) than the dozens of more popular appellations, such as "shortener", "bogeyman", "blood-judge", "bad man", "thief-hanger", Hans, "heads-off", "chopper", "little hammer", Master Hammerling (also a nickname for the devil), "racker", Snip Johnny, "tie-maker", "holy angel", Master Ouch, Master Fix, and, most simply, "butcher".[58]

As in other guilds and brotherhoods, early modern executioners called one another "cousin" and enjoyed common social gatherings, coming together informally at weddings and festivals or in larger numbers at occasional organised assemblies. The most famous German executioner conference, known as the Kohlenberg Court, began in fourteenth-century Basel and recurred irregularly there until the beginning of the seventeenth century. The gathering played out as a typical late medieval "court of equals", combining dispute resolution with comical rituals and copious eating, drinking, and swapping of tales. In this instance the membership comprised not only executioners but also many of the other dishonourable "travelling folk" who had no guild or justice of their own. By the sixteenth century, the assembly was dominated by executioners and sack carriers, but other marginalised men and women continued to participate. According to a 1559 account, the court convened in the square outside the executioner's residence on the Kohlenberg, "beneath a large lime tree [the German tree of justice] and another tall tree here that is called the Vinegar Tree." The presiding judge, elected by the assembly, sat "with his bare feet in a tub of water, summer or winter", and heard cases of defamation and other disputes among his fellow executioners. Upon polling the seven jurors, the judge then pronounced his decision and emptied the tub, and the festivities for the day began. One disgruntled husband, summoned to appear before the court by his wife's executioner paramour, contemptuously described the gathering as "full of foreign ceremonies" and disregarded by all locals, except those up to mischief (including, apparently, his own wife).[59]

Frantz Schmidt's journal does not mention attending the Kohlenberg Court – or any other social occasion, for that matter. Perhaps Heinrich compelled him to come along once to Basel or another assembly. It's more likely that father and son considered such boisterous and indiscriminate mixing with prostitutes and beggars as unseemly, an unwelcome reminder of their craft's lingering shameful associations. The carnivalesque and irregular character of the court also belonged to an earlier time, before the introduction of more sophisticated legal machinery and professionalisation of the executioner craft. Frantz already knew many of his fellow professionals via his father and certainly corresponded with some of them. Celebrating their corporate identity and trade secrets, however, was something that his generation of executioners mostly preferred to do in private, and certainly away from the skinners, tanners, and other disreputable individuals from whom they had worked so hard to distinguish themselves.

The culmination of Frantz Schmidt's apprenticeship returns us to his training with the judgement sword. Unlike axes, which on the Continent were commonly associated with mercenaries and woodsmen, swords in premodern Europe embodied honour and justice. Emperors, princes, and other rulers spoke of their own God-given legal authority in terms of the sword, and the weapon itself played a prominent part in coronation and other formal ceremonies. The right to carry a sword long remained a jealously guarded privilege of nobles alone, an immediately visible display of their high status. Beheading by the sword, consequently, had since Roman times been the privilege of citizens and aristocrats and the universally preferred form of execution, as much for its connotation of honour as for its swiftness.

The executioner's sword itself had become an object of particular symbolic and monetary value. It was large – on average measuring more than forty inches long and weighing about seven pounds – and often impressively ornamented. By the mid-sixteenth century, the typical battlefield sword used by medieval executioners had been mostly replaced by a specially designed weapon, with a flat rather than pointed tip and a more carefully balanced distribution of weight, adapted to the exclusive purpose of beheading. Many such swords have survived to the present and bear witness to the extraordinary craftsmanship and deliberation that went into their creation. Typically, each sword carried a unique inscription, such as "Through justice will the land prosper and thrive; in lawlessness it will not survive", or "Guard thyself from evil deeds, else thy path to the gallows leads", or, more succinctly, "The lords prosecute, I execute".[60] Several swords also bore engraved images of the scales of justice, Christ, or the Madonna and Child, or of the gallows, wheel, or a disembodied head. Some executioner dynasties inscribed the names and dates of each owner, and one family even notched on their sword the number of people it had executed.

Meister Heinrich's judgement sword was thus more than a sign of his technical prowess; it represented his ostracised family's last tenuous link with honour. For his apprentice son, it also stood as a symbol of the new, professional, even respectable executioner, a stark contrast to the mercenary butcher who still lived on in many people's imaginations. As an adult, Frantz wielded a sword designed to his own specifications, proudly borne throughout the entire execution ritual in its own wood and leather sheath and removed only at the ultimate moment of the public drama. In his journal, he would carefully note the exact dates of his *first execution with the sword, first execution with the sword in Nuremberg,* and *first execution with the sword [and the victim] standing.*[61]

In the spring of 1573, two hurdles remained on Frantz Schmidt's path to master executioner status. Like all craftsmen, he needed to spend several years as a journeyman, travelling the countryside, working on a fee basis, and gaining valuable experience along the way. But before he could begin his professional wanderings, he had to pass a master test. By the eighteenth century, Prussia actually required aspiring executioners to pass an extensive written and practical examination, judging whether the applicant could apply torture without breaking bones, burn a corpse completely to ashes, and show proficiency with all the interrogation and execution equipment.[62] The procedure in sixteenth-century Bamberg was much less thorough or formalised, but it remained essential for an apprentice to attain the ritualistic approval of his craft's masters if he hoped to secure a good position in the future.

Frantz's own day of reckoning came on 5 June 1573, when he was nineteen. Five years later, when he began his journal, it was the only exact date he could recall from this period, underscoring its momentous place in his life. With his father at his side, he made the two-day journey to the village of Steinach, forty miles northwest of Bamberg. The condemned was one Lienhardt Russ of Zeyern, whose full description in Frantz's journal is *a thief*. It's possible that some of Heinrich's colleagues or associates came to witness the execution, an otherwise routine hanging, given its momentous nature in the lives of father and son. The form of execution ranked as the least prestigious for a professional, but it was also the least likely to go wrong. What was young Frantz thinking as he led Russ to the gallows, bound his wrists and ankles in the prescribed manner, and moved him up the ladder towards the waiting noose? Did his voice falter as he called for the condemned to speak his final words? Did the assembled crowd of villagers remark on the youth of the executioner or question his skill? About these things we can only speculate. What we do know is this: Frantz completed his task without any apparent misstep. As the body of the condemned man swung lifeless from the gallows, Meister Heinrich or another master strode forward to where young Frantz stood. With ritual aplomb he administered three face-slaps, "according to ancient custom", and then loudly proclaimed to all assembled at the execution that the young man had "executed adroitly, without any mistakes", and should henceforth be acknowledged as a master. Frantz would later receive a notarised certificate (*Meisterbrief*) to show to prospective employers, proclaiming that the new master had performed his task "with all bravery to absolute satisfaction"[63] and was eligible to be hired – and paid – as a master.

As in other crafts, a successful master executioner test often gave way to a festive gathering of family members and friends, all eager to enjoy the hospitality of the proud father. If such a celebration was planned for Frantz, it would most likely have taken place later, in Bamberg.

Half a century after this day, a melancholic bitterness still permeates the recollections of the elderly former executioner as he describes the *great misfortune [that] forced the office of executioner on my innocent father as well as on myself, since as much as I would have liked, I couldn't escape it.*[64] But his account also evinces an unmistakable sense of accomplishment in having spent a lifetime restoring *peace, calm, and unity* to the land. At the age of nineteen, still fresh from *my first execution*, the future Meister Frantz had just begun to experience this complex mix of revulsion and pride regarding his ordained profession. It was a duality of feeling that would propel him up the career ladder in the years following that milestone day, but it would also pit the young executioner against himself and render elusive the genuine personal and professional satisfaction he sought.

THE JOURNEYMAN

Mixing with the world has a marvellously clarifying effect on a man's judgement.
—Michel de Montaigne, "On the Education of Children" (1580)[1]

I must be cruel, only to be kind.
Thus bad begins and worse remains behind.
—William Shakespeare, *Hamlet*, act 3, scene 4, 177–78 (1600)

Formally initiated into the brotherhood of executioners, the nineteen-year-old Frantz Schmidt could now begin building the professional curriculum vitae that might one day secure him a permanent position. Shortly after his professional debut in Steinach in June 1573, the young journeyman was called to the town of Kronach, halfway between Bamberg and Hof, to administer his first *execution with the wheel*. His recording of the occasion is terse, as was his habit during these journeyman years. We learn only that the robber in question, one Barthel Dochendte, was guilty of at least three murders with his unnamed companions, and that his painful final ordeal was preceded by the uneventful hanging of a thief – a double execution and thus another first for the novice executioner. The young Schmidt does not in any way commemorate these novel professional experiences, at least not in writing.

Assisted by his father, Frantz secured an impressive total of seven commissions during his first twelve months on the job. Most of these involved the execution of thieves *with the rope*, all described by Frantz in succinct and emotionless terms. Hanging was a relatively simple, albeit grisly, operation: the young executioner mounted a double ladder with the poor sinner, then simply pushed his victim off. Some jurisdictions used stepstools or chairs, but the platform with the trapdoor did not make its appearance anywhere in Europe before the late eighteenth century. Thus there was no sharp drop to break the neck, but rather prolonged choking, which might be accelerated by the executioner or his assistant pulling on the legs of the convulsing victim, typically wearing special gloves made of dog leather. Once the desperate struggle for survival came to an end, Frantz removed the ladder and left the executed corpse hanging on the gallows until it decayed and dropped into the pit of bones below the gallows.

Three of Frantz's assignments during his first year involved *execution with the wheel*, an extended procedure requiring a much greater degree of physical and emotional stamina on his part. It was also the most explicitly violent, even gruesome, act the young executioner would be required to carry out as a professional. Typically reserved for notorious bandits and other murderers, this method of final dispatch essentially consisted of public torture, akin to the more infamous – and also much rarer – drawing and quartering. But whereas the much more common interrogatory torture of the prison chamber ostensibly sought information leading to conviction or vindication, the very public breaking with the wheel aspired to no more than providing a ritualised outlet for the community's rage and a terrifying warning to any spectators with murderous inclinations.

All three men Frantz executed with the wheel during his first year were multiple murderers, but only Klaus Renckhart from Veilsdorf, the young executioner's seventh victim, merited more than a line or two in his journal. Sometime during the second half of 1574, Meister Heinrich arranged for his son to travel to the village of Greiz, about forty miles northeast of their native Hof. Upon the completion of his four-day journey from Bamberg, Frantz came face-to-face with Renckhart himself, convicted of three murders and numerous robberies. Their initial contact was most likely brief, but during the last hour of the condemned man's life, the journeyman executioner and his victim would be constant companions.

Immediately following the local court's pronouncement of the death sentence, Frantz shepherded the shackled Renckhart to a waiting horse-drawn cart. During their slow procession to the execution site, Frantz administered the court-prescribed number of "nips" with red-hot tongs, ripping flesh from the condemned man's arm or the torso. Frantz rarely comments in his journal on this aspect of the ordeal, but it could not have been more than four nips, which was commonly considered fatal. Upon their arrival at the execution scaffold, Frantz then forced the weakened and bloody Renckhart to strip down to his undergarments, then lie down while the executioner staked his victim to the ground, meticulously inserting slats of wood under each of the joints to facilitate the breaking of bones. The number of blows with a heavy wagon wheel or specially crafted iron bar was also preordained by the

Frantz Schmidt's 1585 execution of the patricide Frantz Seuboldt, from a popular broadsheet. The upper left portrays Seuboldt's "inhuman" ambush and murder of his own father while the latter was setting bird traps. In the forefront, Meister Frantz administers the nips with glowing tongs during the procession to the execution grounds. Upon their arrival at the Raven Stone, Seuboldt is staked out and executed with the wheel, his corpse then hoisted atop the wheel and displayed next to the gallows (in background, with heads on stakes nearby).

court, as was the direction of the procedure. If the judge and jurors had wished to be merciful, Frantz proceeded "from the top down", delivering an initial "blow of mercy" (coup de grâce) to Renckhart's neck or heart before proceeding to shatter the limbs of his corpse. If the judges had deemed the crime especially heinous, the procedure went "from the bottom up", prolonging the agony as long as possible, with Frantz hefting the wagon wheel to deliver thirty or more blows before the condemned murderer expired. Again, Frantz does not remark whether a mercy blow preceded this particular ordeal but it seems unlikely, given the alleged atrocities involved. Finally, the young executioner untied Renckhart's mangled body and placed it atop a wheel on a pole, which he then hoisted to an upright position so that it might serve as a feast for carrion birds and as a graphic admonition to all new arrivals of the authorities' deadly seriousness about law enforcement.

How did Frantz feel about his role in these macabre blood rituals? His journal entries provide little insight, except perhaps in their very brevity. Was his performance during these journeyman years as tentative as his subsequent recording of it? After all, witnessing such gruesome spectacles was quite another thing from perpetrating them with his own hands. Just as important as attaining the appropriate level of technical expertise, he had to develop the psychological fortitude to look into the eyes of condemned criminals like Renckhart before terminating their earthly existence. Did the young journeyman's ambition override his innate distaste for his unsavoury work, or did he find other ways to make the job more palatable? Above all, how would he keep the near-daily violence he administered from consuming him?

The short paragraph that Frantz writes about Renckhart in his journal provides a partial answer. Rather than describe the execution ritual itself, as he often does later in life, the journeyman executioner focuses on Renckhart's crimes, giving most attention to a recent atrocity that clearly chilled the journeyman executioner to the bone. After briefly mentioning the robber's other murders, Frantz recounts how one night Renckhart and a companion attacked an isolated rural home known as the Fox Mill. Upon their break-in, Renckhart *shot the miller dead [and] forced the miller's wife and maid to his will and raped them. He then made them fry an egg in fat and lay it on the dead miller's body [and] forced the miller's wife to join him in eating. Also kicked the miller's body and said, "Miller, how do you like this morsel?"* The robber's shocking violations of all human decency in Frantz's eyes provided all the justification he required in his subsequent administering of *death by the wheel*. This stratagem of recalling and recording the heinous offences that had made necessary the very punishments he carried out was a useful discovery that provided continual reassurance to Frantz throughout his long career.

On the road

From the age of nineteen to twenty-four, Frantz continued to use his parents' home in Bamberg as a base while he travelled the Franconian countryside from one temporary assignment to another. In this respect, his life differed little from the lives of most journeymen his age, all of whom sought to build a reputation and secure a permanent position as a master. Meister Heinrich's name and professional contacts served him well during this period, providing him entrée into several villages in need of an ad hoc executioner for interrogation or punishment. None of these small communities offered Frantz any hope of a permanent position, but collectively they allowed him to earn his keep while gaining invaluable experience.

His journal entries during these years record twenty-nine executions in thirteen towns, most frequently Hollfeld and Forchheim, each less than a two-day journey from his new home (see map on page ix). He also performed three executions in his father's stead in Bamberg, one in 1574, the other two in 1577.[2] In later years, Frantz would sometimes write long, reflective journal entries in which he speculated on such questions as the motives of the people he executed. But in these early years, only the Renckhart execution runs to more than a terse one or two lines. Instead, professional advancement dominated the young journeyman's thoughts and writings, and so he concentrates on documenting the number of executions he performed and the variety of killing methods in his repertoire. Even the briefest hint of introspection would have to wait until he was established and secure.

Like many ambitious young men, Frantz evidently knew – perhaps thanks in part to his father's counsel – that technical proficiency alone would not earn him a coveted permanent position. In the increasingly lucrative, and thus competitive, world of professional executioners, a man also had to cultivate a social network and build a respectable name. Heinrich Schmidt could help his son get a foot in the door, but ultimate success depended on Frantz's own ability to impress influential legal authorities with both his professional skills and his personal integrity. To that end, building a reputation for honesty, reliability, discretion, and even piety went hand in glove with gaining experience at the gallows. In later years, Frantz would improve his reputation by drawing nearer and nearer to respectable society. At the onset of his career, though, his more urgent need was to push away – to the extent possible – his association with disreputable society. This precocious act of self-fashioning made his journeyman years more difficult and lonely – but it also allowed him to establish many of the habits and character traits for which the later Meister Frantz was known and revered.

In his journeys as a "wander bird", Frantz encountered individuals from virtually every social rank. We tend to think of premodern Europe as fairly static, but there was in fact considerable geographical mobility. The young executioner was able to identify most travellers immediately by their attire and means of transportation. Fur-bedecked nobles and patricians in silk travelling cloaks were – as they intended – the most conspicuous, journeying by horse or carriage, usually accompanied by at least a few armed retainers. Merchants, bankers, physicians, and lawyers also typically travelled by horse and dressed in crisp woolen mantles. Frantz himself might have had use of his father's riding horse, but more likely he journeyed as did most other honest folk of modest means, by foot. Along the dirt paths and muddy roads of the Franconian countryside, he would frequently be overtaken and passed by galloping couriers and even plodding transport carts filled with manufactured goods, wine, or foodstuffs. Pilgrims travelling to a religious shrine wrapped themselves in penitential white or sackcloth and moved at a slower gait, while families travelling to a wedding feast or farmers on the way to market hastened along amid boisterous chatter. A young journeyman wearing a modest hat and travelling cloak, perhaps with a walking staff in hand, was one of the most common sights of all.

Rural travel, as Frantz well knew, posed many dangers. Whatever personal encounters he had with highwaymen or other ruffians while under way are lost to history. We do however know of a more insidious threat the young executioner regularly faced and likewise struggled to evade – association with the dishonourable "travelling folk" who also filled the roads.[3] The least marginalised of these were the numerous migrant agricultural workers and travelling tradespeople: pedlars, hawkers, tinkers, pewterers, knife grinders, and ragmen. Executioners themselves, like butchers and tanners, were still widely considered part of this group, as were entertainers of all sorts – acrobats, pipers, puppeteers, actors, and bear baiters. If he mingled in public with any of these individuals during his travels, Frantz risked bringing down on his head the very social stigma he sought to escape.

His deep personal familiarity with the criminal underworld, the so-called thieves' society, put Frantz in an even more uncomfortable spot. Many of his father's assistants came from unsavoury backgrounds, as did of course most of his victims. Like all executioners, Heinrich and Frantz Schmidt were both fluent in *Rotwelsch*, the colourful street slang of vagrants and criminals that combined elements of Yiddish, Gypsy, and assorted German dialects. A denizen of the underworld, for instance, who had "bought the monkey" (was drunk) might be wary of running into a "lover" (police official), especially if he had recently been "fencing" (begging), "bargaining" (swindling), or "burning" (blackmailing).[4] Frantz also knew the signs and symbols that such vagabonds carved or chalked for one another on hospitable houses and inns.[5] The extensive personal contact that young Schmidt had with hardened professionals, albeit not in a social context, meant that in most ways he was more a part of their "wised-up" (*kocheme*) society than the general public's "witless" (*wittische*) world. His familiarity with the denizens of both worlds admittedly gave him an advantage in recognising and steering clear of shady characters, but his years of assisting his father had also taught him that the line between honest and dishonest was neither fixed nor always obvious.

In that respect, the greatest challenge for a young man of the day seeking to establish an upright name came from other young men. Everywhere that Frantz went, he encountered the dominant culture of unmarried males – whether honest journeymen like himself or those engaged in shadowy enterprises – a social world based primarily on

drink, women, and sport. Alcohol in particular constituted a key component of male friendship in early modern Germany and held special significance in the rites of passage among young men. Accompanied by
raunchy songs and poems, the prolific quaffing of beer or wine could
establish the ephemeral bonds of drinking chums or be part of formal
initiation into a local youth group, a military cohort, an occupational association, or even some form of blood brotherhood. Taverns with now-
quaint names such as the Blue Key or the Golden Hatchet were usually
the first stop for all male travellers upon arrival in a village or town, and
buying a round of drinks was a particularly effective way for a newcomer
to command respect and make new friends, at least at a superficial level.

Like today, young male friendships of the era thrived on competition of all sorts. Card playing and gambling were routine. Wrestling or
archery matches provided both a test of physical skill and yet another
opportunity for betting. German men indulged to a legendary degree in
prolonged drinking bouts and "duels" of wine and beer that occasionally resulted in serious internal injuries or, in rare cases, death. The
drunken camaraderie of the taverns often led to much bragging – and
exaggeration – about sexual prowess. And of course the dangerous combination of alcohol and testosterone inevitably sparked violence, not just
brawls and knife fights among the young men themselves but also attacks on others, especially sexual assaults against women.[6]

Participation in this rambunctious world was not an option for an
ambitious young executioner. His efforts to avoid such company, as well
as association with any dishonourable individuals, needed to be relentless and total. The subsequent self-isolation must have been emotionally difficult for Frantz, especially since he had not yet gained the
acceptance of honourable society either. Respectable innkeepers remained wary about housing a man of his background, regardless of
his commission from the prince-bishop or how finely attired or well-
mannered he appeared. On the road, Schmidt could attempt to conceal
his profession, even lie about it, or seek lodging elsewhere, in the house
or barn of a hospitable stranger. Upon his arrival in the village of execution, though, it became impossible to hide his identity from anyone, so
he was effectively excluded from all social gatherings. The only young
males willing to share Frantz's table (and his tavern bill) were the very
individuals he was trying to avoid – beggars, mercenaries, and probable

criminals. His options for female companionship were just as limited: honourable artisans' daughters wanted nothing to do with him, and consorting with prostitutes or other loose women would undermine the very reputation he was seeking to establish.

Thus Frantz did not make any great social sacrifice when he came to what was a remarkable decision for a man of his era: never to drink wine, beer, or alcohol of any kind. It was a vow he apparently kept for the rest of his life and for which he eventually became widely known and admired. Frantz's religious beliefs may have played a role in this choice, but complete abstention from alcohol was rare in the sixteenth century, even among the most godly men and women. Our modern inclination might be to speculate that he had suffered from the embarrassing behaviour or drunken violence of someone close to him – perhaps

Early modern taverns provided young men like Frantz with the opportunity to drink as well as gamble, fight, and pursue sexual exploits. Some moralists considered the taverns "schools of crime", where thefts and other schemes were often planned, while innkeepers acted as fences and prostitutes known as "thief-whores" picked the pockets of unsuspecting and inebriated customers (c.1530).

even his own father. But whatever his religious or emotional reasons, Schmidt's vow not to drink was also a carefully calculated career decision. Early modern Europeans simply assumed that the executioner would drink to excess – a stereotype with a great deal of truth behind it. Compelled to kill and torture their fellow human beings again and again, many in Frantz's profession sought pre-execution courage in a tankard or two of beer or oblivion after the fact in a large quantity of wine. By publicly refuting the legendary fondness of his fellow executioners for the bottle, Frantz found an extraordinary means of underscoring the sobriety, both literal and figurative, of the way he had chosen to live. This jujitsu manoeuvre cleverly took the disadvantage of his de facto social isolation and turned it into a virtue that distinguished him in the eyes of future employers, and perhaps even society at large. The quiet journeyman who sat without companions – or drink – in a far corner of the tavern may have been lonely, but he knew exactly what he was doing.[7]

Violence in the pursuit of truth

To obtain a permanent position, Frantz needed, of course, to prove his proficiency in two particular aspects of law enforcement: interrogation and punishment. Both involved a much greater degree of physical violence than most modern legal authorities would consider permissible (at least on the record). It's reassuring to believe that this contrast is grounded in our own time's greater sensitivity to human suffering and higher respect for human dignity – but the daily headlines regularly mock any smug sense of superiority on this score. The same unstable alchemy of compassion and retribution that fuels modern debates on criminal justice animated the response to crime in Frantz Schmidt's time. Why then was early modern criminal justice itself so much more visibly brutal? And why was a compliant instrument of that state violence like Frantz Schmidt so much in demand?

Again, legal authorities of the day, particularly in "progressive" states such as Nuremberg, struggled in vain to span the chasm between their ambition to practise a new, more effective system of criminal prosecution and their continuing reliance on traditional and largely insufficient means to that end. Despite the imperial codifications of the *Bamber-gensis* and *Carolina*, most local authorities' procedures, personnel, and overall mentality remained grounded in the private accusatorial model of centuries past. In some instances, newly energised criminal courts became tragically susceptible to popular prejudices and personal rival-ries, as in the case of the notorious witch panics of the era. More often, secular authorities simply struggled to conceal their profound inability to prevent crime in the first place or to apprehend criminals after the fact. Frantz's journal is filled with accounts of notorious outlaws who easily evaded authorities, sometimes living *out in the open in a foreign jurisdiction*, until they were at last brought to court by a victim, a victim's family member, or a private posse (*posse comitatus*).[8]

A cool and reliable executioner typically played the pivotal role in making the most of the few opportunities when a suspected culprit ac-tually landed in official custody. He was the one who began the process by obtaining information from recalcitrant suspects, and he was the one who brought it to a close by orchestrating the ritualised public spectacle of punishment. If at least two impartial witnesses aged twelve or older provided testimony, a suspect usually confessed, and Frantz's skills in the torture chamber were not required. Material proof – such as stolen items or a bloody murder weapon – could also make the prosecution's task much easier. Unfortunately, the courts frequently found neither witness nor physical evidence, and the investigation stalled because of the paltry capabilities of pre-nineteenth-century forensic science. In the absence of any other compelling evidence, conviction of the average suspect thus depended almost exclusively on the accused person's self-incrimination. At that point, a professional executioner would be sum-moned. In Bamberg Frantz played the part of the assistant to his father; in those locations he visited on his own, he was in charge.

Like professional interrogators today, Frantz Schmidt and his supe-riors knew the effectiveness of intimidation and other forms of emo-tional pressure. One non-violent but nonetheless psychologically intense method of obtaining a murder confession was the so-called bier test. This ancient Germanic custom, familiar to readers of the *Niebelungen-lied* and other medieval sagas, remained a powerful tool in the professional interrogator's arsenal. Assembling a room full of witnesses, the executioner and his assistant would force the accused – or even a

The ancient bier test as practised by a late medieval court. By the sixteenth century, this last remnant of trial by divine ordeal had lost all official backing, but many people continued to believe that a murder victim's corpse would bleed or move at the touch of its killer's hand (1513).

group of suspects – to approach the victim's corpse on its stretcher and touch it. If the body bled or gave any other sign of guilt (such as apparent movement), the killer would supposedly be compelled to confess.[9]

No jurist considered such an event sufficient or even necessarily credible evidence, but the trauma did often succeed in exposing a guilty conscience. Frantz only writes of one application of the bier test during his career, and it happened long after his journeyman days. The accused Dorothea Hoffmennin vehemently denied strangling her own newborn daughter, but *when the dead child was brought before her, laying its hand on her skin – which she did with a terrified heart – it received a red bruise on the same spot*. Since the young maid kept calm and refused to confess, she was merely *whipped out of town with rods*. The very fear of undergoing such an ordeal nevertheless provided a vulnerability that the experienced executioner might exploit. Years later, Frantz wrote how another suspected murderer incriminated herself by loudly forbidding her accomplice to re-enter the house of the patrician spinster they had just killed in her sleep, fearing that the corpse would "sweat blood" if he approached.[10]

If initial interviews were unsatisfactory and the consulting jurists found sufficient "indices" to begin torture, Frantz's superiors ordered him to "strictly bind and threaten" the suspect, the first of five increasingly severe grades of torture.[11] The journeyman Schmidt left no record of his interrogation method during these years, but it was most likely similar to the well-defined routine he later used in Nuremberg. First he and his assistant would escort the accused from his or her cell to a sealed room with the instruments of torture prominently displayed. In Nuremberg this took place in the "Hole", or dungeon, in a specially designed torture chamber, which was nicknamed "the chapel" because of its arched ceiling (and perhaps to provide a hint of macabre irony). The small, windowless room of approximately six by fifteen feet stood directly beneath a meeting room in the town hall. In the room above sat two patrician jurors, shielded from the gruesome spectacle below, who consulted their case notes and questioned the suspect through a specially designed air duct linked to the chamber.

Even at this point, the executioner relied more on emotional vulnerability and psychological pressure than on sheer physical coercion. In the "chapel", Meister Frantz and his assistant would tightly bind the subject – occasionally on the rack, but usually in a chair bolted to the floor – and then painstakingly describe the function of the torture implements on display. One veteran jurist advised inexperienced executioners such as the young Frantz not to be gentle or humble at this point, "but to employ rumour and speculation . . . saying amazing things [*Wunder-Dinge*]: that he was a great man who had done great deeds . . . learned and practised in his arts, that no person was capable of concealing the truth from his ruses or movements . . . as he had already happily proven to all the world with the most obstinate villains."[12] Perhaps Frantz even learned from his father a version of "good executioner, bad executioner", with the two men alternately threatening and consoling a terrified suspect. Most subjects yielded some kind of confession under such conditions, seeking to avoid both the pain and subsequent social stigma of torture.[13]

For those few other individuals who still resisted, typically hardened robbers, the executioner and his assistant would then begin to apply whatever method of physical coercion their superiors had approved. In Bamberg and Nuremberg the approved options included thumbscrews (usually reserved for female subjects), "Spanish boots" (leg screws), "fire" (candles or torches applied to the subjects' armpits), "water" (today known as waterboarding), "the ladder" (aka the rack; the subject was strapped to a ladder and either stretched or rolled back and forth on a spiked drum), and "the wreath" (aka "the crown": a metal and leather band was placed on the forehead and slowly tightened). The most commonly applied torture in Bamberg and Nuremberg was "the stone", more commonly known as the strappado, in which the subject's hands were bound behind the back and slowly drawn upwards on a pulley, with stones of varying weight pulling down on the feet. Human ingenuity and sadism inevitably produced countless other stylised forms of inflicting pain – the Pomeranian Cap, the Polish Ram, the English Shirt – as well as crude but effective means of degradation, such as forcing victims to eat worms or faeces, or sliding pieces of wood under their fingernails.[14] Frantz Schmidt undoubtedly knew of most, if not all, of these methods. But did he or his father – perhaps out of frustration with a particularly recalcitrant suspect – ever resort to such non-sanctioned techniques? Predictably, both his journal and the official records are mute on this point.

The interrogation technique known as the strappado, showing a suspect before one of the stones is attached to his feet (1513).

On rare occasions, Frantz's instructions prescribed the length of time that duress might be employed, for instance, no more than fifteen minutes for recently delivered mothers. Generally, responsibility for judging the subject's "torturability" (*Foltertauglichkeit*) rested entirely with the executioner. Surgeons and physicians did not attend torture sessions until the practise itself was on the verge of being abolished, two centuries later.[15] In theory, Frantz's non-academic training in human anatomy enabled him to apply sufficient pain without causing serious injury or death. Once he was himself a master, he would be able to call off, postpone, or mitigate torture, though his judgements might occasionally be subject to being overruled. One thieving mercenary who "was already seriously wounded not only on the head but also on both hands and legs" was judged by an older Frantz unlikely to survive a session with the strappado. When the same culprit's testimony under thumbscrews failed to satisfy the executioner's superiors, however, Schmidt was ordered to apply more strenuous means, ultimately two torture sessions with fire and four with the wreath. The accused robber's even more resistant brother-in-law was forced to endure the ladder six times, including frequent torture with wax candles under his left armpit. Not surprisingly, both ultimately confessed and were *executed with the sword out of mercy*.[16]

The executioner also bore primary responsibility for keeping all suspects in relatively good health, both before and after interrogation. Frantz knew well the harsh effects of imprisonment, especially on women, and bemoans in his journal when any suspect was forced to endure "the squalor of incarceration" for many weeks in a tiny cell intended for brief holding before interrogation and sentencing.[17] He personally tended to the broken bones and open wounds of prisoners and brought in nurses for recently delivered child murderers and other ailing women. This paternal concern for the well-being of imprisoned suspects strikes modern sensibilities as contradictory and even cruel, particularly when the individual was purposely given time to heal so that he or she could be effectively tortured or executed. The irony of the situation was not lost on Frantz and his colleagues. One prison chaplain recounted how a barber-surgeon brought in to assist the executioner "remarked to me during the [condemned's] treatment that it troubled him he spent so long healing what Meister Frantz would again ruin."[18]

Delivering a convicted offender in satisfactory condition for public punishment was never a simple matter, even after Frantz had gained years of experience. A farmer arrested and tortured in 1586 on suspicion of having murdered his stepchild had no sooner confessed to the crime when "God immediately provided a visible sign [of his guilt]" and the suspect fell dead, presumably of a heart attack.[19] Torture could also lead to psychological damage, which posed an equal or greater threat of jeopardising a smooth and effective public execution. After one "hard, stubborn thief" was tortured three times with fire in a single session – and continued to swear to God his innocence – he began to behave "very strangely and unruly" in his cell, alternately weeping uncontrollably and lashing out violently, as well as trying to bite the prison keeper. Until then he had "prayed diligently", but now he refused to do so or to speak to any person, instead squatting in a corner of the cell and chanting to himself "Dum diddy lump, dear devil come!"[20]

Young male thieves and robbers, entering the torture chamber with an ample supply of streetwise savvy and bravado, predictably displayed the greatest obstinacy and resilience. Since neither the journal nor the interrogation protocols ever mention comments by the executioner, it's unclear whether Frantz grew more frustrated during especially long torture sessions with stubborn suspects or with his unrelenting patrician superiors. The truculent sixteen-year-old Hensa Kreuzmayer, accused of arson and attempted murder, was tortured repeatedly over the course of a single day – with the strappado, the wreath, and fire – but in the end, the most he would acknowledge was "uttering a sacramental curse out of anger" at various unfriendly villagers.[21] Jörg Mayr, an astonishingly prolific thief of the same age, fought off several similar charges over the course of six weeks before he finally succumbed to despair and literally threw himself on the mercy of the interrogating jurors.[22] Older and more seasoned veterans generally recognised the futility of resistance and broke sooner. After one extended but unsuccessful torture session with a veteran highwayman, Frantz's magisterial superior calmly reassured the suspect that "we will again do with [you] what we want and even have [you] torn to pieces if [you] are not able to confess to having committed a murder", whereupon the suspect recognised the hopelessness of his situation and confessed in full.[23]

How did Frantz himself feel about his role as a professional torturer? As the person with the least seniority, the young journeyman was charged with the most brutal parts of the entire ordeal – pulling the rope of the strappado, turning the screws, burning a screaming subject. Most master executioners supervised the procedure but left the actual dirty work to their more dishonourable assistants. Whether Frantz readily passed on these tasks when he himself became a master is unknown – mainly because in nearly half a century of writing, he seldom explicitly acknowledged his own role in the administration of torture. There is no list of torture sessions alongside his tally of executions and corporal punishments, even though private interrogation was a more frequent and longer-lasting activity for him than both of those public performances combined.[24] If not for the surviving interrogation transcripts, his participation in these monthly, sometimes weekly, procedures would be completely hidden from view.

Was Frantz ashamed of his unsavoury work in the torture chamber or merely reticent about drawing attention to it? The task was in itself no more dishonourable than the public floggings, hangings, or wheel executions that he continued to administer personally until retirement many decades later. Nor, apparently, did he consider such measured violence unjustified. The few times that he writes about torture, Frantz sounds confident that virtually all individuals who made it to this stage, especially the already notorious robbers and thieves, had some degree of culpability. The sole occasion on which Frantz expressed regret about the practise came when the mass murderer Bastian Grübel falsely denounced a companion *out of enmity and [caused] the man [to be] brought into this town and examined by torture in his presence. [He] did him wrong in this for the murders were not true but lies, thinking that by doing the farmer this injustice the murders would not be discovered and that he would himself be released.*[25] The executioner's indignant tone conveys his usual sympathy for all victims as well as an implicit reassurance to himself that unjustified torture remained an anomaly. Otherwise the subject of torture was much more likely to come up in the older Frantz Schmidt's descriptions of the atrocities committed by marauding robbers during their savage home invasions – an interesting evasion on the executioner's part.[26]

Did Frantz really believe the legal axiom of the day that "pain releases truth"? It's hard to say. He nearly always tried to prompt a confession by using psychological pressure and other non-violent methods before he resorted to inflicting physical pain. This suggests that he saw torture as a sometimes necessary evil but hardly considered it an indispensable part of the truth-finding process. His repeated expressions of empathy for a suspect's suffering also make it clear that Frantz Schmidt was no sadist.

Frantz's assessment of the reliability of physical coercion is harder to gauge. He remarks once in passing that an accused child murderer *revealed the truth* under torture but this remains an isolated example.[27] Throughout the journal he displays an apparent credulity about details produced under torture that would have been virtually impossible for a suspect to remember, but even these, he might have countered, did not affect the ultimate question of guilt.

Did Frantz ever worry that a confession obtained under torture might lead to the execution of an innocent person? It's impossible to know for sure. Always sensitive to his place in the social hierarchy and the importance of career advancement, an eager young journeyman could console himself that the responsibility for ordering torture lay with his superiors, whom he was bound by oath (and self-interest) to obey and to please. A more experienced and financially secure executioner might find an even greater number of rationalisations to quiet a nagging conscience: if the accused was not guilty of this crime, he was probably guilty of others; speaking up for a possibly innocent suspect wasn't worth jeopardising both job and family security; his job was to carry out orders, not decide innocence or guilt.

Above all, Frantz did not consider himself the immovable opponent of a tortured subject, fixated on procuring a damning confession at all costs. His official prerogative to halt or forgo torture gave him considerable discretionary powers in cases where he had doubts about culpability, sometimes resulting in complete dismissal of charges. On at least two occasions later in life, for instance, he successfully recommended the release of older women suspected of witchcraft, on the grounds that they could not withstand the physical strain of even the mildest torture.[28] Frantz could also comfort himself with the knowledge that only a tiny minority of the many suspects brought before the council were subjected to torture, that those who were had typically been accused of quite violent crimes, and that even among those who were tortured, only a few suffered more than one session. Finally, he knew that the majority of those tortured would ultimately escape the death penalty, and perhaps one in three would be released with no subsequent punishment whatsoever.[29] This crucial semblance of moderation and due process is particularly helpful in understanding how an otherwise empathetic, intelligent, and pious individual might make peace with his role in routinely perpetrating the abominable personal violation that is torture.

Violence in the pursuit of justice

Frantz's success in carrying out the public spectacle of judicial violence was the sine qua non of his professional reputation. Many premodern criminal punishments appear alternately barbarous or quaint to modern eyes. There seems to be a childlike literalness at work in the way the crime was matched to the punishment, what Jacob Grimm called "a poetry in the law".[30] Some of the essential components – especially collective and public retribution – remained rooted in distant Germanic times, while other ancient influences, notably the *lex talionis*, or Mosaic law ("an eye for an eye"), gained new life thanks to the evangelical reforms of the previous two generations. The religiously charged atmosphere of the day also added a particular urgency to the legal process, since it was believed that unpunished offences might bring down divine wrath on an entire community (*Landstraffe*), in the form of flood, famine, or pestilence. Throughout Frantz Schmidt's life (and well into the eighteenth century), God the Father's keen interest in effective criminal law enforcement remained a frequent catalyst to new law-and-order campaigns and even influenced some legal decisions.

Frantz's ability to effectively administer corporal punishment was a prominent part of his job description. Here the medieval fondness for colourful and "appropriate" public humiliations comes readily to mind: quarrelling housewives adorned with "house dragon" masks or "violins" (elongated wooden shackles around the neck and wrists), fornicating young women forced to carry the "stone of shame" (weighing at least thirty pounds), and of course the stocks, where a variety of exposed malefactors endured verbal abuse, spittle, and occasionally thrown objects.

Among more established members of the community, by contrast, privately negotiated financial settlements remained the norm.

More violent punishments – such as chopping off the two oath fingers (index and middle) of perjurers and tearing out the tongue for blasphemy – had been relatively common before the sixteenth century. But by Frantz's time most German authorities deemed such traditions ineffective and potentially disruptive, because they came across as alternately ludicrous or gratuitously cruel. One Nuremberg jurist considered the brutal practise of eye-gouging (for attempted murder) "a harsher punishment than beheading", and in most parts of the empire it was discontinued by 1600.[31] Similarly gruesome mutilations, such as castration and hand-chopping, were also virtually unheard-of by this time.

Despite these trends, Frantz Schmidt was not spared from administering disfiguring corporal punishments. Bamberg and Nuremberg both maintained the punishment of cutting off perjurers' and recidivists' fingers and casting them in the river, long after other jurisdictions had abandoned the ancient custom. Over the course of his long career, Frantz would stand on Nuremberg's Fleisch (Flesh) Bridge to chop off

By the late sixteenth century, the traditional punishment of eye-gouging had become rare in German lands (c.1540).

the fingers of nine offenders, including prostitutes and procuresses, false gamblers, poachers, and false witnesses. He would also brand a large N (for Nuremberg) on the cheeks of four pimps and con men, clip the ears off four *thief-whores*, and snip the tongue-tip off one blaspheming glazier.[32]

Between the mid-sixteenth-century decline of legal mutilations and the seventeenth-century rise of workhouses and prisons – in other words, Meister Frantz's lifetime – the most common corporal punishment in German lands was banishment, often preceded by flogging with rods. Given the dearth of options for addressing lesser crimes, especially minor theft and sexual offences, Frantz's superiors in Bamberg and later Nuremberg simply adapted this medieval custom to their needs. Banishment became lifelong (instead of one to ten years), now covered "all the towns and fields" of their respective jurisdictions (instead of just the city proper), and was increasingly underscored by a painful public whipping, or at least time in the stocks. In large German towns, flogging out of town became a regular, at times weekly, event. Between the autumn of 1572 and the spring of 1578, Frantz assisted or observed his father's scourging of twelve to fifteen people a year.[33] During his subsequent solo career in Nuremberg, he would himself flog at least 367 individuals, an average of about nine annually, twice that during his peak period of 1579 to 1588. Internal references in the journal indicate that there were still other occasions that Frantz did not include in his tally and many more whippings administered by his assistant.[34] Corporal punishment of all kinds was so frequent in Nuremberg that on one occasion all six of the city's stocks were occupied and Meister Frantz had to bind a recidivist false gambler *in the Calvinist Preacher's chair on the stone bridge* (today's Maxbrücke) and chop off his two oath fingers there, before whipping him out of town once again.[35]

The ritualistic expulsion of undesirable individuals from a city's borders had all the essential components that sixteenth-century magistrates loved: strong assertion of their own authority in the beadle's loud proclamation of the sentence and the churches' ringing of the "poor sinner's bells", the executioner's humiliating stripping of the culprit to the waist (occasionally women were permitted a cloth for modesty), and the culprit's painful whipping at the stocks or during the procession to the city's gate to instil the lesson, as well as an alleged opportunity for

A Nuremberg chronicle portrays Meister Frantz simultaneously whipping four offenders out of town. Note that although the men's backs are completely exposed, they retain their hats, as does Meister Frantz, who also dons a red cape for the occasion (1616).

the offender to reform, or at the very least to avoid further offences within their jurisdiction. As in public executions, the danger of mob violence always loomed. In one flogging of "three pretty young women" in Nuremberg, "an enormous crowd ran [after the procession], so that some were crushed under the Ladies' Gate."[36] Despite the risks, paternalistic rulers found themselves unable to resist the seemingly harmonious blend of retribution and deterrence in these ritualised expulsions – particularly given the absence of viable alternatives.

The flogging itself was typically administered by the executioner's assistant or a journeyman executioner, such as young Frantz Schmidt. In Bamberg Heinrich Schmidt chose to perform the task himself, most likely because he was still paid on a fee basis for his work. Out of deference to his father or based on his own work ethic, Frantz would continue to personally perform (and dutifully record) the floggings he administered long after he began earning an annual salary and could have delegated the unpleasant task. He also chose to employ birch rods, which were reputedly more painful than other instruments of flogging and capable of causing permanent injury, or in rare cases death.[37] Even so, the executioner himself acknowledged the frequent ineffectiveness of these rituals of pain and humiliation, commenting in his journal on the many culprits he confronts who have already been *banished with rods*. His jurist colleagues in Nuremberg similarly advised their Augsburg counterparts to use the punishment sparingly with less hardened culprits such as sturdy beggars and other vagrants, else they risked turning them into professional criminals.[38]

Of course the officially sanctioned violence for which the early modern executioner was most known, and where Frantz's proficiency needed to be the greatest, was in the public execution itself. One early-twentieth-century German historian considered the criminal justice of this period to be typified by "the cruellest and most thoughtless punishments imaginable", but in fact a great amount of thought – specifically about the appropriate level of cruelty or ritualised violence – went into every form and instance of punishment.[39] As in their modification of traditional corporal punishments, secular authorities in the late sixteenth century also sought an unprecedented and delicate balance of severity and mercy in public executions, all aimed at furthering the rule of law and their own authority in enforcing it. Proceedings that gave off the slightest whiff of mob rule or vigilantism – such as the mass executions of Jews or witches – could no longer be tolerated in "advanced" jurisdictions such as Nuremberg. Medieval traditions that opened the magistracy up to ridicule also needed to be eliminated. These included public trials for criminal corpses as well as for murderous and "abominable" animals (which continued in less enlightened areas well into the eighteenth century).[40] A technically proficient and reliable executioner was himself the very embodiment of the sword of justice in action – swift, unwavering, deadly, but never appearing susceptible to arbitrary or gratuitous cruelty.

The new standards that the ambitious Frantz Schmidt had to meet were evident in the transformation of virtually every form of execution in his repertoire. The criminal punishment of women provides an especially vivid example of new adaptations of "simultaneously mild and gruesome" Germanic customs.[41] During the Middle Ages and into Frantz Schmidt's day, most female culprits were punished either by some combination of public humiliation and physical pain or by a financial penalty. Temporary banishment was also a popular option for a variety of offences. In those few cases where a woman was sentenced to death, by contrast, the punishment could be quite horrendous. Since hanging was considered indecent for women (it allowed spectators to see under their skirts) and beheading was typically reserved for honourable men, the most common form of female execution before the sixteenth century was live burial under the gallows. Long before Frantz Schmidt's birth, Nuremberg's leaders declared this punishment "cruel" as well as embarrassingly out of date: "Such a death penalty is [still] practised in few locations within the Holy Empire." Their decision was also influenced by the messiness of live burial, even if expedited by a stake through the heart. One condemned young woman "struggled so that she ripped off large pieces of skin on her arms, hands and feet", ultimately leading Nuremberg's executioner to pardon her and ask magistrates to abolish this form of execution, which they officially did in 1515. Surprisingly, the 1532 *Carolina* retained the punishment of live burial for infanticide – "to thereby prevent such desperate acts" – but the stipulation was rarely enforced.[42]

The form of execution most German authorities substituted for condemned women does not appear much of an improvement to modern eyes. Drowning in a hemp sack was also an ancient Germanic punishment, mentioned as early as Tacitus (A.D. 56–117). Many sixteenth-century authorities found the unseen death struggle in the water an appealing alternative to the visible thrashing about in live burial, which often generated a level of sympathy they wished to avoid. Professional executioners such as Frantz Schmidt, however, found the spectacle of forced drowning just as difficult to manage and in some instances even more prolonged. One condemned woman in 1500 survived long enough underwater to free herself from the sack and swim back to the execution platform from which she had been pushed. Her spirited explanation – "[Because] I drank four [litres] of wine ahead of time . . . the water couldn't come into me" – failed to impress the attending magistrates, who promptly ordered her buried alive. Shortly before Frantz's arrival in Nuremberg, his predecessor's assistant used a long pole to keep the struggling poor sinner from bringing her sack back to the surface, "but the staff broke and an arm came up [out of the water], with much screaming, so that she survived under the water for almost three-quarters of an hour".[43]

Frantz himself does not comment on the relative smoothness of his first drowning execution, a young maid from Lehrberg convicted of

Even in medieval times, live burial of women was considered a horrendous spectacle, often cut short by a stake through the heart of the struggling victim, as in this illustration of the last such execution in Nuremberg in 1522 (1616).

infanticide in 1578.[44] He is unusually forthcoming and even boastful two years later, though, when he and the prison chaplains bring about the abolishment of this form of execution in Nuremberg – a legal precedent gradually imitated throughout the empire. Schmidt's initial appeal to his superiors was shrewdly practical: the Pegnitz River was simply not deep enough in most spots and, in any event, at the moment (mid-January), "completely frozen over". Many councillors resisted any change, countering that women should naturally "sink to the bottom out of meekness" and that the young executioner just needed to do a better job of accelerating the process. When Frantz later proposed that three women convicted of infanticide be beheaded, a punishment unprecedented for women, some councillors called the plan too generous and not enough of a deterrent to this "shocking and too frequent crime" – especially given the large crowd likely to attend the imminent joint execution. Fortunately, Frantz's clerical allies furnished the additional argument that water actually gave power to "the evil spirit", inadvertently prolonging the ordeal. His jurist backers delivered the coup de grâce, acknowledging that drowning was "a hard death" and undoubtedly deserved, but countered that beheading provided a more effectively shocking deterrent, "since in drowning, one can't see how the [condemned] person behaves at the end", while beheading in the open provided a more visible and thus effective "example" to all present. *The bridges, which I had had consecrated, were already prepared for all three to be drowned,* Frantz writes in his journal, when the magistrates finally relented – with the notable condition that afterwards the executioner was to *nail all three heads above the great scaffold.*[45]

This compromise solution for the execution of women provided a template for the rest of Frantz's career, effectively balancing magisterial demands for both "shocking" public examples and smooth, orderly demonstrations of their authority. Nailing heads or limbs of executed

In some jurisdictions, as here in Zurich, the poor sinner was drowned from a boat. In Nuremberg the executioner constructed a temporary scaffolding for this purpose (1586).

culprits to the gallows fulfilled the atavistic bloodlust for retribution and humiliation, while eliminating the public torture aspects of many traditional forms of execution lent the entire procedure a greater legal and even sacred aura. All but two of the poor sinners condemned to be burned at the stake later in Meister Frantz's career were burned only after beheading or were spared the fire altogether.[46] (Burning for witch-craft remained of course pandemic elsewhere in Germany, rarely with strangulation beforehand.) Only one woman was ever again drowned by Frantz – a member of an especially cruel and notorious robber band – and none was ever again buried alive or impaled in Bamberg or Nurem-berg (although both practises survived in some Swiss and Bohemian localities for at least another century).[47] Instead, the heads of female murderers were often posted on the gallows or poles nearby, as were all four limbs of one traitor, sentenced to be drawn and quartered but *exe-cuted with the sword here out of mercy*.[48]

There remained only one traditional form of public execution that regularly placed torture at centre stage: breaking on the wheel. As in infanticide cases, the deep fears and subsequent outrage unleashed by the crimes of brutal robbers and mercenaries often outweighed the risks to a consistent appearance of governmental calm and moderation. Crowds roared in approval as the vicious robber Niklaus Stüller (aka the Black Banger) *was pulled along on a sled at Bamberg, his body torn thrice with red-hot tongs* by the journeyman executioner. Together with his companions, the brothers Phila and Görgla von Sunberg, he had murdered eight people, among them two pregnant women from whom they cut out live babies. According to Stüller, *when Görgla said they had committed a great sin [and] he wanted to take the infants to a priest to be baptised, [his brother] Phila said he would himself be priest and baptise them, took them by the legs and slammed them to the ground*. Stüller's subsequent *death by the wheel* at Frantz's hands seems mild in compari-son to the punishment of his companions, *later drawn and quartered in Coburg* by another executioner.

The ripping of the condemned's flesh with red-hot tongs and metic-ulous breaking on the wheel were the most explicitly violent acts Frantz was required to carry out as a professional. Although the number of nips with burning tongs and the number of blows at the wheel were both carefully prescribed in the death sentence, the executioner appears to have enjoyed some leeway, particularly in severity of the blows. At one point later in his career, Frantz's superiors in Nuremberg actually ordered him "not to go easy on the condemned persons, but rather earnestly seize them with the tongs, so that they experience pain."[49] Yet even in these instances of shocking deeds – such as Hans Dopffer, *who murdered his wife, who was very pregnant* – the presiding judge and jurors often capitulated to requests for a more merciful and honourable beheading, as long as the bodies were later broken and left to rot on a nearby wheel.[50]

As with his torture work, Frantz remained mostly silent about the details of his executions with the wheel – seven during his journeyman years and thirty over the course of his entire career. He only once mentions the number of blows administered and otherwise spends the bulk of each entry recounting the multiple grave crimes of the individual in question.[51] We know from various accounts, however, that the gruesome ordeal could be quite prolonged and that it evoked genuine terror in captured robbers. Meister Frantz himself describes one traumatised condemned man who *had a knife with him [in his cell], stabbed himself twice in the stomach and then threw himself on the knife, but it did not pierce him; also tore his shirt and tried to strangle himself with it, but could not bring it off.* Magister Hagendorn, the chaplain, writes in his journal of another murderous bandit who similarly attempted suicide to avoid his fate by "giving himself three cuts in the body with an instrument he had concealed." Each survived, was nursed back to health by Meister Frantz, and in his time received his prescribed punishment on the Raven Stone.[52]

Although less violent than the wheel, death by hanging was universally considered just as shameful, in some ways even more so. The indignity of publicly choking to death at the end of a rope or chain was bad enough; the subsequent exposure to ravens and other animals was even more shameful. Many master executioners also delegated this distasteful task to subordinates, but until his retirement four decades later, Frantz Schmidt insisted on carrying out with his own hands the most odious parts of an already disreputable profession. Beginning with his very first execution at the age of nineteen, the journal records his hanging of fourteen men from 1573 to 1578 and 172 individuals over the course of his entire career, mostly adult male thieves, but also two

The rare hanging of a nobleman, the finance minister of Augsburg, at the same time as what appears to be a youth. The executioner remains on the double ladder until the victims are dead, while the chaplains celebrate below (1579).

young women and nearly two dozen youths aged eighteen or younger. Frantz was himself taken aback when ordered to hang the two women in 1584 – *it had never before happened* that a woman was hanged in Nuremberg. He appeared even more uncomfortable about the hanging of "unreformable" teenage thieves, but in each instance the diligent professional performed his duty with no reported mishaps.[53]

Meister Frantz, like most in his profession, would also have disdained hanging as not much of a technical challenge. The executioner's job at a hanging amounted to not much more than placing a noose around the condemned man's neck and pushing him off a ladder. In towns without permanent gallows, Frantz was sometimes asked to inspect a temporary structure, but the construction itself was carried out by trained craftsman. As in all executions, it was up to the executioner

to keep the condemned person under control during the entire procedure, wherein the greatest difficulty was usually getting the accused to
mount the ladder to the noose. Nuremberg chronicles show Meister
Frantz and his assistant employing a double ladder for this purpose,
sometimes aided by a pulley, a procedure that culminated in the executioner simply shoving the poor sinner off the other ladder "so that the
sun shines through between the body and the earth."[54] Some executioners sought to make death especially painful or humiliating for the
condemned, hanging them upside down from a chain after strangulation. Nuremberg's gallows actually maintained a special Jews' point at
one corner for this purpose, but it was never used by Meister Frantz,
who instead garrotted one Jew in a chair in front of the gallows (*as a
special favour*) and hanged another "in the Christian way".[55]

In Frantz's first three years as a journeyman, all but one of his
eleven execution jobs involved the two most dishonourable forms of
dispatch, hanging and the wheel. These lowly assignments were an inevitable part of paying his professional dues and building up his credentials in the region. As a result, during the three subsequent years, he
was called on to execute nearly as many individuals with the sword
(ten) as with the rope (eleven) – a clear indicator of his rising status.
Over the course of his long career, in both Bamberg and Nuremberg,
these two forms of capital punishment – hanging and beheading –
would constitute over 90 per cent of his 394 executions.[56]

The growing preference for decapitation was in fact part of a general trend in German lands over the course of Frantz's professional
life, rooted in both the gradual decline of executions for theft (and
thus hangings) and a concurrent rise in mitigation of more extreme
forms of final dispatch. During the first half of Schmidt's career,
hanging was nearly twice as common as beheading; by the early seventeenth century, the proportions had reversed.[57] Popular recognition
of the skill and professional status of the trained executioner rose
accordingly.

Frantz's skill with the sword provided the bedrock of his own professional identity, certainly not his inglorious work as a hangman, a derisive term that he scrupulously avoided. In his own writing, he is always
an *executioner*, a title that emphasises his close association to the law
and courts as opposed to his unsavoury work in the torture chamber or

with the wheel or rope. The two hangings Frantz decides to date during his journeyman years are singled out only because they were *my first execution* (1573) and *my first execution at Nuremberg* (1577). *My first execution with the sword* (1573), on the other hand, is celebrated as a moment of personal achievement, unparalleled by specific commemoration of any other firsts during his career.[58]

The sentence the Romans called *poena capitas* – and professionals like Frantz knew more simply as "capping" – also put the spotlight more fully on the executioner than did hanging.[59] Frantz decided first of all whether the poor sinner would kneel, sit, or stand. Standing subjects, who tended to shift around, posed the greatest challenge to the sword-wielding executioner, and Frantz makes careful note of his five successes with this method, all before he reached the age of thirty.[60] Once his finesse and reputation were established enough to secure a lifelong employment contract, he reverted to the much more common practise of decapitating a subject who knelt or sat. Sitting bound in a judgement chair became more common over the course of Schmidt's career, and was especially preferred for women, who supposedly moved around more at the crucial moment. Following a final prayer from the chaplain, the executioner carefully positioned his feet – not unlike a golfer preparing for a perfectly calibrated swing – and trained his eyes on the middle of the subject's neck. He then raised his blade and struck one graceful blow, typically from behind on the right side, cutting through two cervical vertebrae and completely severing the head from the body. In the words of a common legal formula, "he should chop off his head and with one blow make two pieces of him, so that a wagon wheel might freely pass between head and torso."[61] Following a clean blow, the poor sinner's head plopped serenely at his or her own feet, while the seated torso continued to splatter the executioner and his assistant with blood from the severed neck. Frantz never mentions any especially prodigious feats with the sword – such as lopping off two heads with one swing, as one of his successors did – but he does ruefully note the few occasions when an additional stroke was required to sever the head completely, a dangerous breech in the dramatic narrative, to which we now turn.

Producing a good death

Public executions, like corporal punishments, were meant to accomplish two goals: first, to shock spectators and, second, to reaffirm divine and temporal authority. A steady and reliable executioner played the pivotal role in achieving this delicate balance through his ritualised and regulated application of violence on the state's behalf. The court condemnation, the death procession, and the execution itself constituted three acts in a carefully choreographed morality play, what historian Richard van Dülmen called "the theatre of horror".[62] Each participant – especially the directing executioner – played an integral role in ensuring the production's ultimate success. The "good death" Frantz and his colleagues sought was essentially a drama of religious redemption, in which the poor sinner acknowledged and atoned for his or her crimes, voluntarily served as an admonitory example, and in return was granted a swift death and the promise of salvation. It was, in that sense, the last transaction a condemned prisoner would make in this world.

Let us take the example of Hans Vogel from Rasdorf, *who burned to death an enemy in a stable [and] was my first execution with the sword in Nuremberg* (while still a journeyman) ont 13 August 1577. As in all public performances, the preparation behind the scenes was crucially important. Three days before the day of execution, Vogel was moved to a slightly larger death-row cell. Had he been seriously wounded or otherwise ill, Frantz and perhaps another medical consultant would have tended to him and perhaps requested delays in the execution date until Vogel regained the stamina required for the final hour. For the most part, though, the executioner focused his attention during this period on ensuring the condition of the Raven Stone or other site, procuring all the necessary supplies, and finalising the logistics of the trial and procession to execution.

While awaiting judgement day, Vogel might receive family members and other visitors in the prison or – if he was literate – seek consolation by reading a book or writing farewell letters. He might even reconcile with some of his victims and their relatives, as did a murderer who accepted some oranges and gingerbread from his victim's widow "as a sign that she had forgiven him from the depths of her heart".[63] The most frequent visitors to Vogel's cell during this period would be the prison chaplains. In Nuremberg the two chaplains worked in concert and sometimes in competition, attempting to "soften his heart" with appeals combining elements of fear, sorrow, and hope. If Vogel couldn't read, the clerics would have shown him an illustrated Bible and attempted to teach him the Lord's Prayer as well as the basics of the Lutheran catechism; if he was better schooled, they might engage him in discussions about grace and salvation. Above all, the chaplains – sometimes joined by the gaoler or members of his family – would offer consolation to the poor sinner, singing hymns together and speaking reassuring words, while repeatedly admonishing the stubborn and hard-hearted.

Obviously, a submissive prisoner made for a smoother execution, but the visiting clerics had nobler motives. Dying "in the faith" was of special concern to Frantz's Nuremberg colleague Magister Hagendorn, and in addition to preparing a prisoner to go to the execution site with calm resignation, he hoped to instil in the condemned some degree of piety and understanding. His own journal entries reveal a particular tenderness towards young women convicted of infanticide. He is initially troubled that Margaretha Lindtnerin, condemned in 1615, has learned so little of her catechism, despite over seven weeks of confinement. In the end, however, she obligingly displays all the hallmarks of a good death:

She was very perseverant in her Cross, prayed fervently, and every time that her baby or parents were mentioned, she began to weep bitter tears; had quite resigned herself to her imminent death, strolled out very calmly, enthusiastically blessed those known to her while under way (since she had served here eight whole years at different places and was fairly well known) and fervently prayed with us. When we came with her to the execution site, she started and said, "Oh God, stand by me and help me get through it." Afterwards she repeated it to me, blessed the crowd and asked their forgiveness, [then] she stood there, as if stunned and could not talk until I spoke to her twice or thrice, then she began to talk, again blessed the crowd and asked their forgiveness, [then] commended her soul to the hands of the Almighty, sat down in the chair, and properly presented her neck to the executioner. Since she persevered in the right and true faith until her end, she will also [attain] the end of her faith, which [according to] 1 Peter chapter 1 is the salvation and blessing of souls.[64]

Whatever their success in effecting an internal conversion, the clerics were at minimum expected to sufficiently calm the condemned Vogel for the final component of his preparatory period, the famed "hangman's meal". Ironically, Frantz was not directly involved in this ancient custom (possibly because of its disreputable name), and allowed the prison warden and his wife to oversee its implementation in a special cell with table, chairs, and windows, known in Nuremberg as "the poor sinner's parlour". As in those modern countries that still maintain capital punishment, Vogel could request whatever he wanted for his last meal, including copious quantities of wine. The chaplain Hagendorn attended some of these repasts and was frequently appalled by the boorish and ungodly behaviour he witnessed. One surly robber spat out the warden's wine and demanded warm beer, while another large thief "thought more of the food for his belly than his soul . . . devouring in one hour a large loaf, and in addition two smaller ones, besides other food", in the end consuming so much that his body allegedly "burst asunder in the middle" as it swung from the gallows.[65] Some poor sinners, by contrast (especially distraught young killers of newborns), were unable to eat anything whatsoever.

Once Vogel was adequately satiated (and inebriated), the executioner's assistants helped him put on the white linen execution gown and summoned Frantz, who from this point on oversaw the public spectacle about to unfold. His arrival at the cell was announced by the warden with the customary words, "The executioner is at hand", whereupon Frantz knocked on the door and entered the parlour in his finest attire. After asking the prisoner for forgiveness, he then sipped the traditional St John's drink of peace with Vogel, and engaged in a brief conversation to determine whether he was ready to proceed to the waiting judge and jury.

A few poor sinners were at this point actually jubilant and even giddy about their imminent release from the mortal world, whether out of religious conviction, exasperation, or sheer intoxication. Sometimes Frantz decided that a small concession might be enough to ensure compliance, such as allowing one condemned woman to wear her favourite straw hat to the gallows, or a poacher to wear the wreath sent to him in prison by his sister. He might also ask an assistant to provide more alcohol, sometimes mixed with a sedative he prepared, although this tactic could backfire, leading some women to pass out and making some of the younger men still more aggressive. The highwayman Thomas Ullmann almost beat Frantz's Nuremberg successor to death at this juncture until subdued by the gaoler and several guards. Once confident that Vogel was sufficiently calmed, Frantz and his assistants bound the prisoner's hands with rope (or taffeta cords for women) and proceeded to the first act of the execution drama.[66]

The "blood court", presided over by a patrician judge and jury, was a forum for sentencing, not for deciding guilt or punishment. Vogel's own confession, in this case obtained without torture, had already determined his fate. During the Middle Ages, this judicial pronouncement had been the central moment of the condemnation process, usually taking place in the town square. By the sixteenth century, the subsequent execution now enjoyed this elevated status, with the "court day" itself taking place in a special chamber in the town hall, closed to the public. As in the subsequent procession and execution, the overarching goal of this preliminary stage was to underscore the legitimacy of the proceedings, but in this instance the audience being reassured comprised the executing authorities themselves.

The brisk procedure was accordingly ritualistic, hierarchical, and formal. At the end of Nuremberg's chamber, the judge sat on a raised cushion, holding a white rod in his right hand and in his left a short sword with two gauntlets hanging from the hilt. Six patrician jurors in ornately carved chairs flanked him on either side, like him wearing the customary red and black robes of the blood court. While the executioner and his assistants held the prisoner steady, the scribe read the final confession and its tally of offences, concluding with the formulaic condemnation "Which being against the laws of the Holy Roman Empire, my Lords have decreed and given sentence that he shall be condemned from life to death by [rope/sword/fire/water/the wheel]." Starting with the youngest juror, the judge then serially polled all twelve of his colleagues for their consent, to which each gave the standard reply, "What is legal and just pleases me."

Before confirming the sentence, the judge addressed Vogel directly for the first time, inviting a statement to the court. The submissive poor sinner was not expected to present any sort of defence, but rather to thank the jurors and judge for their just decision and absolve them of any guilt in the violent death they had just endorsed. Those relieved souls whose punishments had been commuted to beheading were often effusive in their gratitude. A few reckless rogues were so bold as to curse the assembled court. Many more terrified prisoners simply stood speechless. Turning to Frantz, the judge then gave the servant of the court his commission: "Executioner, I command you in the name of the Holy Roman Empire, that you carry [the poor sinner] to the place of execution and carry out the aforesaid punishment", whereupon he ceremoniously snapped his white staff of judgement in two and returned the prisoner to the executioner's custody.[67]

The second act of the unfolding drama, the procession to the site of execution, brought the assembled crowd of hundreds or thousands of spectators into the mix. Typically, the execution itself had been publicised by broadsheets and other official proclamations, including the hanging of a blood-red cloth from the town hall parapet. Vogel, his hands still bound in front of him, was expected to walk the mile or so to the gallows. Sometimes, if the condemned suffered from physical exhaustion or an infirmity, Frantz's assistants transported the poor sinner on an elevated chair. This was often the case with the elderly and disabled women such as the swindler Elisabeth Aurholtin, who *had only one leg*.[68] Violent male criminals and those sentenced to torture with hot tongs were bound more firmly and placed in a waiting tumbrel or sled, pulled by a workhorse used by local sanitation workers, known in Nuremberg as a Pappenheimer. Led by two mounted archers and the ornately robed judge, also usually on horseback, Frantz and his assistants worked hard to keep up a steady forward pace while several guards held back the teeming crowd. One or both chaplains walked the entire way, one on either side of the condemned, reading from scripture and praying aloud. The religious aura of the entire procession was more than a veneer, and in Frantz's career only the unconverted Mosche Judt was "led to the gallows without any priests to accompany or console him".[69]

During this phase, the executioner's customary obligation to respect the last wishes of the condemned as well as to avoid alienating the

An execution procession in the inner city of Nuremberg. Here two guards on horseback lead the poor sinner on foot, with a chaplain on either side of him (c.1630).

crowd often required considerable restraint on Frantz's part. Hans Vogel apparently offered little resistance, but the thief and gambling cheat Hans Meller (aka Cavalier Johnny) *said to the jurors as he left the court, "God guard you; for in dealing thus with me you will have to see a black devil one day", and as he was led out to the execution displayed all kinds of arrogance.* Still, the executioner waited patiently while Meller sang not one but two popular death songs at the gallows: "When My Hour Is at Hand" and "Let What God Wills Always Happen". The thieves Utz Mayer (aka the Tricky Tanner) and Georg Sümler (aka Gabby) were similarly *fresh and insolent when being led out, howling,* but also permitted to sing "A Cherry Tree Acorn" before the nooses were put around their necks.[70]

Satisfying his superiors' expectations of a dignified and orderly ceremony put even more pressure on the "theatre of horror's" director. In addition to fending off derisive shouts and thrown objects, the executioner needed to maintain the sombre mood of the proceedings. Frantz was understandably frustrated and embarrassed when one incestuous old couple turned their death procession into a ludicrous race, each attempting to outrun the other: "He was in front at the Ladies' Gate, but from here on she frequently outpaced him."[71] Frantz often laments when a prisoner *behaved very wildly and gave trouble*, but his patience appears to have been especially tried by the arsonist Lienhard Deürlein, *an audacious knave* who continued to drink hard from the bottle during the entire procession. Deürlein bestowed curses – rather than the customary blessings – on those he passed, and upon his arrival at the gallows handed the wine bottle to the chaplain while he urinated in the open. *When his sentence was read to him, he said he was willing to die but asked as a favour that he should be allowed to fence and fight with four of the guards. His request*, Meister Frantz drily notes, *was refused*. According to the scandalised chaplain, Deürlein then seized the bottle again "and this drink lasted so long that at last the executioner struck off his head while the bottle was still at his lips, without his being able to say the words 'Lord, into thy hands I commend my spirit.'"[72]

Outward signs of contrition carried particular significance for Frantz, especially during this third act, at the execution site. He writes with approval when one remorseful murderer *wept all the way until he knelt down* or when a penitent thief *took leave of the world as a Christian*. In stark contrast to his clerical colleagues, he clearly valued such visible evidence of a changed heart more than mastery of the specifics of evangelical doctrine. It's easy to imagine his quiet annoyance when a subdued and contrite Paulus Kraus proclaimed at the gallows ladder that he was about to atone for his sins, only to be loudly corrected by Magister Hagendorn, who pedantically admonished Kraus that "the Lord Christ had already atoned and paid for them [and] he should instead commend his soul to God, His heavenly father".[73]

Last communion represented an especially visible form of submission and Frantz fretted when poor sinners displayed last-minute obstinacy on this score. Vogel readily embraced the sacrament, but on another occasion Hans Schrenker (aka Crawler) consistently refused to receive the Lutheran communion, *because he was a Catholic*. The executioner was relieved, by contrast, that Cunz Rhünagel (aka Rough) *at first refused to receive the sacrament and used very abusive words, but afterwards consented*. Even the robber Georg Prückner, whom Schmidt summed up as *a very bad character [who] had been several times imprisoned in the tower but was released on promise of doing good, in the end repented [and] behaved in a very Christian manner*, receiving communion on the Raven Stone and loudly proclaiming his remorse to the assembled throng.[74]

The single worst death described by Frantz Schmidt later in life was the prolonged ordeal of the notorious highwayman Hans Kolb (aka the Long Brickmaker, aka Brother Standfast):

> *Because he could not escape from prison [here], he bit his left arm, cutting through the veins. When he was healed of this and led out on the last day, he again bit out a piece of his right arm as large as a batzen piece [coin] and an inch deep, thinking he would thus bleed to death . . . [instead,] as a murderer, robber, highwayman, and thief, who stole much many times, executed with the wheel, the four limbs first broken, and lastly as a counterfeiter the body was burnt. He pretended he could not walk so that he had to be carried. Did not pray at all and bade the priest to be silent, saying he knew it all beforehand and did not want to hear it, and that it made his head ache. God knows how he died.*[75]

Virtually all Frantz's acknowledgements of difficult deaths came much later in his career, when he was professionally secure. Even then, he was not always completely forthcoming, especially with those fiascos that might reflect poorly on his own mastery of the situation. Of the prolific thief Georg Mertz (aka the Mallet), for instance, the executioner writes only that the condemned man *behaved strangely as he was led out: shook his head and only laughed, would not pray, only said to the pastors, "My faith has helped me."* The prison chaplain and court notary, by contrast, expanded considerably on the disastrous spectacle. According to Magister Hagendorn, the twenty-two-year-old Mertz insisted on being carried out and executed in his black cap and woollen shirt, promising to go peacefully if he was permitted this last wish.

> But as soon as he left the prison he began to yell and play the fool: "Mine is the day, be comforted dear people," he cried out, with much else, and three times I had to return and help to drive

him along. When we reached the town hall, he repeated the same words with loud cries, so that I had to restrain him and admonish him to be more moderate. Before the court he exhibited himself, grinning crazily, turning first to the right, then to the left, baring his teeth, and twisting his mouth so that I had twice to correct and admonish him . . . When he was sentenced he bowed himself, as if to show reverence to the council, and almost fell in a heap. When we came down with him from the town hall we could scarcely control him. He leapt in the air, raged, and fumed, as if he were raving mad . . . Then he gave orders that they should bring the chair, and when he had seated himself, and was bound, he began to stamp with his feet like a horse, raising and dropping his head, exulting and crying out: "I am comforted: my faith has saved me." He called the people angels, and many times requested that his hat might be removed so that he could see the angels.

During the procession, according to the court notary, Mertz not only forced Frantz's assistants to carry him but also

on the way he kicked the gaolers so cruelly with his feet that they cried out, and frequently let him fall. At the same time he made funny faces, bared his teeth to the people, and thrust his tongue far out of his mouth . . . When he reached the accustomed execution place, and the executioner or hangman told him to climb the ladder, he replied, "Why are you in such a hurry with me? All times are good for hanging – morning or afternoon, late or early. It helps to pass a dull hour." And when he was on the ladder and Magister Hagendorn spoke to him, asking him to whom he was going to commend his poor soul, he gave a mighty leap and burst into laughter, crying, "Priest, what is all this talk? Who else but to my drinking companions, the rope, and the chains?"

Frantz hastened to end this embarrassing display, but the two chaplains continued to exhort the condemned Mertz to repent, only prompting his final words, "I would like to work my jaws much more, but I cannot do so. You can see that I have swallowed a lot of hemp and am likely to be suffocated with it so that I cannot go on talking."[76] Having thoroughly shattered the intended dignity and redemptive message of his own demise, Mertz allegedly died with a smirk on his face.

The greatest terror for any executioner – particularly a young journeyman – was that his own errors might effectively ruin the carefully managed drama of sin and redemption and endanger his own job or worse. The large crowd of spectators – always including many loud drunks among its number – put immense performance pressure on the sword-wielding executioner. Long farewell speeches or songs with multiple verses helped build suspense for the crowd, but also tried the patience and nerves of the waiting professional. One chronicler detected Meister Frantz's eagerness for resolution in the beheading of the murderer Margaretha Böckin, still standing after enduring *her body nipped thrice with red-hot tongs*, but so weak that she could barely talk. "He indicated that he would speak to the people for her [but] had barely said three words when he properly chopped off [her head] and executed her."[77] Elisabeth Mechtlin started out well on the path to a good death, weeping incessantly and informing Magister Hagendorn "that she was glad to leave this vile and wicked world, and would go to her death not otherwise than as to a dance [but] . . . the nearer she approached to death, the more sorrowful and faint-hearted she became." By the time of her execution procession, Mechtlin was screaming and yelling uncontrollably all the way to the gallows. Her continued flailing while in the judgement chair even apparently unnerved a by then very experienced Frantz Schmidt, untypically leading him to require three strokes to dispatch the hysterical woman.[78]

Fortunately, Hans Vogel's execution passed without any incident worthy of note. Bungled beheadings, though, appeared often in early modern chronicles, in Nuremberg several times before and after Frantz Schmidt's tenure. During his own forty-five-year career and 187 recorded *executions with the sword*, Meister Frantz required a second stroke only four times (an impressive success rate of 98 per cent), yet he dutifully acknowledges each mistake in his journal with the simple annotation *botched*.[79] He also refused to fall back on the usual excuses proffered for a bungled beheading: that the devil put three heads in front of him (in which case he was advised to aim for the middle one) or that a poor sinner bewitched him in some other way. Some professionals carried with them a splinter from the judge's broken staff of justice to protect them against just such magical influences, or covered the victim's head with a black cloth to forestall the evil eye. Frantz's well-known temperance had fortunately immunised him from the more mundane explanation favoured by contemporaries, namely the executioner

A botched beheading in the Swiss canton of Chur leads to the crowd's stoning of the bungling executioner. Spectators always reacted violently to miscarried executions, but executioner fatalities remained rare (1575).

"finding heart" for the big moment in the bottle or an alleged "magical drink".[80] Most crucially, his slips did not occur during these journeyman years or even his early career in Nuremberg, but rather long after he had become a locally established and respected figure, his reputation and personal safety both secure.

Another young Nuremberg executioner not long after Meister Frantz's retirement was less fortunate. In 1641 the newcomer Valentin Deuser was to behead child murderer Margaretha Voglin, "an extremely beautiful person of nineteen years". According to one chronicle,

> this poor child was very ill and weak, so that she had to be carried and brought to the gallows, or Raven Stone, and when she sat down on the chair, Meister Valentin circled around her, like a calf around a manger, and with the sword struck a span of wood and a piece of skin as big as a thaler [coin] from her head, knocking her under the chair, and since he hadn't hurt her body and she fell so bravely, [the crowd] asked that she be released.

The inexperienced Deuser refused to pardon her, though, and from underneath the chair she then cried out:

> "Oh, help me for God's sake," which she said often and repeated. Then [the executioner's assistant] grabbed her and set her back on the chair, whereupon the executioner delivered a second blow and [this time] hacked in the neck behind her head, at which she however fell from the chair, still alive, again shouting, "Aiee, God have mercy!" After this the hangman hacked and cut at her head on the ground, for which cruel butchery and shameful execution [he] was surrounded by people who would have stoned him to death had not the archers present come to his aid and protected him from the people, and then stopped his bleeding, which already flowed freely from his head and down both front and back.

This disgraceful performance and the riot it triggered resulted in the young executioner's arrest and subsequent dismissal, despite his claim to have been "blinded or bewitched" by the condemned.[81]

Mishaps leading to mob violence and lynch justice jeopardised the core message of religious redemption and state authority. In some German towns an executioner was permitted three strikes (really) before being grabbed by the crowd and forced to die in place of the poor sinner. Frantz recognised the constant *danger to my life* in every execution, but whether by skill or luck, he himself only faced one such total breakdown in public order – a flogging that turned into a riot and fatal stoning – and that came long after his journeyman years.[82] Every beheading, by contrast, ended like his dispatch of the arsonist Vogel, with Frantz turning to the judge or his representative and asking the question that would complete the legal ritual: "Lord Judge, have I executed well?" "You have executed as judgement and law have required," came the formulaic response, to which the executioner replied, "For that I thank God and my master who has taught me such art."[83] Still at centre stage (literally), Frantz then directed the anticlimactic mopping up of blood and appropriate disposal of the dead man's body and head – always fully aware of the hundreds of eyes still upon him. As Heinrich Schmidt had taught his son, the public performance of the executioner never ended.

The opportunity of a lifetime

The breakthrough moment in Frantz's early career came on 15 January 1577, when he was nearly twenty-three years old. Though some luck was involved, his father's skilful manoeuvring played the larger part. Heinrich Schmidt had early on identified the job of Nuremberg's executioner as a plum position, perhaps the most prestigious in the empire and thus the most promising for restoration of their family's honour. In 1563, after filling in briefly for the frequently absent Conrad Vischer, Heinrich himself applied for the post, only to be brusquely turned away by Nuremberg's councillors.[84] Six months later, when the post again became vacant, Schmidt was again rejected, this time in favour of Vischer, who had returned. Perhaps Heinrich applied once more, upon Vischer's death in June 1565, or a year later when his successor, Gilg Schmidt, passed away. In any event, it was Lienhardt Lippert of Ansbach who eventually secured the coveted position in 1566 and would hold on to it for many years thereafter.

Undeterred, father and son managed to turn this disappointment to their advantage. Within a year of his appointment as Nuremberg's new executioner, Lienhardt Lippert asked the council for permission to marry his housekeeper, who happened to be Frantz's sister, Kunigunda. Exactly when and how this strategic placement occurred is not recorded, but such a fortuitous development was surely not unanticipated by the Schmidts. At first the council sternly refused Lippert's petition, "since he already has a wife" (presumably still in Ansbach), but exhausted by the relentless turnover of the preceding decade, the executioner's superiors allowed him to continue employing "this frivolous wench", as long as there was no public scandal. At some point within the next year and a half, Lippert and Kunigunda Schmidin were privately wed, and in October 1568 the bride gave birth to the first of seven children. Since both divorce and bigamy were unlikely to have been tolerated by Lippert's employers, we must assume a timely end for his estranged spouse during the interim.[85]

Frantz now enjoyed the great benefit of having a relative placed in the very job his father coveted (now on the son's behalf). The eager young journeyman was even luckier in the contrast that he presented to his incorrigible brother-in-law. Determined to avoid more instability in the position, Nuremberg's councillors long tolerated both Lippert's personal and professional shortcomings. Even his third disastrous beheading in a row on 3 December 1569 – this one requiring three strokes – was met with only a mild reprimand, as well as reassurance that the council would always protect Lippert from any mob retribution. In November 1575, however, the executioner suffered a serious fall. Four months later, he claimed that he was too ill to mount the gallows ladder and suggested that his brother-in-law, young Frantz Schmidt, be allowed to act in his place. Instead, the council commuted the punishment to decapitation and ordered Lippert to earn his salary and carry out his duty. Subsequent complaints that he was too weak to torture were similarly batted away, with his assistant ordered to fill in for him indefinitely.[86]

Whether or not Lippert's infirmity was genuine, his sudden (and unapproved) two-week trip to "his father-in-law in Bamberg" in January 1577 required the council to hire "his kinsman, the foreign executioner", for the hanging of the thief Hans Weber.[87] Was this opportunity also engineered by Heinrich Schmidt? In any event, the result was, Frantz later wrote in his journal, *my first execution here*. Over the following sixteen months, the "new, young executioner" dispatched seven more poor sinners on behalf of the city of Nuremberg, all without incident – "very well", according to the court notary – but still on an ad hoc fee basis.[88] Finally presented with an attractive alternative to the trouble-some Lippert, the city's magistrates grew less tenuous in their admon-ishments of the older executioner, warning him that "if he didn't amend his laziness and disorderly life, he would be replaced with another master." Thus, on 25 April 1578, when Lippert informed his superiors that he was too ill to go on, they immediately accepted his resignation, spurned his requests for a pension or housing assistance, and uncere-moniously washed their hands of the twelve-year veteran – who died less than a month later. That same day, they appointed a new master executioner, Frantz Schmidt of Hof.[89]

Two weeks after his appointment, Frantz obtained permission from his new superiors to travel to Bamberg "for four or five days".[90] His cel-ebratory homecoming was a powerful moment for father and son. Frantz had secured the very job that had long eluded his father and taken a momentous step forward in their shared dream of restoring the family's stolen honour. What mixture of pride, envy, and relief did Heinrich ex-perience at learning the news? It was at this point, possibly at his fa-ther's urging, that Frantz decided to keep a journal. After enumerating his previous executions for his father (and claiming that he *can't remem-ber* the corporal punishments), the young executioner came to the pres-ent moment. As usual, Frantz affected an emotionless style, but his joy in this victory shines through the bold letters of his proud pronounce-ment: **Here follow the persons [punished] after I was officially appointed and taken on here in Nuremberg on St Walburga's Day [1 May] in 1578.**

THE MASTER

The conduct of our lives is the true reflection of our thoughts.
— Michel de Montaigne, "On the Education of Children" (1580)[1]

Do, but also seem. Things do not pass for what they are, but for what they
seem. To excel and to know how to show it is to excel twice.
— Baltasar Gracián, *The Art of Worldly Wisdom* (1647)[2]

On 11 October 1593, the notorious forger and con artist Gabriel Wolff met his end at the hands of Meister Frantz. Schmidt marked the occasion with one of the longest entries in his entire journal. Over the course of three decades, Wolff, the well-educated scion of a local citizen family, had perpetrated a series of audacious frauds throughout the noble courts of Europe under multiple aliases – *also known as Glazier; called himself Georg Windholz, secretary to the elector at Berlin; also Jakob Führer, Ernst Haller, and Joachim Fürnberger.* Among Wolff's many swindles, one figures most prominently in the executioner's account: this well-born son of Nuremberg had *borrowed 1,500 ducats from the [city's] Honourable Council by means of a forged letter in the elector's name and under the seal of the Margrave Johann Georg in Berlin.* Other victims of his schemes included *a councillor at Danzig, the count of Öttingen, his lord at Constance, two merchants at Danzig, a [Dutch] master,* and assorted dignitaries in Lisbon, Malta, Venice, Crete, Lübeck, Hamburg, Messina, Vienna, Kraków, Copenhagen, and London. Wolff stole fourteen hundred krona from the duke of Parma and absconded to Constantinople, where he assumed the identity of the recently deceased Jakob Führer, *[taking] the latter's signet ring, books, and clothes, as well as a few thaler*. His roguish journey continued to Italy, where *he slept with and tried to abduct an abbess, but failed; he took, however, from her sister a silver gilt striking clock. On another occasion he took a silver clock from a knight of St John called Master Georg, as well as a horse, and rode away. In Prague, where he was the emperor's personal attendant, being charged with pawning a lady's silver goblets and girdle for 12 fl., he stole [them] and sold them for 40 fl.* Eventually exhausted by his litany of Wolff's crimes and victims, Meister Frantz cuts short his account with the summation: *also practised many other frauds over twenty-four years, causing false seals of gentlemen to be cut [and] wrote many forged documents* – but not before making two more telling comments. First, he notes that Wolff was *fluent in seven languages*. Second, that he was *out of mercy executed with the sword here at Nuremberg, [the body] afterwards burnt. Should have had his right hand cut off first as decided and ordered, but he was subsequently spared this.*[3]

Why did this incorrigible and shameless trickster hold such fascination for his executioner? Certainly Wolff's picaresque adventures rivalled those of any of his literary brethren and undoubtedly supplied the many spectators at his beheading with entertaining stories for years to come. The scale of his thefts was likewise impressive, totalling several thousand gulden (hundreds of times the average artisan's annual earnings), all spent on long years of luxurious living among the rich and powerful of Europe. No doubt many in the crowd who came to witness Wolff's execution felt a frisson of guilty pride that this cunning son of Nuremberg had so magnificently duped the cosmopolitan elite of the day.

Whatever voyeuristic pleasure Meister Frantz may have taken in this celebrated case, there was for him a more serious – and personally significant – moral issue at stake. Born into a rigidly hierarchical society with both innate intelligence and multiple familial advantages, Wolff had chosen to cast aside his privileged position and betray virtually everyone he encountered: his family, his city's leaders, his noble employers, bankers, merchants, abbesses, and so on. More broadly, his treacheries undermined the very tenuous trust that allowed commerce and government to function across the patchwork of kingdoms,

principalities, and city-states that constituted Europe at the time. More
to the point, Wolff's crimes shook to the core the people's confidence in
the ability of their legal officials (and their executioners) to detect and
punish such abuses. For this reason, fraud, particularly of such magnitude, posed a much graver threat to the authority of Frantz Schmidt
and his employers than it would for their modern counterparts – hence
the prescribed punishment of being burned at the stake. Yet in the end,
Wolff's citizenship and family connections – and quite likely his confidence man's way with words – came to his rescue. He was spared the
humiliating and painful punishment of *having his right hand chopped
off*, and he died not in the agony and ignominy of fire, but by the quick
and honourable sword stroke of Meister Frantz. In the words of one
chronicler, "he spoke well".[4]

Frantz Schmidt's consternation over the crime and punishment of
Gabriel Wolff, a case that arose fourteen years after his own appointment in Nuremberg, underscores how little the young executioner's
newfound job security and prosperity did to ease his incessant anxiety
over social rank. Frantz's disquiet was far from unique. As the historian
Stuart Carroll reminds us, honour "is not simply a moral code regulating conduct; like magic or Christianity, it is a world view".[5] As a sub-
scriber to that world view, Frantz experienced a deep inner conflict over
the Wolff case. On the one hand, he felt revulsion for the well-born
Wolff, who squandered all the social advantages that an executioner's
son never enjoyed and behaved in a thoroughly scandalous and immoral
manner *for over twenty-four years*. The scoundrel's decapitation at
Frantz's own hands provided the executioner with welcome reassurance
that justice had finally been served and his own faith in the social order
rewarded. Yet when Wolff was shown mercy – because of his privileged
social status – and spared the court-ordered punishment of having his
hand chopped off, Schmidt directs his anger not at the hypocritical
double standard that made special allowances for him but at one specific instance of unjustified mercy. A lifetime of journal entries reveals
the same consistent deference to the hierarchical status quo itself,
Meister Frantz always making special note when a noble or patrician is
the victim or perpetrator of a crime – hence the lengthy passage on
Wolff – even employing full honourific titles in his private record. Still
shunned by respectable people himself, the ambitious executioner did

not rage against what he saw as an unalterable social reality, but rather sought to continually improve his own place within it. As ever, his progress in achieving that dream would turn on the unlikely prospect of making his own disreputable work the means to that end rather than its chief obstacle.

A man of responsibilities

Frantz's relocation from provincial Hof to urban Bamberg provided but a mild foretaste of the culture shock he faced upon his 1578 arrival in the celebrated imperial city of Nuremberg. With a population of over forty thousand souls inside the city walls and an additional sixty thousand in its surrounding territory of five hundred square miles, the city on the Pegnitz River was one of the largest cosmopolitan centres in the empire, surpassed only by Augsburg, Cologne, and Vienna. The French jurist Jean Bodin called it "the greatest, most famous, and best-ordered of the imperial cities" and local man Johannes Cochlaeus patriotically declared it "the centre of Europe as well as Germany".[6] Other citizens boastingly referred to their beloved home as the Athens of the North, the Venice of the North, or the Florence of the North – not least because of the fame it enjoyed thanks to the celebrated Albrecht Dürer (1471–1528) and a host of other prominent artists and humanists, including Willibald Pirckheimer (1470–1530) and Conrad Celtis (1459–1508).

Even more measured observers acknowledged that Nuremberg was one of the most politically and economically powerful states of the era. Despite officially embracing the Lutheran faith since 1525, the city fathers successfully maintained an advantageous relationship with the Catholic emperors Charles V and Maximilian II, emerging from the Augsburg religious peace of 1555 with the city's political influence unscathed. Nuremberg's banks and mercantile firms competed on a global scale with the Medicis of Florence and the Fuggers of Augsburg, and its printing industry was internationally renowned for its reliable maps and innovative "earth-apples", or globes, based on the latest reports from the New World. The city's craftsmen enjoyed comparable fame for a variety of high-quality manufactured goods and precision instruments,

Nuremberg as viewed from the southeast, with the Kaiserburg looming in the background and the gallows and Raven Stone drawn prominently just outside the city walls (1533).

including clocks, weapons, and navigational tools, as well as ginger-bread and toys (two products for which the city continues to be known today). "What's good comes from Nuremberg" had become a popular adage throughout the empire and abroad, giving the city a level of brand prestige that would be the envy of any modern chamber of commerce.[7]

Frantz Schmidt's lifetime corresponded almost exactly with Nuremberg's zenith of wealth, power, and prestige. As he journeyed there from Bamberg, the newly appointed executioner emerged from the imperial forest a few miles north of the city and caught sight of the familiar but still stunning skyline. Most prominent, high on a hill within the city's walls, stood the majestic Kaiserburg, a towering castle over two hundred feet tall and six hundred feet long – about the size of the Roman Colosseum – that served as the emperor's residence during his visits to the city and was home to the imperial crown jewels until the late eighteenth century. Coming closer, Frantz glimpsed a patchwork of slate roofs descending the flanks of the castle hill – just a few of the hundreds of houses and shops that crowded the city streets below. And in the distance rose the spires of the city's main parish churches – Saint Sebaldus on the northern side of the Pegnitz, and Saint Lorenz, which would become his own congregation, just south of the river. A few miles farther along, young Schmidt passed through the poor outskirts of the city, a district of scattered houses and farms punctuated by patches of forest that might conceal robbers and other rough types. Finally, he arrived at the edge of a moat one hundred feet wide and about as deep. On the far side loomed a massive sandstone wall nearly fifty feet high, ten feet thick, and some seventeen thousand feet long that completely encircled the city and castle. Along this intimidating fortification stood eighty-three soaring towers, spaced approximately 150 feet apart and bristling with armed watchmen. The image of an island fortress was not far from the way Nuremberg's leaders imagined their home, and they would have been pleased at the sense of awe and admiration the city inspired in their new employee.

After arriving at the moat, Frantz paused for inspection at a small guardhouse and then proceeded across the narrow wooden bridge that spanned the water. Next came a larger guardhouse and a more thorough inspection, after which he was allowed to enter whichever of the city's eight massive gates he had selected – probably the northern Vestnertor. Passing through the well-fortified arch, he entered a long, narrow tunnel that took him through the ramparts and finally emerged within the inner city itself. Before him stood a maze of more than five hundred streets and alleys, mostly narrow and crooked, crammed with thousands of structures: stately public buildings, stunningly ornamented patrician houses, modest half-timber artisan residences, and numerous storage barns, stables, makeshift shelters, and commercial stands. The streets, all paved with cobblestones, bustled with vendors, travelling artisans and merchants, maids on errands, loitering youths, playing children, beggars, prostitutes, pickpockets, and rural folk with their livestock – as well as countless horses, dogs, cats, pigs, and rats. Despite the dense concentration of people and animals, Nuremberg's streets were remarkably clean for the era – a stark contrast to the festering ruts of Frantz's boyhood Hof – all thanks to a well-developed water and sewage system (including 118 public wells) and a battery of disposal workers, who dumped waste outside the city walls and sometimes, illegally, into the Pegnitz River. Magistrates still frequently complained about unsightly accumulations of refuse, but by early modern standards, the city appeared quite verdant and lovely, with a number of public parks, gardens, fountains, and decorated squares.

As Frantz knew from previous stays, Nuremberg's governing city council was dominated by a closed circle of forty-two ruling patrician families, and its "senators" highly cherished their homeland's hard-earned reputation as a bastion of law and order. Each of the city's eight districts maintained two district heads, assisted by forty or so municipal guards, known locally as archers, and twenty-four night watchmen.[8] Together with several voluntary street captains, these officials kept stores of weapons, ammunitions, horses, lanterns, ladders, and other supplies, and mobilised able-bodied men in their neighbourhood in the event of fire, enemy attack, or other emergencies. The city government also employed teams of health inspectors and kept a close eye on craft production and prices, with all masters accountable to the city council rather than to independent guilds, as was the custom in most cities of the day.

Most relevant to Frantz Schmidt, Nuremberg maintained an especially active police network, including several paid informers, and boasted the highest capital punishment rate of any city in the empire. Anyone caught wandering the city's streets or alleys after sunset could be imprisoned for suspected burglary, and even such minor infractions as public urination were subject – at least in theory – to a weighty twenty-thaler (17 fl.) fine – twice the annual salary of most domestic servants. According to one admiring (if hyperbolic) English resident, "So trew and Just are they that if you lose a purse with money in the street, Ring, bracelet or such Lyke, you shal be sure to have it again. I would it were so in London."[9] Of course, if all Nuremberg's denizens had truly been this honest, the city would hardly have needed its new executioner's services.

Frantz's immediate superiors were the fourteen city councillors known as the criminal jurors (*Schöffen*). As in all Nuremberg's administrative bodies, the precise composition of this group fluctuated somewhat annually, but all its members were invariably drawn from the same small pool of local patricians and trained jurists. The criminal bureau was managed on a daily basis by a standing judge, typically appointed for life. The patrician Christoph Scheurl, son of the city's most famous jurist, had been serving in this capacity for three years when he appointed "the young executioner from Hof" to his new position. Scheurl would continue in this role for the next fifteen years, until he was succeeded by Alexander Stokamer, who himself served for the following seventeen years. As in his other work relationships, Frantz enjoyed the good fortune of continuity and stability in his superiors.

The financial package that the new executioner had secured in his initial five-year contract was spectacular by the standards of the day. In addition to a weekly salary of 2½ gulden (130 fl. annually), Frantz received a free and spacious lodging (with his own heated bath), a regular supply of wine and firewood, reimbursement for travel and all other job-related expenses, and lifelong tax-free status. He was also to be paid 1 thaler (0.85 fl.) per interrogation session and was permitted to earn supplemental income as both a visiting executioner (with the council's approval) and a medical consultant – the latter generating considerable revenue. His base salary alone put him in the top 5 per cent of earners in Nuremberg and was 60 per cent higher than the salary of his

Nuremberg's magnificent town hall, as seen from the west. Convicted felons waited in the Hole (dungeon) below until their final "trial" in the courtroom on the first floor. The main marketplace is just to the right (south) in this picture (c.1650).

Munich counterpart, making him probably the best-paid executioner in the empire and – at least financially – on par with some medical and legal professionals. On a more personal note, he would earn at least three times as much annually as his own father.[10]

How did a twenty-four-year-old journeyman – albeit one with sterling credentials for his age – achieve such a coup? Once more, timing, character, and contacts were crucial. Nuremberg's leaders were obviously impressed by Frantz's professional experience and expertise, as well as Lienhardt Lippert's recommendation, but it was his reputation for sobriety and reliability, combined with his youth, that likely clinched the offer. Sixteenth-century executioners were not known for their longevity in office, usually owing to a violent disposition or some physical infirmity. Among Frantz's predecessors in Nuremberg, one was executed for treason by his own assistant, another was dismissed after killing his assistant in a dispute over wages, a third was killed in an ambush, a fourth was removed after nearly stabbing a knacker's wife to death, and two others – including Lippert himself – were forced to retire because of old age or serious illnesses.[11] As a young yet accomplished and apparently pious professional, Schmidt promised the stability and seriousness that the office of executioner had hitherto been lacking. His family connections obviously got him a foot in the door, but Frantz made the most of his temporary assignments in Nuremberg, impressing observers with his skill and poise while ingratiating himself with law enforcement superiors during his brief encounters with them.

Masters in any craft were rarely single, and Frantz immediately set out to correct this social deficiency. At some point during the year and a half following his first visit to Nuremberg, the young executioner became acquainted with a woman, nine years his senior, named Maria Beckin. Maria was the daughter of the late Jorg Beck, a longtime warehouse worker, who upon his death in 1561 had left behind a widow and seven children under the age of sixteen.[12] The circumstances of Maria's subsequent courtship by the young man from Hof nearly two decades later are shrouded in mystery. Few respectable women, even of low birth, would have considered marrying an executioner, but a thirty-four-year-old spinster with no dowry and three other eligible sisters at home had few – if any – alternatives. Genuine attraction between the two should not be ruled out, but the match was clearly to their mutual benefit in practical terms, particularly given Frantz's large salary and house. On 15 November 1579, eighteen months after Frantz began his tenure as Nuremberg's permanent executioner, his engagement to Maria Beckin was publicly announced to the congregation of Saint Sebaldus Church. Three weeks later, the city council approved Meister Frantz's request to marry in his new residence – a church ceremony was still out of the question – and on 7 December he and Maria were formally wed.[13]

The municipally owned house that became the newlyweds' home was (and still is) known locally as the Hangman's House (*Henkerhaus*). Most German cities did not allow the executioner to live within the city walls. So even though his house stood in a district filled with other sites of infamy – including a slaughterhouse, the pig market, and a municipal prison – Frantz and his bride would have considered themselves lucky. The original house, built in the fourteenth century, was actually a small three-storey tower (accordingly known as the Hangman's Tower) perched on a small island in the southern outflow of the Pegnitz. In 1457 the city erected a large wooden pedestrian bridge (henceforth known as the Hangman's Bridge) and incorporated the tower into it. Then builders added on to the tower, constructing a long half-timbered house with its foundation set right on the bridge. The expanded residence had provided an exceptionally large space for a young single man, comprising six rooms and an indoor privy: a total of more than sixteen hundred square feet, in an era when the typical family of four managed with a third as much room. Fittingly, the house was at once centrally located and isolated, standing as it did in the middle of the Pegnitz, with the disreputable prison district on one bank and a proper bourgeois neighbourhood on the other. True, Frantz would have to walk past the reeking stalls of the pig market each day to get to the town hall, but he could also gaze without obstruction through his own glazed windows at the opulent structures of the city centre.[14]

Perhaps the young executioner initially continued to share the space with his recently widowed sister and her five surviving children. But such an arrangement would probably not have continued after his marriage to Maria – and certainly not after the birth of their first child, a son named Vitus, on 14 March 1581. Unlike most executioners' children, Vitus was immediately baptised in a church – Saint Sebaldus – as were all of Schmidt's subsequent progeny. Was it significant that Frantz decided not to name his oldest son, or any of Vitus's brothers, after their grandfather Heinrich, a common honourific in the era? Was he perhaps angling for future favours from his father's employer, Bishop Veit of Bamberg, whose name was the German form of Vitus? Or was Schmidt swayed, despite his Protestant faith, by the reputation of Saint Vitus as the patron of healing, the executioner's alternate career? Once more, Frantz's thinking remains hidden from us. His reasons for naming his two subsequent children, by contrast, presents less of a mystery, given that Margaretha (baptised on 25 August 1582) and Jorg (christened on 2 June 1584) ranked among the most popular girl and boy names of the era.

As a new *Hausvater* and a well-paid craft master, Frantz Schmidt finally possessed the social foundation he needed in his quest for respectability. The greater dignity that both he and his superiors sought to bestow on the office of executioner for his public persona, however, would not have been possible without the gradual redefinition of the Nuremberg executioner's job during the generation before him. Some of the executioner's most distasteful and dishonourable responsibilities, such as oversight of the municipal brothel (closed at the insistence of Protestant reformers in 1543), had long ago become obsolete. Other tasks had simply been outsourced to even more disreputable individuals, most notably the job of street cleaning and waste disposal, now overseen by two highly compensated "dung-masters" (also called "night masters").[15]

The executioner's principal assistant, known in Nuremberg as "the Lion" (*Löwe*; a corruption of *lêvjan*, the Gothic word for a bailiff), would play an especially crucial role in helping Frantz pursue his ambition of a respectable life. In exchange for the supplemental income he earned for his various services, the Lion willingly assumed the bulk of the social stigma that earlier executioners had been forced to carry alone. Originally charged only with handing over prisoners condemned by the court, the Lion had, by the time of Frantz's arrival in Nuremberg, assumed oversight of the burning of suicides, the removal of dead animals, and the disposal of spoiled food, oil, and wine (which he usually threw into the Pegnitz). He also continued to serve court summons and assisted the executioner in all tortures, floggings, and executions, occasionally acting as his proxy.[16] Most crucially, the Lion acted as a buffer between Meister Frantz and the many dishonourable individuals connected to his work: knackers, skinners, gravediggers, gaolers, and particularly the municipal archers, infamous for their brutality and corruption in serving as the city's de facto police patrolmen.

Frantz apparently enjoyed a good working relationship with his Lions, remarkably experiencing only one turnover in his forty years of service to Nuremberg. The veteran Augustin Amman already had thirteen years of experience when he began to assist the new young executioner, and Amman continued to fill that role until his retirement (or death) in 1590. His successor, Claus Kohler, worked at Meister Frantz's side for the remainder of Schmidt's career and even continued with the subsequent executioner for three more years, until his own death in 1621.[17] Schmidt no doubt developed a strong professional bond with his Lions. After all, he spent hours each day working with this assistant by his side, more time than he spent with anyone else except perhaps his family members. Moreover, the physical rigour, social sensitivity, and public nature of their job meant that executioner and Lion had to work in a profoundly coordinated, interdependent manner if they were to succeed in their duties. At one point in his journal, Frantz even refers to Nuremberg's *executioners* in the plural, suggesting that he considered his Lion as a partner rather than an underling.[18] Without a reliable and trustworthy Lion, the new executioner knew that his quest for respectability would be doomed from the beginning.

Close working ties did not necessarily translate into close social ties, however. In Bamberg Meister Heinrich's assistant had actually lived with the family, but in Nuremberg the Lion maintained separate quarters in a nearby municipal building. Whatever socialising Frantz's Lions did with the Schmidts, it was discreet and mostly behind closed doors. Two years after Frantz took his first oath of office in Nuremberg's town hall, several new citizens complained about having to take their own oaths next to the dishonourable Lion. The executioner was unable (or unwilling) to protect his faithful colleague from being henceforth banished to a separate annual swearing-in with the hated municipal archers.[19]

Nuremberg also spared its executioner the onus of overseeing its prison system, another time-consuming and odious task standard for many of Frantz's counterparts elsewhere in the empire. The majority of the city's prisons, including the Hole, were intended as holding cells for suspects awaiting judgement, with half of all suspects released within a week, and nine out of ten within a month.[20] Cells in the Luginsland Tower of the imperial castle and within the town hall itself were reserved for the use of patrician prisoners. Six self-standing barracks (designated A to F) were constructed during Frantz's tenure in Nuremberg to house unruly youths and other lesser delinquents. Debtors awaiting financial assistance from their friends and relatives were locked in a specially designated male or female prison. The remaining city towers handled prisoners-of-war and other spillover from the Hole, while a few, like the Frog Tower and Water Tower, simultaneously functioned as long-term insane asylums.[21] (See map on page xi.)

Each prison or tower had its own warden – like Frantz, who reported directly to the criminal bureau – as well as its own attachment of guards (known as "iron masters"). Though not officially dishonourable, prison employees were generally lowborn, poorly paid, and widely disdained. Their reputation for corruption and incompetence was fuelled by the preservation of a medieval funding structure whereby prisoners were expected to pay for their own upkeep, thereby determining the level of "comfort" available. The exorbitant minimum rate of 36 pfennig per day (more than 2 fl. per week) merely assured an inmate of morning soup, a "good piece" of white bread, and a litre of wine. More food and other privileges – an extra blanket or a pillow, access to drinking water, more frequent changing of the excrement bucket – each carried additional charges. Of course, destitute prisoners could not even afford the basic fee, and at the end of their incarceration – regardless of innocence or guilt – their charges were assumed by the city alms bureau or another charity.[22]

For the first twenty years of Frantz Schmidt's work in Nuremberg, he and his Lion worked more often with the longtime warden of the Hole, Hans Öhler, than with any of the other prison heads. Required by law to be both married and resident in the prison, Öhler shared tiny quarters with two successive wives as well as his daughter, son, and two maids. Other than the marriage stipulation, the expectations for any individual willing to undertake such an unattractive position were understandably low. The criminal bureau's sole efforts at better enforcement appear to have been limited to an annual reminder to the warden and his wife that they should carefully explain the required duties to each new staff member.[23] The bureau also frequently admonished – but never dismissed – Öhler for the multiple shortcomings of that same staff, many of whom came from the same disreputable pool as the inmates themselves.

Frantz did not have to wait long to encounter the incompetence (or corruption) of his new associates at the prison. During the night of 20 June 1578, the thief who was to be the new executioner's first victim made a daring escape from the Hole. According to a contemporary account, Hans Reintein got the elderly guard watching him drunk and then fled through a secret underground passage to the imperial castle that he as a mason had helped construct. He used an iron bar to break through any locked doors and to bash a hole in the ceiling of a corridor under Saint Sebaldus Church, through which he ultimately crawled out to freedom.[24] In typical fashion, the guard received a tongue-lashing but kept his job. Two years later, another audacious escape – this one accomplished by an inmate who duped the warden himself out of an iron bar and used it to break into the subterranean passage – merely resulted in another "stern admonishment".[25] Such bold escapes continued to occur throughout Meister Frantz's career, as did frequent inmate suicides and occasional fatal brawls among inmates. The city council invariably responded to such disruptions in muted fashion, merely instructing the warden and his guards to search new prisoners more thoroughly to determine "whether they have a knife, nail, or anything else that they could use to harm themselves or to escape."[26]

Frantz Schmidt was understandably loath to be associated with such disreputable individuals and locations, yet his responsibility for prisoners' physical welfare required him to make frequent visits to the Hole and occasionally to some of the towers. In addition, all the interrogations he performed, whether with torture or without, took place in the Hole, beneath the town hall – a cramped, dirty, dark, and genuinely frightening place that generally conformed to our worst stereotypes of the medieval dungeon. The thirteen holding cells – each about thirty-six square feet, with one narrow wooden bench, a straw bed, and a bucket – could barely accommodate the two prisoners required to share them, let alone a visiting interrogation team of two to five men, who instead stood outside in the corridor to ask their follow-up questions under the dim flicker of a small oil lamp. Primitive coal heating scarcely alleviated the harsh winter cold, nor did the few narrow ventilation shafts to the outside improve the putrid and dank air below. Only those inmates condemned to death enjoyed the slightly larger accommodations of the poor sinners' cells, or during their final three days the relative luxury of the so-called hangman's parlour, the only room in the prison with windows to the outside. Wending his way through the labyrinthine corridors on a near-daily basis – whether to torture a recalcitrant suspect or to heal him – Frantz's greatest consolation was that his visits to this cesspool of sin and misery at least remained hidden from public view.

One disagreeable task that Meister Frantz could not avoid or conceal was the maintenance of the execution site itself, comprising both the gallows and the Raven Stone, a raised platform used for beheadings and for breaking on the wheel. Since 1441, both gallows and stone had been located just outside the portal in the city walls known as the Ladies' Gate, where they remained until the city became part of the duchy of Bavaria nearly four centuries later. By Schmidt's time, the once modest three-legged gallows and adjacent small mound had been transformed into two stately brick edifices, one a solidly built four-beamed scaffold, the other an elevated stage, covered with turf. Law and custom dictated that the execution site remain a horror to behold, adorned as it was by the rotting corpses of one or more thieves that twisted in the breeze for weeks until they dropped off unceremoniously into the pit of bones beneath. Nearby stood a series of sharpened stakes, decorated with decapitated heads and other body parts, accompanied sometimes by the mangled body of a poor sinner broken on the wheel raised high on the instrument of its demise. Popular superstitions abounded over every aspect of the cursed execution ground, its eerie silence broken only by the cawing of hungry ravens and the often-noted whistling of the wind through the ramparts.

The week after his first public performance as Nuremberg's executioner – a triple hanging – Meister Frantz initiated a complete renovation of the existing structure. Over the course of two weeks in late June and early July of 1578, the Lion and his helpers performed the dishonourable task of pulling down and disposing of the old gallows and

Raven Stone. Since anyone who touched an execution structure – even a completely new, untainted one – risked lifelong pollution and bad luck, all the city's masons and carpenters worked on the building project together, thereby dissipating the danger. On the morning of 10 July, 336 masters and journeymen assembled to launch an all-day "gallows festival". It began with a colourful and noisy procession of pipers, drummers, and representatives of all the city's patrician families and crafts, as well as assorted clerics and many others. After solemnly circling the site of the former gallows three times, the craftsmen brought in several wagonloads of stone and wood and set to work.

The infamous site of Nuremberg's gallows (left) and Raven Stone (right) (1648).

With the combination of efficiency and cooperation seen in a modern-day Amish barn-raising, they completed both the gallows and Raven Stone by late that afternoon. Then they sat down with their fellow Nurembergers to enjoy great quantities of food and drink, with the entire day's activities – including the wages of every craftsman – paid for by the city treasury. Twenty-seven years later, in 1605, the ritual would be repeated, as it would every generation or so for the next two centuries.[27]

Maintaining the gallows between such public festivities was a decidedly less festive proposition. Despite the evil spirits and infamy

Nuremberg's gallows, as drawn by a court notary (1583).

associated with the execution grounds, miscreants regularly robbed or otherwise violated the cadavers that hung from the gallows. One nocturnal vandal might slice off the hand, the thumb, or even "the manhood" of an executed man, each believed to possess magical powers. Another would pry loose a head from its stake, perhaps to take home as a gruesome souvenir. Still others broke the ancient taboo for reasons much more mundane. In the autumn of 1588, someone cut down Georg Solen after eight days and later Hans Schnabel after fourteen days, both times in order to remove and make off with the corpse's vest and trousers. Leinhard Bardtmann (aka the Horseman) had only been hanging for three days when *someone cut through his neck, so that the head remained hanging and the body fell to the ground.* Theft was the apparent motive here as well, but in this instance it was triggered by a rumour that the condemned himself had cleverly planted, so as to spare his corpse an extended indignity: *Some wantonous fellows found out and believed that he had much gold sewn in his clothes and thought to get good booty. Nothing was found, however.*[28] The Horseman subsequently received a proper burial, just as he had intended.

Apparently even Meister Frantz and his superiors recoiled at the excessive humiliation of a hanged thief's cadaver. In Solen's case, only the bottom half of his corpse had been removed *and the rest left hanging*, so that *the body was finally thrown into the gallows pit the next day, as it looked too horrible.* And after word circulated that hanged thief Matthes Lenger had been *stripped naked the first night, except for his stockings*, there was such a surge of curious onlookers – especially "cheeky females", according to the prison chaplain – that the city councillors ordered Meister Frantz *to put a shirt and trunk-hose on him.*[29] Whether the executioner delegated this distasteful task, like so many others, to his Lion is not recorded.

A good name

Twenty-four-year-old Frantz Schmidt entered Nuremberg society as an unmarried foreigner, working in a despised profession. That he would confront more than the usual wariness that longtime residents accorded outsiders is an understatement. Even after he took a bride and became locally known, Frantz recognised that to be accepted by the citizens and leaders of Nuremberg, he would not only have to satisfy their standard of propriety but also find incremental ways to formalise and thereby secure his status as an honourable man. "In an honour-based society," the legal historian William Miller has observed, "there is no self-respect independent of the respect of others," and thus every personal interaction remains fraught with the danger of lost honour.[30] Frantz could probably never completely overcome the local animosity towards a foreign-born professional killer, but at least he could grind down the resistance, dim his father's stain of dishonour, and above all provide no ammunition for those who would push him back down into the gutter of society. The campaign would be long and require much patience and perseverance. The young executioner from Hof would need to prove himself as deliberate and precise in this enterprise as he was in his sword strokes on the Raven Stone.

Meister Frantz's deliberate construction of a reputation for himself simultaneously embraced and repudiated the existing social order. He was no rebel; his vision for himself remained framed within the somewhat narrow confines of the conventions of the day. Yet his journal reveals that, like many ambitious individuals, he possessed a social imagination capable of adapting those conventions to fit his own unique circumstances. For most people of the era, one's reputation was inextricably bound up in one's identity, and much of that identity was inherited, including place of origin and social status. For Frantz Schmidt, the importance of such identity was undeniable, but character and deeds – two factors within his own control – determined reputation, not birth. This sharp distinction, while far from universally accepted, at least provided the young foreign executioner with a fighting chance.

The first obstacle Frantz had to overcome was his own foreignness. Specific place of origin – one's town or village – constituted an important part of an early modern person's identity. This made sense, in an era when travel was slow, customs varied widely from region to region, and dozens of distinctive dialects flourished within the boundaries of what we now call Germany, many of them unintelligible to visitors from as little as a few days' journey away. In his journal, Frantz consistently identifies each culprit at the outset by his or her home village or town – *from Bürg* or *of Ansbach*. He himself was long known in Nuremberg as "the executioner from Hof" or "from Bamberg" (even though he had only lived briefly in the latter). A person who could not be literally placed was not only harder for others to remember but also immediately suspect. Although Frantz occasionally forgets or misremembers a proper name in his journal, never – except in the instance of a few itinerant prostitutes – does he fail to record a person's place of origin.

Frantz also recognised that geographical origin always carried a political dimension, identifying an individual as either a native – born in Nuremberg or its surrounding territory – or "a foreigner" – born anywhere else regardless of distance, language, or current residence. Thus, the cowherder Heinz Neuner, who worked as a potter in the Nuremberg suburb of Gostenhof, remained a subject of the nearby margrave of Ansbach and thus just as much a foreigner as *Steffan Rebweller from Marshtall in Savoy . . . and Heinrich Hausmann of Kalka, fourteen miles below Cologne*.[31] Frantz frequently notes – forty-five times in 778 cases – when an individual is not only from Nuremberg but also a citizen, a special legal status granted only to certain residents. Citizenship carried several prerogatives, most notably the right to execution by the sword for capital crimes (as in the instance of swindler Gabriel Wolff) or even mitigation to flogging in the cases of Nuremberg forger Endres Petry or the incestuous Barbara Grimmin (aka Schory Mory).[32] Citizen Margaretha Böckin, convicted of a particularly treacherous murder, merely enjoyed the privilege of being beheaded while standing, having already been *nipped thrice with red-hot tongs and afterwards her [decapitated] head was fixed on a pole above and the body buried under the gallows*.[33]

Of course, a busy metropolis like Nuremberg was filled with immigrants, some of them resident for decades. This aspect of identity was not in itself debilitating, particularly at the lower levels of society. Did Frantz's foreignness exacerbate his isolation? What did he consider home? It's not exactly clear. "The young executioner from Hof" had not lived in his native town for many years and did not display any hesitation whatsoever about flogging malefactors from Hof – some of whom he might even have known. But neither did he express any personal affinity with the city on the Pegnitz that now employed him.[34] Only after ten years on the job in Nuremberg did he begin to refer to *our town* or the murder of *the son of one of our citizens*, and even after that, when it is obvious that he has settled for life, such explicit signs of allegiance remain rare in the journal.[35] The transformation into "Frantz Schmidt of Nuremberg" required time, patience, and more tangible signs of mutual acceptance in his relationship with the city fathers.

Social status, based on family and occupation, obviously posed a much greater problem for the young journeyman. Here Frantz's interpretation of honour and status appear simultaneously alien and familiar to modern sensibilities. Although the victim himself of a capricious prince's life-altering command, he seems not only to accept the idea of upper-class privilege but also to actually believe in its sanctity at a profound level. He invariably writes about his social superiors with a reverence that bespeaks more than mere habit and more even than the caution of a man who knows that his employers might one day read his words. In fact, when Frantz writes of a crime in which a lower-class culprit harms a patrician or noble, he often seems as offended by the mere effrontery of a cross-class transgression as he is by the misdeed itself. He becomes visibly outraged, for instance, when the con artist Gabriel Wolff has the impertinence to defraud the wealthy and highborn of Nuremberg and other cities.[36] And in another entry he seethes with indignation as he describes the murderer of *the nobleman and soldier Albernius von Wisenstein* by *Dominicus Korn, a citizen's child, a mercenary, and whoreson of a tavern keeper.*[37]

For many of us on this side of the French Revolution, it's difficult to understand Meister Frantz's apparently deep belief in the innate superiority of the rich and the noble. Our modern culture of envy presupposes that the inherited wealth and privilege of others can be resented or coveted, but certainly not respected as divinely ordained. For Schmidt and his contemporaries, though, the hierarchy of birth existed as a natural force, like the weather or the plague – capricious, even destructive, but inevitable. It's hardly remarkable that Meister Frantz embraced this status quo. After all, he served as one of the key guardians of this stratified society – and he believed that he had the wit and resolve to achieve his own social ends within its confines. The cost was not negligible: the young executioner suffered daily reminders of his own low status, ranging from casual slights or veiled insults to his formal exclusion from every festival, dance, procession, and other public gathering except those that were directly connected to his unsavoury profession.

A chronicler's portrayal of the 1605 execution of Niklaus von Gülchen, Nuremberg privy councillor, for embezzlement and other offences (1616). In reality, von Gülchen was seated in a judgement chair, not kneeling.

The very men who worked with him on criminal cases – the city physician, the examining magistrates, the court notary – could not freely converse with him in the street or show any other signs of social intimacy. These and other indignities were simply to be borne by Meister Frantz, who likely saw them as the natural lot of someone in his unique social station. Whether these daily affronts caused him anger or shame or despair is known only to him.

One dramatic incident later in Frantz's career reveals the depth of his innate respect for authority and high birth. In December 1605 the noble privy councillor Doctor Niklaus von Gülchen (spelled *Gilgen* by Schmidt) was convicted of defrauding and betraying many prominent Nurembergers and the city itself, in the most infamous governmental scandal in over a century. Though condemned to death, Gülchen received all the privileges of a first-class execution: a comfortable cell in the Luginsland Tower rather than the Hole, special meals, exemption from torture during interrogation (the noble right of *non torquendo*), an honourable death by the sword, and burial in his family plot in Saint Johannis Cemetery.[38] Frantz's deep revulsion seethes throughout the lengthy passage he devotes to Gülchen's diverse *evil deeds*, which included breaking his oaths as a privy councillor, advising opposing parties in many affairs, embezzling from the city treasury, raiding municipal supplies of beer and wine, siring five children by his wife's servant, raping his undermaid, attempting to rape one daughter-in-law and bribing the other one to enter into a long-standing affair, cheating many noble and patrician families, and passing himself off as a doctor by means of a false seal. As in the case of the well-born swindler Gabriel Wolff, it was Gülchen's easy willingness to abuse his privileged position and disgrace his family's honour that particularly outraged Nuremberg's executioner, almost constituting a kind of sacrilege. Yet the prerogatives of rank once more prevailed. Meister Frantz found himself having to negotiate with the condemned nobleman in his cell over the appropriate execution clothing. Schmidt's superiors finally lost patience with Gülchen and provided him a long mourning cloak and a hat from the municipal armoury, which the condemned man burnished with regal aplomb during the public procession to the judgement chair, itself gently draped with a fine black silk cloth.[39]

For the great mass of humanity beneath the aristocracy and patriciate, Frantz Schmidt considered the linking of social status and reputation even more dubious. He was particularly wary of attempts by the craftsmen's guilds to shore up their members' deteriorating rank and influence by vilifying those with dishonourable professions – such as executioners – or with no profession at all. Frantz knew from early on that training or employment in a so-called honourable craft did not in itself make a person honourable. So although he subscribed to the then-universal convention of identifying each culprit in his journal by profession – *a furrier, a farmer, a wire-drawer* – he never states that a particular craft or guild is honourable. In fact, the word "honourable" itself appears only in reference to nobles or patricians, and its counterpart, "dishonourable", is entirely absent from the journal. For Frantz, craft, like place of origin or name, served merely as a neutral way to situate an individual in physical space. In his mind, formal identity of this sort carried no implication of character, good or bad – so that even serial murderer Nickel Schwager's primary designation remains simply *a mason*.[40]

Frantz's distinction between social status and reputation is frequently evident in his combination of a person's professional and criminal identities, as when he writes of *a grocer and murderer, a horseman . . . and a thief, a pedlar and thief,* or more impressively, *a tiler . . . a thief and a cheat at gaming, who also took three wives.* This tendency becomes especially prominent during Frantz's early years in Nuremberg, though he is inconsistent at times, such as in his identification of Georg Götz as *a [municipal] archer, thief, and whoremonger,* and later simply *an archer* – a perfectly understandable omission given the spontaneous nature of his journal keeping.[41] (It's unlikely that the ultimately beheaded Götz developed less of a taste for stealing and loose women during the time between his convictions.) Frantz's growing preference for compound identities – *Michel Gemperlein, a butcher, mercenary, murderer, robber, and thief* – also indicates the maturing executioner's recognition that the old order of identity by craft alone was increasingly meaningless in any moral sense.[42]

Those few instances where Frantz identifies perpetrators exclusively in terms of their offences reveal even more about his own views of morality and character: *a child murderess* (for infanticide); *an arsonist*; or *a heretic* (for incest and for bestiality). Unlike simple fornication or even homicide, crimes of this nature completely obliterated all other aspects of an individual's identity in the executioner's mind. Individuals who had become full-time criminals are thus also sometimes exclusively designated by their chosen professions of *thief* or *robber* – hardly value-neutral terms.

Frantz's refusal to conflate social status and reputation obviously had much to do with his own situation. Even the appellation "Meister Frantz" might reduce him in other's eyes to the level of his odious craft. In general, though, a person's name revealed little about his or her identity, let alone reputation. Noble and patrician names were of course generally self-evident, especially when accompanied in the journal by telltale antecedents, such as "the honourable" or "His Excellency". Jewish names were also easy to identify, as they typically featured first names of Hebrew origin (e.g. Mosche or Moses) and last names intended to serve as a label, such as Judt ("the Jew"). Otherwise, appellations in themselves told little. A Protestant woman might be named after the Blessed Virgin or a saint; a cobbler could be known as Fischer, a longtime Nuremberg family by the name of Frankfurter. Obviously, in actual life certain family names carried more weight than others in some localities, but even the surnames of many Nuremberg patricians also surfaced in the poor rolls and even criminal records.

The one major exception to this ambiguity was when an individual was identified by a nickname or alias. Not everyone who had a nickname engaged in some disreputable activity, but virtually all disreputable individuals had at least one alternate identity. By the time they had become professional criminals, almost all the juvenile thieves Meister Frantz encountered had acquired colourful street names, such as Frog Johnny, the Black Baker, Red Lenny, Corky, Hook, and Shifty. Popular monikers might be based on occupations (the Grocer, the Mason, Baker's Boy), places of origin (the Swissman, Cunz from Pommersbrun), clothing (Green Cap, Cavalier Johnny, Glove George), or combinations thereof (the Fiddling Cobbler, the Woodsman from Lauf, Baiersdorf Blacky). They could be comical (Chicken Leg, Rabbit, Snail), patronising (Gabby, Stuttering Bart, Laddy), or even insulting (Horse Beetle, Raven Fodder). In a decidedly less politically correct age, nicknames often focused on an individual's appearance – Pointy Head, the Long Brickmaker, Red Pete, Lean George, and Little Fatty – or on personal hygiene, such as Dusty.[43] A nickname might also be a play on a given name, as in the case of Katherina Schwertzin (Black) who was known as the Coal Girl.[44] But whatever their origin, nicknames also served an eminently practical purpose: They avoided confusion in a society that overrelied on a few first names (particularly Hans).

For Nuremberg's experienced executioner, the sheer existence of a nickname often implied some association with "loose society", if not the criminal underworld itself. It's less clear that nicknames in themselves carried the same social taint for most common people – depending of course on the nickname. Contemporaries might have been understandably wary of the violent tendencies of men known as Mercenary John, or Scabbard, or somewhat apprehensive about their purses when introduced to the Tricky Tanner or Eight Fingers. There were surely few respectable social or work opportunities for women once their nicknames were revealed to be Playbunny, Furry Kathy, Grinder Girl, or, most jarring, Cunt Annie.[45] No doubt Meister Frantz was aware of a few uncomplimentary, or at least undignified, nicknames for himself, but he declined to preserve them for posterity.

Whatever the circumstances of one's birth or profession (or one's nickname), all of Frantz Schmidt's contemporaries would have agreed that the most reliable indicator of reputation was the company one kept – a fact of considerable comfort to Nuremberg's executioner, who could not choose his origins or even his colleagues but who could choose his friends. But who was included in what must have been a small circle of intimates, given the still-pervasive social constraints he faced? And where did they meet? Certainly not the most frequent site of male sociability, since taverns were generally off-limits to executioners, especially one who didn't himself imbibe or gamble. Public festivals, wedding celebrations, and the like also remained closed to him, as did the homes of learned colleagues or acquaintances, who risked losing their reputations if they were known to associate with an executioner. Given his long tenure, Frantz clearly enjoyed at least an amiable working relationship with some of the city's magistrates, jurists, physicians, and apothecaries. He also maintained a correspondence and perhaps friendship with some other executioners in the area.[46] His relationship with the prison chaplains, by contrast, does not appear to have been particularly close: in their journals, Magister Hagendorn and Magister Müller rarely refer to him by name, instead calling him "the executioner" or "the hangman". Schmidt himself similarly writes impersonally of *the priests*. Whoever Frantz's closest companions were – and we may hope that he enjoyed some of the joys of friendship – their social encounters most likely took place in the privacy of the executioner's house, although being seen there also carried some reputational risk to visitors.

Simply avoiding bad company was a more straightforward matter and one in which the son of Heinrich Schmidt had become well practised. Thanks to the efforts of his Lion, Frantz had minimal direct contact with the municipal archers and other low-level law enforcers, so he avoided the popular animosity roused by their perceived corruption and general thuggishness. The new executioner disciplined without hesitation any begging beadles or municipal archers who consorted with prostitutes or raped young girls in their charge, either by flogging or execution.[47] He impassively notes his own execution of four former colleagues for murder and theft, including the knacker Hans Hammer (aka Pebble; aka Young Cobbler) and the archer Carl Reichardt (aka Eckerlein), who *stole here and everywhere from the executioners and their assistants, also at the knackers' yards where he lodged*. Given the further dishonour such associates indirectly brought on his profession,

Frantz's eagerness to distance himself is understandable. Tellingly, he makes no attempt to convince himself that such miscreants were exceptions among employees of this rank, but to the contrary remarks with surprise when a former beadle convicted of murder strikes him as an otherwise *reputable man*, the condemned man's wheel sentence accordingly mitigated to decapitation.[48]

Among men, association with loose company was an expansive concept but generally implied consorting or even working with professional criminals. Merely casual affiliation with known outlaws might itself provide sufficient grounds for torture in some serious cases. Acknowledged membership in a large robber band was even more damning, so that Meister Frantz can convey with a few words the notoriety of Joachim Waldt (aka the Tutor), *who cruelly stole much and broke into [homes] with some thirty companions*, or Hennsa Walter (aka the Cheesecutter), who was associated with *fourteen of his companions and two whores*. More typically, it is sufficient for him to note that a convicted robber *had many companions*, thereby establishing with one stroke a man's dark reputation as *a rogue* and his subsequently well-deserved execution.[49]

Excessive drinking, gambling, fighting, and consorting with prostitutes were also typically part of a bad male reputation, as was more simply "lewd and lousy language".[50] Given such behaviour's frequency in the larger population, however, it indicated an inclination towards crime but did not constitute evidence in itself. Instead, Frantz used such details to contextualise criminals and frequently to amplify, further underscoring the bad character and just deserts of a man he had just executed. Hans Gerstacker (aka Red) *stole a lot [and] also beat a woman during an argument*. The bag-maker and tollkeeper Andreas Weyr is justly flogged *because he committed lewdness with three common whores; he already [had] a wife; also embezzled from the tolls*.[51]

The executioner remained just as conventional on the question of female reputation. Like males, many of the women Frantz flogged or executed were tainted by their association with known criminals, often as the consort or wife of a notorious robber. If direct complicity in theft or murder was established, the sentence could be more severe, ranging from chopped-off fingers to death by drowning, as in the case of Margaretha Hörnlein, who acted *as an accessory to the murder of the newly*

*born babies who were killed in her house, and gave the murderers and
thieves food so that they might not inform about anything.* Frantz considered women who chose such a lifestyle already immersed in a separate,
shady society made up of thieves, robbers, and murderers. Maria Canterin had already been flogged several times and disfigured for being
the consort of two executed robbers – *Handsome* and *Glove George* –
when she and her current lover, *the Scholar of Bayreuth*, were both executed for new thefts.[52]

Yet whatever her level of involvement in acts of theft or violence, a
woman of ill repute was invariably defined principally by her sexual
deviancy. With a single word, Frantz and his contemporaries could
transform the reputation of any female suspected of promiscuity –
much more effectively than with the frequent curse of *rogue* or
whoremonger for men. Professional prostitutes, "soldiers' consorts", and
other "loose females" (many of them victims of rape or incest) are regularly identified in the executioner's journal as *a common street whore, a
thief-whore,* or simply *a whore.*[53] Like men who beat their own mothers
or who swore at their betters in court, women believed to sleep around
were automatically suspected of still graver offences. Sometimes this
results in a compound designation in Frantz's journal – *three citizen
children and whores; a plumber's daughter [and] a whore; a cook and
whore,* even *an archer's wife and whore* – but more often such women
lose all other identity in the executioner's memory, sometimes even including their very names.[54]

The Reformation's preoccupation with sexual deviance made all
women – married as well as single or widowed – increasingly vulnerable to accusations of promiscuity and its damaging consequences. In
the worst scenarios it was a contributing factor in accusations of
witchcraft and infanticide, the two most common grounds for female
execution during the early modern era. More commonly, any detected
extramarital activity by women led to flogging and banishment or in a
few rare cases – usually exacerbated by theft – execution. While women
overall made up only 10 per cent of the individuals Frantz executed
during his career, they constituted over 80 per cent of those he put in
the stocks and then *whipped out of town with rods* for sexual crimes.[55]

Frantz clearly recognised the double standard applied to men and
women, even noting when men convicted of sexual misdemeanours

received lesser punishments than their female counterparts, including for incest.[56] Yet he appears more amused than compassionate in quoting the lines scrawled on a church wall by the distraught husband of a woman executed for *lewdness and harlotry . . . with twenty-one married men and youths*, including a father and his son: *"Father and son should have been treated as she was, and the panderers also. In the other world I shall summon and appeal to emperor and king because justice has not been done. I, poor man, suffer though innocent. Farewell and good night."*[57] For Nuremberg's executioner, you were the product of your actions, and if those included *losing [your] honour [i.e. virginity] to a mercenary five years ago* or having *three whore's children*, you were *a whore*.[58]

Surprisingly for the era (and for a pious Lutheran executioner), religious identity remained a completely neutral factor in Frantz Schmidt's assessment of personal reputation and character. He shows no open animosity toward the Catholics he executed (whom he never refers to as papists), remarking only upon a special prayer or communion request on the scaffold.[59] Hans Schrenker (aka the Crawler) cheekily attempted to use his Catholic faith as grounds for postponement of his execution, asking at the scaffold to be permitted *to go on a pilgrimage . . . to his confessor, after which he would return (his request was denied)*. Schmidt's unique uses of *heretic* and *godlessness* each refer to the culprit's particular deed, not his or her religious denomination.[60]

Even Jews, who had been ritually humiliated every Good Friday in the Hof of Frantz's youth and officially banned from the city of Nuremberg since 1498, are mentioned more often sympathetically as victims of executed thieves or robbers than as perpetrators.[61] When Meister Frantz was ordered to publicly strangle (out of mercy) the spy and thief Moses the Jew from Otenfoss, he meticulously notes that *it is fifty-four years since a Jew (named Ambsel) was executed*. There is no reference to the "blood pollution" accusations put forward by modern anti-Semites or any suggestion of more serious punishment than flogging for Hay Jud, convicted of *overtak[ing] the Christian women from behind, in his wantonness intending to rape [them] and all the while pressing on them out of brazenness until his nature was satisfied*. Julius Kunrad – a Jew who had converted to Christianity and boasted several powerful sponsors, including the bishop of Würzburg – likewise received the standard flogging and banishment for bigamy and fornication, even though he also had an illegitimate child with *a common [Christian] whore . . . before he was baptised.* When later that same year (and now calling himself Kunrad from Reichensachsen) Kunrad was executed for robbery, multiple thefts, and murder, Schmidt makes no comments about his religious identity except to observe that on the scaffold he *would not receive the [Lutheran] sacrament, but [desired it] in the Catholic way.*[62]

Frantz Schmidt's careful construction of his own good name rendered him understandably sensitive to abuses of reputation. He became especially incensed when confronted with individuals who assumed a name or social status that was not their own – a fairly easy feat in an era before standard means of verifying personal identity.[63] What modern scholars admiringly call "self-fashioning" and what lawyers characterise as "fraudulent imposture" was a deeply serious and troubling matter for Nuremberg's executioner. He is chagrined that Lienhard Dischinger, who *with false letters and seals [passed himself off as] a transplanted schoolmaster or priest,* escaped with a briefly summarised flogging, and reassured that Kunrad Krafft, who committed numerous frauds under a false name and *giving himself out to be [both] a citizen of Forchheim [and] a councillor of Colmutz,* was ultimately beheaded for his lies.[64] Theft of a good name – as in the case of the notorious forger Gabriel Wolff – threatened the bedrock of Schmidt's world view more than the stealing of money or property. When he writes about the weaver's daughter Maria Cordula Hunnerin, who was beheaded for her crimes, it is not her sizeable thefts from former masters that take centre stage but her shameful and scandalous imposture:

> *[she] took up at Altdorf with the son of a cloth manufacturer from Schweinfurt, [and,] giving herself out to be the daughter of the innkeeper at the Black Bear in Bayreuth, hired a carriage, drove to the inn there with her betrothed and a soldier's wife, ordered food and drink to be prepared, pointed out an old man in the inn as her father, then left the inn to fetch her sister, leaving the others sitting in the inn, and the soldier's wife had to pay 32 fl.*[65]

Of course the use of multiple identities was endemic among professional thieves, a practise that further reinforced their disreputable status.

Virtually every one of these individuals whom Frantz encountered in the course of his career boasted at least one alias, and often more. The robber and mercenary Lienhard Kiesswetter *is also known as Lienhart Lubing, Lienhart of Kornstatt, Mosel Lenny, and Sick Lenny*; another young thief already had five aliases by the age of sixteen. An honest man, by contrast, has but one true identity, so Meister Frantz considers it a sign of genuine contrition that Fritz Musterer (aka Little Fritzie; aka Snail) *first told his real name just before being led out [to the gallows], that before he was known as Georg Stengel of Bachhaussen, a thief and robber.* The female consorts of robbers and other professional criminals were likewise known for having multiple aliases, sometimes changing their names as they changed their men. *Thief-whore* Anna Gröschlin (also known as Speedy's Woman) admitted to Frantz that three years previously she *had given herself out as Margaretha Schoberin*, taking the last name of her then consort Georg Schober (as well as assuming a different first name).[66]

Slander, another form of reputational theft, provoked an even stronger emotional response from the status-sensitive executioner, who was himself no stranger to the suffering caused by malicious gossip and prejudice. Many of Frantz's contemporaries shared this point of view, deeming a blow to one's good name more grievous than a wounding of the body. Bastian Grübel (aka Slag) *stole much and besides confessed to twenty murders,* but what most preoccupies Schmidt in his account is how he slandered an enemy, claiming he was an accomplice, which resulted in the innocent man's arrest and torture. Frantz is apparently even more outraged at the former executioner's assistant Friedrich Stigler *for having brought accusations against some citizens' wives here that they were witches . . . However, he wittingly did them wrong* – a serious crime for which Stigler was ultimately beheaded by a disgusted Meister Frantz. Aware of the emotional agony caused by false defamation, Schmidt renders especially harsh judgement on the attempted rapist Valentin Sundermann, who maliciously claimed to have witnessed the mistress of the house *have lewd relations . . . with several journeymen,* and bestows unexpected sympathy on the career thief Georg Mötzela, who languished *in prison for three-quarters of a year because his boy, his whore's nine-year-old brother, accused him of five murders . . . but there was nothing in it.*[67]

Honour could be bestowed or revoked by those in power, men who could be capricious, even cruel. Honesty – and consequently reputation – represented an act of self-determination. By rejecting the caste fatalism of most of his contemporaries and cleaving to a path of forthright action that he hoped would lead to a more honourable position in life, Frantz Schmidt unwittingly embraced a more modern concept of individual identity. This was a strikingly humanist approach for a semi-literate autodidact. His subsequent speculations about human nature and free will shared some important insights with the greatest intellects of the day, despite their raw and fractured form of expression. For Frantz, though, philosophical speculation came in a distant second to his simple, practical objective, and in that respect, establishing an honest reputation was a priority without equal.

The victims' avenger

The essential ingredients for a good name were common knowledge at every level of society. An astute and unscrupulous young man might easily have built a public reputation by manipulating perceptions, achieving the semblance of propriety without actually embracing the principles themselves. As witness to so much human cruelty and deception, it would be understandable if Frantz had become apathetic or even cynical about the criminal justice enterprise and its moral ambiguities. After all, as he well knew, not all evildoers got caught or punished and not all victims were completely blameless in their own misfortunes. Satisfactory performance of his duty, moreover, did not demand any passion for justice or profound belief in the righteousness of his daily work. Early on he might have decided to focus solely on his own self-advancement and the outward conformity it entailed.

A lifetime of journal entries confirms, to the contrary, that Frantz Schmidt was not only a willing executioner but also a passionate one. His outrage at the atrocities committed by robbers and arsonists appears genuine and his commitment to restoring social order likewise heartfelt, not grudging or calculated. His empathy for victims, especially those *robbed of all [their] worldly possessions*, is frequently and convincingly expressed. Rather than suppressing or denying his emotions, in other words, Meister Frantz chose to channel them, providing the only relief he could to the victims of crime – legal retribution.

Frantz's personal definition of justice was highly traditional, and thus distinctly different from that of the imperial law that supposedly guided him.[68] While invoking "ancient custom" and "divine commands", legal and religious reformers of the sixteenth century strove for a new conceptual coherence in criminal law, based on the respective authorities they represented. In this more abstract model, the principal injured parties in a crime were no longer a victim and his or her kin group, but the legal sovereign and God Himself. For Frantz Schmidt, by contrast, all crime remained in essence an act of personal betrayal, either of another individual or of a group. Trust, not obedience to God or state, was the more sacred bond criminals violated, and the greater the degree of that violation, the more infamous the criminal for Meister Frantz.

Learned jurists expanded the definition of treason, for instance, to include not just the betrayal of a superior but a variety of social transgressions they considered rebellions against divinely ordained secular authority itself – the subsequent focus of most new legislation. Yet for Frantz and most of his contemporaries, even political treason continued to be viewed in personal injuries rather than abstract terms. In the ongoing cold war between the city of Nuremberg and the margrave of Ansbach, for instance, both sides regularly employed rangers, spies, and other mercenaries to gather intelligence or to capture agents.[69] His journal entries on these various acts of "treason", however, show no emotion until he comes to the traitor Hans Ramsperger, who

> betrayed many citizens of Nuremberg and poachers, of whom some ten were executed and nothing found on them [i.e. no incriminating evidence]. Also betrayed the town of Nuremberg to the old margrave, revealing where the walls were weakest and most easily stormed and offering if possible to do his best to bring this to pass. Also offered to betray Herr Hans Jacob Haller, at Weyer's house, as well as Herr Schmitter and Master Weyermann or bring them to prison.

Although Ramsperger was ultimately *executed with the sword here out of mercy*, his executioner adds with evident satisfaction that *his body*

A court notary's sketch of the traitor Hans Ramsperger's dismembered limbs and head, publicly displayed at the gallows (1588).

[was then] quartered, and each limb attached to a different corner of the scaffold and the head stuck on a pole above them.[70]

Counterfeiting, another crime elevated by the jurist authors of the *Carolina* to a capital offence against the state (punishable by burning alive), was similarly gauged by Nuremberg's executioner in terms of personal injury. Beyond the insult to Nuremberg's magistracy, he thus finds it difficult to express much outrage at this non-violent crime and reports the offences in the same dry manner as other thefts. Even Nuremberg's leaders displayed some ambivalence about the officially prescribed punishment, consistently commuting the severe sentence of burning alive to decapitation and subsequent burning.[71]

By contrast, descriptions of violations of the master-servant relationship, still another crime the jurists redefined in terms of treason, consistently evoked an emotional reaction in Meister Frantz, but not because he thought they represented some profound threat to the social order. He writes approvingly that a maid who murdered her patrician mistress was given *two nips with burning tongs on both arms as she was led out on a wagon,* and after she was executed with the sword her body *thrown in the gallows pit and her head stuck on an iron over the gallows.*[72] Yet what has really most outraged the executioner is the personal betrayal of a trusting employer, an old lady the culprit stabbed in her own bed at night. Nuremberg's magistrates were predictably more severe with servants who stole large amounts from their masters, and here too Frantz appears more acutely attuned to the degree of personal betrayal involved, Maria Cordula Hunnerin not just *stealing 800 fl. worth in thaler and three kreuzer pieces from the safe box of her master,* but from one *she served for half a year.* Still more treacherously, Hans Merckel (aka Deer John), *who was in service for twenty-two years,* made a career of betraying various masters, *stay[ing] half a year to two years in one place and then leav[ing], taking away with him hose, doublets, boots, woollen shirts, and whatever money he could get.*[73]

Patricide, like regicide, represented the supreme act of treason in a patriarchal society, and here at last Meister Frantz was in complete agreement with the jurists. He was incredulous over the reprehensible behaviour of Peter Köchl, who beat *his own father* severely and repeatedly over the course of many years before ultimately ambushing him on a street *and inflict[ing] seven wounds on him, leaving him for dead.* Köchl was spared the usual execution by wheel only because his father survived the last attack. The patricide Frantz Seuboldt had no such luck, having shown much greater premeditation and malevolence in first attempting to poison his father and finally shooting him from behind some bushes. The motives behind both attacks were never even mentioned by Frantz. Not until much later in life does he openly express sympathy with a woman who attempted to poison her own abusive father on account of the father's being a *violent, wicked man [who] treated her harshly.*[74]

Betrayal of a kinsman or kinswoman in general dismayed Meister Frantz to a much greater degree than all but the most heinous acts of violence, again indicative of a more ancient notion of justice in play. He was appalled that Ulrich Gerstenacker not only killed his own brother but *also drove out with [him] to the woods [where he] slew and murdered him with premeditation* and afterwards pretended it was an accident. Hans Müllner similarly ambushed his own sister in the woods, with the still more disturbing aggravating factors that she was pregnant and he *committed lewdness with her [corpse]*. Can there be any doubt about the just fate for people who were so low as to steal from their own cousins or a young man who *threatened to burn down the houses of his relatives and guardians for refusing him money, though he had formerly squandered it on women and whores?*[75] Most disgracefully, Cunz Nenner

> *stole up to 60 fl. worth [of items] from one of his relatives at Perngau and when the latter thrashed him for it he threatened to burn his house, so that the relative had to agree to pay 50 fl. besides. Also threatened to burn the house of one of his relatives – who, out of pity, had brought up his young daughter in his house for four years – if he did not give the eight-year-old child some wages. Then also threatened one of his relatives at the Rockstock, from whom he had stolen a cow and who had recovered it, that if he did not give him 15 fl. he would burn down his house.*[76]

It was the shameless long-term violation of the sacred blood bond that was at the centre of his description of *Laurenz Schropp, a miller's man from Lichtenau [who] worked for twenty-two years at his cousin's mill, stealing wheat from him, yet by his own account he* only *[!] gained about 400 fl.* (emphasis added) – a considerable amount of money even over the course of more than two decades.[77] "At what price honour or decency?" is the unspoken question of Nuremberg's repulsed executioner.

Always identifying with the victims, Meister Frantz reserved his greatest sympathy for people of inferior status who were abused by those in positions of authority and trust. Attacks against children in particular filled him with a fierce loathing and indignation. Amid the otherwise laconic entries of his early days, Frantz carefully details the thoroughly reprehensible assault of Hans Müllner (aka the Moulder), *who raped a girl of thirteen years of age, filling her mouth with sand so that she might not cry out*. His shock at a similar betrayal of childish trust by Endres Feuerstein is conveyed by listing the respective ages of the five girls the young man raped at his father's private school (six, seven, eight, nine, and twelve) and pointedly adding that *two among them he damaged so [severely] that one could no longer hold any water [and] the city midwives nursed [the other] for a long time, believing she would die.* The more disturbing the outrage, the more specific Frantz becomes about the age of the victim, as in his description of a farmhand who *tried to rape a girl of 3½ [but] the mother came in and prevented him.*[78] The executioner notes with relish that he repeatedly nipped with fiery tongs the robber Georg Taucher, who broke into a house and *murdered a tavern keeper's son . . . cutting his neck and throat, [and] tak[ing] money from the till,* and years later gives the same torturous execution to Georg Müllner (aka Lean George), who, with his companions, broke into a farmer's house at night, cut his throat, and *attack[ed] the same farmer's son (whom the father had hidden in the oven), stabbing him in the thigh and stealing much, so that the farmer's son died eight days later.*[79]

Beyond the brutal violation of childish trust and innocence, the unnatural contrast in age between perpetrator and victim troubled the empathetic executioner. He first establishes that Gabriel Heroldt was *a tailor and citizen and warden of the Frog Tower here at Nuremberg [and] a man of advanced age* before describing Heroldt's full offence, namely that *he violently raped Katherina Reichlin, who was under his charge as a prisoner, and committed lewdness with her. The year previously he tried several times by force to commit lewdness with a girl of thirteen but could not take her honour from her because of her youth.*[80] It is the final blow against the forger and confidence man Kunrad Krafft that he also swindled money from the wardships of children, and likewise fully appropriate that the carpenter Georg Egloff be executed for *deliberately kill[ing] his apprentice, who owed him 9 fl., with his carpenter's file in a beech wood.*[81]

Violence against children in any form was hard enough for Meister Frantz to forgive; violence against one's own flesh and blood remained utterly incomprehensible and unpardonable to him. Throughout his long career, Frantz executed twenty women for infanticide; in every instance he showed himself especially sensitive to the unnatural horror of the deed. Most commonly, he refers to the mother *squeez[ing] [the child's] little neck,* or *crushing the little head,* and in one instance *murderously stabb[ing] [the male child] with a knife in the left breast.*[82] As in Frantz's descriptions of vicious robbers, the contrast of innocence and brutality remains a consistent theme. He vividly re-creates how

Dorothea Meüllin *stopped up the mouth with earth and made a grave with her hand in which she buried the struggling child*. Other *heartless mothers* appear no less brutal: Margaretha Marranti gave birth during the night near a shed by the Pegnitz River and *as soon as [the child] stirred its arms and struggled, she threw it into the water and drowned it*. Other equally disturbing means of disposal included burying in a barn, locking in a trunk, casting into a pile of refuse, or, most shocking, throwing alive into the privy.[83] Having participated in the interrogations of each of these women, some of which included the threat of torture, the executioner knew that many of them were emotionally or mentally disturbed, particularly the murderers of older children, such as Anna Strölin and Anna Freyin. Yet he made no pretence of being concerned about issues of medical or legal competence, and was instead preoccupied with rage at the grisly vision of Strölin, who with *premeditation slew her own child, a boy of six years of age, with an axe*, only sparing her other four children at the last moment.[84]

Attacks on old people and the sick similarly outraged Meister Frantz's sense of basic social trust, as they would anyone in any society. It's not hard to imagine his shock at two drunken journeymen's assault and attempted rape of *an eighty-year-old woman* or other violent incidents where the victim was elderly.[85] Frantz is surprised yet pleased when Hans Hoffman, already banned six times from Nuremberg, was *caught in the act of stealing clothes from the infected people at the Lazareth [hospice] . . . and the Honourable Council ordered the sentence to be read in front of the Lazareth by a town beadle*, after which *he was then led out of the Lazareth and executed here at Nuremberg with the rope*. Such a proceeding, the executioner adds for emphasis, *had never been heard of or seen before*. Yet one week later, on 21 October 1585, four thieves were hanged for the related crime of breaking into the houses of recently dead people, and all but one such offender in subsequent years were similarly dispatched.[86] No such extreme consequences followed for the convicted thief and adulterer Heinz Teurla, but Meister Frantz registers his personal disgust that *he made a child with a poor maid who had no legs*.[87]

Given Frantz's deeply felt sentiments about betrayal and kinship, it is slightly jarring to read his muted account of Georg Preisigel, who *killed his wife and afterwards hanged her to make it look like she had*

The cover illustration of a broadsheet account of a father who strangled his own wife and two small children, then hanged himself (*right*). His corpse was later dragged through the streets of Schaffhausen and then placed atop a wheel at the execution grounds (*left*) (1561).

hanged and killed herself. Also formerly stabbed a man with a skewer; or, still briefer, of Hans Dopffer (aka Schilling) *who with premeditation and for no cause on her part, stabbed and murdered his wife, who was very pregnant.* Meister Frantz by no means condoned spousal murder, but he also showed little interest in probing the basis for domestic disputes (especially during this phase of his career), summarising crimes of this nature with the same brevity normally reserved for mundane thefts. In what should be a sensational case, we hear only that Margaretha Brecht-lin *gave her husband, Hans Prechtel (a carpenter in Gostenhof), insect powder in a porridge, also in eggs and lard, although he did not die at once of it.*[88] The drama of plots interweaving infidelity and greed were left entirely to the popular press and theatre, where they predictably enjoyed great success.[89]

When no threat to life or limb was involved, Meister Frantz's level of interest in victimised spouses sagged even more perceptibly. Adultery, a personal betrayal of a profound nature, might be expected to have raised the executioner's ire. In the sixteenth century, the offence was punishable by flogging and banishment; bigamy was even defined by the *Carolina* and a host of contemporary German law codes as a capital crime (although uniformly punished in Nuremberg the same as adultery). Meister Frantz's flagrant lack of interest in this kind of infidelity, however, is obvious in his terse journal entries, such as *whipped out of town here with rods Peter Rittler from Steinbühl who took two wives,* or – as the case may be – *took three wives;* or *took four wives and impregnated two [of them];* or *took five women in marriage and committed lewdness with them.*[90] In each passage, this supposedly shocking transgression is summarised in a sentence or two, with no attempt on Frantz's part to include the names of all the parties, let alone any of the circumstances. The only time he's moved to write another line of description is when children are known to be involved.[91] Occasionally, in fact, he seems to mention bigamy only as an afterthought, as in the conclusion of the long list of crimes committed by one executed offender, *lastly, tak[ing] a second wife during the life of his first wife, and a third wife during the life of the second, after the death of the first.* He cannot even remember the name *of a farmhand who stole a chain from the gallows at Statt Hilpoltstein and took two wives.*[92]

Should we read into Frantz's seeming indifference to adultery some unhappiness or even strife between the executioner and his own wife, Maria? Or could it suggest implicit evidence of his own infidelity? In view of Frantz's burning preoccupation with appearances, the latter scenario seems unlikely, especially since even a casual relationship could undermine all his years of reputation-building quite literally overnight. As for the happiness or unhappiness of his marriage to Maria, it remains impossible to gauge. The executioner never mentions his family life in the journal, and all we can learn from other sources is that the union produced seven children and lasted twenty-two years, until Maria's death at the age of fifty-five. Whatever form his own marital relationship took, Frantz shared in the common belief of his time that whatever happened within a household – short of murder or potentially fatal violence – remained a strictly private matter. Whether a cuckolded husband wanted to take his adulterous wife back several times or have her imprisoned repeatedly, Frantz considered it their business, requiring official intervention only when it became a public disturbance.[93]

Becoming a Nuremberger

Establishing a good name among wary locals remained a lifelong endeavour for Meister Frantz. Establishing his family's financial security,
by contrast, took nowhere near that long. In December 1579, not yet two
years into his initial contract, Frantz requested a New Year's bonus – a
custom he knew of from his late brother-in-law – which his superiors
readily granted. When he returned the following winter asking for a
significant raise of 0.5 fl. per week, he was rebuffed, first with the
promise of another annual bonus and later with an additional gift of 6
fl.[94] Four years later the young executioner made another attempt at
securing a permanent raise and was again turned away, although this
time with a one-time bonus of 12 fl., equivalent to more than a month's
salary. Undeterred, the young executioner continued to press his claims
and on 25 September 1584 finally achieved his next major career goal:
a guarantee of lifelong employment at the requested higher salary, as
well as a modest pension upon his retirement. By the terms of the contract, Frantz promised

> to be true, obedient, and dutiful to my gracious lords all the days
> of my life and to serve their needs and protect them from harm to
> the best of my abilities . . . never to serve anyone outside of this
> city, no matter where, without permission of the Honourable
> Council, in return for which my lords graciously grant me 3 fl.
> weekly and a New Year's bonus of 6 fl . . . until on account of age
> or other illness or infirmity I can no longer carry out my office.[95]

More to his superiors' relief, the ambitious executioner also swore "never
again to seek any increase in salary" – an oath he assiduously kept for
the next thirty-four years.

Frantz's negotiating talents aside, there are several explanations for
his employers' generous concessions. For many years before Schmidt's
arrival, the city had struggled to find an executioner who was at once
skilful, honest, and reliable. Meister Frantz had proven himself to be all
three, and was still only thirty years old. Nor had it escaped the city
councillors' attention that Meister Heinrich of Bamberg was ailing and
that his exceptionally capable son was a likely candidate to be his

successor.⁹⁶ At a time when Nuremberg's courts were on average sentencing a dozen people a year to death and ordering corporal punishments for twenty more, city leaders dreaded the backlog and legal headaches that would ensue if they lost Schmidt and had to search for a replacement. Whether an outside offer was actually proffered by Bamberg's chamberlain (whom Frantz knew well) or merely implied by the young executioner himself, he achieved his desired outcome.

As is often the case, Frantz's greatest professional success to date was followed by an exceptionally difficult year. First, he was confronted with the unenviable task of torturing and executing his own brother-in-law. Friedrich Werner (aka Potter Freddy) was, by his own account, "bad from youth on", even though his late father had been a well-known citizen and his stepfather a respectable potter. It's not clear from the surviving records how or when such a "truly evil" character ended up marrying Frantz's widowed sister, but the unhappy union does underscore how severely limited the marriage options were for an executioner's daughter. For years the "strong and handsome" mercenary Werner had roamed the countryside "with evil company, committing multiple thefts, burglaries, and home invasions, as well as many robberies."⁹⁷ More gravely, he confessed to three murders, including that of *a boy alone in the Fischbach Wood*, and several attempted murders, the most shocking being the brutal robbing of *a wife in the Schwabach Wood, [whom] he left for dead*.⁹⁸

When finally arrested and brought face-to-face with his brother-in-law in the Nuremberg interrogation chamber, Werner implausibly claimed "he [had] no idea why he [had] been imprisoned." If he was truly an innocent man, the magistrates countered, why then would he be operating under an alias, as he had been in Hersbruck, using the name "Jorg Schmidt"? Meister Frantz's reaction to this particular charge is not recorded, but his anger and shame must have been palpable. On the heels of more denials from Werner, he placed the culprit in the strappado – without the usual warning – and began interrogation "with the small stone". After a torture session of unspecified length, Werner's bravado faded and he eventually confessed to numerous crimes.

It's not hard to infer how Frantz felt about his notorious brother-in-law, a man who had not only committed heinous crimes but also one whose ties to the Schmidt family threatened to destroy the executioner's own carefully nurtured reputation. It's telling to note that although several eyewitness accounts confirmed the kinship between the two men, Frantz himself never once mentions it in his journal entry about the execution. Yet perhaps out of deference to his sister, Frantz dissuaded his superiors from carrying out the unprecedented sentence of "six nips with glowing tongs . . . two in front of the town hall, two in front of St Lorenz Church, and two by St Martha's at the [city's] gate," to be followed by a prolonged death beneath the wheel. So many nips, Schmidt argued, would likely kill the condemned man before he arrived at the execution grounds. The magistrates accordingly consented to only two, as long as the executioner agreed to make "a horrifying example" of Werner. They rejected, however, "with gentle words", the petition of Werner's stepfather and sister to mitigate the wheel sentence to beheading. Thus they compelled the executioner to treat his brother-in-law like any other murdering robber, administering the prescribed two nips while riding the tumbrel to the Raven Stone and then carrying out a brutal execution with the wheel.

On the day of the execution, as Meister Frantz stowed the hot tongs and prepared to stake Werner out, the chaplain asked the poor sinner if he had "any other evil deeds to confess", both to ease his own soul's passing and to prevent suspicion from falling on an innocent person. One chronicler records that Werner then "spoke for a long time at the execution stone with the priests and also with the hangman, who was his brother-in-law." Another account re-creates some of that conversation, reporting that "Meister Frantz, who was his brother-in-law, reassured him that he wanted to help him get through it as quickly as possible," if only Werner would reveal more about his crimes. Instead, the condemned man merely repeated the names of previously executed companions and then declared that he had spoken enough. He directed his final words to Meister Frantz, who stood by, wheel in hand, cryptically asking the executioner to remember him to the daughter of butcher Wolf Kleinlein. Whatever Werner's intended meaning, his brother-in-law swiftly proceeded to administer thirty-one blows with the wheel, demonstrating to all those assembled his complete repudiation of this notorious *murderer and robber*. Frantz Schmidt had worked too hard and come too far to be dragged back into the gutter by such a man.[99]

Within a few months of Werner's execution in February 1585, Frantz

A city chronicler's portrayal of Meister Frantz executing his own brother-in-law, the robber Friedrich Werner (1616).

himself suffered several profoundly personal blows. In the spring, his father, Heinrich, died. No precise record of the death or burial has survived; we know only that it was after 22 February, Meister Heinrich's last public execution, and before 1 May, when his estate was subsequently divided between his daughter in Kulmbach and his son in Nuremberg. Meister Heinrich's long-serving assistant, Hans Reinschmidt, succeeded his master as executioner of Bamberg.[100] Before the month of May was out, Heinrich's widow had also died and Frantz returned to Bamberg to take care of his late stepmother's affairs.[101]

What did it mean to Frantz that his father had died before their shared dream of restored family honour could become a reality? At least Heinrich had survived long enough to witness his son's contract for life with the famous city of Nuremberg, as well as the births of three grandchildren. Unfortunately, Frantz scarcely had time to grieve for his father and stepmother before another calamity struck. That summer, yet another epidemic of the plague hit Nuremberg, this one killing more than five thousand people over the course of the next several months.[102]

Tragically, Frantz's own four-year-old Vitus and three-year-old Margaretha were among the victims. Child deaths were a much more common occurrence in premodern Europe than today, but that did not make them any less painful for their parents. The precise dates of Vitus's and Margaretha's deaths were lost in the confusion of the epidemic, but we do know that sometime in 1585 Frantz bought a family plot in Saint Rochus, one of Nuremberg's more prestigious cemeteries, located just outside the city walls.[103] Perhaps he felt this was as much honour as he could attain for his two little children, lost before their young father could even hope to complete his quest to restore the family name. More we cannot say.

Work for the city's executioner, meanwhile, continued to mount. In 1585 alone, Schmidt would execute eleven people and flog nineteen, as well as undertake numerous interrogations. Overall, during his first decade of work for the city of Nuremberg, Meister Frantz performed 191 floggings, 71 hangings, 48 beheadings, 11 wheel executions, 5 finger-choppings, and 3 ear-clippings. His busiest year was 1588 (13 executions and 27 corporal punishments); his slowest was his first, 1578 (only 4 executions and 13 floggings). On average he put to death 13.4 people annually during this period and administered 20 corporal punishments. The great majority of executions took place in Nuremberg, but Frantz also travelled once or twice a year – always with official permission – to work in rural locations, particularly the towns of Hilpoltstein and Hersbruck, or to perform the occasional freelance interrogation or execution.[104]

At home, grief over the two early deaths gradually yielded to the joys and hectic pace of a newly expanding family. On 21 January 1587, Frantz and Maria were blessed with the birth of a daughter, whom they christened Rosina. Soon "Rosie" and her older brother, Jorg, who had survived the plague, were joined by Maria on 8 June 1588, Frantz Steffan on 16 July 1591, and finally, on 13 December 1596, the baby of the family, Johannes, also known as Frantzenhans.[105] The now bountiful Schmidt household was itself a proclamation of the *Hausvater*'s growing prosperity and prominence in the community. Most artisanal families and a still larger share of poorer households remained considerably smaller, with incomes that could support on average only two or three children.[106] Aged parents also lived with their children in some wealthier households, and the Schmidt family could certainly have afforded this had any of Frantz or Maria's parents still been alive.

The culminating social achievement of Frantz's first two decades in Nuremberg came on 14 July 1593, almost exactly forty years after his family's disgrace at the hands of Margrave Albrecht. Citizenship in an imperial city was a cherished privilege, requiring both significant property and a stellar reputation. It was thus out of reach for most residents of sixteenth-century Nuremberg, including of course all officially disreputable individuals. Shortly after celebrating his fifteenth anniversary as the city's executioner, Frantz Schmidt made the bold move of petitioning the city council for that very status. Taken aback, the magistrates exclaimed that no executioner had ever held citizenship in Nuremberg, to which Meister Frantz countered that he sought the legal status less for the present than for the future, when he hoped his children *would take up another trade* and he himself could retire to pursue a second career. "Since he has to this point performed his office irreproachably," the council declared, the executioner's request was approved and he became one of only 108 individuals granted the status of citizen in Nuremberg that year. Still considered dishonourable, Frantz was ordered to take his oath separately, on the day after thirteen other new citizens. But this was a slight that he could readily endure, given the wide range of legal protections that the ever-more-confident and prosperous executioner had just secured for himself and his progeny.[107] Seven years later, the forty-five-year-old Frantz Schmidt could enter the new century as a full-fledged citizen of one of the greatest cities in the empire, assured of a lifetime of lucrative employment and free housing for himself, his wife, and their five children, aged four to fifteen. It was a remarkable achievement for a hangman's son, but in Meister Frantz's eyes it still fell far short of the ultimate goal.

4

THE SAGE

Just as the Stoics say that vices are introduced for our profit, to give value and assistance to virtue, we can say with better reason and less rashness, that nature has given us pain so that we may appreciate and be thankful for comfort and the absence of pain.

—Michel de Montaigne, "On Experience" (1580)[1]

This my long sufferance, and my day of grace,
They who neglect and scorn, shall never taste;
But hard be hardened, blind be blinded more,
That they may stumble on, and deeper fall;
And none but such from mercy I exclude.

—John Milton, *Paradise Lost*, book 3: 198–202 (1667)

It did not take the veteran Meister Frantz long to conclude that the barber-surgeon Hans Haylandt was *a very bad character*. Shortly before his beheading on 15 March 1597, Haylandt had been convicted of a particularly cold-blooded murder, recounted by his executioner in vivid detail:

> *[Haylandt] and his companion, Killian Ayrer, went out with a youth from Rotenfels who had been servant to a gentleman at Frankfurt, and when they stopped at midnight to drink at the fountain near Eschenburg, Ayrer asked the youth for a ginger, which he gave him, and as the youth was combing his hair, Ayrer slipped something into*

his own food and gave it to [the youth]. When [the youth] couldn't stand out of weakness, [Ayrer] knocked him on the head, so that he fell and said ouch. Haylandt, however, proceeded to cut his throat and robbed him of 200 fl., which money his master at Frankfurt had given him in their presence and asked them both to go with the youth so that he might come safely with the money to Rotenfels, since he knew them both, one from Hamburg, the other from Rotenfels. While home in Frankfurt, they together planned this murderous assault, before they departed, and when they carried out the murder by the fountain they took a stone from a vineyard and tied it with [the youth's] belt to his body, carried the same over a meadow and threw it in the Main so that it sank into the water; the bloody cudgel [they] buried. The next day the lord of Eschenburg wanted to go into his vineyard, thus [his] dogs dug the bloody cudgel back up. He also saw that a stone had been torn from his garden wall, [whereupon] he went in search of the trail and saw that something very bloody had been dragged across the meadow and tossed in the water, and thus found the murder victim. After the two [murderers] divvied up the money, the barber had journeyed to Nuremberg (believing that if he hadn't helped or been present, the deed wouldn't have become public). The murdered youth's father went after him and had him arrested here [in Nuremberg] so that he then had to confess.[2]

This account features all the hallmarks of infamy that Meister Frantz most reviled: a coldly premeditated murder for the sake of money, betrayal of the trust of both the youth and his master, a cowardly ambush, and deliberate desecration of the youth's corpse. It also bears several literary embellishments – in striking contrast to the terse journal entries of Schmidt's youth. The now-middle-aged executioner begins his account by setting the scene, intentionally drawing a tranquil picture of three travelling companions stopping for a midnight snack at an outdoor fountain, in order to heighten the reader's shock over the violent act that comes next. He conveys the sheer perfidy of the deed by choosing details that heighten the contrast between good and evil: the youth readily shared his provisions and innocently combed his hair as Ayrer went about poisoning the food. The blow on the head, the youth's exclamation, and the quick slashing of his throat all vividly recreated a moment of intense violence. To be sure, Meister Frantz was no literary genius – his dialogue ("ouch") could particularly use some work – but by the second half of his life, he had clearly begun to apply his imagination as he recorded the culprits and crimes he encountered. Most significantly, he began to explore in writing the motives behind various actions that in his early days were simply ascribed to bad character or not probed at all.

Why do people do cruel things to one another, and why does God permit it? Frantz did not need to be a theologian, conversant in teachings on theodicy and divine providence, to wonder about the seeming capriciousness of human suffering and death or the inadequacies of human justice. As the executor of that justice, he could take some satisfaction in the punishment, and perhaps even redemption, of evildoers, but he realised long before that the solace offered to victims or the surviving family and friends of those killed was short-lived, incomplete, and often entirely elusive. By the age of forty-six, he had already spent nearly three decades immersed in the dark side of the human condition and was frequently compelled to resort to violence and deceit himself in the interrogation and punishment of those individuals who happened to get caught. Subjected to unceasing cruelty and suffering, Frantz, like any law enforcement official, had to marshal a significant degree of either detachment or personal faith to be able to carry on for so many years. Yet the source of that inner strength, beyond a fervent determination to restore the family's honour, remains the most elusive part of the man's identity.

In addition to his soul-killing work, Frantz Schmidt had other reasons to grow more pessimistic, bitter, and even cynical as he aged. Despite having achieved lifelong economic security and even citizenship, he and his family still suffered exclusion from respectable bourgeois society in ways both subtle and stark. More tragically, the new century had scarcely dawned when the horrors of the world struck at him directly. On 15 February 1600, during the coldest winter on record in Nuremberg, a new outbreak of plague claimed sixteen-year-old Jorg, Frantz's oldest surviving son. Five days later, the grief-stricken Schmidt family followed a funeral cortege to the family plot in Saint Rochus Cemetery, Jorg's coffin borne by his classmates from the Saint Egidien Latin School. Within three weeks, Frantz's wife of just over twenty years, fifty-five-year-old Maria, herself expired, probably felled by the same epidemic that had taken her son and would eventually rob more than two thousand five hundred local residents of their lives. This time "several of [Schmidt's] neighbours, voluntarily, out of goodwill", carried the coffin to the cemetery, indifferent to any dishonour this final act of respect might bring to them. Perhaps such tender, long-desired signs of communal acceptance mitigated the sting of these successive personal blows to Nuremberg's executioner. When Frantz Schmidt walked away from the fresh graves of his wife and young son on 12 March 1600, he was a forty-six-year-old widower with four surviving children between the ages of four and thirteen.[3]

The emotional impact of these two losses must have been staggering, but the bereaved father and husband did not leave a record of his grief; there are no personal references at all in the journal. Whatever his degree of emotional or religious turmoil, Meister Frantz pushed on in his work, six weeks later beheading two thieves and resuming his other duties. Most widowers in his era remarried within a year of their spouse's death, especially if there were still young children at home. Out of grief – or the simple lack of willing prospects – Frantz Schmidt never wed again, relying instead on thirteen-year-old Rosina and twelve-year-old Maria, with the help of a domestic maid, to run the household and look after their younger brothers. The family's isolated mini-society, saddened and diminished in numbers, persevered.

What do faith and redemption mean in such a harsh and unjust world? What roles do divine providence and individual choice play in it all? During the years that follow Frantz's own personal tragedies, a growing fascination with the hows and whys of human behaviour began to dominate his journal entries. As his attempts to find order and meaning among the world's seeming chaos intensified, Frantz increasingly relied on the literary techniques common in the popular crime literature of the day, which he undoubtedly knew well.[4] Seemingly random events became coherent stories, evoking both pathos and resolution. His villains – most commonly bloodthirsty robbers and murderous relatives – were the same as those of the tabloid press of the day. Unlike the writers of cheap broadsheets and popular sermons, however, he neither moralised nor generalised about motives. For Meister Frantz, sin and crime remained profoundly personal, the product of character and choices, not cosmic external forces. His personal interactions with culprits and victims alike undoubtedly reinforced this preference for the concrete over the abstract. They also sensitised him to the individual nature of both sin and redemption. In his full embrace of the Lutheran teaching of salvation by faith alone, the middle-aged Frantz paradoxically became both more judgemental and more forgiving of the poor sinners before him. Would this belief in an ultimately merciful God – the solace of so many converted felons he executed – provide the executioner himself with some comfort amid his many personal travails and solitary quest?

Crimes of malice

As Meister Frantz's journal entries begin to grow in both length and complexity, it becomes clear that there are two standards by which he judged the severity of a crime: first, the degree to which both personal and social trust had been violated, and second, the level of malice that was shown by the perpetrator. Crimes that were premeditated, gratuitously cruel, or otherwise indecent indicated to the executioner that the perpetrator had voluntarily rejected the norms of civilised behaviour and placed himself (or occasionally herself) outside society – had become, in a moral as well as legal sense, an outlaw. Highwaymen and other robbers were, in that respect, the most dramatically antisocial, and therefore culpable, of all the poor sinners who came before Meister Frantz – and subsequently merited the worst torture and punishment when caught. Seemingly ordinary individuals, however, were also capable of exceptionally malicious acts, as Frantz continually discovered throughout his long career. Though not professional outlaws, they were nonetheless guilty of the same wilful rejection of divine and human laws. Like Cain and Satan before them, malicious criminals were defined by their deliberate self-isolation from the norms and comforts of "decent" society – a choice that was incomprehensible to the involuntarily outcast executioner.

The most recurrent example of malice in Frantz's journal is the coldly calculated violation of trust represented by the act of ambush or surprise attack. More dangerous than people who pretended to be something that they were not or those who slandered the innocent, the ambushing murderer repudiated the most basic level of human trust, and therefore decency itself. Whatever the relationship between the individuals in question or the degree of violence involved in such an attack, the reprehensible combination of malice and deceit hit a special nerve with Meister Frantz. The young executioner had encountered this brand of treachery during the first year of his career in the case of the robber Barthel Mussel, who *cut the throat of a man who was sleeping with him on the straw in a stable and took his money*. Thirteen years later, Frantz is equally appalled that Georg Teurla *struck a puppet maker apprentice on the head with a club in a meadow when he told the other there was something in his shoe, [then] stabbed him in the neck with a dagger and quickly covered him up*. In the same vein, Hans Krug *deceptively asked his companion, Simon, to see what kind of shirt he had on and then stabbed him in the neck with a knife he had brought there and hidden on him*.[5] The utter treachery of the act is often underscored by the mundane setting: a man turns and attacks his pregnant sister *on the*

A dastardly ambush of an innocent traveller by two robbers. Note the glee of the perpetrators and the fear of the victim (1543).

road as they returned from their usual work; a forester kills his brother *while driving a sled in the woods*; a woman strikes her friend on the head from behind with an axe, *when [supposedly] looking for lice and stroking her hair*.

As in broadsheet accounts of crime, Frantz's inclusion of descriptive details lent his stories dramatic verisimilitude, while simultaneously conveying the stark cold-bloodedness of the murderers. When a messenger was sent to collect a debt from Lienhard Taller (aka Spit Lenny), the farmer immediately handed over the payment and invited the servant *to spend the night with him, sleeping on a bench in the parlour. While he was sitting and talking to him, [Taller] seized an axe from the wall and gave him two blows on the head, killing him immediately and taking back the money*. Even more chillingly, the mercenary Steffan Stayner calmly *stabbed [a companion] on the left side so that it came out on the right side, [then] afterwards cleaned off his foil before [the other] fell*.[6] One of Frantz's most detailed accounts of an ambush juxtaposes the violence of the attack itself and the perpetrator's ultimate punishment, thereby establishing the familiar equilibrium in cruelty that was the executioner's mainstay:

> *Georg Franck from Poppenreuth, a smith's man and a soldier, persuaded Fair Annala to let him escort her to meet Martin Schönherlin, her betrothed, at Bruck on the Leuth in Hungary. When he, with Christoph Frisch, also a mercenary, had brought her into a wood – the two having made a plot [about her] – Christoph struck her on the head with a stake from behind, so that she fell. [He] then dealt two more blows as she lay there. Franck also struck her once or twice and then cut her throat. They stripped her of everything except her shift and left her lying there, selling the clothes at Durn Hembach for 5 florins . . . Executed here with the wheel, first both arms, the third stroke on the chest, as decreed.*[7]

In these and other ambushes, Schmidt consistently underscores that the evil deed was done *with premeditation*, with malice aforethought – a distinction also stressed by the legal codes and judges of the day.[8] As in most societies today, legal authorities always deemed premeditated murder to be worse than simple manslaughter and accordingly punished it more harshly. The journeyman executioner is clearly appalled when the thief Georg Taucher *murdered a tavern keeper's son [during a break-in] at three o'clock in the morning . . . cutting his neck and throat*, but the crime is made still more reprehensible in that it was done *intentionally with a knife he carried about him for this purpose*. Similarly, when Anna Strölin *slew her own child, a boy of six years of age, with an axe*, or Hans Dopffer *stabbed and murdered his wife, who was very pregnant*, Schmidt feels compelled to stress in each case that the shocking murder was committed *with premeditation*.[9]

For Meister Frantz, the ideal man was honest, pious, loyal, respectful, and brave. Calculating murderers, such as the patricide Frantz Seuboldt, represented the perfect inversion of this heroic type. It was bad enough that Seuboldt, *out of premeditated hate and desire, killed his own father*, but his chosen method was particularly cowardly and unmanly:

> *[He] lay in wait for his very own father (a steward at Osternohe in the castle) upon his fowling ground, hiding behind a rock [and] covering himself with brushwood so that he couldn't be seen. When his father climbed a pole (which they call the ambush tree [under-scoring the irony]) to take down the decoy-bird, he shot him with a round of four bullets, so that he died the next day. Although no one knew who had done it, as he fled from the place and while running [he] dropped and lost a glove, which a tailor at Gräfenberg had patched for him the day before. This [glove] was found by a woman, thereby revealing the deed.*

Seuboldt's treacherous and unnatural deed, despite his careful planning, was uncovered thanks to his own carelessness, a bit of early modern crime detection, and perhaps divine providence. Following his full confession (including that *the year before he had tried to poison [his father] twice, but had not succeeded*) the convicted father-killer *was led out in a wagon here, his body nipped thrice with red-hot tongs, then two of his limbs shattered with the wheel and finally executed with it* – once more, the additional procedural details convey the executioner's sense of justice accomplished.[10] (See the illustration near the beginning of chapter 2, page 47.)

Where and when an ambush took place could further intensify the deed's infamy in Meister Frantz's estimate, again because of the blatant disregard for social norms. His journal entries tend to decry attacks in the woods more for the particular violence involved than for the degree of surprise, perhaps because the area itself was already presumed dangerous. Home invasions by armed bands, by contrast, clearly upset the executioner on a visceral level, and his accounts of these crimes reveal the same sense of personal grief as his anguished descriptions of attacks on children. He accordingly considers nocturnal burglary more serious than simple theft, especially since it might lead to an assault on a startled homeowner. "The night is no friend," warned a contemporary proverb that underscored the particular vulnerability created by darkness in this era before the advent of street lighting. Within the city, the complete curfew after sunset meant that even a thief who snatched people's cloaks from them in the street by night could receive a death sentence. Meister Frantz deplored the murder or assault of a sleeping victim as an especially despicable act that provided compelling evidence of a perpetrator's cowardice and indecency.[11]

Unlike the accidentally fatal blows incurred in the heat of an argument, the violence of malicious murderers also tended to be excessive. Here too, Frantz relies on a few details to convey the cruel nature of such assaults. Elisabeth Rossnerin, *a day labourer and beggar, strangled in a pea field and stabbed with a dagger her [female] companion, also a field worker at Gebersdorf,* all for the sake of 4 pounds 9 pfennigs (approx. 1 fl.). Peter Köchl, eventually convicted of attempted murder, *severely beat his own father with a manure shovel.*[12] Still more brutal, Michel Köller *intentionally threw a rock at the head of a carter servant from Wehr . . . so that he fell from the nag, and took his money from him, but the throw hit him in the shoulders, and when the carter servant armed himself, [Köller] stabbed him repeatedly 32 times in the head with a pocket knife.*[13] Frequently, Meister Frantz employs the number of wounds inflicted as a shorthand for the gratuitous violence of such criminals: Elisabeth Püffin *entered at night the bailiff's house at Velden where she had served for 16 weeks and then the room of his brother-in-law Detzel, a gouty old man with an ear trumpet, giving him about eleven wounds on the head with an [iron] bar.* In a similar act of brutal betrayal, Michel Seitel, a shoemaker's man, broke into *the house of his grandfather's brother, a joiner, and attacked him while he slept, inflicting thirty-eight wounds and holes on his head with a jagged stone and one in the neck with a shoemaker's knife, intending to cut his throat and take the money.*[14]

Like the sensationalist broadsheets that attempted to exploit such atrocities, Frantz's accounts use timeworn dramatic techniques to evoke the terror of the victim, as well as the infamy of the perpetrator. In describing the outrageous assault on the aged patrician spinster Ursula von Ploben by a man and woman let into the house at night by her complicit maid, he succinctly re-creates the perspective of the unwitting victim, startled in her bedchamber by the intruders, who *accosted and smothered her with two pillows over her mouth and wretchedly stabbed her, which lasted almost half an hour, [Ploben] struggling so that they had to smother her three times before she died.*[15]

The father of two teenage girls, Frantz Schmidt was understandably attuned to the terrifying effect of two unrelenting would-be rapists on their victims. Hans Schuster, a barber journeyman,

> *during Holy Week met a married woman from Rückersdorf in front of the village, and accosted the same, attempting to force himself on her. When [she] resisted, [he] struck two blows on her head with his hatchet, threw her to the ground, [and] as she screamed held her mouth shut and stuffed it with much earth or sand until someone came to her assistance; otherwise he would have brought her to his will [i.e. raped her].*

Fifteen-year-old Hans Wadl, arrested on the same day, was just as merciless,

> *accost[ing] four girls in a small wood behind Ostenfoos who were collecting wood, falling on the biggest one, who was in her eleventh year . . . throwing her to the ground and attempting to bring her to his will. When the girl screamed and said she was too young, he replied, "By the sacrament, you have a good sturdy pussy." Throughout her mighty screaming [he] held the girl's mouth shut, took out his knife, [and said] if she would not stop he would stab her, thereupon knocking the girl around, so that two barbers were [later] needed, and he made the girl swear not to tell anyone – not even the devil – anything of it.*[16]

The *Carolina* defined rape as a capital offence, but the crime was both underreported and underpunished. Nuremberg's execution of six rapists during the entire course of the seventeenth century was actually an imperial record.[17] More commonly, as in the case of Wadl, an attacker escaped with mere flogging *out of mercy for his youth*. For Meister Frantz, though, the brutality, vulgarity, and sheer malevolence of these assaults provoked the same profound disdain that he usually reserved for murderous robbers.

To the younger Frantz, the distinction between intended and un-intended violence had been a stark one; later in life, the more seasoned professional showed more interest in weighing and analysing the tangled motives of the unfortunates who came before him. The most common motive for premeditated murders and other attacks, especially among professional robbers, was of course money. Schmidt enjoys pointing out, however, that the hoped-for material gain is often meagre, or occasionally entirely elusive – further emphasizing the sordidness of the crime. The tailor Michael Dietmayr *went for a walk with [a farmer acquaintance] and gave him a blow on the head from behind so that he fell, then gave him two more blows* – all for a total of the 3 fl. 3 pfennigs he found on the dead man. Two industrious robbers repeatedly attacked carters, female bread carriers, and pedlars *although not getting much from them*. Another killed a messenger for 5 orths (1¼ fl.) and some packages with unknown contents (that turned out to be worth little), and embosser Hans Raim was dismayed to find a similarly paltry amount on the woman he had just murdered in cold blood.[18]

Among non-professional criminals, Nuremberg's executioner found a history of personal enmity to be a more common motive for calculated acts of vengeance. Georg Praun (aka Pin George) *was at feud with a farmer and lay in wait for him,* while butcher Hans Kumpler, *on account of a quarrel with the watchman over the village commons, entered [the latter's] house at night to make peace and slew him with his own "dispute hammer"* [Streithammer], *which [Kumpler] took out of his hands.* In his ongoing dispute with a fellow barber journeyman, Andreas Seytzen *threatened to get back at him and give him something to remember, whereupon he stuck his [skin] scraping iron [i.e. razor] into an onion, also cooked plain peas, and breathed on the iron*, presumably intending to infect only his enemy at the public bath where they worked, but instead *over 70 persons in the bath were injured and received French [i.e. syphilitic] sores; [many] also passed out.* Frantz does not note the nature or origin of their feud but he does remark, with some sense of poetic justice, that the vindictive bathman *himself [also] got the sores and lay 8 weeks at home.*[19]

The perceived injustice behind vengeful acts, like the money sometimes gained in murderous assaults, often proved to be quite petty in Meister Frantz's experience. The maid Ursula Becherin *burnt a stable belonging to her master, a farmer on the Marelstein, because the old*

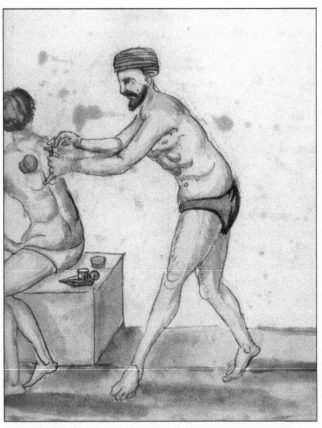

Public baths offered a variety of medical treatments in addition to opportunities for social interactions, including with prostitutes (c.1570).

people were harsh [to her], and in this year 1582 she did the same to her farmer master at Haselhof, burning down a stable because she could do nothing right in their opinion. Anna Bischoffin *burned down a stable at the Kützen farm . . . on account of a purse, which she had mislaid and thought had been stolen from her,* while Cunz Nenner similarly threatened arson *on account of some pigeons taken from him.* Other damning crimes sprang from even pettier origins. Is Schmidt decrying human folly or disproportionate violence when he notes in passing that premeditated assaults might be triggered by *a dispute over a lit torch, on account of a missing spoon,* or because of *a quarrel in a wood about a brooch?*[20]

Money, revenge, and perhaps love were all motives in the plot Kunrad Zwickelsperger and Barbara Wagnerin made to murder her husband:

> *Three times [Zwickelsperger] prompted [Wagnerin] to put insect powder in her husband's food, which she did, putting it in some porridge and even eating three spoonfuls herself, but the husband remained unharmed. He vomited six times and she twice, for – as Zwickelsperger had told her – if she gave him too much he would die, if a little he would only vomit. Zwickelsperger also pledged himself by going to communion not to have relations with any other woman than with her, the carpenter's wife, and she was to go and promise him the same. Also Zwickelsperger gave two fl. to an old sorceress that she might cause the carpenter to be stabbed, struck down, or drowned.*[21]

Whatever the sincerity of the conspirators' affection for each other, the intended victim survived all attempts on his life and saw both of his would-be assassins put to death at the hands of Meister Frantz. Love, or lust, possibly also played a part in Georg Wigliss's deadly assault on a pedlar in the Nuremberg forest, as he not only stole 8 *gulden from him,* but *afterwards took to himself the murdered pedlar's wife, living at Leinburg, and was married to her.*[22] A mutually hatched plot, a murderer's attempt to assuage his own guilt, or a bizarre instance of genuine attraction – Schmidt does not reveal his own take on the murder-marriage, only that Wigliss, a three-time murderer, was executed *with the wheel* next to two hanged thieves.

Bandits and highwaymen embodied the most extreme exemplars of self-indulgent, gratuitous cruelty – evil for its own sake. Though making up less than a tenth of the people Meister Frantz executed, these murderous outlaws dominate his longer accounts and are by far the most vividly drawn characters of the journal.[23] Their attacks on people along the road or in their own homes look less like carefully planned heists than excuses to indulge their sadistic impulses – binding and torturing victims with fire or hot grease, raping them repeatedly, and killing survivors in gruesome ways. Even after encounters with human violations of almost every nature, Frantz is still shaken by a group of sixteen bandits who *attacked people by night . . . bound them, tortured them, and did violence to them, robbing them of money and clothes*.[24] He writes with obvious empathy of two of their victims, *one woman [who] received seventeen wounds, blows, or stabs, of which she died after thirteen weeks; the other had her hand hacked off and died on the third day*.[25] In Frantz's accounts, the stolen property often seemed an afterthought

An eighteenth-century French engraving graphically conveys the cruelty of home invaders and the terror of their helpless victims, particularly in isolated mills (1769).

to the spree of barbarism that preceded it. Men like this revelled in their defilement of all social norms, attempting to outdo one another in their audacity – most inexcusably for Frantz Schmidt when they engaged in the cold-blooded torture and killing of pregnant women, whose foetuses were cut out and murdered before their mothers' eyes. Once more, we should be attuned to the executioner's own need to justify the cruelties he himself later inflicted on such criminals. Although this may sometimes have led Frantz to exaggerate – whether consciously or unconsciously – the violence he describes was indisputably real, as was the genuine terror such outlaws left in their wake.

Nor did atrocities end with the deaths of their victims. Professional robbers, by Schmidt's accounting, were also the most likely to desecrate a corpse. This may seem like a surprising issue of concern for a professional executioner whose job required him to do the same at times, but in fact it's an indicator of the profound seriousness of Christian burial for Meister Frantz and virtually all his contemporaries. Leaving a cadaver hanging from the gallows, exposed on the wheel, or burned to ashes deeply disturbed those who believed in an afterlife and the physical resurrection of the dead. Intentional abuse or neglect of the recently deceased was just as reprehensible. The early image of robber Klaus Renckhart forcing a murdered miller's wife to serve him fried eggs on the dead man's corpse remained unsurpassed in shock value, but typical of such men's disregard for basic human decency.[26] Frantz remarks with dismay whenever murdering robbers stripped their victims' bodies and left them lying by the roadside, sometimes covered with brushwood, other times thrown into a nearby body of water. In the case of Lienhard Taller (aka Spit Lenny), however, it's not clear whether Schmidt is relieved or troubled that the murderer first hid the body of his victim *under some straw in a stable [but] on the next night, with the help of his wife, he carried the [man's] body to a little wood and buried it.*[27]

For Meister Frantz, the ultimate proof that these individuals spurned all social norms could be seen in the way that they treated one another. Unlike some of their literary counterparts, the outlaws in Schmidt's accounts followed no self-imposed code, exhibited no lasting loyalty, and in fact regularly turned on one another. Sometimes the motive was revenge, as when the robber Hans Paier was *betrayed and given to capture by the banished Adam Schiller (whom [Paier] claims no memory of having bewitched in the New Forest so that he would immediately die).* More often it was greed that triggered the conflict, especially during the division of spoils. Hans Georg Schwartzmann (aka the Fat Mercenary; aka the Black Peasant) *quarrelled over the share of the booty with his companions at Fischbach, so that they beat him up and cut up his whore who helped him.* Michel Vogl similarly fought with a longtime accomplice *about a robbery they had committed [together] and tried to stab him, whereupon [Vogl] seized [his associate's] gun and shot him, so that he instantly fell dead.* To demonstrate the utter lack of any honour among thieves, Meister Frantz adds that in this instance the victim's former companion *afterwards stripped and plundered him, taking 40 fl.* Even the robber Christoph Hoffman's accidental shooting of his own companion similarly ended with the former stripping the corpse and dumping the body in some low water.

The infighting among robbers could also be vicious, as when Georg Weyssheubtel *chopped off one hand and almost hacked in two the other arm of one of his companions and then [gave him] a head wound so that he died.* The notoriously brutal Georg Müllner (aka Lean George) not only robbed and killed one former companion but also the next day ambushed and killed the man's wife in a nearby woods, *suffocating her with a kerchief she had round her neck, murdering her, and robbing her of her money and clothes.* Not to be surpassed, the robber Hans Kolb (aka the Long Brickmaker) *stabbed his [own] wife at Büch two years ago [and] later stabbed one of his companions on a road in Franconia . . . Likewise he also cut the ear off his companion's consort in the field.*[28]

Schmidt's anger toward amoral highwaymen was fuelled by the deep frustration that he and other law enforcement officials experienced in preventing or punishing their attacks. His palpable jubilance at the capture and execution of such outlaws is thus understandable. Whenever possible, he cites the names of confederates, particularly if they had already been caught and executed. In his account of the crimes of the robber Hans Hammer (aka Pebble; aka the Young Cobbler), there is a hint of boasting in Frantz's aside that Hammer's numerous accomplices in one especially brutal home invasion had all been executed by him, along with obvious chagrin that *Pebble had still many more companions*, presumably still at large. Frantz records with similar satisfaction that the

companions of Hans Georg Schwartzmann and *his wench* Anna Pintzrinin – namely Chimney Michael, the Scholar of Bayreuth, Spoon Kas-
par, Curly, the Scholar Paulus, Clumsy, Six, and Zulp – *have also since
received their due*. In describing the crimes and executions of the robbers Heinrich Hausmann and Georg Müllner, he goes so far as to provide the full names and/or aliases of forty-nine accomplices. His
rationale for compiling such a list remains mysterious, since all but four
of the culprits remained at large. Perhaps he is making notes in anticipation of future arrests, a kind of wish list for himself and his partners
in law enforcement. It remains in any event an idiosyncratic and unique
gesture.[29]

Crimes of passion

There was a major distinction for Frantz Schmidt between such malicious violations of basic human decency and mere capitulation to human
weakness. Non-fatal and non-violent crimes accordingly received much
less coverage or analysis in his journal. Unless he could identify individuals who were intentionally harmed, Frantz devoted little space or
reflection to property or sexual improprieties, even though together they
composed over three-quarters of the punishments he administered over
the course of his career.[30] Of course Schmidt continued to play the role
of communal avenger in such cases, but the visceral satisfaction so obvious in his accounts of executed robbers is notably lacking. In other
words, containing his outrage did not present much of a challenge in
the majority of his executions and other punishments. In that respect,
Frantz Schmidt came closer to the legal ideal of the executioner as a
steady and dispassionate instrument of state violence.

Frantz's attitude toward non-malicious crimes allowed him to show
greater compassion for the people who committed them. The most for-
givable crimes in his view were those of passion – which by definition
lacked premeditation or malice – particularly one-time explosions of
violence in a moment of rage. Most men in that still tumultuous era,
including Frantz Schmidt, carried a knife or other weapon at all times.
Not surprisingly, drunken or otherwise heated disputes over male honour regularly led not only to fistfights, but also to stabbings or duels,

some of them fatal. The *Carolina* and other criminal codes narrowed the definitions of self-defence and "honourable killing", but as in the American Wild West (and indeed in certain parts of the modern United States), a verbally or physically injured man bore no duty to retreat – to the contrary, self-redress remained an imperative.[31] Victims who had suffered non-fatal wounds typically sought compensation through the age-old practise of private financial settlement (wergild).[32] When angry words led to a dead body, Frantz recognised that justice had to be served, but he tended to treat a killing in the heat of anger as an unfortunate but understandable fact of life.

In his earliest entries, Schmidt laconically notes that a farmer *stabbed a forester*, or a furrier *stabbed a son of the Teutonic Knights.* Occasionally he makes note of the particular insult (*traitor, thief, rogue*), the weapon in question (*knife, axe, hammer, bolt*), or the source of the dispute, often trivial: *for the sake of [a] whore over the payment for a drink; over a kreuzer [0.02 fl.]; or because [his friend] cursed him as a traitor.*[33] Otherwise these accounts have the bored affect of a traffic report.[34] In a world where men must be ever ready to defend their honour, Frantz intimates, there are bound to be accidents, as when the municipal archer Hans Hacker *disarmed [another] archer's son on watch because of cursing, came to words with one another and gave [the other] an accidental blow with a hammer so that he died.*[35] Hacker escaped with a flogging, but Peter Planck's escalating brawl with a prostitute had an even more tragic ending for both. The series of regrettable events, writes Meister Frantz, began when Planck returned home after an evening of heavy drinking:

> As he was walking near the Spitler Gate toward the pig stalls he saw a woman, who was a whore, walking in front of him along Sunderspühl Street and hurried after her. According to his account, she addressed him, asking him to go home with her, and when he refused she said he had to swear by the sacrament or something of this kind. Then, as he sat down, she took away his hat, apparently trying to make a fool of him, and said he had concealed it. He tried to take the hat back from her and they struggled with each other. When he gave her a blow in the face, the whore drew both her knives and stabbed at him. As she went at him, he

picked up some sand and threw it at her; she did likewise, but when she refused to stop trying to stab him, he drew out his knife and stabbed at her, wounding her eye, so that she fell and his knife broke in the act, leaving the shaft in his hand. He knelt on her and snatched the knives from her hands, but his hand was cut by the blade and in rage he drove the knife through her left breast as she lay there.[36]

Sudden anger, fuelled by alcohol and injury (to either honour or person), sparked the violence in cases like these – heat, as opposed to the iciness of calculated treachery.

Succumbing to other passions, particularly sexual desire, likewise appeared inevitable and less grave to Nuremberg's longtime executioner. Flogging for fornication, adultery, or prostitution made up nearly a quarter of Meister Frantz's 384 corporal punishments, yet his records of these events are typically the briefest in the journal – probably

In a universally armed society, even a house servant sweeping away cobwebs kept his personal dagger close at hand (c.1570).

because they were so very commonplace. His most frequent victims were professional prostitutes, denizens of the shadowy world Frantz repudiated at every opportunity. Unlike his clerical colleagues, though, he displays less discomfort over what he terms *lewdness* (*Unzucht*; lit. "undiscipline") than any other form of public scandal. It seems unlikely that the pious Schmidt would have ever denied the sinfulness of extramarital sex, but it is hard to detect more than mild disgust when he writes about the offence, particularly when the activity in question was purely consensual. To the contrary, his language is coarse and very matter-of-fact, his references the briefest in the journal. He even shares a few ribald Chaucerian moments, such as when

> *Sara, a baker at Fach, daughter of the tavern keeper at Heilbron-*
> *ner Hof, called the Furrier, allowed her maid to commit lewdness.*
> *Also incited a smith to have a go with the maid and made him*
> *bring her proof of it, giving her some hairs ripped from [the maid's]*
> *little bush. When the maid cried out, [Sara] held her mouth shut*
> *by sitting with her arse on the mouth and afterwards poured a cold*
> *[glass of] water into it.*[37]

Another passage, part of a digression on the subject of past reprieves, could be right out of the bacchanalian world of Boccaccio's *Decameron*:

> *A farmer from Hersbruck who, after drinking with another farmer*
> *in an inn, rose from his drink to take a piss but [instead] went to his*
> *drinking companion's wife by night, as if he were her husband com-*
> *ing home, lay down in bed and committed lewdness, then got up*
> *and left her, but was recognised as not her husband by the woman*
> *when she looked after him.*[38]

The earthy humour of an executioner who spent most of his time with criminals and lowborn guards should come as no surprise. It also reminds us that Meister Frantz's piety was not equivalent to prudishness and that the rigid sexual standards of his clerical colleagues were not necessarily endorsed by the rest of society, even among the faithful.

Public scandal, more than private sin, remained the graver offence for the status-conscious Schmidt, who considered reputation the most precious possession imaginable. Accordingly, the only flashes of disapproval or even anger over sexual offences come when a perpetrator brought shame on his or her family and community through improper behaviour. Georg Schneck did not just commit adultery but *took in marriage a whore in the New Woods called Dyer Barbie and had a wedding with her.* The thief Peter Hoffman *also deserted his wife and took a consort, then when she died took another and had the banns published at Lauf; when he wasn't permitted [to marry] he took Brigita.*[39]

Surprisingly to modern readers, wedding vows in this era did not have to be pronounced before a pastor or priest to be legally binding. A simple promise exchanged in private or before a few witnesses, followed by sexual consummation, could be considered official. Predictably, a common scandal involved a man who made false vows in order to lure a young woman into bed and then later abandoned her. A young woman who became pregnant in this manner faced a grim set of options: acknowledge the pregnancy and bring shame on herself, her family, and her child; seek an abortion, which was illegal and often deadly; or hide the pregnancy and then abandon the baby. Some women who chose this third option – most of them young, poor, and without family support – laboured alone and in desperation committed infanticide, a crime that if discovered meant certain execution.[40]

In cases of false vows – at least those that did not involve infanticide – Schmidt's sympathies invariably lay with the dishonoured young women and their families, particularly once the affair became public. Meister Frantz writes with contempt of scribe Niklaus Hertzog, who *impregnated a maid at Hof in the Vogtland* [Schmidt's native town], *promised [her] marriage and had public banns announced, then absconded and left her behind,* adding, *also impregnated a maid here at Wehr [and] had a wedding with the same.* He has no patience with the equivocations of the farmhand Georg Schmiedt, *who admitted courting a farmer's daughter, lying with her twenty times, committing lewdness, claiming that he intended to marry her but later denied it.*[41] As in all crimes, deceit and cowardice particularly aroused the executioner's wrath, and he records with satisfaction the few occasions when such cads received their just due from his birch rod.

Other sexual references reflect the same abiding concern with propriety over morality, public embarrassment over private sin. Violating the privacy of the bedchamber, for instance, appears merely distasteful, as when Schmidt flogged the tailor journeyman Veit Heymann and his bride, Margaretha Grossin, *because they committed lewdness and let other maidens watch.* He is somewhat more disgusted with Ameley Schützin and Margaretha Puchfelderin, who prostituted their respective daughters, and Hieronimus Beyhlstein, who pimped for his own wife.[42] Still more scandalously, the clerk Hans Brunnauer

> *during his wife's lifetime committed lewdness with Barbara Kettnerin (also during her husband's life); promised her marriage, consorted with her for three years, went about the country with her for half a year, and had a child with her. Similarly committed lewdness twice with the woman Kettnerin's sister, also several times with the stepmother of the Kettnerin sisters. Also boarded and slept with the wife of a joiner named Thoma for half a year, and promised her marriage and cohabited with her. Also had twin children by a servant during his wife's lifetime.*[43]

And even the world-weary Meister Frantz is taken aback to learn that *Apollonia Groschin provid[ed] her marriage bed for [the confectioner Elisabeth Mechtlin] and herself commit[ted] lewdness – she in a bed with the confectioner and a barber journeyman, called Angelhead, [he] lying in the middle and committing lewdness with both [of them].*[44]

The most serious sexual offences, according to Christian doctrine, were incest and sodomy, both traditionally considered crimes against God and subject to death by fire. The abomination of incest, in particular, supposedly threatened an entire community with divine retribution if not punished. Yet only the case of seventeen-year-old Gertraut Schmidtin, *who lived in lewdness for four years with her own father and brother,* appears to have genuinely shocked Meister Frantz, uniquely prompting him to call her a *heretic.* Still, even here, out of sympathy (and perhaps in recognition of her victim status), he does not dispute the mitigation of her punishment to beheading, while noting that the executioner of Ansbach burned the father and brother alive eight days later at nearby Langenzenn.[45] Frantz also refrains from including any prurient details of the relationship, even though he knew them well from his participation in Schmidtin's interrogation.

One reason for Frantz's exceptional response in this instance was that it was the only case of incest between biological relatives he encountered during his career. Cases of this nature rarely escaped the conspiracy of silence within the early modern household, and thus genuinely shocked most people when they became public. More commonly, incest convictions involved stepfathers and stepdaughters or even one person having sex with two people related to each other (e.g. one woman with two brothers; one man with a woman, her sister, and her stepmother, etc.).[46] Though incomprehensible to most modern sensibilities, incest defined in this second manner was still considered a kind of profound blasphemy and thus usually led to death sentences, though always mitigated in Nuremberg to beheading and occasionally even to flogging.

Typical for the day, the only individuals to escape an incest conviction with banishment were men. Meister Frantz undoubtedly noticed this double standard – which prevailed in virtually all sexual matters – and in fact likely shared it. Sometimes he excuses the discrepancy by distinguishing the level of complicity, as in the case of a father and son who had each been sleeping with their maid: *[they were] unaware of each other's doings*, and therefore merely flogged while she was executed. Kunigunda Küplin, conversely, had been fully cognisant *of what was happening [between her second husband and daughter] and herself [even] arranging it*, and was thus justly condemned to decapitation and posthumous burning. Particularly scandalous behaviour provided a similar justification for magisterial severity. Frantz carefully noted that when Elisabeth Mechtlin *committed lewdness with two biological brothers, [both named] Hans Schneider*, it had been *among the butchers' stalls* (an especially dishonourable place), or that Anna Peyelstainin (aka Cunt Annie) not only *committed lewdness and harlotry with a father and a son, called the Cauldrons, who both had wives and she a husband, [but] similarly with twenty-one married men and youths, her husband helping her.*[47]

Sodomy in the early modern era comprised a variety of offences, ranging from homosexuality to bestiality to other "unnatural" sexual practises (and even heresy).[48] Frantz's first judicial encounter with homosexuality came in 1594, when he burned at the stake Hans Weber,

a fruiterer, otherwise known as the Fat Fruiterer . . . who for three years had practised sodomist lewdness [with Christoph Mayer] and

*was informed on by a hookmaker's apprentice, who caught them
both in the act behind a hedge off a Thon lane. The fruiterer had
practised this for twenty years, namely with the cook Andreas, with
Alexander, also with Georg in the army, and with the baker Toothy
Chris at Lauf, and otherwise with many other baker servants that he
couldn't name. Mayer was first executed with the sword and then
the body burned next to the fruiterer, who was burned alive.*[49]

Two years later, tradesman Hans Wolff Marti, though apparently even
more prolific in same-sex partners and also accused of stabbing the wife
of one of his lovers, was spared burning alive (although the grounds for
such mercy remain unclear).

Contrary to his pervasive fear of robbers and their criminal
underworld, Schmidt's acknowledgement of an apparent homosexual
underground does not appear to have caused him any anxiety. Curiosity, rather – as well as the need to establish an unreformable character
– drives his compulsion to itemise the many alleged partners of both
condemned sodomites. In Marti's case the list is even lengthier:

*having committed sodomist lewdness with [said] mason, also with a
carpenter . . . Also committed such lewdness here and there
throughout the countryside, first with a bargeman at Ibis, also with
another at Brauningen, with a bargeman at Frankfurt, and with a
farmer at Mittenbrück, with a cartman at Witzburg, with a locksmith at Schweinfurt, with a farmer at Windsheim, and with a cartman at Pfaltza, also with a man at Nördlingen, and with a straw
cutter at Salzburg, lastly with a small city guard at Wehr, named
Hans.*[50]

Even though Marti identified his partners in only the vaguest of terms
– either to protect them or because he did not himself know their
names – Meister Frantz did not apply torture to force the suspect to
finger his confederates as witch hunters of the era did. In both instances, Schmidt's tone also remains markedly non-judgemental and
free of derisory language – a sharp contrast to his obvious disgust for
*Georg Schörpff, a heretic who committed lewdness or had relations with
four cows, two calves, and a sheep* and was consequently *executed with*

the sword as a cow pervert at Velln [and] afterwards burned together with a cow with which he'd had sexual relations.[51] Schmidt even mentions a farmer who was accused of *assault[ing] people [and] attempting to commit sodomist lewdness with them* who was merely flogged, his sentence apparently reduced because of the perpetrator's *great drunkenness*.[52] The restraint that Frantz shows when he deals with sodomy shouldn't be interpreted to mean that homosexual activity was either widespread or generally condoned in Meister Frantz's Nuremberg. The severe clerical injunctions against such "abominations" and their cosmic repercussions remain, however, notably absent in Schmidt's writing.

Even if Frantz did consider incest and sodomy to be crimes against God, there's no evidence that he shared the supposedly common belief that such acts invited divine punishment of the entire land (*Landstraffe*) by epidemic, famine, or some other disaster. Outright blasphemy was another matter. Like any other early modern male, God the Father was likely to lash out when His honour was directly challenged, whether by *a common whore* speaking in jest, an archer's son ranting in the midst of an altercation, or a bitter glazier, who *during a great storm, with mighty thunder, blasphemed God in heaven and swore, calling Him (God forgive me for writing it) an old rogue [and saying] the old fool had gambled and lost money at cards [and] now wanted to win it back with dice.* The pious executioner, who even seeks to appease the angry deity in his own private journal, uneasily reports on the blaspheming glazier's *merciful* treatment: merely *placed in the stocks for ¼ hour [and] a piece of the tip of his tongue taken out on the Fleisch Bridge.*[53]

Thefts from a church or monastery, offences that in the Catholic tradition were considered sacrilegious and blasphemous, did not by contrast trouble the Protestant Meister Frantz. He identifies, for instance, Hans Krauss (aka Locksmith John) as *a church thief [who] broke into the church at Endtmannsberg, stole the chalice, and broke open four trunks, stealing the vestments.* But Krauss was hanged the same as any other thief, even despite the additional disclosure that *he also helped ambush and attack people in their houses at night.* The executioner displays the same tone of indifference with the even more prolific church thieves Hans Beütler (aka Skinny) and Hans Georg Schwartzmann (aka the Fat Mercenary). Throughout his journal, rather, it was the thieves' level of activity – *stole often in many places* – that earned them the gallows, not any special reverence for the purloined items themselves.[54]

Crimes of habit

The great majority of the criminal offenders Meister Frantz punished were motivated by neither malice nor other passions. In his experience, most habitual criminals, principally thieves, were not even driven by avarice, the presumed incentive to stealing. Unlike violent robbers or one-time offenders, non-violent thieves in fact tended to display a distinct emotional detachment vis-à-vis their offences. Frantz accordingly displays a similar detachment in his brief journal accounts of the same, only taking pains to note the degree of financial loss entailed. The variety of stolen items is vast, ranging from several hundred gulden in cash to small amounts of money, clothing, bed mattresses, rings, household objects, weapons, chickens, and even honey from unprotected bee-hives. The rustling of horses and cattle proved the most lucrative form of theft; trading in stolen clothing the most common. That all these thefts might be considered equal in severity, let alone punished by death, appears incomprehensible to the modern observer. How could an allegedly pious executioner possibly condone such harshness in punishing non-violent offences, let alone justify his own role in carrying out such severe sentences?

Once more, we must look to Frantz's deep empathy for the victims of crime. In a generally poor society, the loss of a few mantles or a relatively small amount of cash could represent a significant, even devastating, loss for a struggling household. Accordingly, the executioner records thefts of under 50 fl., roughly the annual salary of a schoolmaster, not just more precisely but also with more visceral alarm – reflecting their more immediate implications for specific victims. Clearly Meister Frantz did not consider all thefts equal and he did recognise a greater gravity with large amounts, but his journal's pervasive emphasis on the victim's suffering led to some revealing juxtapositions. While smaller numbers are always specific, sometimes to the pence – reflecting the significance of even a minor amount to a victim who possessed little – large numbers are almost always rounded off into hundreds of florins. In

1609 he recounts how Hans Fratzen *stole ten bed blankets about eigh-teen weeks ago and broke into the hut makers' shelter at Bamberg, stealing 26 fl. worth of clothes,* while in the next passage he simply writes that a well-known cat burglar *stole about 300 fl. worth of silver jewellery.* Frantz similarly devotes a long passage to describing how Maria Cordula Hun-nerin fraudulently ran up an unpaid tavern bill for 32 fl. before noting in passing that later on she stole *800 fl. worth in thaler and three kreuzer pieces from the safe box of her master.*[55]

In another journal entry, the executioner's seemingly compulsive list-ing of multiple thefts in fact serves to underscore both the bad charac-ter of the perpetrator and the great number of his victims: *Simon Starck . . . stole money six times out of the purse of one servant, 1½ fl. from the cooler, and from his farmer 29 fl., which he took back from him, and at Schweinau 5 fl. from a pedlar, about 2 fl. from his cartman, about 1 fl. in sum from an Italian.*[56] Even more bizarre to modern eyes, Frantz's personal identification with crime victims moves him to write passages like the one about Sebastian Fürsetzlich, *who stole money from the purses of carters while they slept at night in inns, namely 80 fl. 6 schilling, 45 fl., 37 fl., 35 fl., 30 fl., 30 fl., 20 fl., 18 fl., 17 fl., 8 fl., 8 fl., 7 fl., 6 fl., 3 fl., 2 fl.*[57] Rather than simply totalling the amounts or copying them in chronological order, Schmidt carefully restructures the thefts in de-scending order of value to convey the crimes' individual financial im-pact on multiple carters as well as the moral case for Fürsetzlich's punishment – albeit in a highly idiosyncratic manner.

Thieves and other non-violent offenders indisputably deserved pun-ishment in Meister Frantz's moral universe, but their crimes, like those of prostitutes and pimps, usually represented the conscious lifestyle choices of weak, rather than malicious, individuals. This attitude repre-sented a divergence from the more sweeping approach of jurists and clerics to all crime. Despite the executioner's exceptional attunement to the losses suffered by their victims, his primary emotional response to the 172 thieves he hanged during his career was less anger than weary resignation. Their own selfish choices had brought them to this moment, and Schmidt never once excused the circumstances behind their thefts. The man born into a gutter-status profession predictably had little sympathy for the many hard-luck stories he encountered in the interrogation chamber. Yet it is neither triumph nor guilt that tinged his accounts of hanging recidivist small-time thieves, but head-shaking sadness. "How could a society hang a man for stealing honey?" we ask from our perspective; "Why does a man repeatedly risk hanging to steal some honey?" wonders Frantz.

The answer to both questions is that stealing had evidently become an unshakeable habit for the offender in question and Frantz Schmidt's superiors had simply reached their point of exasperation. The crucial issue was usually not what a thief had stolen but how often. Virtually all those condemned to die were multiple offenders; many had been arrested, imprisoned, and banished several times. Put another way, most of the individuals ultimately hanged by Meister Frantz had irreversibly transformed themselves in his eyes from people who stole once or twice into professional thieves, "accustomed to the deed".[58] "Obstinate" was the characterisation most common among Nuremberg's obedience-craving magistrates, but the modern language of compulsive behaviour would be closer to the executioner's assessment of many recidivists. He observed that the affluent farmgirl Magdalena Geckenhofferin, *again and again borrowed several mantles, brassieres, and other clothing [and] she even went to communion or to a wedding to snatch the same,* clearly indicating from some kind of internal rather than external stimulus. Meister Frantz thought it obvious that Farmer Heinz Pflügel and his wife, Margaretha, who *had a property worth about 1000 fl. but often busied themselves with thievery,* were likewise motivated by something other than outright deprivation.[59]

Stealing, according to the veteran executioner, was always a choice, but also for many – to use an anachronistic term – an irresistible addiction. Too often, the habit was acquired at an early age. Balthasar Preiss, *child of a [Nuremberg] citizen . . . lay eleven times in the Hole, went several times into the chain gang, was for half a year in the Frog Tower, and [spent] a year in irons in the tower, but would not abandon thieving. When put to some handicraft, ran away and stole.* Meister Frantz himself repeatedly flogged and reprimanded his former colleagues, the municipal archers Georg Götz and Lienhard Hertl, who each spent several years rowing in Venetian galleys; yet both men continued to steal and rob until finally stopped at the gallows. Even career offenders who wanted to rehabilitate themselves were often pulled back into the criminal life against their will. The *old thief father* Simon Gretzelt forty years ago *forswore his thieving*, Frantz writes, and longtime thief Andreas Stayber (aka the Minstrel) *stole many things besides here and there but had given up these practises for five years and wanted to reform* [literally, "become pious"]. The executioner takes no apparent pleasure in recording that in both cases the former thieves' pasts caught up with them: Gretzelt eventually returned to an immoral life, and the Minstrel was sentenced to hang as a consequence of the incriminating testimony of his former companion, the infamous highwayman Hans Kolb.[60]

Habitual stealing by no means equalled skilful stealing. Many thefts were purely crimes of opportunity – a street vendor who turned his back for a moment, clothing left unattended on a washing line, a house left vacant because of a wedding feast. The farmhand Hans Merckel (aka Deer John), *who was in service for 22 years,*

> *used to stay half a year to two years in one place and then leave, taking away with him hose, doublets, boots, woollen shirts, and whatever money he could get. When he drove some sheep to Augsburg for his master and obtained 35 fl. for them, he ran away with the money. Did the same to his master at Amburg, who sent him with 21 fl. and a horse and cart to fetch some white beer from Bohemia; left the horse and ran away with the money. Also stole a pair of hose and a doublet, in the pockets of which were 15 fl., which he was unaware of.*[61]

More simply, a messenger called the Cabbage Farmer *was given a satchel containing silver cutlery and 200 fl. worth of Groshen to carry to Neustadt, [but] he broke into it and sold the silver to the Jews at Furth for 100 fl. in cash,* spending all his proceeds on eating and gambling.[62]

Burglary, because it both violated the home and risked personal contact, presented a greater threat. By late middle age, the veteran executioner had become a connoisseur of such break-ins, rarely the well-conceived and skilfully executed heists of legend. He was amused by the ineptitude of some amateurs, such as Anna Pergmennin, who *sneaked into the house of a schoolmaster at Saint Lorenz [Church], intending to steal but was caught and imprisoned; eight days earlier had been locked in the cellar of Hans Payr, [also] intending to steal.* Erhard

Rössner *one night broke open the locks of twelve shops but couldn't get inside*, while Lienhard Leydtner, a padlock smith, *in the last two years broke into forty-two shops in this town with keys he made for that purpose, thinking to find money, but stole nothing special.*[63] Still more embarrassingly, the shepherd Cunz Pütner

> *had twice concealed himself in Master Fürer's house and tried to break into the office and steal money, but when he had bored seven holes in the door the first time he achieved nothing. [So] he again hid in the house and tried to break into the parlour. When the master heard him and cried out there was a search and [the shepherd's] shoes were found sitting on the floor, he having removed them so as to move silently. He was still hiding in the parlour, though, where he was captured.*[64]

Even the professional burglar Lienhard Gösswein, who *was in possession of many tools, was caught in the cellar of the innkeeper Wastla's house at the Fruit Market, intending to steal.*[65]

Bungled break-ins could also lead to more serious consequences. Lorenz Schober – who, according to Meister Frantz, *stole trifles, namely 12 loaves of bread, 6 cheeses, a shirt and a doublet* –

> *broke into the house of a poor woman at Gründlein, and when she caught him in the act and held him, screaming for help, he drew a knife and stabbed her thrice, the first time in the head, the second time in the left breast, the third in the neck, and left her lying for dead, so that she recovered with difficulty.*[66]

Only the prolific cat burglar Hans Schrenker (aka the Crawler) appears to earn the executioner's professional respect, though not without a hint of mockery:

> *Climbed into the castle at Freienfels, [first] using a ladder over the cowshed, then by a ladder against a tower to the roof, then again by another ladder through a window into a parlour. Broke open a safe box with his cooper's knife and stole about 300 fl. worth of silver jewellery. Then, descending by the ladders as he had climbed,*

went out in front of the castle and hid the jewels under a stone on
the other side of the hill. Entered again by the ladders, broke open
a desk, and stole a bag with 40 fl. Although a sack with 500 fl. lay
close to it, when he was about to take the money such a fear over-
came him that he ran away, thinking for certain that someone was
running after him.[67]

Perhaps in part to relieve the tedium of writing about mediocre
bumblers, Meister Frantz made note of especially ingenious or industrious thieves. One wire-drawer *over the course of a year and a half, used*
specially forged keys to break into the shop of an ironmonger, once or
twice a week, stealing about 21 Ell [approx. 52 feet] of wire, 14 Ell [ap-
prox. *35 feet] of steel, and 40 thousand nails.* The determined Anna Rebbelin *entered houses here more than forty times, and always went up two*
or three flights of stairs into the rooms and stole a great quantity of goods.[68]

Small-time swindlers, a favourite of picaresque literature, particularly intrigued Meister Frantz, probably because of their brazenness.
Christoph Schmiedt (aka Cooper Chris), a longtime thief, most recently *entered eight rooms at the public baths, wearing old clothes, and*
when he went out put on the best [ones] of other people, leaving his old
ones in their place. Margaretha Kleinin, who also regularly worked as a
burglar, *approached people with glasses clattering in small bags, as though*
it were money, [and] convinced people to trust her so that she could steal
from them. Georg Praun *stole 13 thaler [approx. 11 fl.] from the bag of a*
youth from Gräfenberg who was travelling with him, putting stones in their
place, and Hans Weckler similarly *stole 200 fl. from the saddlebag of a*
[fellow] tailor sleeping next to him in a room at an inn in Goldkronach,
afterwards putting sand through the rip so that it had the same weight
again. Fittingly, Meister Frantz adds, Weckler quickly *gambled away the*
money here, being cheated out of it by the roof workers Grumbly and
Rosie, for which he sued them both, and on that account they were both
whipped with rods out of the city – whereupon the two card sharps noti-
fied the authorities of their target's previous theft.[69] Frantz clearly de-
lights in the picaresque staple of thieves who subsequently have their
money stolen by other thieves, and he repeats it often.[70] It wasn't difficult to cheat trusting people, he realised, nor did it require any special
cleverness, just an indifference to other people's suffering.

Large-scale, successful swindlers consequently caused Meister Frantz more consternation, particularly when they audaciously cheated the wellborn, most notably the forger Gabriel Wolff and the treasure hunter Elisabeth Aurholtin. Though scrupulously non-violent, these con artists were also much more calculating – and thus malicious – than common thieves. They also coolly lied, which exacerbated their thefts still further in his eyes. Anna Domiririn, who *often lay in the pesthouse*, nonetheless *intentionally deceived people with fortune-telling and treasure-finding* and thus received a full flogging, even though she *could not walk; had to be led out under the arms of two beadles*. Margaretha Schreinerin, an *old hag about 60 years old, likewise deceived people here and there, by claiming that she had inherited a great fortune* and making multiple bequests to notables around town in exchange for food, drink, and small loans (which she promised to pay back shortly). Despite her age and apparent ill health, she was *burned on both cheeks as a deceiver*. Nor was there any leniency from Meister Frantz or his authorities for Kunrad Krafft, a longtime court clerk whose forgeries and embezzlements over the years ultimately cost him his life.[71]

Mercy and redemption

Whatever the motive or nature of the crime, in Meister Frantz's scheme of justice all offenders had hope. As a believing Lutheran, he accepted that the world was a profoundly evil place and that all men and women would repeatedly succumb to sin over the course of their lifetimes. Admittedly, some fell into much graver transgressions and crimes than others, but the essential message of Christianity for Frantz was the good news of divine forgiveness for all those who sought it. This should not be confused with rehabilitation in the modern, secular sense – after all, sixteenth-century Lutherans believed that the corrupting effects of original sin remained powerful even among the faithful. What Schmidt and his colleagues, both magistrates and chaplains, sought from convicted offenders was acknowledgement of guilt and submission to the authority of God and the state. In return, both the temporal and divine judges held out the promise of absolution and thus redemption.

Mercy, consequently, was the powerful counterpart to punishment in the early modern notion of justice. Frantz shares this reverence, intoning the word ninety-three times in his journal, more than *God* (sixteen times) or *justice* (twice) or *law* (none). Virtually every use of *mercy* in the journal refers to the mitigation of a criminal punishment, but clearly the pious executioner was determined to help poor sinners attain heavenly as well as earthly redemption. The precondition to both was genuine contrition.

Visible signs of remorse thus went a long way with Meister Frantz. He notes with approval that the murderer Michel Vogt *was already out in the woods [and] came back here*, and also that the child murderer Anna Freyin, the thief Hans Helmet, and the murderer Matthias Stertz all voluntarily turned themselves in to authorities (as well as that Stertz *had been a Catholic but turned Lutheran* before his execution). Frantz repeatedly recognised in his journal those souls who *took leave of the world as a Christian*, particularly in his later years.[72] Both the executioner and the prison chaplains took heart that the repentant thief Hans Drechsler (aka the Mountaineer; aka Mercenary John) not only "learned more in the last three days from the chaplains and gaol-keeper than in all his life", but also left the world in an exemplary manner, proclaiming on the scaffold to all assembled, "God bless you and the leaves and the grass, and everything I leave behind! Say a Paternoster for me. Today I shall pray for you in paradise."[73]

Embittered prisoners, particularly violent robbers, who adamantly "didn't want to pray" earned scorn from the chaplains and the executioner.[74] A rebuffed Magister Hagendorn was not above remarking that one recalcitrant thief "carried [a violent fever] with him to the gallows, from which he was not recovered until Meister Frantz hanged a cure about his neck."[75] Both the chaplain and Meister Frantz also knew that condemned culprits frequently exploited their captors' spiritual concerns to forestall the inevitable. After repeated visits to twenty-five-year-old jewel thief Jakob Faber, Magister Hagendorn began to lament the desperate man's obvious insincerity and continued resistance:

> When I came to him, he was ready with all of his old tricks. He mentioned his honourable family, particularly the pleas of his old and helpless mother, and put forward all manner of excuses why

he should continue to live and escape the death penalty. He cared more for his body than his soul and he was troublesome before the council, as with us, though not in the matter of instruction and comfort, for he had studied and learned the catechism in his tender youth, and knew certain psalms likewise, particularly the 6th and 23rd, as well as other prayers, but adhered obstinately to his old ways. Whether we told him sweet or bitter things, his only purpose was to go on living.[76]

Meister Frantz likewise had no tolerance for malefactors who had yet to come to terms with their situation and refused to display the appropriate submission. The notorious Georg Mayer (aka Brains)

often pleaded epilepsy. When he was about to be examined by torture, he fell into a fit and pretended the illness tormented him. As he had been excused three days before on this pretext, he taught his companions to do likewise, so that they would be let off, but when Knau also tried to do this he could not pull it off and when he was detected he admitted [the truth].[77]

Perhaps because of such feigned illnesses, Schmidt displayed no apparent sympathy for condemned poor sinners on account of mental disabilities, even while acknowledging obvious symptoms ranging from confused mumbling at execution to outright psychotic episodes.[78] He was outraged when convicted criminals attempted to game the system for clemency or merely delay, such as the robber Katherina Bücklin (aka Stammering Kathy; aka the Foreigner), who *should have been executed twelve weeks earlier but obtained a respite because of pregnancy, which turned out to be nothing*; or Elisabeth Püffin, also convicted of robbery and attempted murder, who *obtained a respite of 32 weeks on the plea of pregnancy, the committee of sworn women visiting her 18 times* before she was ultimately *executed with the sword*.[79]

In some instances, submission to divine judgement inspired worldly clemency – the judicial *mercy* to which Frantz's journal regularly refers. "In response to his supplications and prayers, and in view of his sufferings under torture", the thief Hans Dietz saw his sentence of hanging mitigated to beheading.[80] More typically, Nuremberg's magistrates showed little concern over spiritual conversion or pain endured, instead exercising their power to forgive only when it would bolster their own standing in the community. When city councillors assembled the morning of an execution to consider whether to punish "by the book" or "by mercy", it was the social standing of the individual before them that carried the most weight, not the apparent state of the poor sinner's soul.[81] In the case of Hans Kornmeyer, "an especially handsome young person of twenty . . . his mother, together with her five children, two of whom are his siblings proper . . . interceded on his behalf, as well as his master [who'd had him arrested] and the entire guild of compass-makers," successfully securing the young thief execution with the sword instead of with the rope.[82] In an even more stunning example of social influence at work, the earring maker Hans Mager and the goldsmith Caspar Lenker, both citizens, received full pardons from their homicide convictions following the intercession of the local guild, the leading goldsmith of Augsburg, and a passing emissary from Lorraine, as well as many friends and relatives.[83]

Nuremberg's criminal records are also filled with pardons of especially well-connected (or especially lucky) prisoners granted at the request of various *illustres personae* passing through town, ranging from the eminent theologian Philipp Melanchthon to the duke of Bavaria.[84] Even children of low-level city employees might benefit from their parents' official status. It probably helped Margaretha Brechtlin, convicted of poisoning her husband, that she was a daughter of the tax collector at the Spitler Gate, so that in the end she was *executed with the sword out of mercy*. Despite their multiple thefts, both a night huntsman's son and a bailiff's son likewise escaped with floggings, and even Georg Christoff (aka Shank), an oft-arrested *thief and chain gang youth*, was aided by his father's position as a municipal archer.[85]

Obviously this magisterial tendency to favour the well connected put poor and foreign individuals at a disadvantage, since they rarely had the same social capital to draw on as citizens and local craftsmen. It also weakened the chaplains' arguments for religious contrition among condemned malefactors, who presumably saw nothing to be gained by even feigning religious conversion. But as the magistrates gradually recognised, any act of leniency on their part invariably made for a smoother and more successful execution ceremony, and eventually their hard position began to soften. Young Hans Kornmeyer repeatedly threw himself down before the court in gratitude for the commuting of his hanging sentence to beheading, while Niklaus Kilian enthusiastically praised the judges for their commutation and left praying Psalm 33, then singing, and in the end "dying joyfully". When the prison chaplain brought the thief Hans Dietz news of his sentence's commutation to beheading,

> he was so delighted and comforted that he kissed the hands of both of us, and also the gaoler's, and most diligently thanked us. Before the court, during the reading of the judgement he wept bitterly, and returned thanks for the merciful sentence. On his way out he sang almost continuously, so that the people, and even the executioner himself, were moved to pity.[86]

The ultimate word on clemency meanwhile became an even more jealously guarded prerogative of the city council itself. Gone were the pre-Reformation days when a nun or young virgin had the power to rescue any condemned person from a deadly fate. Pregnant women still might influence judges in other German lands but the last such account in Nuremberg is the pardon of one bigamist soldier in 1553 because of the intercession of "his [pregnant] first wife and sixteen other women besides."[87] Even in the exceptional 1609 case of Hans Frantz, whose two daughters pleaded with the magistrates that "their bridegrooms would not keep them or marry them if they had to watch their father-in-law hang on the gallows," the result was commutation to beheading, not a full pardon.[88] Folk stories abounded about women who agreed to marry condemned men – most notably the Swabian account of one condemned thief who took a good look at his prospective one-eyed bride, then turned to mount the gallows – but governmental authorities from the mid-sixteenth century refused to cede such power to anyone in actual practise. This included, apparently, the executioner, who in earlier days – as recently as 1525 in Nuremberg – could save a condemned woman by marrying her.[89]

That said, it's likely that Meister Frantz, especially during these later years, had some influence on the mitigation of sentences. Certainly by this time in his life he had become freer in showing his disdain for previous naive acts of official generosity. As a young man,

Frantz merely remarks in a neutral way that a thief *twelve years before had been spared the gallows at Kulmbach.*[90] Over the years, as he saw more of the same people coming before him, his bitterness over misspent mercy came increasingly to the fore. He follows his 1592 lament that convicted robber Stoffel Weber *should have been executed with the sword but he begged off as he was being led out and was punished at a customs house* with a lengthy discourse on other ill-considered reprieves in Nuremberg's recent past. He notes in 1606 that the two Widtmann brothers, ultimately hanged for multiple thefts, *should have been executed two and a half years ago, for they had been condemned to death – and I was at the time sick – but were reprieved.* He never liked that Gabriel Wolff *should have had his right hand cut off first, this being decided and ordered, but was subsequently spared this,* and appears genuinely stunned that *a farmer from Gründla who killed two farmers (he lay in wait for) with an axe was spared by petition.* Not only did such favours cheat the victims, but in the case of professional robbers – such as Michel Gemperlein, who *three years ago should have been executed with the rope for theft but was pardoned* – they led to the suffering of more innocent victims before the criminals were definitively stopped.[91]

The only potentially mitigating factor that moved the mature executioner other than genuine contrition was youth, an increasingly common attribute among those condemned for theft. As a result of the new severity in punishing crimes against property during the second half of the sixteenth century, Meister Frantz's professional tenure coincided exactly with the only period in early modern German history during which minors were executed for crimes other than murder or "crimes against God", such as incest, sodomy, and witchcraft. Non-violent burglary and common theft frequently involved juveniles, with fifteen- to seventeen-year-olds accounting for as many as one in three thieves in some areas. Occasionally the youths, who sometimes operated in organised bands, stole large sums of money, but usually they snatched relatively insignificant items – a bracelet, a pair of trousers, some loaves of bread.[92]

The *Carolina* left much discretion to criminal judges on the question of age in capital punishments, explicitly forbidding only the execution of those under fourteen, but even there permitting some exceptions if the offender was deemed "mature in evil".[93] This appallingly extreme punishment for juvenile theft also shocked Frantz's contemporaries, and Nuremberg's leaders, like those elsewhere in early modern Europe, continued to invoke the mitigating factor of youth in most decisions.[94] In 1605 a seventeen-year-old thief, Michel Brombecker, had his death sentence commuted to two years on a chain gang, but only in response to the appeals of his master "and the entire butcher craft" – once more evidence of the social connections that vagrant and destitute youths crucially lacked.[95] The capital punishment of the scholar youth and citizen's child Julius Tross was similarly reduced to flogging, as were those of the two thieving Wechter brothers and two other youths convicted of brutal rapes (a capital crime).[96] The coach-boy Laurenz Stollman, meanwhile, even though *he had not enjoyed the proceeds of his [latest 150 fl.] theft*, had no apparent local patrons and thus was still executed, albeit *out of mercy with the sword*.[97]

Still, even among those minors with no social capital whatsoever, clemency remained the norm. Eighteen-year-old Hans Beheim had indeed been hanged by Frantz's predecessor for "great thievery". But as recently as the year before Schmidt's arrival in Nuremberg in 1578, three different groups of condemned boy pickpockets aged seven to sixteen years were deemed "too young to hang" and had their sentences reduced to work in a chain gang, followed by flogging and banishment. To drive home both the seriousness of the offence and the generosity of the commutation, the magistrates had one group of boys, "none older than eleven", actually climb the gallows ladder before being pardoned and then forced to stand by and watch their eighteen-year-old leader actually hang. Almost twenty years later, Frantz would hang the adult Steffan Kebweller for running a similar group of young cutpurses, whom he paid the extravagant weekly wages of one thaler (0.85 fl.) plus room and board for their labours; once more, the youths themselves were released.[98]

In fact, all the juveniles ultimately executed for theft in Nuremberg were serial offenders, some having been arrested and released as many as two dozen times. Benedict Fellbinger (aka the Devil's Knave) *had been in the chain gang and lain fifteen times in the Hole, also defied his banishment eleven times*. Every member of one particularly active group of young thieves had supposedly spent at least ten detentions in the begging stockade or dungeon, sometimes followed by a public flogging.

Most important, all juvenile thieves eventually condemned to death had previously received the penultimate punishment of permanent banishment, usually at least two or three times. In every case, final verdicts noted that "such warnings and mild treatment had been received with disdain," and the juveniles continued to return to Nuremberg and steal. At some point, magistrates concludeed that "no improvement is to be hoped for" and clemency on account of youth abruptly ended.[99]

As a result, over the course of his long career, Meister Frantz would himself hang at least twenty-three thieves who were eighteen or younger, including one thirteen-year-old.[100] At Frantz's very first execution in the city of Nuremberg, when he was not yet twenty-four himself, the condemned was in fact one of the youthful pickpockets pardoned just the year before – "a very handsome young person of seventeen", according to one chronicler.[101] How did Frantz feel about this and the many other youthful hangings that would follow? Ever restrained in his expression of outright sentiment, he nonetheless conveys both his initial discomfort and, later, an evolving understanding of human character that provided him with some reassurance in such difficult cases.

During his own youth, Frantz never mentioned the age or youthfulness of any offenders he executed. If it weren't for the city chronicles, which do note the precise ages of the young thieves he hanged, we would not even know that he encountered any juveniles at the scaffold. This reticence is even evident in his account of the extraordinary hanging of seven young thieves, aged thirteen to eighteen, on 11 and 12 February 1584. These five boys and two girls had each been banished multiple times for burglary, and one of the girls, Maria Kürschnerin (aka Constable Mary), had even had her ears cropped by Meister Frantz the year before. The shocking group execution of such young offenders attracted an enormous crowd and made a particular impression on local chroniclers, who recorded the ages of the youths as well as multiple other details (see illustration on page 176). Twenty-nine-year-old Frantz Schmidt, by contrast, notes only that the thieves *had broken into citizens' houses and stolen a considerable amount*. He then adds a single, apparently uneasy observation: that the hanging of women *had never before happened* in Nuremberg. On the equally salient detail of the girls' youth, the journal is silent.[102]

A decade later, Meister Frantz readily acknowledges that the two thieves Hensa Kreuzmayer and Hensa Baur were *both about sixteen years old,* and presumably on that account *out of mercy executed with the sword.* From that point on, he regularly includes the ages of all juveniles executed, without feeling compelled to add any exceptional justification

A Nuremberg chronicle records the unprecedented 1584 hanging of two young women, followed the next day by the hanging of five male youths, all part of a local burglary gang (1616).

other than *stole much*.[103] Both sixteen-year-old Balthasar Preiss and fifteen-year-old Michel König, Schmidt adds, had been given multiple opportunities to reform, but in each instance *would not abandon thieving or could not stop [stealing]*.[104] His 1615 account of another group hanging, this time involving five slightly older thieves, aged eighteen and nineteen, is even less sympathetic:

> *The Big Farmer [aka Klaus Rodtler] stole much with the condemned Devil's Lad and Farmer Cunz, had many other companions, and lay often in the Hole [but] always lied his way out. Bruner [aka Junkman] only gathers purses; since he was released fourteen days ago has stolen about 50 fl. When the three [cutpurses] were executed [last month], he stole two purses during the execution. Riffraff [aka Johann Bauer] also belonged to this company, was often in the Hole and the chain gang. The Weaver [aka Georg Knorr] also lay several times in the Hole, always released on account of his piety. All five thieves executed with the rope.[105]*

What do we make of the mature Frantz's justification for torturing and executing teenagers? Should we read his lengthy protestations of their unreformability as an attempt to convince his own uneasy conscience that the punishments are just? Or had he, like some of the magistrates, grown so frustrated by the young men's repeated offences, so outraged at their disregard for the council's many acts of mercy, that he truly believed they deserved the gallows? Is this evidence of a darkening, even cynical, view of human nature?

Like most people, Meister Frantz appeared to be uncertain whether nature or nurture exerts more influence in the development of children who become career criminals. Clearly he didn't consider lack of access to respectable craft training – a fact of life for him and his own children – to be an acceptable explanation for why a young man might turn to crime. And he had no sympathy at all for those who did have access to training but squandered it. Laurenz Pfeiffer, described by Schmidt as *a grocer and a thief*, was *a young person who attempted to learn the tailor craft but did not do well*, and subsequently took to stealing, as did the burglar Pangratz Paumgartner, *who learned the compassmaking [craft] here from Peter Ziegler*.[106] In fact, the great majority of the juveniles he encountered at the scaffold had received some artisanal training, as had the majority of all the men he executed. Whatever the actual opportunities for employment, these individuals all started out with advantages never enjoyed by an outcast executioner.

Consorting with "bad company" was another frequent catalyst to crime, often establishing a bad or even criminal reputation before the fact. Frantz considers it relevant but not exculpatory that the servant Hans Dorsch was incited to steal large amounts from his long-term master by his cousin and circle of male friends.[107] Spending days and nights with drinking, gambling, and quarrelling men could rarely end well. A youth who wanted to live an honest life had to possess enough self-discipline to avoid the company of dishonest men – a choice the executioner himself had made long before. Military service apparently offered an especially effective education in vice. After serving multiple campaigns in Hungary, the local sons Hans Taumb and Peter Haubmayr fell among professional robbers, and despite multiple arrests and reprieves *both again kept whores as before, putting them in the way of people. As soon as anyone was interested or spoke to them, they pulled [the women out] and blackmailed [the would-be customer], taking all his money or clothes.*[108]

Then as now, Frantz and his contemporaries most often traced the roots of criminal behaviour back to the parents, sometimes attributing the child's perfidy to a faulty upbringing, and other times to an inherited predilection for crime.[109] While Frantz always notes when he flogged or executed a relative of a previously punished criminal, he refrains from interpreting the connection.[110] Given his fierce beliefs about self-determination, and despite his regular encounters with pious and law-abiding parents of deviants, Schmidt appeared to fall more on the nurture side of the debate, blaming some parents for bad upbringing but still holding their grown children accountable. He is clearly disgusted that Hans Ammon (aka the Foreign Tailor) not only robbed churches but also *taught his daughter to steal*, or that Cordula Widtmenin *helped both of her sons in thievery, taking the stolen goods from them.* Parents who prostituted their own daughters or involved their children in counterfeiting were equally reprehensible.[111] And although victimised children might be pitied for their unfortunate backgrounds, that didn't absolve them of responsibility for their own actions, even if they were still relatively young. Bastla Hauck, who was flogged and eventually executed for theft, had watched his own *father and brother [hanged] and [another] brother whipped out of town with rods* for the same crime, yet he refused to mend his own ways.[112] Nor did it make any difference to Meister Frantz that the con artist Elisabeth Aurholtin as a child had been abandoned by her deranged father in some snowy woods, after he had drowned her mother and hanged her brother.[113] Schmidt's genuine sympathy for the little girl of the past would always be outweighed by the undeniable culpability of the present-day woman before him.

Schmidt's insistence on personal accountability did not make him oblivious to the apparently innate origin of some bad character. The robber Hans Rühl *some years ago, while yet a boy, killed another boy of ten by throwing a stone at him and was sent to the chain gang for it, [yet] when he was released he consorted with the knacker [until] he was banished from the town for his evil ways.*[114] Many condemned thieves, despite multiple apprenticeships, continued to steal from an early age, most notably the prolific burglar Jörg Mayr, *who was 17 years old [and] had begun [to steal] eight years ago.*[115] Other young men likewise appeared to Meister Frantz to be overwhelmed by their own violent dispositions, a vulnerability merely exacerbated by drink, bad company, and loose women. Such ne'er-do-wells established their character early in life, including Frantz's own executed brother-in-law Friedrich Werner, who "was bad from youth on and consorted with bad company".[116]

Whatever the respective influence of nature and nurture among criminal offenders, the veteran executioner steadfastly held to his fundamental principle of self-determination. How could it be otherwise for a self-made man who himself had come so far from his cursed origins? Fates were made, not inherited. It was ironic that the notorious *whoremonger and great traitor* Simon Schiller escaped stoning by an angry mob by *jump[ing] into the water [and] crawl[ing] under the millwork*, only to be stoned to death in the same place a year later – but it was his continued wanton ways that determined his end, not the stars, as so many condemned criminals claimed. Frantz's Lutheran acceptance of radical original sin and divine providence in no way released a sinner from personal responsibility in accepting or rejecting God's grace.

Frantz's most recent personal tragedies had the potential to weaken or strengthen his religious faith. The same might be said of his decades of immersion in the world of crime. Frustratingly, we have no idea whatsoever of the religious or philosophical works the self-taught executioner might have turned to for inspiration and consolation, other than the Bible. The most revealing clue we have to the state of his piety at this point of life is a text dated 25 July 1605. The Meistersinger (master singer) schools of German cities represented guild versions of the medieval minstrel tradition, comprised of male members ranked by their respective compositional abilities as apprentices, journeymen, or masters. Composers had to follow strict rules about rhyming, meter, and melody, as well as perform their works a cappella before a panel of master judges. Nearly thirty years after the death of Nuremberg's most famous Meistersinger, Hans Sachs, the city's song guild continued to hold annual open competitions for non-members. Remarkably, the longtime executioner himself, undoubtedly with some assistance, made his own submission. Although his song was most likely never actually performed, it was later included in a published Meistersinger collection of 1617, the year of Meister Frantz's last execution.[117]

Not all historians have accepted the song as the work of the famed executioner, particularly given its linguistic fluency relative to his journal. Upon a close reading, however, the evidence for authorship appears incontestable. The text itself is signed "Meister Franz Schmidt at St Jacob's", the latter a church near the executioner's residence. Schmidt was admittedly an extremely common name of the day, but Franz or Frantz – German for Francis, in veneration of the saint of Assisi – was not, at least not in a Protestant city like Nuremberg. It was also unusual among the *Meisterlieder* for a text to be signed with "Meister" (Frantz's popular honourific) rather than "Magister". The crowning proof that "our" Frantz Schmidt indeed composed the *Meisterlied* is the poet's choice of subject: the alleged correspondence between King Abgar of Edessa and Jesus, a story with particular resonance for the executioner-physician.

According to legend, the Syriac king Abgar V, a contemporary of Jesus, heard stories about the Galilean miracle worker and wrote to him requesting a personal visit. Suffering from leprosy, gout, and other painful ailments, Abgar professed his belief in Jesus' divinity and offered to host the Messiah if he would travel to Edessa (modern-day Şanlıurfa, Turkey) and heal the ailing ruler. Jesus, the received story goes, wrote back to Abgar that he was unable to come himself, but that in recognition of the king's faith, he would send a disciple – Thaddeus Thomas, or Addai in the local tongue. And indeed, shortly after Jesus' ascension, Thomas arrived in Edessa, as his master had promised, and miraculously healed Abgar, who was immediately baptised. The story circulated widely in the ancient world, with the purported letters themselves published in the fourth century by the church historian Eusebius of Caesarea. Over time, an image of Jesus on a cloth, "made not by human hands", became part of the legend and was venerated in the eastern part of the Roman Empire, where it took on still greater liturgical significance.

The story of Abgar and Jesus – which most modern scholars dismiss as spurious – never experienced the same popularity in the western part of the empire, which makes Frantz's selection of it unusual. At the very least, it suggests he had some familiarity with Eusebius's *Ecclesiastical History* (c.323), which the song both names and closely follows in the wording of the two letters. Its central theme of healing clearly appealed to the executioner-physician, who repeats the word *illness* more than any other in the song, both in the physical and spiritual sense. *Impure spirits*, as much as blindness and lameness, *torment people with pain*, and it is *faith*, not *herbs or medicine*, that heals the suffering king. The words *wonders* and *power* also recur frequently, again recalling the spiritual nature of Jesus' healing. Whatever stylistic or theological assistance Frantz received in the composition of the song, the thematic thrust remains entirely his own, fully in keeping with his other writings. If anything, his lifetime of exposure to human cruelties and suffering had merely confirmed the foundational Protestant belief in salvation by grace and faith alone. Sin was inevitable among the fallen human race, but so was divine forgiveness – if one sought it. Criminal punishment offered not just an opportunity for legal expiation but for spiritual redemption, making the executioner a priest of sorts (although, as a Lutheran, Meister Frantz would have rejected identification as an intercessor who had the power to convey divine forgiveness himself).[118] Like a life of sin and crime, submission to divine forgiveness was for him a question of individual choice.

Among the many gospel stories about forgiveness, two in particular apparently found resonance in the pious executioner's journal. The first was that of the Prodigal Son, the well-known parable of a son who immorally squanders his inheritance yet is taken back and embraced by his compassionate father (Luke 15:11–32). Like his biblical counterpart, the thief Georg Schweiger made several regrettable choices, most notably

> *in his youth, together with his brother, first stole 40 fl. from his own flesh-and-blood father. Later, when his father sent him to settle a debt, he kept the money and gambled with it. Lastly, discovering that his father had buried a treasure in a stable behind the house, stole 60 fl. of it. He also had a lawful wife, whom he deserted, and attached himself to two whores, promising marriage to both.*

A popular broadsheet version of the story of the Prodigal Son, with the title character taking his leave on the left, enjoying the high life in the centre, and reduced to feeding swine on the right (c.1570).

Albrecht Dürer's evocative drawings of the bad thief (*left*) and the good thief (*right*) (1505).

Yet rather than forgive his errant offspring, *his father himself had [his son] imprisoned and desired and insisted that his right be exercised, in spite of the fact that he had recovered his money, and paid 2 fl. from it [for the gaol time].*[119] Clearly Frantz believed that Schweiger's father had justifiable grounds for his anger, and the executioner himself does not question the thief's subsequent beheading for his crimes. That the injured father's heart remained hardened against his own prodigal son, however, appeared to him both unnatural and unchristian – an offence of a different order.

The second example comes from the year before Frantz made his submission to the *Meisterlied* contest, following a double execution of thieves. Although also implicit, the contrast in the two malefactors' display of repentance and faith clearly suggested to the evangelical executioner an analogy to the good and bad thieves crucified with Jesus (Luke 23:29–43). Like Dismas, the good thief, who asked the adjacent Christ "to remember me when you come into your kingdom", the shepherd Cunz Pütner showed all the requisite signs of remorse and *died as a Christian*.

His gallows companion Hans Drentz (aka Stretch), by contrast, was a virtual reincarnation of the bad thief (traditionally known as Gestas) who mocked and cursed Jesus as a false prophet from his own cross:

> *[He] would not pray or say a word about God nor confess the name of Christ. When questioned [about God] he always said he knew nothing about Him and could say nothing nor repeat any prayer. A young maid had once given him a shirt and since then he had been unable to pray. The sacrament was not administered to him, therefore he died in his sins and fell down near the gallows as if tormented by a fit. He was a godless man.*[120]

These men had all made their choices, Frantz seems to say, and their subsequent fates were thus of their own design. Every person was destined to sin; to seek or to bestow mercy was a choice. As the widowed father of four persevered in the odious occupation chosen for him – and in his slow but relentless campaign to achieve a status he had chosen for himself – this thought must have offered some reassurance and comfort.

THE HEALER

This policy and reverence of age makes the world bitter to the best of our times; keeps our fortunes from us till our oldness cannot relish them. I begin to find an idle and fond bondage in the oppression of aged tyranny; who sways, not as it hath power, but as it is suffered.

—William Shakespeare, *King Lear*, act 1, scene 2, 46–51 (1606)

The word virtue, I think, presupposes difficulty and struggle, and something that cannot be practised without an adversary. This is perhaps why we call God good, mighty, liberal, and just, but do not call Him virtuous.

—Michel de Montaigne, "On Cruelty" (1580)[1]

Over nearly half a century as an executioner, Meister Frantz Schmidt confronted a bewildering array of human vice and cruelty. Yet in all that time, no culprits provoked a more primal revulsion in Meister Frantz than the sociopathic highwayman Georg Hörnlein of Bruck and his equally depraved henchman Jobst Knau of Bamberg. The executioner's meticulous recounting of their myriad offences – a mere sampling by his own acknowledgement – constitutes the single longest entry in his journal. In the company of other unsavoury associates, most frequently Georg Mayer (aka Brains) from Gostenhof, Hörnlein and Knau roamed the back roads and forests of Franconia for years, assaulting, robbing, and brutally murdering scores of pedlars, wandering journeymen, farmers, and other travellers, including women and youths. After itemising more than a dozen known examples of their perfidy,

Meister Frantz prepares to end the day's entry. But then – we can al-most see him shake his head in exasperation – he changes his mind and goes on to record still more damning examples of the duo's infamy, in-cluding that *they attacked people on the Mögeldorfer meadow and every-where that citizens went for walks . . . as well as attacked eight people on the streets of Heroldsberg, severely wounding a man and a woman and chopping the hand of a carter in two.*

His disgust almost palpable, Schmidt continues with a blow-by-blow account of what he obviously considers to be the most disturbing inci-dents of the robbers' long rampage:

Six weeks ago [Hörnlein] and Knau, together with their compan-ions, were consorting with a common whore, when she gave birth to a son in [Hörnlein's] house, whereupon Knau baptised it, then cut off its little right hand while alive. Afterwards his companion, called Blacky, who acted as godfather, tossed the baby in the air, so that it fell upon the table, and said, "So big must my little godchild grow!" Also exclaimed, "See how the devil runs his trap!" then cut its throat and buried it in his little garden. Over eight days later, when Knau's whore bore a baby boy, Knau wrung its little neck, then Hörnlein cut off its little right hand and later buried it in his shed.

The sheer horror of both moments comes through in Schmidt's writ-ing, as he contrasts the diminutive terms *baby, little neck,* and *little right hand* with the drunken men's cold-blooded mockery of baptism and godfatherly affection. For Frantz, the incident epitomises the pair's utter depravity, and he recalls with undisguised satisfaction the two burning nips that each man received on his arms and legs before suffer-ing a painful execution on the wheel "from the bottom up" on 2 January 1588. Nine days later he executed their accomplice Brains, also with the wheel, and a week after that, he dispatched Hörnlein's wife and ac-complice, Margaretha, employing the supposedly abolished *death with water*, revived one final time by the council – without protest from the executioner – for this especially heinous offence.[2]

But why were these men chopping off babies' hands in the first place? It was not a random atrocity. During Knau's interrogation, which involved repeated applications of the strappado under the supervision of Meister Frantz, the robber claimed that the right hand of a newborn male was widely known to bring good luck, even invisibility, a useful asset for a professional thief. He said that Hörnlein told him he had cut off many babies' hands during his travels and successfully used the "little fingers" as candles during break-ins, "so that no one awoke". (In England this practise was known as the Hand of Glory.)[3] Hörnlein confirmed this account in his own confession under torture, elabourating that the hands must stay buried for eight days, preferably in a stable, after which they may be dug up and carried. He admitted instructing Knau in this practise and giving him one of the hands for his own use, but professed only a modest expertise in any other of the "magical arts". When pressed further, however, Hörnlein conceded that one old woman taught him how to carry a small sack of lead and gunpowder to three successive Sunday masses and thereby gain magical power. He also acknowledged stealing a piece of rope "in broad daylight" from the gallows at a nearby town and carrying it around with his other talismans as protection against gunshot. Challenged by sceptical interrogators, Hörnlein retorted that he even got his two companions to shoot at each other as a test of the charm's power, and since neither was harmed, he won five gulden from each of them.[4]

Magical spells and curses were ubiquitous in Meister Frantz's world. His contemporaries energetically disputed the nature and efficacy of such powers (not to mention their source). But virtually no one challenged the essential mysteriousness of the natural world – and thus the possibility that with certain occult knowledge, human beings might be able to wield some sort of magical power. This fluid and often contradictory quality of pre-eighteenth-century popular beliefs about magic presented Meister Frantz with a predicament. In his sideline as a man of medicine, Schmidt could benefit by exploiting ancient magical beliefs about the "healing power" of the executioner and his equipment. And yet with the European witch craze at its height, a practitioner who bore even a tenuous link to magic faced undeniable danger as well. At once feared and respected – not unlike a powerful wise man or tribal shaman – Frantz was sought out (and well paid) for his healing expertise. But he also risked accusations of incompetence or dark magic from dissatisfied patients or any of his numerous and diverse competitors in a ruthless medical marketplace.

This ambiguous and vulnerable position was of course nothing new to Nuremberg's executioner. Just as he turned governmental demand for pious and responsible state killers to his personal advantage, Meister Frantz also exploited the healing aura surrounding his craft to further advance his quest for respectability – all the while artfully avoiding the wrath of zealous "witch finders" and jealous medical rivals alike. But medicine – as he revealed later in life – had always represented much more to the longtime executioner than a means to an end or a reliable source of supplemental income. Unlike the odious profession foisted upon him, *the doctoring art* was his true vocation. *Almost every person,* Frantz writes, *has an enduring inclination towards a certain thing by which he might earn his keep,* and for him, *Nature [herself] had implanted in me the desire to heal.*[5] More than his role in the redemptive ritual of the execution, his lifelong work in physical healing provided the executioner with a sense of accomplishment, purpose, even restoration. His struggle to secure this professional identity for himself and his sons would in fact shape the final three decades of his life. Whether Meister Frantz's own painstakingly constructed and formidable reputation as an executioner would aid or hinder that final self-fashioning remained to be seen.

Live bodies

All premodern executioners were presumed to possess a certain amount of medical expertise. Some were even appointed to their posts explicitly because of their reputed skills in healing people or animals, typically cows and horses. Nuremberg's magistrates rehired one of Frantz's notoriously dissolute predecessors less than a year after angrily dismissing him expressly "because his doctoring greatly helped many injured and sick people to recover, and since Jörg Unger, the current executioner, is absolutely worthless [in that respect]."[6] In the day of Frantz Schmidt's father, medical consulting had constituted a minor supplement to the salary of most executioners. By the time Frantz himself became professionally

active, fees for healing might constitute as much as half of an executioner's annual income.[7] Following his official retirement in 1618,
Schmidt would become almost completely reliant on earnings from his
medical work, which continued to flourish until his death, several years
later.

The varied and sometimes shadowy array of medical and quasi-
medical services available in the premodern world represented market
competition at its unregulated finest. Academically trained physicians
boasted the highest level of official certification, but their small
numbers and high fees made them inaccessible to the majority of
the population. Guild-trained barber-surgeons, "wound doctors", and
apothecaries enjoyed a similar aura of respectability and were at least
ten times more prevalent than academic physicians in large cities such
as Nuremberg.[8] Typically, these professionals trained as apprentices and
journeymen several years longer than physicians studied at university.
By the late sixteenth century, virtually every German state employed its
own official physicians and barber-surgeons as well as apothecaries and
midwives, imbuing each profession with still greater legitimacy and
credibility.

Of course, institutional endorsements of this nature did not prevent most people from turning to any of a variety of non-sanctioned
"empirics" – pedlars, travelling apothecaries, oculists, Gypsies, and
religious healers – each hawking an assortment of curative powders,
compounds, ointments, and herbs. Physicians of the seventeenth and
eighteenth centuries routinely derided the healing abilities of such
"quacks" and "charlatans", but at least some of these roving practitioners
offered remedies that actually provided relief in certain cases. Sulphur
salves did occasionally clear up skin conditions, and certain herbal con-
coctions did manage to soothe some aching backs. Obviously, the more
sweeping and outlandish claims of itinerant healers were sheer hokum.
But at least these travelling quacks advertised their wares with humour-
ous songs, diverting theatrics, and even the occasional snake-handling
show (to promote a tonic that provided immunity from any bites).

The healing reputation of Meister Frantz lacked any official backing
or carnivalesque promotions, but it unquestionably benefited from the
many folk beliefs surrounding his nefarious profession. Like the "cunning" men and women found in practically every village, executioners

allegedly knew secret recipes and cures for a variety of ailments –
ranging from cancer and kidney failure to toothaches and insomnia –
information typically passed down orally to their young acolytes. The
controversial physician Paracelsus (1493–1541), who publicly rejected
most of what he'd been taught in medical school, famously claimed that
he learned the bulk of his healing remedies and techniques from executioners and cunning people. The Hamburg executioner Meister Valentin Matz was widely reputed "to know herbs and sympathy [healing]
better than many learned doctors."9 Whatever the efficacy of an executioner's treatments, the "sinister charisma" of Frantz and his fellow
practitioners gave them an invaluable advantage in the highly competitive (and highly lucrative) medical marketplace of the day. Sons of executioners frequently profited from the association as well, and were able
to operate prosperous medical practises even if they did not follow their
fathers into the execution profession. Many widows and wives of executioners also did medical work, sometimes competing for patients with
local midwives.10

But how much did Meister Frantz truly know about the art of healing, and where did he learn it? Meister Heinrich certainly would have
taught his son all that he could. But, having grown up as the son of an
honourable tailor, Heinrich would have had to learn the healing arts on
the job, as it were. Once the Schmidts had been accepted into the profession, other executioners probably shared some of their secrets, knowing that direct competition from a geographically distant colleague was
unlikely. The many criminals and vagrants Heinrich and Frantz encountered during their work provided another fecund source of information, often including magical incantations, but this type of healing
ventured into risky territory.

The most valuable resources for a literate executioner were probably
the numerous medical pamphlets and other reference works that
flooded the print marketplace from the early sixteenth century on.11
University-trained physicians just a few generations later would have
been scandalised by the do-it-yourself approach of most popular medical manuals in Frantz Schmidt's day. More shocking still, in many instances the popularisers were themselves members of the medical elite.
The respected physician Johann Weyer (1515–88), today famous as an
early vocal opponent of the witch craze, was better known to fellow

healers of his era for his *Doctoring Book: On Assorted Previously Unknown and Undescribed Illnesses*, which covered treatment for conditions ranging from typhus and syphilis (hardly "unknown" in 1583) to "night attacks" and diarrhoea.[12] Weyer assumed his readers had little or no professional training and describes symptoms and cures in clear, specific, and jargon-free language, supplemented by illustrations of the relevant herbs, medicinal insects, and toads. He also sprinkles biblical references throughout the text, as did most popular authors of the era, beginning with an opening reminder that suffering and illness themselves were the result of Adam and Eve's original fall from grace.

Hans von Gersdorff's *Fieldbook of Wound-Healing*, reprinted several times after its initial 1517 publication, was an even more likely resource for Meister Frantz.[13] Based on the author's extensive experience as a military wound doctor, the 224-page compendium is practically a medical education in itself, beginning with a discussion of the respective roles in health of the four humours, the elements, and the planets, and then offering a step-by-step guide to diagnosing symptoms and applying treatments. Though Gersdorff focused more on external wounds, he also described basic human anatomy, and included several carefully marked illustrations. Like Weyer and other popular authors, he provided illustrations of herbs as well as schematics that show the reader how to construct scalpels, cranial drills, braces for broken limbs, clamps, and even a still. Just as crucially for any non-academically trained healer, the *Fieldbook* included an extensive glossary of Latin medical terms and their German translations, as well as a thorough alphabetical index of symptoms, body parts, and treatments.

In accounting for Meister Frantz's medical success, we should not underestimate the sheer value of listening to patients.[14] A reassuring air of self-confidence and other interpersonal skills could go a long way, particularly since conversation constituted a much more important component of the early modern medical consultation than did physical examination. In the words of one popular manual, "A good case history is already half of the diagnosis."[15] Learning about a patient's occupation, family members, diet, sleeping habits, and more would be useful for any practitioner, but especially for executioners and other folk healers, who could draw on neither the official certification of physicians and barber-surgeons nor the entertaining showmanship of travelling empirics. Meister Frantz could succeed only by painstakingly building up a broad base of loyal patients who felt that he understood them and their ailments. The famed "executioner's touch" may have got some patients through the door, but given the abundance of healing alternatives

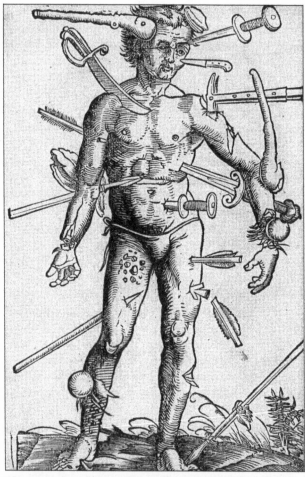

The much-reprinted "wound man" illustration from Hans von Gersdorff's *Fieldbook*, indicating the variety of human-inflicted injuries that executioners and barber-surgeons regularly treated (1517).

available, it would not have kept them coming back had not some successful healing actually occurred.

Genuine skill was especially essential in the executioner's traditional sphere of medical activity, namely "external treatments" such as resetting broken bones, treating severe burns, cauterising the bleeding from amputated limbs, and healing open sores or gunshot wounds. More than a third of the wounds treated by wound doctors and executioners resulted from attacks with knives, swords, or guns.[16] These were areas of demonstrable expertise for Frantz, since his years of work in the torture chamber gave him extensive experience in how to avoid severely wounding subjects during interrogation as well as how to heal them before questioning or public execution. Frantz apparently received no supplemental fee for his work healing prisoners, but some of his fellow executioners earned three or four times as much for healing a criminal suspect as they did for the torture they had just administered.[17]

Schmidt's medical ledgers have not survived. But by his own estimate, in nearly fifty years of medical practise he treated more than fifteen thousand patients in Nuremberg and its surrounding territories.[18] Even accounting for some hyperbole as well as the occasional double-counting (Frantz was never good with numbers), this is a remarkable figure. It means that Meister Frantz saw on average more than three hundred patients a year – at least ten times as many individuals as he tortured or punished. Did this knowledge offer him consolation for the agonies that he intentionally inflicted? Did these nearly daily medical experiences reinforce his already deep compassion for the suffering of crime victims? Undoubtedly his widespread reputation as a successful healer helped mitigate the disdain normally reserved for executioners. But it was not enough in itself to make him or his family honourable.

In this context, the selective way that people of the era interpreted the effect of the executioner's touch appears especially mystifying and capriciously cruel to modern sensibilities. The very individuals who refused to share a table or drink with the publicly reviled executioner, much less allow him into their homes, apparently had no qualms about visiting Frantz in the Hangman's House and allowing him to lay hands on them there.[19] The privacy of such encounters in part accounts for the double standard, but there was apparently no secrecy or shame involved in consulting Meister Frantz for medical reasons. Admittedly,

A wound doctor performs an amputation on an inebriated but still conscious patient. Wound doctors and barber-surgeons constituted Frantz's main competition in the medical marketplace (*c.*1550).

given the nature of his healing expertise, the majority of his patients were soldiers, manual labourers, and farmers. Respectable artisans, however, also consulted him on a regular basis, as did patricians and even some nobles, among them three imperial emissaries, the cathedral provost of Bamberg, and a Teutonic knight, as well as several patrician city councillors and their family members.[20] The steady flow of individuals from all ranks of society into the Hangman's House clearly gives the lie to any absolute marginalisation of the executioner and his family.

On the other hand, this regular contact with people who shunned them in public must have made the Schmidts' unique limbo-like social status even more difficult to bear.

Treating external wounds was also the provenance of barber-surgeons, and this predictably led to frequent disputes between them and executioners, conflicts that usually resulted in governmental intervention. Here too, Frantz's success at building both his personal and professional reputations appears to have staved off the wrath of competitors and the city council alike. He was never once censored by his superiors on this score, and in 1601 they actually referred one man, who complained about a local barber's unsatisfactory healing of his seven-year-old son's right knee, not to the municipal physicians but to Meister Frantz.[21] Eight years later, the barber Hans Duebelius claimed that because Meister Frantz had previously treated an injured innkeeper, the barber guild would consider him dishonourable if he attempted to cure the same man. Councillors reassured Duebelius that he could proceed without fear of contamination, but they also declined to reprimand the executioner for his own medical activity.[22] It's unlikely that Nuremberg's barber-surgeons embraced Frantz as a fellow professional, but neither did they openly challenge either his skills or his obvious clout with the magistracy.

Another potential threat to Frantz's medical success was the rapid ascendancy during his lifetime of the academically trained physician. These professional healers had long occupied the top rung in terms of both prestige and income, but their numbers remained small. Nevertheless, from the late sixteenth century on, they began to assert a new dominance in the medical marketplace. First, they consolidated in German cities, forming quasi-governmental bodies, such as Nuremberg's Collegium Medicum, established in 1592 under the leadership of Dr. Joachim Camerarius. At the same time, physicians convinced secular authorities that the diverse and often "ignorant" methods of "practical healers" – even including guild-certified barbers, apothecaries, and midwives – required closer regulation and supervision. In Nuremberg this meant more restrictions for licensed practitioners and large fines, possibly even banishment, for amateur "tooth breakers", alchemists, wise women, Jews, black magicians, and other empirics.[23]

Fortunately for Frantz Schmidt and his successors, the Collegium

Medicum did not assume oversight of their medical activity, but it did restrict them to treating external injuries, "about which they have some knowledge."[24] Meister Frantz also appears to have successfully avoided the open conflicts with physicians that were common among fellow executioners throughout the empire, including his immediate successors.[25] Surprisingly, Frantz's forensic work brought him into more direct and regular contact with these patrician professionals than with the artisanal barber-surgeons, who were much closer to him in training and expertise. Perhaps the respect Schmidt apparently enjoyed in official circles even encouraged him to daydream about one of his sons pursuing this noble – and as yet unreachable – profession. The day when such a social leap would be possible was closer than he imagined.

Dead bodies

Although much of Meister Frantz's work required him to engage with the living – prisoners, officials, patients, and the like – he also spent a significant amount of time with the dead or, to be more specific, with the cadavers of the poor sinners he had executed. Some of the bodies of those he dispatched received the same treatment as those of any other departed souls, including burial on consecrated ground.[26] The majority, however, met a less happy fate. The corpses of hanged thieves and murderers broken on the wheel of course remained exposed to the elements, their crumbled remains eventually swept into a pit under the gallows. Other cadavers were handed over to the executioner for dissection or other use. In no instance was the body of an executed criminal allowed to go to waste; it functioned instead as evidence of the court's mercy, a gruesome warning, or a useful medical object.

In premodern Europe it was commonly believed – by academic physicians and folk healers alike – that the bodies of the dead possessed tremendous curative powers. This led to a practise that strikes the modern sensibility as bizarre, even disturbing, but that enjoyed widespread acceptance in the era of Meister Frantz: namely the ingestion, wearing, or other medical use of human body parts to heal the sick or injured. Belief in the curative power of various types of human remains can be traced back at least to the time of Pliny the Elder

(A.D. 23–79) and would continue to thrive into the eighteenth century.[27] Despite this tradition's obvious affinity with magic, virtually all medical professionals of the day insisted that the practise had a firm foundation in natural philosophy and human anatomy itself. According to followers of Paracelsus, also known as chemical doctors, human skin, blood, and bones possessed the same healing powers as certain minerals and plants and transferred a curative spiritual force to the ill person. Classically trained Galenist physicians scoffed at such "magical" explanations, and instead insisted that body parts healed the sick by restoring the internal balance of the four humours (blood, phlegm, black bile, and yellow bile). Virtually no healer, formally trained or not, disputed the received wisdom that a recently deceased human body provided a panoply of curative supplies.

Drinking blood, "the noblest of the humours", was considered an especially potent remedy with many uses, among them dissolving blood clots, protecting a patient from painful spleen or coughing, preventing seizures, opening up blocked menstruation, or even curing flatulence.[28] Since the medical establishment believed blood to be continuously concocted by the liver, its supply was also theoretically unlimited, thus diminishing any concern over frequent bloodletting, or phlebotomy, intended to restore the humoural balance. Because age and virility determined the potency of the fluid, the blood of suddenly executed young criminals, whose life force had not yet had a chance to escape, was especially prised. Epileptics, eager to drink the warm and fresh poor sinner's blood, frequently lined up next to the scaffold following a beheading – an alarming scene for us to envision, yet an unremarkable one for Frantz Schmidt and his contemporaries.

Before the mid-seventeenth century, Meister Frantz and his fellow executioners enjoyed a near monopoly on the various human body parts used for popular healing. Many of them ran side businesses supplying apothecaries and other eager customers. The official pharmacopoeia of Nuremberg, stocked largely by the cadavers of executed criminals, included whole and prepared skulls, "human grains" (from ground bones), "marinated human flesh", human fat, salt from human grains, and spirit of human bone (a potion derived from boiling bones). Pregnant women and people suffering from swollen joints or cramps wore specially treated strips of human skin, known as human leather or poor sinners' fat. The healing power of mummy, as preserved human flesh was generically known, even became the focus of a new devotional mysticism devised by the Jesuit Bernard Caesius (1599–1630). There is no way to know how much additional revenue Frantz earned from the human parts trade or to what degree he even engaged in this to-our-eyes ghoulish but lucrative practise.[29]

Inevitably, some healers of the era also promoted various explicitly magical uses for human body parts. One fellow executioner's recipe for treating a bewitched horse called for a powder made out of certain herbs, cow fat, vinegar, and burnt human flesh – all mixed with a shaved stick found on a river's bank before sunset.[30] Academically trained Protestant physicians, eager to debunk Catholic belief in the power of saints' relics, vociferously denied that human body parts had any such supernatural power. They accordingly dismissed as superstition such uncomfortably akin beliefs as the popular claim that the finger or hand of an executed thief would bring good luck in gambling or, if consumed by a cow, provide protection against witchcraft. Catholic authorities in Bavaria similarly professed shock "that many people dare to take things from executed criminals, and seize the chains from the gallows where the criminal was hanged . . . as well as the rope . . . to employ in certain arts," and forbade the use of any such object "to which superstition attributes another effect than it can have naturally."[31] Church leaders of both denominations were even more alarmed by some executioners' attempts to cash in on their magical notoriety. In 1611, for example, Frantz's counterpart in the Bavarian city of Passau began a long-running and especially lucrative practise by selling little folded pieces of magically inscribed paper, known as *Passauer Zettel*, which were reputed to protect the bearer from bullets.

A much more familiar (and still current) use for the cadavers at Meister Frantz's disposal was dissection for anatomical studies.[32] Artists such as Leonardo da Vinci and Michelangelo had long before requested the bodies of the executioner's victims for this purpose – decreed permissible by Pope Sixtus IV in 1482 – but the medical interest in dissection did not really take off until the publication of Andreas Vesalius's remarkable drawings in *De Humani Corporis Fabrica* (Concerning the Construction of the Human Body; 1543). Accompanied by detailed commentary, the twenty-eight-year-old physician's graceful illustrations of skeletal, nervous, muscular, and visceral systems stunned the medical establishment. Almost immediately, medical faculties across Europe began to devote lectures and endowed chairs to the study of human anatomy, convinced by the observations of Vesalius and other pioneers that much of what they had previously taught – received knowledge

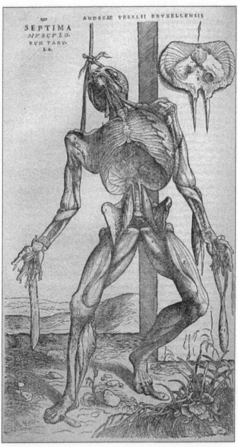

The human muscular system, one of almost two hundred detailed illustrations from Vesalius's 1543 *De Humani Corporis Fabrica*. Note that even the celebrated expert uses a recently hanged criminal as his model.

that dated back to the second-century Greek physician Galen – was inadequate or outright wrong. A century later, eleven German universities, including Altdorf near Nuremberg, boasted their own anatomical theatres, and the practise of medical dissection was ubiquitous.[33]

Demand for the corpses of executed criminals accordingly rose steadily over the course of Meister Frantz's lifetime. By the early seventeenth century, the trade in human cadavers and body parts had reached a feverish pitch. Shortly after Meister Frantz's death, the citizenry and councillors of Munich were scandalised to learn that their appropriately named executioner, Martin Leichnam ("cadaver"), before handing over the corpse of a beheaded child murderer to her parents for Christian burial, had first sold off various body parts, including her heart, which was ground into a curative powder.[34] Medical students from the University of Altdorf apparently always asked Frantz or his successors for permission before taking away executed bodies, but their less scrupulous peers elsewhere frequently staged unauthorised midnight raids of cemeteries and execution grounds. The most infamous body snatcher in the empire was undoubtedly Professor Werner Rolfinck (1599–1673), whose fondness for pilfering the local gallows led his medical students at the University of Jena to coin a new verb for the practise in his honour: "rolfincking".[35]

Meister Frantz's own keen interest in human dissection was uncommon among executioners and offers further evidence of his higher medical ambitions. Since 1548 the Nuremberg city council had restricted "the cutting up of poor executed victims" to a few physicians, and then "so long as only a few persons were present". Three years before Frantz Schmidt's arrival in Nuremberg, Dr. Volker Coiter was permitted to dissect two thieves and give the fat to the executioner for his medical supplies.[36] This traditional division of labour and body uses was probably what city magistrates had in mind when they granted the new executioner's request in July 1578 "to cut up beheaded bodies and take what is useful to him in his medical practise".[37] Yet in his journal's account of how he dealt with the body of beheaded robber Heinz Gorssn (aka Lazy Harry), twenty-four-year-old Frantz is careful to specify *I later dissected [the body]*.[38] Schmidt rarely used the first-person pronoun in his journal, so it seems clear that in this entry the young executioner wished to commemorate a significant personal achieve-ment. He explicitly records only three similar occasions – in 1581, 1584, and 1590 – and the last time clarifies his intentions with the phrase *dissected (adominirt)* or *cut up.* It could be assumed that Frantz had simply appropriated the more serious language of anatomy to de-scribe his own carvings, except that these are the same words he used when he handed over the body of the thief Michel Knüttel to the local physician Dr. Pessler for a full postmortem in 1594. His interest, in other words, was not merely in extracting usable body parts but in ex-ploring human anatomy itself – the same as with any other physician.[39]

Of course there were serious limitations to the discoveries an ama-teur anatomist might make, even one aided by popular versions of Vesa-lius's work and his own healing experience – not to mention a reliable

Volker Coiter (1534–76), municipal physician of Nurem-berg. Coiter, like his successor Joachim Camerarius the Younger (1534–98), was an anatomy enthusiast, at one point even temporarily banished from the city on account of grave robbing (1569).

supply of fresh cadavers. Frantz's curiosity about human anatomy was shaped by the time in which he lived, an era in which most laypeople were fascinated by oddities and anomalies but uninterested in – or unaware of – the possibility of organising their observations into any kind of theoretical system, a pursuit that was left to natural philosophers and theologians. His methodical observation of his victims' bodies, like his interest in their character, also does not surface in the journal until the second half of his life. In his early years, for example, Frantz might note that two brothers and their companion were *three strong young thieves* or note in passing that an executed robber only *has one hand*.[40] We also learn that the barber Balthasar Scherl *was a small person, had a hump in the front and back* and that the beggar Elisabeth Rossnerin *had a crooked neck*.[41] Years later, he writes with an earnest amateur's precision that the beheaded thief Georg Praun (aka Pin George) *had a neck two spans long and two handsbreadth thick [approximately nineteen by eight inches]*, that Laurenz Demer (aka the Long Farmer) *was two fingers less than three Ells in height [i.e., about 7' 4"]*, and that the flogged Simon Starck *has 92 pockmarks* – all facts that could only have been ascertained by his own punctilious postmortem examination.[42] The only time that Meister Frantz's air of scientific dispassion eluded him was following the decapitation of thief Georg Praun, *when his head turned several times [on the stone] as if it wanted to look about it, the tongue moved and the mouth opened as if he wanted to speak, for a good quarter of an hour. I have never seen the likes of this.*[43] Like most early modern chroniclers, the astonished executioner does not offer an explanation, only a wonder worthy of recording.

Black magic

The healing expertise of executioners, as well as their conversancy with the illicit practises of the criminal underworld, lent the profession an aura of authority on the subject of the dark arts. In popular folklore, executioners and their magical swords (drenched in the blood of recently executed young men) could prevail against vampires and werewolves as well as summon spirits of the dead or exorcise ghosts from houses. In one typical folktale of the day, the persistence of an especially vexing house ghost prompts a showdown between a Jesuit exorcist and an executioner, with the latter ultimately claiming victory by trapping the troublesome spirit in a sack and later releasing it into a forest. Dramatic performances of this sort appear but once in the chronicles of sixteenth-century Nuremberg, in 1583, with Frantz a mere spectator to an officially sanctioned demonic exorcism by a Lutheran cleric.[44]

Of course, in the frenzied atmosphere of the pan-European witch craze of approximately 1550 to 1650, any association with magic – even medicinal – could prove quite dangerous. Many people presumed executioners themselves to be "secret sorcerers" and "witch masters", particularly during the peak witch-panic years of the early seventeenth century, when all magical practises came under suspicion of diabolical origin. Though ultimately vindicated, Frantz's Munich counterpart never fully recovered from his 1612 imprisonment for illicit magic (based on evidence brought to the courts by a Jesuit accuser). Even Schmidt's own successor would be admonished for his involvement in "magical business" and threatened with banishment "or worse" should the council learn that he had made any contact with "the evil spirit", Other professionals were less fortunate, most notably the widow of a later Nuremberg Lion, who was convicted and burned alive for witchcraft in the city's only case involving an alleged diabolical pact and sex with the devil.[45]

More typically, professional executioners in Meister Frantz's day served as the indispensable allies of self-proclaimed witch finders. Johann Georg Abriel, Frantz's counterpart in Schongau, and Christoph Hiert of Biberach were themselves highly sought-out experts in finding the so-called witch's mark, and helped to advance many witch hunts in Bavaria and Upper Swabia during the 1590s. Other executioners played similarly pivotal roles in producing confessions under torture and spreading the panic. Southern Germany in fact saw more executions for witchcraft than any other region in Europe – perhaps 40 per cent of the grand total of sixty thousand – and Franconia in particular was ground zero of the witch craze, most infamously as site of the Bamberg and Würzburg panics of 1626–31 that resulted in the executions of more than two thousand people.[46]

In this respect, Frantz and his city represented an oasis of restraint amid the enveloping madness. Until the late sixteenth century, Nurem-berg had witnessed only one execution for magic ever, and that was more properly a case of accidental poisoning by what was intended to be a love potion, nearly six decades before Frantz Schmidt's arrival.[47] By July 1590, though, even the city on the Pegnitz began to show some vulnerability to the hysteria sweeping the region. The city council re-acted swiftly, but in contrast to the leaders of other territories, by ar-resting and imprisoning Friedrich Stigler, a banished Nuremberger and former executioner's assistant in Eichstätt, *for having brought accusa-tions against some citizens' wives here that they were witches and he knew it by their signs . . . also said that they gave magic spells to people.*[48]

Stigler, who boasted considerable expertise from his work with Frantz's counterpart in Eichstätt, claimed to have identified eleven witches just on the street where he resided, specifically five older women and six "apprentice girls". During his interrogation, which in-cluded a session on the strappado under Meister Frantz, the newly ar-rived witch-hunt veteran claimed that he had initially rebuffed all local citizens' appeals for help in detecting witches in Nuremberg, demurring that the city "had its own executioner" for such matters. If this remark was intended to incriminate Frantz Schmidt for being soft on witches, it had the opposite effect on his loyal employers, who likewise regarded all allegations of witchcraft with deep scepticism. Undaunted, Stigler next told how he was finally persuaded by the unrelenting petitioners to share his anti-witchcraft expertise, which he did by selling them small bags of blessed salt, bread, and wax for one ort (¼ fl.) each. According to Stigler, the bags, which he had been taught to make by his execu-tioner master at Abensberg, both protected one from witches and could be used to find the devil's spot on a witch, which – as everyone knew – was impervious to the pain of a needle prick.[49]

The presiding magistrates gave no credence whatsoever to Stigler's "false accusations . . . made out of pure, brazen, wantonness", and showed more concern over his own familiarity with magic, not to men-tion his three wives. More than anything, it was their determination to prevent a local panic that ultimately led them to pronounce a death sentence for the "godless" Stigler, "on account of having given rise to all kinds of unrest, false suspicion, and strife among the citizenry as well as various superstitious, godless spells and conspiracies and other

The burning alive of three accused witches in Baden. The pan-European witch craze coincided almost exactly with Frantz Schmidt's lifetime (1574).

forbidden magical arts and methods elsewhere".[50] On 28 July 1590, he was *out of mercy* beheaded by Meister Frantz.[51]

The Nuremberg government's decisive response to its first serious encounter with witch paranoia received the full support of its executioner. Given the popular association of executioners with the dark arts, Frantz Schmidt had special motivation to see such a disreputable fellow professional punished. That Stigler *wittingly did [the accused women] wrong* earned him still more disdain from the slander-sensitive Meister Frantz. Above all, Nuremberg's executioner appears to have shared the wariness of his superiors towards witch accusations in general, as well as their profound fear of the disorder and lawlessness that inevitably ensued. He followed with amazement, and no doubt disgust, the mass trials and burnings in the Franconian countryside where he had travelled as a journeyman. Like Stigler, Frantz knew from his experience in Bamberg about the methods of witch finders as well as the genuine danger of coerced confessions at the hands of a skilled torturer. The pivotal role of the professional executioner in such spurious proceedings must have been for him a source of discomfort, perhaps even shame.

Over the next two decades, Nuremberg's magistrates continued to fervidly resist the panics seizing neighbouring territories. Less than eighteen months after Stigler's execution, the tortured confession of a suspected witch in the neighbouring margravate of Ansbach led to the arrest of two women from villages in Nuremberg's jurisdiction. After a painstaking investigation of the charges involved in both cases, Nuremberg's jurists found insufficient justification for torture and recommended dismissal of charges. Upon receiving Meister Frantz's further assessment that both women were of too advanced an age to withstand physical coercion anyway, the city council ordered both women released. The following year, when officials of the margravate learned of the covered-up suicide of an alleged witch in Fürth (admittedly within their legal jurisdiction), they not only demanded that her body be exhumed and burned, but also that all her family's property be confiscated. Once more eager to avoid triggering a panic, Nuremberg's jurists countered that neither the charges against her nor the nature of her death could be definitively established, and thus continued to back the aggrieved widower and his son during several additional legal assaults from the margravate. In subsequent years, the council released three Altdorf men after confiscating their "magical books and decks of cards" and summarily dismissed two old women accused separately of employing magical healing. Only the convicted perjurer Hans Rössner, who repeated Friedrich Stigler's mistake of spreading false rumours and accusations of witchcraft, received punishment, although unlike his doomed predecessor he escaped with time in the stocks and lifelong banishment (under threat of execution, should he return).[52]

Neither Meister Frantz nor his superiors denied the efficacy of magic per se, but they focused instead on whether it had been used in conjunction with any harmful deeds, known as *maleficia*. Schmidt impassively notes that Georg Karl Lambrecht, the last poor sinner he executed, *also occupied himself with magic spells,* but since no *maleficia* were established, it was not one of the crimes mentioned in his official verdict.[53] He considers it relevant that Kunrad Zwickelsperger, who *committed lewdness* with the married Barbara Wagnerin, *gave two fl. to an old sorceress that she might cause [Wagnerin's husband] to be stabbed, struck down, or drowned,* but Zwickelsperger's ultimate condemnation is based on the more pertinent evidence that he also convinced his lover to poison her husband repeatedly (as well as that he slept with her mother and three sisters).[54] Often Frantz mentions "magical" curses to establish character and motive for subsequent violent action: a young knacker who publicly *bewitches* his treacherous former companion *so that he would immediately die*; or a village bully who threatens his neighbours that *he would burn their house down [and afterwards] cut off their hands and hide them in his breast.*[55] Anticipating the conclusions of historical anthropologists centuries later, Frantz recognised that such curses and threats often represented the empty bluffs of the powerless. When the arrested thief Anna Pergmennin threatened *that she would fly off next to an old broom-maker hag on a pitchfork,* Schmidt adds sardonically, *but nothing happened.*[56] His apparent openness to the possibility that something might have happened distinguishes his scepticism from ours, but his steadfast imperviousness to witch hysteria matches our own.

The similarity of Frantz Schmidt's outlook to that of contemporary physician Johann Weyer suggests that the executioner was familiar with the latter's *De Praestigiis Daemonarum* (On the Illusions of Demons; first German edition in 1567), either indirectly or through his own reading. The most famous (and consequently vilified) early opponent of the witch craze, Weyer likewise refused to rule out the efficacy of magic, but simultaneously argued that the great majority of self-proclaimed witches were either self-deluded or outright frauds. The remainder were intentional poisoners – a capital crime sufficient unto itself. Like their contemporary Michel de Montaigne, Weyer and Meister Frantz showed acute awareness of the power that emotions could exert on the human imagination, both in the case of alleged victims and alleged perpetrators.

Certainly Meister Frantz recognised the genuine psychological agony of some poor sinners who came before him and had convinced themselves of inescapable diabolical entanglements. During his imprisonment in the Hole, the thief Georg Prückner *claimed that he had received from the night watchman at Kreinberg something against wounds which he must eat – having sworn in return, however, never again to think of God nor pray to Him – which he did and gave himself to the devil. He tried to break out of the Hole and indeed behaved wantonly, as if the evil spirit tormented him.* The executioner's judicious *and indeed . . . as if* succinctly conveys his simultaneous acknowledgement of a diabolical power and his own conviction that Prückner was in fact delusional. Neither Frantz nor his chaplain colleague, Magister Müller – who complained of being kept awake at night two roads away in the Saint Sebaldus parsonage because of Prückner's loud ravings – treated the tormented soul as an actual disciple of Satan, and indeed agreed that he *behaved in a Christian manner [in the end].*[57] Schmidt believed, in other words, that the temptations of a spiritual devil could prey on a weak mind, even if witches' sabbaths and other physical encounters remained pure fantasy. Another disturbed inmate, the thief Lienhard Schwartz, unsuccessfully tried to kill himself in prison, first with a knife and later by hanging with his torn shirt, saying *a voice spoke to him, though he saw nobody, telling him that if he surrendered to him he would soon help him.* Meister Frantz pointedly adds, *at this he fell into repentance, but if the voice had called again it might have happened [otherwise].*[58] On the source or reality of the voice, the executioner remains mute.

Any residual awe of so-called dark magic from his younger days was effectively demolished by Frantz Schmidt's lengthy experience in the torture chamber. He knew intimately of the persistence of countless spurious beliefs among professional criminals, despite not a single example of efficacy. Attempts to acquire invisibility or protection through severed body parts, pieces of the gallows, or other talismans were invariably presented in his journal as evidence of pathetic gullibility. Like disreputable companions and confiscated burglary tools, magical charms could also provide evidence of illicit activities and intentions. During one interrogation, the incorrigible honey thief Peter Hoffman claimed repeatedly that the skull and bones found on him during his arrest were not intended for nefarious purposes, but rather as a means of healing epileptics. (He also denied magically transporting his estranged female companion across great distances, but eventually acknowledged that he had appropriated her undergarments in a failed attempt at love magic designed to bring her back to him.) Schmidt notably declines to make use of such harmless "incantations and conjurations" to further blacken Hoffman's name in his journal, instead mentioning only his multiple thefts and adultery.[59] Even the notorious Georg Karl Lambrecht, pushed hard to admit that "he is himself a true sorcerer and conjurer of devils . . . addicted to the diabolical arts," in the end owns only to buying a charm and some enchanted slips of paper to protect himself against gunshot. Moreover, after having tested one "magically protective" skull on a dog (which promptly died from multiple bullet wounds), he concludes that "the deeds and boasts of these vagabonds were all pretended and imagined [and] he did not desire to have anything further to do with them" – a conclusion his executioner had apparently reached long ago.[60]

The great majority of the so-called magical experts that Meister Frantz Schmidt encountered during his career could be classified quite simply as frauds. He whips out of town Cunz Hoffmann, who *claimed to be a planet reader [i.e. astrologer] and palm reader*, as well as four divining Gypsies, and *the fortune-telling and treasure-finding* Anna Domiririn, who *in one day [obtained] about 60 fl. and five golden rings from Frau Michaela Schmiedin*. Like many travelling folk, the thief and card sharp Hans Meller supplemented his income with occasional commerce in magical objects: among other practises, he was convicted of coating yellow turnips in fat, sticking hair on them, and selling them as mandrakes for healing purposes.[61] The procuress Ursula Grimin (aka Blue) *said she was a cunning woman and could tell which man carried a child*, informing a customer that if he wanted to avoid an unwanted pregnancy, *he had to shove quickly into only her maid; otherwise he had to wait with his paramour until [Grimin] said, "Let's see what my little lamb chop or baby is doing," whereupon she stood before the men, uncovered herself, and said, "Hurrah cunt, gobble up the man."* Frantz's amusement over the gullibility of Grimin's clients is surpassed only by his obvious enjoyment of the relatively innocent fraud of a young shepherd at Weyer, *who for two years pretended to be a ghost in a house, tugging on the people's heads, hair, and feet while they slept, so that he could secretly lie with the farmer's daughter.*[62]

The most shameless – and successful – magical fraud Schmidt

encountered during his executioner days was undoubtedly the one-legged seamstress Elisabeth Aurholtin of Vilseck, who called herself the Digger. Claiming to be "a golden Sunday child", she amassed a fortune of over 4,000 fl. by convincing people of all ranks that she had the ability to locate hidden treasures and liberate them from the dragons, snakes, or dogs who guarded them.[63] The key to her success, in her executioner's assessment, lay not in the *devilish incantations and ceremonies [she employed]* – all ineffectual gibberish – but rather in her evident gift for making the most far-fetched stories sound credible. After listening to her tale of a sunken underwater castle and its iron chest full of treasure, three initially sceptical men spent an entire day digging for a white adder, with which "she would charm the treasure so that it would float on the water." Others wandered the countryside for days with her and her divining rod, apparently undaunted by their persistent lack of success and ready to pay still more for her special services.

Meister Frantz cannot suppress a hint of amazement at the sheer audacity of this gifted con artist or the gullibility of her greedy victims. He describes her most successful scheme in exceptional detail:

This was how she carried out her tricks. When she came into a house and wanted to cheat someone, she used to fall down as if she were ill or in convulsions, claiming afterwards that she had a wise vein hidden in her leg, whereby she could foretell and reveal future events and discover hidden treasures, and that when she entered a house her veins never left her in peace until she announced these things. Also that the realms of earth were opened out before her, and that she saw therein gold and silver, as if looking into a fire. If any doubted, she asked leave to spend the night in the house, so that she could speak with the spirit of the treasure. When this happened, she behaved at night – with her whisperings, questions, and answers – as if someone were speaking to her, and claimed afterwards that it was a poor lost soul in the house that could not enter into bliss until the treasure was dug up. Thus the people let themselves be persuaded by her, believing such tales because of the terrible incantations and assurances which she used, and caused the ground to be dug up. During this digging she would slip a pot full

of coals into the hole and claim that she had dug it up herself.
Then she commanded them to lock it up in a chest for three weeks
and not touch it, and that it would turn to gold when she recovered
it, [but] the coals remained coals.

Predictably, Schmidt is most shocked by Aurholtin's fearless defiance of
the prescribed social hierarchy. She defrauds many well-to-do individuals and even convinces one noble to house her and her small daughter,
and two others to serve as the child's baptismal sponsors. On other occasions she cheekily invokes one of Nuremberg's patrician leaders as a
business reference, claiming to *have drawn a fountain of gold for Mas-*
ter Endres Imhoff out of his yard and had dug up a golden treasure, noth-
ing less than idols of pure gold. Meister Frantz never once takes her
claims to supernatural powers seriously, but he remains in awe of her
prowess as a conjurer of tales.

An executioner's legacy

Until his late fifties, Meister Frantz showed few public signs of weariness in his duties. He travelled less often for work and apparently not at
all after 1611, but he continued to personally administer almost all floggings and other corporal punishments well past the age when most of
his fellow executioners handed over such physically demanding work to
their younger colleagues.[64] The first trace of decline came in February
1611 when he experienced his most dramatically miscarried execution
ever – requiring three strokes to decapitate the incestuous and adulterous Elisabeth Mechtlin. Spectators expressed shock at the fifty-seven-
year-old veteran's "shameful and very heinous" performance.[65] The
executioner's only written acknowledgement of this widely publicised
embarrassment was a single word at the end of the journal entry: *botched.*
The following year, a particularly reviled pimp and government informer
slipped from the executioner's grasp as he was being flogged out of
town and was subsequently stoned to death by an angry mob – resulting
in an official investigation and unprecedented scolding of the veteran
executioner.[66] Two additional botched executions followed, one later
that year on 17 December 1613, the other on 8 February 1614 – neither

of them noted as such in Frantz's journal. There were no apparent calls for the elderly executioner's retirement, however, and he went on to dispatch eighteen more poor sinners over the next thirty-four months.

What turned out to be Meister Frantz's final year on the job began unremarkably, with two successful beheadings and a few floggings. Then, during the night of 31 May, someone – more likely several people – tipped over the Nuremberg gallows.[67] Schmidt makes no mention of the occurrence in his journal, nor did he apparently assign it any significance, assuming it was merely an act of drunken vandalism. Less than a month later, however, he records a more unnerving event that took place during the hanging of rustler Lienhard Kertzenderfer (aka Cow Lenny) on 29 July 1617. According to one chronicler, the executioner's first attempt to mount the gallows was thwarted by "a sudden, stormy wind", which swept the two ladders from the gallows, so that they had to be retrieved and tied fast. Even then Meister Frantz and the *thoroughly besotted poor sinner* could hardly move forward amid the powerful gusts, which "roared and raged so terribly that it blew and threw people to and fro." But at the moment the condemned man, who had refused to pray, was finally dangling from the rope, "the wind calmed and the air became completely still." *Just then a hare came out of nowhere and ran under the gallows and through the crowd*, pursued by a dog "that no one recognised" (and that many spectators took for a demon pursuing the soul of the poor sinner). A shaken but more circumspect Meister Frantz demurred that *what kind of hare it was or what kind of end he had God knows best.*[68]

Seemingly undeterred by omens or by old age, Meister Frantz hanged three more thieves over the next five months and flogged two before coming to what would be the final execution of his career. The prescribed live burning of counterfeiter Georg Karl Lambrecht, on 13 November 1617, was a rare event for Nuremberg and only the second execution by this method that Frantz Schmidt had performed in more than four decades of service. Ever anxious to orchestrate the violence, Nuremberg's council ordered the executioner to speed the condemned man's death either by placing a sack of gunpowder around his neck or by strangling him first, "albeit unnoticed by the crowd".[69] Meister Frantz replied that he preferred strangulation since the gunpowder might either misfire or explode with such force as to endanger those nearby. As usual, the councillors deferred to his expertise, underscoring only that the strangulation had to be done in such a way "so that the crowd doesn't notice". Efficiency rather than mercy drove their decision; the spectators' terror of live burning needed to be preserved.

Lambrecht's execution should have been one of Schmidt's smoothest. During the previous five weeks, according to the prison chaplain, the poor sinner "had talked more with God than with humans", weeping and praying incessantly.[70] After making a full confession and receiving communion in his cell five days before his scheduled execution, Lambrecht had refused "to contaminate or stain his body with food or drink". His final procession was likewise exemplary, the poor sinner alternately praying aloud and asking those he passed for forgiveness. Most important to Meister Frantz, the condemned man made one final confession and plea for forgiveness before kneeling to recite a Paternoster and other prayers.

In the end, Frantz had decided to rely on both a gunpowder sack and secret strangulation, disregarding his own argument to the magistracy. Perhaps he had a premonition that the secret garrotting might fail, but he could not have anticipated that both measures would misfire, producing the agonising and spectacular failure that we witnessed at the book's outset. True to form, Schmidt does not implicate his Lion, Claus Kohler, for the bungled strangulation, either to his superiors or in his private journal. In a bit of deft revisionism, he in fact records the execution as a successful live burning, effectively denying any mishaps whatsoever. He also does not identify the execution as his last – contrary to later manuscript versions of the journal – and soldiers on, even personally administering a flogging three weeks later and another (his last) on 8 January 1618.

The final punctuation to a forty-five-year career was a decidedly anticlimactic affair. On 13 July 1618, the longtime sacristan Lienhard Paumaister reported to the city council that the venerable Meister Frantz was too infirm to carry out either of the two executions planned for the next week. Paumaister did not specify the nature of the illness, but Schmidt himself carefully annotates that it began nine days earlier. When asked to suggest a "competent person" to replace him "until he is returned to health", Frantz remained markedly non-committal, replying that he knew of no one to recommend but that "my lords" might make inquiries at nearby Ansbach or Regensburg. If the veteran executioner intended to keep his options open, these hopes were quickly quashed. Anxious to carry out the impending death sentences of a thief and a child murderer, his superiors acted in typically expedient fashion when a week later they received an unsolicited application from Bernhard Schlegel, the executioner of Amberg, a nearby provincial town. After a cursory look at Schlegel's credentials, they offered him 2½ fl. per week salary plus free lodging. The candidate immediately demanded, with a directness Nuremberg's councillors would come to know well, the same salary as Meister Frantz (3 fl. per week), plus a year's supply of wood and immediate possession of the Hangman's House. Still awaiting a response from Regensburg, the council agreed to Schlegel's terms and had him sworn in as a lifelong employee within two weeks of Meister Frantz's initial message. One week later the new executioner beheaded his first two victims on Nuremberg's Raven Stone.[71] The final entry in Frantz's journal of nearly a half century is typically succinct: *On 4 July [1618] I became ill and on St Laurence's Day [10 August] gave up my service, having held and exercised the office for forty years.*

The apparent ease of Frantz's retirement belies the onset of a power struggle between the old executioner and his replacement that would continue for years to come. The seemingly unsentimental indifference of Meister Frantz's superiors to his forty years of exemplary service likewise obscures their continuing deference to him in that contest, particularly as the favourable contrast to his successor became increasingly obvious. That loyalty was evident from the time of Schlegel's arrival, when Nuremberg's magistrates made only one qualification to his list of demands: that he give Meister Frantz and his family sufficient time to locate another residence and clean out their current home for him. This seemingly reasonable and innocuous compromise would spawn a bitter lifelong feud between the two executioners and their families that would end only when both men were dead.

Within two days of his first executions in Nuremberg, the newly hired Schlegel complained that his temporary lodging in the former pesthouse was still (!) not ready and that staying in an inn presented a great inconvenience and expense. The council immediately responded with a bonus of 12 fl. (one month's salary) and delicately "made inquiries of Meister Frantz" as to when he expected to vacate the Hangman's House. In the first countersalvo of an extended stalling campaign, Schmidt replied that he fully intended to buy a new house but was unable to undertake the task because of his current infirmity. Unwilling to press the venerated veteran, his superiors instead ordered the acceleration of renovations to a large third-floor apartment for the new, married executioner in a building he and his wife would share with twenty single male renters and the occasional chain gang. As a further concession to an apparently indignant Schlegel, the council granted the new executioner several extended leaves during the next few months "to settle his affairs" as well as an additional 12 fl. for moving expenses.[72]

Over the next year, the councillors' annoyance with their new employee grew steadily, as did their appreciation of his predecessor, the realisation gradually dawning that Bernhard Schlegel was no Frantz Schmidt. On the issue of salary alone, Schlegel was unrelenting. Whereas Meister Frantz requested a raise only twice in forty years (the last time in 1584), Meister Bernhard lamented his own inadequate compensation regularly – sometimes several times within a year. Occasionally the council granted him a one-off bonus of 25 fl.; other times they denied his requests outright, with ever more strident language.

One petition for a loan of 60 fl. – likewise refused – suggests that the new executioner was not merely greedy but probably strapped with insurmountable debts, probably brought on by gambling, drinking, or other "frivolous living" – a marked contrast to the sober lifestyle of his esteemed predecessor. Less than a year after his arrival in Nuremberg, Schlegel was summoned before the council: he had taken part in a bar fight at the fencing school, an altercation that began when Schlegel's drinking companion was harassed by fellow craftsmen for sharing a table with the executioner. While dismissing the traditional notion of contagion and reaffirming the respectability of the potter in question, the city fathers also chided Schlegel to "conduct himself more temperately and to not get involved in citizen drinking bouts at public taverns".[73]

Succeeding a venerated icon, famous for his modest living, piety, and sobriety, was bound to be difficult for anyone, but much more so for an outsider widely perceived to be grasping, confrontational, and living beyond his means.[74] The spectre of Meister Frantz clearly haunted Meister Bernhard from the day of his arrival in Nuremberg, and the latter was likely dogged by frequent unflattering comparisons to his predecessor that began to erode public confidence in his professional expertise. Within a few weeks of reprimanding Schlegel for his public fraternising, the city council "fervently admonished" him to do a better job of maintaining order at public executions. Less than a year later he was chided for an especially prolonged hanging, during which Schlegel knocked over the ladders and was stranded on a crossbeam of the gallows while the poor sinner slowly choked in agony, crying out the name of Jesus for several minutes before expiring. Eventually the veteran Lion rescued the bumbling executioner, but only after both received a thorough pelting with frozen mud balls by the outraged crowd.[75]

In 1621, despite grave misgivings, the worn-down city councillors finally conceded the right of citizenship to Schlegel, a privilege that Frantz had won only after fifteen years of service but which Meister Bernhard had requested repeatedly since his arrival in Nuremberg three years earlier.[76] To their dismay, the new executioner's performance on the scaffold showed no improvement. After Schlegel blamed still another bungled execution on the Lion, the council upbraided him and threatened outright dismissal unless he immediately improved his performance and "banish[ed] his gluttonous ways". Aware that his employers were in fact loath to undertake the search for a replacement, Meister Bernhard grudgingly endured their periodic scolding, including humiliating reminders before executions "to take [the matter] earnestly and not to bungle it."[77]

Relentlessly assaulted by unfavourable comparisons to the great Frantz Schmidt, Schlegel took out much of his anger on the former executioner for his continuing resistance to vacating the Hangman's House. Here the new executioner had a legitimate grievance, and it is hard not to sympathise with his frustration about being consistently outmanoeuvred by a wilier and better-connected rival. Perhaps because of Schlegel's frequent complaints on so many other issues, his laments over the Schmidt family's continual squatting in the home that had been promised to him fell on deaf ears for nearly seven years. Possibly the magistrates hoped that the matter might eventually be resolved in relatively easy fashion by the elderly Schmidt's death.

Finally, in the summer of 1625, the devastation of war, an influx of refugees, and the arrival of yet another epidemic triggered a severe housing crisis that forced the city councillors to act against the still vital seventy-one-year-old Meister Frantz. Desperate for emergency hospital space, the councillors evacuated the former pesthouse where Schlegel and his wife had been residing and began the eviction of his predecessor from the Hangman's House, offering to pay all the Schmidt family's moving expenses. Again Frantz repeatedly demurred, claiming that he had been promised the house for life – a dubious assertion that contradicted his own declared intentions to relocate seven years earlier. The tactic nevertheless appeared to work and the councillors directed Schlegel to find alternative housing on his own. When a clerk from the criminal bureau subsequently reported that he found no trace of any such promise in the official records, Schmidt fluently switched tactics. He now claimed to have identified a suitable new house two streets away, on Obere Wöhrdstrasse, but required financial help from the council to cover its yearly mortgage of 75 fl. The residence itself – actually two conjoined houses, owned for the last six decades by a prominent goldsmith – had a steep purchase price of 3,000 fl. and also required a sizeable down payment of over 12.5 per cent. Desperate for resolution, the council did not blanch at the cost but merely verified that the former executioner's investments earned a yearly interest of only 12 fl. before agreeing to grant him an annual stipend of 60 fl. in perpetuity. Shortly after Walpurgis Day (1 May) 1626, Frantz Schmidt finally vacated his home of nearly fifty years and the jubilant Bernhard Schlegel moved in.[78]

Fresh from this victory, Schlegel turned his resentment of the revered Meister Frantz to their competition in the medical sphere. Until then, the new executioner's conflicts had been mostly with local barber-surgeons, who early on complained about his aggressiveness in pursuing their clients.[79] At one point the council admonished him for consulting on a case involving magic and mental illness, reminding him that he was to confine his medical work to "external injuries".[80] Again, Schlegel clearly lacked his predecessor's diplomatic skills, and his professional reputation suffered as a result. On a few occasions, he even suffered the humiliation of having his prognoses formally second-guessed by Meister Frantz.[81] Within a year after taking possession of the Hangman's House, Schlegel complained to the city council that the former executioner was taking away too many of his clients and demanded both a formal sanctioning of Schmidt and the construction of a new entrance for his own patients, away from the dishonourable pig market. Both requests were denied and Schlegel was reminded that "since Frantz Schmidt helped him for many years, he should be able to tolerate him".[82] Rebuffed yet again, the exasperated executioner lodged no more formal complaints against his venerated predecessor but no doubt looked with anticipation towards the old man's imminent demise.

A father's legacy

The single greatest indignity suffered by Schlegel was the moment of ultimate triumph for Meister Frantz and his children. In late spring 1624, while still ensconced in the Hangman's House, Meister Frantz Schmidt wrote to the emperor Ferdinand II (r. 1618–37), requesting a formal restitution of his family's honour. Direct appeals to the imperial court were not unheard-of, but why did Frantz choose this particular moment to seek the final completion of his quest? Perhaps the retired executioner needed such an endorsement to purchase a new house or his sons had requested help in obtaining honourable craft positions. It's possible that Meister Frantz was even thinking of his eleven-year-old granddaughter, who had just moved in with him and his adult children. An even more intriguing question is why he waited six years after his retirement to write such an appeal. Given how important the restoration of family honour was to Schmidt, it's likely that he had been trying to draft and send the missive for some time, but that forces beyond his control – reluctance on the part of his patrician backers or some other local political issue – had until then thwarted him.

Whatever the reason for its timing, this remarkable document – no more than fifteen pages long in its original form – provides not just an old man's summary of his life's work but also a final, telling illustration of the personal networking and powers of persuasion that had made that life such a success. Frantz's petition is a model of rhetorical finesse, skilfully alternating his many accomplishments on behalf of the emperor and his subjects with a personal plea for sympathy over the misfortune suffered by him and his family. Like his *Meisterlied* on the healing of King Abgar, the petition was without a doubt composed with help, probably from a professional notary. The reasoning and sentiments, however, are pure Meister Frantz. After the formulaic obeisance, he begins his appeal by invoking *the responsibility imposed on secular authorities by God Himself to protect the pious [and] law-abiding from all violence and fear [as well as] to punish the unruly and evil with the appropriate severe punishment, so that peace, calm, and unity might be preserved*. Meister Frantz goes on to establish the divine origin of the office of executioner, citing the Old Testament account of the Israelites and their ritualistic execution by stoning as well as the imperial dictates of the *Carolina*. And yet, he writes, despite the legitimacy and necessity of his work, the profession of executioner represented a vocation thrust upon him by an unfortunate incident, *which I cannot refrain from recounting*.

Frantz's subsequent appeal to the emperor's compassion contains the most introspective and personally revealing lines he ever wrote. Finally out of the public spotlight, he is surprisingly frank about the deep shame that has haunted his family ever since Margrave Albrecht callously forced Heinrich Schmidt to perform those long-ago executions on the market square in Hof. Just as unfair, *and as much as I would have liked to shake free of it*, he writes, the family dishonour forced him into the office of executioner as well, a cruel contradiction of his own natural calling to medicine. And now Meister Frantz turns to the final reason his restitution request should be granted: Medicine, he writes, is the vocation he has managed to practise for forty-six years, *next to my difficult profession, helping with my healing over fifteen thousand people in Nuremberg and the surrounding lands – with the help of the most high and eternal God*. Healing is also the trade he has taught to his own children, he writes, *out of true paternal responsibility with good discipline . . . just as my father taught me, despite the difficult and universally despised office forced upon both of us*. Moreover, he has always applied his medicinal learning *in useful and honourable ways*, including the healing of certain highly placed imperial representatives, whom he names in an appendix, together with nearly fifty noble and patrician clients, more than a third of them women.

Only at this point does Meister Frantz return to his forty years of service to the emperor and his Nuremberg representatives in the role of executioner, *which I undertook and administered without the slightest concern for the danger to my life. During that entire time, there were no complaints about me or my executions and I voluntarily left office about six years ago on good terms, on account of my age and infirmity.* An attached recommendation from the Nuremberg city council confirms that Schmidt was *well-known for his calm, retiring life and behaviour as well as his thriving medical practise . . . and his enforcement of imperial law.* In consideration of his many years of service in both law enforcement and medicine, as well as his thirty-one years as a Nuremberg citizen, Frantz Schmidt closes by humbly requesting the restoration of his family name, which will finally lift the stigma he has known all his life and open all honourable professions to his own sons.

Sometime after 9 June 1624, Frantz paid a private courier to carry the sealed petition to the imperial court in Vienna, possibly as part of the city council's regular diplomatic pouch. After only three months, an ornately inscribed and wax-sealed reply arrived at the Hangman's House, also delivered by private courier. The original of Frantz's petition has not survived, but this formal response to it remains preserved in Nuremberg's Staatsarchiv (thanks to Schmidt's immediately filing it with the city's chancery on 10 September).[83] Ferdinand himself had probably never even seen the former executioner's appeal, and the entire affair was likely handled at least a few levels of bureaucracy below the emperor, possibly including the imperial signature itself. Following a reiteration of Frantz's request, though, the brief document culminated in the words he had longed to hear his entire life:

> On account of the subservient petition to us from the highly esteemed mayor and council of the city of Nuremberg, the inherited shame of Frantz Schmidt that prevents him and his heirs from being considered upright or presents other barriers is, out of imperial might and clemency, hereby abolished and dissolved and his honourable status among other reputable people declared and restored.[84]

Little matter that in the end the decision was less influenced by the executioner's heartfelt plea or his long service than by the dignitaries in his corner: Meister Frantz knew the ways of his status-obsessed society. He had achieved his goal; his father's dishonour had been transformed into his sons' honour. It was not the executioner's sword that he would pass on to them but the physician's scalpel.

When the victorious Frantz Schmidt moved into the large new house on nearby Obere Wöhrdstrasse two years later, the seventy-two-year-old paterfamilias brought with him all his surviving progeny – five in total plus one or two servants. Rosina, the oldest and the only child to marry thus far, was now a thirty-nine-year-old widow with a thirteen-year-old daughter. Rosina's wedding fifteen years earlier to Wolf Jacob Pickel, a respectable printer from Frankfurt, had involved a significant dowry and possibly other financial concessions on the part of her executioner father. Two years after their private ceremony, the couple presented Meister Frantz with his first grandchild, Elisabeth, bringing his dream of establishing a line of honourable descendants that much closer to fulfilment.[85] Yet despite Pickel's artisanal standing and financial backing, the foreigner from Frankfurt consistently failed to establish himself in his new home, instead suffering a series of professional setbacks. Shortly after the new grandchild's birth, a loan of 20 fl. from his father-in-law was either squandered or stolen by a would-be business partner and, to Meister Frantz's still greater shame, both Wolf and Rosina were imprisoned for fraud. Only the executioner's direct intervention cleared up the matter, and the young couple was released after five days' incarceration.[86] Four years later, Pickel was still struggling financially and complained to the city council that the local printers refused to accept him because he had married the executioner's daughter. After hearing both sides, the magistrates consulted with the jurists about whether Pickel "can be considered respectable [*redlich*]", and upon receiving word of his good reputation among the printers of Frankfurt, they ordered the Nuremberg printers to accept the newcomer on a probationary basis.[87] Such mandates could still be ignored, but Pickel did not lodge any more formal complaints. However, by 1624 he had either died or absconded. That same year, Rosina herself once again landed in prison on allegedly spurious charges of fornication. After a brief stay she was rescued, as she had been before, through her embarrassed father's intervention.[88] Shortly afterwards, she and her daughter rejoined the Schmidt household.

Meister Frantz's two surviving sons, Frantz Steffan (age thirty-five) and Frantzenhans (age thirty-one), also continued to live with their father and siblings in the reconstituted household. Their occupations are unclear. We know that their father decided early on that neither would follow him into his own dishonourable profession, despite its lucrativeness and his own ability to ensure their placement in Nuremberg or elsewhere. One later source refers to Frantz Steffan as "an upright [*ersam*] young journeyman with no property", but neither his craft nor any actual employment is specified. Given his achievement of journeyman status, it's unlikely that he was hindered by any physical or mental disability. He may well have been simply unable to find gainful employment because of his family background.[89]

Frantzenhans, the baby of the family, also apparently suffered from continued discrimination on the part of Nuremberg's artisans, despite both his father's formal restitution of honour and a 1548 imperial proclamation that had specifically given executioners' sons the right to pursue an honourable craft. Instead, he sought to follow his father into the profession of healing. Just one generation later, a few sons of German executioners would actually be admitted to medical schools and still more would become successful surgeons or physicians during the eighteenth century.[90] This honourable option was not yet open to the sons of Frantz Schmidt, however, so Frantzenhans built on the expertise and client base of his highly respected father, treating broken bones and external wounds, as well as sick or injured animals.

Frantz's daughter Maria, thirty-eight in 1626, had been running the Schmidt household for more than fifteen years – ever since her older sister had left home to marry. The return of Rosina with her daughter probably challenged Maria's dominant role, especially since the older sister had already led her own household as a married woman and mother. We can only wonder if this was a factor in Frantz's decision to purchase two adjoining residences.

As he settled into the house on Obere Wöhrdstrasse, Meister Frantz Schmidt must have felt a great sense of achievement. After years of work and sacrifice – and not a little political manoeuvring – he had finally managed to provide for his family not only an unimpeachably honourable name but also a large and comfortable home in which to enjoy the fruits of their new status. Unfortunately, less than two years later, a tragedy befell the family, one that even the resourceful Frantz could do nothing to prevent. On 10 January 1628, the date of her sixteenth birthday, Schmidt's granddaughter, Elisabeth, died of causes that were not recorded. She was precisely the same age that her uncle

Jörg had been when he died, almost three decades earlier. We can only imagine how this loss must have devastated the entire household. Deprived of the one youthful presence in their midst, the aged Frantz Schmidt and his four adult children accompanied her cortege to the family plot the next morning, Elisabeth's small casket carried by two sacristans and followed by an unknown number of fellow mourners.[91]

Meister Frantz's last years were brightened by one final accomplishment, nearly on a par with his imperial restitution. On 6 February 1632, forty-four-year-old Maria married forty-four-year-old Hans Ammon in a private ceremony at the Schmidt house. Despite Ammon's own modest roots – and his memorable stint as an actor under the name of Peter Leberwurst (Liver sausage) – the groom had by then succeeded in building an enviable reputation for himself among the city's many artists and engravers. For Frantz's daughter to marry such a man marked a greater social achievement than many would have thought possible for the former executioner. As a public symbol that the family had finally been accepted into honourable society, the wedding represented the crowning moment of Frantz's lifelong quest and a definitive reversal of the shame that four generations of Schmidts had been forced to endure.

Yet even this victory was tragically short-lived. Despite its significance, the wedding had taken place quietly. But this time, the absence of a large church ceremony was dictated not by any lingering dishonour of the bride but by the fragile health of the bridegroom. Perhaps the artist suspected that he did not have much time remaining and was mostly intent on passing his inheritance to the personal physician he had come to consider a cherished friend and mentor. After all, the former actor and the retired executioner were both outsiders who had overcome formidable obstacles and ultimately succeeded in their respective quests. Whatever the motivation for Ammon's decision, he never again left the house on Obere Wöhrdstrasse; nineteen days later he was dead.[92] Maria was left with the famous artist's name and property, but no progeny, no grandchildren for her aged father.

The next month, the Swedish king Gustavus II Adolphus and a regiment of his troops marched into Nuremberg's marketplace, cheered by sympathetic Protestant crowds. Since 1618 most German lands had been convulsed by what later became known as the Thirty Years

War – a series of armed conflicts spawned by a toxic mix of religious fervour, dynastic ambition, and self-perpetuating violence. The Swedish intervention of 1630 initially portended a reversal of imperial Catholic gains and an imminent end to nearly a dozen years of warfare and suffering. Instead, the prematurely triumphant entry of Gustavus Adolphus into Nuremberg marked the beginning of the most devastating five years in the city's history and a further extension of the war. Over the months to come, the twenty thousand Swedish troops encamped outside the city walls demanded exorbitant "contributions" from municipal coffers. Still worse, from the magistrates' point of view, Gustavus Adolphus himself was slain in battle at Lützen before the year was out, robbing Protestant forces of their most charismatic leader and bringing the war to a deadlock that doomed central Europe to another sixteen years of bloody conflict. At the same time, Nuremberg itself was struck by the first of three waves of plague, this one killing more than fifteen thousand residents and refugees, among them forty-one-

A funeral procession to the Saint Rochus Cemetery, just southwest of the city's walls. Frantz's grave lies about fifty feet to the left of the cemetery's chapel in the foreground (c.1700).

year-old Frantz Steffan Schmidt, who died on 11 January 1633.[93] He had never married and had resided until his death in the family home. He left behind no children.

Like all Nurembergers, Frantz and his three remaining adult children – Rosina, Maria, and Frantzenhans – welcomed the brief respite from mass graves and quarantines that finally came in the summer of 1633, only to be assaulted the following winter by a still more virulent outbreak of the plague and other epidemics. The year 1634 turned out to be the deadliest in Nuremberg's history, with at least twenty thousand adults and children succumbing to the deadly diseases that thrived in the severely overcrowded city. Appropriately, perhaps, the man who had killed more people with his own hands than any other in the city – possibly in the entire empire – was himself finally consumed by the death around him on Friday June 13 1634, at the age of eighty.[94]

The funeral of Meister Frantz Schmidt, which in calmer times might have been a significant local event, passed barely noticed amid the widespread suffering of that annus horribilis. We know little about the venerated executioner's burial itself, only that the city council unanimously declared that "in view of the imperial restitution of honourable birth", Meister Frantz was allowed to be fully recognised as "respectable" (*kunstreich*). He was buried the day after he died, in the Saint Rochus family plot he had purchased half a century earlier, next to his long-deceased Maria and four dead children. Most important, he was designated in all official records as "Honourable Frantz Schmidt, Physician, in Obere Wöhrd[strasse]", with no reference whatsoever to the more infamous profession of forty-five years that had in the end secured this status.[95] The seemingly impossible dream that had animated his life was at last, in death, a reality, engraved for all posterity to see on his still-legible gravestone.

EPILOGUE

How peaceful in its steadfast ways,
content in deed and work,
lies nestled in Germany's centre,
my dear Nuremberg!
> —Richard Wagner, *Die Meistersinger von Nürnberg*,
> act 3, scene 1 (1868)

If society really believed what it said [about capital punishment as a deterrent], it would exhibit the heads.
> —Albert Camus, "Reflections on the Guillotine" (1957)[1]

The year of Frantz Schmidt's death, 1634, marked the nadir of a particularly tumultuous decade in Nuremberg. Following the peak of prosperity the city reached during the middle years of Schmidt's life, Nuremberg entered a period of gradual, then precipitous, decline. The rise of global trade presented an escalating challenge for the city's merchants and bankers, as did increased competition in high-quality manufacturing from the Netherlands and France. But the resulting rise in inflation and unemployment, while dire, was quickly dwarfed in magnitude by the devastating impact of the Thirty Years War. By the time of the Peace of Westphalia in 1648, more than fifty thousand residents of Nuremberg had died from epidemics or starvation during the previous fifteen years, the municipal government was 7,500,000 fl. in debt, and the celebrated city of Nuremberg had slipped into the decline that would relegate it to the status of a provincial backwater by the eighteenth century. "Nobody won the Thirty Years War," Mack Walker has written, but indisputably Nuremberg was one of the biggest losers of all – a tragic coda to its previous two centuries of glory.[2]

Frantz's personal legacy did not fare much better. Less than a year after his death, forty-seven-year-old Rosina died, possibly as a result of the same epidemic that had killed her aged father, leaving Maria and Frantzenhans as the late executioner's only surviving children. Frantzenhans continued to support the reduced household through the medical consultancy he had inherited from his father. But within months of Meister Frantz's death, the executioner's successor and longtime nemesis Bernhard Schlegel revived his vendetta against his popular predecessor. This time he complained to the city council that Schmidt's son had left him "no one to cure", depriving him of the opportunity to earn "my little piece of bread" from this side occupation. According to Meister Bernhard, the terms of Frantz's imperial restitution did not extend to his offspring, and if the council did not censure his competitor, it should at least compensate Schlegel for the lost income – "especially during these difficult, troubled times." After quickly consulting both its copy of Meister Frantz's restitution and the city's chief jurist, the council rejected Schlegel's petition but granted him a small bonus. A year later, the relentless Meister Bernhard once more lamented that the sole surviving Schmidt male was leaving him "no patients whatsoever", and he repeated his request for official intervention or an appropriate raise in his own salary. Again rebuffed, Schlegel this time informed his employers that the cities of Regensburg and Linz were both looking for full-time executioners, but that an annual raise of 52 fl. – a 35 per cent increase – would keep him in Nuremberg. Exasperated, the city council instructed its criminal bureau either to find another executioner or to settle with the current one, underscoring that "Schmidt's healing cannot be prohibited." Unable to identify an alternate to Schlegel, his employers agreed to a temporary weekly raise "until better times" – albeit considerably less than the always cash-strapped Meister Bernhard had requested. Three years later, in May 1639, Valentin Deuser, "a foreign executioner", was granted permission to heal patients in the city, and before the year was out he had replaced the ailing Bernhard Schlegel on a temporary and then permanent basis as Nuremberg's official executioner. On 29 August 1640, Bernhard Schlegel died and was buried in Saint Rochus Cemetery, not far from the resting place of his reviled predecessor.[3]

Free at last of their longtime persecutor, Frantzenhans and Maria continued their quiet lives in the house on Obere Wöhrdstrasse, with no further appearance in the official record until their deaths. Maria lived until the age of seventy-five, dying in 1664; Frantzenhans persevered alone in the family home for another nineteen years, finally joining his long-deceased siblings and parents at the age of eighty-six.[4] Maria had never remarried, and Frantzenhans remained a bachelor his entire long life. By the time the last of the Schmidt children died, Frantz's only grandchild had been dead for over half a century. There would be no others. The executioner's dream of a line of descendants living respectable, socially unfettered lives, the inspiration of his lifelong struggle for respectability, was never to be.

Meister Frantz's demise also coincided with the end of a golden age for European executioners. The frequency of public executions had already begun to decline during the second half of Schmidt's career, but the destruction and other effects of the Thirty Years War accelerated that process. Everywhere, including in Nuremberg, death sentences became both less common and more likely to be commuted. The rise of discipline houses and workhouses as punishment for habitual non-violent criminals simultaneously reduced the number of executions for theft from one-third to one-tenth of all capital punishments. By 1700 the overall number of executions in German lands had fallen to one-fifth of what it had been a century earlier, a decline that would be even steeper if seventeenth-century executions for the by-then-defunct crime of witchcraft were included. The number of corporal punishments, particularly flogging and mutilation, fell just as dramatically, as did the more gruesome traditional punishments of burning alive, drowning, and death by the wheel. Nuremberg saw only six executions by the wheel during the entire seventeenth century – compared to thirty during Meister Frantz's career alone – and only one, which was preceded by decapitation, during the eighteenth century. Hanging and beheading became the two execution methods of choice, both made more humane by the inventions of the drop door and the guillotine, respectively.[5]

Why did such a remarkable social transformation occur? Modern historians have proposed a wide range of theories. Some posit the widespread development of greater empathy among Europeans in general, part of a profound "civilising process" beginning in the late Middle Ages. Others claim that the emerging states of Europe simply modified their methods of control, replacing capital punishment for nonviolent offences with incarceration or transportation to an overseas colony. Unfortunately for these theories and their popularisers, there is no evidence whatsoever of a shift in popular mentalities regarding human suffering, nor can the development of workhouses and execution methods that did not become dominant until the eighteenth century or later explain the profound changes that began more than a hundred years earlier (especially in Nuremberg, where a discipline house was not established until 1670).[6] To account for the decline in public execution, we must look, rather, to the reasons it became so popular in the first place.

Nuremberg's city councillors and other secular authorities in Europe did not grow soft on crime during the seventeenth century – to the contrary – but they did finally feel secure enough in their legal authority to rely more on public displays of clemency than on carefully choreographed rituals of brutality. Thanks in large part to the work of Meister Frantz and his fellow enforcers, the authority of the state and its judges was now an established reality, as opposed to the not-always-convincing assertion it had been a century before. Professional and sober executioners had become the norm, not the exception, and the public redemption ritual of the scaffold was now firmly enough established in the social consciousness that it did not need to be reiterated at such frequent intervals. Crime continued to flourish and wars consumed ever more victims, but governmental control of criminal justice had become an unquestioned reality.[7]

The precipitous drop in public executions after Meister Frantz's time bestowed a mixed blessing on his professional brethren. In the short term, it spelled a decline in both demand and salary for executioners. In the long term, however, it led to the gradual dismantling of many social barriers for these now more legitimate enforcers/enactors of state justice. By the beginning of the eighteenth century, executioners' sons were regularly accepted into medical schools and other professions. Active executioners themselves could finally practise medicine unencumbered, and Frederick I of Prussia (d. 1713) even appointed the

Berlin executioner, Martin Koblentz, as his court physician – despite vigorous opposition from academic circles. Later, the empress Maria Theresa (d. 1780) herself recognised the new social standing of the executioner, in 1731 issuing an imperial decree that reinstated the honour of all executioners' children and that of executioners themselves, once they had completed their service.

Many of the social prejudices against executioners nevertheless persevered well into the nineteenth century, once more thanks mainly to the craft guilds, which endeavoured to shore up their declining influence – as they had in the sixteenth century – by limiting the social mobility of those who had historically been beneath them. Consequently, many executioner families remained clannish and continued to intermarry. In fact, just two extended dynasties dominated Nuremberg's office of the executioner from the mid-seventeenth to the early nineteenth century. By then, the insidious stigma that had dominated Frantz Schmidt's life had well and truly begun to fade and would one day vanish altogether.[8]

The 1801 publication of Meister Frantz's journal by a local jurist thus came at the very moment that public executioners were fading from the legal scene and becoming ever more prominent in the popular imagination. Local patrician Johann Martin Friedrich von Endter was one of the most outspoken and passionate reformers of Nuremberg's "outdated and draconian" legal system. His manifesto "Thoughts and Recommendations on Nuremberg's Criminal Justice and Its Administration" (1801) proposed reforms based on his own Enlightenment version of the Golden Rule: "As you wish to be judged, so should others be judged." Coming across a manuscript copy of Meister Frantz's "long-forgotten journal" in the city archive, Endter recognised the perfect foil for his soon-to-be-published manifesto. In bringing the work to print, Endter sought "to rescue [Schmidt's book] from obscurity" and in the process reveal how brutally "the misfortunate [were punished] at the hands of our rustic Frantz". His principal target, though, remained the cruelties of the old regime – not "old, honourable Frantz, [who] acted not according to his own feeling and instinct but at the orders of those who put the sword in his hand". After overcoming municipal censors, who feared the journal would present the city in a bad light, the impassioned editor made his final corrections to the text, then abruptly died at the age of thirty-seven, never to know the subsequent success of his proposed legal reforms or his edition of Meister Frantz's journal.[9]

The most vocal admirers of the new publication – in hindsight predictably so – were neither the jurists nor the academics Endter envisioned, but men of letters. Romantic authors in particular embraced the melodramatic figure of the "medieval hangman", an entertaining anachronism in an age of mechanical guillotines and gallows with trapdoors. In an 1810 letter to the folklorists and academics Jacob and Wilhelm Grimm, the poet Ludwig Achim von Arnim wrote enthusiastically of "the well-known annals of the Nuremberg skinner who executed five hundred people."[10] Clearly an object of interest for those celebrated collectors of often grisly folktales, the printed version of Schmidt's journal rapidly made the rounds in the salons and literary circles of German intelligentsia. A certain "Meister Franz" even made an appearance in Clemens Brentano's popular play *The Story of the Sturdy Kasperl and the Beautiful Annerl* (1817), in which the executioner both heals a sick dog and beheads the female protagonist for infanticide. Even Johann Wolfgang von Goethe, the most celebrated German author of the day, embraced the long-shunned figure of the hangman, entering into a lengthy personal friendship with the executioner of Eger, Karl Huss, who shared the poet's geological interests.[11]

Nowhere was the romantic figure of the medieval hangman more fervently embraced than in the revitalised Nuremberg of the nineteenth century. After more than two centuries of obscurity, the old imperial city had been annexed by the prosperous and relatively progressive duchy of Bavaria in 1806. This much-lamented end to Nuremberg's seven centuries of independence had in fact spurred a dramatic economic revival that simultaneously jolted the city out of its old-regime turpitude and unleashed the series of criminal justice reforms long sought by Endter. That the newly progressive city would embrace Meister Frantz's journal is in some ways ironic. Even before the Bavarian Occupation (as it is jokingly still known in Nuremberg), city fathers had abolished judicial torture and public execution and marked the retirement of the last executioner, Albanus Friedrich Deubler, in 1805. Four years later, the municipal discipline- and workhouse was closed and the site converted into the House of Society, a venue for public concerts, lectures, and balls. That same year, the gallows outside the Ladies'

Gate finally collapsed and the entire surrounding area was converted to a park. Even the warden's residence at the formerly dreaded Hole was transformed into a popular pub known as the Green Frog.

How did a sixteenth-century executioner and his not entirely forgotten journal fit into the new Nuremberg? By the middle of the nineteenth century, the city had become internationally famous not just as a manufacturing dynamo but also as a popular tourist destination. Thanks to the efforts of local folk poets such as Johann Konrad Grübel and Johann Heinrich Witschel, the hometown of Albrecht Dürer and Hans Sachs became a powerful symbol of traditional German culture at its most idealised. City fathers lost no time in capitalising on this proto-nationalist cultural windfall for the city on the Pegnitz. During the 1830s and 1840s they purchased and restored a number of historic city buildings, including the former home of Albrecht Dürer, which they converted to a museum. In 1857 Nuremberg became home to the Germanisches Nationalmuseum, today a sprawling collection of artworks and other objects illustrating the magnificence of "Germanic" culture and history. By the time of German unification in 1870, the entire old city, including all the surrounding walls and gates, had been completely restored, and Nuremberg stood supreme among cities of the recently proclaimed Second Empire as the embodiment of a proud German past.[12]

Of course that proud past had a seamy underside as well, and Nuremberg's lucrative heritage industry cashed in on it with new tourist destinations, including a "torture chamber" set up by the local antiquarian Georg Friedrich Geuder in the city's old Frog Tower prison. Taking advantage of continuing popular fascination with the figure of the medieval hangman, Geuder's collection most famously included the iron maiden, a supposedly ancient method of torture and execution said to have been used in a secret court. Both the iron maiden and the secret court were complete fabrications, possibly based on a misinterpretation of old texts, but the exhibit proved highly effective in popularising a Gothic imagining of pre-Enlightenment "justice" and its sinister enforcers. The entire romance of "medieval cruelties" overseen by an executioner in a hood – another nineteenth-century invention – proved irresistible to tourists and novelists alike. Bram Stoker, the author of *Dracula* (1897), visited Nuremberg twice and even incorporated the

Iron Maiden into one of his short stories. The city's torture collection moved to a more prominent location in the so-called Five-Cornered Tower of the imperial castle and later went on an extended tour of Great Britain and North America, prompting even more popular literary works about executioners and a new edition of the Schmidt journal in 1913.[13] Eventually, the Iron Maiden, together with assorted thumbscrews, shackles, executioner swords, and other items – many of them high-quality nineteenth-century forgeries – were auctioned off to private collectors.

By then, the Gothic executioner had become a permanent fixture of modern culture. Only during the past few decades have scholarly accounts fully escaped the gravitational pull of that stereotype, but even the most impressive of these works have been no match in the public arena for the formidable icon created by the Romantics of nearly two centuries ago.[14] Like pirates, witches, and other historical outcasts, executioners have been reclaimed by romance and fantasy writers for

A typical Romantic imagining of medieval criminal justice, including a hooded executioner and his assistants, the Iron Maiden, and a clandestine trial (c.1860).

dramatic purposes, by cartoonists for comical purposes, and by purveyors of popular culture for commercial gain.[15] The modest tourist ventures of nineteenth-century Nuremberg pale in comparison to modern enterprises. Cities across Europe boast well-publicised "historical criminal tours" of dungeons and other sites, and Germany's premier historical reenactment city, Rothenburg ob der Tauber, features a medieval crime museum. These attractions – and I can't claim to have done a systematic survey of them all – run the gamut from legitimate historical presentation to harmless amusement to historical vandalism in the service of profit. The worst of them do no more than exploit the "pornography of suffering and death" that already saturates modern culture.[16]

Even the less titillating and more scholarly treatments of the premodern executioner produce a distancing effect. In Nuremberg, Meister Frantz's residence has recently been transformed into a historical museum of local criminal justice, and the dreaded Hole beneath the town hall has become the site of daily tours through the dungeon's dank cells and torture chamber. The documentation provided in both instances is excellent and the guides are invariably well-informed raconteurs who bravely refrain from passing along the spurious gruesome detail or ghost story. Yet even scrupulous attention to historical accuracy cannot entirely counter the voyeuristic nature of all tourism, the inescapable reduction of all past triumphs and tragedies to a form of entertainment, a diversion from our own "real lives". For most of the smiling tourists who pose in front of the Hangman's House, the emotional and intellectual life of its most famous occupant is not even a tepid afterthought – it is a non sequitur.

More than most of his contemporaries, Meister Frantz Schmidt remains the victim of modern condescension and disgust. The very symbol of a barbarous and ignorant age, he affirms for us the collective social progress of our modern world. To this day, allegedly learned and "scientific" works, such as the social psychologist Steven Pinker's *The Better Angels of Our Nature*, perpetuate the Gothic fantasy of ancien régime cruelty in the service of their own modern, secularist agenda.[17] In distancing Meister Frantz and his fellow executioners from ourselves, we make them safe figures from the world of fairy tales, perpetrators of horrors that cannot touch us, in the process revealing more about our own fears and dreams than about the world we have inherited from them. We view the hooded caricature of modern popular culture with the same patronising amusement as adults watching children at play, all the time confident of our own superior rationality and sophistication.

But is such emotional and intellectual distancing justified? Surely it is not edifying, at least in terms of any genuine understanding of past individuals and societies. Contrary to modernist narratives of the civilising process or gradual conscience formation among later generations, Frantz Schmidt and his contemporaries do not appear to have been more or less prone to cruelty than individuals in the twenty-first century, nor have we seen any evidence of more or less fear, more or less hatred, more or less compassion. It would have surprised the executioner who so closely identified with the victims of crime to hear his society characterised as especially cruel and heartless, particularly once he learned of such unthinkable modern atrocities as genocide, atomic obliteration, and total war. He would admit that the criminal justice of his day could be harsh, but he would recoil at the notion of trials and incarcerations that extended for years, even decades, sometimes involving long periods of isolation. The premodern execution ritual itself, which Michel Foucault characterised as a carnivalesque savouring of human suffering, in fact offers the strongest repudiation of some qualitative shift in popular attitudes, since it was the very cruelty of botched executions – and the suffering they imposed – that was most likely to trigger mob retaliation. There is no defence imaginable today for such abominations as execution with the wheel and judicial torture, but we must recognise that neither was primarily motivated by either mass sadism or pervasive indifference to the suffering of others.

It is not our emotional responses to crime or suffering that separate us from Schmidt's world, but two specific historical developments, one practical and one conceptual. Medieval and early modern judicial mechanisms, as we have seen, were by our standards woefully ineffective. Without modern investigative capabilities, modern technology, and modern alternatives to banishment (i.e. prison), the legal authorities of Frantz Schmidt's day felt compelled to rely on self-incrimination and torture as well as capital punishment for a variety of serious and recidivist offences. Popular fear and magistrates' concerns about their own authority also required some public punishment of those few perpetrators unlucky enough to get caught; "frontier-style" justice was often the result – preferable to lynch mob actions but prone to coercion and other procedural shortcuts.

The even more fundamental distinction between most developed societies today and Nuremberg in the sixteenth century is the notion of inalienable human rights. This other relatively late development in the public sphere, though still contested, provides at least a theoretical and legal basis for limiting state coercion and violence, even in the pursuit of justice. Authoritarian regimes of the past and present recognise no such externally imposed restrictions, nor do they place the sovereignty of the individual on par with, let alone above, the sovereignty of the state. Meister Frantz would have agreed that even apprehended criminals had a right to due process, but the idea that this right included protection of their bodies following incriminating evidence or conviction for a serious offence would have been an incomprehensible concept. Nuremberg's magistrates and their executioner strove for moderation, consistency, and even religious redemption, all in the face of widespread pressure for simple revenge. Abolishing – rather than moderating and standardising – state violence was simply too much of an intellectual jump for them.

The leap backwards for us, by contrast, is neither long nor inconceivable. Procedural enhancements and technological innovations in law enforcement have produced less of a stable or fundamental gap between premodern and modern justice than we would like to admit. Neither death by the wheel nor burning at the stake appears likely to make a comeback in the near future (we hope), but rises in criminality anywhere – real or perceived – still reliably generate popular calls for less constrained means of investigation and harsher punishments of convicted felons. Many modern regimes still employ systematic torture – without any of the legal constraints of sixteenth-century Nuremberg – and other governments (including my own, the United States) have deliberately blurred the line between acceptable and unacceptable coercion during criminal interrogations. Capital punishment is still practised in fifty-eight countries, most prolifically in China and Iran (with combined 2011 execution figures in the thousands), but also in self-proclaimed liberal democracies such as the United States and Japan.[18] Fear of violent attack and frustration with inadequate law enforcement – both legitimate reactions in themselves – appear to be not only constant in human history but also ever on the verge of escalating into overwhelming passions. The abstract legal concept of a set of basic human rights, by contrast, remains relatively new and surprisingly vulnerable to characterisation as a disposable luxury in difficult times, easily outmatched by older, more entrenched primal urges.

Should we be encouraged by the greater limitations on state violence since Meister Frantz's time or disheartened by the fragility of that achievement? The story of Frantz Schmidt offers little of the self-congratulatory reassurance that we have come to expect from this subject. His life in fact provides no straightforward moral for our time. Instead we are limited to sharing the joys and disappointments of one man within the context of his own world. In the judgement of his contemporaries, Meister Frantz fulfilled his duty to provide Nuremberg's citizens with a sense of order and justice. By his own account, he kept his promise to his father, his children, and himself against seemingly insurmountable odds, bolstered by religious faith and by extraordinary success in his self-professed true vocation of healing. We know much too little of Frantz's personal experiences to say whether his was on balance a happy life. But it can be stated with certainty that it was a singularly purposeful life. Perhaps, in a cruel and capricious world, there is hope to be found in one man defying his fate, overcoming universal hostility, and simply persevering amid a series of personal tragedies. Meister Frantz clearly thought so. And that, we can agree with him, is an act of faith worthy of remembrance.

Notes

Abbreviations Used in Notes

Angstmann: Else Angstmann, *Der Henker in der Volksmeinung: Seine Namen und sein Vorkommen in der mündlichen Volksüberlieferung* (Bonn: Fritz Klopp, 1928).

ASB: Amts- und Standbücher; Staatsarchiv Nürnberg, Bestand 52b.

CCC: *Die Peinliche Gerichtsordnung Kaiser Karl V: Constitutio Criminalis Carolina: Die Carolina und ihre Vorgängerinnen. Text, Erläuterung, Geschichte.* Edited by J. Kohler and Willy Scheel (Halle an der Saale: Verlag Buchhandlung des Waisenhauses, 1900).

FSJ: Frantz Schmidt's journal; Stadtbibliothek Nürnberg, Amb 652.2°.

G&T: Johann Glenzdorf and Fritz Treichel, *Henker, Schinder, und arme Sünder*, 2 vols (Bad Münder am Deister: Wilhelm Rost, 1970).

GNM: Germanisches Nationalmuseum Nürnberg.

JHJ: Journal of prison chaplain Johannes Hagendorn (1563–1624). Germanisches Nationalmuseum Nürnberg, 3857 Hs.

Hampe: Theodor Hampe, *Die Nürnberger Malefizbücher als Quellen der reichsstädtischen Sittengeschichte vom 14. bis zum 18. Jahrhundert* (Bamberg: C. C. Buchner, 1927).

Keller: Albrecht Keller. *Der Scharfrichter in der deutschen Kulturgeschichte* (Bonn: K. Schroeder, 1921).

Knapp, *Kriminalrecht*: Hermann Knapp, *Das alte Nürnberger Kriminalrecht* (Berlin: J. Guttentag, 1896).

Knapp, *Loch*: Hermann Knapp. *Das Lochgefängnis, Tortur, und Richtung in Alt-Nürnberg* (Nuremberg: Heerdengen-Barbeck, 1907).

LKAN: Landeskirchlichesarchiv Nürnberg.

MVGN: *Mitteilungen des Vereins für die Geschichte der Stadt Nürnbergs.*

Nowosadtko: Jutta Nowosadtko, *Scharfrichter und Abdecker: Der Alltag zweier "unehrlicher Berufe" in der Frühen Neuzeit* (Paderborn: Ferdinand Schöningh, 1994).

Restitution: Haus-, Hof-, Staatsarchiv Wien. *Restitutionen.* Fasz. 6/S, Franz Schmidt, 1624.

RV: *Ratsverlaß* (decree of Nuremberg city council). Staatsarchiv Nürnberg, Rep. 60a.

StaatsAB: Staatsarchiv Bamberg.

StaatsAN: Staatsarchiv Nürnberg.

StadtAB: Stadtarchiv Bamberg.

StadtAN: Stadtarchiv Nürnberg.

Stuart: Kathy Stuart, *Defiled Trades and Social Outcasts: Honour and Ritual Pollution in Early Modern Germany* (Cambridge, UK, and New York: Cambridge University Press, 1999).

Wilbertz: Gisela Wilbertz. *Scharfrichter und Abdecker im Hochstift Osnabrück: Untersuchungen zur Sozialgeschichte zweier "unehrlichen" Berufe im nordwesten Raum vom 16. bis zum 19. Jahrhundert* (Osnabrück: Wenner, 1979).

Preface

1. Heinrich Sochaczewsky, *Der Scharfrichter von Berlin* (Berlin: A. Weichert, 1889), 297.

2. *JHJ* Nov 13 1617; see also Theodor Hampe, "Die lezte Amstverrichtung des Nürnberger Scharfrichters Franz Schmidt," in *MVGN* 26 (1926): 321ff.

3. Among twentieth-century historians of early modern executioners, characterisations ranged from sociopathic to emotionless to fellow victims of society; Nowosadtko, 352.

4. *Meister Frantzen Nachrichter alhier in Nürnberg, all sein Richten am Leben, so wohl seine Leibs Straffen, so Er verRicht, alleß hierin Ordentlich beschrieben, aus seinem selbst eigenen Buch abschrieben worden,* ed. J.M.F. von Endter (Nuremberg: J.L.S. Lechner, 1801), reprinted with a commentary by Jürgen C. Jacobs and Heinz Rölleke (Dortmund: Harenberg, 1980). *Maister Franntzn Schmidts Nachrichters inn Nürmberg all sein Richten,* ed. Albrecht Keller (Leipzig: Heims, 1913), reprinted with an introduction by Wolfgang Leiser (Neustadt an der Aisch, P.C.W. Schmidt, 1979). The English translation of the latter is *A Hangman's Diary, Being the Journal of Master Franz Schmidt, Public Executioner of Nuremberg, 1573–1617,* trans. C. V. Calvert and A. W. Gruner (New York: D. Appleton, 1928), reprinted (Montclair, NJ: Patterson Smith, 1973).

5. See, for example, the "journals" of Ansbach's executioners from 1575 to 1603 (StaatsAN Rep 132, Nr. 57); in Reutlingen from 1563–68 (*Württembergische Vierteljahrshefte für Landesgeschichte,* 1 [1878], 85–86); Andreas Tinel of Ohlau, c.1600 (cited in Keller, 257); Jacob Steinmayer in Haigerloch, 1764–81 (*Württembergische Vierteljahrshefte für Landesgeschichte,* 4 [1881]: 159ff.); Franz Joseph Wohlmuth in Salzburg (*Das Salzburger Scharfrichtertagebuch,* ed. Peter Putzer [Vienna: Österreichischer Kunst- und Kulturverlag, 1985]); Johann Christian Zippel in Stade (Gisela Wilbertz, "Das Notizbuch des Scharfrichters Johann Christian Zippel in Stade [1766–1782]," in *Stader Jahrbuch,* n.s. 65 [1975]: 59–78). For an overview of early modern executioner registers, see Keller, 248–60.

   At most, about one in three German males was to some degree literate. Hans Jörg Künast, "Getruckt zu Augspurg": *Buchdruck und Buchhandel in Augsburg zwischen 1468 und 1555* (Tübingen: Max Niemeyer, 1997), 11–13; R. A. Houston, *Literacy in Early Modern Europe: Culture and Education, 1500–1800* (Harlow, UK: Pearson Education, 2002), 125ff.

6. The most famous of these were the memoirs of the Sanson executioner dynasty of Paris, collected by Henri Sanson as *Sept générations d'exécuteurs, 1688–1847*, 6 vols. (Paris: Décembre-Alonnier, 1862–63); translated and published in an abbreviated English version (London: Chatto and Windus, 1876). For British examples of the genre, see John Evelyn, *Diary of John Evelyn* (London: Bickers and Bush, 1879); and Stewart P. Evans, *Executioner: The Chronicles of James Berry, Victorian Hangman* (Stroud, UK: Sutton, 2004).

7. In addition to the beginning and end of the journal, as well as the beginning of Schmidt's tenure in Nuremberg: 1573 (2x); 1576 (3x); 1577 (2x); Mar 6 1578; Apr 10 1578; Jul 21 1578; Mar 19 1579; Jan 26 1580; Feb 20 1583; Oct 16 1584; Aug 4 1586; Jul 4 1588; Apr 19 1591; Mar 11 1598; Sep 14 1602; Jun 7 1603; Mar 4 1606; Dec 23 1606.

8. Friedrich Werner, executed Feb 11 1585. The sole exception is a passing reference to *Hans Spiss, my kinsman, who is whipped out of town here with the rods by the Lion* (for abetting an escaping murderer); *FSJ* Jun 7 1603.

9. Keller concludes that "he never succeeds in the ordering of his thoughts" (252).

10. The 1801 version edited by von Endter as well as the 1913 version of Albrecht Keller are based mainly on the late seventeenth-century copy of GNM Bibliothek 2° HS Merkel 32. The working manuscript of von Endtner is found in the StaatsAN: Rep 25: SII. L 25, NR. 12. My own translation of the *FSJ* (forthcoming in print) is based on the copy in the 1634 Stadtchronik of Hans Rigel in the StadtBN, 652 2°. Apparently other copies and fragments were produced during the late seventeenth and eighteenth centuries, of which at least two survive in the Staatsbibliothek Bamberg (SH MSC Hist. 70 and MSC Hist. 83) and two in the GNM (Bibliothek 4° HS 187 514; Archiv, Rst Nürnberg, Gerichtswesen Nr. V1/3).

11. This motive is suggested by both Keller (*Maister Franntzn Schmidts Nachrichters*, Introduction, x–xi) and Nowosadtko ("'Und nun alter, ehrlicher Franz': Die Transformation des Scharfrichtermotivs am Beispiel einer Nurnberger Malefizchronik," *Internationales Archiv für Sozialgeschichte der deutschen Literatur* 31, no. 1 [2006]: 223–45), but neither follows through on the implications for the author's life.

12. Marriage, birth, and death registers, located in the LKAN, have allowed me to reconstruct the externals of Schmidt's origins and family life. Interrogation protocols and other criminal court records, found principally in the Staatsarchiv Nürnberg, have filled in considerable context on his professional activity. Decrees of the Nuremberg council, known as *Ratsverläße*, were the most versatile sources, providing a range of revealing information about both aspects of his life. The decrees also helped shed light on his simultaneous work as a medical consultant, particularly in the years following his retirement as Nuremberg's executioner (only fleetingly mentioned in his journal). Finally, I owe much to the valuable bits of biographical information culled by previous scholars, most notably Albrecht Keller, Wolfgang Leiser, Jürgen C. Jacobs, and Ilse Schumann.

13. For a useful overview, see Julius R. Ruff, *Violence in Early Modern Europe, 1500–1800* (Cambridge, UK: Cambridge University Press, 2001).

1. The Apprentice

1. Collected Works of Erasmus, vol. 25, Literary and Educational Writings, ed. J. K. Sowards (Toronto: University of Toronto Press, 1985), 305.

2. Essays, trans. J. M. Cohen (Harmondsworth, UK, and Baltimore: Penguin, 1958), 116.

3. On the apparent premodern indifference to animal suffering, see, most famously, Robert Darnton's The Great Cat Massacre and Other Episodes in French Cultural History (New York: Vintage, 1985).

4. This reconstruction is based on the common training experiences of the sons of executioner dynasties, as described in Wilbertz, 120–31. Frantz Schmidt does not provide any account of training with his father in the journal other than the June 1573 beginning of his work as a travelling journeyman.

5. This section is especially indebted to the treatment of Arthur E. Imhof, Lost Worlds: How Our European Ancestors Coped with Everyday Life and Why Life Is So Hard Today, trans. Thomas Robisheaux (Charlottesville: University of Virginia Press, 1996), 68–105.

6. For a recent overview, see C. Pfister, "Population of Late Medieval Germany," in Germany: A New Social and Economic History, vol. 1, 1450–1630, ed. Bob Scribner, 213ff.

7. Imhof, Lost Worlds, 72.

8. Imhof, Lost Worlds, 87–88. See also John D. Post, The Last Great Subsistence Crisis in the Western World (Baltimore: Johns Hopkins University Press, 1977). On the Little Ice Age, see Wolfgang Behringer, Kulturgeschichte des Klimas: Von der Eiszeit bis zur globalen Erwärmung (Munich: C. H. Beck, 2007), esp. 120–95.

9. Thomas A. Brady, Jr., German Histories in the Age of Reformations (Cambridge, UK: Cambridge University Press, 2009), 96–97.

10. Brady, German Histories, 97. See also Knapp, Kriminalrecht, 155–60.

11. I am persuaded by the argument of Hillay Zmora, The Feud in Early Modern Germany (Cambridge, UK: Cambridge University Press, 2011). See also his companion volume, State and Nobility in Early Modern Franconia, 1440–1567 (Cambridge, UK: Cambridge University Press, 1997).

12. Decree of August 12, 1522, cited in Monika Spicker-Beck, Räuber, Mordbrenner, umschweifendes Gesind: Zur Kriminalität im 16. Jahrhundert (Freiburg im Breisgau: Rombach, 1995), 25.

13. Hans Jakob Christoffel von Grimmelshausen, An Unabridged Translation of Simplicius Simplicissimus, trans. Monte Adair (Lanham, MD: University Press of America, 1986), 9–10.

14. FSJ Feb 14 1596. More than one in three robbers in one sixteenth-century sample was identified as a landsknecht. Spicker-Beck, Räuber, 68.

15. See Bob Scribner, "The Mordbrenner Panic in Sixteenth Century Germany," in The German Underworld: Deviants and Outcasts in German History, ed. Richard J. Evans (London and New York: Routledge, 1988), 29–56; Gerhard Fritz, Eine Rotte von allerhandt rauberischem Gesindt: Öffentliche Sicherheit in Südwestdeutschland vom Ende des Dreissigjährigen Krieges bis zum Ende des Alten Reiches (Ostfildern J. Thorbecke, 2004), 469–500; and Spicker-Beck, Räuber, esp. 25ff.

16. Imhof, *Lost Worlds*, 4.

17. Angstmann, 85.

18. Other infamous occupations included barbers, beggars, street cleaners, tanners, court servants and archers, shepherds, sow-gelders, privy cleaners, millers, night watchmen, actors, chimney sweeps, and tollkeepers. Nowosadtko, 12–13 and 24–28.

19. "Der Hurenson der Hencker," in 1276 Augsburg Stadtrecht, Keller, 108. The unfree argument falters on the fact that the most common names among executioners were actually from trades and crafts, including Schmidt (smith), Schneider (tailor), and Schreiner (carpenter). A few hangmen may have been condemned criminals but this too seems to have been the exception more than the rule. Angstmann (74–113) is especially influenced by contemporary anthropological research on this subject during the early twentieth century, as well as her findings in the sagas. Some historians even posited, based on Jungian notions of a sacra-lmagical discourse (and no historical evidence), that medieval executioners were the heirs to pagan Germanic priests who led ritual sacrifices and that their subsequent vilification was part of a Christian conversion campaign. Karl von Amira, *Die germanischen Todesstrafen* (Munich: Verlag der Bayerischen Akademie der Wissenschaften, 1922); see also discussion in Nowosadtko, 21–36, and G&T, 14, 38–39.

20. The most celebrated executioner dynasties in early modern Germany were Brand, Döring, Fahner, Fuchs, Gebhardt, Gutschlag, Hellriegel, Hennings, Kaufmann, Konrad, Kühn, Rathmann, Schwanhardt, and Schwarz, G&T, 46; also Stuart, 69.

21. Frantz's account of his father's disgrace is found in *Restitution*, 201r–v, and confirmed in *Enoch Widmans Chronik der Stadt Hof*, ed. Christian Meyer (Hof: Lion, 1893), 430, which does not mention Heinrich Schmidt by name, however, and specifies that the margrave ordered two servants and one gunmaker hanged. The siege of Hof is described in Friedrich Ebert, *Kleine Geschichte der Stadt Hof* (Hof: Hoermann, 1961), 34ff.; E. Dietlein, *Chronik der Stadt Hof*, vol. 1: *Allgemeine Stadtgeschichte bis zum Jahre 1603* (Hof: Hoermann, 1937), 329–94; Kurt Stierstorfer, *Die Belagerung Hofs, 1553* (Hof: Nordoberfränkischen Vereins für Natur, Geschichts-, und Landeskunde, 2003).

22. Hof's baptismal records from this period are not extant. I have based this dating on the journal entry of chaplain Johannes Hagendorn, who upon Meister Frantz's retirement in early August 1618 noted that the executioner had already celebrated his sixty-fourth birthday (*JHJ* 68r). Since Schmidt's 1624 restitution edict does not mention that Frantz was already born at the time of his father's disgrace, this leaves us with a window of roughly November 1553 to July 1554.

23. Ebert, *Kleine Geschichte der Stadt Hof*, 25–27.

24. *Widmans Chronik*, 180, 188.

25. Dietlein, *Chronik*, 434–35.

26. Ilse Schumann, "Der Bamberger Nachrichter Heinrich Schmidt: Eine Ergänzung zu seinem berühmten Sohn Franz," in *Genealogie* 3 (2001): 596–608.

27. Johannes Looshorn, *Die Geschichte des Bisthums Bamberg*, vol 5: *1556–1622* (Bamberg: Handels-Dr., 1903), 106, 148, 217.

28. StaatsAB A231/a, Nr. 1797, 1–Nr. 1809, 1 (Ämterrechnungen, 1573–1584).

29. StadtAB Rep B5, Nr. 80 (1572/73).

30. Stuart, 54–63; G&T, 23; Keller, 120; Wilbertz, 323–24.

31. Whereas Hof was almost exclusively Lutheran, only 14 per cent of Bamberg's population in 1570 was Protestant. Karin Dengler-Schrieber, *Kleine Bamberger Stadtgeschichte* (Regensburg: Friedrich Puslet, 2006), 78.

32. Wilbertz, 319–21.

33. Werner Danckert, *Unehrliche Leute. Die verfemten Berufe*, 2nd ed. (Bern: Francke, 1979), 39ff. On guild moralism, see Mack Walker, *German Home Towns: Community, State, and General Estate, 1648–1871* (Ithaca, NY: Cornell University Press, 1971), 90–107.

34. The Berlin executioner was identified by his grey hat with red trim, and some fourteenth-century executioners apparently wore caps covering their ears but never their faces. In 1543 the city of Frankfurt am Main required its executioner to wear "red, white and green stripes at the top of his vest sleeves" or pay a fine of 20 fl., Keller, 79ff., 121–22; G&T, 26–28; Nowosadtko, 239–48.

35. Wilbertz, 333; Nowosadtko, 266; also Stuart, 3.

36. Carolingian rulers continued to refer to these officials by their Roman name of *carnifices* (literally, flesh-makers) as well as *apparitores* or more simply as knaves (*Knechte*) or lords of the court (*Gerichtsherren*). By the thirteenth century, the chief figure had become the *Fronbote* or beadle (also *Büttel*), called by the *Sachenspiegel* (1224) "a holy emissary" or "knave of God," thereby reinforcing the sacral nature of his duty. There is no mention of a full-time executioner in either the *Sachenspiegel* or *Schwabenspiegel* (1275), G&T, 14. See also Keller, 79–91.

37. *Bambergensis Constitutio Criminalis,* published as *Johann von Schwarzenberg: Bambergische halßgericht und rechtliche Ordnung, Nachdruck der Ausgabe Mainz 1510* (Nuremberg: Verlag Medien & Kultur, 1979), 258b.

38. Stuart, 23–26; Nowosadtko, 50–51, 62; G&T, 9, 15; Keller, 46–47.

39. Stuart, 29ff.

40. *Bambergensis; CCC.*

41. *CCC,* preamble.

42. The term *Nachrichter* was introduced in Nuremberg as early as the thirteenth century but didn't catch on elsewhere until the sixteenth century (cf. articles 86, 96, and 97 of the *CCC*), spreading to the north by the beginning of the seventeenth century. *Scharfrichter*, by contrast, was used early in the sixteenth century in the same way everywhere in German lands. On the multiple regional variations of German names for the executioner, see Angstmann, 4–75, especially 28–31, 36–43, and 45–50; also Keller, 106ff.; and Jacob and Wilhelm Grimm, *Deutsches Wörterbuch* (Leipzig: S. Hirzel, 1877), 4, pt. 2: 990–93; 7: 103–4; and 8: 2196–97.

43. *CCC,* art. 258b.

44. Gerd Schwerhoff, *Köln im Kreuzverhör: Kriminalität, Herrschaft, und Gesellschaft in einer frühneuzeitlichen Stadt* (Bonn: Bouvier, 1991), 155; Schumann, "Heinrich Schmidt Nachrichter," 605; Angstmann, 105.

45. In a late-sixteenth-century sample from Cologne this comprised three-quarters of executions during the period, 85 of 193 executions for theft and 62 for robbery, Schwerhoff, *Köln im Kreuzverhör*, 154.

46. *FSJ* Apr 5 1589.

47. Transportation to foreign colonies was more popular in England during the eighteenth century and France during the nineteenth century. See André Zysberg, "Galley and Hard Labour Convicts in France (1550–1850): From the Galleys to Hard Labour Camps: Essay on a Long Lasting Penal Institution," in *The Emergence of Carceral Institutions: Prisons, Galleys, and Lunatic Asylums, 1550–1900*, ed. Pieter Spierenburg (Rotterdam: Erasmus Universiteit, 1984), esp. 78–85; also Knapp, *Kriminalrecht*, 79–81.

48. On the origin of Nuremberg's discipline- and workhouse, see Joel F. Harrington, "Escape from the Great Confinement: The Genealogy of a German Workhouse," in *Journal of Modern History* 71 (1999): 308–45.

49. *FSJ* Dec 15 1593; Sep 5 1594; Mar 29 1595; May 19 1601; May 28 1595; Nov 22 1603; Aug 17 1599; May 2 1605; Jan 25 1614 (2x); Jul 19 1614; Jan 11 1615; Jan 12 1615. See also Harrington, "Escape from the Great Confinement," 330–32.

50. "Ob Kriegsleute auch in seligem Stande sein können" (1526), in *D. Martin Luthers Werke: Kritische Gesamtausgabe* (Weimar: Herman Böhlau, 1883ff.; reprint, 1964–68), 19:624–26; "Kirchenpostille zum Evangelium am 4. Sonntag nach Trinitatis," ibid., 6:36–42; "Von weltlicher Obrigkeit, wie weit man ihr Gehorsam schuldig sei," ibid., 11:265.

51. *Praxis rerum criminalium, durch den Herrn J. Damhouder, in hoch Teutsche Sprach verwandelt durch M. Beuther von Carlstat* (Frankfurt am Main, 1565), 264ff. Jacob Döpler, *Theatrum poenarum, suppliciorum, et executionum criminalium: oder, Schau-platz derer leibes und lebens-straffen* (Sondershausen, 1693), 1:540.

52. G&T, 23.

53. In Bayreuth on Sep 2 1560; G&T, 5398.

54. *RV* 1313: 14v (Mar 4 1570).

55. Nowosadtko, 196; Wilbertz, 117–20.

56. Keller, 114–15.

57. Keller, 245–46. *Rotwelsch* was a combination of the Latin jargon of wandering monks and students with Hebrew, Yiddish, and Romany (Gypsy). Like English Cockney, the majority of words were created by a change in meaning (through metaphor or "formal techniques such as substitution, affixing, or reversal of consonants, vowels, and syllables"), Robert Jütte, *Poverty and Deviance in Early Modern Europe* (Cambridge, UK: Cambridge University Press, 1995), 182–83; and see also his *Abbild und soziale Wirklichkeit des Bettler- und Gaunertums zu Beginn der Neuzeit: Sozial-, mentalitäts-, und sprachgeschichtliche Studien zum Liber vagatorum (1510)* (Cologne and Vienna: Böhlau, 1988), especially 26–106; also Siegmund A. Wolf, *Wörterbuch des Rotwelschen: Deutsche Gaunersprache* (Mannheim: Bibliographisches Institut, 1956); Ludwig Günther, *Die deutsche Gaunersprache und verwandte Geheim und Berufssprachen* (Wiesbaden: Sändig, 1956).

58. See the fascinating overview of Angstmann, especially 2–73.

59. Jacob Grimm et al., *Weisthümer* (Göttingen: Dieterich, 1840), 1:818–19; Eduard Osenbrüggen, *Studien zur deutschen und schweizerischen Rechtsgeschichte* (Schaffhausen: Fr. Hurter, 1868), 392–403; Keller, 243.
60. Keller, 247–48; G&T, 68–70.
61. *FSJ* 1573; Aug 13 1577; Mar 19 1579.
62. Wilbertz, 123.
63. Based on the 1772 *Meisterbrief* of Johann Michael Edelhäuser, G&T, 99. For the full text of a *Meisterbrief* from 1676, see Keller, 239; also Nowosadtko, 196–97.
64. *Restitution*, 201v–202r.

2. The Journeyman

1. *Essays*, 63.
2. Hollfeld: twice in 1573, once in 1575; Forchheim: four times in 1577, once in 1578; Bamberg: once in 1574, twice in 1577.
3. Harrington, *The Unwanted Child: The Fate of Foundlings, Orphans, and Juvenile Criminals in Early Modern Germany* (Chicago and London: University of Chicago Press, 2009), 78–79. Katherine A. Lynch (*Individuals, Families, and Communities in Europe, 1200–1800: The Urban Foundations of Western Society* [Cambridge, UK: Cambridge University Press, 2003], 38) estimates that migrants constituted 3–8 per cent of most German urban populations.
4. Angstmann, especially 2–73.
5. For examples of these symbols, see Spicker-Beck, *Räuber*, 100ff. See also Florike Egmond, *Underworlds: Organised Crime in the Netherlands, 1650–1800* (Cambridge, UK: Polity Press, 1993); and Carsten Küther, *Menschen auf der Strasse: Vagierende Unterschichten in Bayern, Franken, und Schwaben in der zweiten Hälfte des 18. Jahrhunderts* (Göttingen: Vandenhoeck and Ruprecht, 1983), especially 60–73.
6. Two-thirds of all early modern homicides involved stabbings, most commonly in taverns. Julius R. Ruff, *Violence in Early Modern Europe, 1500–1800* (Cambridge, UK: Cambridge University Press, 2001), 123. On the drinking culture of Meister Frantz's day, see B. Ann Tlusty, *Bacchus and Civic Order: The Culture of Drink in Early Modern Germany* (Charlottesville and London: University Press of Virginia, 2001); B. Ann Tlusty and Beat Kümin, eds., *Public Drinking in the Early Modern World: Voices from the Tavern, 1500–1800*, vols. 1 and 2, *The Holy Roman Empire* (London: Pickering and Chatto, 2011); Marc Forster, "Taverns and Inns in the German Countryside: Male Honour and Public Space," in *Politics and Reformations: Communities, Polities, Nations, and Empires: Essays in Honour of Thomas A. Brady, Jr.*, ed. Christopher Ocker et al. (Leiden: Brill, 2007), 230–50.
7. For a typical reference that Meister Frantz "drank neither wine nor beer," see ASB 210: 248v.
8. *FSJ* Nov 18 1617; Dec 3 1612; Mar 15 1597; Nov 14 1598.
9. In one 1549 account from Nuremberg, a suspected child murderer was confronted with the corpse of a newborn found in the household's common toilet: "When the master of the house said, 'Oh! You innocent baby, if one among us here is guilty [of your murder], then give us a sign,' then supposedly the left arm

of the child immediately lifted up," whereupon the accused maid immediately fainted, ASB 226a: 32v; *FSJ* May 3 1597; StaatsAN 52a, 447: 1155; Ulinka Rublack finds references to the *Bahrprobe* in some seventeenth-century criminal records (*The Crimes of Women in Early Modern Germany* [Oxford, UK: Clarendon Press, 1999], 58) and Robert Zagolla claims that the practise continued in some locations even later (*Folter und Hexenprozess: Die strafrechtliche Spruchpraxis der Juristenfakultät Rostock im 17. Jahrhundert* [Bielefeld: Verlag für Regionalgeschichte, 2007], 220).

10. *FSJ* Jul 6 1592; Jan 16 1616; also *JHJ* Jan 16 1616. Johann Christian Siebenkees, ed. (*Materialien zur nürnbergischen Geschichte* [Nuremberg, 1792], 2:593–98) records two instances of the bier test in sixteenth-century Nuremberg, one in 1576 and one in 1599.

11. E.g., *RV* 1419: 26v. See also Knapp, *Loch*, 25ff.; Zagolla, *Folter und Hexenprozess*, 327–28.

12. Christian Ulrich Grupen, *Observationes Juris Criminalis* (1754), quoted in Keller, 200.

13. Only 1 to 2 per cent of criminal suspects in late-sixteenth-century Cologne were tortured, the great majority of them professional robbers and thieves. Schwerhoff, *Köln im Kreuzverhör*, 109–15; also Stuart, 141–42.

14. G&T, 86–88; Zagolla, *Folter und Hexenprozess*, 399–400.

15. See *CCC*, art. 131, para. 36, on sufficient grounds for torture in infanticide cases; also Rublack, *Crimes of Women*, 54; Wilbertz, 80; and Nowosadtko, 164.

16. *FSJ* May 10 1599; Knapp, *Loch*, 37.

17. *FSJ* Dec 4 1599; Dec 23 1605. See also *RV* 2551: 23r–v (Oct 10 1663).

18. *JHJ* 88v–89r (Feb 8 1614). The interrogators of both Helena Nusslerin (*RV* 1309: 16v [Nov 12 1569]) and of Barbara Schwenderin (*RV* 1142: 31v; 1143: 8r [May 8 1557]) were ordered to wait eight days before further torture. Similarly, Margaretha Voglin was allowed two weeks to grow stronger before her execution was carried out (*RV* 2249: 24v [Feb 19 1641]).

19. StadtAN F1-2/VII (1586).

20. ASB 215: 18.

21. Magistrates accused Kreuzmayer of "many hundred sacramental curses." ASB 212: 121r–122v, 125v–126r; *FSJ* Sep 5 1594.

22. For a detailed analysis of Mayr's case, see Harrington, *Unwanted Child*, 177–227.

23. ASB 215: 332r.

24. It is difficult to estimate how many torture sessions Schmidt took part in per year. Contemporary Ansbach executioners (1575–1600) had an average rate of about one per week, Angstmann, 105.

25. *FSJ* Apr 21 1602.

26. See, for instance, *FSJ* May 25 1581; Feb 20 1582; Aug 4 1586 (2x); Jul 11 1598.

27. *FSJ* Jul 6 1592. On widespread questioning of torture's reliability among contemporary jurists, see Zagolla, *Folter und Hexenprozess*, 34ff.

28. 1588 and 1591, cited in Knapp, *Loch*, 33. On the latitude of executioners in this respect, see Zagolla, *Folter und Hexenprozess*, 367–73; also Joel F. Harrington, "Tortured Truths: The Self-Expositions of a Career Juvenile Criminal in Early Modern Nuremberg," in *German History* 23, no. 2 (2005): 143–71.

29. Based on a sample of 114 torture outcomes from Cologne, 1549–1675, Schwer-hoff, *Köln im Kreuzverhör*, 114–17. In Cologne and Rostock, for instance, six in ten robbers were tortured versus only one in ten homicides, Zagolla, *Folter und Hexenprozess*, 48, 61–63.

30. Jacob Grimm, "Von der Poesie im Recht," first published in 1815.

31. Knapp, *Kriminalrecht*, 60.

32. *FSJ* Aug 13 1578; Oct 9 1578; Nov 9 1579; Feb 7 1581; May 6 1581; Apr 22, 1585; Jun 25 1586; Aug 23 1593; Sep 25 1595; Oct 24 1597; Feb 23 1609; Nov 25 1612; Jan 30 1614. See Jütte, *Poverty and Deviance*, 164ff., on the branding of vagrants during this period. The ear-clippings were on Jan 29 1583; Sep 4 1583; Jan 22 1600; Aug 4 1601; and Dec 9 1600. The sole tongue-trimming was on Apr 19 1591.

   The young journeyman does not record the number or nature of corporal punishments administered during these early years, but he witnessed or assisted his father cutting off at least six ears and two fingers, as well as administering two brandings. In 1576 he notes of the executed Hans Peyhel, *Two years ago at Herzogenaurach I cut off his ears and flogged him with rods*. During the period 1572–1585, Heinrich (or occasionally Frantz Schmidt before 1578) administered 85 floggings, 11 ear-clippings, 3 finger-choppings, and 2 brandings. Schumann, "Heinrich Schmidt Nachrichter," 605.

33. StaatsAB A231/a, Nr. 1797, 1–Nr. 1803,1.

34. Jason P. Coy, *Strangers and Misfits: Banishment, Social Control, and Authority in Early Modern Germany* (Leiden: Brill, 2008), 2–3; Schwerhoff, *Köln im Kreuz-verhör*, 148–53. The use of banishment overall appears to have peaked in German lands during the second half of the sixteenth century. In addition to the unrecorded floggings before 1578, journal references to other whippings are found in *FSJ* Feb 29 1580; Jun 7 1603; and Aug 4 1586.

35. *FSJ* Oct 24 1597.

36. *FSJ* Jan 10 1583.

37. One flogging by Schmidt's predecessor in 1573 resulted in a fatality the next day, Knapp, *Kriminalrecht*, 63.

38. Stuart, 143.

39. Keller, 100.

40. Siebenkees, *Materialien*, 1:543ff; Keller, 189–96; Knapp, *Kriminalrecht*, 52–53. Both traditions continued in some German localities into the eighteenth century.

41. Keller, 7.

42. Siebenkees, *Materialien*, 2:599–600. A 1513 case is cited in Keller, 160. See also G&T, 55–56; Richard van Dülmen, *Theatre of Horror: Crime and Punishment in Early Modern Germany*, trans. Elisabeth Neu (Cambridge, UK: Polity Press, 1990), 88–89; and CCC, arts. 124, 130, and 133.

43. Keller, 185; Knapp, *Kriminalrecht*, 58.

44. *FSJ* Mar 6 1578. For a fuller account of Apollonia Vöglin's ordeal, see Har-rington, *Unwanted Child*, 21–71.

45. *FSJ* Jan 26 1580; jurist opinions cited in Knapp, *Kriminalrecht*, 58.

46. *FSJ* Jul 17 1582; Aug 11 1582; Jul 11 1598; Mar 5 1611; Jul 19 1595; Aug 10 1581; Oct 26 1581; Jun 8 1587; Oct 11 1593.

47. *FSJ* Jan 18 1588.

48. *FSJ* 1573; 1576; Aug 6 1579; Jan 26 1580; Mar 3 1580; Aug 16 1580; Jul 27 1582; Aug 11 1582; Aug 14 1582; Nov 9 1586; Jan 2 1588; May 28 1588; May 5 1590; Jul 7 1590; May 25 1591; Jun 30 1593; Jan 2 1595; Mar 15 1597; Oct 26 1602; Aug 13 1604; Dec 7 1615.

49. *RV* 1551: 5v (Jan 2 1588).

50. *FSJ* Jul 27 1582; Nov 9 1586; Jan 2 1595; Feb 10 1597; Mar 15 1597; Dec 7 1615.

51. *FSJ* Mar 29 1595. Frantz Schmidt only specifies the number of nips four times in his journal: 2 nips: Feb 11 1585; 3 nips: Aug 16 1580 and Oct 23 1589; 4 nips: Mar 5 1612. Again, drawing and quartering for treason, made infamous by Foucault and others, remained an extremely rare form of execution in the early modern era, too much of an anomaly to be useful in any social historical context.

52. *FSJ* May 10 1599; *JHJ* Aug 4 1612.

53. *FSJ* Feb 11 1584; Feb 12 1584; Oct 21 1585; Dec 19 1615. See also above, pages 173–79. The first woman was not hanged in Hamburg until 1619, Aachen in 1662, and Breslau in 1750. Keller, 171; G&T, 55.

54. Cited in Keller, 170. See also *CCC*, arts. 159 and 162; Wilbertz, 86–87.

55. *FSJ* Sep 23 1590; Jul 10 1593; also Knapp, *Kriminalrecht*, 136.

56. *FSJ*: 187 *executions with the sword*; 172 *executions with the rope*. During Heinrich Schmidt's tenure in Bamberg, from late 1572 to early 1585, 105 of 106 executions were either hanging (67) or decapitation (38). Schumann, "Heinrich Schmidt Nachrichter," 605.

57. Overall, decapitations constituted 47.5 per cent (187 of 394) of Frantz Schmidt's capital punishments.

58. *FSJ* Jun 5 1573; 1573; 1576. For Schmidt's references to himself as the *Nachrichter* (never *Henker*), see *Restitution*, 201v–202v.

59. Knapp, *Kriminalrecht*, 52–53; Wilbertz, 87–88.

60. *FSJ* Mar 19 1579; Aug 16 1580; Jul 17 1582; Aug 11 1582; Jul 7 1584.

61. Keller, 157, 160–65.

62. Dülmen, *Theatre of Horror*, especially 5–42.

63. *JHJ* Mar 5 1612, quoted in Hampe, 73.

64. *JHJ* 97r–v (Mar 7 1615); *FSJ* Mar 7 1615. See also Stuart, 175ff., on the importance of a good death on the scaffold.

65. Hampe, 73.

66. Hampe, 69, 75.

67. Hampe, 19; also Richard J. Evans, *Rituals of Retribution: Capital Punishment in Germany, 1600–1987* (Oxford, UK, and New York: Oxford University Press, 1996), 69–70.

68. *FSJ* Feb 9 1598.

69. ASB 226a: 58v; *FSJ* Sep 23 1590.

70. *FSJ* Feb 18 1585; Sep 16 1580; also Dec 19 1615. "Wenn mein Stündlein vorhanden ist" (1562) and "Was mein Gott will" (1554), Jürgen C. Jacobs and Heinz Rölleke, commentary to 1801 version of Schmidt journal, 230.

71. *JHJ* Mar 5 1611.

72. *FSJ* Mar 11 1597; *JHJ* Mar 11 1597. See also Dec 18 1600; Mar 18 1616.

73. *FSJ* Nov 6 1595; Jan 10 1581; 1576; Jul 1 1616; *JHJ* Jul 1 1616.

74. *FSJ* Mar 9 1609; Dec 23 1600; Jul 8 1613.

75. *FSJ* Jul 11 1598.

76. *FSJ* Jan 28 1613; *JHJ* Jan 28 1613; ASB 226: 56r–57v.

77. *FSJ* Aug 16 1580.

78. *JHJ* Feb 28 1611; *FSJ* Feb 28 1611.

79. 1506, 1509, 1540, and Jul 20 1587. *FSJ* Feb 12 1596; Sep 2 1600; Jan 19 1602; Feb 28 1611. Two additional notations of *putzen*, which appear only in the Bamberg manuscript (Dec 17 1612; Feb 8 1614), were clearly the interpolations of a later editor, based on chronicle descriptions, since Schmidt is referred to in the third person. Hampe, 31; also G&T, 73–74.

80. Angstmann, 109–10; Wilbertz, 127–28; Dülmen, *Theatre of Horror*, 231–40; Keller, 230.

81. StaatsAN 52b, 226a: 176; Hampe, 79; *RV* 2250:13r–v, 15r–v (Mar 16 1641), 29r–v (Mar 30 1641), 59r (Apr 1 1641); StadtAN FI-14/IV: 2106–7.

82. *Restitution*, 202v. At another point, Schmidt records that *I executed at some risk* (*FSJ* Jan 12 1591). The stoning of Simon Schiller and his wife took place on Jun 7 1612.

83. G&T, 68; also Angstmann, 109.

84. *RV* 1222: 5r (Apr 14 1563); *RV* 1224: 5r (Jun 28 1563); *RV* 1230: 29v (Dec 9 1563), 38r (Dec 16 1563); *RV* 1250: 31v (Jun 19 1565); *RV* 1263: 20r (Jun 4 1566).

85. *RV* 1264: 17v (Jun 28 1566); *RV* 1268: 8v (Oct 10 1566); *RV* 1274: 2r (Apr 14 1567); *RV* 1275: 14r (Apr 14 1567); *RV* 1280: 24r (Sep 10 1567); *RV* 1280: 25v (Sep 12 1567). The seven children of Lienhardt and Kunigunda Lippert were Michael (baptised Oct 25 1568), Lorentz (Nov 8 1569), Jobst (Dec 27 1570), Conrad (Jul 17 1572), Barbara (Jul 10 1573), Margarethe (Feb 13 1575), and Magdalena (Dec 6 1577). LKAN Taufungen St Sebaldus.

86. *RV* 1310: 24r–v (Dec 3 1569), 29r–v (Dec 7 1569); *RV* 1402: 22r (Oct 24 1576); *RV* 1404: 1r (Dec 6 1576), 39v (Dec 28 1576).

87. *RV* 1405: 24v (Jan 14 1577).

88. ASB 222: 75v (23 Oct 1577).

89. *RV* 1421: 14v (Mar 21 1578); *RV* 1422: 24v (Apr 5 1578), 58r–v (Apr 25 1578), 68r (Apr 29 1578).

90. *RV* 1423: 33v (May 16 1578).

3. *The Master*

1. *Essays*, 76.

2. Baltasar Gracián, *The Art of Worldly Wisdom: A Pocket Oracle*, trans. Christopher Maurer (New York: Doubleday, 1991), 73.

3. *FSJ* Oct 11 1593.

4. StaatsAB A245/I, Nr. 146, 124–125r. For other especially scandalous examples of fraud, see *FSJ* Feb 9 1598; Dec 3 1605; Jul 12 1614; also Knapp, *Kriminalrecht*, 247ff.

5. Stuart Carroll, *Blood and Violence in Early Modern France* (Oxford, UK: Oxford University Press, 2006), 49.

6. *Brevis Germaniae Descriptio,* 74; cited in Klaus Leder, *Kirche und Jugend in Nürnberg und seinem Landgebiet: 1400–1800* (Neustadt an der Aisch: Degener, 1973), 1. My brief description of Nuremberg's appearance is greatly indebted to Gerald Strauss's much more lyrical and evocative description in *Nuremberg in the Sixteenth Century* (New York: John Wiley, 1966), 9–35, which remains the single best English-language overview of daily life in early modern Nuremberg. I have also found the following surveys particularly helpful: Emil Reicke, *Geschichte der Reichsstadt Nürnberg* (Nuremberg: Joh. Phil. Rawschen, 1896; reprint, Neustadt an der Aisch: P.C.W. Schmidt, 1983); Werner Schultheiß, *Kleine Geschichte Nürnbergs,* 3rd ed. (Nuremberg: Lorenz Spindler, 1997); *Nürnberg: Eine europäische Stadt in Mittelalter und Neuzeit,* ed. Helmut Neuhaus (Nuremberg: Selbstverlag des Vereins für Geschichte der Stadt Nürnberg, 2000); and the indispensable reference work *Stadtlexikon Nürnberg,* ed. Michael Diefenbacher and Rudolf Endres (Nuremberg: W. Tümmels Verlag, 2000).

7. Reicke, *Geschichte der Reichsstadt Nürnberg,* 998.

8. Andrea Bendlage, *Henkers Hertzbruder. Das Strafverfolgungspersonal der Reichsstadt Nürnberg im 15. und 16. Jahrhundert* (Constance: UVK, 2003), 28–31.

9. William Smith, "A Description of the Cittie of Nuremberg" (1590), *MVGN* 48 (1958), 222. For information on the informers (*Kundschaftler*) employed by the city, see Bendlage, *Henkers Hertzbruder,* 127–37.

10. During his thirteen years in Bamberg, Heinrich Schmidt's annual income – paid by the execution, not by the week – averaged 50 fl., with a peak of 87 fl. from 1574 to 1575 and a low of 29 fl. the following year. StaatsAB A231/1, Nr. 1797/1. For the details of Frantz's contract, see *RV* 1422: 68r (Apr 29 1578); also Knapp, *Loch,* 61–62. The Bregenz executioner had a base salary of 52 fl. annually plus 1–2 fl. per execution; the Munich executioner was paid 83 fl. annually until 1697; while their Osnabrück counterpart received 2 thaler (1.7 fl.) per execution. Nowosadtko, 65–67; Wilbertz, 101.

11. *RV* 1119: 9v, 11v, 12r, 17r–v, 18r, 20r (Nov 13–15 1554); Knapp, *Loch,* 56–57.

12. StaatsAN 62, 54–79; LKAN Beerdigungen St Lorenz, 57v: "Jorg Peck Pallenpinder bey dem [sh]onnetbadt Sep 16 1560." At least two of the nine children born to Jorg and Margareta Peck died in childhood, possibly others. LKAN Taufungen, St Sebaldus: 93v (Magdalena; Jul 24 1544), 95r (Maria; Sep 20 1545), 96r (Jorg; May 26 1546), 97r (Gertraud; Mar 14 1547), 99r (Sebastian; Aug 10 1549), 104v (Georgius; Dec 1 1551), 105v (Barbara; Oct 6 1552), 107v (Magdalena; Aug 30 1554), 110v (Philipus; Nov 29 1555).

13. LKAN Trauungen, St Sebaldus 1579, 70; *RV* 1430: 34r (Dec 7 1579).

14. *Stadtlexikon Nürnberg,* 437.

15. Ernst Mummenhoff, "Die öffentliche Gesundheits- und Krankenpflege im alten Nürnberg: Das Spital zum Heilige Geist," in *Festschrift zur Eröffnung des Neuen Krankenhauses der Stadt Nürnberg* (Nuremberg, 1898), 6–8; Stuart, 103.

16. G&T, 92. In the late sixteenth century, the Nuremberg Lion earned a base annual salary of 52 fl., Bendlage, *Henkers Hertzbruder,* 36–37, 89.

17. *RV* 1576: 6v, 10v (Nov 11 and 18 1589); StaatsAN 62, 82–145.

18. *FSJ* Aug 16 1597.

19. Knapp, *Loch*, 67.

20. Schwerhoff, *Köln im Kreuzverhör*, 103.

21. Knapp, *Kriminalrecht*, 64–81. On the incarceration of the insane during this period in German history, see H. C. Erik Midelfort, *A History of Madness in Sixteenth-Century Germany* (Stanford, CA: Stanford University Press, 1999), especially 322–84.

22. For instance, a stay of eleven weeks and three days in 1588 cost Christoph Greis-dörffer 13 fl., 2 d. 8 H; paid in full at his release, StaatsAN 54a, II: 340.

23. Öhler was appointed *Lochhirt* on Oct 26 1557 and at a salary of 2 fl. per week was almost as well paid as Frantz Schmidt, *RV* 1148: 24v–25r (Oct 26 1557). On the duties of Nuremberg wardens, see Bendlage, *Henkers Hertzbruder*, 37–42.

24. StaatsAN 52a, 447: 1002 (Jun 23 1578); Knapp, *Loch*, 145–47.

25. Knapp, *Loch*, 20–21.

26. Knapp, *Loch*, 20. *FSJ* Jul 3 1593; Nov 22 1603, Sep 15 1604. See also prison suicides recorded for 1580, 1604, 1611, and 1615, as well as attempted suicides mentioned by Frantz Schmidt, StadtAN F1, 47: 8314, 876r; *FSJ* Jul 11 1598; May 10 1599. In 1604 a convicted murderer stabbed an accused rustler to death in prison (ASB 226: 17r–v).

27. StaatsAN 52a, 447: 1009–10; ASB 226: 23v; *RV* 1775: 13r–v (March 1605). The collective rebuilding of the gallows was prescribed in *CCC*, art. 215. See also Keller, 209ff.; Knapp, *Loch*, 69–70; Dülmen, *Theatre of Horror*, 70–73.

28. *FSJ* Sep 3 1588; Nov 5 1588; Dec 22 1586.

29. *FSJ* Jun 15 1591. Jacobs, commentary to 1801 Schmidt journal, 212.

30. William Ian Miller, *Humiliation: And Other Essays on Honour, Social Discom-fort, and Violence* (Ithaca, NY: Cornell University Press, 1993), 16.

31. *FSJ* Dec 16 1594; Jun 21 1593.

32. *FSJ* Nov 10 1596; Jan 12 1583.

33. *FSJ* Aug 16 1580.

34. *FSJ* Jan 4 1582; Jul 24 1585; Oct 5 1597.

35. *FSJ* Jul 10 1593; and see, e.g., Dec 23 1605.

36. *FSJ* Oct 11 1593; Feb 9 1598; Jul 12 1614.

37. *FSJ* May 12 1584.

38. Knapp, *Kriminalrecht*, 100. For a fuller account, see Wilhelm Fürst, "Der Prozess gegen Nikolaus von Gülchen, Ratskonsulenten und Advokaten zu Nürnberg, 1605," *MVGN* 20 (1913): 139ff.

39. *FSJ* Dec 23 1605.

40. *FSJ* Apr 10 1578; Aug 12 1578; 1576.

41. *FSJ* Apr 15 1578; 1576; Dec 22 1586; Jun 1 1587; Feb 18 1585; May 29 1582. See also Nov 17 1582; Sep 12 1583.

42. *FSJ* Mar 6 1578; Jan 26 1580; Aug 10 1581; Jul 17 1582, Jun 8 1587; Jul 20 1587; Mar 5 1612.

43. ASB 210: 74vff., 112 r; ASB 210: 106r–v. See also Norbert Schindler, "The World of Nicknames: On the Logic of Popular Nomenclature," in *Rebellion, Commu-nity, and Custom in Early Modern Germany*, trans. Pamela E. Selwyn (Cambridge,

UK: Cambridge University Press, 2002), especially 57–62; also F. Bock, "Nürnberger Spitzname von 1200 bis 1800," *MVGN* 45 (1954): 1–147, and Bock, "Nürnberger Spitzname von 1200 bis 1800 – Nachlese," *MVGN* 49 (1959): 1–33. The same naming tendencies were evident in contemporary England: Paul Griffiths, *Lost Londons: Change, Crime, and Control in the Capital City, 1550–1660* (Cambridge, UK: Cambridge University Press, 2008), 179–92.

44. *JHJ* 39v.
45. *FSJ* Jul 19 1614; Jun 22 1616; Sep 16 1580; Aug 4 1612; Aug 23 1594; Nov 21 1589; Aug 16 1587; Apr 30 1596; Jul 4 and Jul 7 1584.
46. Schmidt frequently mentions punishments elsewhere in Franconia that suggest more than word-of-mouth news, for instance, he identifies one condemned thief as *Hans Weber from Neuenstadt, . . . whom I saw whipped with rods out of Neuenkirchen ten years ago* (*FSJ* Aug 4 1586). See also Jan 29 1583; Feb 9 1585; Jun 20 1588; Nov 6 1588; Jan 15 1594; Mar 6 1604.
47. *FSJ* May 29 1582; Nov 17 1582; Sep 12 1583; Dec 4 1583; Jan 9 1581; Jul 23 1583. See also archer Georg Mayr whipped out of town for theft (Aug 11 1586); and Nov 18 1589; Mar 3 1597; Aug 16 1597; May 2 1605; Feb 10 1609; Dec 15 1611. For details on the frequent disciplining of such employees, see Bendlage, *Henkers Hertzbruder*, 165–201, 226–33.
48. *FSJ* Mar 3 1597; Aug 16 1597; May 25 1591.
49. *FSJ* Feb 10 1596; Mar 24 1590.
50. Griffiths, *Lost Londons*, 138; see also 196ff. on contemporary English terms for men of ill repute.
51. *FSJ* May 21 1611; Nov 24 1585.
52. *FSJ* May 24 1580; Apr 15 1581; Dec 20 1582; Nov 19 1584; Aug 14 1584; Mar 16 1585; Nov 17 1586; Nov 21 1586; Jul 14 1593; Jul 26 1593; Oct 9 1593; Nov 10 1597; Dec 14 1601; Mar 3 1604; Feb 12 1605; Nov 11 1615; Dec 8 1615. See also corporal punishments of Sep 8 1590; Jan 18 1588; Dec 9 1600; Apr 21 1601; Jan 27 1586.
53. *FSJ* Oct 9 1578; Oct 15 1579; Oct 31 1579; Oct 20 1580; Jan 9 1581; Jan 31 1581; Feb 7 1581; Feb 21 1581; May 6 1581; Sep 26 1581; Nov 25 1581; Dec 20 1582; Jan 10 1583; Jan 11 1583; Jul 15 1583; Aug 29 1583; Sep 4 1583; Nov 26 1583.
54. *FSJ* Oct 20 1580; Jan 10 1583; Jan 31 1581; Apr 2 1589; Jan 2 1588; Jan 18 1588. See also May 5 1590; Jun 11 1594; Jan 3 1595; Jun 8 1596.
55. On overall criminal pattern for female crime and executions, see Rublack, *Crimes of Women*; Otto Ulbricht, ed., *Von Huren und Rabenmüttern: Weibliche Kriminalität in der frühen Neuzeit* (Vienna, Cologne, and Weimar: Böhlau, 1995); Joel F. Harrington, *Reordering Marriage and Society in Reformation Germany* (Cambridge, UK, and New York: Cambridge University Press, 1995), 228–40; and Schwerhoff, *Köln im Kreuzverhör*, 178–79.
56. *FSJ* Feb 9 1581; Mar 27 1587; Jan 29 1599.
57. *FSJ* Jul 7 1584.
58. *FSJ* Nov 6 1610; Jul 19 1588. See also Laura Gowing, *Domestic Dangers: Women, Words, and Sex in Early Modern London* (Oxford, UK: Oxford University Press, 1996).
59. *FSJ* Jul 3 1593; Dec 4 1599; May 7 1603; Mar 9 1609.

60. *FSJ* Jul 20 1587; Sep 15 1604.
61. Cf. accounts of annual tributes required of Hof's Jews and frequent break-ins to Jewish homes, often leaving bits of pork behind. Dietlein, *Chronik der Stadt Hof,* 267–68; *FSJ* Sep 23 1590; Aug 3 1598; Oct 26 1602.
62. *FSJ* Sep 23 1590; Aug 25 1592; Jul 10 1592; and Jul 10 1593.
63. On this question of fluid early modern identity, see Natalie Zemon Davis, *The Return of Martin Guerre* (Cambridge, MA: Harvard University Press, 1983), and Valentin Groebner, *Who Are You? Identification, Deception, and Surveillance in Early Modern Europe,* trans. Mark Kyburz and John Peck (Cambridge, MA: Zone, 2007).
64. *FSJ* Dec 2 1613; see also Jul 3 1593; Jul 12 1614.
65. *FSJ* Jan 23 1610.
66. *FSJ* Feb 23 1593; May 3 1596; Jul 27 1594; Sep 8 1590.
67. *FSJ* Aug 12 1579; Jul 28 1590; Apr 21 1601. See also Apr 18 1598; Feb 9 1581; Feb 12 1600.
68. *FSJ* Jan 29 1588.
69. *FSJ* Jul 4 1588; Jul 30 1588; Dec 16 1594; Jul 4 1588; Feb 10 1597.
70. *FSJ* May 28 1588.
71. *FSJ* Feb 12 1596; Jul 11 1598; Nov 18 1617; Nov 13 1617.
72. *FSJ* Jan 16 1616. See also Jul 17 1582.
73. *FSJ* Jan 23 1595; Mar 4 1606; May 23 1615; Jun 25 1617; Jan 23 1610; Nov 14 1598.
74. *FSJ* Oct 16 1584; Oct 23 1589; Mar 8 1614. See also Oct 27 1584.
75. *FSJ* Mar 3 1580; Nov 17 1580; Jul 3 1593; Mar 30 1598; Jan 18 1603; Nov 20 1611; Nov 2 1615. See also Apr 29 1600.
76. *FSJ* May 27 1603.
77. *FSJ* Jul 2 1606.
78. *FSJ* Jul 23 1578; Jun 23 1612. See also May 2 1579; Apr 10 1582; Jun 4 1599.
79. *FSJ* Apr 28 1579; Jun 21 1593. See also Feb 28 1615.
80. *FSJ* Nov 18 1589. See also Apr 10 1582; Nov 1 1578; Sep 2 1598.
81. *FSJ* Jul 12 1614; Jan 22 1611.
82. *FSJ* Mar 6 1578; Jul 13 1579; Jan 26 1580; Feb 29 1580; Aug 14 1582; May 5 1590; Jul 7 1590; Mar 15 1597; May 20 1600; Apr 21 1601; Aug 4 1607; Mar 5 1616.
83. *FSJ* Jan 26 1580; May 5 1590; Jul 7 1590; Jun 26 1606; Feb 8 1614.
84. *FSJ* May 17 1606; Aug 4 1607; Dec 6 1580; Nov 17 1584.
85. *FSJ* Jun 11 1585. See also Jun 21 1593; Dec 23 1601; Sep 15 1604; Jul 9 1605; Nov 20 1611; Mar 5 1612; Nov 19 1613.
86. *FSJ* Oct 15 1585; Oct 21 1585; Apr 14 1586; Apr 25 1587; Jul 15 1589.
87. *FSJ* Nov 11 1585.
88. *FSJ* Jun 1 1581; Jul 27 1582; Oct 3 1587.
89. The popular stereotypes of spousal murder in early modern Germany typically contrasted the cool and calculating murdering wife with the violent and passionate husband. See Silke Göttsch, "'Vielmahls aber hätte sie gewünscht einen anderen Mann zu haben,' Gattenmord im 18. Jahrhundert," in Ulbricht, *Von Huren und Rabenmüttern,* 313–34.

90. Two wives: *FSJ* Feb 15 1580; Apr 27 1583; Jul 9 1583; Mar 26 1584; Oct 29 1584; Jun 6 1586; Jul 14 1590. Three wives: Dec 1 1580; Apr 3 1585. Four wives: Apr 3 1585; May 29 1588. Five wives: Nov 5 1595.

91. *FSJ* Jul 28 1590. See also Feb 20 1582; Oct 16 1582; Apr 27 1583; Jul 9 1583; Mar 16 1585; Sep 20 1586; Oct 4 1587; Jul 10 1592; Jul 23 1605; Dec 6 1609.

92. *FSJ* Jul 28 1590. See also Feb 20 1582; Oct 16 1582; Apr 27 1583; Jul 9 1583; Mar 16 1585; Sep 20 1586; Oct 4 1587; Jul 10 1592; Jul 23 1605; Dec 6 1609.

93. *FSJ* Feb 28 1611; Jun 7 1612.

94. *RV* 1431: 37v (Dec 29 1579); *RV* 1456: 46r (Nov 8 1580); *RV* 1458: 25v (Dec 28 1580).

95. StaatsAN 44a, Rst Nbg Losungamt, 35 neue Laden, Nr. 1979; StaatsAN 60c, Nr. 1, 181r; also *RV* 1507: 9v–10r (Aug 19 1584); *RV* 1508: 32r (Sep 25 1584).

96. Shortly after Easter 1582 Frantz requested and received permission to visit his ailing father in Bamberg, *RV* 1475: 23v (Apr 10 1582).

97. ASB 210: 154; also *RV* 1523: 8r–v, 23r, 25r, 31r (Feb 1, 8, 9, 10, 1585). StaatsAN 52a, 447: 1076.

98. *FSJ* Feb 11 1585. See also Jul 23 1584.

99. StaatsAB A245/I, Nr. 146, 106v–107v; StaatsAN 52a, 447: 1076–77. In another passage, Schmidt not only identifies a culprit as a kinsman but also relegates the flogging to his assistant, *FSJ* Jun 7 1603.

100. StaatsAB A231/1, Nr. 1809, 1.

101. StadtsAB B7, Nr. 84 (May 1 1585); StadtsAB B4, Nr. 35, 102r–v (1586); *RV* 1517: 21v–22r (May 25 1585).

102. StadtAN F1–2/VII: 682.

103. St Rochus Planquadrat H5, #654; Ilse Schumann, "Neues zum Nürnberger Nachrichter Franz Schmidt," in *Genealogie* 25, nos. 9–10 (Sep–Oct 2001): 686.

104. Hilpoltstein (*FSJ* Jul 20 1580; Aug 20 1584; Mar 6 1589; Sep 19 1593; Feb 28 1594); Lauf (*FSJ* Aug 4 1590; Jun 8 1596; Jun 4 1599); Sulzbach (*FSJ* Feb 23 1593; Mar 11 1597); Hersbruck (*FSJ* Jul 19 1595; Dec 18 1595; Feb 10 1596; Sep 2 1598); Lichtenau (*FSJ* Apr 18 1598). See also *RV* 1706: 38r (Jan 12 1600).

105. LKAN St Sebaldus, 49v, 50v, 70v.

106. One local study from the period, for instance, found that only one in six poor families had more than three children resident at the same town, while nearly three in four upper-middle-class and wealthy families enjoyed this privilege. On the other hand, based on a sample of 782 executioner families during the early modern period, three boys and three girls was the average among executioner families, Jürgen Schlumbohm, *Lebensläufe, Familien, Höfe: Die Bauern und Heuerleute des osnabrückischen Kirchspiels Belm in proto-industrieller Zeit, 1650–1850* (Göttingen: Vandenhoeck and Ruprecht, 1994), 201, 297; G&T, 45–50.

107. *RV* 1621: 3v, 10v (Jul 14 1593); ASB 308 (Bürgerbuch 1534–1631): 128v.

4. The Sage

1. *Essays*, 398.

2. *FSJ* Mar 15 1597.

3. *RV* 2122: 23r–v (May 19 1631). StaatsAN Rep 65 (Mikrofilm S 0735). The plague and winter of 1600 are recounted in StaatsAN 52b, 226a: 1256–57.

4. See especially the excellent overview of Joy Wiltenburg, *Crime and Culture in Early Modern Germany* (Charlottesville: University of Virginia Press, 2012).

5. *FSJ* 1573; Nov 9 1586; Nov 17 1580; Mar 3 1580; Aug 16 1580; Dec 14 1579.

6. *FSJ* Oct 11 1604; Apr 18 1598.

7. *FSJ* Mar 29 1595.

8. Knapp, *Kriminalrecht*, 179–80.

9. *FSJ* Apr 28 1579; Dec 6 1580; Jul 27 1582.

10. *FSJ* Oct 23 1589. See also Oct 16 1584; Mar 13 1602; Oct 11 1604.

11. *FSJ* Apr 28 1579; Mar 5 1612; Jan 16 1616; Jan 27 1586; Sep 23 1590; May 18 1591; Dec 17 1612. See also 1574; May 25 1581; Feb 20 1582; Aug 4 1586; Dec 22 1587; Jan 5 1587; May 30 1587; Apr 11 1592; Jun 21 1593. On the vulnerability of nighttime, see Craig Koslofsky, *Evening's Empire: A History of the Night in Early Modern Europe* (Cambridge, UK: Cambridge University Press, 2011).

12. *FSJ* Aug 29 1587; Oct 16 1584.

13. *FSJ* Jun 30 1593.

14. *FSJ* Sep 18 1604; Aug 13 1604. See also Jan 2 1588; Jul 10 1593; Feb 28 1615.

15. *FSJ* Jan 16 1616.

16. *FSJ* Jun 4 1599.

17. Four of these included violent robbery (Dülmen, *Theatre of Horror*, appendix, table 5), as did several cases from the sixteenth century. In three instances, the rape of minors resulted in executions (*FSJ* Jul 3 1578; Apr 10 1583; Jun 23, 1612).

18. *FSJ* Mar 13 1602; Aug 22 1587. See also Nov 19 1612; Jun 2 1612; Dec 7 1615.

19. *FSJ* Jun 4 1596; Nov 28 1583; Nov 13 1599.

20. *FSJ* Jul 17 1582; Aug 11 1582; May 27 1603; May 8 1598; May 17 1611; Oct 11 1608.

21. *FSJ* Oct 13 1604.

22. *FSJ* Jul 15 1580.

23. *FSJ* 1578; Jul 15 1580; May 25 1581; Feb 20 1582; Mar 14 1584; Aug 4 1586; Jan 2 1588; Jul 4 1588; Jun 21 1593; Feb 10 1596; Jul 22 1596; Jul 11 1598; Jan 20 1601; Apr 21 1601.

24. *FSJ* May 25 1581.

25. *FSJ* Jul 21 1593. See also three cases in 1573; Jul 15 1580; May 25 1581; Feb 20 1582; Aug 4 1586; Dec 8 1587; Feb 10 1596; Jul 22 1596; Apr 21 1601.

26. *FSJ* 1574.

27. *FSJ* Oct 11 1603. Other examples of corpse desecration are 1574; May 25 1591; Aug 28 1599; Jul 15 1580; Jan 2 1588; Mar 13 1602; Dec 2 1596; Mar 15 1597; Mar 5 1612.

28. *FSJ* May 2 1605; Jul 29 1600; Nov 12 1601; Dec 2 1596; Feb 18 1591; Jun 21 1593; Jul 11 1598. See also 1573; 1574; Feb 11 1585; May 4 1585; May 2 1605.

29. *FSJ* Mar 3 1597; Jul 29 1600; Feb 10 1596; Jan 17 1611; Feb 20 1582; Jul 27 1582.

30. *FSJ*: 300 of 394 capital punishments; 301 of 384 corporal punishments.

31. On the "Code of the West," see especially Richard Maxwell Brown, "Violence," in *The Oxford History of the American West*, ed. Clyde A. Milner II et al.

(Oxford, UK: Oxford University Press, 1994), 393–95. I am indebted to my colleague Dan Usner for this citation.

32. Knapp, *Kriminalrecht*, 170–77, 191–95.
33. *FSJ* Oct 26 1602; Mar 17 1609; May 4 1585. See also Apr 28 1586.
34. *FSJ* 1577; Apr 10 1578; Oct 6 1579; Nov 28 1583; Apr 28 1586; Feb 18 1591; Jun 1 1587; Oct 13 1588; Aug 11 1600; Aug 11 1606. Knapp, *Kriminalrecht*, 31–37. See also Schwerhoff, *Köln im Kreuzverhör*, 265–322.
35. *FSJ* Oct 13 1588.
36. *FSJ* Aug 7 1599.
37. *FSJ* Apr 20 1587.
38. *FSJ* Apr 11 1592.
39. *FSJ* Sep 20 1587; Mar 6 1604.
40. Harrington, *Unwanted Child*, 30–34.
41. *FSJ* Oct 5 1597; Jul 8 1609; also Jul 1 1609.
42. *FSJ* Jan 9 1583; Jul 18 1583; Sep 1 1586; Jul 4 1584; also Jun 16 1585.
43. *FSJ* Jun 28 1614.
44. *FSJ* Feb 22 1611.
45. *FSJ* Jul 20 1587.
46. See Ulinka Rublack "'Viehisch, frech vnd onverschämpt': Inzest in Südwestdeutschland, ca. 1530–1700," in Ulbricht, *Von Huren und Rabenmüttern*, 171–213; also David Warren Sabean, Simon Teuscher, and Jon Mathieu, eds., *Kinship in Europe: Approaches to the Long-Term Development (1300–1900)* (New York: Berghahn, 2007).
47. *FSJ* Jul 23 1605; Jan 29 1599; Mar 5 1611; Feb 28 1611; Jul 7 1584. See also Mar 27 1587; Apr 23 1588; Apr 2 1589; Jun 26 1594; Jun 17 1609.
48. The best work on this subject is Helmut Puff, *Sodomy in Reformation Germany and Switzerland, 1400–1600* (London and Chicago: University of Chicago Press, 2003).
49. *FSJ* Aug 13 1594.
50. *FSJ* Mar 11 1596.
51. *FSJ* Mar 11 1596; Aug 10 1581.
52. *FSJ* Jul 3 1596. For evidence of a surprisingly tolerant atmosphere in this respect, see Maria R. Boes, "On Trial for Sodomy in Early Modern Germany," in *Sodomy in Early Modern Europe*, ed. Tom Betteridge (Manchester, UK: Manchester University Press, 2002), 27–45.
53. *FSJ* Apr 19 1591. See also Jul 15 1584; Oct 13 1587; May 17 1583; Jul 15 1585. On the fear of divine retribution for blasphemy, see Knapp, *Kriminalrecht*, 277–79.
54. *FSJ* Jan 5 1587; Jun 25 1590; Jul 29 1600. See also Aug 12 1600; Jan 19 1602; Apr 21 1601.
55. *FSJ* Feb 10 1609; Mar 9 1609; Jan 23 1610; Jan 19 1602.
56. *FSJ* Oct 1 1605.
57. *FSJ* Jan 27 1586. See also Aug 4 1586; Jan 2 1588; Mar 4 1589; Sep 23 1590.
58. Knapp, *Kriminalrecht*, 119–22. See also 233ff., on the "diebliche Behalten" identified by executing magistrates.
59. *FSJ* Dec 29 1611; Jul 19 1588.

60. *FSJ* Jan 12 1615; Sep 12 1583; Jul 23 1584; Aug 3 1598; Aug 26 1609.
61. *FSJ* Nov 14 1598.
62. *FSJ* Nov 18 1617.
63. *FSJ* Dec 13 1588; Nov 18 1597; Oct 13 1601.
64. *FSJ* Sep 15 1604.
65. *FSJ* Apr 29 1600. See also Jul 1 1616.
66. *FSJ* Oct 25 1597. See also Jun 1 1587.
67. *FSJ* Mar 9 1609.
68. *FSJ* Nov 18 1617; Sep 2 1600. See also Jul 23 1594; Jul 13 1613.
69. *FSJ* Oct 17 1587; Sep 7 1611; Sep 14 1602; Sep 16 1595.
70. *FSJ* Oct 1 1612; Jul 8 1613.
71. *FSJ* Oct 11 1593; Feb 9 1598; Mar 20 1606; Feb 23 1609; Jul 12 1614.
72. *FSJ* May 4 1585; Nov 17 1584; Oct 5 1588; May 7 1603. Explicitly "good deaths" included Jan 10 1581; Nov 6 1595; Dec 23 1600; Sep 15 1605; Sep 18 1605; Jul 8 1613.
73. *JHJ*, quoted in Hampe, 71; *FSJ* Jul 19 1614. See also May 17 1611.
74. *JHJ* 39v.
75. *JHJ*, quoted in Hampe, 19.
76. *JHJ*, quoted in Hampe, 17–18.
77. *FSJ* Jan 11 1588.
78. *FSJ* Jan 28 1613; Jul 8 1613.
79. *FSJ* Feb 20 1582; Sep 18 1604. See also Aug 11 1582; Oct 9 1593.
80. *JHJ* Mar 10 1614.
81. Dülmen, *Theatre of Horror*, 28–32; Schwerhoff, *Köln im Kreuzverhör*, 166ff.
82. StaatsAN 226a, 40v, 77r.; *JHJ* 153r; *FSJ* Mar 15 1610.
83. Hampe, 14–16.
84. Ibid., 83.
85. *FSJ* Oct 3 1588. See also Jul 12 1614; Jun 15 1588; May 23 1597; Dec 18 1593.
86. *JHJ* Mar 10 1614, quoted in Hampe, 16.
87. Quoted in Hampe., 83.
88. *FSJ* Feb 10 1609.
89. Keller, 144–45, 148.
90. *FSJ* Jan 10 1581; also Oct 16 1585.
91. *FSJ* Apr 11 1592; Mar 4 1606; Oct 11 1593; Aug 11 1606; Mar 5 1612. See also Mar 17 1609; Sep 5 1611.
92. See Harrington, *Unwanted Child*, 195–214.
93. *CCC*, art. 179 and art. 14.
94. Harrington, *Unwanted Child*, 221–25.
95. StadtAN F1–14/IV: 1634.
96. *FSJ* May 16 1594; Jul 22 1593; Jun 4 1600; Nov 29 1582.
97. *FSJ* Oct 1 1612.
98. Hampe, 84. The five boys in the first group were forced to watch the execution of their eighteen-year-old leader, Heinrich Lind, before they were publicly flogged and banished. A group of thirteen boys the same year, "of whom none was over twelve years old", was also banished after flogging. StadtAN F1–2/VII: 529; Knapp, *Kriminalrecht*, 9.

99. *FSJ* Jan 25 1614; StaatsAB A245/I Nr. 146, 82v; ASB 210: 86v.

100. *FSJ* Oct 7 1578; Mar 19 1579; Apr 28 1580; Aug 2 1580; Oct 4 1580; Feb 11 1584; Feb 12 1584; Jul 20 1587; May 15 1587; Sep 5 1594; May 3 1597; Jun 16 1604; Jan 12 1615; Dec 19 1615; also ASB 226a: 49r–52v.

101. ASB 226a: 48r; *FSJ* Jan 25 1614.

102. *FSJ* Feb 11 1584; Feb 12 1584.

103. *FSJ* Sep 5 1594; May 3 1597; Jun 16 1604; Feb 28 1615; Dec 14 1615.

104. *FSJ* Jan 12 1615. See also Dec 14 1615.

105. *FSJ* Dec 19 1615; ASB 218: 72vff.

106. *FSJ* Jan 29 1588; Jan 13 1592. See also Feb 11 1584; Feb 12 1584; Jun 5 1593; Jan 12 1615; Dec 14 1615; Dec 19 1615.

107. *FSJ* Oct 25 1615.

108. *FSJ* May 19 1601.

109. Joel F. Harrington, "Bad Parents, the State, and the Early Modern Civilizing Process," in *German History* 16, no. 1 (1998): 16–28.

110. *FSJ* Jan 8 1582; 1574; Apr 15 1578; Mar 6 1606; Apr 2 1590; Jan 14 1584.

111. *FSJ* Dec 12 1598; Mar 6 1606; Jul 18 1583; Sep 1 1586; Jun 7 1612. *RV* 1800: 48v–49r (Mar 14 1607).

112. *FSJ* Jan 14 1584; also Jan 8 1582.

113. ASB 213: 214v.

114. *FSJ* May 2 1605.

115. *FSJ* Jun 16 1604.

116. ASB 210: 154r. *FSJ* Feb 11 1585.

117. Dieter Merzbacher, "Der Nürnberger Scharfrichter Frantz Schmidt – Autor eines Meisterliedes?," in *MVGN* 73 (1986): 63–75.

118. Stuart, 179–80.

119. *FSJ* Apr 2 1590.

120. *FSJ* Sep 15 1604. On the theme of the good and bad thieves in fifteenth- and sixteenth-century art, see Mitchell Merback, *The Thief, the Cross, and the Wheel: Pain and the Spectacle of Punishment in Medieval and Renaissance Europe* (Chicago: University of Chicago Press, 1999), 218–65.

5. The Healer

1. *Essays*, 174.

2. *FSJ* Jan 2 1588; Jan 11 1588; Jan 18 1588.

3. Geoffrey Abbott, *Lords of the Scaffold: A History of the Executioner* (London: Eric Dobby, 1991), 104ff.

4. ASB 210: 289r–v, 292v–293v.

5. *Restitution*, 201v.

6. *RV* 1119: 13r (Jul 22 1555); G&T, 104–6.

7. Nowosadtko, 163. In 1533, Augsburg's retired executioner was unable to support himself as a full-time medical consultant and was forced to ask for his old job back. Stuart, 154.

8. Robert Jütte, *Ärzte, Heiler, und Patienten: Medizinischer Alltag in der frühen Neuzeit* (Munich: Artemis & Winkler, 1991), 18–19.

9. Angstmann, 92; Keller, 226. Paracelsus, *Von dem Fleisch und Mumia*, cited in Stuart, 160.

10. Matthew Ramsey, *Professional and Popular Medicine in France, 1770–1830: The Social World of Medical Practise* (Cambridge, UK: Cambridge University Press, 1988), 27; Nowosadtko, 165.

11. On the proliferation of general medical knowledge among artisanal families, see Michael Hackenberg, "Books in Artisan Homes of Sixteenth-Century Germany," *Journal of Library History* 21 (1986): 72–91.

12. *Artzney Buch: Von etlichen biß anher unbekandten unnd unbeschriebenen Kranckheiten/deren Verzeichnuß im folgenden Blat zu finden* (Frankfurt am Main, 1583).

13. The edition I consulted was *Feldtbuch der Wundartzney, newlich getruckt und gebessert* (Strasbourg, 1528).

14. One popular work, the 1532 *Spiegel der Artzney* of Lorenz Fries, was in fact structured around questions during the consultation. See Claudia Stein, *Negotiating the French Pox in Early Modern Germany* (Farnham, UK: Ashgate, 2009), 48–49.

15. Jütte, *Ärzte*, 108. See also David Gentilcore, *Medical Charlatanism in Early Modern Italy* (Oxford, UK: Oxford University Press, 2006).

16. In a sample of 2,179 cases, 36.6 per cent of the injuries were treated by wound doctors in late-sixteenth-century Cologne. Jütte, *Ärzte*, table 6; G&T, 111.

17. Nowosadtko, 163–66.

18. *Restitution*, 202r.

19. Valentin Deuser was able to obtain an imperial privilege in 1641 that allowed him "to make house calls in any location and practise without hindrance as a wound doctor and barber," G&T, 41.

20. *Restitution*, 203r–v.

21. *RV* 1726: 58r–v (Jul 7 1601).

22. *RV* 1835: 25r (Oct 14 1609).

23. Mummenhoff, "Die öffentliche Gesundheits," 15; L.W.B. Brockliss and Colin Jones, *The Medical World of Early Modern France* (Oxford, UK: Clarendon Press, 1997), 13–14.

24. In 1661 the Nuremberg council answered an angry query from Augsburg physicians about their own executioner's wide-ranging medical activities, stating that such activities were acceptable for executioners, Stuart, 163.

25. G&T, 41. For accounts of conflicts elsewhere, see Wilbertz, 70ff.; Stuart, 164–72; G&T, 109ff.

26. In Nuremberg this was usually Saint Peter's, although sometimes on land within the cemetery that was not consecrated, Knapp, *Loch*, 77.

27. Karl H. Dannenfeldt, "Egyptian Mumia: The Sixteenth Century Experience and Debate," in *Sixteenth Century Journal* 16, no. 2 (1985): 163–80.

28. Stuart, 158–59; Stuart compares the distributing of blood and occasionally body parts to Christian communion, 180.

29. Markwart Herzog, "Scharfrichterliches Medizin. Zu den Beziehungen zwischen Henker und Arzt, Schafott und Medizin," in *Medizinhistorisches Journal* 29 (1994), 330–31; Stuart, 155–60; Nowosadtko, 169–70.

30. Nowosadtko, 179.

31. Stuart, 162; Angstmann, 93.

32. For a different interpretation of the intersection of art and anatomy, see Andrea Carlino, *Books of the Body: Anatomical Ritual and Renaissance Learning*, trans. John Tedeschi and Anne C. Tedeschi (Chicago: University of Chicago Press, 2009).

33. Roy Porter, *Blood and Guts: A Short History of Medicine* (London: Allen Lane, 2002), 53–58.

34. Nowosadtko, 168–69.

35. G&T, 67.

36. Hampe, 79–81.

37. Cited in Knapp, *Kriminalrecht*, 64.

38. *FSJ* Jul 21 1578; *RV* 1425: 48r (Jul 17 1578).

39. *FSJ* Jun 1 1581; Oct 16 1584; Dec 8 1590; Dec 18 1593. Pessler was still dissecting executed criminals in 1641. Knapp, *Kriminalrecht*, 100.

40. *FSJ* Jun 26 1578; Aug 22 1587.

41. *FSJ* Jan 20 1601; Aug 29 1587.

42. *FSJ* Jun 4 1596; Mar 21 1615; Oct 1 1605.

43. *FSJ* Sep 14 1602.

44. Angstmann, 99–101; StaatsAN 42a, 447: 1063 (Aug 7 1583).

45. Döpler, *Theatrum poenarum*, 1:596; Nowosadtko; 183–89; *RV* 2176: 56r (Jul 15 1635); Hartmut H. Kunstmann, *Zauberwahn und Hexenprozess in der Reichsstadt Nürnberg* (Nuremberg: Nürnberg Stadtarchiv, 1970), 94–97.

46. Nowosadtko, 98–117; Zagolla, *Folter und Hexenprozess*, 368; Wolfgang Behringer, *Witchcraft Persecutions in Bavaria: Popular Magic, Religious Zealotry, and Reason of State in Early Modern Europe*, trans. by J. C. Grayson and David Lederer (Cambridge, UK, and New York: Cambridge University Press, 1997), 401, table 13. On the witch craze elsewhere in Franconia, see also Susanne Kleinöder-Strobel, *Die Verfolgung von Zauberei und Hexerei in den fränkischen Markgraftümern im 16. Jahrhundert* (Tübingen: J.C.B. Mohr Siebeck, 2002).

47. Kunstmann, *Zauberwahn*, 39–44.

48. *FSJ* Jul 28 1590.

49. ASB 211: 111r–114r; see also Kunstmann, *Zauberwahn*, 69–78.

50. ASB 211: 111r.

51. *FSJ* Jul 28 1590.

52. Kunstmann, *Zauberwahn*, 78–86. Later in the century, Nuremberg too would succumb to the surrounding mania and execute three men and two women for witchcraft (compared to 4,500 for surrounding Franconia).

53. *FSJ* Nov 13 1617; ASB 217: 326r–v.

54. *FSJ* Oct 13 1604.

55. *FSJ* May 2 1605; Dec 23 1600.

56. *FSJ* Dec 13 1588.

57. *FSJ* Jul 8 1613; *JHJ* Jul 8 1613.

58. *FSJ* May 10 1599.

59. *FSJ* Mar 6 1604; ASB 215, cited in Hampe, 59–60.

60. ASB 218: 324r–342r.

61. *FSJ* Mar 7 1604; Aug 17 1599; Mar 20 1606; Feb 18 1585.

62. *FSJ* Sep 25 1595; Nov 26 1586.

63. *FSJ* Feb 9 1598. On this topic, see the fascinating book by Johannes Dillinger, *Magical Treasure Hunting in Europe and North America: A History* (New York: Palgrave Macmillan, 2011).

64. Between 1601 and 1606, Schmidt travelled at least once a year, and often twice, for executions in Hilpoltstein, Altdorf, Lauf, Salzburg, Lichtenau, and Gräfenberg (*FSJ* Jun 20 1601; Jul 8 1601; Mar 3 1602; May 7 1603; May 27 1603; Jun 16 1604; Aug 13 1604; May 6 1605; May 17 1606). He journeyed to Heroldsberg and Hersbruck in 1609 (Feb 10 and Mar 17), then once to Eschenau on Jan 17 1611. Meister Frantz averaged only two floggings annually during the following seven years, even though there were demonstrably other such corporal punishments administered.

65. ASB 226: 43r-v; *FSJ* Feb 28 1611.

66. StaatsAN 52a, 447: 1413-14; *RV* 1871: 7v, 22v-23v, 25v, 31v-32r.

67. StaatsAN 52a, 447: 1493.

68. Siebenkees, *Materialen,* 4:552; *FSJ* Jul 29 1617.

69. *RV* 1943: 12v, 18r-v, 24v (Nov 10, 12, 13 1617).

70. *JHJ* Nov 13 1617.

71. *RV* 1943: 37v, 58r, 80r, 85r-v (Jul 13, 17, 24, 27 1618); 1953: 10v, 41r, 47r (Aug 1, 10, 12 1618).

72. *RV* 1953: 55v-56r, 72v, 80r (Aug 14, 20, 22 1618); 1954: 33v, 74r (Sep 7 and 21 1618); 1957: 42r (Dec 4 1618).

73. *RV* 1963: 4v, 27r-v, 39r (Apr 29, May 8 and 13 1619).

74. *RV* 2005: 104r-v (Jul 17 1622); 2018: 45v (Jun 23 1623); 2037: 17r (Nov 16 1624); 2038: 32r (Dec 12 1624); 2068: 117r (Apr 17 1627); 2189: 30r-v (Jul 22 1636); 2194: 25r-v (Dec 7 1636); 2214: 36r (May 31 1638).

75. Keller, 174.

76. *RV* 1969: 29v (Oct 22 1619); 1977: 54v (Jun 7 1620); 1991: 35v (Jun 8 1621).

77. *RV* 2052: 92v (Feb 21 1626).

78. *RV* 2044: 29v-30r, 64r-v (Jun 23 and Jul 4 1625); 2045: 13r-v, 41r-v, 71v (Jul 18 and 26, Aug 3 1625); 2047: 16r (Sep 13 1625); 2048: 1v (Oct 6 1625); StadtAN B 14/1 138, 108v-110r: down payment of 373 fl. 27¼ kr.; remainder paid after cleaning of house (Sep 22 1625), StadtAN B1/II, no. 74 (*c*.1626).

79. *RV* 1959: 37v-38r (Jan 23 1619); *RV* 1968: 9r (Sep 18 1619).

80. *RV* 2040: 29v-30r (Feb 10 1625).

81. *RV* 2002: 2r (Apr 4 1622); *RV* 2046: 7r-v (Aug 13 1625).

82. *RV* 2071: 25v (Jun 26 1627); StaatsAN B1/III, Nr. VIa/88.

83. StaatsAN 54a II: Nr. 728.

84. *Restitution,* 209r-211r.; *RV* 2039: 34v (Jan 17 1625).

85. LKAN St Lorenz Taufungen 910 (Jan 4 1612); Schumann, "Franz Schmidt," 678-79.

86. *RV* 1877: 15r, 21r, 31v-32r (Dec 2, 4, and 7 1612).

87. *RV* 1929: 64r (Nov 13 1616); 1931: 49v-49r (Dec 30 1616); 1933: 8v-9r (Feb 8 1617).

88. *RV* 2025: 25v, 37r (Jan 8 and 14 1624). She is initially listed as Rosina Schmidin and later as Rosina Bückhlin; there is no reference to her husband.

89. StaatsAN Rep 65, Nr. 34: 42r, 56r.

90. Between 1680 and 1770, at least nine at University of Ingolstadt alone, G&T, 17–20, 111–12; Nowosadtko, 321ff.

91. *RV* 2122: 23r–v (May 19 1631).

92. *RV* 2131: 74v (Feb 3 1632); LKAN Lorenz 512. *Nürnberger Kunstlerlexikon*, ed. Manfred H. Grieb (Munich: Saur, 2007), 1:24; StaatsAN 65, 20 (Feb 24 1632).

93. LKAN Lorenz 109; StaatsAN Rep 65, Nr. 34: 56.

94. LKAN Lorenz L80, 129; *RV* 2162: 49v (Jun 13 1634).

95. StaatsAN 65, 32: 244.

Epilogue

1. In *Resistance, Rebellion, and Death*, trans. Justin O'Brien (New York: Vintage Books, 1974), 180.

2. Walker, *German Home Towns*, 12.

3. StaatsAN 54a II: Nr. 728; also *RV* 2189: 30r–v (Jul 22 1636); 2194: 25r–v (Dec 7 1636); 2225: 97r (May 10 1639); 2232: 10v–11v (Nov 2 1639); 2243: 91v (Sep 23 1640). By Schlegel's own estimate, he had only ninety-seven clients in Nuremberg, as contrasted with over fifteen hundred in his previous position.

4. Maria died on Apr 12 1664; Frantzenhans on Feb 26 1683 (LKAN Beerditgungen St Lorenz, fol. 311, 328).

5. Evans, *Rituals of Retribution*, 109–49.

6. I am strongly swayed by Richard Evans's devastating criticisms of the teleological and otherwise flawed arguments of Michel Foucault and Philippe Ariès in this respect, although a bit more sympathetic to Norbert Elias, whose "civilizing process" remains valuable in other cultural contexts (*Rituals of Retribution*, 880ff.). Steven Pinker's recent popularisation of the latter, however, unfortunately amplifies one of the weakest components of Elias's theory, namely the alleged rise of empathy during the eighteenth century on. According to Pinker, for instance, "Medieval Christendom was a culture of cruelty," and only with the advent of Enlightenment "humanism" did "people beg[i]n to sympathize with more of their fellow human beings," Steven Pinker, *The Better Angels of Our Nature: Why Violence Has Declined* (New York: Viking, 2011), 132–33. For more nuanced analyses of changes in popular sensibilities regarding public executions, see Pieter Spierenburg, *The Spectacle of Suffering: Executions and the Evolution of Repression* (Cambridge: Cambridge University Press, 1984), and Paul Friedland, *Seeing Justice Done: The Age of Spectacular, Punishment in France* (Oxford: Oxford University Press, 2012), especially 119–91. I am grateful to my colleague Lauren Clay for bringing the second work to my attention.

7. Cf. similar conclusions of Dülmen, *Theatre of Horror*, 133–37.

8. Keller, 262–79; Stuart, 75–82, 227–39; Nowosadtko, 305–16, 333–36; Knapp, *Loch*, 60–61.

9. This section is especially indebted to the excellent treatment of Nowosadtko, "'Und nun alter, ehrlicher Franz.'"

10. Letter dated Sep 3 1810; *Achim von Arnim und Jacob und Wilhelm Grimm*, ed. R. Steig (Stuttgart: J. G. Cotta, 1904), 69–70.

11. G&T, 49; Nowosadtko, "'Und nun alter, ehrlicher Franz,'" 238–41.

12. See especially Stephen Brockmann, *Nuremberg: The Imaginary Capital* (Rochester, NY: Camden House, 2006).

13. See the fascinating historical excursion in Wolfgang Schild, *Die Eiserne Jungfrau: Dichtung und Wahrheit*, Schriftenreiche des Mittelalterlichen Kriminalmuseums Rothenburg ob der Tauber (2001). I thank Dr. Hartmut Frommer for bringing this publication to my attention.

14. For discussions of the twentieth-century historiography of the early modern executioner in Germany, see Wilbertz, 1ff.; Nowosadtko, 3–8; and Stuart, 2–5.

15. Among the multitude of literary works incorporating the "medieval hangman" as a central character, the most successful have been Wilhelm Raabe's *Das letzte Recht* (1862) and *Zum wilden Mann* (written in 1873, published in 1884); and the plays of Gerhart Hauptmann (*Magnus Garbe*, 1914; second version, 1942) and Ruth Schaumann (*Die Zwiebel*, 1943). More recently the figure has become the subject of popular romance novels such as Oliver Pötzsch's *The Hangman's Daughter* (English translation by Lee Chadeayne; Seattle: AmazonCrossing, 2011) or *Der Henker von Nürnberg* (Mannheim: Wellhöfer, 2010), a collection of imaginative short stories edited by Anne Hassel and Ursula Schmid-Spreer.

16. I take this term from Evans, *Rituals of Retribution*, xiii.

17. Pinker, *Better Angels of Our Nature*, especially 129–88.

18. www.amnesty.org/en/death-penalty/numbers.

Acknowledgements

I began writing this book during a blissful fall semester at the American Academy in Berlin and cannot imagine a more ideal incubator for a nascent project. Director Gary Smith and his staff have realised a Platonic ideal of intellectual vitality, providing fellows with long hours of contemplative serenity in a stunning Wannsee villa, incomparable support services, and countless opportunities for intellectual interaction, all topped off by the nightly dining extravaganzas of chef Reinold Kegel. Among the many Academy staff members who contributed to this idyllic environment, Gary Smith, R. Jay Magill, Alissa Burmeister, Malte Mau, and Yolande Korb all deserve special thanks. My family and I were also blessed by an exceptionally convivial cohort of resident fellows, all of whom shared in many hours of lively conversation, urban adventures, and fierce Ping-Pong games (Jochen Hellbeck still owes me a rematch). I am particularly grateful for the friendship and inspiration of Nathan Englander, Rachel Silver, George Packer, and Laura Secor. This book owes a lot as well to the generosity of the universally admired Rick Atkinson, who not only shared with me some wise advice on constructing a narrative, but also the names of his excellent literary agent and his cartographer (but held on to all of those Pulitzers).

During the course of archival work, I benefited considerably from the expert guidance of Dr. Stefan Nöth and Dr. Klaus Rupprecht at the Staatsarchiv Bamberg, Dr. Arnd Kluge of the Hof Stadtarchiv, Dr. Gerhard Rechter and Dr. Gunther Friedrich at the Staatsarchiv Nürnberg, Dr. Andrea Schwarz of the Landeskirchlichesarchiv Nürnberg, Dr. Christine Sauer of the Stadtbibliothek Nürnberg, and

Dr. Horst-Dieter Beyerstedt of the Stadtarchiv Nürnberg. Dr. Martin Baumeister of the Germanisches Nationalmuseum Nürnberg generously devoted an entire morning to discussing and showing me various execution swords, even allowing me to examine closely and wield (at a safe distance) one specimen that might have belonged to Meister Frantz himself. Michaela Ott likewise indulged me with an extended private tour of Nuremberg's *Lochgefängnis* (dungeon), patiently answering my most arcane queries and allowing me to make measurements and take photos of this still chilling venue. Dr. Hartmut Frommer, who has overseen a remarkable transformation of the Hangman's House into an exemplary museum of criminal legal history, has welcomed me repeatedly into his study at the top of the house's tower, shared his vast knowledge of Nuremberg's legal past and Franconian geography, and introduced me to the finer points of Nuremberg's famed sausages.

Back in Nashville, numerous friends and colleagues have helped me see the book to completion. Steve Pryor was the first to read the manuscript as a whole and Holly Tucker braved large chunks at an early stage. Their suggestions improved both the clarity and flow of the narrative considerably. The legal scholar and gifted author Dan Scharfstein lent his keen editorial eye to several chapters and Ellen Fanning gave me a molecular biologist's take on it all. My greatest intellectual debts continue to be to my remarkable colleagues in Vanderbilt's history department, whose breadth of knowledge and unstinting generosity continue to amaze me. By rights I should list them all by name, but in the interest of brevity I will single out Michael Bess, Bill Caferro, Marshall Eakin, Jim Epstein, Peter Lake, Jane Landers, Catherine Molineux, Matt Ramsey, Helmut Smith, and Frank Wcislo. Graduate students Christopher Mapes, Frances Kolb, and Sean Bortz each helped immensely with various editing and illustration tasks. Despite my best efforts, I have been unable to stump Jim Toplon and his crack team at Vanderbilt Interlibrary Loan – and that is no empty boast. I thank my provost, Richard McCarty, and my dean, Carolyn Dever, for their consistent moral and financial support of this project.

Many other friends have contributed to the book in diverse ways. I am particularly grateful to Wolfgang Behringer, Jennifer Bevington, Tom Brady, Joyce Chaplin, Jason Coy, Heiko Droste, Sigrun Haude, Claudia Jarzebowski, Mark Kramer, Paul Kramer and his Narrative

History Workshop, Wendy Lesser, Mary Lindemann, Gary Morsches, Hannah Murphy, Tom Robisheaux, Ulinka Rublack, Thomas Schnalke, Gerd Schwerhoff, Tom Seeman, Richard Sieburth, Phil Soergel, and Jeff Watt. Kathy Stuart, whose work on executioners has guided and inspired me more than any other, saved me a trip to Vienna (not a terrible fate in itself) by sharing her copy of Frantz Schmidt's 1624 imperial restitution. I also wish to acknowledge my great debt to previous scholars of early modern German executioners, evident throughout the endnotes, including authors of a century ago – Albrecht Keller, Theodor Hampe, Else Angstmann, and Hermann Knapp – as well as those of today, especially Jutta Nowosadtko, Richard J. Evans, Wolfgang Schild, Gisela Wilbertz, Ilse Schumann, and the late Richard van Dülmen.

My agent, Rafe Sagalyn, showed faith in me and this project early on and has gently introduced an academic historian to the brave new world of trade publishing. Thomas LeBien, my initial editor at Hill and Wang, likewise reassured me of this book's potential with his enthusiastic encouragement and sage advice. Courtney Hodell, who has seen the work through to press, has been a mentor *sans pareil* (although she has urged me to cut down on the foreign terms). Thanks to the welcoming spirit and creativity of Courtney and her colleagues – particularly Jeff Seroy, Jonathan Lippincott, Debra Helfand, Nick Courage, and Mark Krotov – my experience at Farrar, Straus and Giroux has been an author's dream. The meticulous eye and judicious red pencil of Stephen Wagley elevated my text to a new level of clarity, and the excellent maps of Gene Thorp provide the perfect visual introduction to Frantz Schmidt's world.

Like all my books so far, this one – to my own surprise – ended up being about family as much as anything else. I can only hope that Frantz Schmidt enjoyed a fraction of the love and support from his kin that I have come to rely on from mine. My wife, Beth Monin Harrington, remains my most unsparing editor and most unflagging supporter. Her relentless campaign against the passive voice saw some impressive victories this time around, but mistakes continue to be made (and loving gratitude sincerely expressed). Our children, George and Charlotte, have come to consider Meister Frantz a member of the household and in the process become the country's most knowledgeable middle schoolers on early modern crime and punishment (to the delight of their friends and classmates). The other members of my family have likewise indulged my obsession with this topic and shown no signs of being less than fascinated with my associated discourses. For their kind forbearance, I thank the Lebanon Filloons and Tampa Harringtons as well as the Monins of Sparta, Jonesborough, and Tulsa. Finally, for their lifelong example of selfless love and encouragement, I thank my parents, Jack and Marilyn Harrington. This book is dedicated to my father, with admiration and gratitude for planting and nurturing the seeds of a writing vocation in his eldest son.

Index

Page numbers in *italics* refer to illustrations.

Aachen, 249*n*53

Abgar V, King of Edessa, 180–81, 218

abortion, 157

Abriel, Johann Georg, 203

accusations, false, 121, 142; of murder, 61, 65; of witchcraft, 118, 126, 204–206

Addai, 181

Abensberg, 204

adultery, xiv, 8, 34, 128–30, 157, 158, 209, 211; punishments for, 130, 155; *see also* sexual offences

Alcibiades, Albrecht II, Margrave of Brandenburg-Kulmbach, 17–19, *18*, 21, 38, 136, 219, 243*n21*

aliases, xxv, 91, 115, 132, 153, 159; multiple, 121; *see also specific names*

Altdorf, 206, 262*n64*; University of, 200

Amberg, 214

ambushes, 141–45, *142*, 161; *see also* violence

Amman, Augustin, 102

Ammon, Hans (Maria's husband), 223

Ammon, Hans (aka the Foreign Tailor; robber), 178

amputations, xvii, 26, 64, 92, *194*; cauterising bleeding from, 193; *see also specific body parts*

anatomical study, 39, 59, 191, 197–202; dissection of cadavers for, 196, 198, 200

animals: beheading practiced on, 4, 17; executions of, 161–62; public trials for, 67; sexual offences with, *see*

bestiality; sick or injured, healing of, 222, 232; theft of, 162

Ansbach, *see* Brandenburg-Ansbach.

anti-Semitism, 119

apothecaries, 12, 116, 189, 195, 197

archers, municipal, xiii, 97, 102, 114, 161, 171, 243*n18*; in execution rituals, 80, 87; punishment of, 116, 118, 164

Ariès, Philippe, 263*n6*

Arnim, Ludwig Achim von, 232

arson, 10–12, 60, 114, 148–49; atrocities committed with, 122; *see also* extortion

Art of Wordly Wisdom, The (Gracián), 91

astrologers, 12, 209; *see also* magic

Augsburg, 5, 7, 25, 27, 94, 259*n7*, 260*n24*; corporal punishment in, 67; hangings in, 73; sovereignty of, 26

Aurholtin, Elisabeth (aka the Digger), 80, 168, 179, 210–11

Ayrer, Killian, 137–38

Bachhaussen, 121

Baden, witch craze in, 205

Bamberg, xix, 3–4, 6, 21–25, 28, 32, 43–45, 49, 74, 89, 94, 110, 186, 251*n10*; cathedral provost of, 194; corporal punishments in, 64–66; Heinrich's illness and death in, 131–32, 134, 255*n96*; Lion in, 102; live burials in, 71; religion in, 17, 22, 23, 244*n31*; torture in, 57; witch craze in, 203, 206

Bambergensis (criminal code), 22, 28–29, 55

bandits, *see* robbers

banishment, 26, 31, 32, 65, 66, 118, 119, 152, 204, 248n34; of adulterers, 130; of amateur healers, 195; for false accusations, 206; for fraud, 209; for grave robbing, 201; for incest, 159; of juvenile offenders, 174–75, 179, 258n98; modern alternatives to, 236; temporary, 67; for theft, 164, 179; *see also* transportation to foreign colonies

baptism, 101, 211

barber-surgeons, 12, 59, 189, 191, *194*, 196, 243n18, 260n19; crimes committed by, 137–38, 146, 147, 158; Schlegel's conflicts with, 217; wounds treated by, 146, *192*, 195

Bardtmann, Leinhard (aka the Horseman), 108

Basel, 23, 40

Bauer, Johann (aka Riffraff), 177

Baur, Hensa, 176

Bavaria, 4, 7, 32, 171, 198, 232; witch hunts in, 203

Bayreuth, 21, 35

beadles, 26, 65, 116–17, 128, 168, 244n36

Becherin, Ursula, 148

Beck, Jorg and Margareta, 99, 251n12

Beckin, Maria, *see* Schmidin, Maria

beggars, 10, 14, 41, 52, 67, 96, 243n18

beheadings, *xxiii*, 4, 64, 68, 80, 92, 109, *112*, 133, 135, 202, 212, 249n56; botched, 40, 85–87, *86*, 89, 211, 250n79; before burning, 71; commutation of sentence of, 173; dealing with corpses after, 200; for false accusations, 204–205; for fraud, 120; medical uses of blood from, 197; of minors, 174, 176, 183; position for, 75; privilege of, 42; by Schlegel, 214; sentences mitigated to, 117, 133, 158, 159, 170–72; for sexual offences, 158–60; after torture, 59; of traitors, 123; of women, 69–70, 85, 87, 120, 170, 171, 232; *see also* capital punishment

Beheim, Hans, 174

Bergner, Günther, 19

Berlin, xiii, 91, 231, 244n34

bestiality, 114, 159–61; *see also* sexual offences

Better Angels of Our Nature, The (Pinker), 235

Beütler, Hans (aka Skinny), 161

Beyhlstein, Hieronimus, 158

Biberach, 203

Bible, 77, 180; Luke, 182, 183; Old Testament, 219

bier test, 55–56

bigamy, 89, 119, 130, 172; *see also* adultery

Bischoffin, Anna, 149

Black Death, *see* plague

black magic, *see* magic

blackmail, *see* extortion

blasphemy, 64, 65, 159, 161

Blechschmidt, Anna, 35

blood court, xiv, 79

blood feuds, *see* feuds

Boccaccio, Giovanni, 156

Böckin, Margaretha, 85

Bodin, Jean, 94

body parts: displaying on gallows of, 70–71, 124; medical uses of, 196–98, 200–201, 260n28; trade in, 200

Bohemia, 17, 20

Brandenburg, electorate of, 8

Brandenburg-Ansbach, 89, 109, 158, 206, 214, 240n5, 247n24; margravate of, 21, 30, 110, 123

Brandenburg-Kulmbach, margravate of, 17–21

Brand executioner dynasty, 16

brandings, xvii, 65; *see also* corporal punishment

Braunschweig, 17

Brechtlin, Margaretha, 171

Bregenz, 251n10

Brentano, Clemens, 232

Breslau, 249n53

broadsheets, sensationalist, 146

Brombecker, Michel, 174

Bruck, 185

Brunnauer, Hans, 158

Bücklin, Katherina (aka Stammering Kathy; aka the Foreigner), 170

burial, live, *see* live burial

burning, xv–xvi, 4, 10, 43, 71, 124, 212, 237; posthumous, 92, 101; for sexual offences, 158–60; for witchcraft, 203, 205

butchers, 16, 23, 51, 114, 133, 147, 159, 174

cadavers: dissection of, 196, 198, 200–202; parts of, *see* body parts; trade in, 197, 200; *see also* corpses

Caesius, Bernard, 198

Calvin, John, 13, 33

Camerarius, Joachim, 195, 201

Camus, Albert, 227

Canterin, Maria, 118

capital punishment, 28, 81, 132, 229, 236; decline of, xvii, 229–30; as deterrent, 227; jurisdiction over, 27; of minors, 173–75; modern, xxiv, 78, 237; *see also specific methods of execution*

Carolina, see Constitutio Criminalis Carolina

Carroll, Stuart, 93

castration, 64; *see also* corporal punishment

Catholicism, 17, 36, 94, 161, 169; of condemned, communion for, 82, 119, 120; Gregorian calendar and, xxv–xxvi; holy relics in, 13, 198; and Thirty Years War, 224

Celtis, Conrad, 94

chain gangs, 32, 164, 215; juveniles on, 174, 177, 179

Charles V, Holy Roman Emperor, 9, 28, 94

Chaucer, Geoffrey, 156

childbirth: healers and, *see* midwives; risks of, 5, 12, 35

child murders, 59, 60, *129*, 179; beheading for, 87, 200; bier test for, 56; confessions of, under torture, 62; executions for, 29, 68–71, 117–18, 127–28, 152, 232; of newborns, 13, 77, 114, 118, 186, 246*n9*; premeditated, 144

China, capital punishment in, 237

Christianity, 93, 119–20, 151; communion in, 260*n28*; conversion to, 243*n19*; divine forgiveness in,

168; Evangelical *see* Lutheranism; sexual offences in doctrine of, 158; *see also* Catholicism; Protestantism

Christoff, Georg, 171

Chur (Switzerland), 86

citizenship, 110, 136, 216, 220

civil law, 28

clemency, *see* mercy

cobblers, 23, 114

Coburg, 71

Cochlaeus, Johannes, 94

coercion, physical, *see* torture

Coiter, Volker, 200, *201*

Cologne, 94, 110, 245*n45*, 247*n13*

con artists, 65, 91–92, 127, 168, 179; gullibility of victims of, 210–11

confessions, 213; methods of obtaining, 55–57, 60, 62 (*see also* torture)

Constantinople, 92

Constitutio Criminalis Carolina (Criminal Constitution of Charles V, aka *Carolina*), 28–32, 55, 124, 130, 147, 154, 173, 219

Copenhagen, 91

corporal punishment, xvii, 31, 38, 56, 61, 63–65, 67, 90, 120, 135, 171, 248*n32*, 262*n64*; in Bamberg, xix, 23; for sexual offences, 155–56, 158; *see also specific methods*

corpses, 196–202, 246*n9*; burning of, 43; clothes stolen from, 108, 152; desecration of, 138, 151; left hanging on gallows, 46, 105, 196; lewdness committed with, 126; of murder victims, 56, *56*; public trials for, 67; on Raven Stone, xv; on wheel, 47, 48, *129*, 196; *see also* body parts; cadavers

counterfeiting, xiv, 124, 212

craft guilds, *see* guilds

Crete, 91

crime victims, empathy for, 122–30, 162, 163

criminal justice, evolution of governmental role in, 26–32, 230, 236–38

crop failures *see* famines

Czech Republic, 4

Danzig, 91

death sentences, *see* capital punishment

Decameron (Boccaccio), 156
decapitation, *see* beheading
deceit, 90–93, 111–13, 115, 120–26, 137–45, 157, 167–68, 209–11; in interrogations, 139; *see also* fraud
De Humani Corporis Fabrica (Vesalius), 198–99, *199*
Demer, Laurenz, (aka the Long Farmer), 202
demons, 12, 13
De Praestigiis Daemonarum (Weyer), 207
Deubler, Albanus Friedrich, 232
Deürlein, Lienhard, 82
Deuser, Valentin, 87, 228, 260*n*19
Dietmayr, Michael, 147
Dietz, Hans, 170
Dischinger, Lienhard, 120
discipline houses, *see* workhouses
disreputable occupations, 23, 26, 72, 94, 101, 104, 136, 205, 243*n*18; *see also* honour, *specific occupations*
Dismas, Saint, 183
Dochendte, Barthel, 45
Doctoring Book (Weyer), 191
Domiririn, Anna, 168, 209
Dopffer, Hans, 72, 144
Dorsch, Hans, 178
double standard, 93, 193; sexual, 118, 159
Dracula (Stoker), 233
drawing and quartering, 4, 29, 71, 249*n*51; *see also* capital punishment
Drechsler, Hans (aka the Mountaineer; aka Mercenary John), 169
Drentz, Hans (aka Stretch), 184
drowning: execution by, 68–69, *70*, 117, 186; infanticide by, 128; *see also* capital punishment
drunkenness, 8, 52, 117, 215; of executioners, 86–87; exposure of minors to, 178, 179; lewdness and, 161; of public execution spectators, 85; violence and 153–55
Duebelius, Hans, 195
Dülmen, Richard van, 76
Dürer, Albrecht, 94, *183*, 233
dysentery, 5

ears, cutting off, xvii, 135, 175, 148*n*32; *see also* corporal punishment

earthquakes, 14
Ecclesiastical History (Eusebius), 181
Eger, 232
Egloff, Georg, 127
Eichstätt, 204
Elias, Norbert, 263*n*6
empathy, 230, 263*n*6; for crime victims, 122–30, 162, 163
Endter, Johann Martin Friedrich von, 231–32, 241*n*10
England, 10; transportation to foreign colonies of, 245*n*47
English Shirt, 58; *see also* torture
Enlightenment, 231, 263*n*6
epidemics, 5–6, 12–14, 134–35, 139–40, 161, 225; *see also* plague
Erasmus, Desiderius, 3
Eschenau, 262*n*64
Eusebius of Caesarea, 181
evangelical reforms, 63
Evans, Richard, 263*n*6
exile, internal, *see* banishment
executioners: professionalisation of role of, 26–30; social marginalisation of, 15–16; *see also* Schmidt, Frantz; Schmidt, Heinrich; Schlegel, Bernhard
exorcism, 202–203
extortion, 8, 10–11, 51, 126, 178, 207
eye-gouging, 38, 64, *64*; *see also* corporal punishment

Faber, Jakob, 169
Fahner executioner dynasty, 16
fairies, 12
false witnesses, *see* accusations, false
famines, 6, 13, 14, 63, 161
Fellbinger, Benedict (aka the Devil's Knave), 174
Ferdinand II, Holy Roman Emperor, 218, 220
feuds, 8, 11, 26, 147–48, 214
Feuerstein, Endres, 126
Fieldbook of Wound-Healing (Gersdorff), 191; "wound-man" illustration from, *192*
financial penalties and settlements, 16–27, 64, 67, 154
fingers, chopping off, xvii, 64–65, 117, 135; *see also* corporal punishment

fire, 5, 10–12; execution by, *see* burning; intentionally set, *see* arson; torture with, 58–60

Fleisch (Flesh) Bridge, 64–65

floggings, xvii, 31, 38, 61, 65, 66, 116–19, 135, 154, 202, 211, 212, 262*n*64; of con artists, 168; of juvenile offenders, 174, 178, 179, 258*n*98; Lion as assistant in, 101, 255*n*99; for rape, 147; of recidivists, 164; with rods, banishment preceded by, 10, 56, 65–67, 118, 130, 167, 179, 241*n*8, 248*nn*32, 34; for sexual impropriety, 130, 155, 158, 159, 161; for theft, 171; *see also* corporal punishment

floods, 6, 14, 91

Florence, 94

Forchheim, 49

forensics, 55, 196

forgery, *see* fraud

fornication, *see* sexual offences

fortune-tellers, *see* fraud, magic

Foucault, Michel, 236, 249*n*51, 263*n*6

France, 18, 227, 241*n*6; chain gangs in, 32; transportation to foreign colonies of, 245*n*47

Francis of Assisi, Saint, 180

Franck, Georg, 143

Franconia, 6, 20, 28, 38, 49, 50, 185, 253*n*46; witch craze in, 203, 206

Frankfurt am Main, 137, 244*n*34

Frantz, Hans, 172

fraud, 91–93, 120, 167–68; magical, 209–11; *see also* deceit

Frauentor, *see* Ladies' Gate

Frederick I, King of Prussia, 230–31

French Revolution, 111

Freyin, Anna, 128, 169

Frisch, Christoph, 143

Frog Tower prison (Nuremberg), 103, 164, 233; *see also* prisons

Fröschel, Hans, *xxiii*

Fuchs executioner dynasty, 16

Fuggers, 94

Führer, Jakob, 92

Galen, 197, 200

galley sentences, prisoners condemned to, 32, 33, 164

gallows, 105–108, *106*, *107*; collapse of, 233; displaying of corpses and body parts on, 70–71, 108, 124, 151, 196, *199*, 200; mishaps with, 212; procession to, 80; singing by condemned on, 81; with trapdoors, 232; *see also* hanging

gamblers, 52, 117, 167, 215; false, 65

gaolers/gaols, *see* prisons

Gaunersprache (street cant), *see* Rotwelsch

Geckenhofferin, Magdalena, 164

Gemperlein, Michel, 114, 173

Georg Friedrich, Margrave of Brandenburg-Ansbach and Brandenburg-Kulmbach, 21

Germanisches Nationalmuseum (Nuremberg), 233

Gersdorff, Hans von, 191

Gerstacker, Hans (aka Red), 117

Gerstenacker, Ulrich, 125–26

Gestas, 184

Geuder, Georg Friedrich, 233

ghosts, 12; exorcism of, 202–203; fraudulent, 209

global trade, rise of, 23, 94, 227

God, crimes against, *see* incest; sodomy; witchcraft

Goethe, Johann Wolfgang von, 232

Gösswein, Lienhard, 166

Gostenhof, 110, 185

Götz, Georg, 114, 164

Gracián, Baltasar, 91

Gräfenberg, 262*n*64

grammar schools, 35–36

gravediggers, 16, 102

grave robbing, 201

Green Frog pub (Nuremberg), 233

Gregorian calendar, xxv–xxvi

Greiz, 46

Gretzelt, Simon, 164–65

Grimin, Ursula (aka Blue), 209

Grimm, Jacob, 35, 63, 232

Grimm, Wilhelm, 35, 232

Grimmelshausen, Hans Jakob Christoffel, 9–10

Groschin, Apollonia, 158

Gröschlin, Anna (aka Speedy's woman), 121

Grossin, Margaretha, 158

Grübel, Bastian (aka Slag), 61, 121

Grübel, Johann Konrad, 233

guilds, xiv, 26, 40, 97, 171; dishonourable occupations excluded from and vilified by, 15, 23, 41, 113, 231; of healers, 189, 195; intercession on behalf of condemned by, 171; Meistersingers and, 208

guillotines, 232

Gülchen, Niklaus von, *112*, 112–13

Gustavus II Adolphus, King of Sweden, 223, 224

Gypsies, 16, 189, 209; language of, 51, 245*n57*

Hacker, Hans, 154

Hagendorn, Magister Johannes, xiv, xv, 73, 77, 78, 82–83, 116, 169–70, 243*n*

Haller, Hans Jacob, 123

Hamburg, 91, 190, 249*n53*

Hamlet (Shakespeare), 45

Hammer, Hans (aka Pebble; aka the Young Cobbler), 116, 152

hands, cutting off, 64, 92, 93, 173; of infants, 186, 187

hangings, 4, 32, 38, 61, 68, 72–73, 75, 135, 249*n56*; commutation to beheading of sentence of, 171, 172; decline in, 74; of juvenile offenders, 175, 258*n98*; by lynch mobs, 27; prolonged, 216; slang for, 40; of thieves, 43, 45–46, 72, 82, 89, 128, 149, 161–65, 170, 173–77, *176*, 179, 183–84, 196, 212; of women, 175, *176*, 249*n53*; *see also* capital punishment; gallows

Hangman's Daughter, The (Pötzsch), 264*n15*

Hangman's House (Nuremberg), 100, 193–94, 214–18, 220, 235

hangmen, *see* executioners

Hassel, Anne, 264*n15*

Haubmayr, Peter, 178

Hauck, Bastla, 179

Hauptmann, Gerhart, 264*n15*

Hausmann, Heinrich, 110, 153

Haylandt, Hans, 137–38

healing, 12, 39, 187–96, 217, 222, 238; of broken bones, 193, 222; of burns, 193; dark arts and, 202–11; religious,

189; *see also* apothecaries; barber-surgeons; medicine; midwives; physicians; wound doctors

Hebrew, 245*n57*

Helmet, Hans, 169

Henkerhaus, see Hangman's House (Nuremberg)

Henker von Nürnberg, Der (Hassel and Schmid-Spreer), 264*n15*

heretics, 114, 158, 160

Heroldsberg, 262*n64*

Heroldt, Gabriel, 127

Hersbruck, 135, 262*n64*

Hertl, Lienhard, 164

Hertzog, Niklaus, 157

Heymann, Veit, 158

Hiert, Christoph, 203

highwaymen, *see* robbers

Hilpoltstein, 135, 262*n64*

Hof, 3, 17–23, *20*, 35, 45, 90, 94, 99, 109–10, 119, 219, 243*n21*; Lutheranism in, 36–37, 244*n31*; schools in, 36; sexual offences in, 157; siege of, 17–18

Hoffman, Christoph, 152

Hoffman, Hans, 128

Hoffman, Peter, 157, 208–209

Hoffmann, Cunz, 209

Hoffmennin, Dorothea, 56

Hole, the (Loch Nuremberg prison), 57, 98, 103–104, 112, 208, 233; juveniles in, 174, 177; pub in former warden's residence in, 233; recidivists in, 164, 174, 177; tours of, 235; *see also* prisons

Hollfeld, 49

Holy Roman Empire, 6–8, 79–80, 94

home invasions, 61, 132, 145, *150*, 152, 161; *see also* robbers

homicide, 24; in heat of anger, 154; *see also* manslaughter; murder

homosexuality, *see* sodomy

honour, xvi, xxi–xxiii, 15–16, 19–20, 23–26, 33–42, 50, 61, 72, 93–94, 101, 104, 109–22, 130–33, 136, 205; restitution of, 90, 93, 218–225, 228, 231

Hörnlein, Georg, 185–87

Hörnlein, Margaretha, 117

House of Society (Nuremberg), 232

humiliation, public, 63, 65, 66; of corpses, 108; of executions, 74; of

Jews, 119
humours, 191, 197
Hungary, 143, 178
Hunnerin, Maria Cordula, 120, 125
Huss, Karl, 232
Hussites, 21

impaling, 68–69, 71
incarceration, 31, 59, 65, 164, 229; of
    falsely accused, 121; long-term, 32; as
    modern alternative to banishment,
    236; for theft, 164, 165
incest, 13, 81–82, 110, 114, 118, 119,
    158–59, 161, 173; beheading for, 211;
    execution of minors for, 173; *see also*
    sexual offences
infant and childhood mortality, 5, 35,
    252*n*12
infanticide, *see* child murders
infections, outbreaks of, *see* epidemics
inflation, 6, 8, 30, 227
interrogation, 27, 38, 54–63, 132, 237;
    see also torture
Iran, capital punishment in, 237
Iron Biter, xiv
Iron Maiden, 233–34
Israelites, *see* Jews
Italy, 92

Japan, capital punishment in, 237
Jena, University of, 200
Jesuits, 198, 203
Jesus, 180–81; thieves crucified with,
    183–84
Jews, 16, 23, 165, 195; executions of,
    67, 74, 219; names of, 114; ritual
    humiliation of, 119
Johann Georg, Margrave of
    Brandenburg-Ansbach, 91
journeymen, 51, 222; executioners,
    42–43, 51, 61; murders of, 185
Jud, Hay, 119
juvenile offenders, 73, 173–79,
    258*n*98

Kalka, 110
Kebweller, Steffan, 174
Keller, Albrecht, 241*nn*9–11

Kertzenderfer, Lienard (aka Cow
    Lenny), 212
Kettnerin, Barbara, 158
Kiesswetter, Lienhard (aka Mosel
    Lenny; Sick Lenny), 121
King Lear (Shakespeare), 185
Kleinin, Margaretha, 167
Kleinlein, Wolf, 133
knackers, 4, 99, 102, 116, 179, 207
Knau, Jobst, 185–87
Knüttel, Michel, 201
Koblentz, Martin, 231
Köchl, Peter, 125, 145
Kohlenberg Court, 40–41
Kohler, Claus, 102
Kolb, Hans (aka the Long Brickmaker,
    aka Brother Steadfast), 83, 152
Koller, Claus (Frantz's Lion), 102, 103,
    116, 213; Schlegel and, 216; tasks
    delegated to, 105, 108, 241*n*8
Köller, Michel, 145
König, Michel, 177
Korn, Dominicus, 111
Kornmeyer, Hans, 171, 172
Krafft, Kunrad, 120, 127, 168
Kraków, 91
Kraus, Paulus, 82
Krautz, Julius, xiii
Kreuzmayer, Hensa, 60, 176
Krieger, Hans, xxv
Krieger, Magdalena, xxv
Kronach, 45
Krug, Hans, 142
Kumpler, Hans, 147
Kunrad, Julius, 119–20
Küplin, Kunigunda, 159
Kürschnerin, Maria (aka Constable
    Mary), 175

ladder, *see* rack
Ladies' Gate (Nuremberg), xiv, 66, 82,
    105
Lambrecht, Georg Karl, xiii–xvi, 207,
    209, 212–13
landsknechts, *see* mercenaries
Langenzenn, 158
Latin, 245*n*57
Latin schools, 35–36
Lauf, 262*n*64
lazar houses, 15

Leberwurst, Peter, 223
leg screws, 58
Leichnam, Martin, 200
Leichnam executioner dynasty, 16
Lenger, Matthes, 108
Lenker, Caspar, 171
Leonardo da Vinci, 198
lepers, 15
Letzte Recht, Das (Raabe), 264*n15*
lewdness, *see* sexual offences
lex talionis, 63
Leydtner, Lienhard, 166
Lichtenau, 262*n64*
limbs: cutting off 26; shattering of, with
    wheel, 48; *see also* body parts
Lind, Heinrich, 258*n98*
Lindtnerin, Margaretha, 77–78
Linz, 228
Lions (Nuremberg executioners'
    assistants) 101–103, 105, 108, 116,
    203, 213, 216
Lippert, Lienhardt, 36, 88–90, 99,
    250*n85*
Lippertin, Kunigunda, 250*n85*
Lisbon, 91
literacy, xvi, xvii, 35–36
Little Ice Age, 6
live burial, 29, 68, 69, 71; *see also* capital
    punishment
London, 91, 97
Lord's Prayer, xv, 77
Lübeck, 25, 91
Lubing, Lienhart, 121
Luginsland Tower, 112; *see also* prisons
Luther, Martin, 12, 13, 32–34
Lutheranism, 36–37, 94, 119, 168, 169,
    181; catechism in, 36, 77; communion
    in, 82, 120; exorcism in, 203; original
    sin in, 179; salvation by faith alone in,
    141
Lützen, 224
lynching, 15, 27, 87; *see also* mob
    violence

Mager, Hans, 171
magic, xiv, 12–13, 86–87, 149, 152, 168,
    173, 187–88, 202–11, 217; *see also*
    witchcraft
Magnus Garbe (Hauptmann), 264*n15*
maleficia, 207

Malta, 91
manslaughter, 143
Maria Theresa, Empress of Holy Roman
    Empire, 231
Marranti, Margaretha, 128
Marshtall, 110
Marti, Hans Wolff, 160
Matz, Valentin, 190
Maximilian I, Holy Roman Emperor, 8
Maximilian II, Holy Roman Emperor,
    94
Mayer, Christoph, 159–60
Mayer, Georg (aka Brains), 170, 185,
    186
Mayer, Utz (aka the Tricky Tanner), 81
Mayr, Jörg, 60, 179
Mechtlin, Elisabeth, 85, 158, 159, 211
medicine, 181, 187, 188, 219–20, 228,
    230; *see also* healing
Medicis, 94
Meisterbrief (notarized certificate), 43
Meisterlied, 180–83, 218
Meistersinger von Nürnberg, Die
    (Wagner), 227
Meistersingers, 180
Melanchthon, Philipp, 36, 171
Meller, Hans (aka Cavalier Johnny), 81,
    209
mercenaries, 8–10, *9*, 16, 27, 32, 41, 42,
    52, 119, 123, 178; crimes committed
    by, 10, 59, 71, 111, 114, 121, 132, 143
Merckel, Hans (aka Deer John), 125, 165
mercy, xv, 33, 48, 119, 160, 168–72,
    184, 196, 230; balance of severity
    and, in public executions, 67;
    beheading out of, 59, 71, 92, 123,
    174, 176, 205; divine, xv, 37, 168,
    181; recidivism and, 173, 177; social
    status and, 93, 171; strangulation
    prior to burning as act of, xv, 213;
    for youthful offenders, 147, 173–74,
    176; *see also* mitigation
Mertz, Georg (aka the Mallet), 83–85
Messina, 91
Meüllin, Dorothea, 128
Michelangelo, 198
midwives, 12, 25, 127, 189, 190, 195
military service, *see* mercenaries
Miller, William, 109
Milton, John, 137
minors, *see* juvenile offenders

mitigation of sentences, 14, 74, 169, 172;
to beheading, 117, 133, 158, 159,
170–72; to flogging, 110; *see also* mercy
mob violence, 15, 27, 66, 87–89, 179,
211, 236
Montaigne, Michel de, 3, 45, 91, 137,
185, 207
Mosaic law, 63
Mötzela, Georg, 121
Müller, Magister, 116, 208
Müllner, Georg (aka Lean George), 127,
152, 153
Müllner, Hans (aka the Molder), 126
Munich, 99, 203, 251*n10*
murder, 116, 120, 121, 171; absolution
for, 169; accessories to, 117; by
ambush, *see* ambushes; arson and, 10,
76; attempted, 60, 64, 125, 132, 145,
149, 166, 170; of children, *see* child
murder; committed by minors, 179;
confessions of, 55–56, 60; corpses of
prisoners executed for, 196;
desecration of corpses of victims of,
151; execution of perpetrators by male
relatives of victims of, 26; execution
by wheel for, 45–49, 71; false
accusations of, 61; of family members,
125–26, 128–29, *129*, 254*n89*;
mass, 61; by mercenaries, 132–33;
pardons for, 171; premeditated, *see*
premeditation; rates of, xxiv; for
revenge, 147–48, 151–52; serial, 113;
theft and, 127, 137–38, 142–47, 149,
152, 185; by women, 71
Mussel, Barthel, 142
Musterer, Fritz (aka Little Fritzie; aka
Snail), 121
mutilations, legal, 64, 65; *see also*
corporal punishment

nationalism, German, 21, 233
natural disasters, 12, 13
Nenner, Cunz, 126, 149
Netherlands, 227
Neuner, Heinz, 110
nicknames, xxv, 115
Niebelungenlied, 55
nipping (ripping of flesh with red-hot
tongs), 47, 71–72, 85, 127, 133, 144,
186, 249n51

Nuremberg, xiii–xxiv, 27, 28, 32, 38,
94–135, *95*, 222, 237, 238, 244*n42*,
246*n9*, 251*n6*; citizenship in, 110,
136; Collegium Medicum of, 195–96;
criminal justice in, 54, 230, 231, 235;
curfew in, 145; decline in executions
in, 230; economic decline of, 227;
execution structures in, 105–108,
106–108; healers in, 188–89, 193,
195, 200–201, *201*, 217–220, 228,
260*n24*; Jews banned from, 119;
Meistersingers in, 180; nineteenth-
century, 232–35; ongoing animosity
between Ansbach and, 123; per
capita execution rate in, 30;
pharmacopoeia of, 197; plague in,
134–35, 139–40, 225; prisons in, *see*
prisons; Protestantism of, xxvi, 17,
223; ritual spectacle of public
executions in, 77–88, 230; schools in,
36; sexual offences in, 157, 159, 161;
Staatsarchiv of, 220; in Thirty Years
War, 223–24, 227, 229; town hall of,
98; witch craze in, 204–206
Nusslerin, Helena, 247*n18*

oath-breaking, *see* perjurers
Ohlav, 240*n5*
Öhler, Hans, 103–104
"On Cannibals" (Montaigne), 3
"On Cruelty" (Montaigne), 185
"On the Education of Children"
(Erasmus), 3
"On the Education of Children"
(Montaigne), 45, 91
"On Experience" (Montaigne), 137
original sin, 37, 168, 179
Osnabrück, 251*n10*
Öttingen, count of, 91
Our Lady's Church (Nuremberg), xiv

Paier, Hans, 151–52
pain, stylised forms of inflicting, *see*
torture
panderers, *see* prostitution
Paracelsus, 190; *see also* healing
Paradise Lost (Milton), 137
pardons, *see* mercy
Paris, xvii

Parma, duke of, 91

Passau, 198

passion, crimes of, 153–62

patricide, 125, 144; attempted, 145

Paumaister, Lienhard, 213

Paumgartner, Pangratz, 177

Payr, Hans, 165

Peihelsteinin, Anna, 25

Pergmennin, Anna, 165, 207

perjurers, 64–65, 206

Perpetual Truce (1495), 8

Pessler, Dr., 201

pestilence, *see* epidemics

Peyelstainin, Anna (aka Cunt Annie), 159

Peyhel, Hans, 248*n*32

Pfeiffer, Laurenz, 177

Pflügel, Heinz, 164

Pflügelin, Margaretha, 164

physicians, 12, 50, 59, 116, 191, 195; academically trained, 189, 190; *see also* healing

pickpockets, juvenile, 174, 175; *see also* juvenile offenders

pimps, *see* prostitutes

Pinker, Steven, 235, 265*n*6

Pintzrinin, Anna, 152, 153

Pirckheimer, Willibald, 94

plague, 5, 13, 134–35, 139–40, 225; *see also* epidemics

Planck, Peter, 154–55

Pliny the Elder, 196

Ploben, Ursula von, 146

poachers, 65; *see also* theft

Polish Ram, 58; *see also* torture

Pomeranian Cap, 58

Pötzsch, Oliver, 264*n15*

Prague, 92

Praun, Georg (Pin George), 147, 167, 202

prayer, xv, 184; before executions, 75, 119, 213; mitigation of sentences in response to, 170; petitionary, 13

Preisigel, Georg, 128

Preiss, Balthasar, 164, 177

premeditation, 125–26, 128, 129, 138, 141, 143–44, 147, 149; crimes of passion versus, 153

prisons, 57, 65, 76–79, 98, 102–105, 112, 164, 174, 177, 207, 233, 235; *see also* Frog Tower; Hole, the; Luginsland Tower

procuresses, *see* prostitutes

Prodigal Son, parable of, 182, *182*

property crimes, *see* arson; theft

prostitutes, 16, 23, 53, 65, 111, 116–19, 121, 158, 163, 178, 211; consorting with, 117; punishment of, 155, 156; violence against 154–55

Protestantism, xxv–xxvi, 12–13, 17, 23, 32, 101, 114, 161, 180; foundational beliefs of, 181; Gregorian calendar and, xxv–xxvi; and Thirty Years War, 223, 224; *see also* Lutheranism

Prückner, Georg, 82, 208

Prussia, 8, 43

public baths, 147–48, *148*, 167

public executions, xiii, xxiii, xxiv, 67, 70, 134; abolition of, 232; apprentices' tasks for, 38; behind-the-scenes preparations for, 76–77; decline in frequency of, 229–31; maintenance of order at, 216; methods of, *see specific execution methods*; mob violence and, 66, 87–88; ritual spectacle of, 14–15, 76–88, 236; of torture victims, 39, 60, 193; *see also* capital punishment

Puchfelderin, Margaretha, 158

Püffin, Elisabeth, 145, 170

punishment: capital, *see* capital punishment; corporal, *see* corporal punishment; mercy as counterpart to, 169; ritual public spectacle of, 55, 63–71

Pütner, Cunz, 166, 183

putzen, see beheadings, botched

Raabe, Wilhelm, 264*n15*

rack, 57–59; *see also* torture

Raim, Hans, 147

Ramsperger, Hans, 123–24

rape, 8, 116, 118, 119, 146–47; attempted, 121, 127, 146; child, 126–27; by highwaymen, 150; by minors, 174

Rasdorf, 76

Ratsverläße, 241*n12*

Raven Stone, xv, 47, 72, 76, 83, 105–107, *106*, 109, 133, 214

Rebbelin, Anna, 167

Rebweller, Steffan, 110

recidivists, 31, 32, 64, 65, 164; juvenile, 174, 175, 177

redemption, 168–84; *see also* mercy
Reformation, 22, 36, 118; *see also* Protestantism
Regensburg, 214, 228
regicide, 125
Reichardt, Carl (aka Eckerlein), 116
Reichlin, Katherina, 127
Reichstag, 7
Reinschmidt, Hans, 22, 134
Reintein, Hans, 104
religion, 12–13; instruction in, 36–37; punishment based on, 63; in ritual spectacle of public executions, 80, 82–83; *see also* Catholicism; Protestantism
Renckhart, Klaus, 46–49, 151
repeat offenders, *see* recidivists
reputation, xvi, 53, 87, 113–22, 130; citizenship and, 136; of Frantz's sons-in-law, 221, 223; for honesty, 26, 50, 122; honour based on, 24; impact of association with bad company on, 117–18, 132–33, 178–79; Montaigne on, 3; of Nuremberg as bastion of law and order, 97; of prison employees, 103; professional, 34, 39, 49, 63, 75, 188, 189, 193, 195; religion and, 119–20; of Saint Vitus as patron saint of healers, 101; of Schlegel, 217; for sobriety and reliability, 99; social status and, 109, 113–16, 156; theft of, *see* fraud; honour; slander
Reutlingen, 240n5
revenge, 147–49, 151–52
Rhünagel, Cunz (aka Rough), 82
Rittler, Peter, 130
robbers, 6, 8, 11, 30, 45–49, 51, 60, 71–72, 79, 82–83, 114, 117, 121, 122, 127, 132–33, 137–53, 170–73, 185–87, 242n14; *see also* theft
rods, whipping with, *see* floggings: with rods, banishment preceded by
Rodtler, Klaus (aka the Big Farmer), 177
Rolfinck, Werner, 200
Roman law, 26, 28, 29, 42, 75
Romanticism, nineteenth-century, 24, 232, 234, 234
rope, execution with, *see* hangings
Rössner, Erhard, 165–66
Rössner, Hans, 206
Rossnerin, Elisabeth, 145, 202

Rotenfels, 137
Rothenburg ob der Tauber, 235
Rotwelsch (street cant), xxv, 40, 51, 245n57
Rublack, Ulinka, 247n9
Rühl, Hans, 179
Russ, Lienhardt, 43

Sachs, Hans, 180, 233
sadism, 58, 62; *see also* violence, gratuitous
Saint Egidien Latin School (Nuremberg), 139
Saint Jacob's Church (Nuremberg), 180
Saint Johannis Cemetery (Nuremberg), 112
Saint Lorenz Church (Nuremberg), xiv, 165
Saint Rochus Cemetery (Nuremberg), 135, 139, 225, 229
Saint Sebaldus Church (Nuremberg), xiv, 100, 104, 208
Salzburg, 262n64
Sanson executioner dynasty, xvii, 241n6
Savoy, 110
Saxony, Electoral, 7, 20
Schaumann, Ruth, 264n15
Schmid-Spreer, Ursula, 164n15
Scherl, Balthasar, 202
Scheurl, Christoph, 97–98
Schiller, Adam, 152
Schiller, Simon, 179, 250n82
Schlegel, Bernhard, 214–18, 228
Schmidin, Elisabeth (Frantz's granddaughter), 218, 222–23, 229
Schmidin, Kunigunda (Frantz's sister), 35, 37, 89, 132, 133, 134
Schmidin, Margaretha (Frantz's daughter), 101, 135
Schmidin, Maria (Frantz's daughter), 135, 140, 222, 223, 225, 228, 229
Schmidin, Maria (Frantz's wife), 99–100, 130, 135–36, 139–40, 225
Schmidin, Rosina (Frantz's daughter), 135, 140, 222, 225, 228
Schmidt, Frantz: abstention from alcohol of, 53–54, 86; adult children in household during old age of, 221–23, 225; appointed as Nuremberg's executioner, 88–90,

Schmidt, Frantz (*continued*)
94–97; apprenticeship of, xxii, 3–4, 15, 37–43; assistant of, *see* Koller, Claus; author's discovery of journal of, xv–xxii; birth of, xxii, 5, 8, 20, 28; on blasphemy, 161; brother-in-law tortured and executed by, 132–33; bungling of executions by, xv, 85, 87, 211–13; childhood of, 3–5, 20, 35–44; children of, xxiii, 100–101, 135, 136, 140; citizenship of, 136, 139; corporal punishment administered by, 63–67, 76, 135, 211, 213 (*see also specific forms of punishment*); on crimes of malice, 141–53; on crimes of passion, 153–55; and dark arts, 202–11; death of, 225, 227–29; deaths of family members of, 135, 139–40, 222–25, 228; empathy for victims of crime, 122–30, 162–63; employment contract and salary in Nuremberg of, 98–99, 131–36; executioner relatives of, xviii (*see also* Schmidt, Heinrich); and family's move to Bamberg, 22, 94; father's aid to career advancement of, 45–46, 88–90; and father's death, 134; funeral of, 225; on habitual criminals, 162–68, 172–73; handling of cadavers by, 196–202; healing skills of, xxiii, 15–16, 39, 59, 98, 185–96, 217–20; interrogations by, 55–56, 135 (*see also* torture administered by *below*); journeyman years of, xxii, 42, 45–53, 76, 87; and juvenile offenders, 173–79, 182–83; legacy of, 228; Lutheranism of, 32–34, 36–37, 141, 168; maintenance of execution sites by, 105–108; marriage of, xxii, 99–100, 108; master test passed by, 43–44; *Meisterlied* composed by, 180–83, 218; on mercy and redemption, 168–72, 183–84; modern distancing from, 235–37; neutrality toward religious identity, 119–20; and prison employees, 104–105; professional skills of, xxii, 15, 54–55, 99, 131; publication of journal of, 231–32; public executions carried out by, 67–87, 91–93, 105, 135, 212–13, 229, 230 (*see also specific methods of execution*); reputational theft abhorred by, 120–21; reputation constructed by, 112–17, 120, 122, 133; restoration of family honour by, xxi, xxiv, 20, 94, 134, 218–20, 222, 238; retirement of, 87, 131, 213–14; social status of, xxii–xxiii, 15–17, 34–35, 101, 108–12, 139; successor's animosity toward, 214–18, 228; torture administered by, 57–63 (*see also specific techniques*); and transformation of German criminal law, 26–30; views on women's reputations, 117–19

Schmidt, Frantz Stefan (Frantz's son), 135, 222

Schmidt, Gilg, 88

Schmidt, Heinrich (Frantz's father), xix, xx, xxii, 3–5, 43, 45, 54, 101, 116, 219, 243*n21*, 249*n56*; annual income of, 251*n10*; assistant of, 102; corporal punishment by, 65, 66, 248*n32*; executions per year carried out by, 30; Frantz's apprenticeship with, 37–41, 50, 55, 57; Frantz's career aided by, 88–90; healing skills of, 190; illness and death of, 131–32, 134, 255*n96*; remarriage of, after wife's death, 35; social position of, 15–26; torture techniques used by, 58

Schmidt, Johannes (Frantzenhans; Frantz's son), 135, 222, 225, 228, 229

Schmidt, Jörg (Frantz's son), 101, 135, 139, 140, 222–23

Schmidt, Peter (Frantz's grandfather), 19, 37

Schmidt, Vitus (Frantz's son), 100–101, 135

Schmidtin, Gertraut, 158–59

Schmiedin, Michaela, 209

Schmiedt, Christoph (aka Cooper Chris), 167

Schmiedt, Georg, 157

Schmitter, Herr, 123

Schnabel, Hans, 108

Schneck, Georg, 157

Schober, Georg, 121

Schober, Lorenz, 166

Schoberin, Margaretha, 121

Schongau, 203

Schönherlin, Martin, 143

Schörpff, Georg, 160

Schott, Cunz, 6

Schreinerin, Margaretha, 168
Schrenker, Hans (aka the Crawler), 82, 119, 166–67
Schropp, Laurenz, 126
Schuster, Hans, 146
Schützin, Ameley, 158
Schwager, Nickel, 113
Schwartz executioner dynasty, 16
Schwartz, Lienhard, 208
Schwartzmann, Hans Georg (aka the Fat Mercenary; aka Black Peasant), 152, 153, 161
Schwarzenberg, Johann Freiherr von, 28
Schwenderin, Barbara, 247n18
Schweiger, Georg, 182–83
Schwertzin, Katherina, 115
scourging, *see* flogging
screws, 30, 57–59; *see also* torture
Second Margrave War, 17
Seitel, Michel, 145–46
self-defense, 154
sentencing, 79–80, 132
settlements, financial, *see* financial penalties and settlements
Seuboldt, Frantz, 47, 125, 144
sexual offences, 65, 114, 116–20, 126–30, 149, 155–61, 207, 211; with devil, 203; false accusations of, 121; same-sex, *see* sodomy; violent, *see* rape; *see also* lewdness; *specific acts*
Seytzen, Andreas, 147
Shakespeare, William, 24, 45, 185
Simplicissimus (Grimmelshausen), 9–10
Sixtus IV, Pope, 198
skinners, 102
slander, *see* accusations, false
sleeping victims, 167; murders of, 56, 142, 143, 145–46
smallpox, 5; *see also* epidemics
social status, xxii, 23–24, 111, 195; fraudulent imposture of, 120; privileged, mercy and, 93; reputation and, 109, 113–16, 156
sodomy, 158–61, 173
Solen, George, 108
sorcery, *see* magic
"Spanish boots", 58; *see also* torture
"special interrogation", *see* torture
Spiss, Hans, 241n8
Stade, 240n5
Stadtbibliothek (Nuremberg), xviii, xx

Starck, Simon, 163, 202
Stayber, Andreas (aka the Minstrel), 165
Stayner, Steffan, 143
Steinach, 43, 45
Stengel, Georg, 121
stepmothers, 35
Stertz, Matthias, 169
Stigler, Friedrich, 121, 204–205
stocks, 63, 65, 118, 161, 206; *see also* corporal punishment
Stokamer, Alexander, 98
Stoker, Bram, 233–34
Stollman, Laurenz, 174
stoning, 179, 211, 219, 250n82; *see also* mob violence
strappado, 58–61, 132, 204; *see also* torture
Strauss, Gerald, 251n6
Story of the Sturdy Kasperl and the Beautiful Annerl, The (Brentano), 232
street slang, *see* Rotwelsch
Strölin, Anna, 128, 144
Stüller, Niklaus (aka Black Banger), 71
suicide, 23, 101; of alleged witch, 206; attempted, 208; falsification of, to conceal murder, 129
Sümler, Georg (aka Gabby), 81
sumptuary ordinances, 23, 27
Sunberg, Phila and Görgla, 71
Sundermann, Valentin, 121
swindlers, *see* con artists, fraud
sword, death by, *see* beheading

Tacitus, 68
talismans, 13
Taller, Lienhard (aka Spit Lenny), 143, 151
tanners, 16, 23, 41, 51, 243n18
Taucher, Georg, 127, 144
Taumb, Hans, 178
taverns, 52, 53
Teurla,, Georg, 142
Teurla, Heinz, 128
Teutonic Knights, 154, 194
Thaddeus Thomas, 181
theft, xiv, 10–11, 16, 30–32, 60, 65, 92, 114, 116–21, 124, 128, 162–68, 173, 184, 212; accomplices in, 153–54; bungled, 165–66; from churches and monasteries, 161; from corpses, 108,

theft (*continued*)
152; decline in executions for, 74,
229; execution by wheel for, 45, 72;
hanging for, 43, 45–46, 72, 82, 89,
128, 149, 161–64, 173–77, *176*, 179,
183–84, 196, 212; lack of remorse for,
169; lenient sentences for, 171, 173;
by mercenaries, 132–33; by minors,
173–76, 178–79, 183; murder and,
127, 137–38, 142–47, 149–52, 166,
185–86; nocturnal, 145; non-violent,
162–63; petty, 10, 65, 162–63; by
relatives, 126; sentencing to death
for, 81; by servants, 125; torture to
obtain confessions of, 57, 59–61,
247*n13*

Thirty Years War, 223–24, 227–29
"Thoughts and Recommendations on
Nuremberg's Criminal Justice and Its
Administration" (Endter), 231
thumbscrews, 30, 57–59, 234; *see also*
torture
Thuringians, 20
tongs, red-hot, ripping of flesh with, *see*
nipping
tongue, cutting off or tearing out, xvii,
64, 65, 161
torture, xxiii, 4, 27, 30, 43, 54–63, 74,
141, 187, 234, 236, 237, 247*n13*, *n18*,
24; for association with outlaws, 117;
of brother-in-law, 132; and claims of
magical powers, 208–209; execution
by, *see* wheel, execution by; exemption
of high status prisoners from, 112;
of falsely accused, 121; healing
treatments for victims of, 39, 59,
193; illnesses faked to avoid, 170;
incapacity of executioners to carry
out, 89; judicial, xxiv; Lion as
assistant in, 101; of minors, 177;
mitigation of sentences after, 170;
ordinances regulating use of, 29–31;
psychological damage from, 60; by
soldiers and bandits, 9–10, 150;
techniques of, 57–58 (*see also specific
methods*); threat of, 128; tourist
fascination with, 233–35; in twenty-
first century, 237
traitors, *see* treason
transportation to foreign colonies, 31,
230, 246*n47*

treason, 71, 99, 123–25, 154, 179,
249*n51*
Tross, Julius, 174
trust, violation of, 141–42
typhus, 5

Ullmann, Thomas, 79
unemployment, 8, 10, 30, 227
Unger, Jörg, 188
United States; capital punishment in,
237; coercive interrogation techniques
of, 237; homicide rate in, xxiv; street
slang in, xxv

vagrants, 10, 16, 51, 67, 174, 190
Valkenborch, Lucas I. van, *11*
Veit, Bishop, 101
vengeance, *see* revenge
Venice, 91
Vesalius, Andreas, 198, 201
Vienna, 91, 94
violence, 5, 6, 26; against children,
126–28 (*see also* child murder); in
culture of unmarried young men, 52;
gratuitous, 145–47, 149–52; in heat of
anger, 153–55; of juveniles, 179; law
enforcement to curb, 14–15; of
mercenaries, 8–10; mob, *see* mob
violence; in pursuit of justice, 63–75;
in pursuit of truth, *see* torture; against
women, 125 (*see also* rape)
Vischer, Conrad, 88
Vogel, Hans, 76–82, 85–88
Vogl, Michel, 152
Voglin, Margaretha, 87, 247*n18*
Vogt, Michel, 169
Vogtland, 21
Voltaire, 6
vows, false, 157

Wadl, Hans, 146–47
Wagner, Richard, 227
Wagnerin, Barbara, 149, 206
Waldt, Joachim (aka the Tutor), 117
Walker, Mack, 228
Walter, Hennsa (aka the Cheesecutter),
117
water, torture with, 58; *see also* torture

Weber, Hans, (aka Fat Fruiterer), 89, 159–60

Weber, Stoffel, 173

Weckler, Hans, 167

werewolves, 12

Werner, Friedrich (aka Potter Freddy), 132, 179

Westphalia, Peace of, 227

Weyer, Johann, 190–91, 207

Weyermann, Master, 123

Weyr, Andreas, 117

Weyssheubtel, Georg, 152

wheel, execution by, 33, 40, 45–48, 47, 61, 71–72, 74, 135, 229, 236, 237; corpses displayed on, 47, 48, 129, 151, 196; of highwaymen, 83; for infanticide, 186; mitigation to beheading in, 117; of murderers, 71, 72, 125, 143, 149; nips preceding, 47, 71, 72, 127, 133, 144, 186; sentencing to, 79; site for, see capital punishment, Raven Stone

whipping, see flogging

whores, see prostitutes

Widman, Enoch, 21

Widmänin (Widmenin), Margaretha, xxv

Widmann, Georg, xxv

Widtmann brothers, 173

Widtmenin, Cordula, 178

Wigliss, Georg, 149

Wisenstein, Albernius von, 111

witchcraft, xiv, 12, 13, 30, 55, 203; executions for, 67, 71, 173, 203, 229; false accusations of, 118, 121, 204–206; healing and, 187, 188; opponents of prosecutions for, 190, 207; release of suspects of, 62, 206; torture for confessions of, 160, 203; see also magic

Witschel, Johann Heinrich, 233

Wolff, Gabriel, 91–93, 111, 113, 120, 168, 173

women, 67–71; attempted murder of abusers by, 125; executions of, 67–71, 69, 73, 77–82, 117–19, 232, 249n52; flogging of, 66, 118; hanging of, 175, 176; incarceration of, 59; live burial of, 68, 69; names of, 114; newborns killed by, see infanticide; nicknames of, 115; pregnant, murders of, 71, 72, 126, 128–29, 142–44, 151; public humiliation as punishment for, 63, 67; reputations of, 117–18; vengeance perpetrated by, 148–49; violence against, 125 (see also rape)

workhouses, 65, 229, 230, 232

wound doctors, 191–95, 194, 222, 260n16

wreath, torture with, 58, 59, 60; see also torture

Württemberg, duchy of, 8

Würtzburg, Bishop Veit II von, 22

Würzburg, 17; bishop of, 22, 119; witch craze in, 203

young unmarried men: culture of, 51–52; sexual exploits of, 52, 53; torture of, 60

youths, see juvenile offenders

Zeyern, 43

Ziegler, Peter, 177

Zum wilden Mann (Raabe), 264n15

Zwickelsperger, Kunrad, 149, 207

Zwiebel, Die (Schaumann), 264n15

Illustration Credits

www.vintage-books.co.uk